The Seventh Cadence

JIM WILBOURNE

Published by Emergent Realms

https://www.emergentrealms.com/

Edited by Kate Watts, Spencer Hamilton, Adryanna Monteiro, and Lisa Bryan

Cover Art by Billy Christian

Formatting by Nefarious Press Publishing

To my wife, who is far too indulgent of my flights of fancy

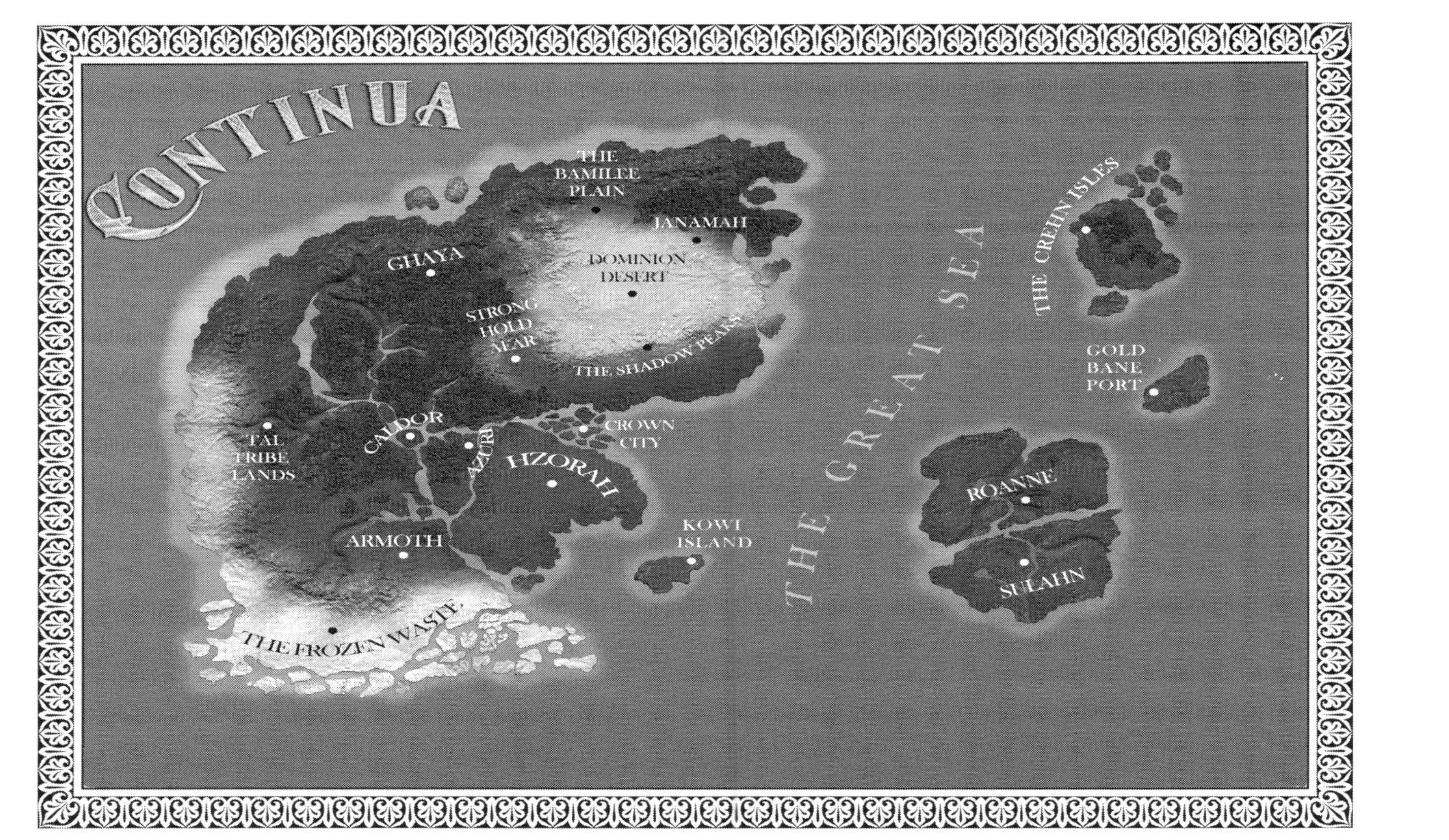
CONTINUA
THE BAMILEE PLAIN
JANAMAH
GHAYA
DOMINION DESERT
STRONG HOLD MAR
THE SHADOW PEAKS
CALDOR
TAL TRIBE LANDS
AZURI
CROWN CITY
HZORAH
ARMOTH
KOWI ISLAND
THE FROZEN WASTE
THE GREAT SEA
THE CREHN ISLES
GOLD BANE PORT
ROANNE
SULAHN

PRELUDE

PRELUDE

Year 200 SA

A long shadow snaked over the plain, passing under smoke and airborne dust, sweeping over blood and sweat and gold-flecked ashes that still glowed even as the fires that had ignited them drifted away. The inferno amassed and expired where the dry grass subsided at the base of lofty rock, and the dead piled where the flames failed to devour them. The Shadow Peaks loomed in the distance, brushing its jagged fingers across the orange and pink sky and flaunting regal indifference to the affairs of men.

King Jeremiah guided Wrathbane across the scorched earth. The horse's head bobbed as it skirted debris—broken spears, remnants of leather armor, and lost swords. Jeremiah held his breath, inhaling only when his lungs burned. One never noticed the stench of war while the battle raged and passion ruled the senses.

We've won, Esther, Jeremiah thought.

High Lord Bendeth, atop his high war horse, emerged from the shadows. Bendeth's squire, with eyes as wide as two full moons, followed just behind on a smaller but respectable gray stallion, his helm lost to battle, and his hair matted with the blood of the enemy. The High Lord paused and allowed his king to approach.

"You've lost your squire," Bendeth said.

King Jeremiah looked behind him to an empty saddle. In the throes of battle, he'd not only lost his sense of self but lost the lad—who had already lost his own mount—as well. The sword in his saddle scabbard was half drawn. Cut off at the wrist, a pale white and blood-streaked hand held fast to the sword's hilt in what appeared to be a final, desperate grab at a weapon before the boy was pulled from Wrathbane and slaughtered by Dominion foot soldiers.

Though only hours past, he couldn't remember if it had been before they'd cleared the southern passage or after. Was it when they'd penetrated the Dominion's piked battalions, or was it when General Ashinn had fallen, leaving his troops irrevocably crippled?

"So I have," Jeremiah said.

Frowning, Jeremiah clenched his horse's reins. *Seth.* That was his name. He'd met him a few days ago. The boy had only seen sixteen years—too young to even take his mark. And now he was gone. *The poor lad.*

Children did not belong in battle. He'd see that changed. He'd see a lot changed.

He looked at Bendeth's squire. "How old are you?"

The squire sat mute on his gray steed, his eyes focused on something distant and invisible.

"Talk when your *king* addresses you, boy," Bendeth barked.

As if just awoken from sleep, the squire blinked. "Sir?"

"His Majesty asked how many years you've seen," Bendeth said. When the squire failed to respond again, he added, "Scorch it, boy! Answer him or I'll have you skinned and pile you with the rest of the Desolate-bound Dominion dogs!"

The squire bowed low in his mount. "I've seen twenty years, Your Majesty."

Old enough to take his mark, King Jeremiah thought. He paused for Esther's reply, but she remained silent, distant. Safe.

He looked into the squire's eyes, saw the unbridled fear that clouded his thoughts and the untapped potential trapped within. *You were right about this, too, love.*

"What's your name?" Jeremiah asked.

"Samuel, Your Majesty. Samuel Tarkus."

"You are relieved of duty," Jeremiah said. "Report to my encampment and tell them the King appoints you for his personal staff."

"Your Majesty?"

"You heard him," Bendeth said. "Fall back to Stronghold Aear. Do as he says."

The squire nodded and guided his steed southeast. "Thank you, Your Majesty."

King Jeremiah sighed and looked to the Shadow Peaks as Squire Samuel Tarkus departed. "Children do not belong in battle."

"I won't pretend like you didn't relieve me of a burden," Bendeth said. "But he was a man. He'd seen twenty years."

"Desolate's Hand was with him. He wouldn't have survived the final push into the desert."

"And *your* apprentice would have? You'll need more than a lone hand in death's valleys."

Jeremiah frowned at the joke. "You were right about my apprentice, and I'm right about yours. He's smart, but he's no warrior. It's not in his blood."

"It's good to see that I'm finally appreciated," Bendeth said, a smile lighting his lips. "Your Majesty."

Ignoring the thin layer of resentment that the words "Your Majesty" carried, Jeremiah urged his horse forward. Bendeth trotted just behind, following him toward the mountains.

High Lord Bendeth was proud. He would have been the Herre—a king in his own right—of the Ehrel tribe had the Ehrel not joined the Hzorah tribe. And though Bendeth bowed to Jeremiah's rule, he did so only because he was bound by the honor of his people. Jeremiah knew no other man more honorable than Bendeth.

He could almost hear her say it: "My brother is headstrong, love. Never mind him."

As they crossed the land, he kept a loose tally of the dead. While it was impossible to truly count, he gave his best guess. Fifteen thousand, more likely twenty. Many of the fallen were the enemy. For every one of the Hzorah troops that had fallen, they'd taken two of the enemy with them. Five thousand at the least. Five thousand men and boys who would never see their families again.

It was a shame, but a necessary act of honor. The Hzorah tribe had given the people the freedom they craved. The *people* had spoken, and his tribe was all too glad to respond to their call. They would not be slaves to the Dominion's prophet—to a regime of magic that had perished with the wizard who wielded it.

Wizard Titan was dead, long dead. And freedom—for the first time in over two hundred years—now lived. They'd won the war. *And I'm finally coming home, Love.*

High Lord Roth joined the procession, with three battalions following a few hundred paces behind. Roth's leather armor shined dark red with blood. His sword, though secured in its scabbard, dripped blood, shaken free by his gray steed's prance.

"The Dominion has fallen back to the Shadow Peaks, Your Majesty," Roth said. "In the west, at least."

"And near Stronghold Gordal?" Jeremiah asked.

"News hasn't reached me that the east has cleared," Roth said. "But I'm confident Captain Rollins has led his troops admirably. The Second League is a fantastic group of soldiers. I can't speak more highly of any battalion."

"Better than your own?" Jeremiah asked.

Roth chuckled. "Though I hate to admit it, yes."

Bendeth sneered. "Allow someone to take their pick of soldiers and of course he'll come up with something better than the stock. It takes a real leader to pull the average into line." He inclined his head toward the Peaks. "While your battalions lounged near the Stronghold, mine are making the final push at the Peaks."

"Had we not," Roth said, his tone hardening, "the soldiers

under your command would have been flanked at both the north and south."

"We were prepared for that," Bendeth said, obstinate as ever.

"Enough," King Jeremiah said. "We all have our part to play."

The sun dipped behind the mountains as they neared the valley. As if Desolate's own hand had carved out the great wall of rock and dirt and snow, the lowlands between the Shadow Peaks twisted between the cliffs. Trees peppered the lands at the valley's mouth but thickened as they entered the heart of the mountains. On the far side, they'd taper again until the vast wilderness beyond the mountains choked the life from the dirt and only sand remained as the world came to an end.

The thick of the valley would slow the Dominion substantially. This would also mean a slowed chase for his troops, but Hzorah soldiers were nothing if not resilient. The Ehrel and many other smaller tribes who'd joined the Hzorah had given rise to the greatest force the world had ever known, proving themselves worthy of the Hzorah tribe's respect.

The chase through the mountains would last days. They would lose men. Not only to small encounters with the Dominion troops as they nipped at their heels, but also to the exhaustion and thirst and dangerous terrain. They had precious little food and water among them, and their nights would be sleepless. At most, there may be an intermittent hour to allow the horses a rest.

The war sparked when Adonijah, his grandfather and warrior king of the Hzorah tribe, eradicated the Dominion from the Hzorah tribe's borders. The war continued as his father, Gillan, forged a pact with the neighboring tribes to help them push out the Dominion's oppression from their lands. And though Gillan died young, Jeremiah carried the torch all the way to the very end of the world. A few more days would be the very least of this war.

"Your Majesty!"

King Jeremiah turned to see a soldier riding through the

ranks. Swords were drawn, then lowered as they recognized the Hzorah mark on his dark leather breastplate. The soldiers parted, allowing him through. As quickly as his horse stopped, he dismounted and bowed.

"Your Majesty," he said, then rose to face his king. He reached into his satchel and pulled forth a small piece of parchment. "An urgent message from the Crown City."

King Jeremiah met High Lord Roth's eyes before reaching down and taking the message from the courier. "It couldn't have waited?"

"I was explicitly instructed to bring you the message no matter where you were, no matter how far I must journey, Your Majesty."

Jeremiah unfolded the parchment and scanned the words. A chill fell over him as if a bitter wind tore over the land and through the cloak and leather armor. He tucked the message under his chest piece.

"I'm going back."

"What?" Bendeth frowned. "Surely, it's not—"

"What's wrong, Your Majesty?" Roth asked.

"It's Esther," Jeremiah said. "She's not well. She's in labor."

"She's not the first woman to have had a child," Bendeth said. "She will be fine."

"She's not fine," Jeremiah said.

"That's the risk that must be taken when giving birth," Bendeth said. "You know that. We have to march on now. It's too late to turn back."

"I'm sure she's fine, Your Majesty," Roth said. "There are great healers at the palace."

"She's *not* fine," Jeremiah said. "This isn't the same. There is something very wrong. She might die."

"Countless things have gone wrong," Bendeth said. "Look around you. Thousands of men died today. And now we have to make sure there will be no more of it."

"She's your *sister*, Bendeth!" Jeremiah glared at Bendeth. "Not some mistress who quelled my lust for a night and carried my bastard. We've won the day. You don't need me to lead the charge."

Bendeth's lip curled. "Esther was a peace offering. You don't have to act as though you care for my sake. Did you lose your honor with your squire? The King must—"

"The *King* must do what he sees fit." As king, Jeremiah could have had Bendeth killed for that remark, but too much death had visited them today. Instead, he turned his horse to the south. Peace offering or not, he loved her. He never thought he would, but he did, and there was little more he could do here with his men. The codes demanded that he stay, but his heart ... his heart said otherwise. "I'm going back. Roth, Bendeth, see to it that the Desolate-bound dogs don't sleep until the wasteland consumes them."

High Lord Roth dipped his head. "Yes, Your Majesty."

High Lord Bendeth refused to speak.

King Jeremiah guided his stallion past his troops. Each man bowed his head as he passed, but Jeremiah did not acknowledge them. His mind was elsewhere. His thoughts belonged to Esther and his second born. With a quick squeeze of his legs, he spurred Wrathbane into a gallop.

Gavini squeezed the cloth, letting the excess water drip back into the basin. He delicately patted away dabs of sweat that beaded on Queen Esther's forehead. Her brow twitched at his touch, but settled as the cool of the cloth briefly drew away the heat of the fever. She struggled for quick, shallow breaths, inhaling sharply.

"Is that better, Majesty?" Gavini asked before setting the cloth across her forehead. "Does the cloth help?"

Queen Esther gave the slightest of nods but didn't speak or open her eyes.

Gavini put aside the basin. He'd mixed in the last of his spice berries with the water in order to help treat the infection, but he hadn't caught the beginnings of the issue in time. He'd given strict instructions to the queen's handmaids to cleanse themselves—particularly their hands—when dealing with her during her pregnancy. He couldn't be sure that they'd followed his instructions, but he suspected that they had not. It was an odd request and may have been forgotten or disregarded as magical superstition.

But it was no superstition. Invisible to all was an array of life that could bring aid or sickness. And though the Hzorah tribe had a somewhat justified resistance to anything that sounded like magic to them, their fear caused them to behave irrationally.

"Majesty, I must listen to your heart," Gavini said.

Again, the queen only nodded, and Gavini bent over her bed and pressed his ear to her chest. Her heartbeat was irregular.

An infection, a fever, rapid breaths and heart rate. *Sepsis*.

Gavini turned and lifted the thick, leather-bound book from within his medicine pack. He thumbed through the pages until he found the entry that matched the symptoms. The prognosis was bleak, but there was a treatment. Unfortunately, that treatment was stored away in another volume—a volume he hadn't seen in years.

Abigail, I wish you were here now. Gavini sighed. *I could sure use you.*

But there was another way.

Gavini shut the book and looked up when he heard someone at the door. Prophet Davin slipped into the queen's palace chambers with deep concern etched on his face. He crossed to the bed with his eyes set on the queen, but he spoke to Gavini.

"How is she?"

"Not well," Gavini said.

The prophet glanced to Gavini, and understanding blanched his expression. "And the child?"

Gavini shook his head. "The infection holds no reservation for youth. By nightfall—"

"Is there anything else?" Prophet Davin asked. "There

must be. I know that there is. There is something you're not saying, something you have not tried. There is still a future. I can see it."

While the gaze of a prophet's foresight rarely concerned itself with the events of one child's birth, this child would be the second born of King Jeremiah and a prince of all the tribes that had united under one banner to fight the Dominion. It was likely that this child's effect on the future was immense.

Gavini crossed the room, considering the implications of the only solution he had. It could work. But not without consequences. He turned back to not only the prophet's expecting gaze but his queen's as well.

"Her birthing pains are still quite far apart," Gavini said. "It is uncertain how long they will continue at this rate, but it may be several hours to two days before she is ready to give birth." Gavini looked apologetically to Queen Esther. "Unfortunately, I don't believe that you have the time. The infection has progressed too far. If I'd caught it sooner … If someone had sent for me—"

"But there *is* a solution," the prophet pushed. "There is something that can make this right."

When Gavini didn't answer, the queen spoke. "Please, Gavini. Tell us what we must do."

Gavini sighed and crossed back to his medicine pack. "I can't make this right. At least, not completely right."

He reached into his pack and pulled out another small leather book. This one was black with gold, embossed lettering. Nearly too thin to be bound, its slim form was disproportionate to the hope it held.

"This is an Abbreviation," Gavini said, looking to Prophet Davin, who'd paled far beyond the natural.

"What's an Abbreviation?" Queen Esther whispered, breaking the silence.

"It's *magic*, Your Majesty," Prophet Davin hissed.

"But the Wizard," the queen said. "He's dead."

"Yes," Gavini said. He glanced down at the small book, a smile touching his lips. "But there are a few things he left behind. A few bits of magic that were preserved. Magic that he etched into existence then packed away to be triggered during times of desperation."

"However," Prophet Davin interrupted, "we do not use these artifacts. They are locked away and safe. Never to be used. The world has seen enough of magic's taint. Fortunately, the King has seen to it that we never have to live under its oppression again. How this *healer* came to find such a thing eludes me."

The queen gasped for breath, then let out a sharp cry. Gavini and Prophet Davin came to her aid.

"The infection?" Prophet Davin asked, gripping her hand.

"No," Gavini said. "A birthing pain." He set aside the small book and picked through his medicine pack once again before producing a small jar. He opened it and pulled out a moist, white leaf. "Open your mouth, Your Majesty."

Through the pain, the queen did as instructed. Gavini placed the small leaf under her tongue. "Resist the urge to swallow. Only hold it there."

After a few moments, the queen settled again. Gavini fetched her a small cup filled with water and allowed her to drink but cautioned her again to not swallow the leaf.

"Please," Gavini said, looking to Prophet Davin, "have someone fetch more water."

The prophet straightened, giving a short glance to the Abbreviation book where it lay. "We will discuss this further when I return."

Gavini watched Prophet Davin leave the room, then turned back to his medicine pack. He had nothing to attend to, but he'd just given the queen of Hzorah a promise of death and preferred not to face her directly. He'd seen death before. He'd delivered harsh news many times. But never to a queen.

"The book," Queen Esther said. "How does it work?"

Gavini paused his work with the pack to glance up at the queen's steady gaze. "Well, as I said, there are some pieces of magic that remained after Wizard Titan left the world. One of them is the magic tied to this book. Prophet Davin is correct,

Majesty. The book that this Abbreviation is tied to is safely away in Caldor. But several books were created so that someone other than Wizard Titan could invoke his power in his name."

"I'm afraid to ask how you came to acquire one," the queen said.

"Then do not, Majesty," Gavini said with a small smile.

"And this Abbreviation ... It will fix me and the baby?" she asked. "It will take away the infection?"

"I'm afraid that it only has the power to save one life," Gavini stepped closer to her. "I can save you, but your child will not live."

Queen Esther looked away, and Gavini felt a pang of regret that he didn't say it as delicately as he could have. But that was the truth of it. He was a man of medicine, but a Keeper first, and his bedside manner left something to be desired.

"And," Gavini continued, "magic has become not only taboo but unlawful. It would be against the will of the king and against the will of the people to use it."

"Then why do you carry it?" Queen Esther looked back to him. "If you know that it's unlawful, why would you have it?"

"Anyone who understands magic would know that it's not something that the common man can create, that it is a tool given only to Wizard Titan. And with his absence, magic is no more." Gavini paused, considering his words. "But anyone who understands magic will also know that it is not explicitly good or evil but a tool. And that there may be a time when that tool can be used to do a greater good."

Prophet Davin slipped back into the room. "I've seen to it that plenty of water will be here for you. I was informed that the palace also has its own birthing amenities. They will also arrive soon ..." He looked between the queen and the healer. "What is it?"

"I want to use the Abbreviation," Queen Esther said.

"But, Your Majesty," Prophet Davin stammered. "It is forbidden. Even for us. It is punishable by death."

"It is a punishment I am willing to take," Queen Esther said.

Prophet Davin stared incredulously. "You would use the magic only to be executed later? To what end?"

"It's not my life I wish to save," she said, then looked at Gavini. "Can you save my child instead? You said it can only save one life. Can it save my child's?"

"It can, Your Majesty," Gavini said.

"I have given the Crown an heir," the queen said. "Gabriel will be strong like his father. And, with this child, I will give the Crown a second. And my son cannot be put to death for the sin of his mother."

Another pain took her, and she cried out. Davin looked at Gavini, his hard expression relenting at seeing his queen in pain.

"The Abbreviation," she said through gritted teeth. "Hurry."

Gavini picked up the small book, but Prophet Davin held up a hand.

"Before you do this, Gavini," Prophet Davin said, "there are conditions."

Gavini nodded. He had expected this. "I understand."

"First, after this is over, you must give me the book. It does not belong here. It's not safe and quite illegal. Second, the consequences for using magic is death. While I am loyal to the laws of the land, I am also loyal to my queen. Therefore, I will not turn you in for this. But you will have to leave Hzorah. And you may never return."

"Done," Gavini said without hesitation.

Prophet Davin stared into Gavini's eyes, as if pondering whether or not the terms he'd given were sufficient. His brow twitched into scowl, and his gaze drifted down to the book with fearful disgust.

"Is that all?" Gavini asked.

"It shouldn't be," the prophet said, then stepped aside.

Gavini opened the book to the second page where the spell form began.

King Jeremiah breathed in the salty air of his city. The sunlight warmed his aching muscles without the oppression of summer's humidity. A cool, gentle breeze carried the murmurs of market trade and spirited away with the hark of freedom.

He was finally home.

He slowed his horse to ride next to Samuel. He'd retrieved the boy from Stronghold Aear to accompany him back south. The journey took several worry-fraught days, and while an entire company of men would have slowed him, a solo ride would have been reckless beyond even his own appetite for danger.

The road opened to a broad avenue where trade wagons could easily access the Crown Palace's storerooms. The delta's streams brought a river taxi filled with men and women—their courtship in full bloom. He smiled at the picture of young love, uncaring as they allowed their passion to carry them into a future of love and prosperity. In that moment, Jeremiah couldn't remember the horrors of battle. None of it could cast a shadow in the radiance of his people's joy.

He looked at the squire. As if too afraid to look at his king directly, Samuel kept his eyes fixed on the palace ahead. The journey had been nearly wordless between them. At first, Jeremiah welcomed the silence. But once the Crown City was within reach, Jeremiah realized that the squire was avoiding him altogether, doing and saying just enough to be compliant but never more.

"You can look at me," Jeremiah said. "Just because I'm the King doesn't mean I'm some god to be revered."

His new apprentice risked a glance. "Yes, Your Majesty."

They trotted on for another moment of silence. Children skirted the horses' paths and Crown City citizens removed their hats out of respect when they realized it was soldiers—if not their king—among them.

"Go on," King Jeremiah said. He looked Samuel in the eye.

"Speak your mind. Perhaps Bendeth didn't allow you to do so, but, under my roof, I expect your honesty."

Samuel looked at Jeremiah. His mouth opened once before it snapped shut.

"I mean it," Jeremiah said. "Speak."

"You left your troops," Samuel said. "You abandoned the battlefield. A man's honor is all that he has. Why would you lose your honor for … for …"

"For a woman?" Jeremiah finished for him and caught the squire's eye long enough to confirm his suspicions. "We'd won, Samuel. They didn't need me for the final push into the mountains. If anything, it's a victory lap and a chance for soldiers to kill a few more men so that they have at least one story for the taverns that isn't tainted by the fearful smell of their own urine."

"High Lord Bendeth won't forget this," Samuel said. "He's a Desolate-bound looger, but he believes in honor."

"'Looger … I keep hearing Bendeth mutter that word. What does it mean?"

"Looger. One who is only interested in one's own affairs." For the first time the entire journey back to the Crown City, the boy perked up. "The etymology of the word is quite interesting, actually. The Ehrel word …" Suddenly aware of himself, Samuel apologized. "I'm sorry. It's not my place to—"

King Jeremiah waved a hand. "I told you to speak your mind, Samuel. I won't punish you for obeying me." He smiled. "You're smart. I like that. You should leave wars to people like me—our kingdom's dolts."

"I studied under High Lord Bendeth's scholar," Samuel said. "I was to replace him, but the kingdom was running short on men to fight."

A moment of silence passed between them.

"Why *did* you leave?" Samuel persisted. "You must know as well as I do that High Lord Bendeth still resents you for taking away his rightful place as a ruler to his people."

"I granted him High Lordship so that he may rule his tribe and region within Hzorah's domain. He still has his authority."

"That means little to the son of a Herre," Samuel said. "The Ehrel tribe are as proud as they are honorable. To be benched second to another ruler is as good as not being a ruler at all. When you left the field—"

"I abandoned the throne to a successor," Jeremiah sighed. "I know that. But I led the winning charge. The soldiers know that. The First League will confirm it. And if Bendeth attempts to challenge me, he'll have the entire Hzorah tribe to fight off." He locked eyes with Samuel. "That is if he manages to strike *me* down first."

Jeremiah didn't like to make threats, especially ones he had no intention to back up with steel. The Hzorah and Ehrel tribes were long rivals, but petty squabbles of land were put aside for the good of their people. He'd thought Bendeth saw the ultimate virtue in that, even if it meant a blow to his own pride.

"He won't forget it," Samuel said as they reached the palace gates. "When the opportunity comes, he'll take what he believes to be his."

King Jeremiah's hand found the hilt of the Crown Sabre. "And when the opportunity comes, I'll welcome his attempt."

King Jeremiah dismounted his horse and handed the reins to a stunned guard before crossing the short bridge that led to the Crown Palace grounds. "He's exhausted. See to it that he is taken care of. Groomed well."

"Your Majesty—" the guard began, but Jeremiah didn't stop to hear the man's response. Two First League guards fell into step in front of and just behind their king, and two runners sprinted ahead to announce his approach.

The party crossed the short bridge that arched over the tributary and split the palace grounds into its own isolated plot of land. Jeremiah focused on the Hzorah mark on the black leather of the First League armor. He traced it with his eyes, focused on the rune's shape to give his mind something other than worry to occupy it.

Behind the thinly overcast sky, the sun had reached high noon, but the palace courtyard lacked the buzz of activity he'd grown accustomed to. There was an eerie quiet. A quiet he hadn't heard over the palace green since he and his father had first conquered the eastern reaches and taken the Crown City for Hzorah. It had been a tranquility born of reverent appreciation of victory—a victory that secured the Hzorah tribe a dominant hand in the war.

Jeremiah glanced to the palace's receiving bay. There were no deliveries. Before he could stop himself, he looked to the banner above the north gate—but there was no banner. It had been lowered. Then, as if his ears had suddenly awoken, he heard the bells. Low in pitch, they droned in a metallic, bittersweet ambivalence.

The king clenched his jaw as pain pierced his heart.

"The bells," Samuel said. "Doesn't that mean …"

At the palace's northern entryway, he saw his son, Gabriel. The child had only seen three years, but he'd already developed a personality that resembled his own—at least that's what everyone who'd known him in his youth constantly reminded him. Gabriel pulled against Marium's hand, eager to rush across the palace green to reunite with his father, but the nursemaid held steadfast. A set of palace workers joined, ready to take his armor and sword, and serve him water after his journey.

Prophet Davin stepped onto the landing, joining Jeremiah's son and nursemaid. In his arms, he cradled an infant wrapped in a light blue swaddle.

"Is that your son, Your Majesty?" Samuel asked.

Jeremiah jogged the remaining distance, leaving Samuel behind. Gabriel broke free of Nurse Marium's hold, and Jeremiah smiled as he scooped up the young prince. The boy giggled and chattered as Jeremiah carried him back to the palace. He humored the babbling child, responding as if he'd truly asked where his father had been all this time.

"Your father had to fight back the bad men! Guess who won? Guess? Your father won!"

But the joy of reuniting with his son was muted by Prophet

Davin's sad gaze. He absently set Gabriel back down before meeting the prophet's eyes. "How is she?"

Prophet Davin shook his head. "I'm sorry."

Jeremiah had known the probability from the moment he'd received the message at the foot of the Shadow Peaks, and he'd prepared himself for the worst in the days he'd journeyed south. He'd seen the solemn gloom about the palace as he approached. He'd heard the bells tolling tragedy. But none of it dampened the impact of the Prophet's words. His chest felt tight under his leather armor, and his stomach felt ready to reject what little he'd eaten.

"But with every tragedy," Prophet Davin said, offering the small infant to his king, "there is a new beginning."

Jeremiah took the child and gazed on his small, soft face. The child slept without acknowledgment of the bells, or the terrible grief, or an absent mother—a mother whose face shared so many of the same features as the child she'd left behind.

"Did she name him before ..." Jeremiah paused, his voice failing him.

"No," Prophet Davin said. "She only left this." Prophet Davin held piece of parchment, folded and sealed. "Her final words for you."

"He's a beautiful child," Nurse Marium said. "And strong. A true blessing. He will be a great warrior like his father."

Jeremiah gave her a courteous but weak smile of thanks. With his free hand, Jeremiah took the note. "Seth. His name is Seth."

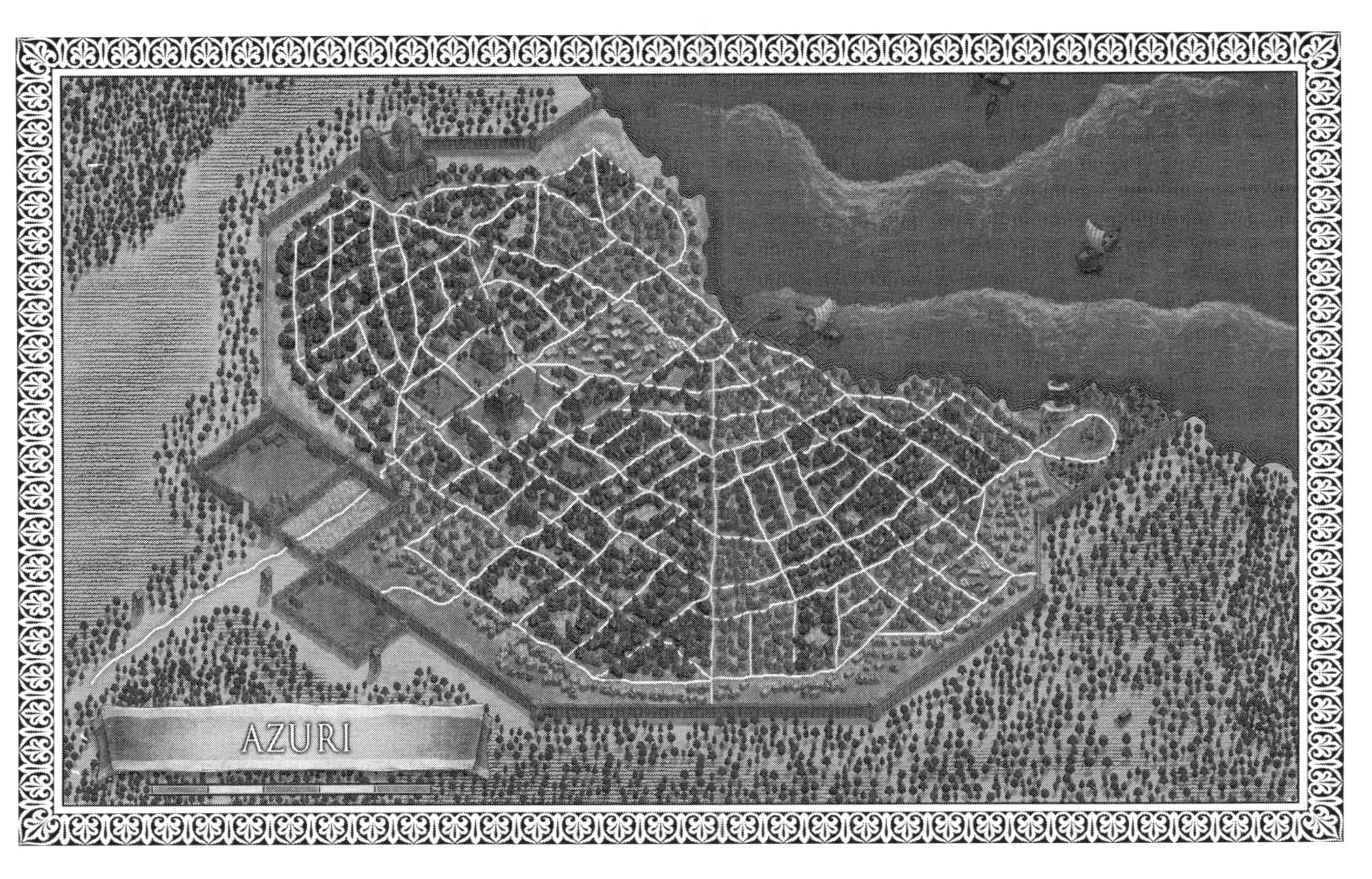

AZURI

The First Movement

ONE

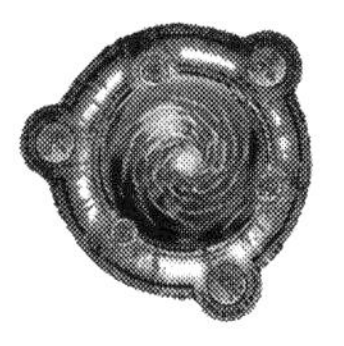

THE MAN IN WHITE

Year 215 SA

Tele focused on the outcropping ahead as her father's last words reverberated through the chambers of her mind. Phantoms of dancing flames and cold, ringing steel haunted the edges of her perception like a mirage amidst the wilds of the desert.

"*You must keep the Covenant safe. Find the true Wizard and deliver it to him! Run, my child! Run!*"

She had to keep moving. She had to escape the Deseran Dominion.

As Tele reached the towering rocks, she allowed her legs to buckle under the shade. Several stone columns stood alone in the immeasurable deposit of sand. Sides worn smooth from ages of erosion, their gray and white hues mingled in layers stacked skyward.

She paused for a moment, unsure if exhaustion had gotten to her head or if she had truly reached her goal. Her perception of time warped against the dreary landscape. The blinding light of the arcing sun served as her only measure of progress.

She rested her back against a column of stone, then leaned forward to remove her pack. Tele swept through its contents, reassuring herself that she hadn't left anything behind since her last inventory. It was an unlikely event, but she couldn't be too careful.

Inside the pack, a faded, gray cloth held the only food she had. She'd been mindful to ration it wisely but feared that eating now would intensify her thirst, and she was already two days dry. At least the pack was lighter without her water reserves.

In her frantic rush to flee, she'd had no time to pack for her long journey. Tele narrowly escaped with her pack and her life. But spending her existence on guard meant having an escape plan. Her rucksack always held the essentials for a quick getaway: water, wafers, a few herbs, some basic tools, and her father's maps. Some of the books her parents had protected for generations were also among her provisions. Their sacred secrets now belonged to her.

She pulled out her favorite—a thick, leather volume with embossed lettering that read: *Small Life*. She opened the cover and removed the parchment inside. Folded over twice and yellow with age, the map was the first one her father had made of the land. She unfolded the map and studied it. The next refuge was a few hours southeast.

Tele gauged an hour to sunset before heading out again. She didn't want to start out too early and risk more of the sun's unrelenting rays. Conversely, she dared not face a night's travel. The setting sun brought a cold as savage as the daytime heat, and she needed time to make camp before the chill.

There were but a few hours near dawn and dusk when travel was safe in the Dominion Desert. Until just a few hours past, she'd kept to that schedule. And she would have continued with it if she hadn't seen … Well, she *thought* she'd seen a Thief-Taker. But now that she thought back to the moment, she couldn't be sure. Perhaps her mind had begun to deceive her.

Her march did well to conserve energy and nourishment, but with a sun-parched canteen, delirium would soon take her completely. As her father had taught her, she used the width of her fingers as a measure of distance. Five fingers spanned where she thought she was and where she and her family had last charted water, meaning five days lay between her position and the next reservoir. Five more days of madness.

Thirty, perhaps forty more days yet, would pass before Tele would reach the desert's edge. And then she'd have to face the dangers of the Shadow Peaks—a place she knew little about—before she could cross into the kingdom of Hzorah. She pushed forward nonetheless, refusing to die without at least attempting to reach freedom.

Beyond Desera's borders existed the hope of finding the Wizard.

She silenced the voice of logistical reason that warned against holding to the illusion of survival. That she would not live to see freedom. That the desert would be her grave.

Delirium from malnutrition and intense heat, Tele thought. *The perfect excuse for irrational hope.*

A sudden gust snatched the map from her hand and cast it into a wild, tumbling flight. The parchment soared high into the air and out of her reach before plunging into a low glide across the ground. Tele threw herself into the effort of catching it. Sudden twists in the wind's heading led to her own clumsy changes in direction. Her swift reactions kicked up clouds of sand that pursued in her wake. The unpredictable dance caught her in misstep several times over before she plucked the map from the sky.

Tele allowed herself a deep breath after retrieving the parchment. She checked it over, ensuring the wind had not carried the ink away with it. Satisfied the map had not been defiled, she folded it once again and placed it in her right trouser pocket.

Another gust tore across the land. Tele shielded her eyes from the fine grains of sand. Her headscarf and loose ends of fabric flapped in accordance. Her back to the wind, she let an arm down to check for a glimpse of the outcropping. If she could find her way back to it, she would be better armed to combat the debris.

Sand hung in the dry air, whirling with the dying current. She stood submerged in the plumes, the sun casting shafts of glimmering light where dust punctuated its cascade. As the sand began to settle, she straightened and brushed at the dust that clung to her tan shirt sleeves. When the outcropping failed to appear before her, she turned to scan for her lost shelter.

A quarter-turn stopped her cold.

In the distance, a man rode toward her on a dappled mare. At least she thought it was a man. Thief-Takers were always men. Draped in white robes, the lone rider swayed with the animal's measured trot.

Cursing her fortune, she continued the search for her rock. As the sand settled, she found the rock and darted in its direction. She quickly scooped up her pack and stuffed the book back inside. In the same motion, Tele swung her pack over her shoulders and turned to face the approaching stranger.

Only his eyes were exposed, golden and gazing intently at her. He closed in, not much more than one hundred paces away. She saw no chance of escape. She could only stand and fight. Without conscious thought, her hand reached for the knife at her belt.

She wasn't sure if the man intended to harm her, but after what had occurred only ten days ago, she held little trust for a stranger in the middle of no-man's-land. Surely he intended to finish the Dominion's deed. Why else would he be making such an odd trek?

Her hunters were relentless and always on the lookout, but they had long ago given up sweeping the land in search of her family. The Thief-Takers who were commissioned to find those like her had many eyes within Desera's borders. Knowing that it was just a matter of time before each fugitive was found out, they sat like perched vultures, waiting for their chance to collect their bounty.

What she couldn't figure out was how this hunter had found her. Well-schooled in the art of evasion, she'd been careful to cover her tracks the entirety of her journey and had only stopped yesterday. Tele knew better than to risk leaving a trail that might not be distorted by the wind. She had crossed dunes with faces that saw little interaction with the common direction of airflow. It slowed her to put so much effort into hiding her path in the sand, but she had had to afford herself the endeavor.

It seemed now that it had all been for nothing.

The horse and rider stopped a few feet in front of her. His eyes, a light golden hue, glowed like nothing she'd seen before. Tele had never encountered someone with an eye color that gave the illusion of luminescence. But she knew what he was.

A seer. That was truly unexpected.

Robes still rippling in the now gentle breeze, his odd calm gave her pause. She didn't hold the element of surprise and often surprise made the difference between winning and losing. At least she had a weapon.

Tele tightened her knife grip.

"I was sent for you," he said. His voice, though slightly muffled through his headpiece, gave no sign of threat. His tones were deep and almost comforting ... Perhaps deceptively so.

"I know," she rasped.

Tele knew better than to let herself be sweet-talked into putting one foot in her grave. She would not give him the satisfaction of an easy capture or kill. She did not admit defeat, but rather, she'd issued a challenge.

"I'm not here to bring trouble," he said, turning his attention to his mare. He whispered a few comforting words to the horse and gave her a gentle pat. Then he dismounted and untied a bag from his mount.

Tele drew her knife. "Stay back. Any closer and I will *make* trouble."

Her blade glinted in the sunlight. She held it between herself and the threat. He turned, the bag already free, and his hands outstretched in clear view.

"Drop it," she said, her eyes unwavering.

He tossed the bag to her feet. It landed with a slosh and displaced a small cloud of sand. Tele took a reflexive step backward. Her knife still raised defensively, she took a quick glance at it: a waterskin.

"Drink," he said evenly. "You look like you need it."

"What's this about?"

"It's water. And you look like you're about to collapse."

Tele looked again at the waterskin that lay at her feet. She desperately needed water, but she couldn't be sure if this was his means of getting an easy capture. The skin's contents could be poisoned.

"You think I'm a fool, don't you? I won't give myself up that easily."

"I don't want to hurt you," the man said, raising his hands to show them weaponless. "I'm here to help you."

"Help me?" Tele glared at him. "I know who you are. You're here to collect your bounty."

"I'm no Thief-Taker. My name is Navid." He tapped his sleeve. "I'm wearing white, and I have no markings to show which Thief-Taker house I represent."

Tele didn't budge. It could be a trick. But she'd never seen a Thief-Taker in white or unmarked. Her brother, Gib, told her that the Thief-Takers of Almirav always showed their markings. Red armbands. It was a symbol of honor among the Deseran bounty hunters, and a fair warning so that their victims died with an understanding of their fate.

"How do I know you don't intend to kill me?"

"I guess you don't," Navid said, "but I can help you. Please, come with me if you wish to escape."

Tele searched Navid's eyes for any hint of deception. She was still unsure of his allegiance. How could he appear like a spirit sent from Desolate and expect her to trust him? Even if Navid truly did come in peace, the fact that he'd found her at all still bothered her. If he was able to track her, certainly her pursuers would be able to as well.

And this was a seer. Tele had limited knowledge about his rare kind, but if he was half the warrior the stories portrayed seers to be, she didn't have a chance to beat him.

But she *could* use him. That's what Gib would do. Or at

least he'd try. If he carried her back to the nearest town, she'd at least have an opportunity to steal a few supplies and make a prepared run for the Deseran border.

This was a chance at survival. A *real* chance.

Tele bent down and retrieved the waterskin, but her eyes never left Navid's, nor did she lower her knife. She tossed it back to his feet. "You first."

With a hint of a smile in his eyes, Navid reached down and picked it up. He pulled down his mouth guard just enough to allow a short stream of water to pour into his mouth, then wiped his chin before replacing the fabric.

He held the skin back out at arm's length, offering it to her. Tele slowly stepped forward and snatched the skin from his grip. He didn't move to grab her, but she backed away again anyway, her knife raised all the while.

She took a slow drink. Warm water trickled into her mouth, not the cool drink she'd wished for, but it didn't taste of taint, either. The eyes of the man in white glowed anew at the acceptance of his gift.

She handed the skin back to him. "Let's go, then."

Tele watched as Navid turned back to his mare. After searching for a moment, he produced a small blood-red book with black lettering that Tele couldn't make out before it edged from her sight.

He walked a few steps forward with the book in his right hand and the waterskin in his left. He held the book high and began a slow, rhythmic chant. The mare gave a skittish shuffle and an alarmed whinny, personifying her own nerves.

In dark contrast to his white robes, a large cloud of sand churned in the distance. It rolled toward them, consuming dunes and swelling into the heavens. Lightning struck, and a weeping howl ushered more loose sand. Rapid gusts spirited past in traceable lines, diminishing the sun.

Tele pulled her headscarf tighter against her mouth and nose. The storms in the Dominion Desert could last for days in the height of summer. Even short-lived sandstorms could be violent. The intensity of the tempest about them was among the strongest she'd encountered and threatened to be the very worst as it was only just beginning to rage.

Tele stood frozen in place as a language impossible for Navid to have known flowed effortlessly from his lips. She couldn't believe it. How had this man learned the runes, and how had he gotten his hands on an Abbreviation?

Tele scanned the land ahead. There was no sign of shelter in sight and the dust had increased in bounds. Soon, she would be blinded by the impending fury.

I could run, Tele thought. *Find the nearest town and steal some supplies. He might even have some gold …*

She eyed the mare reluctantly. She wasn't fond of riding horseback and loathed the animal's continuous sway. She'd never ridden alone, but she was a fast learner. Horses were preferable to capture or death.

Tele gasped when the ground shook. Her balance shifted, and she fell face first into the burning sand. Tele wondered if it was all a dream, a hallucination—if she would open her eyes and wake against the gray and white pillars. She had been exhausted. This was the work of a raving mind starved of rest and nourishment and nothing more.

Tele opened her eyes. Nothing had changed.

Would a hallucinating mind be capable of this consistency?

Through the thickening sandstorm, she watched Navid pour thin streams of water from the skin to a spot before him. The earth's low-pitched rumble rattled Tele's insides, and she felt she might lose whatever bile was left in her stomach. Tele thought the world, angered by her escape of death, had now loosed its wrath and wanted to swallow her.

Navid's chant rose in pitch and speed while the earth's quake did alike in majestic chorus. With the book still held high above his head, he backed away a step. Then another. Then another, until he stood back at Tele's side. He secured the waterskin and caught the horse's reins flapping in the wind before he continued his retreat for a few more paces, the mare taking steps backward in time with him.

Every hair on Tele's body stood straight as a crash of lightning struck where Navid stood moments before. Bathed in blinding light and waves of pelting sand, she lost herself in the turmoil. She could neither see nor hear, but she could feel the heat of it. Tele fell to the ground. She shielded her head and silently prayed for deliverance.

In slow return, Tele's hearing restored, but the ground beneath her continued to vibrate. Face down against the ground, her whole body pulsed. She chanced a glance ahead to where the lightning had struck. Sand still raved in every direction, and the land dipped, forming a crater.

A hand touched Tele's shoulder when she rose to a knee. As if waiting for this moment of contact, the earthquake and savage wind subsided, and the sun reemerged. She shrugged off Navid's hand and continued to her feet. She fixed the bright-eyed madman with a cold glare.

"I'm sorry about the display," he said. "But it's over now."

The bolt's power had carved away the sand spanning fifteen or twenty feet wide with rivets of crystalline rings that radiated outward. Amid the once barren land—at the crater's center—stood a stone archway. It towered several heads taller than her and was as wide as it was tall. The half-circle arch was composed of thirteen large, dark gray stones and displayed an inscription where two sets of six stones met at its zenith.

The runes were in the tongue that Navid had spoken—an ancient language of magic.

Most curious of all was what the archway framed. She saw through to the desert beyond, but the image wavered like ripples on a pond. Sunlight glistened off its surface like a pool of water. She would have named it water if she didn't know better. Water didn't stand vertically in stark defiance to its tendency to flow. But archways also didn't appear where, before, nothing stood. And golden-eyed madmen didn't wander the desert haphazardly. The world had suddenly become an alien place.

"We have to enter." Navid's voice pulled Tele from her trance though his own gaze remained fixed on the archway before them. "The safety we seek lies beyond."

"Enter?" Tele asked. "If anything was the gateway to Desolate … this is it."

He looked at her. "I understand your reluctance, but it's completely safe. Out here though …" He waved his hand across the expanse of wilderness. "Out in this wasteland with whoever pursues you is not."

She couldn't deny that. At the moment, though, it appeared his version of safety involved phenomena that rivaled the great stories of old. Tele's gut screamed for her to turn away, pleaded for her to run until she found the border. But she knew death would find her first.

Only in life was there hope. Only in life could she carry out her father's final requests.

Navid guided the mare down into the pit of sand and to the inscribed side of the rock formation. He stopped short of stepping through the archway and turned to Tele, who hadn't moved.

He tipped his head. "We simply walk through here and on into safety." He gave a pat to the mare's rump. The horse trotted through the archway and disappeared into its shimmering surface. "You see?"

Tele stood in mute shock. She looked to the other side, expecting the horse to reappear. When it did not, she turned her slack-jawed expression back to Navid. "Is it … gone?"

His eyes twinkled. "She has left the wilderness, yes."

"That's impossible," she said. *None of this is possible.*

Her mind refused to accept Navid's defiance of the natural law that mysterious stone arches did not appear from lightning strikes. Perhaps this was something that Wizard Titan could do —but not Navid.

How? That was the question that she fought with. *How could this possibly be?*

"I know you don't understand," he said, "but I can answer your questions once we get to safety."

Without another word, Navid stepped through the archway. The shimmering surface rippled and parted to consume him. Then, he was gone.

And she was alone.

Tele closed the distance to the archway in a few seconds' time. She hadn't expected him to step through so quickly. Just as suddenly as he had appeared, he was gone. She stared at her image in the partially reflective, upright pool. It was truly a marvel. Nothing in all her years compared to what lay before her.

She placed a hand on the surface. It was neither hot nor cold, dry nor wet. The partition blackened under her touch. Darkness spread outward in every direction until it was entirely deep black. She pulled her hand back, and the darkness receded.

She backed away a step so that she could read the runes. "The Gateway."

This spell—all spells—belonged to Wizard Titan. Now that the Wizard had left their world behind, these spells should be useless. This one was different.

An Abbreviation linked to a spell that had a temporal trigger could, in theory, be constructed to remain stable in the Wizard's absence, but that still wouldn't explain how the seer had found it and what he intended to do with it—what he intended to do with her.

Further, it didn't explain how he'd learned to speak the ancient language of magic. She only had a passing understanding of the runes and could only read them as if they were her own language. She had no idea how to pronounce them in their true tongue.

How?

A new thought entered her mind. With Navid gone, she could simply leave. She didn't have the advantage of the horse, nor did she have the man's waterskin, but she wouldn't have to face what was on the other side of the portal. Tele didn't know if the seer would attempt to pursue her, but this was the best chance she had been given since his appearance.

Just five more days. Tele turned from the gateway. *Maybe less.*

She didn't have water, but the seer had given her one good drink. And now that the winds had settled, she might actually have a good night's rest before she set off again. And there was always the chance of finding a water-holding plant even though her father's map had no indication of water between here and the reservoir. He was but human. He could have overlooked that detail.

Delirium from malnutrition and intense heat: the perfect excuse for irrational hope.

Another man on horseback topped a nearby dune. The rider was dressed in dark robes with three red bands across the wrist, forearm and biceps. A red headpiece and the glimmer of polished steel completed his desert wear. A Thief-Taker of the Third House in Almirav dressed in the outfit worn when their bounty was all but theirs.

Catching sight of her, he charged forward.

Tele's breath caught. Uncertainty of Navid's affiliation with Thief-Takers had given her doubt, but she knew this man to truly be one. She would gamble doubt over certain death.

Her resolve established, Tele plunged into her own reflection.

TWO

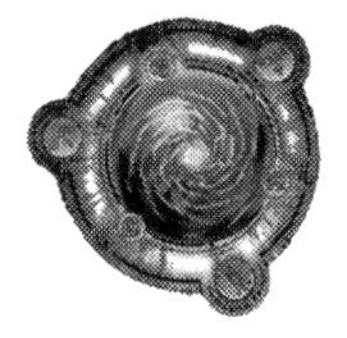

A CURSE

Expecting to feel the familiar rush of water around her body, she found only darkness. Her feet did not feel ground pushing back against her. Her ears could no longer hear the rush of desert air. Thoughts evaded her mental grasp as time came to a standstill.

She merely existed, suspended in nothingness.

Then, Tele saw what looked to be a star flickering in the distance. The pulsating beacon grew larger until it enveloped her. Light polluted her solace. In concert, her hearing restored with a low hum sweeping to a high-pitched ring. Ground formed beneath her feet as her eyes regained focus.

Trees. She saw trees. Tele spun around in a wild effort to regain her heading. An unexpected loss of equilibrium let gravity win, and she fell to the ground.

"Easy now," Navid said, offering her a hand up. "The gateway can be disorienting."

With Navid's assistance, Tele found her way to a sitting position on a forest floor. Navid settled beside her. She turned back to look at the portal, but it was gone. It was as if they'd fallen back into the world through an invisible hole.

"Trees ..." Tele said. "I don't believe it ... Where am I?"

"About fifty days south," he replied. "We are in the Borderland forests."

Fifty days south? Impossible.

Tele gaped at towering oaks and the grassy forest floor. She was certainly no longer in the Deseran wilderness—of that her senses could not argue—but fifty days south? That would place them out of Desera completely and near Hzorah. Her mind failed to swallow the unimaginable state she found herself in. She had never been outside of the Deseran Dominion and now she was suddenly beyond its reach?

Tele scanned her surroundings once more. They sat in a clearing encircled by forest oak. In its center lay a small fire pit littered with ash and a fresh stack of wood beside it. Winter's last breath chilled the air, carrying the smell of new growth and heralding spring's slow approach.

She looked to the sun. Though partially obstructed by the forest canopy, it had not moved since they'd left the Dominion Desert. *Incredible,* Tele thought. *Either the spell transports the caster instantaneously, or it warps the caster's perception of time to such an extent that fifty days feels like an instant.*

"I'm relieved that you came with me," Navid said as he loosened and removed his headpiece. The white guise pulled back to reveal a smile that glowed as brightly as his eyes. Black hair, curling at the ends, fell into place over a sharp jaw and olive skin. He was much younger than she had envisioned. A handsome face that matched her own age. "And I owe you quite the explanation."

"I'd say so," Tele said.

"You're probably hungry," he said and stood. "I tried my hand at catching dinner. Let me check the trap. I'll explain everything I can afterward."

It transports the caster instantaneously, she resolved. *Otherwise, whatever he may have tried to catch in his snare would have rotted before we arrived.*

Navid smiled warmly at her before he disappeared into the trees. The silence following his departure allowed Tele a new rush of bewilderment. She shut her eyes to the world around her.

This was all too overwhelming. The chanting, the wild energy, the gateway marked with the ancient language and its ability to carry them fifty days south in an instant … Her father's tales had come to life. She hadn't doubted that his words were true, but the Wizard had disappeared two centuries ago. Magic was supposed to be impossible.

Tele recalled everything she could about the great Wizard. None of it mentioned gleaming golden eyes. But eyes like Navid's were the distinguishing feature among seers. The wizard was not a seer. No, this was not Wizard Titan.

He'd said his name was Navid.

He could be lying about that, Tele reminded herself. Thief-Takers were cunning, but he didn't wear their markings, and if he was a Thief-Taker, he'd taken her far from Janamah—Desera's city at the edge of the desert. That was the home of Prophet Tristan.

The man who'd killed her family.

She remembered her father's last words to her. They rang with frightening clarity as if she were once again standing before the flames that separated them. The sensation of smoke filling her lungs as she scrambled away into the darkness nearly made her choke again.

"*You must keep the Covenant safe. Find the true Wizard and deliver it to him! Run, my child! Run!*"

This still could all be a ploy. A clever—if not over-elaborate—trick devised by the Thief-Takers to capture her. Even if this Navid didn't appear to be anything like the Thief-Takers she'd encountered before, perhaps they'd somehow placed a seer in their employ to trick her.

Tele stood and scanned the area before approaching and placing a hand on one of the trees. She studied it, recalling her father's notes. *A tapered malt tree, found only in the forests south of the Shadow Peaks.*

The tree was evidence that they were indeed beyond the reaches of the Dominion. If they meant to trick her, they would usher her closer to Prophet Tristan, not entirely outside of his domain. And it didn't seem likely that they would transplant a forest's worth of trees just to capture one rogue Keeper.

The rustling of forest brush interrupted Tele's thoughts, and she straightened at Navid's return. He wore a look of self-satisfaction and carried a large rabbit by the ears in one hand and, in the other, a wire, likely used as a snare. After placing his catch on the ground, he set to preparing the rabbit.

It's unlikely that he is a Thief-Taker, Tele thought, *but he could still be a threat.*

A seer's power was to be feared. She had little chance of survival if it came to a fight. She'd have to avoid direct, physical confrontation and keep what she knew about seers secret. As long as he underestimated her, she had an opening.

Tele watched him struggle with his catch for a moment before deciding to aim for the most direct line of questioning. "How did you perform such sorcery? How did you find me in the middle of a desert? And if you're not out for bounty, what are you after?"

Navid looked surprised and vaguely amused at her rapid string of questions. His gaze turned into a soft smile, then he rose from his task and crossed to his mare. "Well," he began as he freed his saddlebags and rummaged through his belongings. "I'm no Wizard if that's what you're thinking."

She'd already eliminated that possibility, but she had to play the imbecile. "Then what are you?"

"I'm here to help you," Navid continued. "The magic you saw wasn't something I made, but a preserved spell given to me from the prophets who sent me to find you."

"Prophets?" Tele's stomach tightened. "Prophet Tristan sent you to collect me?"

"No. Not Prophet Tristan," Navid said, waving a hand as if to ward off her concerns. "The prophets in the lands outside of the Deseran Dominion. The lands that still work together. They have foreseen Desera bringing war. And they think you can help to thwart the Dominion's threat to the world."

"And how is it that *I'm* to help?"

"I don't know." He fetched a long staff and knife from his saddlebags to skin and gut his catch. "I was sent to retrieve. I was not told why you're needed or your place in this. I was only told to look for you in the Dominion Desert. When I found you, I was instructed that you must come with me of your own accord. I couldn't force you. If I did, existence would fade to Desolate, and the war would be lost before it began."

Tele had no words. While she didn't trust that the prophets outside of Desera were less of a threat than Prophet Tristan, she had at least escaped what was sure to be her final hour. She didn't care about their war, but she did have her father's mandate—the mandate that the Keepers of the Covenant had carried since Wizard Titan had left many years ago. That is what she had to do: find Wizard Titan.

"Are you a seer?" she asked, changing tact.

Navid paused to catch her eye. "I am."

"Is that how you found me, then? You saw me in a vision?"

"Visions didn't aid my search." Navid crossed back to the fire pit and struck a flint stone that he'd pulled from a garment pocket. "I wasn't sure how long it would take to find you, but you seemed to walk right to me."

Tele's question was intended to keep him ignorant of just how much she knew. She knew seers to have talents similar to prophets. It was an ability that was honed for combat rather than premonitions—not visions exactly, but instincts that gave them the ability to intuit what was most advantageous to their immediate survival.

"Is that where you plan to take me then? To these prophets?" Tele asked. "They want to meet me?"

"Yes."

"Why?"

"I'm not entirely certain," Navid said, his attention fixed on his work. "I know that's not the most comforting answer, but it is the most truthful answer I can give. I could guess at their intentions, but—"

"Guess then," Tele said.

He looked at her. "I would guess that they want to protect

you. There are rumors and threats of war about, and they believe that you are somehow connected to it all. But that is only a guess."

Tele wasn't sure that she had anything to do with a war, but prophets differed greatly from seers. While Navid's abilities would be honed for combat, prophets were honed for strategy. Like seers, they did not have visions but a vast capacity for intuition. Prophets understood the flow of time in ways that allowed them to change the fate of nations if they were so inclined.

When sparks caught fire to brush, the seer patiently nursed the hearth with air until it surged with life. He held the staff of rabbit over the fire.

"That book," Tele said. "It was magic. It made that portal. Why bring me here? Why not use it to bring us straight to the prophets?"

"I don't know much about the spells the book contains," Navid said. "I can't even read it. It's in some strange, dead tongue. I only needed to know the key phrases to make it work." He glanced upward. "This is as close as it will let the user get to Caldor."

Most definitely an Abbreviation, Tele thought, but it was a spell she couldn't begin to wrap her head around. The underlying spell forms needed to create magic like the gateway could change everything. Her parents had told her that Wizard Titan had left the world because he felt his magic would cause terrible events in the wrong hands. Maybe he was right. This could certainly be dangerous.

She resisted the temptation to ask the seer to allow her to see the Abbreviation—to touch it. So much of her parents' work had been in service of Wizard Titan and the advancement of magic. She was almost jealous that this man had it in his care.

Tele turned back to the fire. Before her family was murdered, she'd loved fire; how it danced to its own rhythm, bringing warmth and light when everything around her seemed cold and dark. Now, the flames drew out nightmares. She sat, weighing his words, losing herself in flame and steel.

Perhaps this was her chance after all. Navid might be more than a means to an end and a handsome face. If anyone could aid her search for the Wizard, it would be a prophet.

But could she trust the prophets? *They* were the reason her family had journeyed to Desera all those years ago in the first place. After Wizard Titan had disappeared, it wasn't long before the prophets forced the Keepers to disband.

Prophet Tristan wanted her dead. What did these prophets want?

"Here, eat," Navid said, pulling her from her inner thoughts.

She accepted his offering with a forced smile. She ate slowly, savoring the meal. It was the first real meal she had had in days.

"How is it?" Navid asked with a small smile.

"Terrible."

Navid's smile grew large before he took a taste himself. It morphed to a frown of disgust as he chewed.

They ate without speaking. Only the slow crackle of flames and the evening songs of forest birds filled the silence.

When they finished their meals, Navid set to putting his stick away and grooming his mare. He whispered soft words to her and gave gentle pats before rejoining Tele by the fire. He sat quietly, watching the fire and occasionally poking at the burning wood with a long stick.

"What did you steal?" Navid asked.

Tele looked up. "What?"

"You were running from someone. I assume you thought I was a Thief-Taker because you stole something from someone important." He met her eyes. "Is this true?"

"In a way, yes." Tele fixed him with a look that said she didn't intend to say more.

Navid changed course. "Where is your family?"

"Dead."

Navid looked away. "I'm sorry."

Silence reignited.

Tele only had nightmares. Dreams rarely came, but when they did, they were never pleasant. Since childhood, she'd awaken to cold sweats from threats of larger-than-life desert snakes spitting blacker-than-black venom or desert traders stealing her away to slavery in the Bamilee Plain. After many years, Tele considered the nightmares a blessing—an ever-present admonition to stay on guard.

Her sleep pattern already compromised since her flight from the Thief-Takers, Tele insisted on taking the first watch. And though Navid was a seer, she continued her watch through the night. Better she trust herself to the task than a stranger.

Daylight came, and they prepared to leave. When Navid offered her a ride with him on his mare, Tele refused. He offered her a solo ride, too, but Tele had no intention of riding the animal. The route they traversed was smooth and the morning air kept her cool despite the sun's warm rays. And though she'd gotten no sleep whatsoever, the nervous excitement of walking in a new world kept her awake.

"Let me at least carry your pack," he offered.

"No," Tele returned. She didn't intend to sound so cold, but her books were too valuable to be trusted to anyone.

The path twisted with the land, leading into thicker woods. Fallen trees and brush littered their path, remnants from winter's withdrawal, but eventually the road opened to a broader route with less debris. The open path lent less resistance to the rising breeze, and for the first time in a long while, Tele inhaled the fresh air without concern that she might breathe in the desert's dust.

She heard calls from birds and insects that didn't exist in the Dominion Desert and smelled all manner of exotic scents. Some were pleasant, like the white plumes of the Hzorah Acrid, and some foul, like a smell that Navid told her was a skunk. She wasn't completely ignorant of the life forms outside of Desera and recognized many plants that were sketched in her books. Many she didn't recognize, but she hadn't expected to know them all.

Her father had once told her that the number of existing life forms was infinite. He had smiled and said that, of course, this was impossible, but for all practical purposes, it was true. He had worked to catalog many of these creatures, but the more he managed to document, the more he found. His data truly seemed to grow without limit. Most of that information was now lost to flame, save what Tele carried in both her pack and in her mind.

Tele had learned and remembered almost all of her forefathers' work, and she did not forget easily. Her family had told her that her talent for retaining information was unusual. It didn't seem special to her, but her father assured her that her mind worked quite differently than his.

She worked to absorb all she saw in the Borderlands in its true splendor. She would remember it and later record it. Just like her mother and father.

Navid made good on his promise of water not long after they left. What he described as a stream was more like a river. Tele hadn't seen this much flowing water all in one place in nearly three years. It was wide enough that the route had an old wooden bridge spanning across the bend where moss-covered rocks protruded like a misaligned backbone. Vines twisted along the bridge, showing its age and lack of upkeep. Navid stopped before the mouth of the bridge and dismounted.

"I'm going to bathe," he said, grabbing a bundle from the mare's saddle. "Get the itch of sand off of me."

It was a reasonable decision. Tele knew how sand slipped into places you wouldn't expect. Even spending her childhood in the wasteland didn't make the sensation any more comfortable. She felt the itch as well.

Navid pointed to one side of the river bend. "I'll head over there. You can stay on this side and wash if you'd like."

She removed her pack and carefully placed it on a flat rock

that appeared to have been positioned there for this very purpose, and then looked to make sure Navid had cleared the bridge before removing her garments. When she was fully unclothed, she whipped her clothes in the air to loosen the sand, then placed them beside her pack.

Tele dipped a toe into the crystal-clear water and found it just cool enough to be refreshing. She held her breath, then sank into the water. Sand and sweat that had layered on her skin and in her hair loosened and streamed into the distance with the river's perpetual voyage into the unknown. Resurfacing, she allowed herself to bask in the warm morning light.

"Most people gape at large cities, not forests," Navid said from the other side of the bridge. "You're the first person I've met that finds this at all interesting."

Tele tensed, startled that he'd taken this opportunity to talk to her. She forced herself to relax. Calm composure always gave one better odds than fearful agitation. "I've lived most of my life in barren lands, traveling between smaller towns and villages. I've never been in a forest before."

"A nomad?"

"Of sorts."

"Seems odd for someone to live that kind of life in such extreme conditions," Navid said between light splashes of water.

Tele redirected the topic. "And you? You grew up in a forest?"

"No, but I have seen all of what I thought worth seeing," Navid said with a chuckle.

"That so? I'm not sure that anything could be more beautiful. So much life and color and—"

She paused when Navid unexpectedly flashed into view. She'd allowed herself to drift too far. Water fell over his broad chest, and his wet hair clung to a strong jawline and neck.

"Bugs and bears," Navid said, swatting at a fly.

"Yes." Tele turned around as embarrassment warmed her skin. She moved back out of the line of sight. "But all these things live in balance. 'A beautiful web, ever-growing, and spawning more beauty.'"

Tele surprised herself by quoting her texts. Words that, after many years, had grown hollow and void of meaning for her. But after seeing the Borderlands in person, they were more meaningful than ever.

"I see your point," Navid said. "But I'd be lying if I said I preferred this place."

"Where are you from?" Tele asked. She realized she knew nothing about him other than that he was a seer, and he was unreasonably toned for someone who could barely skin a rabbit.

"I was born in the small city of Goil in South Hzorah, near Dunham Lake. Far away from here," Navid said. "After my father became aware of my … abilities, I was sent to Caldor. There, I spent the rest of my childhood. I still live there today."

Tele recognized the last of the places. "Caldor? The trade city?"

"That's right," Navid said. "Seers make people uneasy at best. Terrified, in many cases. The few of us who come into this world are sent to Caldor by agreement between the six lands. There, between the issues of international trade, law, and diplomacy, few people notice or care. And I suppose keeping to ourselves doesn't hurt, either."

Tele hadn't known Navid long, but, as far as she could tell, he didn't appear dangerous. He didn't carry a weapon—one that she could see, anyway—but from what she'd learned from her father, seers deserved to be feared.

"So, you live there alone?" she asked him.

"No. In Caldor, the oldest part of the city is called the Sanctuary Calviere. It's a place where the prophets meet to discuss what they've foreseen for the course of mankind. Seers live together at the Sanctuary and do what we can to pass the time until we are called."

Tele frowned. "Called? Called for what?"

"Duty. There are times when the prophets believe it is important that they … intervene directly."

"I don't understand." Tele's frown deepened, this time truly unsure. Her father had explained to her that seers were taken as children because of how dangerous they could be, but he hadn't said anything about them having any real duties.

Navid paused for a moment as if to find the right words. "Prophets are not rulers. They feel it's not their place to rule … At least, *most* prophets do."

Tele knew he was referring to Prophet Tristan, the High Priest of Desera, as the exception. The Deseran Dominion was ruled by the Creed—their religious order. The Creed was ruled by Prophet Tristan, thereby giving him the role of the people's ultimate authority. The Creed stood as the moral power that dictated the lives of all who lived within the Dominion's swath. To fall from the Creed's favor was to threaten the return of the Great Wizard—of Wizard Titan. The Dominion's prophet intended to see to the Wizard's return by personally leading his people to what he deemed to be righteousness and what Tele deemed to be madness. But even though there were distinct differences in how the Deseran Dominion and the rest of the world regarded their prophets, Tele wasn't sure that the rest of the world's prophets weren't also rulers, albeit in their own covert way.

"Prophets are consulted to help determine the best day to plant and harvest, or when rains and storms will come," Navid continued. "Or when and where disease and natural disasters will occur. But there are times when something specific must be done to avoid calamity. It may not always be clear why, but sometimes there are turning points in time that fountain possibility. Points where existence hinges on a few actions or reactions. It's a balancing act. A very dangerous one."

"What about seers?" Tele asked, feigning ignorance. "They're not the same as prophets, right? They're not used for this?"

Navid gazed forward again. "Seers are feared far more than prophets. In some cases, that fear is manifested in the form of reverence. Seers are cursed, our golden eyes mark us for all to know. This is why we're sent to Caldor where no land is responsible for us. The prophets can help us find our way through the ill hand that Desolate dealt us."

"Surely visions would be valuable to any kingdom. Why would they send you away? How is *that* a curse?"

Navid sighed as if explaining the woes of adulthood to a child. "Seers have been the center of every major war of ages past. Their abilities have destroyed countless innocent people. In order to maintain peace between lands, seers must be sent to Caldor so that no land might use such a weapon against another land. We are strictly forbidden to use our power. And the prophets help us learn to resist it."

"Your visions cause conflict?" Tele smiled to herself. "Do you go about telling others how they might die or the fortunes they will lose?"

"Prophets and seers do not view time in terms of visions. This is a common misconception. It is a sense, an intuition of what is to come. Prophets are valuable because they can see how time flows together for many people on large scales. Seers see how time flows on a small and stochastic level."

"I don't understand." She did, but she had been using most of her questions as an opportunity to gauge how much he would actually say. The best way for him to get the best of her would be to obscure what he knew.

Navid was silent for a time. "It's like … It's like this forest. You say that removing one type of creature might cause the forest to change irrevocably. Prophets might see a change like that coming. A seer would instead notice when an ant dies."

Tele frowned again. It was a terrible analogy. "What?"

"I'm sorry. It's very hard to explain."

Tele refrained from explaining it better herself and looked to where he would be if the bridge didn't separate them. "And my retrieval was worth the risk? Worth tipping the balance? Worth sending a seer into the outside?"

"That's not for me to decide," Navid said. "I'm getting out. Are you ready?"

Tele waded out of the water. "I am. I just need a moment to dry."

Tele squatted by the riverbank, allowing the sun to dry her. Fish that fled when she disturbed water during her bath returned. Tele watched them curiously, remembering the illustrations from her books and trying to spot one she could name, but saw none.

Her memory, though extraordinary, wasn't perfect. She'd taught herself various ways to retain information through mnemonic pattern games. It had taken her years to learn some of the methods she used. Some helped stitch together the abstract and the defined. Some discarded the extraneous from the important. These devices had become a game for her throughout her youth, a way of passing the hours of loneliness while her older brothers sought food and supplies or practiced forms with their father.

Her family's claim to a portion of the Keepers' knowledge meant that she and her brothers were responsible for a wealth of information—research and analysis gathered by generations, showing the natural world as elegant, turning on unvarying laws that yielded accurate predictions.

Tele quickly became proficient in the Keepers' knowledge that her family specialized in, relieving most of the burden from her brothers. Tele held no grudge for her father's lifelong dependence on her. It was more an honor than a burden.

She could still remember her father's voice as if he sat next to her: "If things were different, Tele, you would be very important to the world. Helping others where they can't help themselves. Providing insight to those who have none. Solving problems in the unique ways that only the true Wizard can. That's our role as Keepers of the Covenant."

Fed up with the chill of evaporation and unwilling to risk Navid returning to see her indecent, she dashed back to the rock holding her garments, her flight back doing more to dry her than her shivering squat. She redressed, then sat in the thick grass, watching the river slip and eddy between rocks before falling out of sight.

Tele examined her pack's contents, mentally checking off each item. Everything was in its place. The act was redundant, but it made her feel as if she was doing *something*. Anything to make everything right again.

She pulled out *Small Life*, opened the cover and read the first page for what had to be the thousandth time.

Small Life
The study and findings of Huvil Gavina
regarding living things unseen.
Chronicles: Year 176 SA -

She only wanted to see her father's handwriting once more. Huvil had been her grandfather's name and her father's name, but her father had named his sons Gib and Simon. Both were older than Tele by ten and five years, respectively.

She missed them all more than anything.

Her bath hadn't washed away her sorrow.

"Are you finished?" Navid's voice called from beyond the bridge and bend. "And dressed?"

Tele gave a start and snapped the book shut. Then, remembering the map in her pocket, she reopened the cover and replaced it inside. She tucked the book away inside her pack.

"I am," she called back and stood to watch his approach.

Navid returned, dressed in a new set of clothes. Brown boots, black trousers, and a dark shirt and cowl replaced his all-white robes. The outfit was not at all regal. Tele wasn't sure what the typical dress outside of Desera entailed, but she expected this was not what someone of importance would wear. The clothes didn't diminish his handsome features though. She wasn't sure anything could do that.

"Nice clothes," she said. He frowned and Tele added: "They look good on you." A poor recovery from what sounded like an insult.

Navid took it with grace. He smiled, kneeling down to refill the empty waterskins. "Your compliments flatter me."

She hid her heating face by making to gather her pack.

"Let me get that for you," he said, reaching for the pack himself.

"No!" Tele snatched the pack from his reach and swung it over her shoulders. She combed a stray wisp of brown hair back behind an ear, regaining her composure. "I'm capable of carrying my own things."

"I'm sorry," Navid said, taking a step back. "I didn't mean to imply that you … I'm sorry." Navid turned to his mare who was grazing on the long riverbank grass. He attached his pack to the saddle and led the horse to cross the bridge. "We have a long road ahead. If we continue on this road, we should reach Azuri in the morning where we can gather a few more supplies we'll need before we continue on."

Tele nodded—more to herself than for Navid. She had to continue on. She would learn to live without her family. The void left within her heart didn't need to be filled, it only needed to heal over. And she would be stronger for it in the end.

THREE

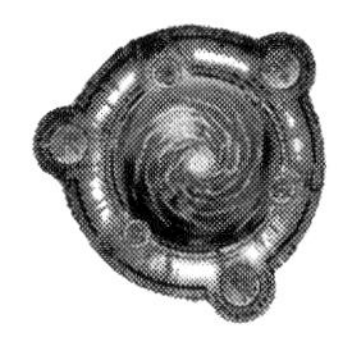

SUSTAINING A NATION

King Jeremiah led Wrathbane onto the long drawbridge. The great city's walls towered high like a mountain of smooth stone set in the mighty river Drunn. Just ahead, three men of the Crown's First League—his personal guard—rode in escort, and behind, another two dozen men followed.

He'd argued against the need for so many men, but General Yix had convinced him that there were enough dangerous men about these days that nearly half of the First League should accompany him to Caldor.

It doesn't have to be this way, a part of him said. *If you'd just take up the Crown Sabre again, you wouldn't need anyone to protect you. Is this what you are now? Is this what you want to be?*

Jeremiah shrugged away the thought. It'd been fifteen years since he'd used the Crown Sabre—fifteen years of peace since the Dominion was driven from their land. If traveling with an escort was what was required to avoid risking all of that, he was willing to do it. Sometimes, the liberty of the powerful must be restrained to bring liberty to all.

The entire journey had taken place on the Crown's riverboats. There was little to no chance of highwaymen, and unless the pirates of the Crehn Isles had suddenly fancied the smaller, riskier exploits of inland river trade, they should have been safe. However, *should be* safe was hardly enough for General Yix. It was hardly enough for any of the First League. Jeremiah only had himself to blame for that. He'd hand-picked every single First League officer personally, and it would seem that he'd outdone himself.

The Caldor gatekeepers bowed as he passed under the shadow of the thick walls. Lanterns suspended from the half-circle gateway lit the cobblestone before them. The city's active buzz reverberated through the gate's tunnel. As they crossed into Caldor's western courtyard, the smell of roasting chicken and potatoes washed over him right as the light bathed them with early spring's subtle warmth. The gate's path opened to a broad avenue, and Prophet Davin and General Yix joined their king to his left and right, respectively.

"Is it possible to ever get used to the sight of this place?" General Yix said, half to himself.

"The awe fades after several weeks within the catacombs," Prophet Davin said. "But as soon as you forget the marvel, you emerge, and your breath is taken again."

"I don't think there's a place more beautiful than the Crown City," General Yix said. "It's my home, and I have enough pride in it for all of us, but *this* place …" He nodded to the rows of mountain-high towers, each challenging the impressiveness of the last. "This place is altogether different."

"The Hzorah Crown City is a city risen by the hands of man," Prophet Davin said. "But Caldor is one risen by the hands of magic."

General Yix shuddered. "Leave it to you, Prophet, to spoil the wine."

Jeremiah chuckled at his men's banter. "Drink up. Even this beauty is worthy of your attention, magic or not."

"Have you decided on how to approach the Ghayan Emperor, Your Majesty?" Prophet Davin asked. "I'm fairly confident that Roanne and Sulahn will be easy to persuade, but Ghaya has a history of being … undiplomatic."

Yix grunted. "Undiplomatic? Looger bastards, more like."

"I haven't," Jeremiah said.

Prophet Davin looked ahead as they passed onto a broad avenue flooded with Caldor citizens. "I still say you ask for supply support rather than ask them to fight. I foresee a more favorable outcome in that."

King Jeremiah nodded. "Even without your foresight, it seems the best solution. I can't see them lifting a sword to help protect us. To them, this isn't their affair."

"Looger bastards," General Yix mumbled again. "The lot of them."

"Even so," Prophet Davin said. "The chances of them agreeing to support you with supplies are almost as slim. Sustaining a nation within the Ghayan reaches is more than a challenge. They have their hands full, and little to spare without a fair trade."

"They'll find themselves in a much more terrible position without Hzorah as a trade partner," Jeremiah said.

"A trade embargo?" Prophet Davin raised his eyebrows. "You plan to give them an ultimatum?"

"Anything short of a threat falls on deaf ears with those ones," General Yix said.

"I don't intend to," Jeremiah said. "Merely a statement of the inevitable. A war of the magnitude we're expecting would cause a period of resource strain and decline."

"And Armoth?" Prophet Davin asked. "Queen Frey is a force of her own."

"Hzorah and Armoth have a strong relationship," Jeremiah said. "Armoth depends on our stability even more than Ghaya."

"That won't necessarily mean she will send her troops in to support *you*, Your Majesty," Prophet Davin said.

Shifting in his saddle, he met the prophet's eyes. He'd seen that look on a number of occasions. Though the Caldor Convention for Peace had forged an era of relative security and prosperity between the dominant lands in the known world, that security was transactional rather than rooted in trust and respect earned through good faith. When Jeremiah said that Hzorah and Armoth had a "strong relationship," Prophet Davin heard: "Armoth will do what they can to preserve their interests."

It was a cynical outlook on things. When given the chance, Jeremiah preferred to believe that many of his constituents acted out of honor. And while their decisions weren't always in *his* best interest, they would do their best to protect the people that the Deseran Dominion threatened.

Jeremiah tore his gaze away from Prophet Davin's to watch the people of Caldor churn about, trading and traveling, moving massive carts of goods from gargantuan store house to store house. The city was a refuge for the broken. If a man dared leave his homeland to find new opportunities, they might inevitably end up here—the great bottleneck of trade. It was thrilling to see a city so alive with commerce and opportunity.

"Your Majesty!" a small voice called.

Jeremiah looked down to see a young girl who'd somehow snaked her way into the procession. She was a Ghayan child and couldn't have seen more than ten years. Her long, auburn hair flowed over an ankle-length, off-white dress that was stained and tattered at the fringes.

A First League officer dismounted and cut her off from his King. "Back. Out of the way, girl!"

Frightened, the child fell back a step. Her eyes shot to the soldier's sword, and she stood petrified.

"Go on, then!" the officer growled.

King Jeremiah dismounted and said, "She's just a child."

"Even a child can be used for evil, Your Majesty," General Yix called from behind.

Jeremiah looked the child over, hesitating. Over the years, there had been several attempts to assassinate him, many of which were under the guise of a victim in distress. On one occasion, during a palace ball he'd attended, a woman tried to lure him into taking her to his bed. Her insistence caught the eye of his guard, and an officer found a knife she'd planned to slip into his back when she had him alone.

It was impossible for a leader to have the full support of a people without any question. Jeremiah wanted to believe the assassins were simply ill, or misinformed, or not informed at all. More often than not, though, it wasn't that they felt hurt by *him*. It was because they still held on to the Dominion's Creed—a religion that rejected his claim to the throne. How could any citizen of Hzorah remain loyal to the Creed after what they had done to their people?

But this child … This child was not a killer.

I have to believe that, Love.

Jeremiah knelt down and smiled at the little girl. "Yes, child?"

"My mother … My mother is sick and needs help."

"I'm not a healer," King Jeremiah said. "Has your mother consulted a healer?"

"Consulted?"

"Visited," Jeremiah smiled reassuringly. "Has she seen a healer?"

The girl shook her head. "We don't have the money."

"Where is your father?" Jeremiah asked. "Is he near?"

The girl didn't respond. She stared at him as if she didn't understand the question. Her eyes welled with tears of fear and confusion. Jeremiah turned to General Yix, who shrugged.

Jeremiah turned back to the girl. "What's your name, child?"

"Emelisse."

"And your mother's name?"

"Sara."

It was strange but not altogether unusual for the Ghayan child and her mother to have names of Hzorah origin. Jeremiah's language—the language the Dominion had forced onto the tribes under his domain—had become the widespread tongue of trade after the Caldor Convention was enacted. Most Ghayans did not change their names, but it wasn't uncommon in the trade city to change one's name to ease the transition into a less homogeneous society.

He gazed into the child's eyes and couldn't help but think of how hard it had been to raise his two boys without Esther.

And while they had become fine young men, it was more to the credit of Marium and Samuel than anything he had done. This child's mother didn't have the luxury of that kind of support.

King Jeremiah stood and pointed to five of the First League officers. "Take the girl back home and help her move her mother to the nearest healer. Inform the healer that I'll be paying for whatever costs her care requires."

The soldiers came forth and followed her back to her family's quarters. Jeremiah mounted his steed and nodded the procession forward. He looked to the street's sidelines and noticed that his arrival had caused many to stop what they were doing to watch in silence.

"You should have kept riding, Your Majesty," General Yix said.

"And leave her mother to die?" King Jeremiah asked.

"It's not because I want you to be cold, Your Majesty," Yix nodded toward the men and women who stood at the street's edge. "But you've opened yourself up to having more people try the same kind of stunt. One child isn't an issue. Dozens of men and women following her lead is."

"It's strange." King Jeremiah met the eyes of several idle observers, for the first time taking in what the people actually looked like since he'd arrived. "So many of them look at the very edge of poverty. Caldor must be the wealthiest city with the most opportunity in all the world."

"No matter how rich a city is," General Yix said, "fill it with the lazy, and you'll have the poor wherever you turn."

"It can't be as simple as that," Jeremiah said.

"It's not," Prophet Davin said. "But he's not entirely wrong. Last I checked, there were many guilds looking for craftsmen and apprentices."

Jeremiah frowned, watching a man in worn out clothing tap a cane near a bowl with two silver coins. "I'm just trying to figure out what could cause such a disproportion."

"Try not to think of it," Prophet Davin said. "There are

people here who are working on the problem. You need to stay focused on our objectives at hand."

Jeremiah didn't answer. Instead he looked forward to where, like a child pressing forth to draw its first breath of life, Sanctuary Calviere crowned from below the horizon. The beautiful white dome emerged like a pearl from the cityscape that birthed it, a stroke of purity amid an array of color.

Prophet Davin was right. He didn't have the capacity to take on the issues of a district he didn't have direct control over. And yet ... He couldn't help but feel he had some obligation to do something. Anything.

One thing at a time, Jeremiah thought. *Emelisse and Sara are all I can do today. When the war is won, and Hzorah is stable, I can turn to the concerns of the north.*

Jeremiah followed two First League officers into the Sanctuary's northern chamber room. Only two others followed—a welcome reduction in numbers.

Several prophets sat at the room's long table. Prophet Lilith from Armoth, alone without Queen Frey, sat quietly, listening intently to the prophets from Roanne and Sulahn in heated discussion, no doubt about what could be done to minimize their people's inadvertent contact. Roanne and Sulahn's councilmen interjected where they could fit a word in.

Jeremiah paused in reflex. He couldn't help but wonder if Sulahn's prophet and councilman carried the terrible plague that ravaged Sulahn into the room with them. It was not the reaction a king should have, but even he could admit his own irrational fear.

Leaving the First League guards at the door, he crossed to the table and took his seat. Prophet Davin sat to his left and slid several sheets of parchment over to him. Jeremiah allowed a quick glance at the talking points Prophet Davin had taken the liberty to record. That was the prophet's way. He took every opportunity to make sure Jeremiah had the leading advantage in the proceedings. However, it often made Jeremiah wonder if the prophet thought him an idiot, unable to carry out a proper meeting without his assistance.

King Jeremiah trusted Prophet Davin far more than his father had. He remembered his father cautioning him against giving the prophet's word too much credence. After all, it was Prophet Odus who led the Dominion into savage tyranny and Prophet Tristan who now threatened the peace of the new world. In the late King Gillan's eyes, all prophets had the same nature. Jeremiah didn't believe in that nonsense. A person should be judged by their own merits, and Prophet Davin had proven to be nothing if not loyal.

"There are more notes," Prophet Davin said, "but I don't think we need them just yet. Today's meeting will only be preliminary."

"Any word on the Ghayan Emperor's arrival?" Jeremiah asked. He stole a glance at the Ghayan Prophet, who sat quietly at the table, uninterested in engaging with the arguments just to the left of him.

"No word." Prophet Davin glanced over his shoulder as if he expected the door to swing open any minute. "At the last report, they hadn't even reached the city. I know we arrived later than we'd hoped, but their Emperor's tardiness is somewhat inexplicable. Their journey is downriver." He glanced to Queen Frey's seat. "The Queen should be here at any moment."

Jeremiah hardly had the opportunity to sit back in his chair before the door opened, and Queen Frey stepped into the room. She wore the traditional Armoth diplomatic outfit—a dress that appeared as though it started from the headpiece. It wrapped across her bosom and midriff in crisscrossing layers of blue and white silks. The dress flowed down to her ankles, ending just above the stilted footwear unique to Armothean women.

Her piercing ice-blue eyes caught his before a sportive smile lit her face. "My, is it hot in here. Don't you think, King Jeremiah? I don't think I will ever grow used to the oppressive heat of Caldor. It tempts one to remove more clothes than … fashionable."

Jeremiah dipped his head respectfully. He hated that she was the only woman that seemed to stir feelings of passion in him. There was something in her bearing that let everyone know how inaccessible she was, and perhaps that alone made her such a force of attraction. That, and the fact that she was painfully beautiful, an attribute that she was not unaware of.

"Dear, Jeremiah," Queen Frey said. "Bashful as ever. You must know by now that I don't bite, at least not when wearing this. Its cut is diplomatic."

Jeremiah forced himself to meet her eyes. "It never hurts to be cautious."

"Wise," she said, gliding to her seat just across from his own. "Have you ever heard the Armothean legend of Omaai and the Great White Wolf?"

"I have not," Jeremiah said.

"I'm no great storyteller," Queen Frey said, "but indulge me. Long ago, before there was an Armoth, our entire land was covered in ice, and the great white wolves were kings of the land. The only true rivals to the wolves were men. Every time a man saw a white wolf, he would try to kill it before it could carry away his wife's children. And that was the way it was: the white wolf hunted, and man fought them off.

"That is, until a brave young warrior girl by the name of Omaai came. Omaai was a special girl. It was said her very gaze could melt the heart of any man, and her touch could melt ice like fire. Though Omaai was as clever as any man, many men disregarded her as a true warrior.

"One day, while hunting for food, Omaai and a man who journeyed with her crossed paths with the king of the white wolves. Omaai warned her companion to disregard anything the wolf says as a lie, for the great white wolves cannot be trusted."

Jeremiah raised his eyebrows. "The wolves could talk?" When the Queen frowned at him for the interruption, Jeremiah added, "I'm sorry. Please continue."

"As the wolf king approached the camp, Omaai and her companion wielded their spears. 'Back!' they said. 'You have no business here. Back or we will slay you!'

"The wolf paused and said, 'There are many wolves who surround your camp. You have already lost. But I am willing to spare your lives if you answer correctly my riddle.'

"'Don't listen to him,' Omaai told her companion. 'Cast your spear into his side so that we will be rid of him.' But he did not listen. Instead, he entertained the wolf king's request. 'Tell me your riddle,' said he.

"The wolf king paced in the snow. His eyes gleamed, and he smiled a wicked smile. Then, he spoke. 'What is a warrior with sight half as keen, a grip half as strong, and a sprint half as swift?'"

The queen paused and smiled at Jeremiah as if to give him the room to answer the riddle. When Jeremiah shrugged, the queen's smile grew before she continued the tale.

"The man puzzled over the words. Then, overcome with his own cleverness, said to the wolf king: 'a warrior woman.' The wolf king stopped pacing just before the man. 'No,' the wolf king growled. 'You.'

"Quick as lightning, the wolf leapt at the man. Before Omaai could raise her spear, the beast cut out the man's eye with a mighty paw. With the other paw, he cut off the man's right arm. And with his powerful jaws, he bit off the man's leg. Omaai drove her spear into the wolf king's side, killing him."

When Queen Frey paused, Jeremiah frowned. "Is that it?"

Queen Frey raised her eyebrows. "Should there be more? The moral is quite clear. If you fail to be cautious, you may be overthrown by your enemy."

"It seems to me," Jeremiah said, "that it's a story about why you shouldn't disregard the wisdom of women."

Queen Frey's eyes grew. "Is *that* what you got from the tale? Strange. But I suppose your interpretation is equally relevant."

The queen continued to hold his gaze before he broke away in favor of his notes. He had never met a woman so bullish. If she lived in Hzorah, her prospects would be limited.

However, her land had different customs. In fact, all of the leaders at the table were of a different mind. And if Jeremiah didn't tread carefully and consider their needs, he would lose their support.

Prophet Davin stood. "A moment, fair leaders." The room quieted, allowing Prophet Davin to speak. "Though the Ghayan Emperor has yet to arrive, I believe it's imperative that we begin proceedings. Today is merely a first look at the issues. Tomorrow, when the Emperor has arrived, we can work toward solutions."

The Prophet Davin looked at Ghaya's Prophet Tsubasa. He nodded in agreement.

"There are perilous times ahead," Prophet Davin continued. "We've all foreseen a great calamity. While we cannot yet see what will bring these troubles, we know that it is undoubtedly rooted in the Deseran army rising in the Dominion Desert."

Jeremiah glanced to his right in time to see a whisper exchanged between the Roanne councilman and his Prophet. It wasn't likely that he'd gain a significant measure of support for Roanne, but together, they may build a naval force strong enough to prevent an attack on their shores or mobilize offensively to bring the battle to Desera.

"Hzorah has prospered under the Caldor Convention for Peace and has largely integrated the land's various tribes. We've worked to strengthen trade agreements between our High Lords, and we've extended invitations to traders to freely move across our borders to further encourage inter-kingdom trade."

"And queendom," Queen Frey whispered.

Jeremiah glanced at her, but no one else appeared to catch her insertion. She sat mute, as if she hadn't said a word. Jeremiah turned his attention back to his Prophet.

"Unfortunately, Prophet Tristan has refused to participate with the Caldor Convention, and now, fifteen years after they were forced from our lands, has built a rather formidable army.

"This army almost certainly is a strain on their stability.

They haven't had the support of trade with the rest of the world—"

"Except the Crehn Isles," Frey whispered again.

"And half of their land is desert."

"The other half probably arable but strained for water."

Jeremiah glanced her way again. Frey gave him a teasing smile before she turned away and assumed the poise of a seasoned ruler.

"If I could interrupt," Sulahn's Councilman said, then stood. His dark eyes matched his ebony skin and stood out in stark contrast to his ornate white clothing. "We all know where this is going. There's no need to blanket it in formalities. You need help defending against their army. They're moving toward Hzorah first."

"If that's not their exclusive target," Roanne's Councilman joined in. Like Sulahn's representative, his skin was dark brown, but his eyes were green. He also stood, revealing white garb tailored with an eye for simplicity. "Roanne has its own battles." The Sulahn Councilman shot him an irked look but didn't interrupt. "We simply do not have the resources to spare."

"Nor does Sulahn," the other Councilman said, then looked at Jeremiah. "Perhaps if you'd sent aid to *us* before the Sundering, we would have had the resources to spare."

The comment was a cheap jab. Hzorah was a small tribe beneath the heel of the Dominion at the time. But King Jeremiah knew he couldn't dignify it with a response. It wouldn't lead to what they both wanted.

"We can assist now," Jeremiah said. "At least we can after this is done with." He looked at Ghaya's Prophet. "Is there anything that you can spare? Men? Supplies? We've dealt with the Dominion before. Prophet Tristan and his friars have the people there devoted by both duty and religion. They won't stop until the entire world adopts their ways. The *entire* world."

Jeremiah hoped that his plea on religious ideals would spur unrest in Prophet Tsubasa. Their devotion to the Ghayan deities would be eradicated if the Dominion had its way.

Instead, the Prophet barely blinked, as if he didn't understand Jeremiah's words. But the Ghayan prophet knew his tongue. He was a prophet, after all.

Prophet Tsubasa crossed his arms. "Ghaya can defend its lands. We are mountain folk. The Deseran Prophet and his people are flatlanders. They would fail."

"But you will have lost a valuable trading partner," Queen Frey said. "*Two* partners, in fact."

Jeremiah looked at Queen Frey with a bit of surprise. Queen Frey gave a quick nod, confirming her support.

"Armoth is not a land of warriors, but we'll send what we can. We will also assist with metal for your weapons and armor by providing extra shipments." She caught Jeremiah's eye. "Provided that you waive the import tariff."

Jeremiah wanted to breathe a sigh of relief, but he held his countenance. "I believe we can make some adjustments." He looked back to the others. "I'm willing to make concessions to stop Prophet Tristan's terror. Your lands have never fought their kind. You didn't see how their dogma was used to strip us of our lands and enslave the weakest of us. All of the Prophets have felt a great calamity ready to strike. *This* is that calamity. *This* is the fight that will redirect our peoples to prosperity."

His passion kindled, King Jeremiah's gaze swept the table, but he only saw the formal, aloof masks of the world's most powerful men.

Prophet Davin put a hand to his shoulder to signal his time to speak. "There is a storm coming. Consult your advisors, then return with your offers. We will hear them out. With your help, the Hzorah Crown Kingdom will stop the Deseran Dominion once and for all."

After Jeremiah presented his case, the leaders remained for a moment to discuss the agenda and scheduling of the summit over the next several days, but Jeremiah could hardly focus on details that felt trivial compared to the imminent crisis of the Dominion's return.

Jeremiah left the room feeling both spent and motivated to re-engage with the leaders. He paused at the door's entry and gave respectful nods to each of them as they left. Prophet Davin was the last one out, carrying the stack of documents he'd brought into the meeting that had ultimately gone unused.

"That didn't go as well as I'd hoped," Jeremiah said. "I expected a hard sell, but not a blatant disregard for the threat."

"It went exactly as well as I'd hoped," Prophet Davin said as they began down the Sanctuary's long halls toward the Hzorah quarters. "From their standing, Desera wants one thing: Hzorah. That is the land they lost to the Dominion War, and that's why Prophet Tristan is moving his forces to the Shadow Peaks rather than the Ghayan mountains or sending a fleet of ships to Roanne."

"Hzorah is just the first on his list of conquests," Jeremiah said. "If they manage to take back Hzorah, it will only be a matter of time before they look elsewhere. Even Queen Frey knows that."

"She also knows that her lands would be the next logical place to invade," the prophet said. "The others have plenty of time. Additionally, the Hzorah Crown is a relatively new kingdom. I believe they are wary of sending direct support in the form of troops when our nation is so new. They see us as fragile and liable to fall back into disparate tribes at the lightest fracture."

As they crossed the Sanctuary, Jeremiah spotted a half-dozen seers proceeding down a corridor. Their kind was a rarity to see. He himself had only observed an adult seer a handful of times when he'd journeyed to Caldor. Locked away in quiet service to the prophets, the dangerous, living weapons were allowed to live out their days in isolation.

It had crossed his mind that perhaps now would be the time to employ seers in defense of the stability they'd gained over the past several years, but he dared not voice it. Reopening that option would inevitably lead to another request for their service and then another—each time becoming easier to justify their use.

No. Like the Crown Sabre, there were some weapons that were best never used again.

King Jeremiah paused at the door of his guest room. "We should meet with my advisors and discuss what we're willing to offer Ghaya and Roanne for their assistance."

"That's scheduled for tomorrow afternoon after they make offers in tomorrow morning's meeting." The prophet shuffled his documents, tidying them. "And many of your advisors are engaged with other meetings regarding trade."

"Isn't this more important?" Jeremiah asked.

Prophet Davin met Jeremiah's eyes. "There are many matters we must address over the next week. We don't often have the opportunity to meet all of the leaders at once. We have to take advantage of this and do the most good. The Dominion won't attack before the week's done. We have the time."

King Jeremiah nodded, conceding to the Prophet's good sense. He was right. There was a lot they could accomplish over the next several days. And as long as they obtained military support from either Ghaya or Roanne, they'd easily have the might to stamp out the Dominion's army. Wary or not, he'd do his best to see that they understood the value of trusting him in this.

Prophet Davin gave Jeremiah a reassuring pat on the shoulder. "Get some rest. Tomorrow will be a long day."

Jeremiah gave him a short smile before Prophet Davin turned and left him alone in the Hzorah diplomatic wing of the Sanctuary. His father had been convinced that the prophets were just as dangerous as the seers, and he wasn't alone in that belief. High Lord Bendeth had sneered when he'd informed the court that he'd be taking the prophet with him. And though the prophet had always been a firm ally to King Jeremiah's efforts, as he watched the man go, he couldn't help but remember his father's warning once again.

He waited until the prophet disappeared down the hall before he turned and entered the guestrooms. Closing the door behind him, he crossed into the drawing room. He didn't know how they managed to capture the smell of his chambers back home, but it smelled like the Crown City mixed with the lavender of the palace candle wax.

An arrangement of chairs circled a small table. He stripped off his coat and draped it over the back of the chair. On the far side before the bedroom's doorway, sat a tall bottle of Erida Velvet and several glasses. Jeremiah indulged with a half-glass.

He circled the table. Set under a layer of glass, a map of the known world stared back at him in incredible detail. The mountains, the colors to indicate regional differences, even the details of the Hzorah Crown City's delta were crafted with expert precision.

He intended to spend a bit of time over the next few years showing his sons the world. While he wasn't sure that Gabriel would be interested in geography, Seth was quite the academic. And he was certain that if he could frame the lands in terms of battlefield strategy, even Gabriel would find the tour inspiring.

A few years ago, he'd taken Gabriel to Stronghold Aear and the Shadow Peaks. He'd never forget the moment he'd shared with his son as he described how the final battle was fought just days before the birth of his younger brother. Even with the suppressed memories that had been unearthed with the journey, his son's awe was more than worth the pain.

Gabriel would be king someday. Seeing the broader world beyond the former tribe lands that now made up the great nation of Hzorah would be an advantage he and his father had never had.

A knock at his room door startled him. Jeremiah turned to eye the door, and the knock repeated once more before he crossed to the entryway and opened it.

Queen Frey stood there. She'd refreshed herself with a different dress, a purple and white gown of casual royalty but no less elegant. She stared at him as if he should have expected her.

Jeremiah frowned. "Am I in the wrong wing, or are you?"

"Neither of us are," she said, then glanced past him. "Are you going to invite me in? Unless, of course, you have a woman here. I wouldn't want to interrupt your—"

Jeremiah's cheeks warmed. "There's no one here. But why are you?"

"My, did my wolf story frighten you that much?" The queen smiled. "I'm not here to eat you. I wanted to talk about our arrangement."

Jeremiah shifted. "This is rather … informal. Wouldn't you prefer—"

"If I preferred it, I would have done it. Please, Your Majesty, indulge me. My time is a limited resource."

Jeremiah stepped aside, and Queen Frey glided in. He followed her into the drawing room where, without hesitation, she crossed to the far table and helped herself to a glass of erida. He wasn't sure he would ever get used to how forward she and her people were.

"Time is a limited resource …" Jeremiah mused. "My prophet says otherwise. We have the whole week."

"*You* have the week," she said, turning back to him and crossing to the center of the room. "I, however, will be leaving tonight."

"Tonight? Why? There's so much to discuss."

"My prophetess and advisors are all quite capable without me. But then, they're all women." The queen raised an eyebrow at him. "How many of your advisors are women?"

Jeremiah didn't have to take a moment to count, but the question caught him off guard. "None of them."

"And, thus, you will never know the brisk efficiency of the female mind." She sat across from him. "You should reconsider who you allow to carry out your business."

Jeremiah sighed and sat. He didn't want to play this game. Armoth was a matriarchy, and it seemed the queen delighted in sharing the virtues of such a system. Instead of engaging with her comment, he changed the subject. "Your offer of aid is appreciated. We need all the help we can get. Is there anything I can do to expedite the process? Or, better yet, to encourage more aid?"

"Is there anything I can do to get you to abolish the tariff on mined imports?"

"The tariff is there to encourage internal growth."

"The crop share treaty is quite functional without a tariff," the queen said. "Both of our lands are well fed. There are fewer hungry every day."

"The mined imports are different," Jeremiah said. "They're comparatively unessential and incur more upkeep on trade routes."

The queen gave him a pointed look as if she wanted him to know that she withheld more damning evidence. "There are … other arrangements that can be made. I'm sure you recall your father's idea."

Jeremiah's jaw tightened. "I remember."

"He was so intrigued when he learned about the Ghayan way. How they reward power." She refused to break her eye contact with him as she savored the taste of her erida.

It took all of Jeremiah's focus to maintain his composure. He'd always tried to be a tolerant man, but the Ghayan power structure had always struck him as … distasteful. In Ghaya, power was often rewarded and sealed with a marriage. If a man were to surpass his station, another marriage was expected. The Ghayan emperor had nine wives.

"I'm a married man," Jeremiah said flatly.

"*Were* a married man," Queen Frey corrected.

"And I have children and responsibilities," he continued. "I can't walk away from that."

"Your children have both seen several years. Your eldest must be practically a man now, and your second born is right behind him." She sat straight and leaned in to meet his eyes. "No one is asking you to walk away from anything. And what about your responsibility to your people? A marriage between the King of Hzorah and the Queen of Armoth would unite our people. We would be a force unparalleled. My men would fight for you if you were my husband. Without that, they're no more impassioned than mercenaries. And that's what you need, Jeremiah, is it not? Passion?"

Jeremiah stood. "It's late …"

"Hardly," Queen Frey stood. "But I'll leave. I have other

matters to address before my departure. Promise that you'll at least think on it. Our people would have everything to gain. You do love your people, Jeremiah?"

"Of course, I do."

"And I love mine." Queen Frey placed her half-empty glass on the table before crossing in front of him on her way to the door. She stopped just before him, close. "You'll think about it?"

Jeremiah managed a nod. Satisfied, the queen let herself out. He stepped to the door after she shut it and listened, making sure he heard her footsteps disappear down the hall. When they faded, he crossed back to the table, dumped her erida into his chamber vat, and collapsed onto a white, cushioned chair.

The encounter had taken him off guard. The woman was insane. How could she think it was decent to come to his chambers this way? Furthermore, how could she think it decent to make such a proposition? It was the Armoth way for a woman to make such a proposal, but he still didn't like *how* she made it.

Gabriel was less than a year away from being old enough to take the crown. If Jeremiah married Frey, his sons might lose their birthright if they had a child. And even if they didn't lose their birthright, would Frey's people allow themselves to be ruled by a man?

How could she think I'd think this was a good idea?

Because he needed allies.

She was right about one thing: this kind of arrangement would easily secure their position as the most powerful kingdom in the world. Desera wouldn't be able to conquer them. They'd have the army and the resources to prevent that. Ghaya would be forced to concede to more favorable trade agreements. Roanne and Sulahn … Well, they had their own problems.

Was it not his responsibility to protect his people from the Deseran Dominion? Gabriel might lose his birthright, but was what *he* wanted more important than what his people needed?

Agreeing to this union would guarantee they'd win this war, and it wasn't so different from what his grandfather had done to forge the nation of Hzorah. Jeremiah's union with his beloved Esther had been the result his father's deft negotiations to keep the tribes united as one under the banner of Hzorah.

When he thought of it that way, it seemed insane not to take the offer. Yet, when considered his heart …

What should I do, Love? Jeremiah asked Esther, but she remained ever silent, distant. Safe.

Prophet Davin hurried down the corridor that led to Time's Alcove. He passed under long rows of Hzorah-made candles set on walls textured with Ghayan molding. He ventured deep within the Sanctuary where few had ever explored its depths. The prophets and seers were the only people who frequented its deep layers, and seers had taken the responsibility of its upkeep in order to preserve its sanctity.

At the end of the hall, before the door of his destination, four seers sat in a small wall nook, immersed in their duties of cataloging reports and records received over the past several months. It was a time intensive and thankless task. The nations involved in the Caldor Convention for Peace took for granted how much paperwork the treaty generated.

Davin smiled to himself. Frair, Mason, Kikoda, and Balimerre. He'd known each of them since they were young—when he was a much younger man himself. They'd seen nearly thirty years now, and they'd become the very model of excellence, helping guide the younger seers in the Sanctuary to quell their abilities and live in peace. They'd found an important place in the sanctuary, studying the histories and aiding the short memories of diplomats as they discussed new treaties.

"Prophet Davin," Mason said as he looked up from his book. His companions repeated the greetings in turn.

"Seers Frair, Mason, Kikoda, Balimerre." Davin smiled. "I trust your studies are going well."

"They have," Frair said. "How were your travels, Prophet? Is Hzorah faring well?"

"As well as can be expected with the rumors of war about," Prophet Davin answered. "I see a plentiful harvest. But at the eve of a war on the northern plains, there may be shortages."

"Prophet Davin," Balimerre said tentatively. "Have you heard from Seer Navid? Has he found the key that you were looking for?"

Davin shook his head. "He has, though he has not yet confirmed my forethought. I expect to hear from him soon. It wouldn't be like him to not to send a message ahead, though it may arrive only a day or so before his own arrival."

"But he found the woman?" Kikoda brushed a stray wisp of hair away from her face. "You've seen that much?"

"I have," Prophet Davin said. "Beyond that … Well, he's very much capable. I wouldn't have sent him if I didn't trust that he was the one to successfully complete the task. I—"

Davin hesitated. He was often blunt with his ability's foretellings—a habit he'd attempted to eliminate for many years unsuccessfully. It would seem that age did not immediately translate to wisdom.

Balimerre shrugged. "There's no need to explain yourself, Prophet Davin. We understand."

"He's young," Mason said. "Younger than I."

"But age does not matter in this," Balimerre said.

"In fact," Frair added, "that may be his advantage. This woman is likely to be near his age. Perhaps that will help her trust him in a way that she wouldn't trust an older Seer."

"Perhaps," Prophet Davin said.

Seer Navid's age wasn't the metric he'd used to determine Navid's chances of success. It was, rather, how the current of time bent around him. And it was the fact that he was able to give Navid a personal stake in his quest. Davin wasn't sure why, but Navid's fate—his ability as a seer—was coiled and knotted around this woman. If Navid completed his mission as instructed, he could not only save Hzorah from the tragedy of war, but he would gain his life back—somehow untangle himself from the curse of his ability, something that these four seers would never be able to do. Davin didn't understand how it was to happen; his senses couldn't see that far down time's river.

"I must leave you to your duties," Prophet Davin said. "My constituents await my arrival. Seer Kikoda, please be sure to meet with Prophet Tsubasa and his Emperor. There are several records they'd like you to pull to help them adjust their seasonal trade schedule."

"Of course, Prophet Davin," Kikoda said. "As soon as I finish here, I'll meet them in Ghaya's guestrooms."

He and the seers traded parting words, and Davin entered Time's Alcove. He took in the room as he shut the door behind him. The small, cozy chamber was far from glamorous and was purely functional. Dim and unadorned, there was only the matter at hand to occupy the mind.

Prophet Lilith sat closest to the door. She raised an eyebrow as he stepped to the table. "You're late, Prophet Davin." In Armothean style, her tone juxtaposed cold superiority and playful jabbing. "Next time, I'll have my chamberman take his time with my hair."

"I apologize," Prophet Davin said, moving to the head of the table. "My king requested a word with me. Our time here is short, and the danger threatening our lands is vast. I presume we can set aside formalities."

"Agreed," Prophet Tsubasa said in his thick Ghayan accent.

Davin looked at Prophet Nafis and Prophet Kafeel of Roanne and Sulahn, respectively. Both Prophets inclined their heads in silent approval.

"The intervention is in motion," Prophet Davin said. "Seer Navid has left with the *Gateway Abbreviation.* I haven't heard word yet, but my forethought is that he's intercepted the young woman by now. I can sense her drawing near."

"I, too, sense it," Prophet Tsubasa said. "I can now see what you see. Time warps in her presence. She is integral to this."

"Yes," Prophet Kafeel said. "Even the course of my people has already been affected by her. She is dangerous."

"Women with power would surprise you," Prophet Lilith said. "You so rarely grant it within Sulahnese society that you would have no other way to resolve her significance than to call her dangerous."

Prophet Kafeel gave her a pointed look. "You know that I don't mean it this way."

"Of course," she said. "Clearly, I mock unfairly."

It *was* odd. Not that she was a woman, but that she carried so much potential singularly within. Navid was a crucial player, but this woman … she carried something he'd never felt before. Her ripples throughout time's rapids reminded him of … something … No. Someone. The healer at his queen's deathbed. *Odd.*

"Still," Prophet Nafis said. "You've allowed a seer out into the world—an element of chaos. The way that they see time is different. They don't have a clear trajectory."

"Navid maintains control," Prophet Davin said. "We've seen other seers slip under pressure, but Navid has held through all the trials."

"Agreed," Tsubasa said. "His progress has been more than sufficient, but his control under the stresses of reality may prove differently."

"Let's not forget why we're doing this," Davin said. "The Dominion's Creed can't be reasoned with. They may have their eyes toward Hzorah now, but eventually, Prophet Tristan will turn to Ghaya. To Armoth, Roanne, and Sulahn. He won't accept your people's ways. Your customs, your religion, your whole way of life will be stripped away either by compromise or by force. And compromise is not an option your emperor appreciates."

"This is a war of ideals," Lilith said. "Make no mistake; it's a war for resources as well, but Tristan is not a tolerant man."

"And though Wizard Titan couldn't cure the plague at the time," Davin said, looking to Prophet Kafeel, "perhaps this woman will be able to find a way. She may be the very last

Keeper of the Covenant that exists. She is the only one who can heal the magic in the Tal's forests."

Prophet Davin surprised himself with that. He'd spoken the foretelling before he'd even realized he'd had the forethought. He so rarely had forethoughts that were so acutely specific to an individual. A true Keeper of the Covenant. He shuddered to consider what that would mean when she arrived at the Sanctuary, but they had no other choice.

Prophet Tsubasa nodded. "I foresee Prophet Davin's plan to have the outcomes we expect. I believe we would be wise to stay on course now that it has been put into motion."

"I, too, agree," Lilith said. "We cannot allow the Seed to fall into the hands of the Dominion. We will send her to the Tal."

Kafeel sat back in his chair. "I foresee potential where without this woman there is none. I agree."

Nafis took a deep breath, considering. "I agree. We continue forward. I am not convinced she can truly solve the problem with the Tal or prevent war from befalling us, but when this Keeper arrives, we will assess her usefulness."

"Good," Prophet Davin said, allowing his shoulders to relax. He sat in his chair. For a fleeting moment, he was concerned that the prophets would want to attempt an alternative option, an option that had been put to rest many years ago. Magic's consequences were too great. Wizard Titan could never return.

Seer Navid had found the woman. He was sure of that. But personal incentives of the mission—the part he hadn't discussed with the prophets—still hung in balance. He couldn't quite sense its odds of success, but there was little room for error. He simply had to return home. Azuri wasn't the most direct route back to Caldor, but it wasn't wildly off course.

"Before we adjourn," Davin said, "should we address the issues surrounding the Crehn Isles?"

"We should." Kafeel sighed. It was a subject that was both important and tiring for Roanne.

"Excellent," Davin said. "For that, I have a different plan."

FOUR

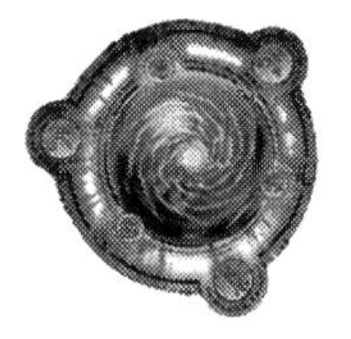

KRUV HOUSE

"They're the finest silks in the land. Yes, yes, the finest! I assure you of that," the peddler said. He was an older man with black-and-white stubble and gray-streaked hair. He pulled forth a roll of sky-blue silks from a sack he kept handy in the jockey box of his canvas-roofed carriage. His hands shook, making a less-than-steady display of his prized goods. "Take a look yourself. You'll see. You'll see."

While Navid endured the man's sales pitch, Tele peered inside the cart. In addition to the silks, he carried pottery and woodwork of varying degrees of quality. Some of it was even broken. She looked back to his sly smile, and he grinned at her as if he were judging her weight in gold.

"I'm sorry," Navid said, waving away his offer. "We are pressed to make good time."

"But …" He stopped, and a brief touch of what looked to be panic flashed across his face so fast that Tele barely caught before it morphed into a smile. "Yes, of course, sir. I'm sure you have much to attend to. Yes, of course."

A child that had seen about six or seven years and looked like the very image of the peddler's past self, appeared behind the man. His hair was close-cut and his eyes gleamed with joy and mischief. He looked a touch too thin, and Tele wondered if they made enough of a living out on the road. Tele was no stranger to sparse eating. She could almost see herself in his eyes.

The man stuffed away his goods and made to continue forward.

"Wait," Tele said.

The peddler paused but avoided looking at her. His eyes darted in every direction to avoid eye contact.

"Do you have anything tailored to my size that I can wear?" she asked.

"I'm sorry, uh, madam." His eyes crossed hers for a moment then darted away again. "I'm afraid I sold all my clothes to the last town, Azuri. Lots of wares in town. Yes, yes. Lots of wares."

He urged his horse down the road as if eager to be away from whatever trouble she and Navid brought with them. As he and his son rode away, Tele turned to Navid.

"Are all the peddlers in Hzorah so odd?"

Navid refused to meet her gaze. He shrugged. "Perhaps. I rarely interact with them in Caldor."

Tele turned back to watch as the small boy's head popped up from the rear of the carriage. He ducked away again when she caught his eye.

Within an hour of their encounter, they cleared the trees and entered Azuri. The town bustled with the late morning's tasks. Men and women crossed back and forth between buildings, some holding bundles, some holding jars. Others stood outside shops and called quick advertisements for all manner of goods to those passing by. Many granted them an unnaturally wide passage after observing the pair.

"There's a tavern ahead," Navid told her, adjusting his cowl as he guided his mare through the town's foot traffic. "I know the innkeeper. We should be able to get a meal and a room there."

Tele nodded. The sooner they were away from the crowds, the better. Tele's experience with the outside world had been an exercise in covert maneuvering throughout her youth. The

Dominion Desert often failed to provide for her family's every need, and when it became necessary to venture into a city, she and her brothers preferred an approach that avoided being seen at all. Giving the people here a chance to look her over was profoundly uncomfortable. She had to keep reminding herself that she wasn't a target here. There were no Thief-Takers waiting to capture her.

At the next block, they rounded a corner that opened to a dead-end street and a courtyard bordered by several double-rise buildings. Large signs hung outside each structure. It was the first written building description she'd seen in the town. The closest building displayed a wooden sign, painted red with bold lettering inscribed: KRUV.

Navid paused at the entrance.

"Is this the wrong place?" Tele asked.

Slowly, he shook his head and took a deep breath. "No. This is the place."

A stable hand took their horse, and after waiting for his mare to disappear into the rear stables, Navid led them through the entrance.

Inside, the tavern was brightly lit, and though the wooden walls were unpainted, they were coated with a varnish finish—polished and clean with an unnaturally vibrant shine unlike anything she'd ever seen. A dozen tables sat in two tidy rows of six, half of which were occupied by patrons.

As they stepped inside, the patrons quieted, leaving behind an eerie silence that contrasted harshly against an otherwise cheerful establishment.

The serving girl nearest them flashed a pleasant smile before she finished taking orders for three ornately dressed men. She shuffled over to them, her long green skirts licking the legs of tables as she carved her way to the entry.

"Welcome! I'm Amie Kruv. You're looking for rooms?"

Blonde curls bounced with her cheerful greeting. Both serving girls in the tavern's dining hall matched in outfit and likeness. Sisters, Tele guessed.

"Yes, please," Navid said. "I have an account with Caldor.

This is my friend, Tele. We're on an urgent journey and will only be staying a night. Please bill her stay to my account."

"A pleasure." The girl curtsied and smiled. Turning to Tele, she repeated the formality. "Please, have a seat, and I'll see to your orders."

"Is Master Kruv in?" Navid asked as Amie guided them to the table in the far corner of the room. Navid set his packs down beside them and they took seats opposite each other.

"Yes, Father is in the kitchens. I can fetch him if you'd like." Amie smiled as they settled into their table. "Would you like the house soup? The first batch is just finished and fresh."

Navid looked at Tele for approval. She gave another single nod. She had no preference; she only wanted a full stomach.

"That sounds wonderful, Amie. Thank you," Navid said.

After a final smile of approval, Amie whisked off into the kitchens through a swinging door. Navid turned to watch her leave.

"She's … she's a sweet girl," Navid said, his voice cracking almost imperceptibly.

"Her curls are a little too cheery for my mood."

Navid chuckled nervously. "You can't hold a girl's hair against her. A poor judge of character."

Tele let a smile edge onto her face but didn't allow her brow to rise. "You're right, but I'm not in the mood to be cheered. My stomach won't let me see the nice things."

"I know the feeling," Navid said, sitting back in his seat and rubbing his thighs.

Tele watched Navid carefully. Her time as a Deseran outlaw afforded her few glimpses into the behaviors of those outside of her immediate family. But she had enough experience to know when someone was nervous or anxious. She'd seen her brothers wear the same uncomfortable expression numerous times as they guided her through the streets of Janamah—the Deseran Dominion's great capital city—always looking over their shoulders, watching for danger.

Navid was anxious.

Tele glanced around the tavern again. The west-facing

windows looked out into the courtyard where finely dressed residents crossed to their destinations. A roar of laughter erupted from the table of three men. Amie, who had delivered their ale, scurried back to the kitchens with a red-faced look of embarrassment.

The Kruv House appeared to have all the trappings of an upstanding establishment and lacked the rough crowd Tele's mother had always warned her about. But she hadn't forgotten the strange behavior of the peddler and the townsfolk who'd given them more than a moment's glance, or how the atmosphere of the tavern had changed as they entered. Everyone here knew that she didn't belong here. She was a stranger in their midst. Tele had spent her life either hiding or on the run and knew the dangers of staying in one place for too long.

"How many more days until we reach Caldor?" Tele asked, sinking deeper into her seat.

Navid adjusted his cowl again, eyes glowing in the dim light of the corner table. "Not long. Three days at best, a week if we take it slow. The city is conveniently between nations within the borderlands. The gateway placed us close. It'll be an easy journey from here out. The roads are well-traveled and direct."

"Good," Tele said. "I say we leave after our meal and make better time. I don't think we should stay longer than we have to. And I don't need a bed."

"We'll need supplies and another horse," Navid pointed out.

"I hope you have a fine amount of silver or whatever they except for money here," Tele said. "And I can't walk around like *this*, either. I don't fit in here wearing my desert garb. I'll be the talk of the town by day's end. It wouldn't be smart to cause unrest. We should leave. *Now*."

"Right ..." Navid said as if distracted. "We'll find something more fitting for you. A green dress to match your eyes would suit."

Tele deepened her frown. "Sorry, not my style."

The kitchen door swept open, and a tall, heavyset man

stepped into the common. He was rosy-faced with a well-kept, blond beard and short, nearly shaven hair. He wore a dirty white apron with a pocket that held a clean white rag. He scanned the room and quickly spotted Navid.

"Navid …" He closed the distance, ignoring his rag to wipe his hands on the flap of his apron as he glanced around the room nervously.

Navid stood. "Master Kruv, it's good to see you again."

Master Kruv gave a sharp gesture, encouraging Navid to sit back down. After Navid complied, Master Kruv positioned himself like a wall between the table and the rest of the dining hall. "It's been …"

"Too long." Navid smiled. Remembering himself, he turned to Tele. "This is my friend, Tele. We're on our way to Caldor, and I couldn't pass up letting her experience your fine establishment."

"A *friend*?" Master Kruv asked as though he didn't believe it. He then looked at Tele as if expecting her to shape-shift into a wolf. When she failed to meet his expectations, he cleared his throat. "You won't be disappointed, Madam. The house soup is excellent. It's been known to keep travelers full for a week." Master Kruv immediately moved his attention back to Navid. "What's going on? I've haven't seen you in … And you come back …" He paused. "Tell me you're not bringing trouble." He looked back to Tele. "No offense, Madam."

Tele looked away.

"That's what we're trying to avoid," Navid said and sat forward in his chair. "We're leaving at first light, but we'll need a second horse, some clothing and food—"

"Some weapons," Tele said. "Knives."

Navid frowned at Tele, his eyes flashing.

Master Kruv stood a little straighter. "I can direct you to someone who can provide you a fine set. You can pick a horse from my stables, and Amie can help you gather supplies in the city."

Rather than feeling relieved that they'd found someone who was willing to help them on their way, Tele felt profoundly uneasy. While his offer was a generosity beyond reason, Master Kruv sounded as if he'd say anything to get the two of them out of his hair as soon as possible.

"Thank you," Navid said. "I really appreciate your help."

Master Kruv gave a sad sigh. "I'll add it to Caldor's account? You have a pass?"

"Yes, please," Navid said, his voice taking a tone of disappointment. "I appreciate this. Please, give an extra silver to those who gather the supplies on my account."

"I'll see it done," Master Kruv said. He eyed Tele again as if recognizing her need to blend in. "And I'll have Amie bring something for Madam Tele to change into for now. You must be eager to wear something a bit more comfortable and fitting."

Tele shifted. "I am."

Master Kruv smiled sadly and departed through the kitchen door.

"You could try a little tact," Navid said. "If you sound like you plan to kill everyone you meet, this won't go easy."

Tele was not in the mood for pleasantries, but she supposed that she could have been a bit less blunt. "And what about you? You said you knew this innkeeper. I assumed your relationship was amiable. This was not a friendly transaction."

Navid swallowed. "Right. Well, we're getting the supplies we need. That is what's most important."

Tele glanced around the tavern. A few onlookers turned away when she caught them staring. "Can a seer predict which one of them is going to alert the town that a stranger is among them?"

"It's not right for a seer to use his power."

Tele eyed him. "Even in this? I can't imagine a better use."

"It's dangerous," Navid said.

It's a waste, Tele thought.

The swinging door opened once again, and Amie approached with a green bundle of garments. She placed them on the table and smiled at Tele.

"We're about the same size," Amie said. "I hope this will do for now."

Tele was probably several fingers taller than the girl, but tried a bit of the tact Navid had prescribed and smiled half-heartedly. "Thank you, Amie," she said before the girl was again beyond the swinging doors.

"See," Navid said. "She's not so bad. You'll do well gathering the supplies with her."

"Me?" Tele crossed her arms. "I'm not going to spend the day with her."

"It won't take the whole day. Would you rather pick the horse?"

"We can do without another horse."

"Not if we want to make good time."

After an awkward moment of silence, Amie's sister passed through the swinging door carrying a tray with two bowls of steaming soup. She set the tray before them and looked at Navid. Her expression paled.

"Is there … is there anything else I can get for you two?" she asked, then looked away from Navid. "Some ale?"

"I think Tele will want to leave to gather supplies after we eat," Navid said.

She nodded without meeting their eyes and went back to the kitchens.

They clearly don't want us here, Tele thought. How could Navid think this would be a good idea? The inn was nice. It wasn't smart to go where people knew you when you're attempting to travel unnoticed. It was especially stupid to go someplace where they actively disliked you.

Navid pulled free a folded piece of parchment from his trousers' pocket and slid it across the table to Tele. "These are my passage rights from Caldor. With it, you'll be able to purchase any supplies you need. Amie will help you. She should know the town well."

Tele unfolded it. It held a red, circular seal with the words "Sanctuary Calviere" written inside the stamp. She folded it again and placed it atop the bundle of clothing she had received.

"I'll make my way without sweet Amie," Tele said, a statement made out of annoyance rather than logical sense. She didn't care to have an escort but supposed blending in would be an easier task if she looked like she knew where she was going rather than wandering around, hoping to find what she needed.

Amie entered then, cheerful as ever. "Father told me you need an escort around Azuri. What supplies do you need to gather? I know all the best shops."

"Well ..." Tele put on her most convincing smile. "I'll need to take a few moments to really sort it out in my head. I think by the time I finish this soup, I should know."

Amie watched Tele and Navid as they took their first sip. The soup was as good as it smelled. Tele closed her eyes in satisfaction. It warmed her insides, and she savored the small meaty chunks. She opened her eyes again to find Amie still staring at her with a hopeful grin.

"It's delicious, right?" She placed two keys on the table. "These are your room keys. If you'd like, I can have someone put your things in your room."

"We can manage," Tele answered for the both of them.

"Great! Well, I'll be around when you're ready." Amie disappeared behind the swinging kitchen door.

Tele made quick work of the soup. Flavors deliciously melded, she thought Master Kruv might be correct about it filling her for a week. She felt renewed. It had been a long while since she'd had a proper meal.

Letting her spoon rest on the lip of the empty bowl, she again peered around the room, observing the occupants. The three in fine dress were engaged in a game of cards while, at another table, a man and woman spoke in hushed tones. The couple stole quick glances in her direction every so often before conversing once more.

"I'm heading back to stow my things," Navid said.

Tele stood, shouldered her pack, and stuffed the dress and parchment under her arm. "Alright."

She followed Navid out of the common and toward the Kruv House rooms. She found the door with a marking that matched the five geometrically arranged dots etched on the broad side of the key.

"I'll meet with you later after you've gone out with Amie?" Navid said.

Tele nodded, and Navid slipped into his room. Tele unlocked her room door and stepped inside.

The accommodations were nicer than she expected. The room was decently sized, windowless, and shared the same polished look of the common. Two candles hung on the wall above a small desk and chair. A bed was positioned in the corner, and a red and blue quilt and a water basin with a towel sat against the opposite corner.

She dropped her bag beside the bed and unfolded the bundle of clothes given to her—a green dress the match of Amie's. Amie must have thought it would be cute for them to match. Desolate's Hand had dealt her a raw deal. At least she would be able to buy something more practical when she went out with the girl.

Tele stripped down and packed away her clothes before replacing them with a thin but soft shift and the lightly worn green dress. There was no glass to see her reflection, but as she gazed down on herself in an outfit that was so far removed from the flatly masculine garments of her desert life, she didn't recognize herself.

Would her brothers have recognized her like this? Her mother and father? Would they approve? Far removed from the coarse tans she'd lived her whole life accustomed to, the dress was a vibrant reminder of the life that was torn from her —a life that was forever lost.

Who was Tele Gavina in the absence of her family, of her Dominion Desert, of the constant threat of the bounty on her head?

She lowered herself to the floor and clutched her pack.

Without her family, Tele was alone. But she was still a Keeper, and it was her duty to protect the knowledge her family had left to her.

That was who she was now. Nothing more, nothing less.

Navid shut his room's door behind him as he stepped out into the Kruv House guestroom hall. He waited until he saw Tele follow Amie out the tavern's door, then entered the common room and sat at the table where his unfinished soup awaited him. He sank into his seat as if it were a loving embrace.

Though Master Kruv had made many changes to the Kruv House since he was last here, the chairs felt the same. The rooms were the same. The feeling was the same: home.

But his curse still needled him. The town was at unrest. There was danger about.

Time always seemed to slip for Navid. A jittering in the corner of his mind's eye like an incessant itch that could never be soothed. Years of meditation had taught him to ignore it, but the itch was always there, waiting to be scratched.

He knew the itch to be Desolate's call—the temptation to use his ability—and it would become too distracting if he didn't shut it out. He needed his wits about him for this. He needed to focus. Navid shut his eyes and clutched his soup spoon, letting his mantra fill his mind.

To allow it to take him was to take a path of evil. To allow it to control him was to take a path to destruction.

Navid opened his eyes. The itch was gone, and Mara, Amie's sister—his sister—was there.

"Are you finished?" she asked, refusing to meet his eyes.

"I—"

"I never thought I'd see you again," she said. "When you left, I couldn't sleep for months. I know it wasn't your fault, but I can't tell you how much it hurt. I couldn't go a day without thinking of you, and that made me furious. And a year later, when I didn't think of you for a day … Well, that hurt even more." Mara looked at him, her sharp blue eyes hard with pain.

"Mara, I …" Navid swallowed. He hadn't seen his sisters in years, and in all that time, he'd only thought of how hard it was for *him*. He hadn't thought much about how they must have felt. "I'm sorry. I didn't want to leave. If I could make it right—"

"I know," she said, then lifted the bowl from the table. "I know you couldn't control what happened. I don't blame you. At least, I don't anymore. I just thought you should know."

Before Navid could respond, Mara turned and walked away. She pushed the swinging door in and brushed past her father. His father. Master Kruv stepped out of her way. When he caught Navid's eye, he approached his table.

"Your friend is … different," Master Kruv said and sat down.

Navid nodded. "She is." He recalled her holding her knife at him, ready to cut his throat, the fierce energy of her green eyes locked with his. "If you're worried about Amie—"

Master Kruv waved a hand. "I'm more worried about Tele. Amie's been a handful lately."

"She looks just like Mara," Navid said. "They could almost be twins."

Master Kruv let on a small smile that withered as he sighed. "Why are you here, Navid? I know you didn't come to Azuri to chat about my daughters. What's this really about? I thought you weren't allowed to come back."

"Things have changed," Navid said.

It was an understatement if he'd ever uttered one. He'd only seen seven years when he was taken to Caldor and forced to leave his family—the Kruvs—behind. He wished he could go back to that moment at Dunham Lake and take back what had happened, somehow stop his curse from surfacing.

"Mara was a mess when you left," Master Kruv said. "I thank Desolate's Hand that you left before Amie really knew you. Why come back to reopen old wounds?" Master Kruv sighed when Navid looked away. "I'd be the first one to welcome you back, Navid, but my family could be arrested for housing you."

"There's a war on the horizon," Navid said. "The Deseran Dominion is gathering their forces at the Shadow Peaks. I'm not sure how they're doing it. Moving so many soldiers across the Dominion Desert would be a logistical feat that I can't even imagine."

"I know about the Dominion and the coming war. Even the deaf know about it." Master Kruv crossed his arms and leaned back in the chair. "What's this have to do with you?"

"Prophet Davin sent me to find Tele. And to find you."

Master Kruv smiled and a short chuckle escaped him. "Find me? Because they want me to host the Dominion? Or perhaps they want me to make them a fine roast."

Navid knew how it sounded. It sounded the same to him when he was summoned before the Prophet Davin at Sanctuary Calviere. But the prophets would know about this. They could see how time moved, knew what pieces to move into place to stem the flow to calamity. He had to trust them.

"I was given a prophecy," Navid said. "I was told that I had to find a woman wandering alone in the Dominion Desert, that she must journey with me to Caldor, but only of her own accord. And I was told that I must 'find what I had lost.' I found the woman. Now I must find what I've lost."

"You found her in the desert?" Master Kruv's eyes widened. "You went into the Dominion wilds?"

Navid nodded. "I wish I could explain it all to you, but that's the short of it. The Prophet told me that if I did this, I would prevent the world from falling into darkness, and I'd be rewarded with my freedom. He said I'd be *free* of my curse."

Master Kruv shook his head. "You're a seer, Navid. I wish it weren't so, but it is. It can't be changed."

"Prophet Davin said it *can* be changed," Navid said, leaning forward. "I just had to find what I'd lost. I've only lost one thing in life—my family."

"So that's why you're here." Master Kruv shook his head before looking out to his patrons.

"That's why I'm here." Navid smiled. "You see? Everything can go back to normal. I've found the woman. I found you. The war will end before it starts, and I'll be *free*, Father. Free to come home."

"Navid …" Master Kruv sighed. "Scorch it, I didn't think it would be like this. It's not right."

Navid frowned. He'd thought his father would be happier. He'd been cursed, but this changed everything. Shouldn't his father rejoice in that? "I don't understand. I thought you'd be happy."

"Navid, nothing would make me happier than to be able to welcome you home. You know that." Master Kruv stroked his chin. "But … I'm not your father."

What? Navid's face twisted in confusion. "I know it's been a long time, but—"

"No, Navid. Listen," Master Kruv sighed. "When you were a child—no more than a few months—I took you in as a ward. I didn't feel right about raising you any different from my daughters, so I raised you as if you were my own."

Navid was speechless. He'd known he'd been different. Master Kruv, Mara, and Amie all had fairer skin and blonde hair, but he'd seen families with children that didn't quite the look the same as their parents. After his curse revealed itself, he'd ascribed his differences to his affliction.

But never had he even considered … "Why didn't you tell me?"

"We thought it would be better to wait until you were old enough to understand," Master Kruv said. "And then when you were taken away … Well, it didn't matter much then. I didn't think I'd ever see you again."

Navid turned in his seat and peered around. "Where's Mother?"

"She …" Master Kruv paused and swallowed. "Navid, she passed not long after you left. The healer said the winter's sickness had taken her, but I knew better than that. Her heart was broken. You were her only son. She didn't carry you, but she loved you more than anything."

Navid let his face drop into his hands but held back his emotions. Everything he'd known had been a lie. He'd lost it all years ago in childhood, but to lose it again tore his heart apart. Why hadn't they just told him? Who was he?

Countless memories flashed before his mind's eye. The Kruvs had been a loving family, full of joy and laughter. Even after he'd been taken to Caldor, he'd held fast to those warm memories. They kept him grounded when he lost sight of his own identity, when he didn't know what made him special among a Sanctuary of kids just like him.

And though Madam Kruv had died long ago, Navid had lived all those years believing that even though he was gone, their family still had each other. His leaving had broken their family in countless ways, and him returning to Azuri tore at the stitches of a deep and miserable wound.

He should have never come back. He couldn't be a Kruv anymore. And as much as it pained him, he put away that hope and faced the new reality of his existence.

"I met your mother," Master Kruv said. "When you were brought to my door, she carried you, wrapped in cloth, red-faced and crying. She was with three big men who seemed to be escorting her to my door against her will. I didn't learn her given name. But her family name was Tevaad."

Tevaad. Navid let the name fill his thoughts. He wasn't Navid Kruv. He was Navid Tevaad. "Do you know where I can find her?"

Master Kruv gave a solemn shake of his head. "A few days after you were left in my care, they found a woman dead in the fields just outside of the eastern side of Azuri. Several stab wounds—a murder. No one knew who she was, but I stepped outside of the inn as they carted her through the streets and to the morgue. It was her. They asked for family to claim the body, but no one claimed her. I almost claimed her out of respect, but thought better of it. Whoever had killed her might target anyone who claimed her next."

Navid swallowed hard, trying to digest what Master Kruv

told him. Who would have wanted his mother dead? Where had she come from? Why had no one claimed her?

"Do you know where I might be able to find a Tevaad? What about my father?"

Master Kruv stroked his chin. "I don't know of any Tevaads in or around Azuri. Sounds like an East Hzorah name. The Hzorah Guard only found her body. I didn't hear anything about another murder."

"So he's still alive …" Navid whispered.

"I don't know that," Master Kruv said, leaning in. "Navid, I don't know anything more than what I've told you. Your father might be alive, or he might've been killed elsewhere. *He* could have been the one who murdered your mother. I don't know for sure."

Navid nodded absently. Prophet Davin had sent him to find what he'd lost. His mother had been killed, but his father was alive. He *had* to be alive. Otherwise, there would be no prophecy to fulfill.

Navid Tevaad, the cursed.

But he wouldn't be cursed if he found his birth father. He was out there somewhere, perhaps in East Hzorah. After Navid safely reached Caldor with Tele, Prophet Davin was sure to allow Navid to venture back out to find his father. It wasn't just for Navid. It was for peace.

Master Kruv placed a hand on Navid's. "I know this is surprising. I'm sorry I had to tell you this way."

Navid shook his head, stood, and forced a half-smile. "No. It's fine. I should have known. I was the only one with olive skin and dark hair. I was the fool for not figuring it out earlier."

"Navid …" Master Kruv stood and met his eyes. "You don't—"

"No," Navid waved his hand. "It's fine. We should probably find a horse to buy."

Master Kruv stood and untied his apron. "I think I know just the one."

FIVE

A MONSTER

Azuri's streets were quieter now. Morning errands were nearing completion and shop owners were retreating to tend to businesses before foot traffic increased again come evening. Tele was happy about that. Fewer people who might recognize her from earlier and better service in the shops.

"I hear the highwaymen are becoming more of a problem lately," Amie said as she led Tele to their first stop. "Did you see any on the road?"

"No," Tele said. "We were lucky to not encounter any real danger on our journey here."

"And Navid ..." Amie bit her lip. "How long have you known him? He's so very handsome, isn't he? You're lucky to be with him."

"*With* him?" Tele nearly missed a step. She almost had to stop herself from laughing aloud. "No, we're not together in that way, Amie. He's escorting me to Caldor."

Amie stopped before a shop entrance. "Still, lucky," she muttered and pushed the door in.

The sound of a bell above the door announced their arrival. The shop was filled with a variety of clothing, organized by season and size. A short, middle-aged lady dressed in a blue-and-white knee-length dress with a measuring rope draped across her shoulders, hopped up from behind a large stack of clothing in the far-left corner. She hurried over, a broad smile on her face.

"Amie! Lovely to see you, child." She greeted Amie with open arms.

The two embraced, and the shopkeeper gave her a peck on the cheek. Amie stepped back and gestured toward Tele in introduction.

"Aunt Bell, this is Tele," Amie said. "She's looking for new clothes. Her traveling clothes are quite worn."

The lady looked Tele up and down, appraising her in Amie's too-short dress. "How terrible …" She took Tele's hand. "My name is Bell. Please, come in."

Bell guided them deeper into the shop. She stopped at the shop's center and began taking Tele's measurements. She was quick, whispering numbers to herself as she pulled at Tele's limbs and spun her around to check her dimensions.

Amie plopped down on a chair beside a large body-length mirror and smiled. "I think green is her color, don't you, Aunt Bell?"

After the woman completed her measurements, she stepped back to take stock. "Yes … it does match her eyes." She placed a hand under her chin and an index finger across her lips. "Where are you from, child?"

Tele was surprised by the question and more than a little alarmed. Admitting she was from Desera wouldn't be the best idea. It might invite questions she couldn't give answers to. She instead decided to go with where her forefathers had lived. "Hzorah."

"Yes," Bell said impatiently, "but where in Hzorah, child?"

"Goil in South Hzorah near Dunham Lake," Tele said, immediately regretting her choice. She should have picked a place she knew better. Unfortunately, there was no other place in Hzorah she knew besides Azuri, and she couldn't possibly pass for living in the large Crown city. "I travel a lot. I don't stay in one place very long."

At least that much was true.

"Well …" Bell looked surprised for a moment, but turned on her heel and approached a stack of clothing a few paces away. "I don't have many in the South Hzorah cut, but I might have …"

Her voice trailed off as she ducked behind the wall of clothing. She came up again with a green dress, a different cut than the one Tele currently wore, more suited to a lady of higher class.

Tele began to protest, but Amie piped in. "Oh, Tele, it's beautiful! Do try it on!"

Amie hopped up and pulled Tele by the arm toward the left side of the shop to a white partition. Bell trailed behind and handed the dress to Tele when they stopped. With a sigh, Tele passed behind the curtain.

"Can you find me something better suited to traveling?" Tele said, pulling off Amie's dress. "Something brown or black. No dresses."

"Of course, child," Bell called back to her. "Amie, dear. How's your father?"

"He's fine," Amie said. "Still has me tied to the inn like a dog as if someone will spirit me away if I spend a second out of his sight."

"With the highwaymen, can you blame him?"

"I do, in fact."

Tele struggled with the dress, unused to anything of the like. She stepped from behind the partition to find Amie holding up a mirror that cut off her body from view, leaving just her head exposed.

"Tele!" Amie exclaimed. "You have to get this dress. You just must!"

Tele eyed herself curiously in the mirror. Her face reddened at the amount of cleavage the dress left exposed. She would have never imagined herself wearing this, but now the image burned into her mind.

"I don't know …" Tele said. "This isn't … me."

"Nonsense, child!" Bell appeared from behind another

stack of clothing and shuffled over. She held several bundles of clothing—folded browns, greens, and blacks. "It fits you admirably. But if you insist … These are all more suited for traveling. Utilitarian, comfortable … not dresses."

"Excellent," Tele said. "I'll take those instead."

"Oh, come now, Tele. You're getting them for free." Amie looked at Bell, who wore a frown. "She has a voucher from Caldor."

Bell's expression transformed to an eager smile. "I have some other fine garments that will fit you very well!"

"Fine," Tele said, growing annoyed. "I'll get the dress, but I'm on a long journey and must travel light. I can't afford to carry much."

Amie wore a look of victory. Bell, a look of satisfaction.

"Please, let me note the purchases in my log to Caldor," Bell said. She made her way to the back room after taking the Caldor Pass from Tele.

"I knew you'd love the dress, Tele," Amie said, smiling widely.

Tele couldn't help but feel like the two had worked together to make a sale. No matter. As Amie had pointed out, it came at no cost except, perhaps, her own embarrassment.

Bell returned moments later with a parchment and the clothes. "A notary of purchase for Caldor," she said and gave them to Tele.

Amie and Bell again hugged, and they were out of the shop. Once outside, Tele realized she'd forgotten to change out of the fancy dress. She called to Amie to go back, but she was already entering another shop.

It won't be the world's end if I'm seen in something extravagant, Tele thought. But when she saw how people reacted so strongly to her new attire, she decided that she'd been wrong. The reactions to her desert clothing had come at far fewer intervals and with much less exploratory regard.

Amie led Tele on a path that zig-zagged from shop to shop. It seemed that Amie was intent on taking advantage of the Caldor Pass's credit to find the most expensive shops in Azuri.

Tele had given up protest. In the end, though, Amie had ensured that Tele had a pack and waterskin of great quality. She'd found rare herbs that were many times more expensive in Desera. The girl knew the town's shops well. Tele couldn't have asked for a better guide in that respect.

The end of the street they traveled spanned a market where Tele gathered wafers, hard cheese, and nuts that would expire slowly and provide the energy they needed to survive. Each merchant had taken the Caldor Pass without question. Most tried to sell her more items when they realized Tele had a voucher of unlimited funds. Some tried before they knew she had the pass. Tele blamed the ridiculous dress for that. Her new pack, stuffed to the brim, weighed on her shoulders, and the dress's hem dragged at her feet, threatening to trip her in their haste if she didn't clear it from the ground.

The only items left unretrieved were the knives Tele wanted. Amie backtracked to a street that veered off the main road where they'd gathered other supplies. It was a quieter street, home to three shops. These shops did not display signs announcing to customers what they sold. They were subdued, foreboding.

Amie came to a stop at the entrance of a shop. She turned to face Tele and crossed her arms. "Tele, you shouldn't be buying knives. Father says that weapons are nothing but trouble, and you're only inviting evil when you carry them."

"Evil invites itself to my door whether I want it or not," Tele said.

Amie didn't respond beyond a disappointed frown. She turned, opened the door, and led Tele inside. Unlike the shops she'd visited previously, it was dark, with candles haphazardly placed on shelves scattered throughout the store. Swords and daggers of various lengths, axes unintended for lumber use, and scythes that looked sharper than needed in the farmlands all hung from the walls.

Three men were speaking in the back of the store. Dressed in all black, one of them leaned over a counter, his arms supporting his weight. The flickering candlelight cast shadows that made parts of him seem to disappear. Beside him stood another man of the same attire, but in gray. He leaned lazily against the table with his arms folded, looking directly at the two girls who wandered in.

"The man is dangerous. I've gone to the council and they won't do a thing about it," the man in black was saying to the shopkeeper behind the counter. "They talk as if he's harmless! How much longer before his meddling hurts someone else? How much longer before Desolate's Hand lifts, and he burns down the whole bloody forest?"

The shop door shut behind Tele and Amie and the man in black gave a start. He turned to see them, then exhaled audibly before turning back to the shopkeep. "Listen, me and Jarvis are gonna do something about it." He gestured to the man in gray. "Domis and his brother are in, too. You in or not?"

The young and balding shopkeeper wrung his hands as he paced in a circle. His eyes darted between the two men in black and gray. "This can't come back to me, you hear? I have a business, a family. I can't be going about like you two. I—"

"Listen," the man in black interrupted, his voice quieter. "You don't gotta do nothing but lend us the torches. We'll do the rest. Don't you want your family to sleep safe at night? Don't you want …" The man paused and turned to look at Tele and Amie for a moment. He turned back to the shopkeep. "We'll be back in an hour. Remember what I said, Tajit. It's only a matter of time. Witchcraft ain't no good."

The man in black signaled to his gray accomplice. They headed toward the shop's exit. The one in black gave Tele and Amie a smile as he passed. The one in gray, a frown.

"See?" Amie said. "Trouble."

Tele didn't argue. Instead, she approached the counter. "Hello, I'm looking to purchase."

"Oh …" He looked at her, surprised, as if he hadn't seen them enter. He continued wringing his hands for a moment before forcing them down at his sides. "What do you need? Nothing but weapons here …"

"My guide told me that—" Tele gestured to her side, but

Amie wasn't there. She turned to look behind her. Amie still stood at the front, her arms crossed, holding herself close. She looked ready to run out of the shop at any moment. Tele turned back to the shop's owner. "I was told I could find good weapons here."

"Weapons?"

Tele frowned. "That *is* what you sell here, no?"

"What would you need of weapons? Is there someone bothering you? You should talk to the Crown's Guard. They will help you. You know, when I was younger, there was a particularly nasty bully who—"

Tele held up a hand. "I'm sorry … Tajit, is it?" The man nodded. "Tajit, I need two daggers and two knives of shorter length. Well balanced, sharp, fourth degree Hzorah steel."

"Madam," Tajit said, taken aback. "I can't sell you weapons of that caliber without a directive from the crown. I'm not that kind of shopkeep. Bribes won't work. No, Madam, I'm sorry."

He pulled out a rag and polished a clean spot on his table. Tele looked back to Amie, who still stood nervously at the front of the shop. Tele set the Caldor Pass on the table.

Tajit halted his needless cleaning. He looked up to Tele. "Madam … This is … You're from the Sanctuary? But your eyes … They're—"

"I'm on my way there as soon as I can get those knives." Tele leaned forward and added, "Please, don't delay me."

The man gave a weak smile and bowed before exiting to the back. Tele let herself relax. She wasn't sure how much weight the Caldor Pass held, but every merchant in the town had no trouble accepting it for any expense.

Tele turned to Amie again. Amie gazed back, her eyes pleading for Tele to hurry. Tele smiled in reassurance and leaned against the table. She hoped it would relax Amie to see her a little less uptight. The girl was afraid. She had probably never been inside the shop before, and the place didn't hold the same welcoming quality as the other places they'd visited.

Tele heard a scream. Instinctively, she reached for a dagger that wasn't there. "What was that?"

"The surgeries …" Amie said. "They have them on this street … They almost never live." Another scream sounded. Amie put her hands over her ears and shut her eyes.

Tele allowed herself to breathe, relieved that the sounds weren't an immediate threat. And yet, empathy for Amie's fear washed over her. Tele's experience with danger had steeled her, but she still remembered how it felt to stand alone with her fears, wishing Simon would just hurry and get on with his heist so they could go back home.

Tajit entered from the back with a leather bundle in hand. He set it before her and unrolled it. Inside were four blades held secure by leather holsters. Two for stabbing, two for cutting. Tele pulled free the two longer daggers and spun them in her hands, a skill she'd practiced for years with her brothers. The daggers were incredibly well-balanced. She wished she could thank the blacksmith who'd forged them.

"These will do," she said and placed the daggers back. She folded the leather roll and placed it under her arm. "I'm sorry, but I couldn't help but overhear about some trouble someone is causing the town. Should I be concerned?"

Tajit cringed. "Oh, no … That was just about old Gavini. He's always up to some sort of trouble. 'Experiments,' he calls them. Don't you worry. Those men were just blowing off steam. They don't mean any harm." He displayed an unconvincing smile.

"Right. Thank you for the supplies, Tajit," Tele said. Tajit bowed and wrung his hands once more.

Tele turned to see Amie still at the front of the shop. When Tele approached, Amie pulled open the door and dashed outside.

She turned to Tele as they exited. "Are we done here?" Amie held herself tight again, looking around as if she expected a chilling wind to pass.

"Yes," Tele said. "I believe I have all that I need."

"Good," Amie said.

Amie led them back to the main street where her mood lightened. "I love the springtime," Amie said. "The air always smells best in the spring, don't you think?"

"It does," Tele said absently. She wondered if the two men in the shop were as harmless as Tajit had said and if the old man, Gavini, was just a meddling old man or someone else entirely.

"Winter in Azuri held shorter than was expected, just as the prophet said," Amie continued.

"I noticed," Tele replied. It was odd that this Gavini would use a term like "experiment." It wasn't that no one knew what the word meant … Still, it was odd.

"I heard that the winters in Goil are rather mild, is that true?" Amie asked.

"I suppose …" Tele didn't want to jump to conclusions, but who else would even use such a word? What did the man mean about Witchcraft? *This isn't my problem. I can't afford to get distracted.*

Amie stopped before Tele once more and crossed her arms. She wore the same motherly look she had before they entered the armory. "You're not from Goil, Tele. The winters there are horrible, and Dunham Lake isn't anywhere near Goil. Dunham Lake is by Azuri."

"So?" Tele said. It was a poor rebuttal. Amie's confrontation caught her unguarded.

"So, admit it. You're not from South Hzorah. I'm not a fool."

Tele sighed. She'd been foiled by her own ignorance of Hzorah. She supposed that it wouldn't also foil her ability to get to Caldor if one adolescent in Azuri knew where she was from. And who would believe her?

"Amie, I'm sorry. I didn't want to lie to you, but you must understand that Navid's charge to get me safely to Caldor is of grave importance."

"Why did you lie? Where are you from?"

Tele sighed. "I'm from Desera."

"Is *that* why you wanted knives? To kill us?" Amie took on an expression that bordered on hatred.

Tele was shocked. "To kill you? Of course not. Why would I want to kill you?"

Amie's expression darkened. "Hzorah has a prophet too, you know. I've heard the talk. That Desera is mounting an army. That you hate us for turning our back on the Creed. Why would you want to hurt us? We haven't done anything to you."

Mounting an army? Life as an outlaw lacked the luxury of being on top of current events. The news she *did* hear was mostly from fleeting conversations in the towns. Navid had said that Desera was to bring war to the other kingdoms, but he hadn't said that Desera was already mounting an army for attack. If Desera was already preparing to make a move, how would her going to Caldor change anything?

"I don't know that I can answer that either, Amie, but I promise that I'm not here to hurt you or hurt anyone." Tele wasn't sure that she knew anything anymore. It had seemed simple. Go to Caldor and no war. But was it really that simple? The Prophets had surely made a mistake.

Amie huffed, turned and began walking again. "I don't understand why you want those weapons if you're *not* bad. Not that it's any of my business ..."

No, it's not, Tele thought as she walked just behind Amie. But the girl had a strange way of making her feel guilty about her purchase. "Sometimes you fight so that you don't have to."

Amie looked at Tele. "I don't understand."

"Pray that you never have to," Tele said.

The walk back to the Kruv House stretched silence thin. Tele could almost feel the tension of the absence of conversation. Tele hadn't intended to upset Amie. She had thought Tele was something she wasn't and had withdrawn into herself. When they finally arrived at the inn, Amie made her way back to the kitchens with her eyes at her feet and without a parting word.

The Kruv house common had transformed from a quiet

dining hall into a bustling establishment. Where before there were only six tables, there were now many more, closer together, to accommodate the crowd. More servers bussed tables, and the candles were lit in anticipation of the setting sun. Most of the patrons were the upper-class type, predominantly male. Only a few tables in a far corner were occupied by less lavishly dressed townsfolk.

Uninterested in the notion of a crowded common, Tele made for her rooms.

"Madam Tele," Master Kruv's voice called from behind. Tele turned to the man cleaning a table. He motioned for her to sit with a swing of his apron rag. "Please, sit. Have a drink. I insist."

Tele turned back reluctantly. She didn't want to join the common or have a drink, but the man had allowed her to stay at his inn. He had even given his own daughter's clothes for her to wear, and his daughter had just helped her find supplies. She, at the very least, owed him a moment.

Tele approached the table and sat with Master Kruv. "I think I upset Amie."

"Amie's at that age," Master Kruv said. "But she's always been a bit dramatic. I used to tell my wife that she would do well as a performer if she could focus that energy. She didn't make things difficult for you, did she?"

"No, not at all," Tele said. "I think she just expected me to be … different somehow."

"She fancies Navid." Master Kruv laughed. "Perhaps she feels you're a threat."

Tele smiled. "Please, assure her I don't intend to woo him."

Master Kruv laughed again. "I will."

"So …" Tele thumbed her cup, trying desperately to find words to fill the uncomfortable silence. "So, have you known Navid long?"

"Quite long." Master Kruv straightened and looked beyond Tele. "I raised him. At least until he'd seen several years. Then he was taken …"

"You're his father?" Tele raised her eyebrows. "I guess I understand why he wanted to stay here."

"I raised him," Master Kruv said, "but I'm not sure who his father is. He was brought to me as an infant."

"I see." Tele wasn't familiar with what was normal or acceptable in Hzorah, but she was almost certain that Master Kruv's tone implied that the circumstances around Navid's parentage was an uncomfortable subject.

Mara approached the table with two glasses of ale. She glared at Tele. Tele guessed that Amie had relayed her disappointment to her sister.

"I think you raised a fine man. He got me here safely," Tele said. She took a drink of the ale and was surprised at the fruity flavor.

"I don't think I can take much of the credit. He's spent more time in Caldor than under my roof." Master Kruv took a swig before continuing. "Is there anything else you'll be needing? I have the horses you and Navid wanted. Did you get all the supplies you need? Anything for your room?"

"No, nothing," Tele said. She paused, considering. "Do you know someone named Gavini?"

Master Kruv raised a shocked brow before gesturing for Tele to keep her voice down. "Only been in town a few hours and you already know about Gavini? Did Amie tell you about him?"

"I overheard someone talking about him and his … experiments," Tele said.

"The man does odd things," he said before glancing about the tavern. "He used to work in the medicine house in town for a small fee. He managed to save lives that the other healers couldn't. I first met him there. There was a fight in my common between two brutes. One of them had a knife. Stabbed the other man five times in the gut. Desolate's Hand must have been with the man because he's still alive today."

He pointed a thumb to a table to their left where a large man ate quietly.

"But it wasn't just healing." Master Kruv gestured around

the room. "He made my walls shine. I barely have to clean them. Stains don't stick." He placed an elbow on the table. "I run an establishment that attracts a crowd with heavier pockets, but that wasn't always so. His … well, I don't know what to call it … experiment, I suppose. His experiment made my walls shine, and it attracts a lot of attention. The merchants love it. The lords who pass through love it. They say it makes them feel more comfortable than the dark taverns they usually have to stay in when on the road."

"How did he make the walls shine?" Tele asked.

"I'm not really sure," he said. "He asked if he could clean the common for a few marks, and I agreed. I couldn't pass up the offer. My wife wanted to have some time out with the family together, so I had a good excuse to give in to that request and at a price I found hard to turn down. When I returned, the common's walls were shining.

"Not long after, I began getting more and more customers who enjoyed the look. I went to find the man to ask him how much he would charge to do my guest rooms with the same treatment and he said he'd do it for free—provided I did something for him."

"What did he want?" Tele asked, curious.

Master Kruv grinned. "He wanted my daughters to learn to read. Oddest thing …"

"Indeed, odd," Tele said, finding herself instantly liking this Gavini.

"I took my daughters to his cabin in the woods twice a week so that he could teach them. I even became interested in learning more myself. My wife was always the smart one. I've picked up on a few words and phrases over my years, but the idea of learning how to read well became a personal goal. What's funny is that my learning to read enabled me to improve my inn further. Doing him a 'favor' only resulted in my family prospering. My daughters learning to read will ensure them skills that they can use to petition for a higher mark than I could."

"Mark?" Tele asked. "More money?"

Master Kruv frowned. "No, no … Not that kind of mark." He pulled up his sleeve to reveal a blue and red tattoo of a crest. Under it was a red tattoo that resembled a building. Beneath the building was the word KRUV. "My daughters will be able to receive a greater mark if they decide."

"Ah, I understand." At least she thought she did.

"Not long after I stopped visiting Gavini," he continued, "a few children began exploring the woods around his cabin. You know how children are … they're always curious. One of them got into one of Gavini's … experiments he'd left outside. Gavini was inside and heard the girl scream. He ran out to see Domis Kemp's daughter burned by some sort of liquid. Gavini rushed the girl to town to seek help. She died that night in the medicine house."

Master Kruv finished his ale and sat back. "Since then," he said, "everyone in and around Azuri has stayed clear of Gavini's place. They wouldn't go near the man if you paid them. I even caution my daughters not to go back there. The man has done a lot of good things, but …"

"You don't want anyone hurt," Tele finished.

Master Kruv nodded solemnly. "I'm sorry, Madam—"

"Please, it's Tele."

"Yes." He smiled and bowed. "Tele, I must get back to the kitchens. Don't hesitate to let me know if there is anything I can do for you. You won't be disturbed here."

Tele returned his smile and Master Kruv retreated back behind the common's swinging door.

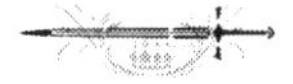

The last of the sun had disappeared when Tele exited the Kruv House common for her room. The men who occupied the hall drank heavily and gambled heavier. When one game ended, those at the table would immediately set up another round of cards while the losing party would request another round of ale.

And then there were those who used the time between

rounds to make drunken conversations with the available women. One such man had spotted Tele and stumbled over to make her acquaintance, complimenting her fine dress. She opted out by downing the remainder of her ale and making toward the tavern's guest rooms before he reached her table.

Navid had asked her to stay out of trouble and that's exactly what she intended to do. Her experience in Desera meant a low profile would likely result in living another day. Navid was certainly keeping out of sight. She hadn't caught a glimpse of him since morning. Much longer and Tele would have to leave without him. She didn't know where she might go, but she knew that staying here for much longer was too dangerous a prospect.

In her room, Tele placed a fresh piece of parchment on the open desk. She had only been in Hzorah for a day, and she'd already seen so many new things. A firsthand account of her experiences, while they were still fresh, would undoubtedly be valuable for her notes.

The room was quiet—no one to disturb her work. She would be able to get a good portion of it done before she slept. Tele dipped the pen in the ink basin and began to write.

After my father, mother, and older brothers—
Huvil, Abigail, Gib, and Simon,
respectively—died

She paused, looking at the words. They were cold and distant, as if she wasn't the one who'd actually lived through the tragedy. How had she so easily slipped into the role of a Keeper of the Covenant? Her family wasn't a curiosity to be accounted for.

Tele had dreamed of having the opportunity to expand her parents' work. Her mother and father had built their knowledge on the shoulders of their own parents' work, and so on back to the beginning of the Covenant. Magic was not a solo endeavor. The Keepers of the Covenant were a vital part.

When her family died that night in the Deseran wasteland,

the torch had been passed down to her. She was the last protector of the knowledge held by her family—a living vessel of said knowledge. Like the Keepers before her, she'd vowed to protect the Covenant. Staying alive was no longer just instinct. It was imperative for allowing the piece she held to pass to the great Wizard … *If* she could find him.

Tele sat back in her chair. It was her duty to deliver her part of the Covenant to Wizard Titan and, thus far, she had not made any progress in that effort. She wasn't even sure if the man was alive—though he was said to be immortal—and she didn't know if the prophets who'd sent for her would know where the Wizard would be.

But they *did* know where she was.

Maybe they know who I am … what I am, Tele thought. *Maybe they know where the Wizard is and they want to recommission the Keepers.*

It made sense. What other purposes would they have for her?

Leaning back into her work, she set the pen to paper once more. She tried to write on, but another thought obstructed her intent. Those men were going to hurt the Gavini fellow. The man in gray, Domis, had all but said it with his eyes. And when Master Kruv told her that Domis' daughter had died, she understood why. Tele's father had said he'd do anything to protect her. That a father would do anything to right a wrong to his child.

Tele redoubled her pen grip. *That's not my problem right now.*

Amie had thought Tele was a monster—a Dominion zealot who intended to kill them. Tele's denial of it didn't make a difference to Amie. Tele had arrived from nowhere, bought weapons, and claimed herself of Deseran origin. Amie saw a woman of violence. Tele only wanted to help, but she couldn't begin to explain to Amie the gravity of her lot in life.

Tele sat back again. Was she really any different than what Amie thought? She'd killed men in the past, and yet she felt justified in her actions. Killing without remorse was the trait of a monster. She'd had remorse, but that didn't stop her from doing it again and again to survive the Dominion wilderness—to keep the Thief-Takers who hunted them from taking her family's work and giving it to Prophet Tristan.

And then there was Gavini. She had walked out of the armory and hadn't even tried to stop those men. She could have at least said something. She'd told herself that it was not her battle, but was that as bad as killing him herself?

I don't know that they will actually do anything, Tele thought. *They could just be blowing off steam like the shopkeeper said they were. Perhaps Domis' look of hatred is as far as he'd take it.*

But Gavini and his "experiments"—a term that was often used by many Keepers—could be something more. The man in the shop had called it Witchcraft, but people were always afraid of things they didn't understand. That was why the Keepers had been banished so many years ago.

Gavini had worked in the medicine house, and though he wasn't a healer, he was able to save lives that many healers couldn't. And he could read and was obviously well educated despite being poor enough to ask Master Kruv for work. That wasn't a common pairing from what she understood of the world outside of her lifelong isolation.

Tele didn't know for sure, but if Gavini was a Keeper of the Covenant ...

Tele set down the pen. She *could* do something about those men. She certainly wished someone could have helped her family when the Thief-Takers finally caught them. And if Gavini was a Keeper, then she *had* to do something. Even if those men had no bite to their threats, she should at least verify that that was the truth. She should at least warn Gavini that tensions were rising.

Maybe I am a monster. Tele thought, standing. *But I don't have to be the kind anyone expects.*

SIX

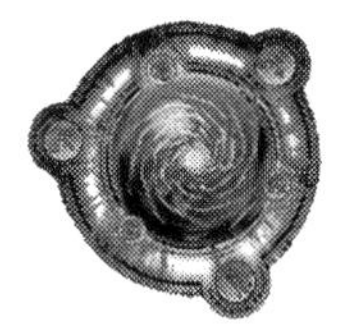

TO FLAME AND STEEL

Tele scanned the Kruv House common. A harpist had joined the tavern, entertaining with a skilled performance. With practiced finesse, he plucked out a tune that was unfamiliar to her but held the audience enraptured. When his eyes passed over Tele, he let a smile grace his face and winked as he flawlessly dipped into an arpeggiated sweep.

Master Kruv was nowhere to be found.

She turned to the kitchen door. Pushing it open just enough to peek inside, she called into the room beyond, "Master Kruv?"

A serving girl she didn't recognize pulled the door open with a nimble foot, exposing Tele. Tele stood, blocking the girl's path. The girl shifted the weight of her tray.

"I'm sorry," Tele said, moving aside to let her pass. The girl smiled politely and crossed into the common.

Tele slipped into the kitchens before the door closed. She looked around at various stations where cooks tended a brick oven and cut meat on long counters. Two young men, maneuvering a large jug, passed her. Tele pressed against the wall, allowing them to pass, then turned to meet Mara's frown.

"Are you lost?" Mara asked, balancing her own tray. "Or are you here to upset my sister?"

Tele scowled. "No, I'm looking for your father. I need to speak with him."

"He's out seeing to a shipment at the docks." Mara brushed past her. "Patrons are not allowed back here. Please show yourself out." Without another word, Mara backed through the swinging door.

"Please, Mara," Tele beckoned, but Mara ignored her to smile at the table she attended.

Tele cursed her fortune and surveyed the common again, hoping to find that Master Kruv had returned, despite what Mara had told her. Sure enough, the common had not changed, save the harpist, who now sang as he played an anthem.

Tele made for the exit. She shut the tavern door behind her, dampening the sound of the harpist's victorious song. The warm, humid early night air carried the smell of hearth and ale. The streets were aglow with the light of a nearly full moon, its image reflecting in the window glass of the surrounding buildings.

Tele shut her eyes to the world around her. Master Kruv had said that no one was willing to go near the Gavini place. Someone had to know where to find him, but was it really a good idea to go door-to-door searching for someone the town feared?

There has to be another way.

"Going somewhere?"

Tele turned at the unexpected inquiry. She sighed in relief when she saw that it was only Amie sitting under the pale moonlight, staring into the heavens.

"Father says the streets can be dangerous at night," Amie said. "That sometimes thieves lurk, searching to take what isn't theirs to take." She cocked her head at Tele. "Is that why you're going out? To join them?"

Tele frowned, then let a hint of a smile creep onto her face. "No."

Amie stared her down. "Is that funny to you?"

Tele turned away as her smile widened. Amie's jab

reminded her of her brother, Gib. He had always tried to push her over the edge with his constant shots at any of her shortcomings. Though passive-aggressive, Amie's words were the first that brought her any true comfort. As if a little piece of him still lived.

"I'm sorry. You just reminded me of someone," Tele said.

"Well," Amie said, "have a pleasant night walk."

Tele turned back to Amie, her composure reformed. She squatted down to Amie's level and the serving girl eyed her suspiciously.

"Amie, I'm sorry I upset you earlier."

Amie looked away. "Right."

"Listen," Tele said. "I need your help. I need to find someone."

Amie turned back, then shook her head before looking away again. "I'm not sure I want to help you dull your knives."

Tele sighed. Gib would have had quite the competition with this one. "I'm not trying to hurt anyone. Do you remember those men in the armory earlier? The ones at the counter when we arrived?"

Amie looked back again, eyes narrowed. "Yes. The ones who wanted trouble?"

"Right. You closed your eyes and ears after the—" Tele paused when Amie showed a sign of discomfort. "The noise. The shopkeeper told me they were talking about a man named Gavini."

Amie sat in attention. "Gavini?"

"Yes. Your father told me about him. How he helped your family. How he taught you how to read. Amie, I'm afraid those men are going to hurt Gavini. I want to help, but I don't know how to find him. If I can get to his place, I can warn him before it's too late. Can you help me?"

Amie looked down. "Father has forbidden me from going back to Gavini's cabin. He says it's too dangerous … and he's right. Lana died there."

Tele placed a hand on Amie's shoulder. "Amie, everyone

here fears the man. They think he's trouble. But I know that you know that that just isn't true. He's a good man, isn't he?"

Amie nodded, but didn't look up.

"I need your help. I can't help him without you. Please, just tell me where to go. I just want to do the right thing."

Amie looked at Tele, her eyes searching. She looked away again before she stood and approached the tavern door. Of course Amie wouldn't go. She respected her father far too much, but she could have at least told Tele where to go.

Amie paused before entering the Kruv House. Tele was surprised to see her face bearing determined mischief.

"Meet me around back in ten minutes." She looked down at Tele and let on a half-smile. "And pray Desolate's Hand delivers us on time."

Amie opened the door and departed.

Tele smiled. Gib's match, indeed.

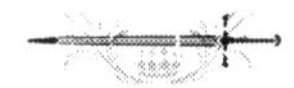

In a narrow alley, Tele leaned against the rear wall of the Kruv House. Beside her was a locked metal gate, and beyond, stalls to each side of the stable sheltered the horses of the Kruv House visitors. The smell of manure became the foremost sensation, reminding her of Janamah—the capital city in Desera. She imagined that one of these animals would be the one Navid planned for her to ride. Though a few of the horses looked nearly identical, she thought she recognized Gilly happily chewing in a corner stall.

A shuffle of footsteps drew Tele's attention. Amie, lantern held before her in one hand, emerged from the Kruv House's rear exit. She'd changed from her green dress to tan trousers and a white shirt. She glanced in Tele's direction before pulling open a stall and ducking inside. Amie reemerged with a brown and white horse in tow. When she approached the gate where Tele stood, she smiled.

"Ready?" Amie asked as she dragged a saddle from under a shelf.

"Is that horse really necessary?" Tele asked.

"Yes, it's necessary," Amie said and unlocked the outside gate. "Don't you want to get to Gavini's before those men do?"

Tele frowned. "I suppose. But shouldn't we take the horse Navid and I arrived with?"

"That would be smart if I actually knew that horse," Amie said. "It's smarter to ride a horse I know than one I don't."

Can't argue with that, Tele thought.

Amie led the horse into the dark alley and motioned for Tele to help her toss the saddle over the horse's back. Tele complied, holding it steady as Amie buckled the mount in place. Amie gave the horse a gentle rub and a few comforting words before she stepped onto a mounting platform and pulled herself into the stirrups.

"Alright then," Amie said. "Hop on."

Tele stepped onto the platform. She too had changed and no longer wore the dress that Amie had coaxed her into purchasing. She now wore the new travel garb. Wearing the dress for a time was … interesting, but it was ultimately impractical. She would give it to Amie before she left. Amie would, at least, appreciate it.

"I hate riding these things," Tele muttered and mounted behind Amie, shifting to sit comfortably astraddle.

"Not a thing," Amie said. "*He's* a horse. His name is Dasher." She led Dasher into the open street.

"Is this your father's horse?"

"No," Amie said. "He belongs to one of my father's regulars. He'll be here half the night drinking and won't even notice him gone."

"What if he decides to leave early?" Tele asked. "I don't want to get you into trouble."

"Well, then …" Amie said, looking back. "We'll just have to be sure to be quick. And if we aren't fast enough, maybe you'll get a chance to use those knives after all. I hear he's good with a sword and quite violent when he's angry."

Amie brought the horse to a gallop. In spite of Tele's prior experience with Navid, she still held tightly to Amie's waist, fighting nausea. They followed the now-vacant streets out past the city's edge, through an open field, and into the dark wood.

They slowed to a trot as the path grew narrow and the trees consumed them. The road was not like the well-traveled route Navid had used to bring her to Azuri. The thick brush and trees grew wild, uncarved by farmers and traders making rounds. Moonlight did little to guide them. Its shafts of white light were strangled by the unchecked reach of plant life. Were it not for the lantern light, Tele was sure they would have struck low-hanging branches that appeared as the trail bent along the winding path.

"I'm sorry for accusing you of being evil," Amie said, breaking the silence. "You might not be. I just don't think weapons are any good. You're just so … pretty … You could be a princess. Weapons are unbecoming of you."

Tele was surprised by both the apology and the compliment. She stared at Amie's gently bouncing curls a moment before she replied, "You can't expect one's looks to be a reflection of her true nature."

"I still think you shouldn't have bought those knives," Amie said. "I'm not wrong about that."

Tele smiled. "I hope you're right."

"Gavini means a great deal to me," Amie said. "Father told me once that we'd nearly lost the inn before Gavini made our walls shine."

"Did he ever tell you how he accomplished such a thing?" Tele asked.

"No, but he always seemed to know a lot about the strangest things. He said that he would teach me as much as he could—how to read, how to use numbers, how to ask good questions.

"Then the accident with Lana happened and Father wouldn't let me return. Gavini came to the inn and begged my father to let me and Mara return, but Father refused. Father said he didn't hate Gavini … just that he didn't know what he would do if he lost us."

"Your father cares for you deeply. Were it my daughter, I think I would do the same. Wouldn't you?"

Amie didn't answer.

The path eventually opened to a small clearing. Surrounded by patches of dirt and knee-high grass was a small, wooden cabin. Smoke floated out of its chimney, and the warm glow of candlelight flickered in the single, small window near the door.

"Is this it?" Tele asked.

Amie dismounted. "This is Gavini's."

Tele slipped off the horse and glanced around the clearing. It was encircled by trees, interrupted only by the path behind them. Behind the cabin was a large fire pit and a cauldron. Several other metallic tools sat on a workbench along with a few glass bowls and beakers. Further back was a small well and several small cages.

Her body almost tingled as she looked over his odd assortment of tools. What was he doing out here? What kind of experimentation was he engaged in? Even as the tide of excitement rushed in to replace her doubt, she tried to temper her expectations.

There could be a simpler explanation. Perhaps he merely loves to collect oddities.

Amie smiled and started toward the cabin door. Tele followed a few steps behind, allowing Amie to take the lead. Instead of knocking, Amie opened the door and stepped inside. More cautious than Amie's presumption of welcome, Tele stood in the entryway.

The cabin was lined with shelves that collected tools, parchment, dishes, and plants without any apparent care for organization. Below the shelves were various chests and wooden crates, each nearly overflowing with their own miscellaneous contents. A cot was against the rear wall and next to it, a small table. At the table, hunched over a glass dish of blue liquid, was a man.

"Gavini!" Amie said. "I've—"

Gavini raised a finger without turning, apparently

unalarmed by their intrusion. He lifted a small cylindrical shape with a wooden casing and put it to his eye. He leaned in closer, examining the contents of the dish before setting it down and lifting a pen out of an inkwell and scribbling a few notes.

Tele's stomach fluttered. The tool he'd used was a hand lens. Tele had never seen one in person before. Even her father hadn't owned one, and most of his research had required it. Her father had lost his lens when he'd fled Prophet Tristan's palace in Janamah. The skill it took to grind a lens with optical precision … The glass was priceless.

Gavini dropped the quill back into the ink basin before turning in his chair. An unkempt gray-and-white beard fell over his dark green shirt. Bright blue eyes met them, and his mustache twitched.

Amie rushed forward and collapsed onto his chest. "Oh, Gavini! I've missed you so! How are you feeling? Are your knees still giving you trouble? The winter must have been awful out here, all alone."

"I'm fine, child," Gavini said. His voice was weathered and mature. "It's so good to see you." He appraised her. "You've grown into a beautiful woman."

Amie's neck reddened. "It hasn't been that long since you've seen me."

"You see yourself everyday," Gavini said. "Several months has changed you. You've grown more lovely, and I have grown infinitely more frightful."

"Nonsense," Amie said. Her voice cracked, and she wiped at her eyes with the sleeve of her blouse.

"It's all sense," Gavini said. "And who is this?"

Amie turned back toward Tele who still stood at the entry. "This is Tele."

"Come, child," Gavini said. "My vision isn't sharp. Step into the light."

Tele stepped into the cabin. The floor creaked as she entered as if to acknowledge her presence. Gavini stood and waved her forward.

"Gavini, this is Tele," Amie said. "She's a guest at my father's inn."

Tele walked to the middle of the cabin. "Hello. I'm sorry to have interrupted your work. Is that a genuine hand lens?"

Gavini turned and picked up the hand lens from the table. He held it out for Tele to inspect. Tele stepped closer and took it. The lens had a wooden frame with rounded grooves and a split that allowed for it to twist—a focal point adjustment.

"I haven't met anyone who could identify one in years," Gavini said. He appraised her curiously. "Tele, is it?"

She nodded. "Tele Gavina."

Gavini's eyes lit with renewed curiosity. "Gavina … Where are you from, child?"

Tele glanced at Amie who nodded reassuringly. "Desera."

"Where are your parents?" he asked. "Did they travel here with you?"

"No, they …" Tele glanced down at the hand lens. "They recently passed. Thief-Takers."

Gavini stepped back and sat back down in his chair. "I see."

Amie looked at Gavini then to Tele, confused. "Gavini, we came here to warn you. Tele heard something in town about Lana's father and some other men. They want to hurt you."

"Everyone in Azuri is uncomfortable with me just outside their city," Gavini said. "That hasn't been lost on me."

"It's urgent," Tele said. "They are coming here tonight. They gathered men and torches. I think they plan to burn your cabin down with you inside. You have to leave right now."

"And why, child," Gavini said, "do you care whether an old man lives or dies? Don't you have more important matters to attend to?"

Tele did have important matters. She had to find some place to bunker down. Prophet Tristan's Thief-Takers had seen her before she walked through the gateway that had spirited her to Hzorah. They would know she was alive and would pursue.

But if what she thought about Gavini was true …

"You're a Keeper of the Covenant, aren't you?" Tele asked Gavini bluntly. "That's how you own a hand lens. That's why you're hiding in the woods alone."

Gavini met her eyes. "A Keeper? That's a dangerous accusation. You must want me dead too if you're not a Keeper yourself. And if you are a Keeper, then you've made a dangerous mistake if I'm not one."

Tele stepped to the table and pointed out a few objects amongst the clutter. She wasn't wrong. She knew that now. "That's a radial rule. This is a thermoscope. And this," Tele said as she lifted the black, leather-bound book he'd been writing in and flipped to the first page. "This is—"

Tele froze when she read the few words on the page.

Element and Reaction.
The study and findings of Gavini Gavina
regarding material interaction and reaction.

"Gavina?" Tele looked up from the page. "Your name is Gavini Gavina."

"I'm aware," Gavini said with a smile. "Rolls off the tongue, don't you think?"

"But that means …"

"I'm your uncle," Gavini said. "Huvil, your father, is my brother."

Tele stood speechless, staring into the eyes of the old man. Her parents would have known many if not all of the Keepers, and it stood to reason that many of them would have been related. After all, her parents had passed their knowledge down to her instead of finding another.

She recalled her father saying something idly about his brother. He'd never referred to him directly, but she'd known that he wasn't the only child of his family. Why hadn't he told her more about him? And why hadn't she even thought to ask?

There was probably a multitude of topics she'd never thought to broach with her parents. There was always later that night or tomorrow.

"So," Amie said. "This is … unexpected."

Gavini broke away from Tele's gaze to look to Amie. "It was a long time ago, before you were born." He looked back to Tele. "Gib must have only seen two years, maybe three years? How is—"

"Dead," Tele said. "Simon as well. I'm the only one left."

"I'm very sorry, child," Gavini said.

"Speaking of dead," Amie said, "we came here because people want *you* dead, Gavini. We have to get out of here."

"And go where?" Gavini asked. "It's not just the Kemps who want me dead. No one in town would offer me refuge. They'll find me eventually. I'm an old man, Amie. Too old to run."

"You're not too old," Amie said, half stomping her foot. "We brought a horse. You can ride it. We'll take you to my father's inn."

"Your father doesn't want me there." He looked at Amie pointedly. "I'm sure he'd be very upset if he knew you were here. I'm sure he doesn't."

"He doesn't," Amie said, almost ashamed. "But that doesn't matter. What matters is making sure you're safe."

"What matters," Gavini said, "is making sure that *you* are safe. I've seen many wonderful years, more than my share. If they don't kill me today, they will tomorrow. It's only a matter of time and has been for many years now. What happened to Lana was only the catalyst for what many have wanted to do for a very long time."

"You could come with me," Tele said.

Amie's eyes widened. "To Caldor?"

Tele shot Amie a venomous glare. She hadn't planned to tell him that detail, lest she scare him from coming. "There's someone who's taking me there. The Prophets think that I'm important somehow. They sent a man named Navid all the way to the Dominion Desert to find me. I think they want to gather the Keepers of the Covenant."

"The Prophets," Gavini said, "are the very reason we hide

in the first place. They scattered us across the land and forced us into hiding."

"I know," Tele said.

She herself hadn't fully intended to go to Caldor. She still planned to leave Navid the first opportunity she had. With Gavini along, someone she could actually trust, she'd be able to rebuild a life for herself and find a way to bring the Wizard back.

"You don't have to come with me," Tele said. "But you can at least escape. You have a better chance at life coming with us than not."

Amie nodded. "Please, Gavini."

Gavini stood, using the table for support. "Hand me that pack over there."

Amie's expression lit with joy. And she rushed over to the large pack in the cabin's corner. She handed it to Gavini, and he began placing table items inside. He pointed to various places in the room and asked Amie and Tele to help him retrieve tools, papers, and small, loosely bound books. Tele scanned the room, looking for anything that might be important to take. Her gaze fell on a small rack holding vials of colored liquid.

"What about these?" she asked.

"Too fragile," he said. "They might break."

"And these here?" Tele asked, pointing to a set of delicate, metallic tools that she'd never seen before.

"Unimportant," he said.

"And this?" Tele asked. She held the hand lens. "It's small."

Gavini smiled. "Why don't you hold on to that one. Hand me that staff there."

Tele nodded and pocketed the lens before retrieving his tall walking stick. She stuffed a few more items that appeared to have some sort of value in her pockets, though she couldn't be sure. She didn't know how accessible many of these objects were in Hzorah.

When Gavini was satisfied with what he'd gathered, the pack's buckle almost didn't latch. Even then, he'd only packed a small portion of the tools and notes scattered about. With a momentary gaze of discontent, he turned to the door. Tele shouldered the pack, and Amie took his arm as they exited the cabin.

Outside, smoke drifted into the dark sky. The smell of pitch hung thick in the air and the footfalls and chatter of men drawing near rang beyond the tree line.

Tele turned back to Gavini and Amie. "They're coming from the path. We should hide in the woods."

"The woods are thick." Amie's face puckered. "And there are ticks in there."

"By all means, Amie," Tele said, "feel free to stand here and wait for the men to come."

It was a harsh quip considering her fear, but there wasn't time to coddle the girl. Amie nodded her understanding and moved to follow Tele into the woods behind the cabin. Tele resisted the urge to jog, and instead, slowed and took Gavini's other arm.

The clearing in the woods had seemed quaint when she'd first arrived. Now that their rush to escape was slowed by Gavini's aging knees, the clearing felt unnecessarily vast. Tele urged Gavini forward, trying her best not to push him so fast that he lost his footing. If he fell out here, they'd be caught for sure.

I'm not going to lose the last vestige of my family. Not again. Not tonight.

Tele glanced over her shoulder as they reached the thick brush. Several men were beginning to materialize from the path. She let Gavini's pack drop from her shoulder and shoved it at Amie.

"Here," she said. "Take this." She then reached for Gavini's staff. "May I?"

He handed her the stick. His weight sagged, and Amie adjusted her footing to keep him upright.

"What are you doing?" Amie demanded.

"Buying you some time," Tele said. "Get as far into the woods as you can. Find a place to hide if you can. Better yet, find a way back to the path. I'll keep them from searching for you, then meet you with the horse."

"There's six of them!" Amie said, looking to the cabin.

"Right," Tele said. "So, you'd better get moving."

Amie hesitated a brief moment before Tele barked a sharp, "Go!"

When Amie left, Tele rushed forward and paused to press herself against the wall of the cabin, just out of sight. Five men gathered there, all wielding torches. Tajit, the armory's shopkeeper, wasn't with them. The quiet man in gray—Domis—was. He inspected the horse Tele and Amie had ridden. The man in black stood in front of the men, appraising the cabin with two torches.

Another man stepped out of the cabin and took the second torch from the man in black. "There's no one in there, Ronzit," he said to the man in black. "There's a warm bowl of stew inside. Looks like he just scorching left."

"Last I heard, the man was half-crippled. He couldn't have gotten far," Ronzit said. "Domis, Nithin, you're with me. You three, burn this place down. The old man won't need it where he's going."

Thirty seconds. The forest was thick, and Amie and Gavini should have been completely out of sight by now. Tele stepped away from the cabin as the men took their torches to it. She held Gavini's staff before her, steeling herself to be the mountain between them and Gavini.

"What do we have here?" Ronzit said as he walked toward her with Domis and Nithin just behind him. "What are you doing out here, girl? Who's your father? He won't be pleased to know his daughter is wandering about the woods near a murderer's cabin."

"Stay back," Tele warned.

"We don't want any trouble with you," Ronzit said continuing toward her. "Put down that stick, and we'll see to it you get back home safely."

"Stay *back*. I won't say it again."

Nithin chuckled as he stepped up beside the ringleader. "Put the stick down. Who are you? Rohan's girl?"

He stepped toward her, and Tele struck. The man yelped as his torch fell to the ground. He clutched his hand, cradling it against his chest. She'd given the strike a bit too much force and had broken his hand for sure. *Good.*

"Bloody sitter!" Nithin snarled. He gritted his teeth and fell to a knee.

Tele didn't care what he called her just now. *A minute of time bought. Amie and Gavini should be nearing either a safe hiding place or the road.*

"Alright, girl. Enough," Ronzit said after stomping out the torch fire before it caught the whole clearing ablaze.

Ronzit reached for her staff. Tele knocked his hand away and landed a swift crack to his right ankle. He dropped his torch and stumbled backward. Domis leapt for her. Tele stepped aside, then used the length of the staff to push him down.

Tele moved for the others before they could recover. These men were not soldiers. They didn't even appear to have any comprehensive experience in a fight. She'd swept them aside easily. Gib and Simon's training had more than prepared her for the likes of these men.

The front of the small home was already engulfed in flames, and the other three men were making their way around the cabin. She paused, staring at the destruction of so much of Gavini's work, hearing her mother's desperate cries and her father's pleading words in the inferno.

Tele broke free of the spell and ran after the three arsonists. With several swift attacks, she reduced the men to crumpled, wailing boys, begging for mercy.

The heat of the flames almost burned her skin. Like a forest in a drought, the cabin welcomed the fire. Smoke billowed into the air, blocking out the moonlight and allowing the flickering fire to cast phantoms across the clearing.

A minute and thirty seconds, almost two minutes. Gavini and Amie should be safe by now. Transfixed, she backed away from the burning cabin and absently grabbed Dasher's reins.

Domis stumbled into the clearing, followed by a limping Ronzit. When Domis made to go after her, Ronzit grabbed him by the arm, holding him back.

"Let the sitter go," he said. "We got to finish what we started here."

Domis stared at her another moment before trotting back to a fallen torch and setting fire to the cabin's rear.

"Go home, girl," Ronzit said. "And if we find you clucked about what you saw here, we'll burn your house next." He turned away and took up his own torch.

Tele led the horse away from the clearing and to the path. She paused, looking back to the burning home—Gavini's home. Wood snapped as the flames ate away at the cabin's frame.

Run, my child. Run!

Tele turned and ran.

Smoke was the only thing Tele could smell even though she was now far away from the burning cabin. Amie was quieter than Tele had ever thought possible. Gavini sat behind Amie on the horse, and Tele walked alongside them. The horse's footfalls on the cobblestone streets rang out, setting the tempo for the steady hum of the dkricas.

"My family died that way," Tele whispered as they approached the Kruv House. Amie looked back at her with watering eyes. "They died victim to flame and steel and men who let hate destroy who they once were."

Amie looked forward again. "I hope you find them and make them pay for what they've done."

Mara sat outside the Kruv House stables. When they approached, she stood. Amie dismounted and ran into her sister's arms.

"They tried to kill him!" Amie cried, her voice muffled

against Mara's shoulder. "They burned his house to the ground. Everything is gone."

"They're just things, child," Gavini said and smiled down to Mara. "It's good to see you again, Mara."

Mara looked at Gavini with shock, then to Tele. "Ever since you arrived, you've brought nothing but trouble. It's good to see you don't intend to keep that pattern."

"I wouldn't be so sure," Gavini said. "Have you ever tried to help a crippled, old man off of a horse?"

Mara smiled and took Gavini's hand. Tele stepped up to assist and the two of them eased him to the ground.

"See? Trouble," Gavini said, then winked at Amie. Amie smiled despite her tears.

Mara pulled her sister close again and took Gavini's hand. "Come now, let's go inside. Then you can explain what's going on." She walked them back through the stables toward the inn's rear door. She turned back to look at Tele. "See to it that the horse is returned … *please.*"

Tele stood alone in the late-night silence. She turned to Dasher. "Of course, Desolate's Hand left me with you." The horse didn't respond. "Well, come on then. Let's get you back in your stall."

Tele struggled with the saddle's buckle before the mount fell to the side. The horse, startled by the noise and still spooked from the fire, shuffled at the impact.

"Shh, I'm sorry." Tele patted the horse on his nose, comforting.

She put away the saddle and led Dasher back to his stall. "Goodnight," she said and closed the gate. She shook her head. She was talking to a horse. Exhaustion was clearly getting to her.

A mixture of raucous laughter and joyous song leaked from behind the inn's door. The Kruv House was full of patrons who, by any good sense, should be home with their families. The tavern seemed the nightlife center of activities for the sleepless.

Tele stood before the Kruv house entrance. She would

simply skirt past and into the guest rooms. She pushed open the door and immediately set to her plan. But, in an unfortunate pass of attention, Tele caught eyes with the performing musician. The harpist abruptly ended his upbeat song and stood to look at the newcomer. The first to truly notice her, he called out with concern. "Are you alright, Madam?"

The hall fell silent and all eyes turned to examine what had disturbed the performer enough to actually pause his song. Tele had hardly been noticed before. Now, with her clothes ashen from the thick smoke of the burning cabin, all eyes stared. The inn's crowd had increased even at this late hour. As quickly as the silence fell, whispers broke out among the tavern guests.

Unwilling to remain the inn's spectacle, Tele turned and headed for the guest rooms. The crowded common parted to make room for the disheveled arrival. When she exited the common and entered the empty guest hall, the talk grew louder and, undoubtedly, reactionary.

Finding her room, she fished her key from the inner pocket of her shirt and unlocked the door. The room's candles had burned to half length. The parchment and pen still lay on the desk. She desperately craved a bath, but didn't want to be so rude as to ask for a tub this late into the night. She crossed over to the water basin and soaked the white towel in the lukewarm water and wiped the fire dust from her face.

Tele began to feel the prod of irritation with how poorly she'd done so far with going unnoticed. Already, she'd caught the attention of several angry, torch-wielding men, and now she'd alerted the whole tavern of her presence—many of which were likely town gossips.

I can't stay much longer, she thought as she began the task of removing her outfit and scrubbing her skin with the char-stained cloth before slipping on a fresh set of traveling clothes. *I should take this opportunity to strike out on my own.*

She still had the Caldor Pass and all of the supplies that she'd purchased. It would take Navid some time to return to Caldor and longer yet for word of this particular voucher's invalidation to reach the shops across the continent. By then, she could amass quite the stockpile of tools and supplies, enough to kickstart the production of her own food and water, thereby eliminating the need for the pass.

Tele fished out the items she'd stuffed in her pockets and slid them into her packs wherever they would fit. But she paused when she came to the hand lens. She studied the careful woodwork that encompassed the glass. It was absolutely beautiful, with intricate designs that required an impossibly steady hand. Her father had often wished he could get his hands on one. If not to continue his work with *Small Life*, then to show Tele the wonders of the world invisible to the naked eye.

If she left now, she'd never get to know her uncle. She'd never be able to ensure his safety. She wouldn't be able to ensure that the knowledge he had acquired and protected would not be lost forever.

A knock on her door caused Tele to jump.

"Tele!" Amie called from outside.

"Just a moment!" She scooped up the items on the bed and shoved them into her pack then opened the door. "Yes?"

"Meet us in room six," Amie said. "The room with the six dots." She pointed to her left. "It's right here—"

"Yes, I can count," Tele said, frowning.

"Hurry," Amie said, then turned on heel and darted away.

Tele shut the door and turned back to her supplies. It would only be a moment before she was ready to leave. She hadn't completely organized all her supplies, but that could wait until after she'd escaped.

She allowed her thumb to absently rub the shell of the hand lens as she considered the consequences of the junction before her. And with a sigh of resolution, Tele knew exactly what she must do.

SEVEN

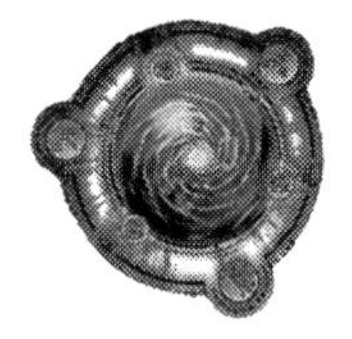

THE COVENANT

Tele gathered her hair into a tight bun before knocking on the room door. Amie answered it and stepped aside so that Tele could enter a room that was practically identical to her own. Gavini sat on the bed, shuffling through items in his pack. When he looked up and saw her step into the room, he smiled.

"I'll go get Mara," Amie announced, then left them alone.

Gavini gave an empty spot on the bed a soft pat, an invitation for her to join him. Tele crossed to the bed and sat down. She scanned the room nervously before meeting Gavini's expectant gaze.

"You look so much like your mother," he said.

Tele flushed. "Don't we all look like our respective mothers?"

"Hardly," Gavini said. "My mother—your grandmother—was far more stern. She had a gaze that could break steel. Much like you do, in fact."

Tele looked away. She didn't intend to stare daggers, but good cheer was something she thought she'd never again experience. Not after all that had happened to her. She'd lost everything. That is, she'd lost everything until she'd found Gavini.

"It was a compliment," Gavini said.

"Thank you."

He placed a hand on hers. Tele flinched at the unexpected gesture of comfort but relaxed when he squeezed a measure of condolence. They sat silent for a moment while time allowed Tele to relax.

"Did you manage to save any of your parents' work?"

Tele nodded. "Thief-Takers caught up with us. I managed to escape with a pack of their most prized work. A few volumes of each of their studies. Their latest work, I left behind. I couldn't possibly take it all." Like a scab torn from a wound, the terror and pain of it all rushed back. She steeled herself against it. "It burned with them, I suspect."

"I'm so sorry, child," Gavini cooed. "I don't know of another Keeper who's still alive today. Besides you and me."

Tele suspected the same. In Desera, a world away, they'd once banded with other Keepers in the wilderness, but the Thief-Takers had whittled them down until only her family remained.

"I'm supposed to find the Wizard," Tele said. "My father believed that he was still alive somewhere. After Navid—"

"Navid?"

"The seer that found me in the desert," Tele answered. "When he brought me here, I thought I'd eventually find someplace to hide. I didn't intend to go with him to Caldor. Now that I've found you, perhaps we can find the Wizard together."

"The prophets sent a *seer* to find you?" Gavini asked.

Tele frowned. "Yes."

Gavini slowly nodded, considering. "Before when you said that you planned to journey to Caldor, I thought you were simply desperate to find answers. But now that I know that the prophets are the desperate ones …"

"Wait," Tele said. "You're actually considering going to meet with the prophets? You were right about what you said before. They took everything from us. They'll do it again." She paused before deciding to admit her plan. "I considered leaving immediately now that you are safe. It would be better than risking the unknown of the prophets."

Gavini gave her a compassionate smile. "The prophets don't send seers to retrieve people for them on a whim. In fact, if they were truly concerned about you, they'd likely send him to kill you instead. I think we should go. I believe this is much bigger than we think it is."

A soft knock sounded at the door, and Amie stepped in before waiting to be invited inside. Mara followed, carrying a small tray, and shut the door behind them.

"No one saw us bring you in," Mara said. "I think we're safe."

Amie sat on the floor before Gavini's feet and pulled her legs tight against her body. Mara set the tray on the desk against the wall, then gave a small cup from the tray to Gavini.

"I brought tea," Mara said. "It's still a bit hot."

"Thank you, child," Gavini said. He took a small sip. "You still brew an exceptional cup of tea; exactly the way I like."

Mara concealed her smile as she backed away and leaned against the room's wall. Tele studied the two girls. They shared so much in common physically—blue eyes, blonde hair—and if they were closer together in age, she'd wager them to be twins. But their personalities were like night and day, except for one thing: their admiration of this man.

She saw the smile in Gavini's eyes and knew that he and Mara were intimately connected. The way she had been with her parents.

"So," Amie said. "What do we do now?"

"Unfortunately," Gavini said, "we're not safe yet. I can't stay here. I'd be putting you and your family in great danger."

"You're going then?" Amie asked. "To Caldor?"

Gavini nodded, looking Tele in the eye. "Yes."

"But … but …" Amie shook her head as she frowned at the space between her feet. "Back at the cabin. You said you didn't want to go to Caldor because of the prophets. I don't understand."

"It's a long and difficult story, but I believe I can tell it simply." Gavini straightened and wrapped both his hands around the cup of tea. "A few hundred years ago, before

Wizard Titan disappeared, he brought together the greatest minds in all the world to a place he called the Sanctuary Calviere. There, he established the Keepers of the Covenant—an order of individuals whose primary goal was to learn about the natural world and how it functioned."

"But why?" Amie asked. "Why would a Wizard want that?"

"Magic, dear, is fundamentally connected to the natural world," Gavini said.

Tele opened her mouth to add in a more specific explanation, but Mara cut in first.

"Understanding the world you're tasked to manipulate is the core principle for magic to function with any proper depth," Mara said. She shut her eyes and a small smile formed on her lips. "Understand nature and you understand how to write a spell to control it."

Tele raised her eyebrows, stunned at Mara's grasp of the connection between the Keepers and the Wizard. Mara stood against the wall with her eyes still closed. She looked calmer at that moment than Tele had ever seen her—as if she were finally in her element.

Gavini nodded. "Precisely. Well said, Mara."

Amie cocked her head in curiosity. "So, you helped the Wizard learn so that his magic could do more things. What happened?"

"The prophets forced us out of the Sanctuary when Wizard Titan left," Gavini said. "We were the arbiters of truth and the scholars of the vast libraries kept there, and they took that away from us." Gavini paused, then looked at Tele. "Did your parents tell you how they came to be in Desera?"

"They told me about Prophet Tristan and how he betrayed them by misusing their work for evil." Tele folded her arms. "Otherwise, they hardly discussed it. I don't think they liked remembering those days."

"It goes back a bit further," Gavini said. "After the prophets forced us out of the Sanctuary, Prophet Odus—the rogue prophet of what is now Hzorah—invited us to work with him in the Hzorah Crown city. Back then, the Dominion ruled here."

Tele nodded, recalling some of what her parents had told her. "Before the Hzorah Tribe and other surrounding tribes joined together and pushed them out of their lands and into the desert."

"Correct. Prophet Odus believed that the Keepers still had value despite what the other lands believed. The Dominion's Creed is a religion that holds the Wizard up as a god. To them, if the Wizard wanted us to study the natural world, it wasn't a prophet's place to stop them. And then the war came."

"The Dominion War?" Amie asked.

"The Dominion War," Gavini confirmed. He took a slow sip from the teacup before continuing. "When the Hzorah Tribe gathered the strength of the various surrounding tribes to take back their lands from the Dominion's rule here, Prophet Odus was pushed into the desert. The Hzorah Tribe and their kings were strictly opposed to magic. They'd lived under the thumb of the Creed and wanted nothing to do with them or the Wizard they revered.

"Many of the Keepers decided to return to hiding. We preferred to attempt to continue our work alone in isolation than risk death in the wilderness with the Dominion. Some of us decided to risk the journey in hopes that they'd be able to work together, with the protection of the Dominion. I chose to be in the former group." He looked at Tele. "My brother—your father—chose the latter."

Mara's eyes shot open. "Brother?" She looked at Tele, her eyes narrowing with focused understanding.

"That was my mother and father's decision until Prophet Tristan came to power," Tele said, continuing where Gavini left off. "After Prophet Odus died, there was a short time of peace for the Keepers in Desera, but not for long. Prophet Tristan had a different idea of what the Keepers' knowledge should be used for. When the Keepers in Desera found out about his plans—"

"You fled." Amie gasped. "But I don't understand why

you'd want to talk to the prophets now. If you're not safe with them, why would you be now?"

"Apparently," Tele said, "the prophets must be getting desperate. They sent a seer to find me."

"If Navid's true purpose is to bring you to Caldor," Gavini said, "the Keepers have a chance to reform."

Tele awoke to a room pitched in darkness. Left lit, the candles had burned out while she slept, leaving behind the faint smell of a night filled with wild fire. She felt along the edge of the bed and slowly approached the desk. After rummaging inside its drawers, she produced a candle and striking stone. She lit the new candle, placed it in the candle holder above and squinted, allowing her eyes to adjust to the small, first light.

Tele dressed in one of the new outfits she'd purchased. She slipped the two longer daggers she'd acquired into the holsters of her belt and checked them for accessibility and quick release. She inspected herself in the mirror. Though the new clothes were alike in color, her old clothes had been long and loose enough to conceal her weapons. These were not tailored with that intention. With a pack over each shoulder and Amie's green dress under her arm, she doused the candle and exited the room for the final time.

The common appeared the same as it had when she and Navid first arrived—completely reset from the previous night crowd. It was empty, save a quiet couple who didn't appear to notice her entry.

Navid must still be in his room. She hoped that he would be ready to leave soon. She wanted to be away from Azuri. Her short stay gave her more than she wanted to see of the town and left her with memories that would haunt her into Desolate.

As Tele settled into the same far table from the day before, she saw Amie peek outside the kitchens. When she spotted Tele, she disappeared beyond. The swinging door hadn't stilled before she reappeared, carrying a tray of food. Tele avoided her gaze as she crossed to her table.

Amie slid the tray onto the table. "Good morning. I …" She cleared her throat. "I told the Crown's Guard about the fire. They asked if I knew anything about it, but I said I didn't." She rubbed her shoulder and looked away. "They said that they would look into it."

"How are you doing, though?" Tele asked.

"Tired." Amie's eyes met Tele's for the first time. "And sad. And angry."

"What about Mara? Your family?"

"Mara is fine. She's always fine." Amie sat across from Tele. "She's helping Gavini get ready. We didn't tell Father. Mara insisted that I not say anything. I wasn't supposed to be there. I guess they'll find out about it eventually. Word gets around fast here."

Tele looked down at the plate of rice and chicken. "I hope that now that those men have what they think they wanted, they won't cause you any more problems."

Amie shot to her feet, surprising Tele. She tucked her loose hair behind her ears and smoothed her already neat dress. Tele turned to see Navid nearly at the table.

"Good morning, Navid. How was your rest?" Amie asked.

Navid's dim-eyed gaze crossed Tele's before he answered. "It was good, Amie. Thank you. We should be leaving very soon. Is your father available?"

Amie curtsied. "He is. I will tell him you are here and ready for departure. Please, eat." Amie shared a look with Tele before she left them.

Navid collapsed into the seat Amie had just abandoned. He placed his elbows on the table, held his head in his hands, and massaged his eyes and temples. "Amie looks tired."

"So do you." Tele picked up a spoon. "She had a long night."

He looked at her. "I didn't think that it would be so taxing to guide you around Azuri."

"I think we were both surprised at how taxing it would be,"

Tele said. She took to eating when Navid frowned. "I found everything we need for the journey. Did you gather the horse we needed?"

Navid lifted his own fork. "I did. Our time here was as expedient as I'd hoped. The next leg of our journey should be similarly brisk."

Tele glanced toward the Kruv House rooms and saw Mara helping Gavini from his room and down the hall toward the rear stables. Tele would have to give up her horse for him, which she was more than willing to do, but their pace would be affected.

"About the journey," Tele began. "While you were gone, I—"

"Sleep well?" Master Kruv lumbered in, wiping sweat from his glistening brow with the lip if his apron. He gave Tele a slight bow.

"Well enough," Navid said.

Master Kruv looked at Navid thoughtfully. "Did you decide to … try my ale?"

Navid nodded, meeting Master Kruv's gaze. "I did."

Tele cocked her head at the exchange. It was an odd thing to ask, but when she saw the look in Master Kruv's gaze, she recognized it as something familiar—something she longed for—the approving gaze of a father.

"Very good, then," Master Kruv said as he wiped his hands with the flap of his apron. "Amie said you're looking to leave now. I'd recommend catching a river boat, but there have been delays. No ships have docked the river port for the past five days."

Navid frowned. "Five days?"

"Is that odd?" Tele asked.

Master Kruv grunted. "I'd say so."

"The Drunn River is a channel composed of waters flowing from the mountains in Ghaya, past Caldor, and into Hzorah. It's a primary highway of import and export," Navid explained.

Master Kruv sighed. "Are you sure you don't want to stay

longer?"

"I'm sure," Navid said. "It is imperative that we arrive in good time."

"I'll have Mara waiting for you in the stables with your horses," Master Kruv said with a slight bow.

Navid stood and gave the innkeeper an embrace. "Thank you, Master Kruv. I really appreciate your hospitality. We will meet again, I'm sure."

Master Kruv smiled and said, "Come thirsty," before he exited the common.

Tele stood and passed him a pack. "I think we have everything we need. But there's just one other matter."

Navid paused in confusion at the Kruv House stable's entry. Tele crossed into the stable and stood next to an old man who sat next to Mara on a small wooden bench. Both Mara and the man met his eyes.

"Who's this?" Navid asked. He looked at the old man. He couldn't have seen less than fifty years. There was a sturdy staff on his lap. He was probably half-crippled. Torn between sympathy and confusion, Navid ran his fingers through his hair. "What's this about?"

"This," Mara said, "is Gavini."

"And he's coming with us," Tele added.

"No," Navid frowned at Tele. "He's not coming with us."

Navid's instructions were quite explicit. Find Tele and bring her back to Caldor. Find what he'd lost and he would be free from his curse. This man was neither.

"He is," Tele said. She faced him with an iron gaze, and—despite her testing his resolve—there was a fierce beauty in the way she stood her ground.

"Tele," Navid said, "we don't even know this man. He could—"

"Attack us with his walking stick?" Tele finished. "Or

perhaps he'd bore us to death with lengthy descriptions of days gone by?"

Navid sighed, unamused. "But why?"

It was an apt question. Tele was secretive to a fault. She had been more than willing to simply pass by Azuri without resting here for a night. It seemed strange for her to take an interest in a random man's welfare.

"Have you tasted my potato soup?" the old man asked, filling the uncomfortable silence. His eyes sparkled and he smiled warmly. "I promise to make you some. It's quite delightful. And I do have stories. Hopefully best to pass the time rather than dilate it."

"He's a good man," Mara said. She stepped up to him. "He helped my—our family a lot over the years, but there are people in this town who'd like to see him dead. Please, Navid."

"And I'm not leaving without him," Tele added.

Navid opened his mouth to protest again, but Amie stepped into the stables. She carried two large packs—one over her shoulder and the other she dragged behind her.

"I've got all your things," Amie said. "And I tried to pack a bit extra for you to—" She paused when she saw Navid. "Oh. Hello."

"Both of these bags are his?" Navid asked. *This is ridiculous.*

"He had *one* bag," Mara said sternly.

"This one is his," Amie said, letting the bag she'd shouldered fall to the floor. "This one" —she pulled the other beside her—"is mine."

"Yours?" Navid asked. "You're bringing the town?"

"Please let me go with you," Amie pleaded. "I won't be a bother. I'll help with whatever you need. I'll keep the horses clean and fed. I'll help cook. I'll—"

Gavini held up a hand. "Amie, I can't let you come, child."

"But I can help!" Amie said.

"Amie," Mara said. "You can't go."

Amie rounded on her sister. "You're *not* mother. You may want to stay here and play innkeeper for the rest of your life, but I don't." She turned back to Navid. "Take me with you. Please!"

Navid stared into her pleading eyes, a look he'd almost forgotten from his youth. She would look at him with those big, blue eyes and insist to be carried.

"Amie—" Mara growled.

"Come, child," Gavini said. He held out his hand, and Amie approached him, taking it. "If I could take both of you with me, I would," Gavini said, looking at both Amie and Mara in turn. "But the both of you are safest here with your father. Master Kruv has worked his fingers to the bone to make a proper life for the both of you. You'd be a fool to leave that."

"But—"

"Listen." Gavini pulled Amie closer. "I'll be fine. And so will you *if* you stay out of trouble and mind your father."

Amie released a small cry as she sat next to the man and hugged him. Though her hair fell over her face, Navid could see tears pouring down her cheeks.

"Now, now, child," Gavini soothed. "No reason to cry over an old man."

Navid watched quietly as Gavini comforted the girl he'd once believed to be his younger sister. Even though he knew the truth now—knew that he could no longer be a Kruv, he still felt a strong connection to the only family outside of the Sanctuary he'd ever known.

Whoever this Gavini was, he obviously felt the same sort of connection. Navid could clearly see that this man wasn't a threat to him, Tele, or the prophecy he'd been tasked to fulfill. He didn't know why this man wanted to go to Caldor, but wasn't the city a refuge—a place for new beginnings? Just because he was old didn't mean he didn't deserve that opportunity. Navid could be giving him a death sentence if what Mara said was true.

He met Mara's gaze. She sighed, spreading her arms. "Well, Navid? You said that you wanted to make things right with us. This is it."

"I suppose," Navid said. "Gavini can come with us."

"Good," Tele said, as if Navid hadn't made any real decision at all. "Which one of these horses is ours?"

Navid helped Tele load Gavini's things onto Gilly then helped Gavini mount her. He placed his own things on Kemper—the new, larger, deep-black steed—and proceeded to lead the horses into the quiet alley.

There were quiet goodbyes. Amie's were tearful. Mara's, like Tele's, were almost stoic. Gavini's were warm and sincere. But, inexplicably, Navid's eyes remained dry until, Mara took his hand, and placed something small and cold into it.

When Navid looked down, he saw a silver pendant on a silver chain. The pendant, round and just smaller than a coin, had an impression of a tree and a hammer adorning its textured face.

"What's this?" he asked her.

"When you left," Mara said, staring down at his hand. "When they sent you away, I didn't understand why. I don't think I remember ever crying so much. I don't think I've even cried since. Father gave this to me. He said that your mother had left it with you when you came to us in the night. He said it would keep you close to my heart." She looked up to his eyes. "You should have it back."

Navid shook his head. "No, Mara …"

"Yes," she said. "Father told me what he said to you. And what you were looking for. Maybe this will remind you not to lose hope. Please, take it."

Navid's hand closed around the pendant. "Thank you, Mara. This means so much to me."

She gave him a gentle smile. "And no matter what happens, you still have a home here. Never forget that."

EIGHT

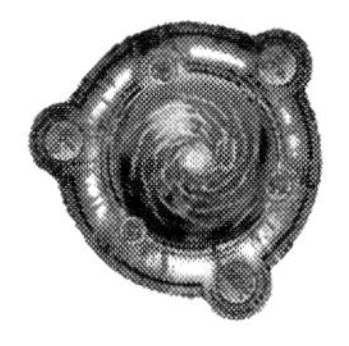

ELEMENT AND REACTION

Once out of Azuri and again on a broad route that led into the thickly wooded Borderland Forests, the road bent steadily south and eventually met a wide river that flowed opposite their direction. Navid took the lead, allowing Tele and Gavini to trail behind. The two spoke quietly behind him, but instead of eavesdropping, he turned his attention inward—cycling between worries of what he'd learned in Azuri and lengths of meditation to calm the torrent of thoughts that threatened to engulf him.

Navid Tevaad. Not Navid Kruv. The sound of it was completely foreign to him. Then again, there was a rhythm to it that felt natural. Both thoughts hung in conflict, yet they were equally true. He still felt like a Kruv, but at the same time, he felt like he had met himself for the very first time. A spark of exhilaration in finding a new piece of himself tarnished by the loss of the parts he never wanted to lose.

As dusk fell, they reached a fork in the road. One direction kept pace with the Drunn river while the other split off, penetrating deeper into the woods.

"This route here," Navid said, pointing back toward the fork that pulled away from the river. "It leads to a clearing.

Some traders use it as a common rest stop. There's a wide fire pit and log benches. We should stop there."

After they reached the clearing, Navid helped Gavini down from the mare and onto one of the hardened logs. He then led Kemper to the riverbank and allowed him to take a drink. Tele followed his lead, edging Gilly to the bank where soft soil peppered with moss-covered rocks formed a depression—a respite from the river's steadfast flow.

Tele knelt beside Navid with her waterskin. He glanced to her, still upset that she'd gone and found them a new traveling companion without consulting him first, then threatened not to continue their journey without him. It wasn't like her. At least, he didn't think it was like her. They'd only just met. The memory of her pointing her knife at him flashed into his memory once more. *I really don't know this woman. She could be as crazy as she is headstrong.*

"I'll go and collect some firewood," Navid said. "Can you groom the horses?"

She shook her head. "I'd rather you do the grooming. I'll gather wood."

Navid raised his eyebrows. Despite traveling the entire day, Tele had refused to ride the horses. Of course, Gavini needed to ride, so one of them would have had to walk, but Navid offered to trade with Tele more than once throughout the day. Each time, she refused. And now she was offering to walk some more. He suddenly wondered what he would have heard if he'd eavesdropped earlier in their day.

"Alright," Navid said. "There's a hatchet in my pack."

Tele stood and moved out into the thick of the forest, and Navid brought the horses around. He retrieved the horse brush from the saddlebag and started with Kemper.

"Do you have a pot?" Gavini asked from behind him.

Navid paused his grooming to turn to the old man. He was fishing items out of his pack and humming softly as he arranged them at the base of the tree. Navid turned his attention back to Kemper when the steed nuzzled his hand to continue.

"There's a small one with my things," Navid said.

"Mind fetching it for me?"

Navid did mind. His journey hadn't gone as smoothly as he'd hoped. It'd given him more questions than answers, and now, he had an old man along that could barely walk—a man that shouldn't even be with them.

He took a deep breath. He was allowing himself to become agitated, and with agitation came the itch of his curse. It needled him now, more like the painful prick of thorns than the gentle tickle he was accustomed to ignoring.

He stepped over to his bags and fetched the pot and walked it over to Gavini. "What do you need with it? If you intend to relieve yourself, I much rather it done on the ground."

The man waggled a small potato. "For cooking. I promised you my potato soup. I like to keep my promises."

Navid set the pot down in front of the man and returned to the horses. "Thank you."

"Of course," Gavini said.

Navid gave Kemper a gentle pat before he began grooming him again. The steed's previous owner had used the horse primarily for short distance travel, but he'd continued much farther without resistance. Even his mare from Caldor was not accustomed to long journeys. Neither were particularly fast, but strong enough. They deserved a good grooming for their steady work.

"Seems like I forgot my salt."

Navid turned to Gavini rummaging through his belongings again. He pulled out a thin, metallic vile, unstopped it, and poured several white grains into his hand. He licked his hand and smiled.

"Never mind," he said. "False alarm."

Navid moved to Gilly and started her grooming. When he stretched to reach the arch of the mare's back, the small pendant softly tapped his chest, making him aware of its presence. It was as if his father reached out to him through time to remind him that he was still there, waiting for him.

Navid touched the pendant through his shirt, pressing the

cool, smooth metal against his chest. His heart pulsed against it as he closed his eyes. *I'll find you. I know you're out there.*

Even as he promised himself he'd find his father, there was another part of him that reminded him how impossible of a feat this might be. He had no solid information on where his father was. What was he truly supposed to do? Go from jeweler to jeweler across Hzorah, asking if they remember the man or woman who had purchased the pendant? It was as silly an idea as was the story it reminded him of. *Ridley and the Seven Pearls:* a tale of a young street urchin who traveled the East Hzorah shores with a pearl the size of a loaf of bread in search of the oyster that made it.

"Because she's my niece," Gavini said.

Pulled from his thoughts, Navid turned to Gavini. "What?"

"You asked Tele back at the Kruv House stables why she would want to bring me along." He looked up from peeling a potato to meet Navid's eyes. "It's because I'm her uncle. Were I not, I'm not sure she would have even considered it."

Navid stood mute, and Gavini resumed peeling the potato. It was strange that Tele had insisted that they bring this man along. And though he hadn't pressed her for an explanation, he was still curious. This, however, was quite unexpected.

"So," Gavini continued, "you were a ward of the Kruvs?"

The man said it as if the whole world should know. The second surprise from him. If you were to ask a superstitious man, a third surprise was due. Depending on whether or not that man was an optimist or a pessimist, the surprise would be either fantastic or devastating.

"Don't look so surprised," Gavini said and dropped a potato in the pot. He grabbed another and set to peeling it. "Mara told me."

"Yes," Navid said. "I was. Until I was taken to Caldor."

"Because you're a seer," Gavini finished. "I presume you've told Tele about the Kruvs."

"No," Navid admitted. He sat across from Gavini. "And I'd appreciate it if you didn't tell her."

"You want me to lie to my niece?" Gavini asked, dropping the last potato into the pot.

"I want you to avoid telling her," Navid said. "That's not a lie."

"I can do that," Gavini said with a curious smile. "But why is it so important to you that I don't? The Kruvs are a wonderful family. It's nothing to be ashamed of."

"I'm not ashamed," Navid said. "I couldn't have asked for better. But, Tele is … Well, you've met her. If she knew that we stopped in Azuri because of the Kruvs and not for supplies … Well, I don't know what she'd do. She didn't want to stop there. I don't want to give her another reason to reconsider coming with me. It's too risky."

"Have you ever courted a woman, son?" Gavini asked.

Taken aback, Navid shook his head. "No. I'm a Seer. We're not allowed to take a wife. It's too dangerous."

"Lying to a woman is the most dangerous thing you could ever do." A wisp of a smile touched Gavini's lips when he looked up at Navid. "Nothing has been or ever will be more risky than that, and you're dancing close to the fire."

"Fire doesn't begin to cover it," Navid said. "She's head-strong, suspicious of everyone, and she already tried to kill me once—"

"You've really thought hard about why you don't like my niece," Gavini said.

Navid took a breath before continuing. "I just have to bring her safely to Caldor. After that, you can tell her whatever you feel you need to."

"I appreciate your dedication to her welfare," Gavini said.

Navid stood at the sound of crunching leaves, and Tele's figure appeared between the trees. She carried more than an armful of thick branches and dropped them beside the small fire pit.

She looked at the both of them as she used her pants to clean the dirt from her hands. "I hope you two are getting along."

Gavini smiled as he crushed a green plant between his

fingers and dumped it into the pot. "Navid was just telling me about the time you tried to kill him."

Tele flushed before she turned away to grab a hatchet. "He's a seer. I'm sure he would have held his ground."

"Like I told you before," Navid said, "seers don't use their power. There is a long history of seers who fail to—"

"And I," Tele interrupted, "told you that it was a waste." She held up the hatchet. "Imagine if people insisted that hatchets shouldn't be used because sometimes a finger gets severed."

"That's rather reductionist," Navid said. "Seers and hatchets are very different. Seers have sentience, volition."

"As does the wielder of the hatchet," Tele said. "I could choose to cut that log over there." She used the hatchet to point into the forest, then turned it back toward Navid. "I could choose to use it as a weapon."

"You don't know what it's like to be a seer," Navid said. "You don't understand the temptation."

"I'm beginning to get an idea." Tele turned and headed back toward the woods. "I have a log to chop."

When Tele was out of earshot, Navid turned to Gavini. "I hope you saw what I saw."

"I saw," Gavini chuckled, then pointed to the pot. "Mind filling this with water? Not entirely. About three fingers above what's inside."

Grateful for a change of subject, Navid nodded, pulled a small cup from his pack, and carried the pot to the Drunn. He found a patch of water at the bank that flowed against rock rather than dirt and collected enough to submerge the vegetables.

He paused to take a relaxing breath as the itch of his curse played on his senses. *To allow it to take me is to take a path of evil. To allow it to control me is to take a path to destruction.*

He had always been calm and patient, but Tele could be exhausting. It wasn't that she was a bad person. It was her lack of—

Navid stood when he spotted something in the distance.

Like a glass attempting to signal a passing vessel, the light of the setting sun reflected off its surface. He squinted, trying to see what it was. As it drew near, he frowned in confusion.

Ice.

When Tele returned to camp with the first short stack of firewood, Navid wasn't there. When she returned with the final stack, he'd worked with Gavini to set up camp and a meal. They cooked in relative silence, allowing Tele to slip into a state of routine action so that the core of her thinking mind could rest.

When Tele felt relaxed enough to break her meditation, her inquisitive nature took hold, and she questioned Navid about some of the lingering mysteries of her new world, firing off question after question that he answered with ease. Tele listened, determined not to be caught in a lie—as she had been with Amie—that might prove disastrous.

She asked Navid about the basic relationships between various lands, what the people were like, and how common men lived from region to region. Gavini volunteered his knowledge where Navid lacked. Each answer sparked a dozen new questions, and she found that she was painfully ignorant of the world she'd found herself a part of.

"What about the Hzorah mark?" Tele asked, changing the subject from the Hzorah-Armoth crop share treaty. "Master Kruv said that his daughters would receive a better mark than he had. What is the significance of such a thing?"

Navid swallowed his final spoonful of soup. "By King Jeremiah's directive, Hzorah has its citizens marked with the seal of the Crown. Your occupation, if you have one, is also marked. It's a means of assuring that you are a subject of the Crown and that you are competent in your trade."

"And everyone is marked this way?" Tele asked.

"Everyone in Hzorah that has seen two decades," Navid said, pulling up his sleeve. His arm didn't have a mark as

Master Kruv's had. "I was young when I left Hzorah—too young to be marked. Caldor is not a part of Hzorah or any nation. Caldor is Caldor. And it must be an independent territory in order to hold peace and balance between kingdoms."

Tele thought the idea of marking citizens to be odd. It seemed practical to an extent, but she couldn't help thinking of cattle. Tele wouldn't want to feel like she was merely a dumb beast to be branded, prodded, and corralled into submission.

"Those men who wanted you dead," Tele asked, turning to Gavini. "It must be somewhat commonplace that accidents happen, even horrible accidents. Why had those men directed so much of their anger to you? What did you ever do to them?"

Gavini looked at her. "As I alluded to yesterday evening, the Dominion War was not only a conflict against Dominion occupation, but a resistance to an entire ideology."

Navid nodded in confirmation. "The Dominion's Creed insists on the conversion of all people to their ideals. Only then will the Wizard return to our world. The Creed as a religion wasn't dangerous until the Wizard disappeared—at least as far as I understand it."

"I believe that once Wizard Titan left," Gavini said, "the Creed faced an existential crisis. Without out their deity among them, they were forced to rethink their ideas. Unfortunately, the prevailing belief was that Wizard Titan left because no one else believed in him. Therefore, for him to return, he must be believed in by all.

"Because the Creed was the dominating force where the Hzorah, Ehrel, and other tribes resided, that meant the Creed needed to strip them of their cultures and beliefs so that they could be reforged for the Dominion to fulfill their new goal."

"So when the tribes joined together," Tele said, "they had but one thing in common: their mutual hate of the Creed."

"And all they associated with the Creed," Gavini said. "The Wizard Titan, magic, Keepers, seers, and even prophets to some extent."

Tele nodded, taking in the madness of it all. It was a case

study in over-correction. The Creed couldn't reckon with the cognitive dissonance of Wizard Titan's exit and therefore doubled down on their beliefs in a way that threatened the freedom of other peoples. Then, in response, Hzorah united themselves around the idea that anything that reminded them of the Creed should be exorcised from their lands. This time, threatening the freedom of their own people to such an extent that they marked each other to verify that they held the same beliefs.

Tele stood, exhausted with the folly of her new world. "I'll take first watch."

"Good enough," Navid said. He offered Gavini a hand. "I made you a bed near the fire."

Gavini accepted the leverage to help him stand, and they walked together to the bed. "Thank you. I'd just like a few moments with my niece. Can you bring my pack over here?"

Navid nodded and retrieved the pack for him, then bid them both a good night after making Tele promise to wake him for his watch. As Navid settled under his blanket, Tele sat against the thick, gnarled trunk of a bowing oak.

"He has a way of getting under my skin," Tele said.

"Oh?" Gavini asked as he picked through his pack.

"Did you hear what he said about his power? About it being evil? That's so incredibly naive."

"You should try being patient with him. His understanding of his abilities is different from yours."

She folded her arms and exhaled. She supposed that she was still a bit worked up about Amie and her insinuations that she was somehow evil because she was willing to protect herself—to keep the knowledge passed down to her safe.

"I suppose I could *try* being nicer."

"Think of it as an experiment if it helps," Gavini said. "You're a woman forged out of a very abnormal circumstance. Perhaps you should reframe your relationship with him and the world around you. 'How would someone act and react if they hadn't been subject to your unusual set of experiences?'"

"I suppose."

Tele's life before had been quite unusual compared to anyone's she'd met in Hzorah. And if she had any chance of surviving, she'd need to learn how to fit into this new world. She didn't know what 'normal' was, but she should at least try.

"I have something for you," Gavini pulled a black book from his pack and handed it to her. "I believe you'll get a bit more use out of it than I will."

It was the leather-bound book from the cabin. Tele opened the cover to the first page.

Element and Reaction
The study and findings of Gavini Gavina
regarding material interaction and reaction.

She turned the page.

For Mara and Amie
To keep safe until the day comes when he returns
to us.

The shifting glow of firelight gave the aging, bound parchment a glowing animation. Tele leaned forward, staring at the text as the words sank in and disparate connections that she'd failed to resolve came together.

"Master Kruv told me that you wanted to teach his daughters to read," Tele said. She looked at Gavini. "You intended for Amie and Mara to hold the Covenant."

Gavini nodded. "I'm an old man, Tele. I lived alone. For all that I knew, I was the very end of my line."

It made sense. Tele's parents passed their knowledge down to her and her siblings. With Tele's family in Desera and every known Keeper either dead or killed, Gavini would need to find someone else to carry his yoke. Someone he could trust in full.

"When I first met those girls," Gavini said. "They were much as they are now: passionate, sharp, thirsty for knowledge. Such raw intelligence—it couldn't be wasted. I saw Mara and Amie as a way to keep my covenant alive. Master Kruv saw my simple request for Amie and Mara to learn to read as just that: a simple request. In truth, my plan for Amie and Mara would be more payment than Master Kruv could realize."

"They were a hedge," Tele said. "A way for you to ensure that if you died, the Keepers would live on."

"Exactly," Gavini said. "Mara is older, and her mind is a bit more analytical, so I focused on her education first. I understood how to teach her. Amie, on the other hand is a bit more—"

"Flighty?" Tele finished.

"Unfocused," Gavini corrected. "But she's no less intelligent. With my time short, I had to focus on what I understood first. If the very worst occurred, I knew Mara could continue her education."

Tele remembered how Mara seemed to understand more about magic than she should at the Kruv House. She'd explained an idea that Tele often found hard to even articulate to herself.

"Apart from the obvious concerns of safety, this is why I couldn't allow Amie—or Mara for that matter—to come along." He took Tele's hand. "Tele, we are about to walk into a lion's den. The prophets wield as much power as kings. They wouldn't frame it in such a way, but they do. I told you at the Kruv House that I thought the Keepers had a chance to reform, but I don't know what the prophets truly have in mind.

"I'm going with you because I thought I might be able to help. I knew Hzorah's prophet. Our time together was amicable before he found out that I was a Keeper. My hope is that I can help you navigate what is to come. But if I can't, Mara and Amie are all that is left."

Tele looked back down at *Element and Reaction*, at the worlds that reinforced the beliefs her own father had held:

> *To keep safe until the day comes when he returns*
> *to us.*

"You believe that Wizard Titan still exists," Tele whispered. "My parents believed the same thing. I was never so sure."

"Wizard Titan was immortal," Gavini said. "I'm not sure that dying was something he was capable of. I can't explain what happened to him. He didn't tell the Keepers alive at the time of his plans, but I have no reason to believe that he died."

In a way, Gavini's belief in Wizard Titan's potential to return wasn't unlike the Creed's. The dividing line was what he was willing to do to reinforce his beliefs.

"If the Kruv girls are our backup plan, you should have left this book with them. And I should have left my books with them."

Gavini shook his head. "Mara has absorbed much of the Keeper knowledge. She will be fine. Unfortunately, your father didn't study much of what I did. I had certain advantages my brother didn't. I was passed along a broader scope than he was." He smiled and nudged her affectionately. "And while your family battled snakes in the wilderness, I discovered a new world of possibility. I hope you can keep up."

Tele smiled as she turned to the next page in the book. "Dear Uncle, I hope *you* can keep up."

General Darius Gareth kicked at rubble and ash with a polished boot as he made way across the charred heap that was once the Keeper's cabin. His deep-black cloak rippled in the breeze. The wind loosed and churned ash that clung to the fabric of his Dominion uniform. Battle-hardened, he was accustomed to getting his hands dirty but still retained a low tolerance for filth. Now, he stood right in the belly of filth—filth of the worst kind.

His eyes flicked to the two imbeciles that had earned his ire. Anger did little good held inside. It was always best to let it out. If he let too much build inside, the anger became furious and unfocused. If he let it out in small, calculated, razor-sharp acts, he'd get the satisfaction he needed.

In youth, he had held fast to anger, and rarely did it aid him aside from spending far too many nights in a dark military cell. The Deseran Dominion army looked down on the lack of control amongst their enlisted, and Gareth's wealth of bitter contempt seeped from his pores, following him like phantoms until his wrath exploded.

But things were different now. His superiors had seen his skill and rewarded his persistence. It was those phantoms that whispered incentive, spurring him to push harder yet. Exciting his need for justice. He heeded that wisdom, made it his own, and rose above the rest—the ignoramuses who thought playing soldier a game. A role to fill until your time passed.

Gareth had seen the game of war. He had seen the wounded writhing in pain. Sat by his father's side as he drew his last, weak breath of life stolen by the blasphemous, his gut ripped clean by the heathen sword wielded by an ungrateful rebel. He had seen his mother weeping, pulling at him to look away lest his young soul taint. But he held steadfast, looking on. He would remember every detail. He would remember who had done it.

I have only to get my hands on the boy. And when I do, I'll be rewarded for it.

He turned back to the soldiers waiting patiently for direction. Lieutenant Damien Farrin, his right hand, stood straight-backed and at the ready. His vigilant, blue-eyed gaze watched over Gareth; his loyalty to the Creed watched over Desera. It was his loyalty more so than his attentiveness that warranted Gareth's trust. The man would walk straight into Desolate without a second thought if it meant a victory for the true path. Men like Lieutenant Farrin were rare. Many would swear their loyalty to the Creed up and down until faced with their own mortality. Damien Farrin *meant* it.

Beside Farrin stood his left hand, Lieutenant Cassius Owen. He was a weasel of a man: lanky, under-muscled, strange white hair shaved into a mohawk that was common to his kind. And appointed, not chosen. His constant and insincere groveling for the Creed, Prophet Tristan, and himself didn't fool Gareth. The man was Bamilee, a coward. Why Prophet Tristan appointed Owen over his own selection was beyond him, but it wasn't his place to question the Creed's great prophet.

At their feet knelt the two lowlifes who had carried out the deed. Their faces were so low to the ground that he fought the urge to march over and kick them in. He compromised with a visual and smiled. With a quick flick of his finger, he summoned Farrin forward. Owen fell in behind, close to heel. A fist and knee to the ground, they bowed.

"My General." Farrin's grizzled appellation cut through the whistle of wind.

"My General." Owen's youthful, almost sing-song timbre from behind.

He would kill Owen one day. He knew it.

He rested his hand on his father's sabre.

IN GOOD TIME, GARETH.

"Owen." Gareth clasped his hands behind his back. "Be so kind to usher our guests over."

Without reply, Owen hopped to his feet, nearly skipping to task. *The Desolate-bound fool.*

"At ease, Lieutenant." Gareth said.

Farrin rose to his feet and clasped his hands behind him. Gareth watched Owen over Farrin's shoulder. The way he pulled his sword in the least graceful way for a man of his rank and how his less-than-commanding air could barely frighten a mouse *vexed* him.

"How long until I finally kill him, Farrin?" Gareth asked. "A week? Tell me once again why I tolerate him."

"Because Prophet Tristan has appointed him, My General."

"Yes, yes." Gareth directed his attention to Farrin as Owen finally got the two moving. "And you found nothing … Nothing at all?"

"Nothing, My General," Farrin replied. "Nothing salvageable."

"On your knees before the General, you Desolate-bound

savages." Owen said as he approached Gareth. The two knelt and Owen looked at Gareth triumphantly. Gareth frowned and Owen shrank away before assuming a position behind the two.

Gareth squatted to meet their eyes. He looked at the one in black first. "Ronzit, yes?" The man nodded, meeting his eyes before glancing back to the ground. Gareth then looked toward the one in gray. "And Domis, yes?" Domis met his eyes with a dark coldness, holding his gaze, unlike the first man.

He stood, looking over their heads and out to the towering trees. "Can you tell me what you were instructed to do? I find my memory may have failed me."

Ronzit looked at Domis before he spoke. "We were told to kill Gavini."

"Use his title when you address the General, you buffoon!" Owen hissed.

Gareth raised a hand and glared at Owen. "Was that what you were told? *Exactly?*"

"We were told to kill him," Ronzit said.

"Hmm ..." Gareth stroked his gray beard. "So, instead of following orders, you went and set fire to the place ... Am I correct? Arson was *not* included on the task list, yes?"

"No, but—"

"And yet," Gareth continued, "I stand here in a shell of a house, dirtying my boots on ash."

"We had to burn it," Domis spoke up, his voice strong and sharp with self-righteousness. "The man commanded sorcery. It took my daughter. We could not allow such wickedness to remain intact."

Gareth sneered at the notion. The irony of it nearly made him laugh. Here stood two men of the Hzorah Crown—the most wicked of all lands—claiming that they had done what they had to do in order to purge the wicked. In fact, he may have laughed at their ignorance in matters of magic if Hzorah hadn't used their ignorance as justification to spark a bloody war.

"Did you take anything from the house?"

"My General?" Ronzit asked.

"Did you *take* anything from the *house*?" he repeated again with a touch of menace.

"No … no, we took nothing!" Ronzit offered eagerly.

Gareth looked long and hard into his eyes, judging. The man would say anything to spare his life, but he saw no lies in him—not in this.

Prophet Tristan had wanted the Keeper eliminated, but the knowledge the old man had stored and cultivated over the years was valuable. And now, because of the bastards before him, the Keeper's records were destroyed. But if the rumors he'd heard in Azuri were true, there was still hope that some of that knowledge could be recovered.

"Very good. Farrin, please assist Owen in their execution."

Farrin grabbed Ronzit.

"No!" Ronzit pleaded. "We didn't take anything from the house! We swear! We killed him just as you asked! He's dead!"

Domis knelt, unmoving.

"Yes, that and more." Gareth swept a hand across the scene of waste.

"We weren't told *not* to burn the house." Ronzit continued his desperate petition. "We didn't know! What can we do to make it up to you? We can do more. We can!"

"Silence!" Gareth barked and Ronzit's mouth snapped shut. Domis held his head high. The man was bold. Gareth had to give him that.

He squatted close to Ronzit—close enough to smell the man's rancid breaths. "Do you know why you're going to die today?" Ronzit didn't answer. Gareth turned to look at Domis who continued studying the ground. "No? Well, it's not because you failed to follow your orders. You killed the man just as instructed. Though burning the house was not what we wanted, I suppose this is our fault. Perhaps we should have been more specific. I hadn't expected a Hzorah half-wit to be quite so inventive. No, it's not because you burned the house. And no, it is not because you're a Hzorah heathen that I no longer have use for. It is none of these." Gareth inched closer yet. "The reason you are going to die today is because you are a traitor."

Ronzit looked shocked. "A traitor? General, we did as you said. We told no one of your instructions. No one knows. No one!"

This time, Gareth did laugh. "You are mistaken, Ronzit. Not for betraying me but for betraying Hzorah. You betrayed your own homeland for silver. I cannot allow a traitor to live." He glanced at Owen, making sure the pitiful excuse for a soldier heard his point. "You betrayed your own. How could I trust you to not do the same to me? Hmm?" Ronzit worked his mouth, but no words came. Gareth smiled. "See? You don't even trust yourself. You are vermin, and so you will die like vermin."

Gareth gave a slight nod to his right hand before turning to continue his search. Behind, he heard the sound of sword to flesh and blood chilling screams loosed then abruptly cut off. He smiled to himself.

VERY GOOD, GARETH. VERY GOOD.

Yes. He had done good.

Amie squinted against the glare of the sun. Of course she picked the spot facing west. She kicked herself for such a stupid selection. But then, she didn't have much of a choice. The path ended on the west side of Gavini's cabin. She would have had to come in through the woods otherwise. Circling around the clearing of the Gavini plot may have risked her being spotted.

Despite the sun, her eyes went wide when the two soldiers dressed in unfamiliar black-and-gray uniforms pulled swords. One cut into Domis and Ronzit. The other hesitated, allowing the first man to do the deed.

She nearly screamed when red spilled across their fronts. She choked back tears, fighting to keep her position hidden. A few dull thwacks ended the terrible screams. She squeezed her eyes shut as her breaths quickened. She was dizzy. She thought she might faint.

A hand grabbed her shoulder. Before she could cry out, another hand clasped over her mouth, muffling her high pitched wail. She struggled, and through the tears she saw the man with the gray beard look in her direction. The direction of her and her captor.

"Shh! Be still!"

Mara's voice.

Amie shut her eyes and ceased her struggle. Breathing heavier still, she slouched back into her sister's embrace. It wasn't one of those horrible men. It was just Mara.

But what was Mara doing out here? Had she followed her? She pulled at the hand at her mouth, loosing its grip.

"Mara!" she exclaimed in whisper. She looked back at her sister's frown-drawn brow. "What—"

Rustling from the soldiers in the clearing cut her words short. She turned back to the soldiers and stilled her tongue. The man with the gray beard and a healed-over forehead scar had squatted down, beginning to pick through some wood.

She turned back to Mara. "What are you doing here?"

"What am *I* doing here?" Mara said. "What are *you* doing here?"

"I ..."

Amie had had a hundred reasons why she'd wanted to come back. To check see if Gavini or Tele had returned for some reason, or maybe to see if the Hzorah Guard had investigated the fire as they'd promised. But if she was honest with herself, she was here because Tele and Navid had been *doing* something, taking action. She'd felt a momentum she'd always craved, but now that they were gone—and Gavini with them—she felt a void. And she was expected to return to her mundane life as if nothing had happened.

But she couldn't say any of that to Mara. She wouldn't understand.

"I ... I was checking to see if everything was ... you know ... safe."

Mara's expression didn't shift. "Amie, Father has told you countless times not to come over here. And after what happened, you should know moreover that his words ring true!"

"He's told you no less!" Amie snapped. She wasn't going to back down this time. "Why are *you* here?"

Mara eyed her, her expression softening a hint before she spoke. "I'm here to look for something."

"What?" Amie mocked. "You forgot your scarf?"

"No, you dolt." Any hint of Mara's wrath relenting had disappeared.

Mara looked up and over Amie's head, and Amie instinctively looked back to the Gavini plot as well. The man with the beard had changed position, still searching.

"Looks like they're looking for something, too," Amie said. "What are you looking for?"

"A book."

"What?"

"Never mind. I don't think anyone is going to find anything in that mess," Mara said. "We should go back."

"So, you came all the way here to look for a *book*? What kind of book?"

Amie's curiosity was aroused. What book would be so important to risk coming all the way out here? Mara wasn't nearly as prone to risking Father's wrath as she was. In fact, Mara seemed to act as though she was their mother more and more every day—the way she liked to order her around. She didn't mind when Father did it. When Mara did, it wrinkled her mood.

"I said never mind." Mara turned and pushed through the brush. "Come on, before we're caught. You don't want to end up like those two, do you?"

No, she most certainly did not.

As she followed Mara through the thick wood and back onto the path, the image of the soldier cutting into Lana's father flashed into her head. Amie tried to banish the image from her mind, but like a red erida on fine white carpets, it would not wash away.

She wanted to believe that he got what he deserved for trying to hurt Gavini, but she knew in her heart that his horrible death had been the result of his own horrible actions. Violence sires violence. And that soldier's actions would only birth another act of violence. *No. There was a better way. He shouldn't have died like that.*

NINE

A NIGHTMARE

Jeremiah clasped his hands behind his back as he walked around the watchtower's apex. The tower spiraled into the air, hundreds of spans above the city floor, supported by the Sanctuary below. The view overlooked Caldor and functioned as one of the many guard towers within the city's walls.

The cool spring air felt as if winter threatened to reemerge, but as far as he knew, winter didn't touch the great city the way it did in his homeland. Set in the heart of the hot and humid Borderland Forests, the temperature here remained relatively warm. Jeremiah breathed it in—a refreshing chill after the grand effort of the climb to the tower's peak.

He preferred to start the day's meetings at dawn, but the first session wasn't scheduled for another few hours. Prophet Davin had explained to him that though they were all in the same place, Sulahn, Roanne, and Ghaya's leaders were all experiencing a very different sleep cycle than his own. He could barely comprehend why. Sunrise was sunrise. However, Davin insisted that sunrise for him was at a different time than it was for these other lands. For Sulahn and Roanne, their day had begun hours ago. For Ghaya, it had yet to start. It was a strange marvel of time and geography.

As he overlooked Caldor from a height he'd never experienced, the wonder of time was somehow dwarfed by one of architecture. Prophet Davin had encouraged him to leave his chambers and experience the city's sights while he waited.

Gabriel would love this. So would you, love.

He watched the Caldor Guardsmen observe the skies through their spyglass several strides away. One man signaled for Chief Guardsman Ruggles and pointed out something in the distance. Ruggles appeared surprised at what he saw but not alarmed. Jeremiah imagined that in a city of this scale they saw a number of strange happenings.

"What did you see?" King Jeremiah asked the chief guardsman as he rejoined them. The officer had been giving him and General Yix a tour of their operations. Jeremiah was fascinated by the inner workings of their remarkable city, and General Yix was interested in discovering what he could incorporate into the Crown City's guard.

"Looks like a large flock of birds of some sort," Guardsman Ruggles said. "With spring the flocks come."

"Are they a problem?" Jeremiah asked, giving General Yix a knowing glance. The portsmen at the Crown City's docks often submitted requests for assistance in dealing with the gulls. It seemed silly until Jeremiah ventured to the ports himself and witnessed their ability to raise havoc.

"Mildly," the officer replied.

"Mildly?" General Yix repeated. "They're almost as bad as the rats in the Hzorah Crown City."

"Rats aren't terribly troublesome either," Ruggles said.

General Yix crossed his arms. "How do you manage it?"

"*We* don't," Ruggles said. "There are safeguards in Caldor that manage certain susceptibilities without much intervention."

"Mind sharing?" General Yix pressed. "We could use a safeguard or two ourselves."

"I wish I could," Ruggles said. "Unfortunately, I don't quite understand it. The city is … Well, the city seems to handle certain things on its own."

King Jeremiah frowned. "On its own?"

"Right," the Guardsman said. "The city is so large that it'd be unmanageable without it doing some of the work for us. The Prophets have tried to explain some of it to me, but it's above me. I think it's above them, too. It boils down to what Wizard Titan left behind to protect the city."

"Magic," General Yix growled.

"Precisely," Ruggles said.

The guardsmen called Ruggles over once again, and as he walked back to his post near the spyglass, Jeremiah turned to General Yix. "Amazing, isn't it?"

"I prefer the Crown City, Your Majesty," Yix said. "Handcrafted architecture, beautiful women, the great sea behind it all. And no magic."

Jeremiah was ever-inspired by the Crown City, but Caldor was something altogether different. It took his breath and demanded more. Around every corner there was something new to discover—a spectacle unlike anything else in the world.

Caldor was built before Jeremiah was born, while Wizard Titan still walked the earth, but his father often talked at length about the famine and starvation that swept the land as the population multiplied. Caldor had ended the cycle, giving shelter to many. The systems in place—systems that even Jeremiah didn't understand—helped feed the millions who lived here. And millions more could live here before its capacity was truly tested.

Jeremiah understood Yix's distaste for magic. He shared it. But for all the harm that the Dominion and Prophet Tristan caused in the name of Wizard Titan, there was at least this one testament to what magic could have been.

"Remind me to introduce you to my son when we return to the Crown City. He has the same expression about his face anytime magic is mentioned."

"Smart boy," Yix said, his expression giving way to a smile. "I hear the prince is good with the sword. I've even heard that he's better than you. Perhaps I can convince him to come down and show our ranks a thing or two about handling a weapon."

"A warrior king isn't what Hzorah needs right now."

Jeremiah had purposefully prevented Gabriel from spending time with military men. The boy had that spark in his eye when he talked about war and fighting. He'd taught his son what he knew, but he'd done so in isolation. Apart from his physical and weapons training, it was mostly conceptual—where to deploy troops, when to retreat, how to avoid entrapment. High Lord Bendeth had criticized Jeremiah for withholding his knowledge about the brutal arts, insisting that it would be a disservice to his son in the end. But Jeremiah stood by his decision to prevent Gabriel from dwelling on such things before he had sound reason to engage in such dark matters.

"They're still fretting over that scorching spyglass," Yix said. He nodded back toward the lookout station.

King Jeremiah turned to see Chief Guardsman Ruggles tense and confused. He looked to the sky and watched as the birds approached.

Were they birds? They were certainly larger than any bird he'd ever seen.

He crossed back to the post and tapped the commanding officer on the shoulder. "Is something wrong?"

"The birds …" Ruggles shifted. "They're not birds."

"Birds that aren't birds?" Jeremiah raised his eyebrows. "I'm not sure I understand what you mean."

"They're—"

"Step aside." General Yix crossed in front of the guardsmen and searched through the spyglass himself. "You men almost had me convinced you had some scorching sense. Birds that aren't—" He froze. "Wisdoms! How … What is that?"

Jeremiah stepped closer to his general. "What do you see?"

Yix withdrew. His eyes were fixed between awe and fear. "I don't know. They're … huge."

Jeremiah looked through the spyglass and scanned the skies. He saw a great flying beast, but it had no feathers, only white, reptilian skin stretched over large wings. The beast opened its mouth to reveal monstrous teeth. Mists collected as it inhaled then its head lurched forward. Something white sprayed with tremendous force from its mouth.

Was that ice? *Wisdoms. How?*

Jeremiah backed away from the spyglass and a guardsman quickly took his place. He stepped to the wall and squinted into the distance. He could just barely make out the white beasts against the darkening sky. Clouds swirled behind them, darkening into tumbling gray masses. There had to be at least two dozen, perhaps more.

Then he heard the screams—distant and barely audible, but they shot shivers down his spine.

General Yix stepped up beside him. "May I suggest we leave the tower, Your Majesty? Whatever that is, it's coming this way. You're not safe here."

"I was just about the suggest the same thing," Ruggles said.

King Jeremiah nodded, finally tearing his gaze away from the phenomena. "Right. Let's go."

Jeremiah rushed down the winding stairwell just behind General Yix.

"Mind sharing what you saw in that spyglass?" Yix asked.

"What?" Jeremiah huffed. "You saw it yourself."

"Time hasn't been good to these eyes," Yix said. "I don't trust them as much as I used to."

"I think they were giant hawks, or bats, or flying lizards? They didn't have feathers."

"So, my eyes aren't as bad as I thought they were."

"No."

King Jeremiah's mind raced, trying to place what he saw into some sort of framework he could understand. No marvel should surprise him after what he'd seen of the city. But this … this was overwhelming. The guard hadn't seen it coming, which meant it was unexpected, probably unprecedented.

"Have you heard of anything like this before?" Jeremiah asked Yix as they stepped onto the final landing.

"I'm a warrior, not a scholar, Your Majesty," General Yix

said. "But what I saw, even if a rarity, would be known far and wide if only to frighten young children into staying in bed at night." He turned to his king. "I think you should return to the Crown City."

Jeremiah clenched his jaw. There was still so much to accomplish. Leaving was not an option. Too much was at stake.

A Hzorah soldier approached and saluted. "General. Your Majesty. I was just coming up to find you."

"Walk and talk, Lieutenant," Yix said as he brushed by him.

"The mother and child you asked us to help have been assisted," the soldier said as he followed in their wake. "She's on her way to recovery. Uh, sir, why the rush?"

"Ever seen a nightmare, Lieutenant?" Yix asked without looking back.

"Sir?"

"That scorching prophet should have said something about this," Yix growled. "What's he bloody doing here if he can't even warn us about flying lizards attacking the city his king is visiting?"

General Yix led them toward the sanctuary's northern chamber room and stepped in. At the intrusion, the prophets stood. Queen Frey was absent, but the Ghayan emperor had arrived. He, too, stood, his hands appearing out of the long sleeves of red and gold robes. Unlike the other leaders, his guards accompanied him. They pulled their swords, prepared for Hzorah's general to attack.

"General," Prophet Davin said. He frowned after he met Jeremiah's eyes. "What's wrong?"

"You don't know?" General Yix asked. "Wisdoms! Get off your ass and do some prophesying."

Jeremiah stepped up to the table. "There's something coming. Sky beasts. They're causing havoc in the city."

Prophet Davin turned back to the other prophets who shared looks of bewilderment. He turned back to Jeremiah. "You saw this?"

Wisdoms. Something like this should have been sensed. Moreover, it shouldn't have been missed by *five* prophets. This was wrong. This wasn't supposed to happen.

A Ghayan soldier sprinted into the room followed by Sulahnese and Armothean soldiers. The Ghayan spoke in the language of his people, but the urgency in his voice bespoke his warning.

"The city is under attack," the Armothean soldier said to Prophet Lilith.

"From the north?" Prophet Vanik asked the Armothean soldier, abandoning his native tongue. He leaned on the table next to the Ghayan Emperor. "What banner do they fly?"

The Armothean soldier didn't answer. He looked at Prophet Lilith, unsure if he was clear to answer the questions of a foreign Prophet.

"Well?" Prophet Lilith asked as her scowl deepened.

"From the North," the Armothean guardsman confirmed. "And South, East, and West. From every direction."

"How many soldiers?" Lilith asked.

"I … There are none, Prophet." The man's voice wavered in fear. "The attacks appear to be from the skies. These flying creatures are attacking of their own will."

"Take me to see," Prophet Lilith said, and rushed out of the room with the soldier.

King Jeremiah and General Yix stepped aside as a flood of prophets and guardsmen rushed out of the room. King Jeremiah met his general's eyes as the leaders filed between them.

"I'd like to see this up close for myself," King Jeremiah said.

"Me too."

A pale Prophet Davin stepped between them. "Perhaps a measure of caution is best. I did not foresee—"

"Perhaps," General Yix interrupted, "your usefulness has run its course. *I* will protect my King."

Prophet Davin's mouth hung open as he looked between them. Jeremiah sighed in an effort to calm his nerves, but the instinct for action coursed through his veins. For so long, he ruled in peace. Strange how easily his warrior's instincts were awoken.

"Normally, Prophet Davin, I'd agree with you. But your guidance has been compromised." He turned to Yix. "Let's move."

King Jeremiah took the lead and marched for Hzorah's wing of the Sanctuary. Outside of the northern chamber room was the large central cavity of the Sanctuary. Its dome stretched many spans above them, echoing the jumble of footsteps as the Sanctuary's heart came to life. Behind, General Yix barked orders to his officers. Flurries of armored and uniformed bodies swarmed the great enclosure, and three men of the First League came to Jeremiah's side.

The noise of it all dimmed as Jeremiah entered Hzorah's wing. Near the end of the hall, he stopped at his suite and opened the door.

"Bring my armor and sword," Jeremiah said as he stripped off his coat and trousers. He replaced them with the proper undergarments for his leather armor and turned to the First League soldier who helped him step into his leather-padded greaves. "What's the plan, General?"

General Yix clasped his hands behind his back. "With your permission, I'd like authorization to aid the Caldor guard. These three," Yix said, inclining his head to the soldiers that dressed Jeremiah, "can help you escape. I imagine the western passage will be the safest. It'll take you away from Hzorah and deeper into the Borderlands, but the thick of the forest will conceal you from the skies."

"Permission granted," King Jeremiah said, as the soldiers secured his breastplate. "But don't get yourself killed."

"You take all the scorching fun out of being a warrior, Majesty." General Yix smirked.

"The unfortunate duty of my post."

Yix saluted before leaving the room, and Jeremiah turned his attention to the First League soldiers who were securing his weapons—a dagger at one hip and a sword at the other. The weight of the sword still felt wrong. There was no other sword like the Crown Sabre. He never intended to wield the weapon again, and, if Hzorah stopped Desera's tropes at the Shadow Peaks, perhaps he could keep his word. But in light of what he'd seen in the spyglass, he wished he had it now.

You never did like that sword, love.

"You're clear, Your Majesty," one of the soldiers said. "From here, the most direct way to the city's western passage is underground. The staff tunnels run in all four cardinal directions. We'd only need to find the appropriate one. Each one ultimately emerges in the city. They're typically sealed from the outside but can be opened from the inside for emergencies."

"Very good," King Jeremiah said before leading the soldiers out of his room. The once quiet hallways had lost their serenity as the Sanctuary became aware of the chaos outside. "And where in the Sanctuary can we go for the best view of these creatures?"

"Majesty?"

"You don't think I'm going to leave without getting a good look at what actually happened here?"

"But General Yix—"

"Doesn't always have to have all the fun," Jeremiah interrupted, then sighed, taking on a serious tone. "I need to understand what these creatures are and if they're a threat to my people."

"There are passages coming up to the left that are designated to the Caldor Guard—they lead to the same tower you visited this morning, but that one is sure to be too crowded to use," the First League Officer said. "But there are other lower towers what could give us a proper viewing position."

"Perfect," Jeremiah said. "Let's have a proper look at this nightmare."

Jeremiah leaned over the tower wall. Far below, hundreds of men and women ran through the streets, screaming and shouting. People dropped food and clothing in their rush. Families huddled together in packs, holding each other's hands as they weaved through the panicked throng. He then scanned the skies, hoping to catch a glimpse of one of the beasts he'd seen in the spyglass, but saw nothing. The balcony wasn't as high as the lookout from before, and much of the city was out of his sight. Furthermore, several of the buildings were taller here.

And, despite the madness all around him, he couldn't help but gasp at the vast scale of the city around him.

"Majesty?"

King Jeremiah turned to the officer that stood behind him on the wide landing. Though stark still and attentive, the man bled nervous caution. "Yes?"

"I know this isn't my place, but I feel I must advise that we carry on with General Yix's plan."

Sighing, Jeremiah turned back to his observation. He knew the officer was right, but he didn't want to admit it. He just couldn't bring himself to leave without a good look at the creatures. Even if it didn't serve to help his people, the marvel of it must be worth the attempt.

The shouting and running swarmed and melded. Buzzing like a massive nest of hornets, the sound penetrated to his very core and pressed against his instinct to flee.

His mind suddenly turned to the young girl who'd approached him on the streets. Emelisse. He silently prayed for her safety. He'd pushed aside the concerns of the city, hoping that one small act might make a difference. In odd counterpart, he now did the same, worrying for the safety of one wide-eyed girl and her sick mother.

Just as Jeremiah was about to turn to leave, a shadow cast them in darkness. He turned, shielding his eyes against the sun to see a pale white wing sweep across the sky. Its full form came into view as the wind carried it down between the city's tall buildings. Its lizard-like head turned, and King Jeremiah looked deep into an ice blue eye.

The creature slowed, spreading its terrible wings and extending talons like a hawk searching for a perch. There was only one place the creature could land—the balcony.

"Majesty!" the officer cried out and grabbed his shoulder.

Awed to a standstill, Jeremiah watched as the beast caught the lip of balcony wall. The tower's stonework crumbled under the unnatural load but held, giving only dust and scant chips of rock.

"Majesty!"

Though the soldier's words were loud in his ears, he barely noticed them. He was transfixed by the beauty of the lizard before him. Its icy, pale scales, long neck, and leathery wings were a vision out of a dream, not a nightmare. The reptile grunted and chirped and breathed an eerie mist about them that tumbled and swirled as if alive.

Jeremiah watched, even as several of his officers took hold of him, pulling him away from the balcony. Jeremiah wished dearly that his sons, Gabriel and Seth, could be here to see the sight. He'd never seen anything so wild, so fearsome, so … magnificent. For years he'd been called Majesty. Never in his life had he felt so undeserving of the title.

It's beautiful, love.

As his men pulled him off the balcony, the creature reared its head and released a thick cloud of powder-white snow. The creature's cold fog engulfed him, obscuring the city beyond, deadening the wailing of men, women, and children, isolating him from the world around him. There was only the king and the beast. And then even the beast disappeared.

There was the faint glow of fire and the taste of ash in his mouth. The screams were no longer of panic but of war. Wrathbane was under him, riding hard across the North Hzorah Plain, and the gentle tap of the Crown Sabre against his leg comforted him.

He swiped his hand mace to the right, cutting the throat of a Dominion soldier as he sped through the ranks of the Deseran troops. He would not waste the Sabre on petty game. He would only draw it when he reached his goal.

The smoke ahead thinned and cleared. Before him stood the man he'd come for: General Darius Gareth, the Desolate-bound bastard who'd killed his father.

With practiced grace, Wrathbane slowed just enough to allow Jeremiah to jump off the horse. Well, not jump, so much as gracefully fall. Tucking and covering his head, he tumbled across the fertile soil, rolling into the second cadence on bended knee.

Jeremiah stood, staring Gareth in the eye. The man's dark glare was like a stone wall, daring him to climb out of the prison the Dominion had risen around his people. His black cloak beat with the dust and smoke, pulling away to reveal his sword. He drew it in invitation.

King Jeremiah pulled the Crown Sabre free and brandished it, allowing the blade to breathe in the chaos of battle. Then, he charged. Gareth did not flee. He waited for the king's attack, welcomed it. Jeremiah flowed into the first cadence—his preferred attacking stance—with perfect battle form, but as he approached the ground shook. He lost his footing, stumbled and caught himself. The ground between them splintered. Fresh earth fell into the breach. The world exhaled, and pale white mists rose out of the growing chasm.

As King Jeremiah straightened, a canyon lay before him so vast that the Dominion General was but a fleck against a distant horizon. The horizon faded away. The canyon dissolved. The ground beneath his feet drew away beyond the icy mists. The mist disappeared, leaving only darkness before even the darkness was no more.

But Esther was there. He took her hand and stepped into Desolate to remain together forever. Ever silent, distant. Safe.

CALDOR

THE SECOND MOVEMENT

TEN

AN ORPHAN

Prince Gabriel slouched further into his chair. It was plenty comfortable. In fact, save King Jeremiah's, it was probably one of the plushest chairs in the whole palace. But it didn't matter how soft a chair was: if you sat in it for too long, it was bound to grow uncomfortable.

More so than the fact that he had sat in the chair for far too long was his agitation with the fool Lords that surrounded him. The amount of squabbling in which these grown men reveled seemed beyond the limits of anyone their age and compounded his discomfort. And they called *him* a child.

His father would be displeased to see him slouching, and even though he didn't turn to look, he was relatively certain his tutor was giving him a look that said, 'when the meeting is over, we are going to have a long talk about how to act like a proper gentleman.' Gabriel had sat through many lectures of the same sentiment and he wondered if the man ever tired of giving it.

One more year. Repeating that thought was how he got himself through it. One more year and he could finally do what he was supposed to do—what he should be doing *now* instead of wasting his time listening to the Desolate-bound.

His father insisted on his education. According to his tutors, this meant he needed to know the ins and outs of

Hzorah's entire political landscape and have just as strong a hold on the inner workings of the other six kingdoms in the world. Gabriel would have picked almost any other subject to be well versed in. Masonry, blacksmithing, woodwork, glass, even farming would be preferable. Something worthy of his time. Something that actually got things done. All that ever happened in the court was circular debates that would lead to few actual changes.

Gabriel already knew what he was good at, and it wasn't sitting around listening to bureaucratic dribble. He was an excellent swordsman and archer. He even held his own as a pikeman. He was a warrior, and he should be doing what a real leader should be doing in a time like this: actually *leading* his men to victory. And save what little his father had taught him about battlefield strategy, he'd resisted the idea of allowing Gabriel to learn from his generals. Gabriel had hardly even *seen* them in person.

The Deseran Dominion had clear and hostile intentions. War was all but inevitable now, and Hzorah would be their first target. It only made sense. The Dominion viewed Hzorah as the root of all the Dominion's problems. But the rest of the world knew better. Refusing to cooperate with the rest of civilization was the root of the Dominion's problems.

What was created with the establishment of Caldor was clearly working. Over two-hundred years under the Caldor Convention for Peace had proven that the world was capable of long-term cooperation. Gabriel's tutors had made sure to chisel that deep into his head. Every nation was growing. Hzorah smithed more steel than ever before, and Armoth quarried more ore consequently. Ghaya produced copious amounts of livestock, furs, and silks, and the Crehn Isles—when the pirates were kept at bay—exported the finest fish. There was no getting Roanne and Sulahn working together, but at least they traded with everyone else.

Desera was the only wet gauntlet.

If it were up to him, he would be doing what his father should be doing, what his father *used* to do: in the army camps showing his troops that he was there to lead them to victory should the Dominion make its move. His bloodline was praised as some of the greatest warriors who had ever lived. He grew up with stories of how his father had survived the impossible and stories of his grandfather doing the same. Somehow, between then and now, his father had grown soft. In an era where Hzorah knew a few years of peace, his warrior heritage was reduced to this: bureaucratic dribble.

Now, at the end of his day in court, there was but one more messenger before he could retire for the evening. Then he could finally get out of this stiff court and get some practice in. Spring had come in strong, and he wanted to absorb as much sun as he could.

From his slouching, he looked to the mosaic painted on the ceiling above. The story it depicted told of how the Hzorah Crown unified scattered tribes and pushed out the Dominion. This was the war that liberated the people of Hzorah to live their lives free of the zealots who enforced the outdated practices of the Creed. Practices that held tightly to the hope of the return of a long dead Wizard.

The court's ceiling carved over in an oval-shaped dome until it reached walls trimmed in gold and black swirls that interlocked in four repeating patterns. The walls themselves were a soft pearl color except where large, wooden double doors cut the room in half at the widest points of the room's elliptical design.

"A message from Caldor, issued by the Crown's Prophet Davin," called the court's announcer. "Please step forward."

The man wasn't a messenger, but a soldier. One of his father's personal guard. His father had grown soft indeed, allowing such a well-trained warrior be subject to a task unsuited to his skills. Gabriel sat up straight, though. He was curious when his father would finally return. He had finally made several shaft shots in a row and could now do it rather consistently. He would beat his father in contest this year at the solstice festival.

The man stepped forward. He didn't carry a physical

message, as was often sent when official word from his father intended for the Crown's Lords needed immediate attention. It was usually best to not risk allowing a messenger to change or leave out any part of the message whether by accident or intent. His father had told him how he'd made that mistake twice and did not intend to make it again.

But then his father had also told him that there were times when a message was so sensitive that it could only be memorized. Some information was too dangerous to risk finding its way to enemy hands.

The soldier stepped up to a chest-high podium atop the petitioner's landing. He looked weary, as if he had traveled hard to reach them. Caldor was at least two weeks west of the Hzorah Crown on horseback and only when traveled at breakneck speeds was it possible to reach it in any sort of haste.

"My Lords," he began, "I have come with the gravest of news."

A murmur slipped through the court. Gabriel caught one man's comment—one of the Crown's relay men to his right: "I heard he killed three fast stallions getting here. Three!" And another to his left: "Sending a soldier is an outright waste of resources. I've been talking the like for weeks now!"

As the chatter died down, he continued, "After the arrival of King Jeremiah, Caldor was ravaged by a storm." Another wave passed through, this time louder and to greater alarm. Gabriel sat straighter in his chair and the soldier continued. "By some strange change in weather, the city was covered in ice like no winter I have ever seen. Caldor has fallen … King Jeremiah has … fallen."

This time, the ripple of alarm was accompanied by several low lords finding their feet and shouting their disbelief. Runners stopped in their tracks, taking in the news before leaving the hall to deliver messages.

Gabriel sat without words. His father was dead? *His* father was dead? The man who had survived many great battles under the cause of the Hzorah Crown was dead? The man who taught him how to draw a bow, how to hold a sword, that honor was paramount... was dead?

Gabriel swallowed hard. The voices around him began to grow quiet and dull as the messenger's words rained thick its horror. He could only hear his breathing, his heart pumping, his reality shattering.

The sounds of the court flooded back in as a hand found his shoulder. "I'm sorry, my boy." It was his tutor, Samuel. Gabriel turned to see him standing over his shoulder, his eyes rimmed with sincere remorse. "I'm so very sorry."

Gabriel shoved off his hand as he stood and backed away from him. He didn't mean to react aggressively, but he didn't want anyone to touch him. He turned to more eyes looking at him like he was a lost orphan. And they weren't wrong. His mother had died giving birth to his younger brother and now his father had died as well. He was an orphan.

He took a step backward from their gazes and into a server behind him. The server's tray, pitcher, and cups clattered to the floor, drawing yet more eyes to him before they returned to their debating. Samuel placed a hand on his plush chair. "Please, Gabriel. Sit. I will have—"

"No …" Gabriel found his voice. "No …" He brushed past Samuel and ran for the door. Samuel called after him, but he ignored it. He pushed the court's doors open and stepped outside.

And then he ran.

Gabriel pushed past the guards on the outside of the court doors. He pushed past petitioners who wouldn't see the council until the following day. He charged into a wild sprint down the Great Hall that crossed from one end of the palace to the next.

Like the courtroom he'd been in before, the walls were a pearl, but only where the gray of darker marble prevented a homogeneous mix. Columns of opaque and ridged gold doubled the wall's support of the high curved ceiling, and windows set on the right wall let in shafts of warm sunlight from the western horizon. Gabriel had walked this hall countless times. It was this very hall where he'd taken his first steps and, when he became practiced, where he'd ran carelessly between the waiting arms of his mother and father.

He shook off the memory and continued running. His mother had been gone for years now and he hardly felt the distant longing for her. He really only had a few murky memories of her face; one of which was that moment in this very hallway. He'd only seen three years—too young to really hold on to the pain. Too young to pass blame to his brother.

Forcing his eyes shut, he ran on. He didn't want to see the phantoms. He didn't want to look upon the halls that his father would now haunt forever just like the memory of his mother did now. He wanted to shut it out. He wanted to keep running. He wanted out of the palace.

Gabriel opened his eyes just as he came to the palace's center where the Great Hall intercepted the South Hall and North Hall. He'd ran the length so many times that he'd timed it perfectly even from behind his grief. He looked back down the Great Hall. Several runners were looking in his direction. To the side, between columns and walls, they continued at a brisk walk, offset by Gabriel's blind charge. He turned back ahead, unwilling to meet their eyes. They looked at him as if he'd lost his wits; soon they'd look at him as if he'd lost his father.

Not only did the intersection act as a junction between halls but also between floors. The circular crossroads featured two grand and wide set staircases that spiraled in a double helix to the next landing. Gabriel cut to the nearest set of stairs. Each led to the same level. The second stairway was a pure redundancy for the purposes of symmetrical design.

Vaulting up the stairs and holding onto the broad railing, he remembered the first time he'd fallen down them. He had only seen four years but was confident that he'd mastered the incline. He'd dashed ahead of his father who held Seth in his arms. His father had told him to stop, but he didn't listen. Only two steps down, he'd slipped and fell several more before he stopped. His father called for help, afraid that the worst had happened ...

Gabriel cleared the stairway and continued down the next hall. The floor was much of the same but without the golden columns and supported a lower hanging, flat ceiling. Soft carpets cushioned his footfalls, leaving the memory of his passage behind like winter snow. He remembered his father drawing in that carpet when he had seen twelve years. With his finger, King Jeremiah drew out features of the Hzorah terrain and played out battles that he and his own father had won. He would bring marbles and position them in place of regiments to illustrate proper flanking, inverted wedges, and encirclement tactics.

Near the end of the hall, he stopped. The last door, set at the end of the hall, was the King's chamber. He stood there, half expecting his father to step out. He shut his eyes and swore that he'd never blow off a lesson again if his father would just walk out and show that he wasn't gone. And he meant it.

He opened his eyes to no such result.

He pushed open the door directly to his right and was greeted with the warm lilac scent of his room's scented candles. A luxury—and unnecessary with the daylight spilling generously through the wide set windows on the far side of the room—but they were in no short supply at the Hzorah Crown Palace and Gabriel couldn't burn them faster than they were stocked.

Panting from the continuous run and pace of his broken heart, he stood just inside his chambers with his head bowed. He didn't want to cry. He'd cried for less, though it had been years since he last remembered doing so. He *did* want to yell. And with that singular, empowering thought, he did.

"Gabe?"

Gabriel looked across the room to see Seth sitting on his bed. Looking up from his reading, his eyes met Gabriel's. Trouser-less, he still wore a shirt in the midday cut under a messy mop of hair far past needing a proper trim. He and his brother shared the room. It was plenty big enough for the both of them—bigger than many families in Hzorah had for their entire homes.

Gabriel never complained about sharing the room even though the palace had enough rooms to easily have one to himself. His father had told them that it was important that they learn to share and get along and that when he was of age, he would get his own room. It didn't make sense to him, but Samuel and Nurse Marium had insisted that his father had his reasons.

His father …

Gabriel needed to clear his head. He needed to find release. He grabbed his bow that sat, leaning against his bureau.

"Archer court. Now," he said, then turned on heel and slipped back out into the hall.

Gabriel charged back down the hall without waiting for his brother's response. He knew he would follow. He always did. He and Seth were close, and Gabriel was often in the mood to chew bark after a day in the court. Seth always helped defuse his anger. Gabriel knew it was because Seth genuinely cared for him, but he couldn't help but feel some of it was rooted in the guilt of not having to carry the same burden of the Crown as Gabriel.

He could hear Seth's light but rapid steps catching up to him as he began back down the palace stairs. Seth took to them, mirroring his descent on the opposite set. Seth did this often. He enjoyed the effect, and it made for a far more enjoyable race when you're taking a wager on who would reach the bottom first. Gabriel would usually win, but it was one of the few contests in which he held the upper hand with his brother.

Other than his bow being the closest weapon within reach at the moment, he had intentionally grabbed for it. He found his sword to be a greater release of his frustrations, but Seth didn't care for dueling. Gabriel couldn't imagine why, though. Seth was by far his better. And Gabriel wasn't by *any* stretch incapable. He imagined that most boys his age would proudly display a banner saying that he could out-duel than his older brother. Seth, instead, shied away from it, saying it wasn't much fun.

This pushed Gabriel to practice his swordsmanship even further. He'd practiced relentlessly, becoming far better than his own instructors. Still, he couldn't beat Seth. Though his pride was on the line, Gabriel still tried to be a good brother and pushed Seth to compete at the upcoming festival, but he would have no part in it. Seth, trying to be a good brother in turn, still practiced with him occasionally and even let him win sometimes. Gabriel hated when he did that.

Gabriel took to the South hall that led to the palace grounds. Seth, catching up to his side, fell in step with his brother's brisk pace. He could feel Seth's eyes on him, burning with expectancy. This was usually the point when Gabriel started spilling what was wrong with the Crown's council and how half of Hzorah could burn before they passed an ordinance to put out the fire. This time, he didn't have a complaint with the council. At least not one that could wink in the shadow of what was most important.

How was he going to tell him that their father was dead?

Gabriel didn't want to believe it himself. He'd trade anything, even himself for it not to be true. But any sort of wishing and wanting wouldn't change the truth. The faster he accepted it, the faster he could pull his emotions together. The rational part of him knew that. So why couldn't he bring his heart around?

"So …" Seth's voice cut past his thoughts. "Bad day in court?"

Gabriel kept walking. Though his brother would likely take his demeanor as outrage, he was actually trying to out-march the inevitable. He had to tell him the truth. He just didn't want to yet. Maybe if he could hold off long enough, he wouldn't have to.

No. He should hear it from me.

They'd passed the Crown's garden and reached the archer court before Seth spoke again. "Samuel and Marium want to go fishing upriver soon. It's getting really nice out. I think we'll make some nice catches."

Gabriel listened but didn't respond. He walked straight to the furthest target range, pulled an arrow from the large black bin sitting next to an 'X' burned into the grass that marked the proper shooting distance.

"Samuel said that if I do good on my lessons in the coming months, maybe we'll actually get separate rooms," Seth continued. "That's been a long time coming, right?"

Gabriel grunted an uninterested response as he eyed the target in the distance, contemplating his shot. He and his brother *would* be getting separate rooms, but not for the reason Seth imagined.

He pulled the arrow taut and level with his eye. His bow was the exact right resistance and proportions for him. Though many bows were now fashioned in standard sizes, as commissioned by his father three years prior, a proper bowman always had his bow set to fit his arm span and strength.

"With all the talk about the Deseran Dominion threatening the Hzorah Crown, Marium is doubling up on my studying of that area," Seth said as he pulled his own arrow and nocked it.

Threatening? How understated. Gabriel frowned deeper as he lined up his shot. The target's center wobbled under the arrow's point. He held his breath, letting his hands guide him to a clean shot.

"From what Nurse Marium has taught me so far," Seth said, drawing to take his shot. "I don't see how they really stand a chance against us. Father is strong."

Was, Gabriel thought.

Gabriel freed the arrow. He turned to Seth before it missed its mark, too high from the target's center. He didn't need to see it for himself. He knew where it would land. Seth's comment had wavered his focus … or rather, Gabriel had *let* Seth's comment waver his focus. He couldn't make excuses for his missed shot. Excuses never won a battle.

"Father is dead."

Seth let his tension on the bow falter before he pulled back again and let his arrow fly. "Shove off, Gabe. That's not funny." He turned from his near perfect shot and looked at Gabriel without amusement in his expression. He reached past him and grabbed another arrow from the barrel and took aim again.

Gabriel watched as he took another shot. He didn't want to try to convince Seth of their father's death. Just saying it aloud twisted his gut and thinned his breathing. But he *had* said it out loud, and now the reality of it began to set in.

Seth cursed another less than perfect shot before turning back and renewing his disapproving glower. "What?" he demanded. "You didn't really think I'd find that funny, did you?"

"Seth, I …" Gabriel stabbed the end of his bow deep into the ground, letting silence soften words that wouldn't come easy. "A member of the Crown's Guard reported in before I left the court. He told of a violent storm that tore through Caldor. He said that Father was killed in it."

Seth's expression didn't change as he continued to stare razors into him. His light brown eyes—lighter now since winter—seemed to change. They dimmed under the slow realization of the truth behind Gabriel's words.

"Father is … dead?"

Gabriel answered with a look to the ground and a slow nod.

The silence wore on several moments longer before Gabriel lifted his bow from the dirt and nocked another arrow. He drew it tight and aimed, this time envisioning the Desolate-bound Prophet behind the Dominion's insanity as the target instead of the bright red dot. He could see Prophet Tristan standing there—at least what he imagined him to look like—smugly challenging him then laughing at his weakness. The arrow escaped his grip.

Perfect shot.

"So, you will be king now," Seth said, half-whispering.

Gabriel turned to him as if he'd blasphemed rather than stated the obvious. He knew that he would have to take the throne but had mostly avoided thinking of it. He may as well have been given a death sentence. He'd seen the life of a king. How his father had been reduced from a great warrior to a figurehead of limited power. How putting down the sword and taking up a pen had taken a piece of him away. He saw it in his eyes every time his father taught him in his younger years. How much he missed that life and how it pained him that he would never have it back.

That would be his life now.

"I'm *not* going to be king." Gabriel snatched another arrow and aimed again. "Not yet anyway. I've only seen seventeen years. I have a few months to go yet before I come of age. For all I know, the council will find a way to break the Crown by then."

His response was only partially wish fulfillment. It was true that by his father's own directive, all successors to the Crown would need to see eighteen years before being allowed to rule—a full two years younger than the kingdom's recognized age of adulthood. Until then, the High Lords would share power, and Gabriel could only watch. But he also knew that the Hzorah Lords would eat up the opportunity to control Hzorah as they saw fit without the Crown's directive. Even more likely, they'd vie for power themselves. Either was good enough for Gabriel. He knew where he belonged, and it was not on a throne.

Gabriel took a shot that fell wide of his intended shaft shot before turning back to his brother's tearful eyes. Seth dipped his head, embarrassed of his crying. Gabriel pulled him into a comforting embrace. He understood his brother's grief. Though he didn't feel like crying, he still felt the gravity of sorrow in the pit of his gut.

"I will avenge him, Seth," Gabriel whispered. "By the Crown, I will."

"Gabriel!"

Nurse Marium's voice cut through their moment. They split apart and Gabriel prepared for the tongue lashing that would follow. *Perfect.*

"I have been searching the palace from top to bottom for

you! Running away and leaving the court like that in the middle like some sort of … I should have known to look here first …" She continued her rant and briskly stalked across the yard. She held her long sky-blue skirts clutched in her hands; her wrinkles intensified by her disposition under a gray and black-striped bun of hair. "And at such a time as this … you march right off."

As expected, the news must have swept the palace. Odds were that everyone in the palace had heard it by now. Gabriel dreaded this the most. It was hard enough that his father would never return. It was even harder knowing he was the sad sack of the palace. No matter how well he carried himself, whispers would follow in the wake of his passing.

She stopped just short of trampling them and looked Gabriel up and down before turning to Seth. "Come now," she said, pulling him under her wing and taking Gabriel's place for comfort. She looked back up to Gabriel, her face now more understanding. She whispered something in Seth's ear and smiled a small, tight-lipped smile. Seth nodded and turned to leave, looking back at his brother as he left.

Marium turned back to Gabriel. Her eyes still held compassion, but her lips had tightened to show her usual stern attitude she dished out generously when Gabriel balked at his duties. "I know that this must be hard for you boys, so I will spare you the usual lecture I grow tired of giving. You are nearly of age to be king yourself." She paused, letting her brow furrow in resistance to what she might say. "But you are still young yet. It's not fair to be given this lot, but you must be strong for your kingdom. King Jeremiah was a good king and beloved by his people. We need a king that will be strong. You must not give them reason to doubt their trust in you."

Gabriel looked away. He *was* strong. He would just never have the chance to prove it while chained to a throne. He was not the king now, but Seth was right. He would be king if the High Lords kept the Crown from dissolving.

"There will be a dinner this evening," Nurse Marium continued. "I expect you to attend. Had you stayed long enough, you would have heard of it yourself. The High and Low Lords will want to share their condolences as well as the diplomats who are currently visiting the palace."

She eyed him, searching for argument. When he didn't rise to opposition, she continued. "I know that you don't care for formal events, but it's important that you present yourself in a manner appropriate for a king. Your legacy as king begins today." She paused again for a response and, again, Gabriel remained silent. "The dinner will be in three hours. Please, Gabriel, do *not* be late." She turned and whisked away without waiting for his response.

Gabriel let a sigh escape as he watched her go. He didn't want to go to a dinner, especially one that would parade him as kingdom-stooge and orphan of the year. Marium was right about one thing, though: Hzorah did need a strong king. A king who could lead his people to victory.

Gabriel pulled another arrow and took aim. He vowed right then and there that he would be *that* king. If he was forced to take the Crown, he would do everything in his power to lead his people to victory on the battlefield. He would not hide behind a throne as his armies died on the field. He would show his men strength and bring glory to the Crown once more.

Gabriel released the arrow. It struck, just south of shafting.

ELEVEN

CRACKS ON THE SURFACE

"Do you think it's frozen solid?" Tele asked, gazing at the great city before her.

She shifted in her mount. Gilly, while smaller than Navid's horse, competently carried her and Gavini while Navid rode on Kemper. Though she had insisted that she'd rather walk, Navid insisted that she learn to ride, and she couldn't argue that learning to ride was without value.

Navid had spent nearly an hour correcting posture and explaining the basics before having her bring the mare to a slow walk. Tele thought back to how she'd entertained the idea of stealing Navid's horse when they'd first met. She realized now that she wouldn't have made it very far.

She looked at Navid, his expression a blank disbelief. When he didn't answer her question, she turned back to the spectacle. Tele had seen things she hadn't thought possible after meeting Navid: A gateway capable of linking distant places. The Borderland Forest was far grander than she could have imagined—even with the sketches drawn by her Father. Caldor was far more shocking.

Navid spoke true when he said it was like a crown jewel towering higher than any tree. Before, she had the sense that Navid exaggerated the truth out of patronage to his home. His words had understated the city's majesty completely. It wasn't the sheer size of Caldor that left her and Navid dumbfounded, however. It was the ice that encased it.

The ice covered every inch visible. Her father had told her of the white crystalline water that formed in place of rainfall when conditions were right. He had said that they could rage like powerful dust storms, covering the land in frozen water many feet deep. But this was different: only the city and the water surrounding it was frozen while the ground on which they stood remained untouched by the phenomena.

Caldor was dead-still, quiet. Circular in form with towering golden walls and spires reaching into the heavens, it rested on land surrounded by water. Several trade ships, half-sunken into the frozen moat, protruded at high angles, captured in mid-descent. The trees ended a few thousand paces before the city, leaving a broad clearing for the forest's man-made jewel to rest.

The city Navid had described before they arrived seemed terrifying in its own right. She had never been to a place of such a grand scale. She found large numbers of people unsettling. Seeing it like this, however, was little comfort. A stilled city carried its own set of anxieties.

The Drunn river flowed outward from the water surrounding the city. When they had tried to fish the previous day, they'd seen frozen chunks floating on the water. But here, the water appeared entirely frozen, meaning that, somehow, under ice perhaps, the water still flowed.

She eyed Navid once again, hoping for a response. When he continued to sit quietly atop his mount, she tried for his attention again. "What do you think could have caused it?"

As if waking from a dream, he shook his head. "I can't imagine … The climate here doesn't succumb to snowfall any time of the year. This is impossible."

"Clearly not. What do we do now?" Tele asked.

"We should check for survivors," Gavini said.

Tele sighed. "And then what? We can't save a whole city."

"Well, I don't know what else to do," Navid said.

"We don't know that things aren't fine inside the walls," Gavini said.

"The walls …" Tele's eyes narrowed, straining to make out what lay ahead. "Do they post guards on them? Someone tasked to keep watch from above?"

"Yes," Navid replied.

"There are none. I don't think things are fine inside."

"Let me know if you come up with a better plan." Navid gave his steed a gentle kick forward.

Tele urged Gilly into a trot behind him. Protesting wouldn't be much help. She didn't have a better plan. She had nowhere else to go. Tele had placed all her chips in favor of Caldor and it seemed she had no luck in gambling.

Someone had better be alive in there, she thought. *Someone has to be.*

With every step, the pressure changed. The frozen city sapped the very heat from the surrounding air. And the air, humid behind and chilled ahead, caked into a swirling fog. Tele found herself pulling her arms tight around her, letting her reins dangle and trusting the dappled mare to stay on course.

Tingles of chills and dread crawled up the nape of her neck as she and Gavini caught up alongside Navid. Tele looked to his hard expression. She couldn't read his thoughts, but his eyes looked as cold as the city beyond. She pulled Gilly close to his steed, hoping to share in their warmth, thankful for Gavini's warmth behind her.

By the time they reached the clearing, her cloak had been freed and wrapped close around her. Navid had done likewise, and Gavini pressed close against her. She tried the method she'd always used on colder nights in the Dominion Desert: holding her breath for a few moments, think of being warmer until she felt it, then breathing again. It never worked more than a few seconds at a time, but it was always a precious few moments of relief.

"Do you think it's frozen enough to cross?" Tele asked.

They paused at the edge of the motionless water and Tele looked to the great bridge drawn tight against the city wall.

Caldor's walls towered higher than she thought it was from a distance. She felt minuscule—a dizzying effect.

"I'm not sure," Navid said, staring at the water's edge.

Gavini shrugged from atop the horse. "It's usually risky to try crossing without having a core sample to verify the ice's thickness."

Tele looked around for a time, searching for a rock or something to test the fragility of what they faced. Nothing of substantial weight seemed readily available. She dismounted, placed a foot over the edge, and stomped hard. It felt solid, but Tele was still unsure.

"Hand me your pack," she said.

Navid untied the one on the right side of his saddle. She took it and tested its weight. It wasn't as heavy as either of them and certainly not as heavy as either of the horses, but it had nothing vital inside. It would have to do. Re-approaching the breach, she spun in place three times before releasing the pack with as much strength as she could. A soft thud sounded as the pack landed and slid a few feet further before resting gently on its side.

"Well," Tele began, turning back to Navid and Gavini. "I'm still not sure if it's safe to cross, but if we want that pack back, we're going to have to try."

A small, uncertain nod was Navid's only response.

Tele found Navid's recent lack of nerve disparaging. It was partly his level assurance that had edged her into the unknown at their meeting. Now, at the sight of his beloved Caldor in icy ruin, he faltered.

"Have either of you ever crossed a frozen lake?" she asked before turning back to the chasm before her.

Her tone shifted light and conversational with the intention of pulling Navid another step closer to optimism. She had looked forward to reaching Caldor for many days and, frozen or not, she wasn't going to let ice keep her from reaching her goal.

"Crossed? No," Navid said.

"But you have walked on ice?"

"Yes."

Tele looked at him as he sided with her. "Any tips?"

"Don't slip."

Tele sighed in resignation. She had tried. Navid was no child, and she wasn't about to hold his hand. Still, she couldn't help but empathize with him. She understood a bit of what he was feeling—the pain and shock. The faces of those she had lost flashed in her mind's eye—fire, ice, it all came to the same end—and she pushed them away. It would do little to have two souls bleeding together. He needed time, and she would give it.

"I can hobble across," Gavini said. "I'm slower than gluan sap, but we're best served distributing our weight."

Navid nodded and moved to help Gavini down from the horse.

"Is it even worth bringing the horses in?" Tele asked.

"It could take two days to walk from one side of Caldor to the other," Navid said. He gave Gavini his walking stick. "Due to our … circumstances—"

"My hobbling."

"— we may have a difficult time reaching the sanctuary."

Tele turned back to the great moat of ice before them. "Ready, girl?" she asked Gilly. She still felt a bit silly talking to the horse, but she'd learned during their journey that Gilly appreciated acknowledgment.

She placed her faith in uncertain ground and stepped forward. When the ice didn't break, she let her heart slow before taking another step. Gilly followed in reined tow, treading lightly. Each pace brought a high-pressured heart pulse and a release of breath unconsciously held. She kept a close watch at the ice before her, searching for thinning and cracks on the surface.

Tele reached the pack she'd thrown soon enough. She bent over, grasped its strap and swung it over her shoulder, then made a careful about face to check if Navid and Gavini had followed. They were just behind with Kemper near halfway between the shore and where she now stood.

Navid's expression had shifted from wary to focused as he

walked with Gavini, ready to assist him if his legs failed. Tele smiled. He hadn't lost so much nerve as she'd feared.

Another half circle and a tug on her horse's leads saw her off again. She counted her breaths as they escaped in thick clouds, feeling confident enough in their passage to breathe evenly. Only a few hundred paces more and she'd be done with the worst of it. At least she *hoped* this was the worst of it.

Taking her eyes off her feet, she eyed the golden walls before her. What did those walls hide? How bad was it really inside? Had she traveled all this way only to find a dead end?

Her father's final words to her had been a plea for her to preserve the knowledge her family had taught her. Had Navid not arrived in the Dominion Desert to help her when he had, she almost certainly wouldn't have survived. When she'd found Gavini, she'd even allowed herself to hope again—that with his help, she might be able to actually reform the Keepers.

I'm so close.

A loud snap and the slosh of displaced water caught her attention. She whirled at the alarm, looking behind her. Kemper danced nervously, backing away with a whiny at the breach in ice. Navid and Gavini had disappeared, swallowed into the Drunn's frozen depths.

Navid twisted in the dark water. The ice above masked the sun, giving the water a quality like traveling through the magic gateway he'd used to find Tele. Completely submerged, he only had the dim light from the ice breach above and a stream of bubbles that escaped from his mouth to orient him.

The curse coursed through his blood and pulsed in painful waves. Like a wedge shoved between his mind and the piece of himself he'd locked away over years of careful training, his curse hammered, desperate to escape Navid's strict partition.

Thump.

Navid shut his eyes. *To allow it to take me is to take a path of evil. To allow it to control me is to take a path to destruction.*

Thump. Thump. Thump.

He kicked his legs, swimming up to the surface. *To allow it to take me is to take a path of evil. To allow—*

Thump. Thump. Thump. Thump. Thump!

Fractured by panic, by fear, by danger, Navid's veil of control shattered. Awareness filled him as his mind—his very soul—opened and breathed.

He sensed danger—an intuition granted by his curse that was far beyond the simple awareness of the present. He turned about in the water. There was something in the river, something monstrous. It was suddenly as obvious as it would be if he could see it right in front of him. If he didn't get out of the water, it would hunt him down and kill him.

What was once deep within now enveloped his being, giving him direction and pointing him to safety.

Sensing deliverance above, he looked to the surface. But something else tugged at his awareness. With the blight of his curse guiding him, he swam down into the depths, searching for redemption.

Navid reached out and took Gavini's hand.

Tele's chin met ice after taking her first fretted step toward Navid's rescue. She pushed herself up on all fours and began scrambling toward the ice breach. Kemper, a contrasting black against the pale white ice, still pranced. If Navid weighed enough to break through the ice, then certainly his steed would make matters worse moving about as he was.

She slowed when nearing where the water bridge had fragmented, fearing that she would trigger more breaking. As she inched further, the ice stung her bare hands. The wind cut through her, invoking shivers and leaving her face numb.

Tele slowly peered into the frigid, black deep. The waters rippled, churned and lapped over edge, but she couldn't see him. She leaned in closer, looking for signs of life: air gathering in bubbles or shadows of movement.

Nothing.

Without warning, Navid's head broke the surface. She recoiled, startled by his sudden rise. Navid cast a hand atop the solid ice and pulled Gavini above the water with his other. Tele regained her wits, clutched Gavini's upper arms, and pulled with the entirety of her strength. She slid toward the freezing water. Grounding her boots, she worked to add friction.

Now that his torso was above the surface, Gavini swung a leg out of the water and leveraged the rest of himself onto the ice. Tele backed away, more out of fear of falling in herself than to give Gavini room to recover. He shivered violently, near convulsion, as he fell to his side.

"Keep moving!" Navid shouted. "Before the ice breaks!"

"Come on. Hurry," Tele said, pulling him again. Gavini assisted as much as he could as Tele pulled him away from the break.

Another crack cut through the frozen surface. It splintered and branched, growing outward like a tree. Chunks of ice broke away in the shadow of their flight, widening the liquid rift. When the sounds of encroaching death ended, she turned, still sliding backward. The watery abyss had more than tripled in size.

Frozen ice churned in the aftermath of severed stasis. Kemper stood on land, grazing the dying grass along the bank. And Navid … Where was he?

Navid's ankle erupted with pain. Something razor sharp clamped down and pulled him down into the depths. As he sank, the light of the surface dimmed, and he pressed his lips tight to preserve the last remnants of air that he'd managed to claim before he was snatched away.

The curse ran through his nerves, permeating every facet of his awareness. Every ripple of water over his skin, every twist of his limbs as he descended, every fragment of material —dead or alive—brushed against his senses as his mind structured and restructured the chances of his survival with every passing moment.

He needed air. But instead of a frantic struggle, he relaxed. It wasn't a calm resignation to the inevitable, but a tactical shift to patience. The more he struggled, the more of his breath he'd waste. The truth of it barely registered as his reasoning. In fact, it wasn't *his* reasoning as he understood it. It was a curse-driven instinct. His ability as a seer had taken control of his actions, and even as he fought to regain control, the power within him took the opportunity to fill every crevice of his being.

Navid's descent slowed and he sensed the swirl of countless particles of debris, disrupted from his journey to the bottom and whatever-monster-gripped-him's movements. It was too dark to see the globs of swirling dirt, but his curse made its presence known to him and he shut his eyes to keep them from agitation.

Sensing and opening of deliverance, his hand gripped something blunt—a handle—a hammer long ago lost to the depths of time.

Navid curled about, positioning his body to wield the tool against the creature's grip. He cocked his arm, giving his trajectory as long a path to accelerate as possible, sensing how much harder it would be to retaliate through the water. His ability guiding him, he struck.

Heart pounding and breathing wildly, Tele allowed herself to lie back against the cold ice. She looked at Gavini a span away. Hair streaked with frost and panting, he curled into a warmer position. Tele scooted closer to him and tried to offer some warmth. He felt as cold as the ice beneath her. He needed to get dry.

She turned back to the ice breach beyond and felt a weight in her stomach as she watched for the seer.

But Navid was gone.

"Come on," she said. "We need to get to the other side and find warmth and dry clothes."

Gavini nodded without looking at her, his teeth chattering. She helped him to his feet, and they turned toward the golden walls. Labored step after labored step, they continued, stopping only to grab Navid's pack and Gilly's reins.

Fearing the risk of triggering another collapse of ice, they left Kemper behind. They could make due with the provisions Gilly carried, and Kemper—who'd crossed back to the grassy river bank—looked delighted not to be walking across the frozen hazard. Tele even thought she saw him smile.

Guilt overcame Tele as shivers ran the length of her spine, knowing that Gavini's condition was far worse, knowing that Navid had suffered a fate far worse than she'd ever faced.

Every few steps, she asked Gavini if he would be alright. His response was a stiff nod from his hunched posture. His legs shuttered at each footfall, but Tele feared that adding his weight to Gilly's might place too much pressure on one spot of ice—ice that had proven to be inconsistently thick.

Tele hadn't felt so cold since the nights following her family's death. Her possessions, insufficient for the harsh exposure to the elements, left her freezing and frightened, praying for a chance at survival.

And as she looked to Caldor, its walls stretched wide with their approach and obstructed the world from view. Ice locked in a frame of disquiet; it held the last chance to rebuild her life. Within, she would find answers; she had to find something. Tele held tightly to the hope of Caldor, even as that hope began to wear thin.

A splash from behind gripped her attention.

She turned. Crawling onto the solid ice was Navid.

To Tele's great relief, they crossed the icy gulf without further mishap, but Gavini and Navid's conditions had intensified. Though the drawbridge was contracted, Navid pointed them toward an alternate entrance set within the Caldor wall. The archway leading into the city curved several spans taller than needed for a horse and rider but still appeared small compared to the walls it breached.

She helped Gavini keep his footing as they hobbled onto land and toward the smaller gate where a half-frozen dock extended over the ice below. Upon reaching its mouth, Tele left Navid and Gavini to lean against the city wall while she checked for signs of a Caldor guard or anyone who might help … or worse: deny them access.

Peering inside the dark corridor lined with blue-gray stone that seemed to prevent the very light that leaked in from reflecting back out, she saw only the dim outline of a gateway the match of the one she stood before. Though too dark to see the length of the access way, the arch's size implied its true distance. The walls were thicker than she would have thought practical. A barrier half its girth would prove virtually indestructible.

As Tele expected, there was no one to be seen at the entrance. She was glad for it. She'd spent most of her life avoiding contact with those outside of her family. A city as large as Caldor may have been more disturbing than bearable. Caldor appeared abandoned—or unstable enough to leave its walls unchecked. The eerie silence magnified what would otherwise go unnoticed: the continual drip of water letting go of sharp edges where icicles came to a point, the quiet whistling as air shifted pressure between cold and hot.

She turned back to her companions who'd both sank to sitting, still shivering.

"Well?" Navid asked through quivering teeth.

Tele looked back once more before returning to them. "Frightfully quiet."

Supporting Gavini with one arm and leading the mare with the other, she guided them back toward the open gate. Gavini slid down again within the opening while she began rummaging through a pack. She pulled free two sets of dry clothes and presented a pair to each of them. "Here, put these on. You need to get out of those clothes."

Navid took the clothes and met her regard. A flash of

golden appreciation passed through his eyes.

"I want to thank you for saving Gavini," Tele said. She paused, trying to keep her voice from sounding wooden. "Sincerely, I do. I feel as though a simple 'thank you' is insufficient."

Navid shook his head. "Think nothing of it. I didn't do much to save him."

That was anything but true. It had been dangerous for him to attempt to assist Gavini. He almost didn't come back up. She'd even accepted his death before he resurfaced. And though she hated to admit it, that acceptance hadn't come easily.

Instead of arguing the point, she simply nodded. "I'm going to see how bad it really is in there."

He too nodded, already pulling his wet garments off.

Tele turned to the light at the end of the tunnel. The darkness disoriented, casting doubt at the safety of each step forward. She thought of the magic gateway that had connected the Dominion Desert to the Borderlands. The gateway spell had been a darkness unfathomable, but this tunnel was dark enough to elicit a similar sense of isolation.

Trusting that a slow and cautious advance would reduce the odds of stumbling, she pushed forward. The far gate grew larger until its light touched her path, allowing her to move faster without the fear of stumbling. When she reached the end, she peered beyond the threshold.

There was no one to greet their passage. No soldier stood patrol nor officer to question their entry. There weren't even locals or merchants or children or animals. There was only the cool air pushing fine snow across a snow-packed courtyard. Four great pillars stretched upward from each of the yard's four corners, each iced over and planted within the cold white dust that seemed—though she couldn't see much beyond the immediate surroundings—to desecrate the Caldor's innards as thickly as its outside. At the pillar's base lay half-covered banners of reds and grays and greens and blues, their designs unclear as they lay frozen and tattered.

Where the courtyard ended, the streets began, marked by a slope in the snowbank along the edge of the field. Where there weren't streets, there were buildings. Buildings stacked on top of buildings and buildings on top of that, reaching out from behind their shorter counterparts. None looked to have the exact same make or design, but they all were taller than two landings. She had never seen buildings of this size other than the Shrine of the Creed in Desera which, until today, was the largest structure she thought could be built. Though it appeared that each building sat separate, had they passages between that would make the Shrine seem tiny by scale—as tiny as she felt right now.

Just as suggested from the outside, Caldor's insides were as frozen as the outsides. Broken windows and scattered debris, both wading in the iced water and tumbling about in drifts of wind, told the story of a storm beyond the typical. Tales would spread across the land and through time about a storm like this. As legend usually did, the tales would attempt to break free of its proper proportions, though Tele found it hard to envision how one might bring exaggeration to an unmatched catastrophe.

Navid stepped to her side, surprising her. He supported Gavini, who, like Navid, had changed into their drier clothes. She looked to his slack-jawed expression.

"I don't understand how or why …" His voice trailed off as he took in his surroundings.

"I've never seen a storm like this before," Gavini said. "And this region hardly has the conditions for a snowfall. Conditions for a blizzard are unheard of."

"I spent all my life in a desert," Tele admitted. "I had no idea that storms could be *this* bad."

"They're not," Gavini said. "Not like this."

"How far is the sanctuary from here?" Tele asked.

Navid shook his head. "I've never entered from this gate, and I'm not exactly sure how to get from here to a place I know well. But the Sanctuary is near the center of Caldor. It's almost exactly centered, and Caldor is almost exactly circular.

We're at the edge now. Provided we reach a primary road, we should find it with little effort as far as navigation is concerned."

Tele caught on that he was worried about the efforts needed in order to get to the center outside of navigation. The ice and snow that lined the streets might manifest as treacherous.

"Why is no one at the wall?" Tele asked. "Surely the guard wouldn't have abandoned the place entirely."

"It's possible that their efforts are allocated elsewhere," Gavini said, and Navid nodded his grim confirmation of the possibility.

Gilly nuzzled Tele's shoulder from behind. Surprised, she returned his affection with gentle pats. She looked at Navid and Gavini. "Both of you should ride if Gilly can handle it. Until you feel properly warmed."

"We'll both ride," Navid said before leading the mare out into the open. He offered Gavini his assistance up before he climbed up and took the reins.

Mounted high on the mare, Tele caught a glimpse of the blood that soaked through the cloth on Navid's ankle. "Navid! Your ankle! What happened?"

Navid glanced down at the injury. "Just a wound I got under the ice. Something … something attacked me."

"Do you need me to look at it?" Tele asked.

"No, no," he said, waving off her concern. "I used my old shirt to constrict the bleeding. I'll bandage it properly when we get to the Sanctuary."

Reluctantly, Tele nodded, hoping Navid didn't underestimate the wound. She didn't know what attacked him under the ice, but she wouldn't be surprised if there were krokuden in these waters, and their bone-crushing jaws could inflict an injury that was not easily disregarded.

Just beyond the clearing, they turned onto a narrow street between two rows of buildings layered in snow. Where one structure ended, another began, giving the feeling that they each shared a wall with the next. Nearly featureless, aside from simple numbering and color, the road stretched onward in a stale indistinguishable row.

"I don't understand," Tele said, stepping high to trudge through the snow. "I'd imagine you'd get lost without the colors and numbers."

"Though it happens," Navid said, "unique structures aren't always the goal for Caldor. In other areas, the buildings are more varied, but here in the outer ring, the buildings are mostly for storage. Caldor functions as the foundation for trade. Nations stock certain exports in many of these buildings, and they receive credit in exchange. A primary reason for Caldor's size is to be a bottleneck for supply and demand. It balances each kingdom so that all can grow."

Tele wasn't entirely sure how it worked and decided it best to not question further. She didn't want another lecture on trade. Her stomach for it was small, and she had had her fill. Her travels with the two after they left Azuri was full of explanations just like this one. Even as she found the world outside of the Dominion to be less mysterious, other things still troubled her.

In the nights prior to their arrival, she had spent her watch reading the book Gavini had shared with her. At first, due to its title, she thought it was about fire, water, air, and land. The elements of the world she saw around her now, save fire. After the first night's reading, she found that it was less of that and more of things she had never before encountered.

The book contained a careful examination of the material world and what it was really made of—how it could be manipulated and to what consequence. How different compounds of matter combine to create something new, how they can break apart into their component parts, and the energy taxed to achieve the desired result.

Tele had spent her shift of the night's watch reading *Element and Reaction* and talking with Gavini to reinforce the concepts presented. The book completely changed the way she thought everything around her could be classified. It was perhaps the most progressive and thought-provoking work she'd ever encountered. Even thinking of it now sent her reeling down gaps in her knowledge that she hadn't even known were there.

If Gavini intended to teach Amie and Mara what he knew, he would have had to begin preparing them for the knowledge ever since he'd met them. Her own knowledge of medicines from her mother and the works in her father's *Small Life* gave some foresight to what *Element and Reaction* meant, but she couldn't imagine learning it without some sort of foundation to build on.

Tele felt like she saw new colors. She found correlations between what she knew and what she recently found that she didn't. Where she learned new concepts, she created new connections that were unrealized by Gavini himself, then spent the night discussing them with her uncle. The world felt infinitely larger, and Tele found hope in the possibilities left untapped.

Though any failure to comprehend what she was learning aggravated Tele, Gavini had been patient with her when she couldn't grasp a particular concept. He was ever kind, helping her build new models and systems of understanding. She loved him for that patience. It left her with an emotion she hadn't felt since her parents had died.

But now, with Caldor in ruins, her hope had withdrawn. Was there anything left for her if she left Caldor with no direction?

No. The Prophets must know something, Tele thought as she gazed ahead at the lifeless city. *They have to be alive.*

Turning from the veering path of the Caldor street, Navid directed them to a main road. Larger than life, the road stretched into the distance, cutting through the city like a gaping canyon with towering walls of ornate buildings. Like route they left behind, it was thick with snow, giving under the weight of Gilly and her two riders no more than a foot.

Mixed into the hard snow lie the remains of thousands of fallen men. Death peppered into the distance. Soldier and commoner alike, they lay time-locked in a frozen river of carnage.

TWELVE

A SORROWFUL DUET

A shiver snaked down Navid's spine—a reaction to both the chill and slaughter.

"Navid, what happened here?" Tele asked. "Why didn't anyone find shelter?"

"I don't know …" He swallowed, his voice suddenly dry. He'd lived here since early childhood, and nothing like this had ever happened. It had never once snowed. "There has to be someone alive … someone in the Sanctuary Calviere."

Navid tried to fathom how fast the snow would have had to fall to catch thousands in its fury. And with so many buildings, there were plenty of places to take refuge. Aside from the seeming impossibility of such a rapid storm, anything with this much power shouldn't be so highly concentrated.

Furthermore, a storm of the like should not occur near the borderlands at all. There were blizzards in the Ghayan highlands, in the frozen waste, and even in Hzorah. Here, the climate was far too mild.

The soldiers also didn't make any sense. Steel cannot fight back the weather, no matter how unnatural. It looked as if in the midst of a great battle snow had fallen in such a rapid downpour that they were consumed within moments. Navid had feared what would happen if the Dominion army threatened the peace of the lands outside Desera. Perhaps there existed far more frightening eventualities.

Their path straight and uninhibited by the living, Navid pushed Gilly on faster. The white graveyard paving their route continued onward without interval. Gilly avoided stepping on the fallen without direction from Navid, all the while moving faster toward their end.

He pointed toward the emerald green dome in the distance. "The Sanctuary is that place there. We'll find answers there, if there are any. There are snow tracks here and there along the road. I think there are people still in the city."

"How many do you think are still here?" Tele asked.

Navid sighed. "I don't know. It's hard to tell."

All those people—forever gone. Prophet Davin had given him strict instructions on how to carry out his task. Maybe he'd done something wrong. This whole thing could be *his* fault.

Navid felt the itch of his curse surface again, but resisted it. Guilt tarried with the prick of his taint and the throbbing from his injured ankle. He'd allowed himself to slip. He'd lost control. The curse had taken him.

He had long ago mastered his control on his curse. At least he *thought* he had. Like a partition he'd reinforced over years of continual maintenance, the impulse to fall into the spell of the seer's ability had dimmed to a faint tickle at the bottom of his awareness. Even now he felt it simmer beyond his reach, as if it hadn't just broken down the barriers he'd erected over the years.

I failed, Navid thought. *In my search and in the purity of my soul.*

The buildings to either side of the broad street grew larger and more ornate while the number of the fallen thinned. Great spires cut into the sky with sharp edges while others arched lower in domes and spirals of bright colors that glowed as if they had no ice dulling their hues. Smaller buildings, wedged between each great tower, crowded into whatever space could be afforded within the shadow of their larger counterparts.

Massive in size and deceptively distant by illusion, the Sanctuary always neared slower than what felt natural. Much like the outer walls of Caldor, it inflated to encompass their field of view.

Please be alive in there, Navid prayed. *Someone. Anyone.*

Navid brought the mare to a halt a few hundred feet before the reach of the Sanctuary's silver-worked gate. Tele approached it and touched the detailed metal work. Twists and spirals intertwined into a weave of metallic vines that interlocked in a wonderfully complex pattern. She stepped slowly, letting her hand glide across the gate and drinking greedily of its creator's artistic vision.

"It's beautiful," Tele said. "I've never seen anything like it."

"Metalwork is a craft of Hzorah," Gavini said. "The design, however, is after a traditional Sulahnese pattern. This city was meant to represent all people. The result is often magnificent."

Navid looked to the ground. Pacing the pristine set of snow, footsteps trailed in and out of the Sanctuary's open threshold. The prints were varied in size and texture. Someone had been here recently, or perhaps was still here. There were survivors.

"Do you think they're still here?" Tele asked as she stepped up to him. She squatted beside the tracks Navid studied.

"It's a safe bet," Navid said, nodding to himself. He winced but withheld showing how much his ankle really hurt when he dismounted. "I don't think the Sanctuary would be abandoned entirely."

"Well, no better time to find some answers, no?" Gavini said as Tele helped him off of Gilly's back.

Stepping in a high march to cut through the snow, they led the mare to the gate and secured her reins. Though the gates cut off less than a third of what could be seen beyond its metal workings, seeing the Sanctuary Calviere's courtyard without obstruction was breathtaking. The snow and ice covered the trees, statues, and shrubbery in a way that only increased the beauty of what lie underneath. All pointing to the entryway ahead, the shapes complemented rather than distracted from the destination they outlined. Cast in white, the marvel of it was renewed.

At the end of the path sat two large oak doors. Its borders were sectioned into thirteen stones in an arc—just like the Gateway spell—a detail he'd only just realized now that he'd used the magical text to retrieve Tele. Much larger and wooden in its center rather than the upright pool, the similarity to the Gateway remained disturbing even with what was dissimilar.

The writing on the arch was of similar form as well.

"What does it say?" Tele asked.

"I don't know," Navid said. "It's in a language long forgotten. A language only used by the great Wizard himself."

"'In knowledge there is power. In truth there is freedom,'" Gavini said. When he caught Navid's wide-eyed disbelief, he added: "I've studied the ancient tongues."

Carved into the aged and ringed oak canvas of the double doors were figures of man and beast dancing between scenes of peace, war, birth, and death. They spiraled in cycles that encircled a tall dark figure in the center of it all. His hands were outstretched and welcoming, his eyes sad and distant.

"Wizard Titan," Navid pointed at the carving in the middle. "That's who it's supposed to be."

Tele looked back at the carving once more before she found Navid's eyes. "He looks … sad."

"Seems fitting, now," Navid said. "Help me with the doors?"

Tele nodded and leveraged herself against the cold wood. Together, they pushed. The heavy doors resisted at first but, once moving, they continued with ease. The carving of the Wizard Titan cut cleanly down the middle as the two doors opened into the sanctuary.

Inside, candles lined an expansive hallway with red and gold carpets that were soiled from heavy, wet traffic—a sign of life. The sanctuary was being used and often. By who, though, was a matter that still needed an answer.

Navid stepped into the mouth of the building and began a slow, limping march toward the belly of the structure. The walls were lined with tapestries woven in a style akin to the entry. The ceiling arched in the same manner as did the doorway behind. The candles were only aflame along the right side of the corridor, casting their shadows long against the opposite wall. Tall doors paced the hall's stretch to either side at intervals of fifty feet or so. Navid passed them all, his attention focused on the door at the hall's end.

Double doors, not unlike the ones they'd first encountered, barred the hall from the heart of the sanctuary. Its carvings voiced a similar tone to the one behind them, but with the difference being its centerpiece. Instead of the single man—the Wizard—holding his hands outward in welcome, there was instead seven figures, each sharing the weight of what looked to be Caldor's walls.

Navid stopped before the second set of doors and looked at her. "Ready for answers?"

Tele pulled free the long daggers holstered at her belt. "I am now."

Navid nodded before turning to push the door open. Tele aided his effort. With the same brief resistance, accompanied by a short creak, the doors opened.

Within was a large open chamber with high ceilings that arched over in a circular dome. Under its shelter were hundreds of men and women. Some were soldiers, others were Caldor locals. Most lay on pallets lining the walls and snaking in toward the room's middle in manageable rows. The number of those standing were few, the number injured were many.

Tele lowered her weapons and Navid scanned the room, meeting set after set of tired eyes. Some looked to him with a glimmer of hope on their faces only to melt away under the heat of disappointment when they didn't recognize their faces. Others, children mostly, only looked in fear, their eyes taking in Tele's glower and sharpened steel as a threat to the little they had left.

A few cries rose up at the surprise entry. The desperate shrill of infants swept across the chamber in waves, bouncing off the cavernous dome in terrible chorus. The guardians who sat with the young survivors hushed them, comforting—their voices a sorrowful duet.

A soldier approached. His black and gold uniform was damp from melted snow. The man was tall, taller than Navid, and a few decades his senior. His eyes were set in dark circles and his dark blond, gray-streaked hair touched his shoulders. Multi-colored stripes cutting down the side of his right arm marked him of high rank—a Hzorah soldier.

"Is this the refuge you were assigned to?" The man's dark tone addressed Navid as he stopped before them. He paused, staring into Navid's eyes. "You're a seer!"

"I'm aware," Navid said. "I'm Seer Navid. I have returned from a journey and must speak with Prophet Davin."

"I'm General Yix of the Hzorah First League," The man said as his brow furrowed. "The prophets—" He looked at Tele, taking stock of her daggers. He then looked at Gavini and raised his eyebrows. "A lot has happened since the attack."

"Attack?" Navid's scowl deepened. "There was an attack on Caldor? By who? And the dead and snow … what happened here?"

"Please, Seer Navid. Follow me."

General Yix led Tele, Navid, and Gavini across the open floor toward another doorway set at the opposite side of their entry. Tele passed row upon row of refugees, each examining her behind sullen faces. Men tended wounds of the injured. Others rationed food, stepping between the victims and distributing measures of bread.

Many children sat alone without the comfort of loving arms, though some huddled close to women who couldn't possibly have mothered them but accepted them for orphans. The children's lost eyes were the most disheartening—the ones who were old enough to comprehend the enormity of what had transpired. Many of them laughed and played as if the world had not just been turned on its head.

She forced her gaze forward. The eyes she met sought

answers from her that she couldn't give. The questions that never had an easy answer.

"Have you seen her?" A man scrambled from his pallet toward them.

Tele slowed, turning to the sudden question. A young man, his clothes were torn and soiled—his eyes, deep black as his newly stubbled face.

"Please," he cried and reached out, grabbing hold of Tele's trousers in both hands. "Please, have you seen her? She has to be— Did you tell her I'm sorry? Did you tell her? Did you?"

Another man, aproned in the garb of a healer, took hold of his arms, pulling him away from her. The man put little into fighting back, his energy focused on Tele's eyes.

"Did you see her? Did you see Sara? Did you see her? Tell her I'm sorry. Tell her I tried … Tell her!"

Tele stood unmoving. She watched him being pulled back to his pallet. He eventually redirected his questioning to the man who guided him, repeating the plea. The man's voice faded to whispering. He sat with the assistance of his handler. Pulling his legs in close, he fell silent under shudders.

Tele flinched when a hand found her shoulder. She turned to Gavini's gaze.

"Come," Gavini said. "He will be fine."

They continued on, and Tele redirected her attention to the doorway ahead, ignoring the calamities that surrounded it. The door, single and wooden, was not as large as the grand doors marking the Sanctuary's entrance but was still several heads taller than any man she'd ever seen. General Yix took hold of its metal ring and pulled it open just wide enough for each of them to pass through before he walked through himself.

Inside was a well-lit hall the better size of any room she'd ever seen. Tall, grounded candles set in glass cornered the walls and disrupting shadows. A stretch of table, carved and jointed with darkly stained wood, sat center. Its length dominating the hall's reach. Fourteen chairs rimmed the table with seven to each side and none at its head.

Several men, well armored with dark brown leather layered over deep black fabrics and mail bore the Hzorah crest and stood idle at the room's far side. Their attention perked at the unexpected entry, then relaxed at the sight of General Yix in lead. Among them rested a body under a shroud.

General Yix sent one of the soldiers to find a proper binding for Navid's leg and tasked another to help him into a chair. The first soldier returned in short order and set to binding his wound.

"What happened?" Navid asked, wincing as the Hzorah soldier cleaned his ankle. "How did so many die in the face of an impossible storm? Why didn't the prophets see this coming?"

General Yix circled the large table, brushing his hand over its smooth surface before looking to Navid again. "They came from the sky. Perhaps a hundred or more. Large, white, winged creatures that breathed ice and snow. They were larger than anything I've ever seen take flight. Terrible beasts that hungered for destruction. They reduced my men bit by scorching bit. Armed civilians stormed the Sanctuary, killing everyone they found."

Tele looked at Navid. He didn't appear to be listening, his gaze searching Desolate as the soldier worked on his ankle. He rejoined the world after the General paused his tale.

"The other seers ..." Navid said. "Are they safe?"

"I don't know exactly what happened in the Sanctuary. Much of it I've pieced together with my men. But some of it doesn't make sense. It appears that the prophets and seers pushed for an alternate exit."

Navid's eyes lit with hope. "There's a small escape shaft near the south side of the Sanctuary. A ladder leads to the surface. It allows one person to climb at a time."

General Yix rubbed his chin. "Makes sense. We found what looked to be a frantic escape toward the end of the Sanctuary. Damaged walls, blood, corpses. They all fell... The seers with them."

Navid began shaking his head. "No ..."

"The Caldor guard and Hzorah's First League battled the beasts," General Yix said, "but with the creatures spewing ice and attacking from above, we found ourselves overwhelmed. Three-hundred bloody bowmen and not even a scratch on the beasts. Then, as suddenly as they had come, they left."

"Peculiar," Gavini said. "But not an entirely unreasonable response." He looked at Tele. "Yes?"

Tele straightened. She had spent the last few weeks absorbing Gavini's vast collection of notes. He'd been by her side, instructing her, filling in the gaps. But Gavini still relied on her to be the expert in her father's work.

She nodded. "There are avian varieties that flock and attack as one. When satisfied, they will retreat as one as well."

Gavini nodded. "Go on, General."

"When the threat passed, I sent my men—those of us left, anyway—to search and rescue with the remaining Caldor Guard. The Sanctuary Calviere is one of several places we have refugees."

Tele shook her head. "So all of the prophets—"

"Dead," General Yix said.

"And King Jeremiah?" Navid asked as he stood and tested placing weight on his ankle.

"He has fallen," General Yix said. He lifted his arm, gesturing toward the shrouded body the Hzorah soldiers now guarded. They hung their heads low at the mention of their fallen leader.

"I left His Majesty in the care of some the First League's finest men. He was to escape into the Borderlands." He pointed upward and his voice grew hoarse with pain. "We found him frozen on a Sanctuary balcony. Scorch it! If I'd known he would have done something so scorching stupid, I would have seen to his escape myself …"

"Don't blame yourself, General," Gavini said.

"I do."

"Don't."

General Yix frowned at Navid. "Who's the old man?"

"What happens now?" Navid asked, ignoring the inquiry.

"The Hzorah Crown has lost its ruler," Yix crossed his arms. "I'm returning to Hzorah with His Majesty's body now that we've finally gathered the supplies we need. His body must be returned to his homeland."

"Can't you stay and aid us?" Navid asked. "Or at least send someone back to help once you arrive in the Crown City?"

"It's not up to me to send aid," General Yix said. "If the High Lords see fit, they will. I promise to impress upon them the need of Caldor, but I can't promise that they will respond to the need."

"Then who will?" Navid asked. "Armoth is the only nation that may lend any aid. But Roanne, Sulahn, or the Crehn Isles? They are an ocean divided and would be far too slow. And Ghaya? Their Emperor has kept their kingdom nearly as removed as the Desolate-bound Dominion!"

Tele crossed her arms as reverberating silence washed through the hall, growing thick and uncomfortable. Navid rested his palms against the grand table, his head bowed. Gavini stepped close to Navid's side and gave his shoulder a gentle squeeze. She grappled with comforting words, trying to find the right ones to share with Navid. She wanted to say something that would help his grief, but couldn't. What did one say to someone whose entire life was destroyed?

What could anyone have said to her when she lost her family? Nothing.

The room's door opened, and an officer stepped inside. "General? We finished today's sweep of the Fato district. I appreciate you holding the Sanctuary in my absence."

"No bother," General Yix said. "You won't believe what just arrived."

The officer looked between Tele and Gavini, his eyebrows raised. When Navid turned to him, he cocked his head. "You're—"

"Seer Navid."

"You're the one that Prophet Davin sent to the Dominion Desert," the officer said, appraising the seer. "He asked me to watch for your return—to make sure I alerted him as soon as you arrived. He—"

"I already informed him," General Yix said.

"Right. I'm Chief Guardsman Ruggles." Ruggles inclined his head respectfully. "Quite honestly, we have no protocol for what we're dealing with. I've assumed command."

Yix pointed with his thumb. "You'll have to ask him if you want to know what's next. This is his city, and me and my men have stayed longer than we should've." He looked at the guardsman. "Mind taking over here?"

The Chief Guardsman nodded, and General Yix saluted before he and his men reverently carried the king's shrouded body out of the room.

"I can't believe it," Navid said. "I can't believe this is happening."

Neither could Tele. In her most optimistic moments, she'd hoped that they'd help her and Gavini reform the Keepers of the Covenant. But this … This wasn't the way she'd imagined this happening at all—the death, the destruction.

Her father had dreamed of a world that was different. A world where the Keepers could help people. He'd told her that this was the reason why the Keepers had to keep the Covenant alive, that one day the world would need them, and they would be there to answer the call.

Well, I'm here, Tele thought as the memory of the man who'd begged for her help chilled her thoughts. *And there is certainly a need.*

Tele turned to Gavini. "We have to try to help. There are so many people here. We can help heal them."

Gavini smiled warmly. "How much did your mother teach you about medicine?"

"Not enough to be her equal," Tele said. "But enough to be useful."

"Good," Gavini said. "If we work together, we can probably do some good."

Ruggles led them out of the room and back into the large

chamber. "If you two have experience with healing, we could sure use a hand. Frankly, I'm in over my head here."

Tele nodded. "There doesn't appear to be a healer here, and there's no sensible arrangement or approach to treatment."

"We split off the infected into their own chambers," Ruggles said. He pointed off toward an entryway. "Down that way is a long stretch of rooms full of sick civilians, some guardsmen." He pointed the opposite direction to another doorway. "We've begun stockpiling as many supplies as we can down that way. Grains, meat, water, bandages, whatever we think might be useful."

"That's a good start," Gavini said. "See if your men can track down some antiseptics, white rull leaves, spice berries ..."

"Ginger," Tele added. "Perhaps some passion bark."

Guardsman Ruggles stared blankly. "Uh ..."

"Oh, right," Tele said. "I don't think you call it passion bark here. In Hzorah, the trees are called elkan trees—so you'll want to look for elkan bark."

"We'll do our best," Ruggles said.

"We should split up," Gavini said. He looked at Chief Guardsman Ruggles. "Perhaps you can have a guardsman help me?"

"That would be Guardsman Anders. He's no healer, but he's done reasonably well here, and knows better than anyone what injuries each person has."

"I'll take him." Gavini then looked at Tele. "Why don't you and Navid see what you can do about the infected?"

Navid, as if he'd suddenly awoke, looked up. "Me?"

"Provided your name has not changed," Gavini said, winking.

Navid nodded slowly, still lost within his own home.

"Come on," Tele said. "I'll teach you what you need to know."

THIRTEEN

THE CROWN SABRE

"Mushrooms, stuffed with cheese and breaded, My Prince." The young server smiled warmly at Gabriel, a look that conveyed both respect and said 'I'm sorry for your loss' at the same time. His name was Winston, the usual server he and Seth received.

"Thank you," Gabriel said, and Seth repeated the formality as the dishes were set before them.

It was almost exactly as Gabriel had envisioned the dinner to be. The People's Hall was chosen to host the event, an appropriate selection given how large the room was and the symbolic meaning it held for Hzorah. The hall was one of the most ornate of all the Palace, typically reserved for the most formal of occasions.

Conversation between various Lords, guild masters who had no formal land holding title, and their wives and immediate families conversed at a reserved volume. Reverence to their fallen leader pulsed throughout the room, lending a vibe Gabriel found intolerable. Eyes lingered in his direction longer than usual. He'd grown up knowing and experiencing a certain level of attention among those who frequented the court. This sort of attention was worse. It was the kind of attention you gave to a beggar outside the palace gate. Gabriel half-entertained the idea of walking the room with his chalice, pleading for alms to see their reaction.

Gazes also fell across the room's head. His father's seat at the Crown table was empty now and would remain until Gabriel was crowned. There were strict stipulations and traditions set down by his forefathers that the palace staff would never cross or change. Here, just like the court, the chairs and tables were arranged in a very particular manner. The staff never failed to position them in the correct place. So particular, in fact, that Gabriel would wager against anyone that he could run in and out between the tables blindfolded.

If I'm forced to take the Crown, Gabriel thought. *I'll at least give the palace a good shake.*

In the far corner, most distant from where he and Seth sat, were several distinguished military men. The table next to them seated a few Admirals, representing the Crown's small navy. They were the quietest of the tables, passing only a few words between solitary grazing of appetizers.

Seth craned to see the soldiers over the sea of heads that divided them. "Do you know any of them, Gabe? Samuel has told me of some of their accomplishments, but I don't know their faces. Do you ever see them in court?"

"No," Gabriel said. His father had never allowed him to spend time with the officers. It had vexed him to no end that he was forced to sit through hours of court proceedings while the real men did all the work out on the field.

The focus of the room felt odd to Gabriel. Who was in charge? The council would lead the proceedings of the court themselves, but what about formal events? They were always led by his father.

Gabriel thought to what Marium had said about Hzorah needing to see a strong leader. Was he supposed to take the lead? Gabriel wondered if the eyes on him were of this nature instead.

He turned his attention back to Seth. "Do you think they're expecting me to say something?"

"I don't know. What did Marium tell you to do?"

"Nothing." Gabriel pulled his chalice close and watched the swirling red liquid. "Nothing except to be here."

"Then I guess, no?" Seth's reply was dry of confidence. "It is strange … to eat without anyone saying anything to make it formal."

Gabriel scanned the room for a hint of who would be taking the reins.

The hall's doors parted and High Lord Bendeth of West Hzorah, his uncle, glided inside under a long black cloak. Trailing behind were his wife and three children. His wife, Lesia, rarely made an appearance in the palace and looked out of place where her husband was far too comfortable. He clasped hands with officials as he passed them and signaled greetings to those beyond his waking path.

After settling her children as best she could, Lady Bendeth sat and shook nervously as she awaited her husband. Gabriel thought she always looked ready to crack to pieces if anything fell out of sorts. Tomas and Doran waved fervently in Gabriel and Seth's direction. Seth returned their waves while Gabriel merely smiled and nodded to them. Both had not seen more than thirteen years, the youngest only seeing seven. The eldest of the set, Cainan, returned Gabriel's nod—a fair show of respect when usually he afforded none.

The brothers shared each other's sandy blond hair and color-filled cheeks against pale white skin. They also shared a general appreciation for mischief. Cainan had long crossed the line of appreciation and was really just an ass. While their mother rarely ventured out of the Bendeth manor, her three children visited the palace frequently when their father made the journey. Gabriel prayed their stay would be brief. He was not in the mood to entertain their games.

The doors opened again, and Samuel slipped into the hall. He made for a vacant chair across from Gabriel. After graciously accepting a cup of wine from Winston, he sat quietly, looking between the two princes.

"I'm not certain I can express how sorry I am for your loss," Samuel said. His expression displayed a true sense of remorse. He looked between the both of them before accepting a waiting plate from Winston, who waited patiently over his right shoulder.

"What happens now … now that …" Seth frowned. "Now that Father is—"

"We don't have to talk about that now, Seth," Gabriel said. He didn't like seeing his brother hurt this way. It was better not to get him worked up in public.

"Seth," Samuel said. He watched until Seth looked up from his plate. "You don't have to worry about a thing. There is nothing we can do to bring your father back, but the Crown will hold strong."

Seth didn't say anything. He instead turned back to his plate, dispassionately entertaining the flavors with a silver fork.

"I just want both of you to know that everything will be fine," Samuel concluded.

Gabriel grunted. "I don't think we should get ahead of ourselves."

Samuel granted him a hard look. "Speaking of getting ahead of ourselves: you stormed out rather inappropriately today in court. Now, I do understand your pain, but your reputation as a ruler begins today. It began the moment your father died. You must know that the Hzorah Lords will give you a run if you give them reason to believe you are unfit. The people of the Crown are loyal, but do not give them reason to believe you are dishonorable. You will be crushed under the shift of power."

"I don't want the Crown," Gabriel said. He leaned in, making eye contact to show Samuel just how much he meant it. "I've been subject to the droll incompetence of the court for half the year now, and I've never seen a poorer lot. And the Lords …" Gabriel waved a fork around, gesturing abstractly to those around him. "If you ask me, they would have killed Father long ago if it weren't for them being cowards themselves, trembling atop their riches." From the corner of his eye, he saw Seth begin to fidget with his fork nervously. "I have half the year yet until I'm old enough to take the Crown. How long until I end up with a knife in my back?"

Samuel looked at Seth a moment before redirecting his glower. "Gabriel, that is quite enough."

"How is it that I'm the only one who sees the Desolate-bound Lords for what they are?" Gabriel continued. He'd reached his limit of unneeded absurdity.

Samuel looked nervously around the room, as if hoping Gabriel's speech hadn't fallen from the eaves and into unintended ears. He glared back at Gabriel after assessing that his rant had gone unheard. "Have you had your fill?"

Gabriel sat back and pulled his chalice close to take a drink of apathy. He felt a tinge of satisfaction that he'd gotten his say. He knew that it wouldn't sway Samuel, but it felt good, nonetheless.

"Yes."

"After your grand exit," Samuel said with a darker disposition, "another messenger followed in his wake. He was a Dominion carrier sent to request an audience with the king and his court for talks of diplomacy."

"What?" Gabriel asked, incredulously. "Why would they send a bloody diplomat? They must know we're not so daft as to really believe they want to make friends with us."

"Manners, Gabriel," Samuel said, correcting his language.

"Proper manners would be to leave us be …" Seth muttered over his fork.

"Proper manners would be to shove off," Gabriel concluded.

"Manners!" Samuel rebuked. "The diplomat will be arriving by high noon in a week's time."

Gabriel scoffed. "Their mounts must have wings."

Samuel opened his mouth to respond but closed it again as a hush fell over the room. High Lord Bendeth stood regally, his gaze passing over the hall as he waited for the last few conversations to fade. He gripped his chalice in a heavily-ringed right hand and gently stroked its rim with his equally-ringed left.

When all eyes were upon him, he smiled sorrowfully and

sighed. "Today is a day of tragic loss. A tragic loss for me and my family. A tragic loss for two young boys who now mourn deeply. And, indeed, a tragic loss for all of Hzorah and the people of the Crown." Bendeth paused as he appraised the reaction of those gathered. A few quietly voiced their agreement, but the majority merely nodded.

"Near fifteen years past," he began again, "I saw the death of my beloved sister, Esther of house Bendeth. She was strong, courageous, and gave the Crown two boys." He let an arm guide the attention of the room toward the table where the two princes sat. "I've watched these two scamper the palace, fall and scrape their knees and cry out for a mother who was no longer there. Now, when they need their father most—during the prime of their adolescence—they must go without."

Gabriel shifted, hoping to quell his agitation. The audience watched with that look he hated. For a moment, he considered standing and shouting at them. Instead, he averted his eyes, but the feeling didn't diminish.

Lord Bendeth turned around to address those behind him. "Just like Prince Gabriel and Prince Seth, Hzorah is without Father and Mother. We mourn the loss of a fearless bloodline that united the tribes of the delta and the lands beyond and uprooted the tyranny of the Dominion. We lie awake in our beds, fearing for our children as that very same foe sits at our door like the midnight wolf, pacing and yearning to devour whoever might open the door.

"I look to the faces of my young boys—the very future of our land—and question if there will be a Hzorah for them to call home. Too many have died to have it taken from us in the hour of our weakness." After passing the chalice to his left hand, he raised a fist. "The Crown must rise up and let evil know that we are a nation of strength. That we are a nation undivided. And we will not be moved!"

The tables roared with applause as High Lord Bendeth stood, fist in air and a look of righteous indignation to support it. Gabriel and his brother remained seated. Samuel looked downward and rubbed his forehead, muttering something that

Gabriel couldn't hear over the cheer. When he finally looked up, his face was grave.

As the hall settled, Bendeth changed his expression to a smile. "We have some of the finest leaders Hzorah has ever had. Caring and ambitious leaders. The Bendeth guilds are providing housing, furniture, and supplies." He cast hand to the Eddings' table where Lady Eddings sat with a well-pronounced frown. "And High Lord Eddings has offered to redouble his efforts and provide our soldiers with the finest of Hzorah smithed steel. This, of course, comes at a cost to the Eddings guild, but they do this knowing that their part will bring Hzorah victory and give our sons and daughters the greatest chance of driving back the enemy."

Lady Eddings somehow managed to darken her expression. Lord Eddings was no less amused. Gabriel looked at Samuel, who appeared just as displeased. While Lord Bendeth continued his speech, Gabriel took the opportunity to gauge the room. Like the Eddings table, the Roth and Laonne tables carried the same burden of disapproval. The other tables, however, were rapt in the High Lord's speech.

Something was happening. Gabriel knew that much. But *what* exactly pulled such unrest among the High Lords?

" ... and as we look out to the North, with stakes driven into the ground and even our wounded persevering on bended knee, our children's children will tell of how Hzorah drove our adversaries back into the waste from whence they came." Lord Bendeth held his chalice high and his wife, rather gracelessly, leaped for her own. Lady Bendeth raised hers high above her head with an unsure hand, allowing small waves of light red liquid slip over the edge and down her trembling arm. "From out of darkness and into light, to the Hzorah Crown!"

"The Crown!" the entire hall echoed as each member raised their own cups.

The other High Lords remained reserved, refusing to join him.

Lord Bendeth found his seat again and the hall found new

life, the collective voice sounding more hopeful than before. Gabriel slid down into his chair.

"I guess Uncle Bendy took care of that one for me," Gabriel said. He looked at his brother, but Seth didn't reply. Seth pulled at a small red thread in the hem of his dinner coat, wrapping it around an index finger and unraveling it again.

"High Lord Bendeth is—" Samuel began, but cut his words short as Lord and Lady Bendeth, and their children with them, approached the princes' table. Several other tables followed their lead. Samuel leaned in close. "You boys must continue on firm standing and represent yourself well. The Crown's High and Low Lords will want to pass their consolations formally. Look sharp!"

Samuel stood and bowed to Bendeth as he stopped before the table. Gabriel looked at Bendeth a moment before a jerk of the head from Samuel prompted him to stand as well. Gabriel dropped his fork and stood.

"My boy," Bendeth said. He ignored the hand Gabriel held out for him and pulled him into a full hug. Samuel raised an eyebrow as Gabriel recovered from the surprise. Bendeth spoke softly in his ear, "I am beyond words for your loss. But know that I will *always* be here for you during your darkest hour." Lord Bendeth pulled back from the embrace and held him at arm's length. "Promise me that you'll come to me if you need anything?" When Gabriel didn't answer immediately, he repeated his beckoning. "You hear? Anything at all!"

Gabriel wanted to say, 'What would I *need* from you?' but a glance to Samuel admonished any thoughts of an honest response. "Of course."

"That's my boy!" Bendeth beamed and moved to Seth, repeating the gesture. Samuel nodded his approval to Gabriel's words.

"It's good to see you well, Gabriel," Lady Bendeth said. She held a hand over her mouth and one over her heart—both fighting tremors. Her eyes looked past him, though, as if she had trouble placing where he stood before her. She stepped past him following Lord Bendeth as if chained by the hip.

Gabriel watched her go. He swore she looked deranged several degrees further every time he saw her.

Gabriel yelped at a sharp pain in his shoulder. He turned to Cainan and two giggling, blond-haired menaces.

Cainan shook a limp fist. "Bulkin' up for winter, m'lord?" he said, taking a mocking, ratty tone. Tomas and Doran nearly doubled over in fits of laughter.

Gabriel frowned and rubbed a sure-to-bruise shoulder. "Shove off, Cainan before I—" A short and insistent throat clear from his instructor caught him mid-sentence. Cainan beamed at the reaction he'd churned. "Look, get out of here."

"My Lord," Cainan bowed and followed after his mother.

"My Lord," Tomas mimicked the gesture.

Doran pulled on his ears and stuck out his tongue.

Gabriel looked at Samuel again who cleared a half-smile from his face. Gabriel's mouth tightened as he repressed his want to retaliate. Samuel tilted his head slightly toward the next approaching High Lord.

The condolences continued similarly, though High Lords Laonne, Eddings, and Roth's families restrained themselves from striking the prince, and other Low Lords and Ladies gave their good wishes before the procession ended. Gabriel's responses to each slowly glossed from thoughtful to routine. Each Lord had little to add that the last hadn't and, consequently, neither did Gabriel. Seth at least seemed to glean some sort of comfort from the words. Gabriel forced himself to halfheartedly feign good cheer just for that alone.

"They really did love Father," Seth said as they were finally able to take their seats once more. Winston cleared the half-eaten dishes while another server slid rice in sugar and cream to replace them.

Before Gabriel could respond, Samuel said, "Why, of course they did. Your father was the single greatest king Hzorah has ever seen." He left out the fact that Hzorah had only seen three kings, but Gabriel decided it best to preserve his brother's positive outlook.

"You know," came a voice. "King Jeremiah would often

frequent my quarters when I was in the Crown's Palace or when he passed through my district."

Gabriel turned to hear High Lord Bendeth confiding in a small group of Low Lords and Guild Masters.

"He cared deeply for his people and he always made certain I knew it." Bendeth bowed his head solemnly. "He said that ever since dear Esther passed into Desolate, he found little comfort. That the days were cold and the nights were colder without her wisdom to light his way. Still, he persevered.

"I know it's not proper to talk of your king in such a way, but he would want his people to know much he cared. He made me promise that I would not allow our great land fall prey to those who hate. I told him I would never let that happen, of course. House Bendeth is forever honored to have provided heirs to the throne, but for him to continue to find goodness with House Bendeth—even after the passing of my dear sister? Well, that, my friends, is the greatest honor."

"Gabe?"

"What?" Gabriel's attention snapped back to his table and Seth's questioning gaze. "What?"

"The Solstice Festival. You said you'd nearly perfected your shot."

"Right, yes," Gabriel said. "Samuel, have I done my duty here? The day's events have left me spent."

Samuel sighed but nodded. "You are not needed any longer. I'm sure everyone will understand your need to retire."

Gabriel stood to leave.

"But," Samuel continued, catching him with a stern eye. "It is imperative that you attend court tomorrow. Please do not make me have to exhaust the staff searching for you. Your rep—"

"My reputation as king has already begun. I know, please spare me." Gabriel raised his hand. "By my word, I'll be there."

Gabriel snapped the collar of his dinner coat shut against the chill of the exterior passage. Spring had indeed come, but winter still breathed upon the night. The rain fell in a chorus of light pelts, driving a song of various pitches between wood, metal, and rock. The tones reverberated harmonically in an even rainfall—a phenomena intentionally designed to pleasantly caress the ear. In a rain like tonight's, it sang discord.

He turned left, toward the bridge that crossed over a canal and separated this part of the palace from the primary keep. The canal flowed east from the river Drunn and split across the delta on which the Hzorah Crown city sat. His hands dug deep into his shallow coat pockets and he walked briskly to keep his blood flowing warm.

His exit from his father's memorial dinner was hardly noticed among the hall's talk. He'd caught the eye of one table who signaled for his approach, but he slipped by, pretending he'd not seen their invitation.

Before he rounded the corner, he heard the voice of one the palace servers. " … and then, right out of the dark, the soldier says the king is dead. At least that's what Finnian said when—" The server cut his story short as Gabriel turned and crossed onto the bridge.

They both turned to face him, undoubtedly fearful that they'd been caught gossiping in the shadows during work hours. He didn't stop to reprimand them. He didn't care what they did. Gabriel avoided giving orders to anyone who served at the palace. It wasn't his place. There were others who governed the palace staff and, frankly, he didn't much care what the workers did. Their eyes shifted from fearful to apologetic to sympathetic all within the span of his passing. Gabriel picked up his pace.

The edging sunset across the western horizon cast long shadows over the Hzorah Crown. The city extended across the delta, spliced by canals both natural and constructed. By convenience of the Crown's locale, the city played to the land, using the water as primary passages throughout.

A strong back and high endurance went far within the

Crown. Taxis powering long canoes profited considerably during the warmer months and well into winter. Only the coldest of days froze the streams. Salters were always in high demand. Sifting for salt was as large a business as fish, if not larger. When the canals didn't need it, meat did. High Lord Roth acquired most of his wealth through salt sifting.

Gabriel grimaced at the thought of the High Lords. Roth had softened as much as his father had. And between Lord Eddings' ever-present concern with his finances and his wife's covetous gawking, the entire experience had whittled his patience down to wisps. Gabriel was far from physically exhausted. He'd left because he had exhausted his tolerance.

High Lord Bendeth's speech still rung in his ears. He'd said all the right things. In fact, Gabriel couldn't have done a better job. It was exactly the kind of speech that *should* be given at a time like this. But for some reason, the speech fell silent on the ears of the other High Lords. Something had happened tonight … he just couldn't place what.

What he *could* place was the speech he overheard afterward: lies.

Gabriel couldn't imagine his father confiding in Lord Bendeth. He was his father's brother-in-law, but King Jeremiah rarely had anything good to say about Bendeth in private. His father wouldn't *confide* in him. Those who listened to Bendeth's reflections wouldn't have known, and they gulped down his tales like fine ale.

He couldn't deal with it—with the looks, the whispers, the lies, the ignorance. It all ground at his well-being. This was how it was going to be. This was kingship. He spat.

The halls were silent within in the primary keep. A member of the palace staff zig-zagged far ahead with a thin torch, opening the small shafts in the hall's columns and lighting the candles inside them. The design was said to be sleek, ingenious, and the first of its kind. Common rooms of new buildings and houses now used a similar construct to light their rooms. Gabriel walked briskly to keep the hall's memories out of step, letting each light pass by like street wicks.

He took the same grand stairway up to his family's private wing. He stopped before the entry of his father's study. The door sat open with the soft glow of fresh lit candles that sweated the scent of Hzorah pine. Gabriel thought for the briefest instant that he saw his father sitting behind the large wooden desk, hunched over a small stack of parchment. The illusion was cast by shadows, and once he realized its true form—the combination of a high-backed chair and a thick coat of bear hide—he wished it would reform so that he could have that small spark of hope once more.

He crossed inside. The hearth against the western wall warmed the room, though there was no king to enjoy the luxury. It was a waste. The Crown's staff stuck to such strict routine that even this continued senselessly. The room was lined with stained birch. The shelves behind the desk held many objects: books, stacks of parchment, trinkets collected and passed from father to son. Most beautiful of all was the Crown's Sabre.

Gabriel rounded the desk and stood before the sword in its ruby red and silver-plated sheath. He let his eyes brush over the slightly curved form and slip between the ridges of design and embossed runes that wrapped the blade from tip to cross guard. The metal-wound hilt was stained midnight black and extended to allow both single-handed and double-handed techniques.

The Crown Sabre had belonged to his grandfather first; forged by the most talented smiths of the era, shaped, balanced, and hardened with fourth-degree Hzorah steel—the highest grade of steel in all the world. This was a weapon far beyond the common. It was a sword that had inspired legends, capable of defeating even a seer.

He reached out, first letting his hand wrap around the hilt and then his other lifted the blade from its stand. He stared at it, tightening his grip and preparing to let the blade breathe once more. Then he paused, remembering that last time he'd attempted to pull free the blade seven years past.

"*Gabriel!*"

Gabriel nearly dropped the sword as he spun to face his father. King Jeremiah stood with a frown creasing his face and the hearth casting him in a long shimmering shadow. Gabriel stood frozen with his muscles tight and ready to pull the sword free of its scabbard. In five quick strides, his father crossed to stand directly in front of him. His giant form breathed heavily under the thin shirt he often wore to his chambers at night. He placed a proportionately large hand between Gabriel's, grabbing the sabre in the middle.

Gabriel looked up into his father's disapproving eyes. "Father … I …" He tried to summon words, but they wouldn't form. "I …"

"I have told you not to touch this sword. Have I not?"

Gabriel cringed at the rhetorical question. His father knew the answer. Why ask it? "Yes."

"And why have I found you sneaking about, touching things you know well not to touch?"

Gabriel's mouth hung open. He struggled to find an answer that his father would find acceptable, but there simply wasn't one. He hated feeling trapped like this, knowing that if he lied, it would most definitely be nonsense. If he answered honestly, his father would be displeased. And every time Gabriel looked like an imbecile—just as he looked now—with his mouth drying.

But he had asked him. He'd responded this way countless times before. It never smoothed things. And the way his father looked at him, saying 'I don't know' may not be good enough. He decided that he would take a chance with his real reasoning.

"Because I want to learn to fight."

King Jeremiah raised an eyebrow at the response then lifted the sabre from Gabriel's hands. "You are never to touch this sword, Gabriel. Never."

He placed the Crown Sabre back on the stand.

Gabriel hung his head, ashamed at his actions as his father crossed the room. He heard a wall panel slide open, and he lifted his head. His father turned back around, his hands clutching another sword. It was near the same as the Crown Sabre, save for length.

King Jeremiah crossed back and stood before him. "You will meet me at the south garden tomorrow morning before the sun rises. And you will bring this with you. Is that understood?"

Gabriel stared at the sword, how delicately wound the hilt was and the intricate embossing that snaked around its sheath. It was a beautiful sabre. He couldn't be serious.

"Father … What … I …"

The king gestured with the sword for Gabriel to take it. He reached out with caution, still half expecting his father to pull it back at the last moment and have a laugh at his belief in an obvious joke. When he took hold of it, his father let go then turned and headed for the study's exit. He stopped just before the entry and turned back.

"You best get some sleep, Son. Tomorrow will be a long day."

"Gabriel?"

Gabriel spun to Samuel's intrusion on his musing. He turned back and placed the sword on the stand before facing his tutor. Samuel glided into the room, ignoring the fact that Gabriel had been snooping in his father's study. He pulled a long iron spike from under the hearth and shuffled the logs, redoubling the flame.

"No need to be so jumpy, Gabriel," he said as he replaced the iron and turned to face him again. "All of this is yours now. Yesterday I might have reprimanded you, but today … Well, today everything has changed." Samuel appraised him for a moment before leaning back against the study's wall. "This must be all very confusing for you."

Gabriel ignored the lead. "Did the High Lords mourn my early departure? Did Bendeth comfort them with fake stories of how Father cried on his shoulder?"

"Bendeth delivered quite the performance," Samuel said, "but I fear there is more than goodwill fueling his intentions. Bendeth has played his card for the Crown. His tongue speaks easy but is slick with acid. He does this knowing you are far too inexperienced to see a play even when it is done right before your eyes."

Gabriel frowned as the image of the unsettled Lords passed over his mind's eye once more. Then he smirked. "Bendeth can't hold a sword to me. I don't think he's lifted one since youth. He's weak. I don't think I have to worry about him."

"There are battles that are won without ever lifting a sword," Samuel said.

"How about I grab a sword and you make a speech, and then we'll decide who wins?" Gabriel scoffed.

Samuel frowned at him. "You miss my point."

"I caught your point. Be careful of Bendeth."

"This is a dangerous game you find yourself in, Gabriel." He let his feet take his weight from the wall. "You must not let your words flow without careful assessment. All that you do and say will be scrutinized. This will not be the same life you lived the day before."

"I hardly consider molasses-paced litigation and tea parties dangerous, Samuel," Gabriel smirked. "Drawing a bath requires more tact. What will they do? Talk me to death?"

"You, yourself, said that you foresee a knife in your back."

"Not from Bendeth. Lady Eddings, however ..." Gabriel chuckled. "I'd bet she'd live here as a runner if someone asked her."

"Well," Samuel began, unamused. "No matter who, you must practice caution. We will wait for your father's advisor to arrive from Caldor before we make any moves. It is imperative that we not make any rash decisions."

As Samuel waited for his agreement, Gabriel wondered what he meant by *we*. Samuel wasn't the one who had to make any of these decisions. "Prophet Davin? I was thinking he might be the first to go once I'm king."

"He is a trusted advisor," Samuel said. "You would benefit from his skill."

"I don't need to tell you how the people of the Crown feel about magic, Samuel. And I don't trust it either."

"Prophets don't cast spells."

"May as well," Gabriel snapped. "And with Prophet Tristan threatening us? How do you think it looks that I have my own Prophet whispering in my ear?"

"Prophet Davin is a good man. He has done a lot for the Crown."

"And how did his skill prevent Father from dying?"

"You presume to accuse him for your father's death?"

"I presume that he didn't prevent it."

Samuel sighed and rubbed his forehead. "Please Gabriel, don't be foolish. Do not allow your new authority to lead you to haughtiness. We can help you."

Haughtiness? Gabriel frowned. He didn't remember asking to become king, and he couldn't recall anyone asking *him* who he'd like his advisors to be. He felt rage tasting the air, but decided to sidestep its hunger. "Goodnight, Samuel." He stepped past him and headed for the entryway.

"Please be on time tomorrow, Gabriel!" his tutor called from behind.

Gabriel waved his assurances.

FOURTEEN

THE HEART OF THE EDIFICE

Navid knelt over the large basin, filling another glass jar with water. Tapped from Caldor's aqueduct, a large, metal faucet streamed water into the oversized tub. He watched the water cascade as his mind streamed from fear to panic.

The prophets—dead.

His fellow seers—dead.

His mother—dead.

He stepped back and began screwing on the jar's cap. Slick from water, the jar slipped from his grasp and shattered on the stone floor.

"Scorch it!"

He stood there, staring at a hundred shards of glass. That was his life. Broken. Utterly broken. Everything and everyone he'd known was gone. *Everything.*

He pulled another jar from the shelf behind him, filled and sealed it, and placed it in a pack. He also grabbed a scrubbing stone and several towels. Navid wasn't entirely sure he'd gotten everything they needed from the store rooms. Tele had simply asked him to find supplies to care for the injured, but he had never actually cared for someone who was sick. At least not beyond fetching things for them when they'd asked. He was practically useless.

There had always been a healer on staff at the Sanctuary. And now even he was gone.

Navid shouldered the pack and swept up the glass so that someone wouldn't happen on it barefoot. Who might come in here barefoot, he didn't know, but that was what one did. The cleaners—

The cleaners were gone, too. *Everyone*.

What perplexed him was General Yix's comment about *how* everyone had died. Armed civilians stormed the Sanctuary? Who in their right mind would do that when the city is under attack?

He shook his head. Perhaps no one had their wits about them. Everyone must have panicked. It wasn't unheard of that people would riot or act irrationally during a catastrophe.

But to murder all those people …

The hour passed as Navid drifted in a fog of disillusion. He followed Tele's instruction without question. Lift her up … Set her down gently … Hold this … Hand me the gauze … She needs water, quickly …

They moved from room to room, attending to sickest refugees first. Tele led the charge. She treated each citizen with professional aptitude. Were Navid not so absorbed in his cocoon of misery, he would have found her fluid efficiency beautiful.

Presently, they stood before a room with a modest bed and a small window. Two candles were burned near to their end, but they kept the room illuminated as the evening wore on. The room was thick with the stench of vomit, and the sick patient lay in the bed, wrapped in a brown blanket.

Unlike the other rooms, this one had something different: another person—a small child. She hopped up from the floor as he and Tele entered and curtsied.

"Hello," she said. "Are you the healers?"

Tele smiled. "Yes. Is this your mother?"

The child nodded. "She's sick. She was getting better, but now she's worse."

Navid crossed to the basin, opened his jug, and filled it with water. He then crossed to the window and opened it. He breathed in the fresh air as it rushed in to replace the stench of stale breath. When he turned back to Tele, she was kneeling beside the girl, inspecting her eyes.

"What's your name?" She asked her.

"Emelisse."

"Have you been sleeping, Emelisse?"

Emelisse shook her head. "Not really."

Navid approached the bedside. Frail from malnourishment, the woman's sunken face was likely the picture of youth a few weeks prior. When Tele circled the bed and felt her forehead, she stirred, and her eyes fluttered.

"She's too hot," Tele said, then felt her neck. "Swollen."

"Will she be alright?" Navid asked.

"Most likely," Tele said. "She has a viral infection."

"Viral?" Navid frowned.

"A type of plague," Tele said. "Like a tiny bug. Well, not a bug, but small, nearly invisible. A kind of proto-life."

Navid didn't have a proper response. They'd visited several rooms already, and Tele always had some strange, outlandish description of sickness that he'd never heard before. "So, what do we do?"

"She needs to stay hydrated," Tele said as she opened the woman's mouth. "Her mouth and skin are dry." She inclined her head to the small table beside the bed that held a bowl of fluid. "She hasn't been holding much of her fluids."

The woman coughed. Navid and Tele stepped back. By pure reflex, Navid covered his mouth and nose.

"A virus can spread through the Sanctuary like a wildfire," Tele said. "We need to be extra careful when we leave this room to disinfect ourselves."

Navid's throat felt like it was closing. He imagined Tele's "bugs" crawling down his throat. "Shouldn't we get out of here? Can't we get sick, too?"

Tele looked at him. "Someone has to take that risk. Wet a cloth. We need to clean her."

They spent the next few minutes washing the woman, replacing her bedding, and disposing of the soiled blankets. Afterward, Tele used a few pillows to help the woman sit upright and gave her a small cup of water.

Tele turned to Navid. "Hopefully, the guardsmen find all the supplies we need. That'll certainly help if there are a lot more people like this."

"Finding the supplies won't be as difficult as actually accessing them," Navid said. "The snow and ice out there are more than they're equipped to handle. There's never been a need to prepare for this kind of disaster."

"We have medicine at our house," Emelisse said, yawning. "It was working, and she was almost better until we had to leave when the guardsmen came."

Navid and Tele turned to the child who sat patiently on the floor. Tele approached and sat beside her.

"Your house is clear of the snow?" Tele asked.

Emelisse nodded. "We lived in Raslowe. Number twenty-eight."

Tele looked at Navid. "Do you know where that is?"

He nodded and crossed his arms. "The Raslowe district is in the south-west region of the city. It's about a two-hour walk from here. I'm not sure how long it'll take now, and the guardsmen have already left again to do another sweep of the city."

Tele stood. "Then maybe we can go."

"I'm not sure," Navid said. "It would be dangerous. There's a lot of ice out there. Some of it can fall on us. We could get stuck."

"But I don't know if we'll get the supplies we asked for with this run," Tele said. She stepped closer to him. "If we get this medicine, we might be able to stop the sickness before it becomes a bigger problem." She lowered her voice as she gripped his arm. "And the girl … she might already …"

Navid glanced behind her to Emelisse. Her skin was rather pale, and children her age were often bursting with energy. This one barely fidgeted.

She was right. If more of the Sanctuary's displaced citizens were to become sick, they'd have a much bigger problem on their hands. Controlling a plague in the city was difficult enough. Even the prophets had a hard time staying a step ahead. But now they had no prophets, and Caldor was more vulnerable than ever.

Someone has to take that risk.

"Alright," Navid said. "We'll go."

Navid took Tele's hand as she helped him hopped over another patch of slush that obstructed the streets of the Raslowe district. He winced as he caught his fall on his injured ankle. He wasn't sure why, but for some reason, the city's ice melted in uneven chunks. Tele explained that it had to do with cloud cover, the sun's respective angle, and the density of the buildings, but Navid barely grasped the concept.

Instead of uncomfortable silence, Navid took the opportunity to question Tele about her knowledge of healing. While some of what she said was just as perplexing, he had a much better time following her when she talked of sutures and medicines.

Navid stopped before the large light gray building and turned back to look at Tele. She studied the building as if attempting to deconstruct it. The building rose into the sky like the majority of the buildings in Caldor. The smooth stone-like material that wrapped it uniformly was only broken by strips of glass that allowed the people who resided in the housing sunlight.

"People live in these?" she asked.

Navid shrugged. "Yes. Is that surprising?"

"With a city this large, you'd expect that there'd be enough room for everyone to have their own place to live instead of living stacked on top of each other."

"It's probably not what you're used to," Navid said, gazing upward at the building. "But it's actually practical for a city of this size. It allows for resource efficiency. Spread out, people have a tendency to waste more either carelessly or inadvertently. It facilitates transportation. If this city was more like Azuri, it would have taken the better part of the day to reach this region. Consequently, the city would need to be several times larger if it were to accommodate a population of its size."

"Its former size," Tele corrected.

She stepped up to the structure and placed a hand on its smooth walls. She let her hand glide along the building as she stepped carefully across the tightly packed snow. Tele turned back and caught his eye.

"Let's have a look?" she asked.

Navid wanted to tell her that her comment was insensitive and irreverent. He'd lost everything in the catastrophe. Thousands of people had shared his loss. But when she looked at him, he forgot all of that. He was starting to come to a certain understanding of her. Like Mara, she was a bit more matter-of-fact. It wasn't that she didn't care. She just didn't communicate her concern in a way that he was used to.

He'd spent most of his youth in Caldor where his councilors—the prophets—had relied on him to share his feelings and thoughts so that they could help him tame his curse. After years of meditation and communication, he'd learned to be better than his ability's predisposition. Talking to Tele was the antithesis of that, and he was beginning to appreciate it.

Navid led the way to the building's entryway. The primary doorway was without barrier, but the snow and ice had fallen thick enough that it was nearly a waist-high drop down into the common house. After Navid dropped in—this time taking care to lead with his good leg—he turned and offered Tele a hand down. She took it but didn't lean on him as she jumped in.

It was quiet inside. Usually, one could hear the soft crying of a child or perhaps the hardy laughter of several people enjoying each other's company. Or, at least, the soft hum of the city beyond. No more. And though Navid had often felt isolated and confined in the Sanctuary, wanting nothing more than to be allowed the simple freedom to walk Caldor's streets unrestricted, having to walk amongst the horrors of the dead made him wish he could lock himself away.

Navid started toward the stairwell. "Twenty-eight should be on the second floor."

They climbed the stairs and, eight doors down, they came to number twenty-eight—a nondescript door of pale gray. Navid tried the door's handle, but it was locked.

"Excellent," he said, backing up to study the situation. "It's locked."

Tele kicked the door. It rattled on its hinges but remained shut. Another two kicks and the door swung inward.

"Wow," Navid said. He pointed to the left to the home's front window. "I was going to suggest a window."

Tele shrugged. "In my experience, you usually want to avoid shattering glass. You're more likely to hurt yourself."

"In your experience?"

Tele stepped inside. "This isn't the first time I've broken in someplace. Prophet Tristan wasn't fond of feeding his outlaws well."

Navid followed her inside. A table with two chairs was pushed against the wall of the room. A small wash bucket sat under a silver facet and a few porcelain plates and vessels were stacked beside a tall, black cupboard.

"Do you know where people in Caldor like to keep their medicines?" Tele asked as she walked to the far side of the room toward the back rooms.

"Maybe in the back with their beds," Navid said.

Tele disappeared through the doorway, and something caught Navid's eye from across the room. He moved to the table and lifted a parchment. Once folded and sealed, the Hzorah Crest stamped the note as an official document.

"Found it," Tele said as she came back into the room. "What's that?"

Navid looked up to see Tele carrying a small drum under an arm. He flashed the parchment so that she could see the crest. "Looks like King Jeremiah paid for the medicine while he was here."

"That makes sense," Tele said. "Because this is enough medicine to cure a small village. That healer took advantage of the king's account. It's lucky he did. This is more than I'd hoped for."

Tele set the drum of medicine on the table and unstopped the cork. She took a whiff of the contents, and her face contorted.

"That will do it," she said as she jammed the cork back into place. "Smells aged. Probably took advantage of this moment to offload some overstock. It won't be the best brew, but it'll keep us ahead of the virus while we wait for fresh supplies."

"Good," Navid said. "So, it was worth it?"

"Well worth it," Tele said.

Navid smiled and let his pack fall from his shoulders. He pulled out a waterskin and took a short drink before handing it to Tele. "I need to rest my foot a moment before we head back out."

Tele nodded her agreement before she took a drink of her own. Then Navid noticed something brown poking out of the pockets of her pants—something he was sure hadn't been there during their walk here.

He nodded toward it. "What's in your pocket?"

She pulled out a small ragdoll, aged and full of patches. "It was on a small bed in the back. I think it belongs to Emelisse. She said she hasn't been sleeping." She looked at him shyly. "Do you think it'll help?"

"I think so."

Navid thought he saw a hint of a smile on her lips as she stuffed the doll back in her pocket. She took another drink from the waterskin before handing it back to him.

"It must be hard for you," she said. "Seeing your home this way and everyone you knew …"

"Yes," Navid said. "It is."

She nodded. "It hurts."

Navid was painfully aware of Tele's shared trauma. When he'd found her, she was completely alone. When he'd asked her about her family, she'd said they were dead. Worst of all, when she'd found a family member, he'd tried to keep them apart.

"I'm sorry for trying to keep you from bringing your uncle along with us."

Tele looked at him sharply. "How'd you know he's my uncle?"

"He told me," Navid said.

"Oh."

"If I'd known that at the time …" Navid shook his head. "Well, I guess I can't honestly say that I would have been less resistant to the idea. But I understand now. How you needed him."

"Like you were with the Kruvs?"

Navid froze. "You knew about that?"

Tele smirked. "You're not the only person who finds things out. Master Kruv told me you were his ward. It was important enough for you to see them that we stopped there instead of going straight to Caldor."

"It was a bit more complicated than that," Navid said. He shifted uncomfortably.

"I know how important family is," Tele said.

"They're not my family."

"Close enough. Why didn't you just tell me?"

He frowned at her. "Why didn't I just tell you? I almost didn't get you to stay at the Kruv House for the night. The whole journey, I was terrified you might up and spirit away before we even arrived here. I thought that if I told you, you'd think I was … weak."

"*And* back in the forest," Tele said, "You told me that you grew up in *Goil* near Dunham Lake." Tele fixed him with a razor-sharp gaze. "Imagine my surprise when I regurgitated that same nonsense to Amie, and she caught me in a lie."

Navid's cheeks warmed as he looked away from her. "Right."

"Right."

"So," Navid said. "We should do something about our mutual mistrust. I propose we start fresh. Give each other a chance? Maybe lie a little less?"

Tele let on a beautiful, mischievous smile. "Perhaps just a little. I do love that look you get when you've been caught in a lie."

Navid struggled to suppress a smile. "I'm serious. From now on, we both make an effort to be friendly. Forthcoming. Honest—to an extent. Deal?"

She held out her hand to him. "Deal."

He took it and was suddenly aware of how sweaty his palms had become. Tele didn't comment on it. Instead, she said, "Good. And while we're being honest. I should let you know that I'm not accustomed to this whole … friend thing. I'll probably need a bit of help."

He smiled. "I can do that. I'll brief you on the finer details on our way back."

Tele held the shallow bowl to the woman's lips. Her face contorted as she sipped the medicine. Tele couldn't help but frown in sympathy. She'd nearly gagged when she first smelled the brew. But the woman finished it all without complaint.

"I've left you quite a bit of water here by your bedside," Tele said as she stood and put the bowl aside. "And there's a bit of bread and almonds here while we find someone to handle the cooking. I'm sure you'd enjoy a hearty soup."

The frail woman slowly nodded then her thin, hoarse voice managed a "thank you."

"What is your name?" Navid asked.

"Sara," she whispered.

"Well, Sara, I must insist that you stay in bed," Navid said. "If you need something, please send your daughter to find someone. You need to keep your strength."

Tele turned to Emilesse. The child sat on the floor, her back against the wall and her weary eyes red from tears and exhaustion. She knelt beside her and smiled.

"I brought you something, too." Tele pulled the doll from her pocket and offered it to her.

"Lord Nibbles!" Emilesse squealed. She took the doll and hugged it close. "I missed you so!"

"He missed you too," Tele said. "He was wide awake on your bed. I don't think he's slept in several days."

"He has a hard time sleeping without me," Emilesse said. She smiled at Tele. "Thank you."

Tele gave the girl a small, tight-lipped smile before standing again and turning back to Navid. He looked at her with his own half-smile. Tele stepped back to the bed and began gathering supplies. "Let's move on."

"You're a marvel," Navid said as he began packing his own pack.

"I know," Tele said. She turned away from him to hide a warm blush. "But we still have a lot of work to do. Ruggles said there were other areas of the city where they kept survivors, didn't he?"

"Yes," Navid said as he shouldered his pack. "But we have our hands full here as it is."

Tele nodded and followed Navid to the door. He was probably right. She was getting a bit ahead of herself. She wasn't sure if any of the other outposts had healers, but she was the healer here even if she was unqualified by normal standards.

There was a part of her that felt guilty. She wanted to say that she had to help as many people as she could because that was her altruistic nature, but that wasn't completely true. Sure, she didn't want anyone to die. And even if things were different, she would still help. It was for this, after all, that the Keepers existed: Helping others where they can't help themselves. Providing insight to those who have none.

Solving problems in the unique ways that only the true Wizard can.

But a piece of her did this because when she was focused on healing—when she was in the moment—she forgot about what had happened. She didn't see flames, hear her father's last words, or smell pitch and burning flesh as she fled the campsite.

Navid led them back into the Sanctuary's wide chamber. Since they'd begun working, Gavini had assisted guardsmen Ruggles and Anders in re-ordering the injured by the severity of their injuries. Those who'd suffered no more than minor scuffs and bruises were moved away from those with more urgent concerns. Gavini and Anders assessed and treated each before guardsmen moved the party to their own room so that she and Gavini could follow up on their treatment later.

Tele surveyed the progress. It was slow but steady. All of the critically injured had been attended to. Guardsman Anders knelt beside a small boy. The child's mother stroked his head, cooing softly while Anders and another guardsman gently wrapped the child's arm in thick gray bandages.

Gavini was nowhere to be found.

"Tele!" Guardsman Ruggles approached from across the chamber. "Gavini has been searching for you. He asked me to send you to him when I found you."

Navid knelt and retrieved the medicine from his pack. "We left the Sanctuary for a bit of an errand." He stood and held up the prize. "There's a woman who's severely sick. Tele thinks it could spread if we're not careful."

Ruggles's eyes widened and looked toward Tele. "Anders has already identified several people who aren't injured but are ill and a few others who are both. This will help?"

Tele nodded. "Provided the illness is viral like the woman we identified. Can you show me where you moved them? I might be able to ascertain their condition."

"Of course," Ruggles said. "But Gavini—"

"This is a bit more important," Tele said. "I'm sure he'll understand."

Navid turned to her. "Why don't you go, and I'll handle it. This is why you showed me the symptoms, right? You can't be everywhere at once."

Tele hesitated. "But—"

"Go on," Navid insisted. "The Sanctuary won't collapse if you step away for one moment."

She nodded. "Alright. Lead the way."

The Sanctuary's massive size didn't truly sink in until Guardsman Ruggles lead Tele into the heart of the edifice. The Guardsman pointed out where each wing led as they passed long passageways that tunneled into the deep recesses of the home of the seers.

How one managed to navigate such a large enclosure without getting lost mystified her. Without the open air above, the Sanctuary disoriented, squashing any hope of Tele finding her way back to its entry without assistance. Navid's childhood in the place must have been terrifying.

Once Tele realized the enormity of the space, she set her mind to at least try to remember the route they'd taken. She wasn't adept at spatial mapping. Her brothers had been so much better at it.

Guardsman Ruggles stopped just outside a large door and inclined his head. "He's in there. I should probably get back."

Tele considered asking the man if he had a map of the place. Instead, she nodded. "Thank you."

Ruggles smiled before turning and leaving. Once he'd disappeared around a corner, Tele turned back to the door. The same inscription from the Sanctuary's entrance marked the doorway.

She whispered the words to herself. "In knowledge there is power. In truth there is freedom."

She opened the door and stepped inside a small, dark room, lit by one freshly lit candle. Gavini sat in a chair to one side of the room. Leaning on his staff for assistance, he rose and smiled.

"I thought I'd lost you," he said. "Where'd you disappear to?"

"Navid and I left to find some supplies," Tele said. "Why are you this deep in the Sanctuary? There are still others that could use our help. Shouldn't we be helping them?"

"Most of the severely injured have been assisted, and Guardsman Anders learns fast. His father was a healer. They will be fine for a moment." His eyes twinkled in the dim candlelight. "Until then, I thought it important that I show you something very special."

Gavini turned to the wall just before them. Though mostly wooden, a large, smooth, metal panel was etched into the wall from floor to ceiling.

He placed a hand on it. "*Ret'en.*"

The panel faded away, revealing an even smaller, round room. Gavini stepped inside and turned to Tele. He waved her in.

Tele stepped inside, turning around to see that the panel had reappeared. Now sealed inside an even smaller room, Gavini spoke again. "*Nescht.*"

Tele's stomach lurched as if she were falling. She gripped the wall. "What's happening?"

"We're moving," Gavini said. "You feel it at the initial acceleration. But once we're going, it doesn't feel like anything. This is a small room that can move to different places in the Sanctuary."

Tele let go of the wall, noticing that Gavini was right. The feeling had only lasted a moment. And now that the initial fear of it was passed, Tele was astounded. "Where is it taking us?"

"That," Gavini said as he touched the panel again, "is what I want to show you. *Ret'en.*"

This time, the entire room dissipated, revealing a much larger circular room. Lit from above, the ceiling glowed, illuminating the room as if it were open to daylight. Desks and large instruments populated the room. Most were tools she'd never seen before. Others appeared to be larger versions of things she'd only imagined she might one day see. For example—

Tele hurried to a long, black cylindrical tube. She resisted the urge to look into its eyepiece. "Is this … Is this a magnifier?"

"One of the largest in the world. Perhaps the only of its kind."

Tele turned to him. "*One* of the largest?"

He tapped his staff on the floor. "There's a few dozen floors beneath us. The Sanctuary below is as vast as it is above. There are things here that have not been touched in two hundred years."

Two hundred years. Since Wizard Titan disappeared. "This is where the Keepers worked."

Gavini nodded as he crossed the room. "This is where the magic happened."

Tele allowed her attention to wander from place to place, examining each object in the room, taking note of what it was or might be. Several tables were piled high with books, several others supported objects so alien she couldn't begin to imagine what they were.

Her parents would have died to see this place. They'd worked their entire lives to ensure that one day the keepers could return to it. And here she stood, living that very dream.

"There's one more thing I want to show you before I leave," Gavini said as he reached the room's perimeter. He touched the wall. "*Evres*."

Tele gasped when the ceiling's glow dimmed, and the walls disappeared. Beyond, the inky blackness meshed with the light of orbs that drifted around the room. She approached the void, curiously stepping to Gavini's side. When she drew closer, she realized that the walls had not disappeared. Instead, they'd become transparent. And beyond was …

"Water," Tele whispered.

She gazed into the deep as a large school of fish approached. In united charge, they danced, flitting this way and that, swimming so close that they seemed to almost enter the room before they turned away again. Tele followed them as they circled the large room, probing the invisible barrier that prevented their advance.

It was so beautiful that she felt a lump press against her throat. "It's …"

"Breathtaking," Gavini finished. "With every great tragedy, there is a fleeting wisp of opportunity. It's time for the Keepers to continue their work. Will you help me?"

Tele dried her eyes with her sleeve before she turned back to him. "Of course, I will."

FIFTEEN

BIRTHRIGHT

"Gabe," Seth whispered. "You awake?"

"I am," Gabriel said, but didn't stir. He hadn't slept.

"Sleep well?"

"Hardly."

"Same."

Gabriel remembered his father's words: "When you have truly defeated your enemy, they cannot escape you. Though they may live to see another day, nightmares will haunt them to their deathbeds."

Silence set in again, then Gabriel heard a shuffling of sheets before his brother's footsteps neared his bed. Seth continued past and stopped before the bedroom door.

"Don't need to piss anymore?" Gabriel asked.

"No … just …" Seth turned. "I just don't want to walk out past Father's door."

Were things different, Gabriel would have laughed and asked what he'd done to warrant avoiding Father's wrath. No more.

Gabriel rolled over and sat up. "Are you okay?"

"Yes," he said, crossing his arms. "No … I'm scared. You heard the stories from the new messengers that came in. How there were white beasts spitting ice. What's stopping that from happening to us. Right here?"

Gabriel hadn't even considered that. Over the past few days, four other messengers had come from Caldor, bringing dozens of disturbing and often conflicting reports. One of which had said that the snow storms in Caldor had been caused by giant lizards. An absurdity if he'd ever heard one. "It's just one report. Some said it was a blizzard. Some said there were soldiers in the streets. Sounds like a lot of frightened men who are grasping to explain what happened. But even if there *were* beasts like that, don't you think they would have done it by now if they really wanted to?"

"And Prophet Davin is dead ..." Seth said.

That was the one thing that all of the messengers had reported. All the prophets that met in Caldor had died in the storm.

"That Prophet was useless. He didn't help Father in Caldor, and I don't see how he would help us now. We can't use evil to fight evil."

"You really think he's evil?" Seth asked. "Father trusted him. Shouldn't we?"

"Maybe if he didn't, he'd still be alive."

"What does someone like a prophet have to do to earn our trust?"

"I don't scorching know, Seth. Just go back to bed."

Seth nodded and looked to his feet. "Someone's coming," he said and then darted back to his bed and sunk in under his blankets.

Gabriel let himself fall back against his pillow. Their father had only journeyed to Caldor at Prophet Davin's urging. When Gabriel asked him if it was really necessary, his father assured him that six prophets were better than one. A useless lot they were and just as blind as the rest of the world.

They were a dead lot now, save one. Prophet Tristan would be next. Gabriel would see to that.

The room door opened and Nurse Marium swept inside.

She made for Gabriel's bedside. "Come on now, up you go! Come on."

Gabriel sat up, covering himself with the bed sheet. "Whatever happened to knocking?"

"You've nothing I haven't seen before." She waved off his question before turning and gliding to his closet. "I think you should wear something red. Something that shows passion and authority. Something …" She looked over her shoulder at him. "Come now, up!"

"Court's morning session doesn't start for another hour. I have time." Gabriel dropped back into his bed.

"The diplomat has arrived earlier than expected," Marium said as she combed through layers of clothes.

That got his attention. They weren't due to arrive for another few days.

Nurse Marium pulled free a red and silver morning coat. "The High Lords are quite eager to hear what he has to say. I don't think you'll want to crawl in last. King Jeremiah never did. I can only imagine they'll want to start as soon as they are all together." Her back to him, she held the coat out at arm's length. "This coat will do grand, no?"

"Sure," Gabriel mumbled.

Marium turned around, her glare a picture of austerity. "Gabriel, if I have to tell you to rise once more, I'll pull you out and drag you to the courtroom myself. These bones aren't as young as they used to be, but I assure you: I will see it done." To punctuate her threat, she tossed the outfit atop him. "Hurry now. Samuel awaits you."

Gabriel heard the room door shut from under the garment. He pulled it aside and sat up again, this time letting his feet touch the floor. "And now they steal my sleep. I don't see negotiations going well. Maybe I should kill him and get it over with."

"You're not supposed to kill a diplomat," Seth piped in. Gabriel turned an annoyed scowl to his brother who sat in the warmth of his blankets. "Well, that's what Nurse Marium said anyway. It's not good practice."

"It's also not good practice to wake a prince any earlier than necessary," Gabriel said as he put on and buttoned his shirt. He pulled on his trousers and slipped on his boots before turning back to Seth. "I expect today to be a riot. Have your bow ready."

Seth smiled and sunk in under his covers. Gabriel grabbed the morning jacket Marium had picked and left the room.

"Boo!"

Gabriel stopped cold as Tomas and Doran fell atop one another, giggling at their attempt to startle him.

He shut his eyes along with clenched fists and teeth. "Shove off!" He pushed them aside hard enough so that they knew he was serious, but not so hard as to truly harm them. They shouted in protest, but then fell in behind as if it hadn't phased them. He focused his gaze to the end of the hall as sporadic footfalls danced just behind him.

"Wouldn't you rather go play with someone who actually has time?" Gabriel said as they pursued him down the spiral staircase. "Seth is awake. What about your fool brother?"

"Cainan left," Tomas said.

Gabriel half-smiled, remembering Cainan's jab during his father's memorial dinner. "I hope my shoulder broke his hand."

"Cainan went to war," Doran said in a near sing-song tone.

"What?" Gabriel turned on them, causing Doran to slip down the last stair in an attempt to slow. Gabriel caught his arm. "What did you say?"

Doran's face twisted in pain. "Let go, Gabe! You're hurting me!"

Gabriel complied, allowing him to back away with a tear-rimmed expression. Tomas, dropping to the landing, put himself between his brother and Gabriel.

"What's up your ass?" Tomas demanded and stepped in closer. "It's not like you have to go out there and die while we sit back in *our* palace."

Gabriel's eyes narrowed, and Tomas flinched into a defensive pose with arms raised and ready.

"There you are, Gabriel," Samuel's voice chimed in from behind. Gabriel turned to see Samuel waving him forward from the mouth of the Great Hall. "Come now, hurry!"

Gabriel looked back to the Bendeth boys, delivering one last heated glare before leaving them at the foot of the stairway. Samuel continued to wave him forward and gently smiled as he grew closer. He placed a hand on Gabriel's back and guided him at a brisk pace toward the main court.

"Now, I know that the Diplomat's early arrival is unexpected," Samuel began in a lecturing tone, "but this is likely done to push us further off guard. We are without Prophet Davin and we must do our very best to present our confidence. It's likely that they don't know about the attack in Caldor yet.

"Of course, you really don't have to do anything but sit and listen, but I say this in case he tries to address you directly. I don't mean to say that he will, but we must be ready for any eventuality. I can't predict what he will say or do, but I can tell you that your response to this must align with the tactic of stonewall confidence."

Samuel stopped just before the court doorway and held him at arm's length "Is that understood?"

Gabriel nodded slowly. "Yes."

"Excellent," Samuel turned and opened the court doors.

The court buzzed with collective anticipation. Whispers passed back and forth between High and Low Lords and parchment rustled in an attempt to find organization. Gabriel's entrance hardly shifted the commotion. His father's entrances always seemed to garnish a great deal of attention. Gabriel was just short of ignored.

He glided around the edge of the room with Samuel shadowing him from behind and found his usual chair in the court. The seat was designated for his learning purposes and was partially set off from the court's proceedings. As he settled in, a court attendant placed several pieces of parchment, a pen, and a small jar of ink before him. Blank and meant for note-taking, Gabriel rarely used them except to express his artistic view of the proceedings. The High Lords had quite large heads according to his characters. It was one of the few things that made the court's proceedings not feel as if they lasted into eternity.

There were more Low Lords in attendance than usual. Low Lords had more involved duties with their districts on a day-to-day scale. This required them to spend more time within their own courts where petitions were passed from commoner to Guild, Guild to Lord, and then passed back down as directives. Those courts would be at a standstill as their leaders crowded the palace. It seemed that everyone who was close enough to make it into the Crown City wanted to hear this diplomat for themselves.

High Lord Bendeth was in deep discussion with one of his Low Lords. Though he continued speaking, Gabriel's entrance hadn't flanked his notice. Bendeth watched as he settled in, the Lord beside him scribbling intently to keep up with the High Lord's stream of remarks. Gabriel pretended to ignore the attention.

Scanning the room, he caught High Lord Roth's eye. Roth inclined his head in the slightest of bows, letting a small smile edge onto his hard expression. The smile was one of reassurance, similar to his sentiments from the memorial dinner.

The Court Announcer nodded as a runner whispered in his ear before dashing back out. The Announcer tidied his parchment then stood, facing the High and Low Lord end of the chamber. "High and Low Lords of the Hzorah Crown, diplomat of the Deseran Dominion: Eidin Carowin."

The hall's doors opened again, and several of the Crown's Guard escorted a tall man with a gray beard under sharp, observant eyes. He wore a neutral gray uniform that held no ornamentation and boots of polished black. He approached the podium and placed his hands behind his back.

The court's assembly showed no sign of stirring, save what seemed to be a synchronized leaning forward to give their guest a proper appraisal. The diplomat did not shy away from the judgment. Instead, he seemed to challenge it, giving each of them his own raptor glare. When Carowin's gaze crossed Gabriel's, he felt something decidedly dangerous.

"People of the Hzorah Crown," he began, "I have come with good tidings. The Creed has seen the suffering of your people, of all people. We have seen how man wanders without direction, shackled to an allegiance to Caldor. We have come to help guide you to a better life."

The court crescendoed from whispers to shouts of outrage. Lord Bendeth stood and waved his arms in an attempt to pull the court back to order. The court complied reluctantly.

Bendeth leaned in, measuring Carowin's demeanor. "With little due respect, Diplomat Carowin, you have shown us no such evidence. You have mounted an army that journeys steadily toward the Shadow Peaks—a threat we cannot ignore." Bendeth paused, allowing the court to quietly agree. "Surely, Diplomat Carowin, you cannot expect us to believe you intend us good will."

The diplomat smiled. "All things work to the advantage of those who follow in the Creed's true path. Fate has brought Caldor to heel, knowing that it has outgrown the vision originally intended for it. If the Great Wizard Titan could see the result of his creation, he would be most displeased."

So, he knew. Gabriel thought. But just because he knew what happened in Caldor doesn't mean he knows what happened to his father.

"The Wizard is dead!" High Lord Laonne shouted. "This man speaks insanity!"

"We have moved our army as a precaution," Carowin continued, ignoring him. "We come, praying that the Crown will see that they must rejoin with the Creed and restore us to the once proud people we were before the Hzorah tribe split us in two. We only hope that you see the light and that you join the true path once more."

More shouts erupted from the Lords and several took to their feet. A few even shouted for his execution where he stood. The Guard within the chambers shifted nervously, unsure if they were required to carry out the Lords' will. Carowin stood stone still, his expression cool as it was the moment he'd entered the court.

So much for stonewall confidence on our part, Gabriel thought. It had taken just a few words of grand posturing from the diplomat to make the Low Lords melt into their emotions. *Of course, the diplomat's words are ridiculous. They're zealots. What else should we expect?*

Again, Bendeth worked to quiet the court. Gabriel turned to Samuel, checking if his expression had anything to say on the matter. Samuel turned to meet his eyes. His expression echoed his own thoughts.

"Where is your King?" Carowin asked. He scanned the room. "Is the prospect of peace so unimportant to him? Could he not give the Creed that much respect?"

Gabriel tensed, hoping that Bendeth had the good sense to avoid the question.

"Is that all, Diplomat Carowin?" Bendeth asked, his voice taking a tone of condescension.

"We, of course, don't expect this decision to come easily," Carowin said, giving Bendeth a self-satisfied smile. "You have spent more than a decade playing at being a sovereign nation and nearly two decades without the Creed within your lands. We only ask that you surrender now and spare your people the pain of another war. I come with open arms to accept the lost fold. I beg of you: do not ignore the call of your true purpose. We will be forced to take action so that Wizard Titan may return to us." He scanned the crowd, his gaze crossing the lords and ending on Gabriel. "Your time has come. Choose."

Whispers, laughter, shouting, and curses all followed the diplomat as he bowed and exited the court. Runners were summoned to carry news of what transpired. One Low Lord toppled his drink, bringing forth a rush of servers to clear away its disorder.

Gabriel turned to Samuel again. "That Desolate-bound fool. Where does he get off with demands like that?"

Samuel shook his head, still focused on to the chaos beyond.

We can't surrender, Gabriel clenched his fists. *Weakness is not the Crown's way. Weakness didn't rid us of the Creed. Give the Creed a handhold and they will take the whole scorching mountain.*

Gabriel turned back to see Bendeth, still standing in place with hands outstretched and leaning over the table that kept him at bay from the waist down. He did not whisper, laugh, or shout. He watched the door where the diplomat had entered before, eyes narrowed and thoughtful. Several of his districts whispered intently at him, but his attention to the door beyond remained unwavering.

Bendeth's calm matched that of his father in matters of great weight. Gabriel knew that his father would not be reduced to the behavior that filled the court. He'd seen how his father handled dire news. His father did not allow his serenity to crumble under pressures that would drive most men to take up arms.

Perhaps Bendeth *was* the king that Hzorah needed.

On the other hand, the court wouldn't have behaved this way if King Jeremiah was present. Bendeth had a flair for theatrics and seemed to purposely allow the court to crumble to dysfunction.

At long last, Bendeth raised a hand, calling for order. The other High Lords brought their party's discussions to an end. With order again restored, the court took to a silence that was as unsettling as the diplomat's demands.

"High Lords," Bendeth said, "please state your case. High Lord Eddings?"

Eddings stood and stroked his beard. "The Shadow Peaks lie just north of my lands. I fear my people are in the greatest danger as we would be the first to feel the impact of conflict. Though our lands have been the epicenter of many of our greatest victories during the Dominion Wars, much of that land has been worked into farmland. If the Dominion brings the battle to our door, many of my people will lose their investments with those who lose their lives. We cannot allow the Deseran hoard to pass beyond Stronghold Aear."

High Lord Laonne stood. "Are you asserting that we accept

his terms? That after all Hzorah has been through to rid ourselves of the Creed, we just let them waltz back into our lands?"

Eddings's face grew red. "Lord Laonne, with all due respect, you have all of Hzorah between you and the Dominion …"

"Do you really think *that* is what this is about?" Laonne shot back. "My decision would hold just as firm if it was Armoth attacking from the south."

"I think you misunderstand, Lord Laonne." Roth was standing now. "Perhaps there is a compromise to be reached."

"Bah!" Laonne threw up his arms. "Better luck reasoning with rocks!"

"It is not just North Hzorah that will suffer," Eddings said, sweeping an arm, "but all of the Crown. Near three-quarters of the Hzorah food supply comes from those lands. And the crop-share agreement between Hzorah and Armoth depends on that supply."

"So, we roll over on our backs, then. We let them take all that we have worked for?" Laonne pointed at Lord Bendeth. "You said how we must be undivided. How we must show the Dominion our strength. How—"

"There is more than one way to use strength," High Lord Roth interjected. "We must find a way to come to some sort of agreement. We can't be divided in this. Perhaps there is something that they want. Something that they need that will cool their lust."

"What they want," Lord Bendeth said, "is submission. What they want is dominance. What they want is the Crown." He pointed to the king's empty seat. "I believe that no matter our decision, we roll the dice." He raised a hand to Roth's party. "On one hand, we try to reason with them and risk losing control of our lands and all that we believe. And on the other," he repeated the gesture to Laonne. "we fight and risk our people starving."

Murmurs between the Low Lords rippled from wall to wall.

Bendeth turned and looked straight at Gabriel. "Prince Gabriel."

Gabriel, taken by surprise, straightened from his slouching. He'd never been addressed directly during court before.

Bendeth dipped his head. "We have not heard your opinion on this. Tell us. What do *you* think should be done?"

"I …" Gabriel took in all the eyes that turned to him. He felt his mouth and throat dry to cracking. "Well …" He looked at Samuel who gave him a small, short shake of the head. "I don't believe that this is something that I should decide. My time has not yet come."

"Don't be modest," Bendeth said. He gestured toward his father's empty seat again. "You will sit here before another year is seen. A few months will make little difference between now and then. This is the Crown. This is your *birthright.* It is only reasonable that you weigh in. The Deseran Dominion wants what is left to your care. Truly, if anyone is to decide what is to become of it, it would be you."

Gabriel glanced from Roth to Laonne. Both wore expressions of expectant agreement. He looked toward Eddings, whose eyes pleaded for him to see things his way. It was Eddings' people who were caught in the crossfire. Gabriel's first reaction was that of Laonne's, but as king, it would be his duty to protect his people from harm.

For the past few months, he'd been angry with his father for being disinterested in taking direct action and fighting back the Dominion horde. But now that the options were laid before him directly, he saw how either decision risked destroying everything, Gabriel finally understood how his father could hesitate to do what should be an obvious decision.

No matter which course Gabriel took, there would be a loss. Choose war: lose many lives to battle and possibly starvation. Choose compromise: lose the life for which they'd fought many years to obtain … lose the respect of his warrior heritage.

I don't know which is the correct course. He thought as he looked at Samuel. *But only one will buy us time.*

"I think …" His voice came out as a hoarse whisper. He cleared his throat and tried again. "I think we send a message and call for another meeting. One in which we can further discuss alternative solutions."

Laonne cast his hands upward in frustration, as if Gabriel's words had doomed them to eternal servitude. Roth nodded in agreement. Eddings took to consulting his Low Lords, and Bendeth slipped him a half smile before turning back to those assembled.

"The court will see recess until after midday," Bendeth said, piling his parchment. "Roth, send your best runner to my ready room. I will prepare a message for him to deliver."

The Court Announcer stood, somewhat thrown from the break of protocol, and repeated the High Lord's recess plea in his usual stately manor. The court released some of its pent-up chaos as they began reshuffling parchment and conversation sparked anew between Low Lords. Many eyes tried for furtive glances in Gabriel's direction. They spanned between agreement and deep mistrust.

He attempted to slip low enough in his chair to avoid their furtive glances, glancing down at the empty parchment before him. He didn't know what answer would make everyone agree—the answer his father often seemed to have. Gabriel had given the most neutral response possible, and he still suffered whiplash. Maybe he should have stuck to his gut feeling. Maybe fighting was the right course. It was the course that his father and father's father took so many years ago. But how could he ignore the suffering of an entire district of the Crown?

Gabriel felt Samuel's hand rest gently on his shoulder. He looked up to meet his eyes. "You did well, Gabriel." He smiled reassuringly. "You should go get something to eat before the recess concludes."

"Right." He stood, his stomach feeling suddenly hollow, and caught Bendeth's wry half-smile once more before he turned and exited the court.

SIXTEEN

THE SEVENTH CADENCE

Gabriel left the court but avoided the Great Hall by exiting the palace altogether and crossing the courtyard, taking a less direct but more isolated path to the Breakfast Hall. He squinted his eyes in response to an early spring sunrise.

Outside, a long line of Crown City citizens idled at the palace dispensary, awaiting food. The Crown Palace left its wasted food here and was accessible to anyone who arrived to take it. His father had issued that change. He'd said that the palace may never produce enough to feed all the poor in the Crown City but throwing it away or selling what's left helped no one.

As Gabriel approached, the citizens looked at him then away as if he didn't exist. News of his father's death would surely have swept the city. Even the poorest and homeless knew by now, but Gabriel's father had kept him out of the public eye, and there was little to hint that their future king was among them save his clothes, but he could easily be the son of a local Low Lord. Gabriel brisked passed them. He preferred the silence to whispers.

After crossing the courtyard, he re-entered the Great Hall and headed toward the Breakfast Hall. Now that the immediate shock of actually being asked his opinion had receded, anger now filled in to replace it. Where did Bendeth get off asking him out of nowhere to comment on what should be done? It was not the way things were supposed to happen, at least not until he'd become king. His thoughts were irrelevant.

It was as Samuel warned. This was another jab at his competence as a leader. High Lord Bendeth was trying to show that Gabriel lacked the strength to wear the Crown. Catching him off guard like this was a low blow, one he wasn't sure he'd completely evaded.

Gabriel crossed into the East Hall from which the Breakfast Hall branched. A stream of Hzorah Low Lords trickled inside, chattering amongst themselves about the morning's discussions of diplomacy. They must have taken several of the smaller, crossing halls that interconnected the four primary branches of the palace's center keep. What those halls lacked in grandeur, they replaced with expedience.

He crossed back into the Great Hall, hiding from view. With the line inching forward, it would be some time before no one waited outside, and he could enter unnoticed.

What am I doing? His father had never hidden from the High or Low Lords. He never hid from anyone. But here, he hid like some sort of … coward.

And there it was: cowardice. Just like Bendeth was trying to show the world.

He squeezed his eyes shut and gave the Hall's wall blunted smack. He'd never wanted the crown. He just wanted to be a warrior. His father had known his skills; the entire palace knew where he really belonged. But now he hid, fighting to convince himself to face the dull and riddled sword of politics.

He didn't know how to fight that war, but he did know how to fight in battle. That was the difference. He wouldn't be acting this way if it were a real battle.

Gabriel turned and headed for the palace kitchens. At least there, talk of litigation or debates of economic upheaval would be scarce. There was the rest of his life for that.

The kitchens were among many rooms and vaults that

slipped unnoticed to one who didn't care to seek them out. They rested underneath the palace's first floor along with store areas, staff quarters, and various utilitarian chambers that would detract from the clean beauty of the palace above.

Halls crossed beneath the palace in an intricate web. Stairwells climbed hallowed walls and ended behind panels of the upper palace to give the staff quick, unnoticed access to wherever they were needed.

In some ways, the staff had their own palace—a shadow palace that had its own community set off from the pruned formality of what most thought of as the Crown's epicenter.

Gabriel knew the palace's unseen web of rooms and hallways as well as he knew the ones above. In youth, he'd taken to exploring every corner of his home and by the time he'd seen seven years, he'd discovered the entire manor.

Marium found it unfit for a young prince to spend time where the royal family didn't belong, but his father never rebuked his efforts to find adventure within the safe limits of the palace. Nevertheless, throughout childhood when Marium caught Gabriel below, it resulted in a sharp lecture and an escort to the surface.

Gabriel had long outgrown those days, and the staff now seemed to find his presence warming where the High and Low Lords seemed to ignore their existence. They still treated him as their prince, but he had the sense that he'd gained a bit of respect by not pretending the caverns beneath his feet did not support the palace above.

Without exception, the kitchens roared with the continuous clang of pots stirred and pans grating above caged flames. The sweet and savory vapors slipped between the cracks of the kitchen door and beckoned him closer to their den of fulfillment. At that moment, Gabriel thought he might be willing to walk straight into Desolate's cold clutches if that's what lies beyond those doors. And then, he wished it, knowing that beyond Desolate's door was eternal peace.

He pushed into the kitchen to take that release, but inside was the kitchen he'd always known. The cooks stepped in stride with the high tempo of demand, knowing that it was neither High nor Low Lord that pushed them to perform at such velocity, but rather the hardened spoon of Prisha, the head cook.

"Is that an open flame, Kas?" Prisha's voice cut through the chaos in casual reprimand. She weaved between cooks and preparation tables with her signature long wooden spoon clutched in her right hand. She wore her white hair in a tight bun just above her neck and black apron over long flowing skirts.

Spotting Gabriel, Prisha rolled her eyes before checking a large brick oven.

"You." She pointed at the young cook who was tending the oven. "Go upstairs and get my son. Tell him the prince is in the kitchens."

Perhaps unsure how to respond, the cook saluted and turned. It took several near spills and apologies before he reached one of the kitchen's stairwells and slipped into the palace innards.

Prisha crossed over to Gabriel. "They always send the new blood to my kitchens. *My* kitchens. As if I don't have enough to do."

Gabriel chuckled. "They know you're the best."

"Poor boy doesn't know a paddle from a sail." She used her wooden spoon to wave at the brick oven. "A good thing you came and gave him a chance to do something he can handle. He was going to ruin that turn pie. Best I use him as a runner than a cook."

"Maybe he can be reassigned," Gabriel said. "With all the chaos down here, you could use a few runners."

"And you!" Prisha turned her wooden spoon to Gabriel, pointing it to his chest like a rapier. "You need to let someone know when you aren't going to a meal. I had a whole table set for you and your brother. Had I known I didn't have to prepare it, we wouldn't need runners!"

Gabriel held up his hands in surrender. "My apologies, Prisha. I just wanted a meal away from the Lords. And if Seth attends, I'm sure he'll take care of it. He's seen fourteen years. I don't need to tell you of the appetite he's gained."

"You don't." She turned and hammered her spoon near a ceramic tray before crossing back into her domain. "Eat this. And be happy you get anything at all."

"Yes ma'am," Gabriel saluted and lifted the tray of fried potato, green pepper and north melon. He walked to an unused, corner cutting table and settled into a tall chair against the wall.

Two cooks, Peer and Ricci, shuffled toward him, sharing the burden of a large tray of to-be-baked food. They wore the typical white of the cooking staff from head to toe. The Hzorah Mark was the only bit of color added to their attire in a small black patch across the heart.

"Time news reaches North Hzorah, those who can afford it will migrate south," Ricci, the younger cook, said. A grunt landed the tray on the oven's open lip. "And we don't need any more Desolate-bound northerners around here. I swear the sun sets half-speed there."

"That's even if they can make it down here alive," Peer said, turning to retrieve a long, wooden peel. He began dishing food into the oven. "My son's been telling me the highwaymen have been as rampant as ever. The Crown's Guard can't track them, and they appear out of nowhere in all sorts of places. The whole world's gone crazy."

"Crazy? Let me tell you crazy," Ricci said as he circled Peer. He checked for Pisha before leaning back against the kitchen wall. He then spotted Gabriel, but Gabriel passively popped more food in his mouth before leaning back himself. "Just a little over a week ago, my uncle was found dead in the middle of the woods outside Azuri. There was a house there—it belonged to some local looney—but it was burned to the ground, too."

"If you ask me, that's not highwaymen work." Peer dished in another tray of food. "That's the work of someone with a vendetta. The whole world, I tell you!"

Ricci turned to Gabriel again. "Well? What do *you* think?

What are you and the Lords planning to do about all this mess?"

Peer cut in. "Now, Ricci, you don't have to go—"

"No," Ricci said, approaching Gabriel's makeshift table before turning back to his older counterpart. "We've got just as much rights to know as anyone else." He looked back to Gabriel. "What then? What are we supposed to do?"

Gabriel gave a small shrug. "The food's good. I'd say keep making it."

Ricci frowned. "What?"

"I appreciate your concerns, and I'll do what I can to make it right," Gabriel said, defaulting to the words of his father. It sounded outright ridiculous falling from his lips. He didn't even believe himself.

"I don't really get how it's that complicated," Ricci said. "People are dying. We need to stop it. Simple as that."

It was that simple, or at least it should be. Gabriel had heard of the highwaymen problem. It was a big enough issue that it had been brought all the way to the Crown. So far, there hadn't been a coordinated effort to stop it.

He hadn't heard of the house burning down, but bad things happened all the time across Hzorah. His father had told him that there was no way he could stop all the hurt or punish all those who wronged the innocent. This, he'd said, was the paradox of being king. Even with the power of armies at his command, knowing what he could change and what he couldn't was a constant consideration. Knowing which actions were truly worth taking, which battles were most worth the fight.

Gabriel opened his mouth to pull another response out of Desolate.

"Those turkeys aren't going to carve themselves, you know," Prisha said, appearing behind the two cooks. They spun, surprised.

Ricci spread his arms. "We were just trying to figure out what—"

"I'm sure Prince Gabriel is working hard to fix your problems," Prisha said. Her eyes narrowed and she pointed her wooden spoon at him. "It's not your place to confront," she repeated the gesture at Peer. "Yours, either."

"Mother," Winston said, coming up behind her, two trays balancing on each arm. "What should I do with these?"

"We weren't trying to antagonize anyone," Ricci said. He turned to Gabriel for backup. "Right?"

"Put it aside for the leftover dispensary," Prisha to said Winston without letting her attention falter from her targets.

"We weren't though, right?" Ricci pleaded. "We're on the brink of war and nobody knows nothing. We need answers."

"But, Mother, Prince Gabriel is right here. I can just give it to him."

"Put it *aside*." Prisha waved her spoon between the two cooks. "If I ever find you two falling out of line again, I'll carve *you*. Turkey, go!" Without another word, the two cooks hurried off.

"You know," Gabriel said. "It wasn't a big deal. They're only worried. They *should* be asking questions. I know I would." His eyes met a raised eyebrow. "And am."

"Well, you keep asking those questions, Prince Gabriel," Prisha said. "But for now, leave the questioning in the courts and the cooking in the kitchen." She turned to her son. "*Dispensary*, Winston."

Gabriel watched Prisha stride back into the kitchens before turning to meet Winston's eyes. He pointed to the tray in front of him. "She's right. Give it to the dispensary. I'm nearly full anyway."

He looked down to the elegantly positioned food and nodded. He turned to go but stopped and turned back again. "Don't let Ricci get to you. He has a big mouth, but the staff has confidence in you. We think you'll make a great king."

"All the staff?" Gabriel asked.

"Well," Winston said, shifting his weight. "I guess that's a general statement, but I don't think that many people here doubt your abilities. We know you'll bring us victory. Victory is a part of your bloodline. So, don't worry about that."

"Thank you, Winston," Gabriel said.

Winston smiled and said, "You're welcome," before turning and disappearing deep within the kitchens.

The sun sat just above the western tree line, and the water between patches of canal rippled its reflection when Gabriel finally left the court. He ambled through the brown, ankle-high grass with a bow in one hand and a quiver of new arrows in the other. The archer court was empty when he'd gone there, but a gardener told him that Seth was in an adjacent court near the south garden.

As Gabriel neared the line of ten-foot hedges that separated the archer court from the south garden, he could see forms through the still leafless branches. He passed through an open patch and spotted his brother, Tomas, Doran, and another man in the court's center. Seth sat off to one side while Doran watched his older brother duel with the man from the opposite side.

Seth's head perked when he saw him approach, and Gabriel gave him short nod and smile. He sat on the ground where his brother watched. "Who's that?"

"Tomas and Doran's new tutor," Seth said. "Apparently, Uncle Bendeth found someone who was both well-educated and skilled with the sword. I think he's even an advisor."

Gabriel watched them practice a basic thrust and parry repeatedly as they stepped in clockwise circles. The man was obviously holding back and with good reason. Tomas's stance was sloppy, and his skill was less than adept. Gabriel blamed youth for the stance but blamed nature for his talent. Even the clumsy could learn to hold his own with the sword.

"He seems competent," Gabriel said. The man was certainly more fighter than his own tutor. He'd never even seen Samuel use a sword even though he claimed to have seen battle.

Seth shrugged. "What happened with the diplomat?"

Gabriel sighed. "He was an imbecile. He seriously thought that Hzorah would consider full surrender. Of course, I can't blame the messenger for the message."

"And what did the Lords do?"

"Uncle Bendeth asked *me* what to do."

Seth turned, frowning. "You can't be serious."

"Samuel told me to not get involved," Gabriel said, "so I just suggested we send a runner to tell him to come back for another meeting."

"And he came back?"

Gabriel shook his head. "When the runner left, the diplomat somehow managed to disappear. They sent a messenger to his camp. So far, no report."

Seth nodded, examining his hands.

"What about you?" Gabriel asked. "How are you holding up?"

"I'm alright," Seth said, not looking up. "Just … none of this feels real. Like a dream."

Gabriel pulled his knees close. "I think this is exactly what reality feels like. I think everything before was a dream. A beautiful dream that we're all just waking from. After you wake, reality is confusing at first. But then you smell the air and you look at yourself in a glass and you feel the pain of existence."

"The sixth cadence's forms always follow the fifth's, Tomas!" the tutor shouted, tucking his practice staff under an arm. "You fight as if you want to die. Fourth, fifth, and sixth. Four, five, six. Four, five, six." He clapped his hands in time as if conducting a choir. "Can you even count, boy?" He pulled his staff and held it between them. "Again!"

Tomas did as instructed—but not without reddening with embarrassment or anger—pulling into a defensive form. His tutor lurched forward and Tomas responded in the fourth cadence. The man spun, striking again and forcing Tomas into the fifth, then the sixth. He fell back just long enough to redouble the advance.

In classic form, they danced from cadence to cadence.

Fourth, fifth, sixth, and repeated until the repetition caught up with Tomas's poor form. He fell back to the seventh cadence.

Catching him by the sleeve, the tutor struck him hard across the face, grounding him. Gabriel and Doran stood simultaneously. He felt his breath quicken at the injustice. Tomas was sloppy, slow, and weak—and annoying—but he'd made the correct move. Moving to an extension—in this case, paired with a seventh cadence form—was his only real chance to break the pattern long enough to calibrate his footing.

Gabriel had underestimated Tomas's intuition. He had a long way to go, but he knew the sword well enough to know that continuing that pattern would have led to his downfall in a real battle. A student should never be punished for breaking form when breaking form is the only thing you could do.

At least, that's what his father had once said.

"Are you that daft, boy?" The tutor towered over him. "Or do you just enjoy a swift backhand?"

Tomas didn't answer.

"The seventh cadence is preferable to death," Gabriel said, intentionally louder than necessary.

The tutor turned, starring Gabriel in the eye. "What did you say?"

"Tomas did the right thing." He pointed to Tomas. "You were crushing him. He did the only thing that could pull him back from the brink."

The tutor's eyes narrowed as he stepped in front of Tomas. "Sixth always follows the fifth or you risk being gutted. Don't be foolish—"

"You're wrong. There are no absolutes in battle," Gabriel said, once again finding himself repeating an adage from his father. He shifted, looking around the tutor. "You did the right thing, Tomas."

The tutor leaned to mirror Gabriel. "This is my class, Prince Gabriel. And in *my* class, you follow the forms. They're what will keep you alive in battle, not reckless tactics. I think you'd best stick to tea parties."

"How about this?" Gabriel said, standing. "If you can bring me to defeat, right here and now, I'll admit you're right."

"I don't think—"

"So, I was right?" Gabriel said. "You admit your error?"

"Alright, then. I accept your challenge." The tutor turned on heel and thrust an expectant hand to Tomas who knelt on the ground. Tomas lifted his hand to take it, but the tutor slapped the hand away. "No, fool boy, your staff. Give me your staff." Tomas did as he was told, and the tutor tossed the staff to Gabriel.

Gabriel clenched his teeth. He knew that even in the most appropriate of settings, this was far out of line. A prince doesn't challenge a citizen to a duel. You just don't. Even if there isn't real steel involved.

But this is what Gabriel wanted. He didn't want the crown. He wanted to be a warrior. He didn't want the world to respect him for his position, but for his ability to protect and serve. Gabriel pulled off his coat.

"Gabe," Seth said. "You don't have to do this."

"No," he said. "I think I do." He dropped the coat to the ground and lifted the too-small staff to point back. "Well? Come on, then!"

Gabriel fell back into a defensive form as the man charged him. He pushed back, feeling out his opponent's strength. The tutor—pushed off balance—backed away, letting their staffs separate for only an instant before he went back on the offensive.

His strength was comparable, if not stronger than his own. This would a be a duel of skill rather than wearing strength. The tutor's confidence in his own movements told Gabriel that much within seconds. It didn't shake his nerves, however. It excited him.

Staffs spun between their skilled hands, stopping only when they collided. The sound of each wooden crack quickened his heart and each thwack sent ripples up his arms and through his body. The sensation was incomparable.

He let his frustrations pour from his heart and into the staff.

The anger, the fear, the doubt—it all glowed within like hot embers. For the first time since his father had last danced with him, he felt … *alive.*

The forms were reflexive to Gabriel, near familiar as walking. Like harp and songstress, they melded—their strikes the rhythm, their bodies ascending and descending runs. Gabriel let the music run wild within him, but it always manifested as controlled skill to those who looked on.

They separated, giving quarter. The tutor's lips curled into a smile. "Show me, my prince, how your unorthodox ways win the war. Show me the true path to victory."

"Gabriel," Seth said, calling from the side. "Stand down. It's pointless."

Pointless as the war being thrust upon his shoulders? Pointless as those who would die to the north in the name of his family? Pointless as holding a warrior captive to the crown?

Pointless as his father dying?

Gabriel had been questioned, gamed, and backed into corners one too many times. If there was ever a situation where he had the bearing to push back, it was now. He was sick of whispers and plotting and slow litigation. He was taking action, and it felt good.

Gabriel charged the first cadence. The man warded and dodged, backing away and then letting his guard relax. His lips twisted into a wicked smile.

"You see, boys?" the tutor said as he effortlessly warded a few more of Gabriel's advances. "Men act as though they know the sword, but when placed against a true swordsman, their poor skill reveals itself."

Gabriel's breaths quickened. He was *not* poorly skilled. He could hold his own and he would win. He just had to find the tutor's point of weakness. Every man had a flaw in their form. It was up to the warrior to spot it before his opponent did.

The tutor took his turn to advance an attack. He stepped lightly, pulling strength from Gabriel's counters. Gabriel cleared a leg sweep, only to have to duck a slash to his throat. He fell back and the tutor redoubled his advance.

Fourth. Fifth. Sixth.

Fourth. Fifth. Sixth.

Fourth. Fifth. Sixth.

Fourth.

Fifth.

Sixth.

Fourth.

Fifth.

Sixth.

Fourth.

Fifth.

Seventh.

The tutor took a swipe at his midriff and missed by less than a span as Gabriel arced to wider ground. Gabriel spun again and fell into form. He allowed a smug smile as his opponent cursed. Gabriel had only just warmed and already he'd gotten what he wanted: proof that he was right.

"No fair!" Tomas called. "He broke form!"

Rage crossing his face, the tutor charged. Wood struck wood, cracking in an ever-increasing pace. Gabriel sidestepped and spun; attacked and followed through. He let the staff slip around his fingers as it whirled, the momentum of battle giving it flight.

Gabriel saw the flaw. The man kept his centerline well-guarded as would any swordsman with experience, but he was slow to defend his lower left. Most fighters had this flaw. It was an awkward lower defense for the right-handed. He had only to focus there, wait for an opening, and he'd have him. He would win.

Another attack put Gabriel on the defensive. He allowed himself to be pushed back. He had to let the man fall into a comfortable rhythm before he could break it with his own.

Then, his moment came. Caught in a position where his defense would falter, Gabriel began an aggressive advance, wearing the man down just enough for him to yearn for respite. He swept the staff in a clean, controlled curve where his defenses were weakest. He made contact, just hard enough to bring the man to a knee.

Gabriel pulled the staff to the kill zone under the man's chin.

The tutor stiffened, his eyes resting on the staff before him then following it up to Gabriel's eyes.

"My, my," Gabriel smiled. "What a turn of the tide—"

A sharp pain jolted Gabriel's skull. He cried out and backed away reflexively. Another pain struck his chest and he found himself on his back, lungs empty. As the pain receded, he opened his eyes to the tutor's staff against his neck and his form haloed by the western sun.

"What a turn of the tide, indeed," the tutor said again. He tapped his staff to Gabriel's exposed neck flesh. "Well then, Prince Gabriel, I would appreciate an admittance of defeat and a proper apology."

Air finally retaking his lungs, Gabriel said: "You're the best, and I apologize."

He didn't mean it.

The tutor smiled again, taking in the moment. "Tomas! Doran! Gather your things. We're done here." He turned and retrieved the staff Gabriel had dropped.

Gabriel didn't stand as the three sauntered away. He pressed a hand against his head and found a small bit of blood in his hair. *What happened? I'd won … I'd almost won.*

"Tomas threw a rock at your head," Seth said. He extended a hand to his brother.

"Why would he do that?" Gabriel took the assistance and rose to his feet. He felt the bruise again. "I was trying to help him out."

"Maybe he didn't *want* your help."

"Maybe."

His father had taught him never to expect an opponent to play by strict rules. How things were always done wasn't always the right approach. And in his confidence, he'd let his guard down, violating very point he'd tried to make.

Father had said nothing of his cousins betraying him when

you stood up for them. There were no rules in war, but he'd thought there was respect among peers. He would have won if he'd not been stabbed in the back … or rather, stoned in the head.

But troops were different. They only had incentive to be on his side. He didn't belong here in the palace where even the Lords could not work together. He needed to be where he could actually enact change. Leading troops to war might be the only thing he could even be effective in as king; not playing with the likes of Bendeth's spawn.

SEVENTEEN

A BEAUTIFUL WEB, EVER-GROWING

"Lie him here," Tele said.

Navid and Guardsman Anders carried the man to the empty pallet that Tele indicated. While they set him down and arranged him, Tele took advantage of the time to begin pulling out supplies. Before Tele could request it, Navid immediately set to stopping the outpour of blood.

The man winced and, when Tele looked to his expression, she realized it was the same man who'd approached her in a panic when they'd first entered the sanctuary. "I thought someone was looking after him."

"Someone was," Anders said. "But the guardsmen are trying to take what I taught them—what you taught me—to the other outposts."

Tele nodded. The number of stranded citizens the Caldor Guard found every day would have been overwhelming if it weren't for the other four outposts easing the load on the sanctuary. She had yet to visit any of the other four locations were the injured had gathered. She'd entertained the idea, but Gavini had impressed upon her the utility of delegation. Chief Guardsman Ruggles would ask for her help if he required it.

"Let me take that," she told Navid, slipping in to take his

place at the injury. "Can you make a paste from the elkan bark. Two hand—"

"Two handfuls of elkan bark, half as much water, a sprinkling of yarrow," Navid recited as he worked. He swiftly crushed then mixed the ingredients. "Apply a thin layer to the gauze. Elevate the victim's wound above the heart." He looked at Anders and sat the victim up. "Hold the gauze to the wound and apply pressure." Navid followed through on the task before turning to Anders again. "Mind preparing another? This one's bound to become blood-soaked."

Anders nodded and set to it while Navid maintained his hold on the wound.

Tele set back and allowed her hands to rest in her lap. "Excellent work."

Navid looked at her, his golden eyes aglow. "I have an excellent teacher."

Tele smiled. She was happy to find that Navid was a quick learner under pressure. While his knowledge of international law and relations were far out of her experience and what she studied with Gavini were far out of his, healing had become a bridge—a middle ground between their interests and a platform of communication.

She'd taken Gavini's suggestion of treating her interactions with Navid as an experiment. She didn't have the experiences most people had to inform cordial relations, but she quickly learned that if she treated Navid similarly to how she'd treated her own family, their relationship seemed to develop naturally as if by magic. The problem only arose when she tried to place how she should interact with him specifically. There was hierarchy and social patterns in a family—in hers anyway—but Navid didn't appear to fill any of the roles she'd typically casted as "family."

He wasn't at all like her father—save his caring nature. Gavini was more like that to her. And that seemed to make sense considering that Huvil and Gavini were brothers. Of course they'd share some of the same qualities. Tele and her mother, Abigail, had been more alike than different in both appearance and personality. But Navid wasn't like her mother, either. *Where does he belong?*

Amie had reminded her of her brother Gib. And Simon … well, she wasn't sure that she'd met anyone like him yet. Neither of them were like Navid.

Tele observed as Navid continued to care for the man. She watched him change the gauze, withholding her suggestions so that he could focus and think through each step on his own. If he needed help, she'd be there to intervene.

I'll just have to develop a new kind of relationship, Tele thought. *I just need a model to work from, an example.*

It was the unfortunate result of her isolation with only a few personalities to serve as an example of how to get along with people. She'd never had a friend outside of her family. What was the most natural thing in the world for so many, she found to be entirely foreign. And, if she was honest, she wasn't very good at it.

After changing the gauze four times over, the coagulant in the medicine restrained the bleeding and Navid set to bandaging the wound.

"Desolate's Hand was with you," Navid said to the man. "Were we not here when you ran headfirst into the wall, you might have bled out."

"I don't know. I—" Dazed, he looked up to Navid in horror. He tried to back away, but Guardsman Anders held him in place.

"Whoa, now," Anders said. "Stay still."

"You … He's a seer!"

"Hold still—"

"Get your cursed hands away from me, seer!"

Tele moved in as Navid resigned. She took hold of the bandage and completed the work. Her stomach turned as she tried to suppress the urge to choke the man.

Most of her time with Navid had been in isolation—away from the broader population as they traveled. The Kruvs and Gavini had treated Navid like a person. Even the Guardsmen seemed friendly with him. But this was the first time she'd seen someone react so violently to what his golden eyes meant.

Since they'd decided to be friends, she did notice that others looked at him cautiously. That the sick and wounded preferred to talk to her and ignore that he was with her. That rooms would fall silent when they entered them. And now that she thought of it, she remembered how the peddler had reacted before they reached Azuri and how the town's people had reacted to them on the streets and in the inn.

She'd assumed that they were reacting to her. Her lifelong experience as an outlaw had naturally led her to that conclusion. But now she realized that the reaction was to Navid, not her. If anything, the only reaction to her was why she insisted on keeping his company.

She turned to look at Navid. He'd busied himself with cleaning up the supplies while Tele finished the job he'd started. The man had called him cursed. He didn't know Navid, but he was afraid of him. He didn't know how much Navid resisted that part of himself. He didn't know how he'd risked his life to save her uncle.

Tele looked back to the man as she completed the binding. "This *seer's* hand just saved your life. Something Desolate's Hand was all but willing to do. Perhaps you should think before you call his hands *cursed*."

The man teetered between shock and shame as he stared at her. "You sound like … Sara!" He gripped her shoulders. "Have you seen her?"

"What?"

"Sara. My wife."

"Isn't that the woman with the child?" Navid asked. "Emelisse."

The man's eyes grew wide. "Emelisse! Yes! Where are they?"

Tele turned to Navid. "I'm inclined not to help him after what he said to you."

Navid smiled weakly as he stood. He gave Anders a nod and together they helped the man to his feet. Tele stood and followed Navid and the guardsman. They supported his unsteady legs as they made their way back to the rooms where they'd quarantined the sick. The man was lucky that they'd found the medicine to help his wife recover, had they not, Tele wouldn't have allowed him into the private rooms.

When they entered the room with his family, Emelisse raced to embrace her father. He apologized for abandoning them. Sara, still weak, gave him a welcoming smile.

Navid joined Tele at the room's entry. "I couldn't put my family back together, but at least we reunited this one."

Tele watched Navid smile as the family held each other close, how he derived so much joy from what he'd done even though the man had out-right insulted him. It made her feel good to see him smile that way.

That's the model—the feeling I can build our relationship on. It wasn't the same foundation she'd built her other relationships on, but it was a good start. It just *felt* right.

Navid looked at her, his golden eyes glowing with satisfaction. "We should leave them to it. We have others to attend to."

Tele gave him a small smile before they turned away.

Navid shook his hands over the wash basin before turning to find a clean cloth to dry his hands. He'd never heard someone scream so loud in his life, and he vowed to never again reset a broken leg if he could avoid it.

"I think she'll be alright," Gavini said, entering the washroom behind him. He set his walking stick against the wall before washing his hands. "I would have preferred it if she'd stayed off of the leg, but getting that woman to stay put is like reasoning with a winking blume."

"I asked the guardsmen and a few refugees to make sure someone is there to help her if she needs it," Navid said. "She isn't inclined to ask for help herself."

"If she doesn't stay off that leg," Gavini said, turning to grab his own cloth from the shelf behind them, "she'll do more damage. I described that reality to her. Hopefully, the image I put in her head will do to keep her in line." He smiled at Navid. "You know, you'd make a fine healer. You learn fast; you care."

"Thank you," Navid said.

"And pardon me for saying," Gavini said. "but that's not exactly something I ever imagined saying to a seer. Putting the words 'healer' and 'seer' so close together only seemed to work when you said something like, 'Someone find a healer! A seer cut off my arm!'"

A destructive monster. Cursed. Navid bowed his head.

"Hmm. I suppose that wasn't the best joke for the moment. I apologize." Gavini retrieved his walking stick. "What I'm saying is that if you'd like to learn, there's more that I can show you."

The thought of becoming a healer had never seriously entered Navid's head. Since he'd manifested his ability as a seer, he knew that he wouldn't be able to do the things that a normal man could. There had been times when he'd dreamed of being a tradesman, but he'd long ago put those dreams away with childhood.

"It's too dangerous for a seer to become a healer," Navid said.

"There are several dozen people today who might be inclined to disagree," Gavini said.

Gavini hadn't seen it. But how could he expect him to? Every person he'd treated with Gavini accepted the help, but not before staring at his golden eyes in fear. They knew what he was, and if there had been any other way for them, they would have taken it.

And as much as Navid wished they were wrong for it, they weren't. After years of holding a tight rein on his ability, the itch had snaked its way to the surface at the first threat of danger. He'd kept control since the incident on the ice, but that day had proven how fragile his control really was.

Navid shook his head. "It wouldn't be right."

Gavini watched him for a moment before sighing. "Well, if

you change your mind, I'm more than willing to help. It's the least I can do after you saved my life."

"Have you seen Tele?" Navid asked, eager to redirect the conversation away from that day.

"I'd wager she's exactly where I left her this afternoon," Gavini said. "I told her to get some rest, but there's little chance of that now."

Navid nodded. "Right. Maybe I can get her to come up."

"And perhaps bring her something to eat?" Gavini smiled and gave Navid a friendly pat on the shoulder before he exited the room.

Navid followed him out, stopping at the storeroom that served as a makeshift kitchen until the Sanctuary's actual kitchen was staffed again. As he prepared an assortment of dried fruit and rice that had been prepared that morning by a few willing guardsmen, he wondered if it was even possible for Caldor to reconstruct with so many now dead or seriously injured. Caldor's function depended on the interconnectivity of its people. With those ties severed, it could take years before order was re-established, and years more before all the damage was repaired.

When he left the storeroom, Navid ventured deeper into the Sanctuary where Gavini had found the strange, moving room. Navid had lived here most of his life, and he'd never thought much of the room. The seers were given a reasonable amount of freedom to roam the Sanctuary—save the prophet's wing, deeper within Time's Alcove. Though this part of the Sanctuary wasn't restricted from his access, he hadn't explored this particular section with great detail.

Navid and the other seers his age had combed the building. After he'd settled in, it was a way to cure boredom between his studies. Once he'd grown accustomed to his life here, he rarely bothered to wander the unused halls. The seers had everything they needed in their own corner of the Sanctuary.

Once a seer had sufficiently mastered their control on the curse, they were allowed to leave the Sanctuary within certain boundaries. However, when they realized how much people feared to interact with them outside the Sanctuary, they tended to make their visits outside few and far between.

When Navid entered the room, he touched the large silver panel and entered the smaller room that moved—Tele had named it a "lift"— and, a moment later, the room opened to the large circular room that he still barely believed had been below his feet all these years.

The strange, glowing ceiling lights were dim, giving off just enough light for him to safely cross the room where Tele's silhouette sat in a large round chair facing the glass wall. Beyond was an endless void of water. The depths stretched on, wrapping them in darkness between star-like orbs.

Tele sat in the chair that was more amorphous cushion than furniture. She'd wrapped herself in a warm blanket and held a piece of parchment pressed against a large book. A half-page of notes had been taken, but now her pen hovered over the page, its ink drying while she stared into the water.

Navid turned to the water and frowned, trying to see what she was seeing. "What are you looking at?"

"Patience," Tele said without looking away. "It'll come back."

"I brought you something to eat." He set the bowl on the table next to her cushion. "I think Gavini was worried you'd starve yourself if we allowed you to stay down here any longer without checking on you."

Still focused on her task, she simply said, "Thank you."

Navid sat on the floor next to Tele and waited. As he watched the waters, he remembered sinking into its depths when the ice broke beneath him. The cold had seized his muscles, penetrating to his bones. Unbridled panic had taken him by the throat. The low rumbling sound of the water's tendrils slipping around his body shuddered as the world opened to swallow him whole.

But that all disappeared when he'd lost control.

Navid imagined the deep disappointing gaze of Prophet Davin. He swallowed and a chill rippled down to his toes. The

Prophet had trusted him, and he couldn't even maintain control after getting a little wet.

Navid Tevaad, the cursed. He shut his eyes and pushed away the darkness that threatened to engulf him. Seers in ages past had lost control, killing hundreds in a mad attempt to protect themselves or others, or whatever perverse reasoning they used to take what they wanted. Under the water, he'd felt his curse break through. It'd saved him and Gavini, but next time, saving himself might mean taking lives. *I can't lose control again. I won't.*

He turned his attention to Tele. It looked as if she were afraid to blink. "How long have you been here? Have you gotten any rest?"

"I found several books full of fish with illustrations on the table over there," Tele said. "I've been using them to help me identify some of the fish I've seen so far. There are hundreds that my father hadn't yet cataloged. To his credit, the Dominion Desert wasn't the ideal place to carry out an investigation of the world's water dwellers, but I'd assumed that he had cataloged a majority in his notes. He hadn't even begun to —" She paused, turning to him. "I'm sorry. I'm probably boring you."

"'A beautiful web, ever-growing, and spawning more beauty,'" Navid smiled at her. "Your words. That's what you told me when we'd first met."

A small smile found its way to her lips as she looked down to her parchment. "It was something my father had written."

"I wish I could have met him," Navid said. "He seemed like a wonderful man."

"He was," Tele said. "My whole family was wonderful."

They sat quietly a while longer before Tele broke the silence again.

"Did you ever meet your family?" Tele asked. "Not that the Kruvs aren't your family—"

"No," he sighed. "Actually, that was the whole reason I took us through Azuri to begin with. Prophet Davin had told me that I needed to 'find what I had lost.' And if I did, I would be free from my curse—free from being a seer. I went through

Azuri, hoping to reunite with my parents only to find that I was a ward, not a Kruv. So, I asked him if he knew of my family, if he could help me find them."

"And?"

"And he couldn't." Navid looked at her. "My mother died not long after she left me with him. My father …" He turned back to the water and touched his chest, feeling the small pendant that hung around his neck. "No one knows who or where he is."

"How?" Tele asked, risking a quick glance at him before she looked back to the water. "How could finding your parents make you something other than a seer?"

Navid opened his mouth, but paused, realizing that his only real justification for believing the prophet was that he was a prophet. They knew these things. "Well … I don't know, exactly."

"Has anyone ever stopped being a seer?"

"Well, no … not that I've ever heard of."

"Huh."

Navid frowned at her. "Are you saying that he lied to me? To what purpose? I would have gone to find you regardless if Prophet Davin hadn't told me I could also find my parents and be free from my curse."

"I'm not saying he lied to you," Tele said. "I'm just saying it's odd that he didn't tell you how that might happen. It's never happened before. If he knew that spending the day with your parents was the solution to fixing this whole …" She waved a hand vaguely in the direction of the Sanctuary above. "… seer operation, then why not do it to all seers? It would save the world a whole lot of effort and dread."

Navid looked away from her, embarrassed. He'd been so excited at the prospect of seeing the Kruvs again, of becoming a Kruv again, he hadn't even stopped to think about how it all made sense. Maybe it had all been a lie to get him to skip to task without protest.

He had worked hard in his time at the Sanctuary. He'd done his meditations and duties here. He'd devoted everything to stopping his curse from bringing harm. And it wasn't uncommon for one of the prophets to point out Navid to a new, young seer child as an example of good behavior.

But under the waters of Caldor, he'd snapped like a twig. Maybe they'd known he was weak and lied to him.

It was not like the prophets to lie about something like this. They'd made sure to let him know that his curse would be a lifetime commitment to the Sanctuary. But if retrieving Tele was really so important, and if they'd known that in a moment of weakness, all his training would dissolve, perhaps this was the only thing they could do for the greater good of the world.

Navid sat in silence, feeling ill to his stomach as he considered the possibility that maybe nothing would change. He'd be forever cursed. He'd known that was his fate for years and had grown used to it, but it felt as if the reality of it hit him anew all over again.

"I'll help you find him," Tele said.

Navid looked at her. "You will?"

She nodded. "Eventually, the city will have to begin rebuilding. They won't need us here forever. When the time comes, I'll help you. Who knows? Maybe finding your father *will* save you from your curse."

Navid didn't know what to say. "Thank you."

"For the record: I don't think you're cursed at all. You're just different. Forget everything that the prophets told you. Forget everything that you've read about seers. Forget all of it. The prophets, the seers … They're all dead now. You are the only one who can decide if you are cursed. *You*."

Navid wanted to believe that. He really, truly did. But he knew better. He knew what he was. And to deny that would only bring him further pain.

Tele stood suddenly and approached the glass wall. As she did, her blanket fell away, revealing a stunning green evening gown. Navid had only seen her in her travel clothing. Even when they'd arrived in Caldor, she'd continued wearing it. He hadn't even imagined that she could look any different than the mysterious desert traveler that he'd met in the wilderness.

But now, standing before an expanse of black and blue, she was arresting, magnificent.

"There," she pointed. "It's coming again."

Navid stood and approached the glass. A blurry shadow took shape and lightened as it grew into a pale white mass of scales. It drifted near, turning so that he could see the entire length of it. It was larger than any creature he'd ever seen and filled the entirety of his vision. The animal's wings were tucked flush against its body. Its tail flexed broad and powerful, propelling itself through the abyss.

"What is it?" Navid whispered.

"I don't know," Tele said. "Some sort of massive freshwater lizard."

"It's beautiful."

"Beautiful."

He looked at her. She smiled as she studied it before she caught him watching her.

She frowned at him. "You're missing it."

Navid didn't feel as though he was truly missing out on what was most beautiful in the room, but he turned his attention back to the creature.

Tele turned away and fetched her blanket. She tossed it over her shoulders, then gathered the parchment and dipped the pin in a rogue ink jar before scribbling a few notes. "A guardsman offered to wash my clothes after noticing I hadn't changed in a while. I bought this so Amie would stop pestering me about it, and the fabric does little to keep me warm."

"I think you look beautiful in it," Navid said.

"Thank you," she said with a coy smile. "But I think I prefer function over form." She inclined her head toward the creature just outside the room. "Describe as much as you can about it. I'll take notes."

The lights in the room dimmed further as Navid squinted into the darkness. His curse flared in step with a sudden realization that perhaps this is what had grabbed hold of him under the water. He tried to shrug off the chilling fear of confronting it again even from behind the glass.

"It's gray … or perhaps white. Scaled like a lizard but with wings like a bird. There are powerful claws on its legs like a falcon. And—"

Navid's jaw dropped.

"And what?"

"Look!" Navid pointed as Tele came to his side.

They watched together as the reptile became transparent, its body becoming hazy. Then, like a phantom, it dissolved.

"Curious," Tele said. "That's what happened last time."

"How can it do that?"

"I'm not sure," Tele said. "It's unlike any organism I've ever seen. It doesn't seem possible."

Navid suddenly understood why Tele had sequestered herself away when she wasn't helping with the injured. This was something fantastic, novel. "Will it come back?"

"This is the second time that this has happened," she said, looking down to her notes, already engulfed in her thoughts again. "So perhaps if we wait long enough, we'll see it again."

"Can you eat while we wait?" Navid asked, inclining his head to the untouched bowl he'd brought down for her. "I'd make me feel a lot better about it. I'll keep watch for you."

She looked to the bowl as if seeing it for the first time. "Oh. Right. Thank you." And to Navid's relief, she took it this time.

As the memory of the creature swam in his mind, the itch of his curse pricked at his nerves. And without understanding how or why, he knew without a doubt that this was indeed the creature that had pulled him into the deep, that had shattered his ability to control his curse.

Brushing away the feeling with the mental repetition of his mantra, he turned to watch as Tele ate the meal he'd brought down for her. "Is it good?"

"Absolutely," Tele said. "Had I known it wasn't your rabbit dish, I may have indulged when you brought it down."

Navid laughed as he settled before the veil of glass to wait for the lizard to reappear.

EIGHTEEN

A KERNEL OF HOPE

Unable to sleep, Navid opened his eyes. Cast in the cold, silver light of moonlight through the tall skylights above, the room felt frozen, time-locked. The three beds to the left of his were pristine, untouched since they were last used by his seer brothers. The bed just to his left had been Balimerre's—his dorm's older mentor. The other two had belonged to Maeko and Bhasim—the only two seers his same age in the Sanctuary.

Of Ghayan and Sulahnese descent respectively, Maeko and Bhasim had been the first two people he'd ever met who didn't share his Hzorah heritage. Plucked from every corner of the world, the Sanctuary's seers—his brothers and sisters—were not family by blood but by circumstance and by curse. The world beyond these walls feared them, but inside was acceptance.

That was forever gone now.

Navid turned away, choosing to face his dormitory's wall rather than the empty beds. It had taken days for him to accept that his entire life had been stripped away. Now that denial had burned away, he was left with sadness.

When he finally shut his eyes again, he saw Tele. A picture of powerful grace in her elegant dress, she gazed into waters of the Drunn river with intelligent, green eyes. He smiled, remembering her fascination and complete dedication to studying the world around her.

Armed with insatiable curiosity, she denied even sleep in order to fulfill her purpose. And *she* had promised to help him find his father. If she gave even a fraction of the effort she put into solving the puzzles here, he'd find his father for sure. He'd lost what he'd thought to be true with the Kruvs and he'd lost his family at the Sanctuary. Her promise to help him was the only thing that burned through the crushing darkness—a beam of hope in a world of disillusion and despair.

He allowed the vision of her to fill his mind's eye, replaying the evening in his head. He rewatched her as she scratched notes onto parchment, and circled a table full of opened books, searching for a reference that matched her observations. Tele belonged there. Hidden away for years, the room had waited patiently for her to—

Navid opened his eyes and sat up in sudden realization. He'd lived most of life in the Sanctuary, and he'd never given that room a second glance. If that was what was hidden in the open, what was hidden in the restricted regions of the Sanctuary—in Time's Alcove?

The prophets had given the seers the freedom to go anywhere in the Sanctuary except for their private rooms. There were records there about the seers. Balimerre had said so once, saying that the careful record keeping allowed the prophets to track the progress of the seers with their meditations so that they might guide them to better suppress the darkness inside.

With the prophets gone, there was no one to deny him access. Navid had never entertained the idea of violating the rules the prophets put in place for him. Even now, something inside him warned against it.

But they might have records about my father, Navid thought.

He didn't know where to begin looking for his father. The only trail he had to follow had ended cold, leaving him with just a small necklace and no one else to turn to. If there was something—anything that could lead him to his father, he'd be able to fulfill the prophecy. He'd be free of his curse.

Navid stood, pulled on his shoes, and left the memories behind.

Navid walked down Time's Alcove's unfamiliar hall. There were eight entryways that lined the hall—four to either side—leading into the private chambers of the prophets. He wasn't sure which chamber belonged to which prophet or why there were eight. Only three prophets frequented the Sanctuary. Hzorah, Armoth, and Ghaya were the only lands close enough to Caldor to make recurrent visits practical. With Roanne, Sulahn, and the Crehn Isles separated by the Great Sea, their prophet's visits were far between. And, of course, Desera's prophet—Prophet Tristan—remained secluded, beyond the reaches of the Dominion Desert.

That only accounted for seven of the eight. Navid stopped before the final room. None of his studies had said there had been an eighth prophet. Who was this for?

He looked to the end of the hall where a final entryway sat secluded. He turned away from the missing prophet's chambers and approached it. The door wasn't labeled, but it was built wider with dark cherry wood, distinguishing itself from the rest. Taking in a breath of courage, he pushed open the door and stepped inside.

Like the chambers of his dormitory, a wide, foggy skylight opened to the night sky above, letting moonlight fill the room with pale light. Remnants from the disaster that decimated the city, layers of snow rimmed the edges of the ceiling glass and reminded him of the Drunn's ice-covered depths. To one side of the expansive room were a set of doors that led deeper into the Alcove. To the other, a long stretch of books, neatly kept before a long empty table.

Navid crossed to the books. The shelves holding them aloft were labeled by region, then further labeled by year. The books alternated between record and prediction, cataloging the guarded knowledge of the prophets.

Before he could talk himself out of it, he scanned the shelves until he found what he was looking for—a large dark brown volume entitled *Era of Calviere, Year 205 SA*. He pulled the heavy book from the shelf and placed it on the room's table.

He opened the cover and found that the prophets had taken the time to include a directory to preface the book. His finger ran along the names until he found his own: Navid Tevaad. His heart raced as he began turning pages to find his record, careful not to break the delicate pages of older accounts.

Navid paused at Maeko's name. His birthplace was listed along with parents. It went on to chronicle the date of his arrival at the Sanctuary, his appearance, his demeanor, and a careful account of his progress. It was just like Balimerre had said.

A few more pages and he found his own. Like Maeko's, it listed his home: Azuri. It showed his arrival date, his appearance, demeanor, and a monthly account of his development. It did not, however, list his parents. That was instead filled with one hope-crushing word.

Unknown.

"You didn't tell me you were a night reader."

Navid started and looked up. At a doorway on the far side of the room, Gavini stood smiling at him, a walking stick in one hand, and a book in the other. Navid closed the book on the table and straightened.

Gavini stepped into the room. "No need to feel ashamed, Navid. I'm not here to limit your access. In fact, I encourage your exploration." He smiled as he approached the table. "We're all struggling to put the world back together."

Navid nodded. "I still don't understand *how* it fell apart."

"Mmm," Gavini mused and leaned on his staff. "I have a scant theory. What were you looking for?"

"What?"

Gavini nodded toward the book in front of him. "In the Sanctuary records. What were you searching for? These volumes are a bit heavy for late night perusal."

Navid let his hand rest on the book's cover. "I was hoping there was a record of who my father was."

"And?"

"Nothing."

"I see," Gavini said. He lifted the book in his own hand. "I've been doing some searching myself. I may just have found something that'll help solve the mystery of why the prophets sent you to retrieve Tele."

Tele sidestepped, moving from a volume she'd found in the Keeper's library that detailed differentials for magnetic flux to Gavini's *Element and Reaction*. There were clear similarities between the results of the two journals, and she wasn't sure if Gavini's work had been informed by this one or if they'd come to much the same conclusions independently. Due to Gavini's assumptive tone within his own reports, she guessed the former.

She moved yet again to her own notes and compiled what she'd absorbed into a new set of data, collapsing the work into a single, masterful set of equations. When she finished, she set the pen aside, collapsed into a chair, and gazed at her work, trying to visualize what the assortment of symbols meant visually. She frowned as if a serious brow would force her mind to grasp the scope of the collection.

I need to sleep, Tele thought. She'd known that for days. And she *did* sleep; she just didn't get enough of it. She knew well that she needed at least five hours to work at a steady efficiency. She'd whittled that down to four hours when her family had died, then again to three when they'd arrived in Caldor.

Knowing that she needed more sleep and *actually getting* more of it felt irreconcilable. After helping refugees for several hours a day, she filled the rest of her waking time below the

Sanctuary, studying the texts there, attempting to absorb as much knowledge as she possibly could. And while her talent for detailed memorization served her well, understanding what she retained was a separate process. Tele tried to keep the two as balanced as possible.

Letting her notes rest in her lap, she turned to the walls but resisted the temptation to make them transparent. If she did that, she wouldn't finish her notes. She'd be up all night observing the life there. And waiting for the strange, aquatic reptile to return.

Tele stood and paced, letting her mind clear. She watched her dress's skirts flow across the lab floor in the wall's reflection. While she had been resistant to wearing it, she now had a certain appreciation for its design. It allowed for a certain amount of unrestricted freedom and it was easier to equip than the layers she usually wore. Testing its usefulness in this setting was worth the effort. She was supposed to be learning how to adapt to common life, after all.

She paused before a tall, silver water tank and looked at herself in the distorted reflection. Amie had been right about it looking good on her. Tele turned to see what she looked like from the rear. The outfit was far from what she'd consider practical in her former life—a life where stark practicality and invisibility were a matter of survival. Now, far from the reaches of Prophet Tristan, Tele felt free to be noticed.

Navid had certainly noticed. Before she could rein in her imagination, it drifted to her accidental encounter during her river bath. Her stomach warmed and tingled as she vividly recalled contour of him.

Tele turned when the lift at the room's center opened. A refugee stepped off the platform with a bucket, mop, and a pack over her shoulder, stuffed to bulging. She gaped at the room, before looking to Tele.

"Can I help you?" Tele asked.

She lifted the bucket. "I was given the chore of custodial duties now that the Sanctuary staff is mostly gone. A Guardsman told me to clean here next, but I never …" She trailed off before she shook her head, regaining composure. "Oh! And …"

The woman set down the bucket and mop and crossed the room while removing her pack to dig inside. She pulled out Tele's travel clothes and handed them to her. "Some of the Guardsmen asked me to bring these to you."

Tele looked down at the muted tans of practicality, of invisibility. "Thank you."

The woman smiled and crossed back to her bucket. "Don't mind me. I'll be in and out quickly."

Tele set the clothes on the table and retrieved her notes. She went back to *Element and Reaction* and began reading the next passage. After a length of notes about endothermic and exothermic reactions, methods of calculating when they'd occur, and a rather well-developed hypothesis of why they occur, Gavini had moved on to attempting several spell forms that might express their use in magical application.

The runes that Gavini used to construct these spells matched those that she'd seen on the gateway. While she understood some of those runes, these were much more complex, but with some work, she was able to decipher their meaning.

The more difficult task was learning how to pronounce them. Her parents hadn't taught her how to speak the old tongue. Luckily, she'd found a few volumes in the vaults that gave some phonetic translations for certain rune constructions. She hadn't absorbed enough of it to reconstruct the tongue—her research had been too scattered to properly learn anything. There was just so much to discover.

I have to focus on one thing at a time, Tele told herself. *Navid used the* Gateway Abbreviation *to activate the spell. He'd spoken the runes.*

She shut her eyes and tried to relive what he'd said, but she'd been so overwhelmed by the seismic activity that she couldn't recall any of it. She saw him in her mind's eye, standing within the fury, his hair tumbling in the wind … his disarming smile … the warm glow in his eyes …

Focus! She reprimanded herself for getting distracted. *This is important.* But then she found herself distracted by …

That smell … Tele turned to the woman. "The bucket. What's in the bucket?"

The woman paused, confused. "In the bucket?"

"Yes. In the bucket. What are you using to clean the floors?"

"It's what the palace has on hand." She looked down at it. "It's not the most pleasant-smelling cleaning water, but—"

"Take it back up," Tele said. "Find soap and water. This is a lab, and that mixture is highly reactive."

"It's what everyone uses," the woman said. "Hzorah uses it to great success. It's an excellent cleaner, and even other lands are—"

"My lab is different," Tele interrupted. "Do you know how that chemical will react to ammonia?"

"I—"

"Do you know how much ammonia is down here?"

"Well, no. I don't."

Tele crossed the room and pointed to a fair sized vile of pale liquid. "This is more than enough of it. If it were to accidentally react with the chemicals in your bucket, you'd turn the entire room into a death chamber."

The custodian shook her head. "I'm sorry. I wasn't aware."

"Just get it out of here."

The woman flushed red before gathering her things and exiting on the lift. Tele rubbed her eyes as she moved back to the table. She was beginning to get a headache.

Several minutes later, the lift descended again, and Gavini and Navid stepped off the platform.

"What did you do to the custodian?" Gavini asked. "She hurried past us in a huff of fury."

Tele sighed. "I told her to use soap and water to clean. Not the cleaning agent she was using." When Gavini gave her a knowing look, she added: "I suppose that I could have informed her with a more … gentle tone."

"She looked like she might cry," Navid said. "You still haven't slept have you?"

Tele turned to her notes and tidied them. "What makes you think that?"

"The more exhausted you are," Navid said, "the more likely you are to point a knife at me. Or make someone cry."

Tele turned to face him. "Alright. I can't disagree with you there. I'll apologize."

"You should really get more sleep, Tele." Navid crossed his arms. "I'm worried about you. You can't keep pushing yourself like this. Upsetting the new Sanctuary staff will be the least of what might go wrong."

Navid wasn't wrong about that. Tele could feel her thoughts beginning to scatter, her strangle on her emotions unraveling. She needed to rest.

"I hope you didn't come down merely to harass me about sleeping," Tele said. "I'm fine."

"Gavini has an idea about what really happened here in Caldor."

That caught Tele's attention. "Really?"

Gavini nodded. "I suspect that the creatures that attacked the city are somehow linked to magic."

Tele turned away and approached the glass partition. She placed a hand on the surface and whispered the word to herself. "Magic ..."

"But how?" Navid asked. "How did the prophets not see it coming? The prophets are sensitive to calamity. They prepare each land for coming disasters. In some cases, they've even come up with a way to solve it. Nothing like this could have been overlooked. They even knew about the Deseran Dominion preparing an army to attack Hzorah. Why didn't they do anything to stop it? Or at least warn the city's forces?"

"That," Gavini said, "is a critical point of evidence to my theory. A ripple in time."

"I'm afraid I don't understand," Navid said.

"These creatures were not of this world," Gavini continued. “There was an event—an event of constructed magic—that distorted their ability to see it coming.”

“You’re saying,” Navid said, “that some magic was triggered to cloud their vision of the future?”

“Yes and no.” He straightened. “Magic events *themselves* cloud the future. They create ripples through Desolate, distorting time and its potential eventualities. Pulling potential—the energy that fuels magic—from Desolate and into existence rattles the continuum of what is and what isn’t. It creates a ripple effect that affects the very fabric of existence. As the event of magic settles, it clears again. Much like when you disturb a basin of water. Your view through it becomes distorted until the ripples settle. The distortion is clearly noticeable, but it doesn’t happen until the magic is triggered.”

Navid sighed. “I’m trying to follow you. I really am. But this is all so confusing.”

Tele turned back to them. “Navid, remember what you told me when we first met? How removing one creature from the Borderland Forests might ripple outward and change the ecosystem to varying degrees?”

Navid rubbed his chin. “Yes.”

“This is similar. This is a ripple effect.” She crossed back to them. “Imagine if you were walking down a forest path and every step you took, the forest changed. A tree appeared right before you. A nest of hornets appeared underfoot. It would be disorienting and deeply troubling.

“Magic causing a ripple in time is like this for the prophets. They can see the flow of time, but magic creates events that break causality—like a tree appearing out of nowhere. Nothing makes sense anymore, and the flow of time distorts as reality rushes to catch up and mend the causal discrepancies.”

Gavini nodded. “That’s a much too literal description, but I think it describes the problem well enough for the purposes of understanding the issue.”

“So, what triggered the magic?” Navid asked.

Gavini shrugged. “It could have been a timed spell, but that doesn’t seem likely as I can’t imagine what purpose the spell would have served. More likely, the creatures existed for some time now, since before Wizard Titan left, and only now revealed themselves."

It was far from secret how powerful the Wizard had been. The very city they now stood in had been built by him without a single hand tasked to help. It was as if—according to the Prophets—the city had risen from out of the forests itself. With powers so vast, even this fell within that realm of possibility.

"So, the creatures are magical," Tele mused as she looked back to the glass and rested a finger across her lips. "I hadn't considered the possibility of that, but it certainly helps explain how the one we saw could simply disappear."

"Actually, that's only the beginning." Gavini said. "I wanted to show you something else." He set a fair-sized book before her. "I had to do a bit of digging. But I found it."

Tele read the title. *The Seed*. She looked at Gavini. "What is the Seed?"

"The Seed is the spell Wizard Titan constructed in order to escape the bounds of time and space. It's how he left the world as we know it."

"I'm not sure I understand what that means," Tele said.

Gavini eased down into a chair. "Well, according to this, it's a rather unique bit of magic. It was constructed in order to contain Titan's power. In order to do that, it draws on life itself—all life—to remain stable. That's how it maintains its power while Titan is absent. Otherwise, the spell would have ceased to function as soon as Titan tried to contain himself within it."

"The gateway book," Tele said, looking to Navid. "I think it's using a clever design to continue to function without Wizard Titan's power. I haven't studied it, but I'm assuming it works because of a temporal trigger. Somehow, a spell was constructed that loops back on itself in time, continuously feeding on Titan's power from a certain instance long ago. Though the Wizard is gone, the spell is fueled by Titan's power from the time it was made—a clever loophole by creation of a literal loop."

Navid shrugged. "Tele, I honestly can't pretend to follow you."

"A brilliant deduction, Tele," Gavini said. "I once had an abbreviation that worked that way, but I haven't seen it in quite some time. However, the Seed is different. I believe Titan found a different work-around for this spell because his standby method failed."

Tele crossed her arms. "So, where is this Seed?"

"With the Tal tribe," Gavini said. He tapped the book's cover with a finger. "The prophets were diligent enough to record what they knew of the Seed."

"The Tal?" Navid asked. "I've never heard of such a people."

"Nor would you have if the prophets had not fallen and fate had not brought us together," Gavini said. "That was the next part of Wizard Titan's plan. He enlisted the help of a remote people to protect his vessel. As long as the Seed remains hidden away and untapped, the Tal are protected from the wider world. One can only find them under two conditions. First, they must know that they exist. And second, they must approach without ill intent in their hearts."

"That seems like a rather subjective standard." Tele frowned.

"I agree," Gavini said. "It would be rather simple to sidestep if one was clever enough. But here's where things get interesting …" Gavini revealed a ledger he'd carried in under his arm. "It appears that there has been correspondence recently between the prophets and the Tal."

Tele took the ledger out of Gavini's hands and began scanning it as Gavini went on. "They've reported back to the prophets that something has gone wrong with the Seed and has requested that they send a Keeper to them to repair the problem."

Tele's attention left the parchment to meet Gavini's gaze. "Me?"

Gavini nodded. "I can only assume so. The prophets exerted a great effort to find you in a vast wasteland. They enlisted the help of a seer and they allowed him to use a powerful spell to locate and retrieve you. *This* must have been the reason. But, as fate would have it, they perished before they could tell you what they needed of you."

Tele's mind reeled as she tried to absorb everything her uncle told her. Her parents hadn't thought that Wizard Titan's disappearance was truly a disappearance at all. Even her father's dying wish was for her to find the Wizard.

"*You must keep the Covenant safe. Find the true Wizard and deliver it to him! Run, my child! Run!*"

"Do you know how to repair the Seed?" Tele asked Gavini. "What's wrong with it?"

"I'm afraid not," Gavini said. "The magic of the Seed is far beyond my knowledge. From what is written, it appears that the influence the Seed exerts on the forest is deteriorating, but it neglects to describe *what* that influence is."

"Maybe they didn't need to describe what was already understood between them. They probably didn't expect that they'd have to leave a note behind for us." Tele opened the book Gavini had found and flipped through the pages aimlessly. "And how are we supposed to find—"

She paused when she reached a map. To the left side, along the shore of a vast ocean was marked The Backbone. To the right, a great city: Caldor. And in between, outlined with a red circle in the corner of the vast borderland forests, was the Tal, nestled between the two branching legs of the Everwisp River.

Navid stepped close behind her. "That's deep into the Borderlands. Those reaches are largely unexplored and uninhabited. Or so I thought."

Tele tapped the page and looked at Navid. "How far away is that?"

"I'm not entirely sure," Navid said, frowning. "Could be anywhere from twenty to forty days, depending on the terrain."

"Terrain isn't going to be a problem." Gavini smiled. "I believe you have something that will get you there rather quickly."

"The Gateway." Navid's golden eyes brightened. "The book is in my pack. I'll go get it."

When Navid ascended out of the room, Gavini turned to Tele. He watched her for a moment, a curious smile spreading across his face. Tele suppressed a smile.

"What?" she asked.

"You didn't strike me as someone who might wear a dress," he said.

Tele shrugged. "I had to wear something while my clothes were being cleaned."

"It's striking how much you resemble your mother," Gavini said. He folded his hands and looked about the room. "I'd always dreamed of bringing her and your father here. The work we could have done together, the discoveries we could have made ..." He trailed off before catching Tele's eye. "Even without Wizard Titan, we could have changed the world."

"'Helping others where they can't help themselves,'" Tele said, quoting her father. "'Providing insight to those who have none. Solving problems in the unique ways that only the true Wizard can.'"

Gavini smiled. "'That's our role as Keepers of the Covenant.' I'm pleased that Abigail and Huvil taught you so well. When we decided to go to Caldor, I wasn't entirely sure what we'd find, but I knew that I had to do what I could to protect you. When we arrived, in the aftermath of such ravage destruction, my first instinct was to help. It made me remember how important the Keepers are—how much good we could do. Amidst all the pain and loss, we've been given a kernel of hope. Out of which, a new era can grow. The Keepers can finally return."

The lift opened and Navid rushed in with his pack. He stopped before them, his eyes wide and wild, clutching the pack in trembling hands. As if attempting to speak, he opened his mouth but said nothing.

"What's wrong?" Tele asked.

"It's gone." Navid's voice trembled. "The Gateway spell. It's gone."

Tele and Gavini shared a confused look. "How?" she asked. "It's been in your pack all this time."

"I know," Navid said. "The last time I used it was to bring you to the Borderlands. I haven't so much as *looked* at it since." He turned the pack inside out, spilling its contents across the floor. "I kept it in this compartment here." He lifted a flap and pulled out a thin wooden block the size of the book. "When I checked for it upstairs, this was what filled the space."

"Is anything else missing?" Gavini asked.

Navid rummaged around the pack, opening a few other compartments. "A few things. Some ointments, a flask … That's it, I believe."

Tele felt chilled to the bone. How could this have happened? They'd kept to themselves for the majority of the journey. Only in Caldor had they left their possessions unattended.

Tele caught Navid's eyes. "Maybe it was one of the refugees?"

"Perhaps," Gavini said. "I'm not sure that any of them would know where to find the seer's rooms."

"They wouldn't have been looking for them in particular," Tele said. "It could have been purely coincidental."

"Wouldn't the Guardsmen have known if anyone was wandering the halls?" Gavini rubbed his chin.

"I don't know," Tele said. "I'm not really sure if they've kept them strictly isolated from the rest of the Sanctuary. I've been so absorbed with treating them and my work down here that I didn't even think to consider that."

"I can have Guardsman Ruggles assist us in a search," Gavini said.

Tele looked at Navid who stood frozen, mute. She crossed over to him. "Navid?"

His spell broken, Navid looked at her before shaking his head, the wooden block still clutched in his hand. "I don't understand."

"I don't either," Tele placed a hand on his arm. "We'll do a search of the Sanctuary and see what we come up with."

Tele rubbed her eyes as she sat back in the chair. She'd resigned herself to a mere hour of sleep, and it hadn't been nearly enough to keep herself working at full efficiency. The distant memory of a fully rested state tempted her to shut her eyes for just a moment, but before she could give in to the temptation, the lift opened, and she heard Gavini and Navid step off of the platform behind her.

"Nothing," Navid breathed. "They haven't found any sign of the book."

Too tired to stand, she merely shifted in the large, amorphous seat so that she could see them. "Did they question any of the refugees?"

"About two dozen of them," Navid said. "All of the ones who have been given a measure of freedom to move about the Sanctuary to assist the guardsmen. I feel almost sick. I barely slept—"

Tele resisted the urge to remark on what barely sleeping *really* was. "What's the next step?"

"Well," Gavini said. "Chief Guardsman Ruggles appointed three of his guardsmen to the task of continuing the search after I impressed upon him the seriousness of the matter, but he couldn't spare more men than that to the effort."

Tele was surprised the guardsman could afford even that. He'd been split one hundred different ways as of late, and she was certain he'd lost just as much sleep as she had. "That sounds reasonable."

"And what about your search?" Navid asked Tele. "Were you able to find anything in that book about what the prophets or the Tal expected you to do?"

She rubbed her temples. "Simply put: no."

"Humor an old man, and complicate your answer for me?" Gavini asked with a facetious smile.

Tele shut *The Seed* and let it rest in her lap. "This book confirms what we talked about. The Wizard using a spell to functionally end his immortality, how he tasked the Tal people to protect the vessel he'd used to contain his magic. But this text is frightfully thin on any specifics about how the spell functions. But I suppose it did reveal a few details of interest. Chief among them is that the Seed has a Dissolution."

Navid's expression twisted in confusion. "A what?"

"A trigger to end the spell," Tele said. Unsettled by her simplification, she added, "in this case, at least."

"Hmm." Navid ran a hand through his hair. "Is that what you think the Tal wanted?"

Tele shook her head. "I'm almost certain they wanted the exact opposite. But, as I said, I have no direction on how to perform a repair on a spell, especially one of this complexity."

"Nor do I," Gavini said. "Which severely limits our options to two paths: do nothing or invoke the Dissolution. Does the text give a description of what happens if we do the latter?"

"Again," Tele said. "It is vague on the specifics—likely because the prophets don't understand the magic involved themselves—but it does involve the magic contained within the Seed returning to a physical form. A reincarnation of Titan of sorts. In the prophets' notes, it appears that the reincarnation is placed within an already living vessel."

"Meaning the return of Wizard Titan," Gavini said.

"In a sense," Tele said. "It won't literally be the same person but a continuation of his magic. Just in case a great enough need arose."

Navid, shifting his gaze between the two of them, broke his silence. "I'm experienced with magic, but does this constitute a 'great enough need?' The Wizard left under mysterious circumstances, but who would do that to themselves without a very good reason? Maybe he didn't want to be reincarnated. Maybe this isn't the reason the Dissolution exists."

"I'm not sure a greater need could arise," Tele said. "There's war brewing from the Dominion in order to bring the Wizard back to life, there's great lizards encasing entire cities in ice roving the land, and for the first time in perhaps all of history, we have no prophets to help us see our way to the other side of all this."

Gavini nodded. "I'm afraid I agree. Times are desperate."

Navid sighed. "Right. Of course, you're right."

"But I don't think we should wait to see what the guardsmen uncover to take the leap and journey to the Tal," Gavini said. "There's a good chance that they find The Gateway book, but there's also a chance that they don't. The Sanctuary is vast and it could very well take months to find a single object if it's well hidden. And that's time we can't afford to lose."

"It could take some time to reach the Tal," Navid said. "No one has properly mapped that area of the world. We know that it's there, but it's thickly forested, and all who have ventured there have never returned."

Tele nodded looking back to Navid. "So it takes us a bit longer to get there. And it's potentially life threateningly dangerous. Seems like that's where we thrive as of late." She smiled as Navid met her eyes. "Come now, don't tell me you're too tired. I *did* promise to make trouble for you when we first met."

Slowly, Navid smiled. "We'll go. But only after you get some sleep."

NINETEEN

A SHADOW AMONGST THE DARKNESS

General Darius Gareth studied the maps spread before him. A single thick candle aided the war tent's skylight as the sun sunk beneath the horizon. He chewed a strip of re-hydrated lamb while he listened to the rising, insect drone of the dkrica's song.

He looked to his guard, who shifted, allowing his other leg to take the burden of his post. He'd been on duty for the past three hours and it was near time for his shift to end. *I may as well make use of him.*

"Get me a second candle," Gareth said, turning his attention back to the maps. He heard his leather armor squeak in compliance before cool air slipped into the tent to replace his departure.

His gaze traced the curved spine of the Shadow Peaks. His troops were nearly in position. Nearly twenty thousand men would end there, but he only needed ten thousand to begin his campaign. His last relay reported a headcount of seventy-eight hundred.

Prophet Tristan took special care to ration their forces in small intervals as to not attract the attention of the prophets until it was too late. This also meant the supply strain across the desert would grow in a manageable measure. Beyond that, there was said to be places within the Dominion Desert where misstep and overweight could trigger a whirlpool of sand, swallowing up all within. Gareth had not seen such a phenomenon himself, but he saw little reason to test his doubt.

Ten years since the Dominion began planning. Ten months since their troops finally began moving. Ten hours since Gareth smelled the first, sweet fragrance of revenge.

Hzorah was more troublesome than he'd imagined. The whole kingdom was full of the wicked. In his days within their borders, he'd not met one soul who was loyal to the Creed. Prophet Tristan had warned him of such infidelity, but he hadn't believed it. *How could so many turn their backs to the Wizard?*

Even Azuri had been corrupted. Most of the city had been of the Ehrel tribe, and they too had been stripped of their beliefs.

He'd had to make some changes.

He left Lieutenant Farrin and Owen behind in Azuri with a few men to root out the rest of Domis and Ronzit's families. Forced to speak at sword point, they would reveal what they knew of the rumors he'd heard of the old Keeper and the family who was sympathetic to him. The man was old and alone. He'd have sought out someone who he could trust with his life's work and trained them to continue where he would leave off. While it was preferable to have the Keeper's knowledge in a format that didn't require food and water, that option had been taken from him, and his prophet had left him instructions to retrieve the knowledge even if it required bringing back the Keeper himself.

Gareth had hesitated to delegate the task to someone else, but there were other preparations to be made, and he couldn't possibly handle them all himself. Prophet Tristan had explicitly instructed Owen's placement as his left hand, and while Gareth could not—would not—defy a direct order from his prophet, he didn't have to keep the Bamilee lapdog at his side either. At least he had Lieutenant Farrin to spearhead the mission. With him along, even Owen couldn't botch the job.

Then Gareth smiled, remembering his meeting with the

Hzorah Lords. Disguised as a diplomat, he'd walked among them without fear of them attempting to kill him on the spot. It was unnecessary for him to go himself, but he'd wanted to see the prince and High Lords' faces and dedicate them to memory. He'd watched their eyes sink back in terror. He saw clenched fists and sweaty brows and the soft grinding of teeth. Hung thick as morning fog, he could have breathed their fear. And that in itself could have been reason enough to risk going before them.

And then he saw him—the heir of the heathen who'd stolen his father away from him. It'd taken all his will to not draw the steel of a bumbling Hzorah guard and strike him down at that very moment. But he'd heeded the wisdom and held his peace like a well-behaved diplomat should.

He'd spoken lightly, despite the broiling inside. A glance in the fool prince's direction made him question if the boy was listening at all. He just sat there like he was king of the world. As if Desolate had given him birthright to power. He would soon see true power.

And I'll be the one to show him, he thought as he absently caressed his sheathed sword.

YOU WILL HAVE YOUR REWARD, GARETH.

He would have his. He nodded, agreeing with the phantom's wisdom.

"My General?" a voice from outside the tent interrupted his thoughts.

"Enter."

A ranked soldier crossed inside and fell to a knee and fist. "My General, the Crown has sent a messenger in response to your visit."

"A negotiator?" Gareth leaned back, taking in the news.

"I do not believe so, My General." He kept his gaze to the ground. "Just a simple messenger, it would appear."

"Send him in."

"Yes, My General," the officer said before rising and exiting the tent.

Gareth stood and began pacing. He'd known that this

would come, but it was still, to an extent, unnerving. He'd given an ultimatum; one that was undeniably vile.

The people of Hzorah were wicked and they had pride in their wickedness, but after the attack on Caldor, he could only see them backing down. It would wound their ego, but it was the only course that would save their land. They would surrender if they cared at all for their people. The Creed's purpose could not be stopped.

To ensure that they would see reason, he'd given them a short span of time to respond. No time to overthink or puff up their chests. No time to gather the opinions of other officials throughout the land.

Gareth had been raised to believe that the wicked would see the light when it was placed before them so clearly. The wisdom had told him otherwise, but he had to believe it. It was the only thing the phantoms were wrong about.

He'd told Prophet Tristan as much. The prophet only smiled and said, "We can only hope you are correct, General." His smile and tone said he didn't believe Gareth.

He took another turn around the tent before he stopped to lean over the maps once more. His eyes fell over the lands of Ghaya and Armoth where there would be other Dominion missionaries. Gareth himself was only one piece of the grand design. He was the primary piece, but still just one. The Creed would break the world and give rise to the Great Wizard. The Wizard would see that they'd changed their ways and come back to them.

He had to believe it.

"Enter!" Gareth said, hearing the escort outside before they announced themselves. He moved to the center of the tent where he could hold the dominant position.

His officer led a young man inside. His eyes were wide—a mix of awe and fear. Gareth had seen that look a thousand times over. From new recruits to the Desolate-bound he'd tasked in Azuri, they all shared the same expression when met with men who had noble cause. He watched as the boy wagged his fingers, fighting desperately to find his courage.

Gareth held his amusement behind dark eyes. "What message has the Crown delivered? I do hope it is of good report."

"The Crown requested—" He paused, swallowing to moisten a cracking voice. "The Crown has requested a second meeting in which the Lords might discuss further terms of diplomacy."

Gareth's amusement wavered. Hzorah was trying to delay their decision. He'd shown them the light and they'd rejected it. Just like the wisdoms said they would.

The image of the young prince flashed in his mind's eye once more. This was *his* doing. He knew it.

He turned his back to the messenger. He shut his eyes and pulled a fist to his chest. "When is this meeting to occur?"

"In two weeks."

His fist shook. It was right again. It was always right. He'd opened himself to follow wisdom, but for one belief. And even in this most basic of truths, he was wrong. Hzorah had no heart for its people.

Pulling his belt knife, Gareth turned and lunged. His blade found the messenger's throat and slid deep into his airway. He caught the man by his shirt, keeping him from falling to the tent floor. His life warmed his hand and trailed his forearm.

He pulled the wide-eyed youth close. "Tell the Crown I have a message."

Gareth pulled and sawed, wrenching the knife up under the soft of the man's chin and to the point of his jaw-bone. With a swift jerk, he pulled the knife free. The man sunk heavier against his grip, and Gareth finally allowed gravity's pull. Thrashing about, the messenger stained his tent. He cocked his head and watched as the man descended into Desolate.

Filth. And now that filth had stained his tent. *What a waste.*

VERY GOOD.

He didn't allow the wisdom the satisfaction of agreement. Instead, he turned to his officer who simply watched with raised eyebrows.

"Permission to speak freely, My General?" he said.

Gareth grunted approval before turning to find his damp towel.

"Have you ever heard the saying 'Don't kill the messenger?'"

"I will *not*," Gareth said, wiping away the filth that stained his arm, "be played for a fool by the wicked. I did as Prophet Tristan asked. I gave them a chance to surrender. I'm no longer responsible for their fate."

The soft sound of fabric ushered in another soldier. "My General—" He paused in knee-jerk reaction to the unexpected corpse. "My General, the candle supply has been depleted."

Like lightning, Gareth turned, letting another knife fly. It tore into the tent fabric just right of the guard's head. He let the last few raging breaths pant from his lungs as the two soldiers watched in shock. And then there was silence.

He turned back around and dabbed his forehead with the cleanest part of the reddened brown cloth. He allowed the wisdom to refill him, letting it push out the anger. The wisdom had proven itself true once again. He hated it, but it was correct. He would never doubt it again.

His nerves calmed, he turned back to his audience. "Remove this filth from my tent. Be sure that he's returned to the palace immediately. I don't want them thinking we didn't respond in a timely manner."

"Yes, My General," the officer and guard said.

Gareth tossed the tainted cloth aside and slid back into his chair. The two men shuffled the dead weight from the tent. He pulled his ink and parchment from below the table and dipped his pen. First a message to Prophet Tristan, then one to his troops. It was time to take action.

It was time for revenge.

Gabriel kicked off the sheets after thirty minutes of wishing didn't close the curtains on the far wall. Though his window faced the west, the sun's light felt omnipresent. Gabriel rolled onto his feet. He was going to be late.

He slipped on the same trousers and shirt from the night before and masked its age with a new morning coat of navy blue. No one seemed to notice when he did this. Either they feared to point it out or didn't care to. No one noticed except Marium. It was best he leave before she decided to pay a visit and pick clothes for him.

The halls were deadly still with evening candles still lit and a hint of morning dew where windows invited fresh air. Gabriel halted as a small group of Low Lords crossed from the breakfast hall and toward the court. They chatted around the topic of West Hzorah wheat and the allocation of resources.

He suddenly had second thoughts about the Breakfast Hall. Risking Prisha's wrath seemed somehow preferable to eating with the Lords. Worse yet, he wasn't keen on sitting across from the new Bendeth advisor and his cheating pupils. Finding the nearest hidden panel, Gabriel pushed it inward and stepped into the landing beyond.

He descended into the palace innards between two narrow-set walls, his hands sliding along them for balance. The right wall was lined with inset candles at about every ten steps or so, unlit now that the early morning sun poured down the passage from the skylight above.

Gabriel cut right after reaching the hall below. As expected, the scent of tasteful bliss strengthened, and he swallowed in anticipation of fulfillment. He pushed the kitchen door open and stepped inside.

Silence greeted him. Not complete silence, but the silence of a staff disheartened.

Gabriel took hold of the sleeve of one of the passing cooks. "What's going on?"

The man turned. It was Peer, the same older cook from the previous day. His lips were half-pursed, and his eyes darted as if searching for safety. "The court, Prince Gabriel. The High Lords have declared a draft of fifty percent of all youths who've seen sixteen years."

"A draft?" Gabriel questioned the man's certainty. The Crown has never once forced a citizen into war. By the very nature of their people, the army was sizable with many who wished to keep their people safe. "Why a draft?"

The man only shook his head with mouth ajar as if to respond: 'you're the leader, not me.'

Why wasn't I informed? An order must have been issued that night, outside of the court's proceedings. *They could have awoken me.*

King Jeremiah had limited their forces to only men who had seen enough years to have taken their mark. Drafting young men who hadn't seen twenty years directly contradicted a Directive from the Crown.

But did his father's word hold any sway now, especially now that they were in a time of war?

"Did any of the kitchen staff get drafted?" Gabriel asked. "Any of the staff's children?"

He pointed across the kitchen to where a small congregation of workers stood, encircling what he guessed were the workers who'd been affected. Gabriel thanked the man before letting go of his sleeve.

He drifted across the kitchen, frowning as he heard a mix of whispers and weeping. The group was tightly packed, huddling close in a protective cocoon. He touched shoulders and wedged between layers of kitchen staff until he reached the center.

In the middle, Prisha sat on a short stool. She held her wooden spoon in one hand and a tear-stained cloth in the other. Gabriel turned to the cook beside him. The man averted his eyes before turning and making his way through the throng of comforters.

Gabriel stepped into the center and knelt to meet the head cook's eyes. He took her hand before she looked at him. "Prisha, I'm so sorry about this."

Prisha shook her head. "No, no. It's not your fault. What must be, must be." She dabbed her eyes. "But I'm afraid. He has known nothing but the palace. He knows nothing but food.

He cannot fight. I've seen him run from bugs … I …" Her words slipped into tears.

Gabriel fought for the right thing to say. What would his father say? "I will do everything I can to make sure your son is placed somewhere where he'll be safe. Even the army needs cooks."

Prisha let go of a small chuckle between tears before she nodded. He rubbed her hand before standing. He'd never seen her in a state like this. In a few days' time, Prisha's whole world had changed. *His* whole world had changed. And there was nothing he could do about it.

No, there was something he could do.

It was as if for the first time since his father died, he had a moment of stark clarity. He felt as though he knew what he had to do all along, but now that someone close to him had been hurt by this war, he knew with absolute certainty.

Gabriel pushed back through the onlookers and crossed the kitchen to where a few cooks packed preserves. "Excuse me," he said, catching their attention. They turned, two women and one man—all three somewhat surprised at the interruption. "I need to grab some bread and some meat. Wait. Maybe some preserves—some food that won't easily spoil. I'll need enough fill a large pack."

The cooks shared a look before one took the lead. "Go grab some bread and grains," she said, nodding to the cook to her right. "You, jerky and dried fruit." They both complied. She turned and pulled three jars from the shelf. "Is three fine?"

Gabriel nodded.

"Why the food?" she asked. "We're not feeding you good enough in the kitchen?"

"No," he said, shifting his weight. "I lost a bet with a couple of the guards. Said I couldn't make two shaft shots in a row. I thought I could win it, but I didn't. I lost. So, I owe them some extra food. They really just want the preserves, but I figured I'd do them one better, you know?"

"Of course," she said.

The other two returned with their portions wrapped in

sheets of thin cloth. Gabriel thanked them and tucked the food under his arms. He crossed the kitchen again and found a sizeable wheat sack. He placed the food inside and shouldered it.

After looking back for a short moment, Gabriel turned and headed for the kitchen's exit.

He took an uncommon route back to his room. The first portion was spent within the servant halls, the second in the secondary halls. Not only did the route save a bit of time, but also saved him from interacting with anyone who might be crossing the palace.

He immediately began pulling clothes from his closet when he entered his room. Why did he have so many fancy clothes? He almost always avoided them to a piece. Why would they keep stocking them?

He stuffed the plainest wears he could find in the sack. Then turned to survey the room, looking for anything else he might need. His eyes caught Seth's in the far corner. He held a book which he closed.

"Where are you off to?" Seth's eyes narrowed, taking some of their youthful glow with it.

Gabriel stood paralyzed for a moment. He didn't even notice Seth when he entered. He shuffled through a dozen different responses before he settled on one. He may as well stay consistent. "I'm off to settle a bet."

"You're leaving, aren't you?" Seth said, looking down at the sack.

Gabriel turned and stuffed a small pillow inside to top off the contents. So much for leaving by cover of alibi. "I am."

"You can't leave Gabe, what—"

"I *can* leave, and I *will*!" He rounded on his brother, then exhaled, calming. "I have to. You've seen me in the court. I'm useless there. I have no skill as a king aside from filling out a chair. I only belong one place and that's out on the field."

Seth's scowl deepened. "But Father wouldn't approve."

"Well, Father's dead now, isn't he?"

Seth fell silent at that.

Gabriel sighed, and let the sack sink to the floor. He crossed the room. Leaning against the wall where Seth sat, he slid down beside him. "I'm sorry, but Father isn't here to stop me, and I think that might be the best thing that could have happened to me. I'm supposed to be king, right? Shouldn't a king actually lead his men to victory instead of staying behind? Father did it. Father's father did it. How can I send my men to die if I'm not willing to suffer the same fate?"

Seth held fast to his tongue, looking away.

"You're going to cluck, aren't you?" Gabriel said.

"No," Seth said.

Gabriel stood and placed a hand on his brother's shoulder. "Look, you don't have to worry about me. I'm not going to die out there. I promise you that. But I'd rather die in battle than waste my talents listening to petty affairs and power games. I have to do this. For the good of Hzorah. For the honor of our name." He pulled his brother into an embrace. "I love you, Seth."

"I love you, too," he said.

Letting go, Gabriel crossed back to his sack and shouldered it once more. He took in the room again, halfway searching for a way that he could make this moment seem a bit less uncomfortable. "I'll see you soon," he said and then exited.

He closed the door behind him and began his death march, letting the hall's silence give rise to guilt. He knew that what he told his brother was fluff—what every warrior tells his family before he steps out the door to never see them again. If Seth had half a mind, he'd know it himself. But he knew that if he didn't do this, he'd regret it forever. He couldn't turn back.

Gabriel stopped before his father's study. He peered inside to the hollow vessel. The fire wasn't lit. He crossed inside, breathing in a fresh pine scent. Standing before the Crown Sabre once more, he lifted it from its stand.

This was the sword that was passed down to him. This was the sword wielded to drive back the same horde that threatened them now. Gabriel was going to make sure that the Desolate-bound Creed was pushed out. If he didn't, all that his forefathers had done would be for nothing. This was his duty.

The sword deserved to be put into play again. He'd never seen a finer weapon. It was made for what he was about to do. It was a waste to leave it here as a trophy, a mockery of what it once was. His father would have to forgive him this. He slipped it down the side of the sack then left the study behind.

Gabriel emerged from the service passages near the transport yard on the western side of the Crown Palace. He crossed between barrels and crates holding palace supplies and paused at the edge of the last shipment, just out of sight to the distributors and workers beyond.

The men passed barrels from the cart to the delivery bay, griping about the draft as they worked. The barrels were small enough for a single person to shoulder or stash underarm—likely wine or erida barrels from the north. Gabriel arched around the edge of the loading bay's supply line, just behind the last layer.

If he waltzed out of the front door, the palace guard would note his leaving, and Samuel would send for his retrieval before he'd put a good distance between them. There was the chance that they wouldn't find him, but if they did, Gabriel wouldn't have the upper hand if he tried for it a second time.

But the wine cart could be his ticket out.

Once he disappeared, an extensive search of the palace proper would be the first move. That could take hours before they even considered spreading wide. The princes had rarely ventured outside of the palace grounds, so they wouldn't anticipate this. Hours in a cart meant an accelerated pace in a not-so-obvious hiding spot. Not to mention a free ride back north.

Gabriel rounded the delivery bay where two horses stood, waiting for their payload to be relieved. There was no driver in the box seat. That was one concern cleared. And because of how the cart was covered—shielding a direct line of sight from the box seats to the payload—they wouldn't be able to look back and see him.

He approached the horses slowly. Horses unaccustomed to war could easily be spooked, especially from strangers. He had to proceed carefully and win their trust if he wanted to get in close without the workers noticing.

"Hello, boy," Gabriel whispered in his sweetest voice. The horses perked, though their expressions were somewhat wary. "How are you?"

As they relaxed, he took another step forward. He held out a hand and offered them a sniff. His presence accepted, he followed with comforting pats, reassuring them of his good intentions.

"I'll be back with your note," a man with the loading staff said.

"Alright, thank you," another replied.

Gabriel peered around each side of the cart. He pulled back when he saw the two drivers coming from the left. Crouched, he slowly rounded to the right of the carriage and circled opposite their approach. He waited until he heard the first take to the mounting steps before he swung his sack up into the rear of the cart. It landed softly, which meant it was lined with padding. Lucky.

When the two had both taken their seats on the cart, Gabriel slowly stepped onto the rear cart mounting step. A creak of stress whispered in response. He clenched his teeth as he waited for the worst, but the drivers didn't respond to the noise. He pulled himself the rest of way into the cart.

Shaded from the warm spring sun, the cart was cool and dark. The cart bed was lined in a layer of bale hay that pricked at Gabriel's skin, but he could care less. He'd done it. Now he'd just have to sit and wait. He settled in, lying on his stomach.

"Excuse me," a voice called from the cart's rear. It was a palace counter. "I'm sorry, but I think we might have missed a barrel. Our count was thirty-nine of the Erida Velvet."

Gabriel lay frozen. The cart slightly swayed as a driver dismounted. Footsteps crossed around on the left. He took in a fist full of hay as he waited for the cart's gate to open and reveal his hiding spot.

"No bother!" another voice called. "We found it misplaced with the Erida West Cherry."

"Very good. I'm sorry about that," the counter said. "I should have known it was a miscount."

"It's fine." The steps rounded back again, and the driver mounted.

Gabriel exhaled, and the cart swayed as it pulled away from the palace yard. He shifted to kneeling so that he could see out of the rear. His home was already beginning to shrink with distance.

"This will be the last one, I think," one driver said to the other. "From what I'm hearing about this war, I don't think trade can be sustained."

The other grunted. "They took my son already. The boy's only sixteen. What else can they take from me now?"

It was louder this time, like glass breaking.

Amie opened her eyes, taking in the darkness around her. She'd tried to ignore it before. She had rolled over and discounted it as wind. She knew what her father or sister would say if she tried to wake them. It was always the same thing. And they were always right.

But this time was different. She was sure of it. The wind rarely broke glass and the nearest tree was on the far side of the courtyard adjacent to the inn.

The wind can't be that strong tonight.

Amie pulled off her blanket and rushed the window. One landing up, her family's rooms overlooked Azuri where most constructs were only one landing. She peered down to the empty street below. A few leaves lie scattered and waiting to be swept away with the morning traffic. They were dead still, weighed down by the late-night rain.

Clutching the hem of her nightgown, she turned back to see her sister's even breathing. She knew that if she woke her, she would be angry. It was usually best not to poke the bear and Mara could be a real bear when awoken unnecessarily. Her father would be asleep at this hour. If she went to him, he would be far less likely to respond with anger, but he wouldn't exactly be happy with her, either.

Amie had nearly seen seventeen years, and she was certainly capable of investigating on her own.

She tiptoed across the cool wooden floor and pressed herself against the bedroom door. Ear flush to the wood, Amie strained to hear if any other movement came from the outside. She pulled back. Nothing. She caught sight of one of Gavini's tall walking sticks leaning against the door frame and grabbed it. Wild dog, rat, or spider: she'd have a better chance fending them off with a good stick.

The door softly creaked as she pulled it in, and the hall's cool air flooded her room, washing over her feet. Amie shivered before stepping out into the hall and shutting the door behind her. Shielding her torso from the torrent of chill, she took her first step into the dark passage.

Light slipped from under the doors that lined the hall on both sides. Unlike the first landing, all of the upper rooms had windows. Aside from the personal quarters of her family, all the inn's rooms were completely empty tonight. The sound couldn't have been a tenant.

The hall's end was a shadow amongst the darkness, forming a rectangle of blackness to mark the stairwell's descent. It seemed to pulse an agitated rhythm as she drew near—a beat matching the racing pump of her heart. Amie knew that darkness itself was not evil, but that thought didn't calm her base instincts at the sight of the void.

Amie jumped at the sound of scraping and crunching. Glass sliding across an open floor, and boots crunching that glass in the darkness. Shuffles and footsteps. There were people inside, not a wild animal. People!

She raised her stick, winding up to strike the first person up the stairs.

What was she thinking? That she could take on whoever was down there? She'd never fought anyone before, and childhood scuffles with Mara counted for little. She needed help.

A silent but swift turnaround faced her in the direction of

hope. If she could wake her family without arousing the attention of who had violated their home, there would be a fighting chance. Her father was a big man. This was the best move.

The footsteps reached the stairs and Amie froze. The intruder climbed rapidly, taking each step as lightly as his wear allowed. She told her feet to keep moving, but instead, she turned around and found herself face to face with her threat.

Tall and slender, his form broke the stairwell darkness. He halted when he spotted her. She could scarcely make out a wrinkled brow and surprised eyes. Shaven on both sides, his white, spiky hair stood straight up.

Amie knew this man. He was one of the men who she'd seen at Gavini's. He was one of the terrible men who had killed Ronzit and Lana Kemp's father over the ashes.

No. He hadn't killed them. It was that other soldier who had done the killing.

She raised the stick again as she backed away. She had to do something. There was no doubt in her mind that he would try to hurt her. He may not have killed Lana's father, but he hadn't stopped the other soldier either.

The man stepped forward.

Amie screamed.

He ran for her then. Amie reared and swung her stick. She closed her eyes at the sound of cracking. Too late, she realized she'd completely missed and hit the corridor wall. Before she could take another swing, he grabbed her.

Amie wrenched her body, trying to escape his vices. A hand over her mouth and nose muffled a renewed effort at raising an alarm. He dragged her back toward the stairwell as she flailed. His hand restricted her breathing. She fought panic, but it won out as tears joined her effort.

Through the struggle, Amie saw her father lunge into the hallway. An instant later, Mara was also in the corridor. Amie caught her father's attention and tried to scream again. Her father made for her, his eyes ablaze with fury.

Several men flooded the hallway from behind, cutting the vision of her family away from her. Her captor pulled her into the stairwell. Amie shut her eyes as the sound of crashing and grunting poured from the landing above. The walls shook and a few men howled before only the cries of Father and Mara blended with the shuffling of feet.

Amie wailed in protest, a new wave of terror invigorating her. Catching her legs, the man carried her down into the inn's common. At the base of the stairs, he let her feet touch the ground. He pushed her into a tight grip of another uniformed chest. Six inches of steel pressed tight against the soft of her neck.

Amie opened her mouth to scream again.

"You scream and I take your voice," the new soldier said, his breath rancid with ale.

Amie opted to keep herself intact, but it didn't stop the tears from flowing. He slowly backed her from the stairs as his accomplices followed. Another soldier man-handled Mara down the steps. Her father was carried down between three men who struggled to keep balance under his dead weight.

"Is he dead?" the spiky-haired man asked in a strange, foreign accent.

"No, just out cold. Put up a good struggle, this one," said the one holding her father's legs.

"Good. Get them outside before he wakes," he hissed, backing away to give his men room.

The inn's door crashed open when the man restraining her sister shouldered it. The soldiers passed through one by one into the night. Amie's captor pulled her along and out into the light spring drizzle. They crossed into the alley near the rear of the inn. Outside were several horses, a large carriage, and two others. Another soldier and a woman.

Lana's mother.

And beside her, the soldier who'd killed Lana's father.

Without warning, Amie was shoved in the direction of another one of the men. Before she could find her balance, he caught her. He wrenched her into the same submissive position she'd been in a moment before.

The soldier turned to Lana's mother. "This is them?"

"This is them." She crossed her arms. "They were the ones who knew that man. I upheld my end. Now, let me go."

The soldier turned and gave a quick signal. Another opened the carriage's rear gate then stood back. They dropped her father inside and shoved him into the rear. Mara went in next.

Amie was nearly dragged to the mouth of the carriage. It was more of a cage than a carriage—something fit for a prisoner. Amie considered protesting, but the blade to her throat still promised an ill consequence. She went in face forward. The soldier pushed her deeper inside before shutting the gate.

Amie immediately crawled to the barred, carriage window. She peered out the small opening. The soldier—the one who'd killed those two men at Gavini's plot—pulled a small leather belt from his pocket and held it before the woman.

"I suggest you start wearing your prayer belt. Perhaps when the Creed returns, you will be spared any additional pain for the sins of your people."

Lana's mother eyed the small brown strap before accepting the offer. Amie heard the soft clank of the buckle as the woman secured it around her neck. She slowly let her hands fall back to her sides and straightened in pride despite the act of submission.

The soldier raised a hand and sounded a sharp whistle. His men took to their mounts as he took hold of the reins of his own gray stallion. He pulled himself into the stirrups.

"See to it you don't speak of this," he said. "I would hate to see your children fall victim to the same fate as your husband."

The woman's expression darkened before her eyes found her feet. "No one will hear of it."

The soldier tossed a brown sack at the woman's feet. It clanked against the cobblestone alley. "For your troubles," he said before pulling his horse forward and into the lead.

The woman quickly scooped up the sack and held it close to her bosom. Then she stood there, watching as Amie's cage tugged into motion.

The Crown City

The Third Movement

TWENTY

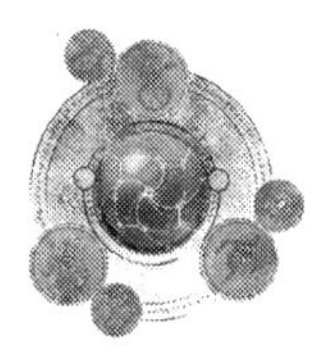

TO LIVE WITH HONOR AND TO DIE WITH HONOR

"Sixty-two eighty-five!"

Gabriel stood, shouldered the sack filled with his belongings, and walked toward the open door. Once inside, a man behind the parchment laden desk looked up at him. Blond with grayed sideburns, the man scribbled a few early notes. Without bothering to look back up, he gestured for Gabriel to sit.

Gabriel set his sack beside the seat and sat on the small wooden chair, straight-backed and waiting for orders. He glanced around the cramped office. The building had obviously been constructed in haste out in the middle of the North Hzorah fields to accommodate the encampment, but the officer had already made it his own. He'd decorated the walls with three Border Guard medals of stationary honor and two paintings, one that appeared to be the officer's mother. The other was Gabriel's father.

The man paused for a brief second to look at him before returning to his reports. "Can you read?"

"No, sir."

A lie, but the more he did to avoid suspicion, the smoother this would go. It'd been that way since he'd left, moving from one trader's wagon to another. None of them questioned if he was Hzorah's prince, especially in the ragged state he'd fixed himself in, but he'd landed on a faux personal history that was, so far, believable enough to anyone who questioned.

"Family name?" the officer asked.

"None, sir."

The officer raised his eyebrows.

"I'm an orphan," Gabriel added, sticking to script. "I don't know who my parents were."

The officer continued staring a moment before he took to scribing once more. "Trade?"

"None, sir," Gabriel said. "That's why I enlisted. I had nowhere to go."

"So …" The man set the pen in its holster and met his eyes. "How is it that an orphan without a trade got so good with the sword and bow?"

"I lived in an orphanage," Gabriel said, reciting more of his contrived backstory. "We were allowed outside to play twice a day. We often dueled with twigs and sticks. As for the bow, I think I was just lucky."

"No such thing," the officer grunted and lifted a sheet from his desk. "Says here that you shot better than most trained soldiers, and you dueled like a master swordsman. You lost twice, but your form was impeccable. That's not luck. That's genius."

Better than most soldiers? Gabriel thought. *Are the troops really that under-trained*?

Perhaps he should have held back a bit more. He'd faked the two losses he'd earned. He'd thought that doing too well would draw attention, but dueling was already second nature only to walking for him and tripping realistically when the path is swept smooth is a difficult feat.

"Not only that," the officer continued, "you're tall, strong. You could really do well on the field."

"Thank you, sir," Gabriel said, trying to sound both appreciative and inconspicuous.

The man eyed him for a moment longer before lifting his pen again. "I'm assigning you to the Second League. The

Crown places great value in young men like you. We take note of those with potential. You'll be with the best recruits out here under the watch of Captain Alden. Keep up what you did out there in the evaluations and you'll do good. Slack off, and Captain Alden will use you as his mopper."

"Thank you, sir."

"My name is Lieutenant Gaphe," he said, standing and giving direction with an outstretched arm. "If you would step this way, Gabriel."

Gabriel walked with Lieutenant Gaphe out of the makeshift office and into the North Hzorah flats. The air was cool—at least, cooler than it'd been the past several days—and smelled of soil and dew with the occasional hint of dung. A fleet of horse-drawn carts waited to taxi new soldiers to their proper camps. Gaphe waved at the nearest cart.

"New recruit for the Second League," Lieutenant Gaphe said as he climbed into the cart's rear. The driver nodded and headed for the encampment as soon as they were settled.

"You ever been to the plains before?" Lieutenant Gaphe asked.

"No, sir," Gabriel said. He'd been to the plains when he was young, but it wouldn't fit the role he'd cast for himself.

Gaphe pointed northeast to a flag in the distance. "Up there. That's where King Jeremiah made his final stand. Deserves more than just a flag. It deserves a statue, but King Jeremiah wouldn't have it. And over there," he continued, "are the Shadow Peaks. Over those mountains is where the Desolate-bound wait to make their move."

He pointed to the mountain range further north, belting the earth from the sky. The mountains were staggered in height. Some spots were little more than exaggerated hills guarded by a small watchtower and early-response camps. They were much more grand further north and south, but here, in the middle, they tapered.

"And there," he said, pointing east to a large, dark-brown structure with high walls, "is Stronghold Aear. That's usually where the farmers go to do business but has taken on its original purpose now that the Deseran threat has returned. Our Generals issue commands from the stronghold, hold prisoners of war for questioning, and it functions as a last stand when our troops are pushed back south."

Gabriel nodded attentively, though he already knew these details—a perk of growing up a warrior's son. He tried to play out some of the stories his father had shared with him. It was a bit easier to imagine now that he rode into the same battlefield as some of them took place.

He turned back to survey the troops that sprawled across the countryside. "How many troops have arrived?"

"Over ten-thousand," Lieutenant Gaphe said. "And twice as many more to come at the very least."

Gabriel had never seen so many people all together in one spot. He took a mental note of what ten thousand people looked like. It would be useful on the field, something you couldn't teach without first-hand experience.

"If you don't mind my asking, Lieutenant," Gabriel said. "You're older. Why enlist? I'm sure there's a lot of younger men who'd be fit for the job."

Lieutenant Gaphe smiled. "I've been in the military for nearly thirty years."

"You fought in the Dominion War?"

He nodded. "Not everyone who enters and stays moves to a high rank. Most do, but not all. I was never the best soldier. I just didn't happen to die." He looked at Gabriel. "Don't worry about dying, though. You're in good hands with Captain Alden. He should be a General. I'm sure he will be one day."

"You could have gone home," Gabriel said. "You could have started a new life. You didn't have to stay all this time."

"It's all I know," Lieutenant Gaphe said. "And I'm happy here. I feel like I'm useful. I don't have any money or land. At least here, I'm doing something good. That's why you're here, no?"

"It is," Gabriel said, then smiled.

The cart circled the massive camp, then stopped after

reaching the northeastern reaches. Gabriel stood and stepped off the cart. "Thank you, sir."

Gaphe nodded. "The red flag with two stars is the Second League encampment. May Desolate's Hand deliver you safe." The cart pulled away and circled back to pass a train of larger carts filled with men his age.

Gabriel spotted the flag and trotted over to the collection of tents. A crowd of about thirty or forty stood in front of the flag watching two others fight. They'd found their way to the ground already, and the larger one was on top, handing it to the other recruit's face.

No one stopped it.

Gabriel pushed through the crowd, then dropped his sack to pull them apart. The soldier on top was solid, but Gabriel managed to pull him off before two others found their senses and helped him. The man jerked and shouted, demanding to be allowed to dole out his justice. When two others helped up the soldier on the ground, Gabriel let him go.

He reeled, fists clenched and ready to transfer his fury to whoever had stepped into his warpath. His coat had been torn and his blond hair crazed in the scuffle. A blue vein bulged between his livid eyes and—

It was *Cainan.*

Cainan relaxed his guard a bit in concordant recognition. "What—"

"A *word*," Gabriel said, cutting him off.

He took a fistful of Cainan's coat and redirected him away from the crowd. Surprisingly, Cainan didn't resist, allowing himself to be tugged along for a few paces before he shook off Gabriel's grip.

"What kind of shoved-up outfit are you wearing?" Cainan asked.

Gabriel ignored him. Of course Cainan would have ended up here. Where else would he have gone, save the shipyard? *Ten thousand men and the first one I run into is someone who knows me.*

"What are you doing here?" Cainan said, then caught him by the shoulder.

"The same reason you're here. To fight for our people."

Cainan scoffed. "I'm sure."

"Look," Gabriel said, glancing about to make sure no one had stumbled into earshot. "You can't tell anyone who I am."

Cainan frowned before his eyes grew wide. "You didn't … You really *are* as daft as you look."

"Shove off, Cainan," Gabriel said. "You know I've always intended to be a warrior. Don't act surprised."

"I suppose you think you're noble," Cainan said, crossing his arms. "That coming here somehow makes you a better man."

Gabriel ignored the jab. "What will it take to keep you from clucking?"

"Oh, I don't intend to say anything," Cainan said. "You may think you're better than us. That you'll show us you're better, prancing about, playing at soldier. But you'll bleed and die just like the rest of us. That's punishment enough."

"I don't think I'm better," Gabriel said. "I'm here out of respect for the Crown. Seems like you have none. You forget that *I'm* the one who holds it."

"Not yet," Cainan said. He lifted a thumb over his shoulder. "And not out here. I'll keep quiet. I'm glad to. But stay out of my way."

"I won't let you lay into another soldier."

"The looger deserved it," Cainan said. "Talk to him yourself and maybe you'll be itching to finish the job."

Cainan turned and stalked away.

As the crowd dispersed, Gabriel walked back to find the victim of Cainan's assault. The man sat just outside a tent with his head bowed between his legs and dripping blood that collected on the patch of dirt between his feet.

Gabriel sat next to him. "You alright?" The man nodded but didn't look at Gabriel. "What's your name?"

He turned a good eye to Gabriel. His expression softened. "Fabi."

"I'm Gabriel. Do you need anything? Water?"

Fabi shrugged but didn't answer. He stared at the space

between the ground and his boots. His dark hair was matted with dirt and his clothes were ragged, barely fit for a mopper. Gabriel's own clothes weren't as prim as they were back at the palace, but at least they were proper for society.

"He's no good at answerin' questions." a recruit sitting nearby said. He had light brown hair and blue eyes and looked of North or West Hzorah origin. His dialect spoke more of the North. "I've been askin' him the same sort since you pulled the bastard off him." He extended a hand. "I'm Mel."

Gabriel accepted the handshake, then slid out of the way as another recruit came back, and knelt with medical supplies. The dark-haired medic—likely a southerner—worked quickly, skillfully damping the bleeding before applying a light-gray ointment where the bruising puffed. Fabi's face contorted, but he didn't cry out.

"You got shoved right good," he said, pulling the wrapping gauze tight around his head. "This has a salve on it that will aid the healing. My father made half his fortune off this one mixture. It's half-a-miracle. Which explains the half-fortune."

Gabriel sat uncomfortably as he waited for the aid to finish. He felt helpless. He should do more, but he didn't know anything about being a medic. Just stop the bleeding and pray Desolate's Hand didn't pull you under.

"I'm Gabriel," he said, hoping it would settle his restlessness.

"Good for you," the medic recruit said without looking up. He leaned back and inspected his work. "You'll be alright," he said before gathering the leftover supplies and walking away.

"What's his problem? I pulled—" Gabriel paused, he didn't want to give away that he knew Cainan. It would only add pathways that led back to the Crown. "I pulled the scorching bastard off him."

"That's Aeron," Mel said. "Merchant's son. He don't trust blonds much. And that brute ain't doin' much to change that."

Gabriel frowned. "Blonds?"

Mel waggled his hands over his head. "Ain't used a lookin' glass, have you? Your hair."

"I know what my hair looks like," Gabriel said. "What does it have to do with anything?"

Mel held his hands open. "We all got our ways. I'm not sayin' I agree, but that's just how most merchants are. Thinks they're all loogers. Out for no one but themselves."

Would a looger save someone from a beating? Gabriel thought but didn't bother voicing it. Mel was right. People had their prejudices, no matter how strange or unfounded.

Gabriel turned back to Fabi. "Where are you from?"

"Around."

"I'm guessing you don't care for blonds either?" Gabriel said. "Or is this just how you treat everyone who steps in to save you?"

"I don't have a home," Fabi said.

"An orphan?"

"Highwayman," Mel piped in.

Gabriel was taken aback. "You're a highwayman? You steal from caravans and the like?"

"I'm *not* a highwayman," Fabi said, suddenly finding his voice through grid-locked teeth. "I'm a soldier. My *father's* a highwayman."

Mel smirked. "That blond one that whipped you don't see no difference."

Fabi shot him a look. "Shove off."

"How'd you end up here?" Gabriel said, interjecting what might end up another fight. One bad eye was already enough trouble.

"My father insisted I join them on raids," Fabi said. "But I'm not a thief. I won't be. I don't want to hurt those people. So when I heard about the call to arms, I left. I don't have any skills but with a knife. Short of a butcher, this might be the only thing I'm suited for."

Gabriel nodded. He understood why Cainan nearly ended him. The Crown was hearing an earful about the highwaymen problem and West Hzorah had seen the worst of it. Bendeth's and Roth's guard worked tirelessly, patrolling the roads, but couldn't seem to catch up with the footpads. It left a sour taste on the Bendeth name and dishonor wasn't a flavor their family wanted dripping from the tongues of the citizens.

"You might not want cross paths with him again," Gabriel said. "I managed to get him off you, but I can't promise I can do it again."

"I don't need your help," Fabi said. "I can handle myself."

Gabriel didn't want to risk another stab at Fabi's pride. He should have been a bit more careful about how he'd phrased his advice. He imagined Samuel scrutinizing his approach to diplomacy.

"Roundup!" a voice called from the distance.

Mel stood. "That's rations. Blonds ain't allowed, though."

Gabriel frowned. "What?"

"Ain't heard a joke before?" Mel asked, then strolled off the join the massing soldiers.

Gabriel wandered around the Second League plot—one hand holding his sack over his shoulder and the other balancing his food—searching for a place to sit. At home, it'd always been easy: sit where you were assigned. Here, there was a certain level of chaos that he was unaccustomed to. He'd never imagined the camps to be the same as life at the palace. In fact, that was what he found alluring about being a soldier. But he'd imagined there would be more standards.

Not long after taking his ration of bread, pale root, and water, he'd stumbled across arguments, wrestling, and men who sat alone crying. Other than a general sense of groupings, the soldiers were allowed to move about the encampment freely within the confines of their league.

The Second League had the smallest plot of land. Set off to the north, the league was the shore to an ocean of men. Gabriel had seen roughly this many people all together during the solstice festival when at least a fraction of the Crown City and some of the surrounding towns came into the city for the festivities, congregating primarily in the city green.

The sun fell to the western horizon with reluctance. The days had begun to grow long, and Gabriel's sense of daylight felt skewed against the reality of time. Men were distributing wood for fires that would keep the camp aglow late into the evening.

Gabriel approached the Second League's firepit. He spotted Fabi sitting alone. He settled next to him and greeted him warmly. Fabi didn't look up at him, and Gabriel didn't push him. Fabi didn't really know Gabriel. The only reason Gabriel sat next to him was because he didn't really know anyone either, and he at least knew something about Fabi.

Moments later, others in the Second League crowded in. Cainan took to the opposite side of the pit's circle, shooting Gabriel a look that beckoned him to choose his side. Had this been the Crown Palace, Gabriel may have joined him. Of all the men and women that frequented the dinners and events at the palace, Cainan was perhaps the most like himself. They'd both wanted the life of a warrior. They'd both practiced themselves soar to become the very best.

But sometime during the last year or so, Cainan had taken a turn. He wasn't the same cousin he'd grown up with. He'd become cold and arrogant. As if High Lord Bendeth had left the worst stench of himself on his son to linger in his absence.

Gabriel turned from Cainan's gaze. This was an opportunity to rediscover himself—to fulfill his true purpose. Having this version of Cainan around tainted that for Gabriel.

You wanted me to stay out of your way? Gabriel thought, frowning. *Well, you have it.*

"The ol' crew's back together!" Mel said from behind. He flopped down beside Gabriel, his gaze catching his glower. In mock fear, Mel raised his hands. "Hold up now. That don't mean I'm next, do it? I ain't a highwayman. I never stole anything. Put down that scowl, we can talk this through!" Before Gabriel could reply Mel laughed and gave a quick wink. "You wouldn't spot a joke if it sat on your knee."

"Perhaps if they were funny ..." Gabriel said, looking away to catch Fabi's good eye. Fabi looked down, his lips pursed.

"I'm plenty funny," Mel said. "You just ain't got the bones."

Aeron settled next to Fabi. "How's the eye?"

"Better," Fabi said.

"Good," Aeron broke off a piece of bread and wet it with some of the water from his skin. "I'll change it before it gets too dark and again in the morning. It won't heal up for a week, but you'll find the pain won't be a bother."

Fabi nodded.

"What's the medicine called?" Gabriel asked.

Aeron didn't look up at him. "Osemer."

"How's it made?"

"I can't tell you. Family secret. Mind your food."

"You ain't gotta be so hard on him," Mel said. "He's a blond, but he's got morals. He's named after the prince, after all. Right, Gabriel?"

Gabriel froze. "Uhh—"

Aeron looked up then. "I don't care who he was named after. I've never met a blond who didn't have an ulterior motive. You'll have to excuse me if I don't skip to his drum."

A few other men settled in, and Mel leaned in close to Gabriel pointing each of them out. "That there's Lurin and Bear. Bear's from up my way. Lurin's from South Hzorah, I think." He pointed again. "That's Jae from somewhere out west. And them two is Urwell and Paitin. They're some Low Lord's second cousins down south near Armoth, and I ain't never seen brothers who look just the same like that."

"Identical twins," Gabriel said. He looked at each man in turn, trying to memorize their names. They were all about his age, none of them could have seen more than twenty-five years. "There's only ten of us?"

Mel's mouth dropped open, then he clapped him on the back. "You ain't tell me you can count, too. Scorch it, Gabriel! What other secrets you hiding?"

"How about how much he spent on that sword in his sack?" Cainan dropped his bowl between his legs and leaned back on his log, grinning wickedly. "Must have cost you a fortune."

Gabriel glanced down where the hilt of the Crown Sabre protruded from the top of the sack. "Nothing."

"Really?" Cainan raised his eyebrows. "So, it's just a *family* relic?"

"You blonds always end up on top," Aeron said. "Getting rich while the commoners fall behind. There's no way you got that without being a looger and a cheat. Who'd you cheat for the sword?"

"No one," Gabriel said, then made to cover it. "I won it in a bet on the way here."

"They have bets at your banquets?" Aeron mocked.

"Whatever you think you know about me isn't true," Gabriel said. "I don't have a family. I'm an orphan. Blonds get dead parents sometimes too."

Cainan snorted from across the fire.

"That's shoved," Mel said. "How'd you end up here?"

"Too old to stay at the safe house," Gabriel said. "They don't let you stay there forever. Eventually, you have to make your own way. I don't have any skills except fighting, so I enlisted."

"Man," Mel said. "I can't imagine growing up without no parents. That's just …"

"It's fine," Gabriel said. "You don't need to feel bad for me. I don't know anything different. That's just how life is."

"If you need a place to go after all this," Mel said between chewing his pale root, "you can come with me. We ain't got much back home. Just a farm. But you can have a bed in the stables if you carry your load. Me and Pa could use another strong arm. My sister's lame, so she can't do much."

That took a kick at Gabriel's gut. Mel should be at home to help out. "Thanks, Mel. Truly."

"I don't think we'll be going back home," Fabi said.

"We have the best chance to go home in the Second League," Aeron said. "At least we're a skilled bunch. Those other poor bastards don't have much of a shot."

"War isn't an easy effort," Gabriel said. "You have to prepare for the worst, but you hope for the best. If you walk into it with a broken spirit, you're already dead."

"I'm not a philosopher," Fabi said. "I simply accept the reality of it all."

"You can't think like that."

"I'm sure they taught you to be hopeful at the orphanage," Fabi said. "That Ma and Pa would come back for you one day. But you can't live like that forever. You have to wake up. *This* is reality. That life in the orphanage was a dream. You'll never make it in the world if you don't figure that out."

Gabriel watched as Fabi stood and walked away, disappearing between tents. He looked down at the cup of water in his hand.

"He's still gettin' over a headache," Mel said. "Don't take it strong."

Gabriel shook his head. "No. He's right. It was a dream. And it's time to wake up."

"One!"

Gabriel dropped to a prone position, his arms holding him inches from a mouth full of wet dirt. The line of recruits next to him mirrored his stance in perfect time.

"Two!"

He shifted into a squat. His boots sank into the mud, staining his clothes and splattering his face.

"Three!"

Gabriel stood, perfectly still, awaiting the cycle to begin again. He was tired. Less than three days in and Captain Alden had put them through their paces. Gabriel had never felt so sore, tired, and *alive*.

It took some time to adjust to being looked at, talked to, and treated just like a commoner. It was jarring. He'd taken princedom for granted, *especially* the food. But now that he'd lived in the skin of Gabriel, the Orphan from Nowhere and of

Nothing, he discovered a new sense of freedom. He could finally be his own man without any expectations.

"Rest!" Captain Aldan said, circling the rear of the company. He sloshed through the mud, taking the opportunity to meet the eyes of each Second League soldier who awaited his command. "I'm sure you're envious. That you wished you performed a bit less admirably in your review. That your aim was less sure or you'd been born with a limp." He pointed back toward the camp. "I bet you'd give anything to be back there, warm, comfortable. Maybe play a hand or two of dice. You'd lose, but at least you didn't have to be like those poor Second League men. Up on a hill in the mud and rain."

The company stood silent. No one agreed with him, but no one objected either.

"Those men," Captain Alden continued, "aren't the best. And the price you pay for not being the best is death. Because in war, the difference between life and death is this right here." He paused, sweeping a hand at the ground they stood on before pointing back again. "And that, over there. Excellence verses mediocrity."

He turned and crossed back to the other side.

"Even though you are 'the best' by the standards of your evaluations," he continued, "I'm still not sure I can call you 'the best' by mine, not yet. I don't think of my company as the Second League—the soldiers who didn't make it into the King's personal guard. Because out here, we're second to *none*. We're a wolf pack, focused and strong. We train harder because it's our job to win the wars we start. Everyone else is little more than a distraction.

"I'm sure," he said, stopping again and turning on heel, "that you find that belittling—possibly even cruel—to dismiss the lives of so many men as trivial, as pawns in a blood game. But all men must play their role in life." He paused near Gabriel and turned to the soldier two down from his right. "Tell me, soldier. What does it mean to be a Hzorah Warrior?"

"Captain?" Urwell said, his voice half-failing him.

"I'm sure you heard my question," Captain Alden said. "Go on. Answer."

"To protect the people of Hzorah."

"Wrong," Captain Alden said. He stepped in front of the next soldier. "What does it mean to be a Hzorah Warrior?"

Lurin stood straighter. "Fighting fearlessly. Marching straight in—"

"Wrong," Captain Alden said again. He stepped in front of Gabriel and looked him in the eye. "Tell me. What does it mean to be a Hzorah Warrior?"

Gabriel met his eyes. "To live with honor and to die with honor."

Captain Alden smiled a moment before stepping away. "'To live with honor and to die with honor.' King Jeremiah *himself* told me that. Our every action is to the end of honor. Through times of great wealth and times of poverty, through health and sickness, through life and in death, we maintain our honor. Yes, we protect, and yes, we fight with great courage. But all of that is to the end of honor. We want our fathers to end their lives with dignity. We want our sons to begin theirs with a chance."

He looked at Gabriel again. "If you live and die with honor, you are a true Hzorah Warrior. And I'll test your honor at every step. Stay vigilant. Your time has come."

TWENTY-ONE

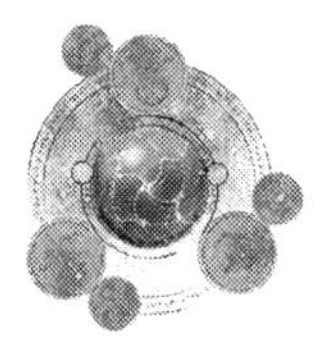

THE TAL

Tele rubbed her hands to bring them warmth as she crouched before a fist-sized, fire red, bulbous plant. Lowering herself down to eye level with the oddity, she smiled. This was a marvelous find.

Over several days of travel, the Borderlands had transformed from a trailblazed woodland to an untouched reserve of natural life. No settlements, no trails, no sign that anyone had even ventured this far into the west at all. Trees grew close together and climbed into the sky, allowing thick patches of moss along for the ride. Branches and vines crisscrossed from the understory and up through the canopy, establishing a network of greens and browns.

And the *sounds*. Though it could easily become a disregarded background of birds, insects, and distant rumblings of thunder, when she closed her eyes and really listened, the inkling of patterns began to emerge. More times than she could count, she had been tempted to stop and take notes so that she might reconstruct how it all connected.

And now that nightfall neared again, they'd made camp in a small clearing on the forest floor. While Navid arranged a firepit, Tele, as she'd preferred during their travels, had gone in search of firewood. Not that she expected to find anything usable.

As if to affront her efforts to commit *Element and Reaction* to memory, Desolate's Hand had spent the last few days throwing every misfortune at them possible. Yesterday's had been heavy rainfall, forcing her to keep her books in her pack as the shelter they'd put together wasn't completely moisture proof, and she wasn't willing to risk the texts being tarnished before she was sure she could reproduce them.

The rain had receded early that morning, but starting a fire would be a chore. It was already a grand effort when the brush and branches were relatively dry—not that dry was an attribute to be expected here—but the moss and fungus that layered the bark of the trees acted to snuff out the spark of flint.

On one hand, Tele found the resistance to fire brilliant. A wildfire in the Borderlands would destroy large swaths of land, and over countless years of adaptation, the plant life had managed to raise a defense that could slow the flames until the rains inevitably came again. But, on the other hand, it was dark this deep in the forest, especially at night, and without fire to give light to their surroundings, Tele couldn't study.

But now she'd found something that would change all that.

"Aren't you just resplendent?" Tele asked the plant before she carefully reached out and plucked it from the soil. She glanced about and found three others and picked them as well. She then slipped them into her pockets and picked up her stack of branches before turning back to camp.

She returned to find Navid arranging a few thicker bits of wood from a newly fallen tree they'd come across just an hour before. He'd scraped off most of the moss so they'd at least have a shot at catching fire. Tele dropped her pile of wood beside his and helped him add the lighter brush to the mix.

"It's still pretty wet," Navid said, as he retrieved his flint stones from his pack. "I'm not sure that we'll have any luck tonight."

"I thought so, too," Tele said and pulled the red bulbs from her pockets. "Until I found these."

Navid frowned at the strange spherical plants. "What are those?"

"Kipado," Tele said. "I've never seen them in real life before. They're common in Ghaya. According to my father's notes, the Ghayan people often use them to help start fires when they're on their spirit quests."

"How?"

Tele smiled. "Observe."

Just hard enough so that they would burst, Tele threw the plants into the firepit. With a crack, the firepit burst into flames. Navid fell backward as the sudden burst of heat took him by surprise. *Success.*

"That ..." Navid said. "Was ... amazing! How does it work?"

"I don't know." Tele drew closer to the fire and warmed her hands. "There hasn't been a proper extensive study on them. But now that I've begun studying my uncle's work, I think I have an idea."

Navid sat next to Tele as she pulled *Element and Reaction* from her pack and opened it to one of the sections she'd book-marked. He leaned in close as she explained how she thought it might be two chemicals within the plant's bulb that ignite when combined. "It's called an exothermic reaction."

"Why would a plant do that?" Navid asked.

Tele thought for a moment. "Well, I don't know for sure ... but from what I know about other plants and some animals, I'd start with the guess that it's a defense mechanism."

"A defense mechanism that kills it?" Navid looked skeptical.

"It's not uncommon that a plant will sacrifice itself." Tele said. "The individual plant may parish, but the species gains a lot. The animal that trampled or tried to eat it learns its lesson quickly. And the rest of the kipado won't have to encounter that danger. Oh!" Tele flipped to the end of the book where her newest set of notes were. She pointed out runes she'd been constructing in an effort to learn how to construct spell forms. "Look at these. I'm getting better."

Navid carefully took the book from her hands and scanned her work. He tapped one of the runes. "I remember this one." He pointed out another. "And this. Your penmanship is fantastic. These runes look hard to draw."

"Right," Tele said, taking back the book. She took pleasure in the compliment but stored it away to revel in the pleasure of it later. She then pointed to another rune. "So, this one might be similar to the last three runes." She turned the volume so that Navid could see it in the firelight.

Navid squinted at the page. "They may be. What does that flourish mean?"

Tele flipped back a few pages to where she'd last seen it. "There was another … Yes, this one here." She pointed to another rune—a simple rune that tied one concept to another but was nonspecific in how those ideas were ordered. "I think this calls for a soft palette sound with a higher intonation."

"Right."

"I wish we had the *Gateway Abbreviation,*" Tele said. "I could use what you learned from that book as a stronger reference. It's exponentially slower this way."

She heard him swallow before he whispered, "I'm sorry."

"I'm not blaming you." She sighed and shook her head. "I'm just perturbed from the rain and the cold and every branch that insists on whipping me in the face when I'd thought I'd pushed it away."

"I thought you *liked* the forest."

She looked to his amused smile and was forced to suppress her own as she gave him a warning look. "Don't push it, Navid. I will bite your whole head off."

He let go of a warm chuckle. "I can't stop it from raining or do much about the overgrowth, but I can help with the cold."

He shifted a bit closer, put an arm around her, and drew her close. She stiffened.

"Am I making you uncomfortable?"

"No," she said a bit too quickly. "You just surprised me. This actually makes it better."

"Good."

Tele forced her muscles to relax as she sank into his side hug. Alarm melted away and cozy warmth took its place. She sighed, feeling a certain sense of security she hadn't allowed herself in weeks. She'd almost forgotten what it felt like to not be continuously on guard or to have someone that she trusted enough to sit so close.

Though the lack of fire over the past few nights had been its own problem, Tele wasn't quick to forget the horrors the flames sparked within her mind. They'd sat in comfortable silence while the sounds of the forest enveloped them—a welcome respite from the living nightmare. But now that she'd gotten a fire going, it all came back again. But Navid's kind embrace helped a bit. And that was ... nice.

"I couldn't find any reference to the creature that lived in the waters beneath Caldor," Tele said, distracting herself from her memories. "I've never encountered an animal that has never been named. So, I've decided to name it."

"Oh?"

"It's a good opportunity for me to practice using the ancient tongue I'm learning to construct a word based on what I know about the language so far. It's a good first step to mastering a language if you can create a word that feels native to it. And I've never named an animal before. I'd be lying if I said that the vanity of it isn't enticing."

"So," Navid said. "What will you name it?"

"Dragon."

Navid let out a soft "hmm" in response. Tele felt the tone resonate through his chest, almost harmonious with the beating of his heart.

"I like it," he said.

Tele smiled. She liked it too, but it was nice to hear that someone else agreed. As much as she loved her role as a

Keeper, there was a certain sense of isolation she felt in her duty. She'd never really felt that sensation until her family had passed on into Desolate. It had abated when she met Gavini, but now that she'd had to leave Caldor, she was alone with her thoughts.

No, she wasn't alone. Navid was with her. He continued to help her decode the ancient language of magic even though he admitted over-and-over that it was over his head. It wasn't that she needed him to do the work for her. But having him to talk to while she reasoned through the process somehow made it easier.

He gave so much of his attention selflessly that she felt a sting of guilt in her gut when she realized that he was likely just as alone with his thoughts as she was. They'd made an agreement to be friends. And Navid had been a shining example of what that meant. It was her turn.

"What are you thinking about?" Tele asked.

There was a short paused before he replied. "Nothing."

"Liar. We made a deal not to lie to each other anymore—to be forthright. Remember?" She felt him nod. "Well?"

"I'm just thinking about what my parents must have been like." He grunted a short chuckle. "It sounds as absurd saying it aloud as I thought it would."

Tele pulled away from him so that she could turn to look him in the eye. "That's not absurd. Do you know how much time I spend thinking of my parents?"

Navid looked away from her gaze. "Master Kruv told me how I was left at his doorstep and how my mother was found dead not long after—a murder." He swallowed before continuing. "I don't understand why anyone would want her dead."

Tele came up with a half-dozen reasons right then but didn't voice them. She may not be a good friend, but she'd had a family and she knew that probably wouldn't be what Navid needed. The question was likely rhetorical. "I don't know either."

"From the moment I was born, I've been carted about and

traded between one guardian or another. All with the intent to 'save my life.' It's not that I'm ungrateful. I just wish I had control for once."

Tele nodded, acknowledging his pain.

"And what about you?" Navid asked. "What's on your mind?"

"We just talked about what's on my mind."

"No," Navid said. "We talked about your work. That's just the surface. What's really troubling you?"

"I could go on for hours about all the little things. But we're so close to accomplishing the one thing I was born to do that, for once, I'm actually more excited than afraid." It wasn't really the truth, but Tele didn't think Navid really needed to hear the truth right now—pact or not.

Tele leaned back against him again, and she shut her eyes. "We're going to win this."

She felt him nod, wordlessly. Reassured, Tele relaxed into his warmth. And when sleep took her, she dreamed. Not of steel, not of flame, not of death.

Only him.

Navid shielded his eyes as he and Tele crossed out of the forest. The sun's light was intense compared to what they'd grown used to for the last few days of travel. In the thick of the Borderland forests, the sun had been snuffed out to such an extent that even high noon was no brighter than dusk on an open field.

But the grounds outside the forest halted not far from the treeline. A few dozen strides further brought them to the edge of a cliff. And far below, a large lake fed by a river far in the distance flooded the landscape. Navid let out a breath of awe as he took in the arresting view of cliffside grays and browns under the forest greens leading to perfectly reflective lake.

"That explains the sound of water I heard," Tele said as

she knelt near the cliff's brink. She pointed where the river fed into the lake. "That looks like a major river."

Navid nodded. "It's likely an offshoot of the Everwisp river. I think we're in the Tal tribe lands."

"I think I could spend a thousand lifetimes here and never tire of this view," Tele said before she stood and caught him in her gaze.

Navid smiled. "After this is over, maybe we can come back here and truly enjoy it."

"Perhaps," she said, returning his smile, and crossing back to the forest.

Navid followed her back through the treeline and into the stifling darkness. And after some time pushing their way through the untouched brush, they came to a narrow path that was clearly man-made. However, the clearing brought little light to their way. Navid filled the void by answering Tele's questions about what he knew of the Borderlands, but it wasn't long before Tele brought them to a halt.

"What's wrong?" Navid asked.

"Nothing …" she said, frowning. "I just thought I heard … It's nothing. What were you saying?"

"That there were agreements made—the Imperial Expansion Pact—that prohibited the further expansion of any land beyond its natural borders. It allowed all unsettled lands to remain untouched. The prophets always taught us that it was a foresighted effort to ensure that the balance struck between developed and undeveloped lands remained the same. And that may still be true. But now I'm starting to believe there were other motives at play. For example—"

Tele snatched his arm. Before Navid could ask what was wrong, she held a finger to her lips and pointed ahead.

"It changed," she whispered.

Navid squinted where she was pointing. "What?"

"The trees. They're different now. They moved."

With the little light that they had, Navid couldn't see what she'd seen. He wasn't even sure *she* could see what she thought she could see. They'd been in the forest for some time, and it could be that her mind was making up changes.

Sharp pricks trickled down his spine. It had always been there—perhaps in response to the potential danger all around them at all times this deep in the Borderlands—but now it intensified in urgent warning. He gritted his teeth against the feeling.

Tele gasped just as he saw it.

The vines were growing. The branches were growing. Like dark and gnarled fingers, the overgrowth began to reach out toward them at a slow but steady rate.

"What's happening?" Navid asked.

"I don't know, but I don't think—"

Tele yelped and stepped back. At her feet, a root had emerged from the path. It slowly recoiled as if it were a wooden snake.

"It stung me," Tele hissed.

"Maybe we shouldn't wait to see what else they might do."

Tele nodded, and together they turned and hastened down the path. As if excited by their speed, the plant life grew faster. And while the growth couldn't keep up with them, it grew from all sides, prompting them to quicken into a dangerous sprint.

Navid risked look behind them. A mass of vines and branches warped and bent to reach them in a steady pursuit. Before he could turn back to focus on the path ahead, his foot caught on something in the path and he went down. Hard.

He was only momentarily stunned before he came to his senses. All around him, thin vines broke free from the forest floor and rushed to wrap around them. A thicker root grasped his ankle and squeezed, shackling him to the ground.

As panic took him, the itch of his curse ignited with hot need. Navid jerked, ripping his torso free from a hundred strands of green before its web could thicken to trap him in place, but the root held steadfast. Just as he cried out for Tele's help, a thick vine wrapped over his mouth.

Tele descended over him with a hatchet. She hacked away

at the vines and then the root that held his ankle before she pulled him to his feet.

"Consider keeping up," she growled.

Navid limped behind her, trying to regain the feeling in his leg. The load of their packs were beginning to weigh on him at this pace. "We can't keep running. It's closing in from all sides. And eventually we'll have to slow down."

"The cliff," Tele said. "If we can get to the cliff, we can jump off and escape."

"That's crazy. The drop has to be—"

A vine shot at them from behind, passing just between them and narrowly missing his cheek.

Tele took his arm. "Should I wait for an alternative, or are we moving forward with my plan?"

Navid swallowed and his curse rattled his skull. "No. Let's do your plan."

Another vine wrapped around Tele's arm, and she cut it away quickly with a dagger. She fell behind Navid a step as her second blade was freed and she took to hacking away at the vines and branches that encroached at their rear.

Navid paused. Reaching for the knife at his belt.

"No!" Tele said. "Keep moving. I'm right behind you."

Following her instructions, Navid pushed on but couldn't help but turn to check that she didn't need his help. The itch had stopped being merely an irritant and had evolved into a chaotic venom that rippled over his skin, seeped deep into his muscles, and gouged with sharp talons. It demanded his attention, refusing to be ignored.

Finally, they broke free of the forest and onto the clearing of the cliff face. Panting, Navid turned to check that they'd truly escaped the danger. To his horror, Tele continued to battle the multitude of arms that extended beyond the dark boundary. Even as they encircled her, she fought back like a furious ball of energy. But she could only be in so many places at once, and the weapons at the forest's disposal appeared infinite. For every branch she cut away, two replaced it. Eventually she'd be completely encased in an arboreal cocoon.

"What are you waiting for?" she cried out to him. "Jump!"

In his mind's eye, he saw himself turn, take a running start, and leap from the rock face. Tele did the same, after making just enough of an opening to dash into the open air.

But none of that happened. Navid was anchored in place. It was a simple plan, and it would likely work. But Navid knew that he was but a hair's width away from his curse overpowering his will just like it had done outside of Caldor's walls.

He could not let that happen again. He could not fail his training.

To allow it to take me is to take a path of evil.

"Navid! Quickly!"

To allow it to control me is to—

"Nav—"

With a sudden snap, the tangle of vines and branches constricted and trapped Tele in their clutches. Her face went pale then a slight shade of violet. Petrified, Navid watched helplessly as their eyes locked. The pain of betrayal filled her gaze before her eyes rolled back in her head and she went limp in the grip of the wilds.

A whistle and soft thud pulled Navid back to reality. Gradually, the plant life receded, gently dropping Tele to the ground. Beyond her—as if he'd materialized from thin air—stood a tall, bare-chested man. Shaved on both sides, his wild, white hair spiked in a single line from his forehead to the base of his neck. His chest and arms were covered in lines of paint that striped up to his face. Thin straps secured his biceps and coiled down to his wrists.

Around him, several others rose from the tall grass. Some were male, some female, but they all had the same outlandish look. Navid's breath caught at the sight of their long daggers that curved half-circle at their ends. One of them spun his casually as he eyed them with heightened curiosity.

"You have crossed into the lands of the Tal," the man at their center said. His voice had the deep accent of an unfamiliar tongue. "Your life is now forfeit."

As Navid stood frozen with fear in the high grass before a line of dark, red-barked trees. Spears, daggers, and several Tal men and women stood between him and a safe escape. The evening sun stole between the gaps of thick forest canopy, its arms crossing out to lick the earth beneath it. The grass stretched upward to join with the rays as if in joyous union with heaven and earth. The smell of wild things misted just above the threshold of his senses. The aggressive contrast of beauty and danger tried to split his focus. And though the shearing pain of his curse had abated, its warning was all too clear: there was no bluff to the man's words.

His life hung in a thin balance.

"I am Navid Tevaad," he said, raising his voice and speaking slowly to increase his clarity. "We are here in response to your message with the prophets in Caldor." One of them whispered a few words to the rest. A few of the Guardians redoubled their blade grip, all of them stiffened noticeably. He was treading over hot water. "I only want to help."

Again, one of them whispered to the others, and again they all reacted the same, though this time with greater intensity. The speaker stepped forward through the grass. About ten paces short of them, he stopped. His eyes stared intently at him before he looked toward Tele at his feet and slowly knelt down to her side and felt the side of her neck. He waved over his men and said a few words in a language Navid couldn't understand. Four of them approached and lifted Tele.

"I am Tal Aval," the speaker said, then turned back and crossed to the tree line. "If you come to bring evil, you will die. We will talk to the elders. Follow."

Navid followed Tal Aval into the woods. The others followed up the rear, chatting away in their strange language. He looked at Tele. The men were gentle enough with her body, but he didn't know these people. He didn't know what they'd do with her. She deserved a respectful end.

Navid made to catch up with Tal Aval, but before he drew too close, a few of his Tal companions blocked his path with spears. The warning glint in their eyes was clear. He was to go no closer.

"My friend," Navid called to Tal Aval. "What are you going to do with her body?"

Tal Aval continued forward but took a moment to look back to him. "She is still alive but will die if she does not see our healers. Do not slow us or she will die from the poison of the ardya."

Relief filled his heart. He was so happy that she was alive that he caught himself smiling. *At least she's true to her word,* Navid thought. *There's been nothing* but *trouble.*

But that relief quickly gave way to a wave of concern. She could still die yet. Navid could only hope these people could help her before it was too late.

In the near distance, Navid saw a small light coming from the ground. He frowned at the mystery and, in response, another light appeared higher up. Then another and another. In a chain reaction, the forest began to glow in beautiful shades of color.

As they crossed into the light, Navid saw that the sources of the light came from the vast networks of fungi that carpeted the ground and draped the trees. He turned about in the path, taking in the epic splendor that was hidden away from the rest of civilization.

They paused before a large tree, and when Tal Aval touched it, branches grew out of the ground and encircled them. At first Navid panicked, but instead of constricting, the branches joined, forming about them like a large, human-sized nest.

He gasped and stumbled as the ground shifted and began to rise. Catching himself at the edge of the wooded nest, Navid watched the ground fall away as they rose into the air, carried by a sprouting tree trunk. Soon the forest floor disappeared as they passed into the forest heights. Expectant of their passing, trees and branches illuminated in brilliant colors and leaned away from the path of their ascent.

After several minutes of growth, Navid squinted against the sun as the living platform crossed out of the thick, and the sky opened up above. And there, spread before him, was an entire village.

His Tal escort proceeded forward when the branches receded, but Navid hesitated. If they were truly in the treetops, what was holding everything aloft?

"Come," Tal Aval said. "We must speak to the elders."

After watching several of them step onto what appeared to be solid, grass-covered ground, Navid took a tentative step forward. Solid. There wasn't even a hint that what he stood on was any less solid than the forest floor below.

Navid followed the Tal into the maze of trees. Like the ground below, the village looked like a forest, except that it was far more sparsely wooded, allowing large courtyards and avenues of space for the people who milled about.

Several small children with the same stark-white, flared hairstyle as the men and women darted between trees and dwellings that appeared almost organic to the landscape. One screamed when she was caught in the path of the only child with a long twig. She fell to the ground in fits of giggles, playing dead.

Tal Aval cut directly into the heart of the community. A few of their escorts peeled off, leaving a lean group that didn't interrupt the village's order. Navid surveyed the village, catching the eye of a few villagers who seemed near homogeneous in their appearance. Man, woman, and child all had the same strange, white hair and nearly the same dress.

Navid averted his eyes when he caught groups of young females, conversing amongst themselves, as bare-chested as the men. It would appear that modesty wasn't valued here. He'd learned of many peoples in the known world. None of which looked favorably on such unabashed appearances.

Don't they think to cover themselves?

Navid suddenly felt ignorant for jumping to judgment. He'd thought of himself as well-cultured, but there were obviously more people to be known. There were few who actually attempted to map the Borderland forests. All who tried, almost to a man, never returned. It'd become a fool's task—a task he'd suddenly become apart of.

The path into the village center was well-worn by traffic and became increasingly grassless as they neared their destination. The village center opened up to a wide circle of dark brown dirt with a stone well in its center. Ten paths branched outward from the village center, all foot-worn like the path they'd taken.

Tal Aval paused before the well and the rest of the company halted. He turned to Navid. "You wait here. What is your friend's name?"

Navid swallowed. "Tele. Will you be able to save her?"

Tal Aval's dark expression softened if only just a touch. "I cannot make that promise. I can only promise that we will do all that we can to keep her alive."

Navid managed a short nod of acknowledgment and the four who carried Tele followed Tal Aval into a large hut. Like the shelters that surrounded him, the hut she disappeared into was nest-like in appearance. It wasn't like anything Navid was used to. Smooth outer walls and sloping roofs were replaced with organic structures, as if a giant bird hand constructed a fully enclosed home of branches and vines and leaves.

Please, Navid thought. *Please let them be able to help her.*

It was his fault that she'd gotten hurt. He was the one who hesitated and failed to carry out their plan. Tele had almost died so that Navid could have a clear shot at escape. She should have taken the leap instead. Then it would be him instead of her.

A man in a distinctly different dress slowly approached the village center. He wore black bands and paint and what looked like an ankle-length skirt. Two others wearing the same deep black outfit drew near on the paths to either side. Navid turned, watching others surround the village center at the same slow rate, one from each path.

The itch of his curse flared. *To allow it to take me is to take a path of evil.*

In perfect sync, the Tal people in black stopped just inside of the circle. Five were men and five were women. Long, curved daggers hung at their sides. They made no move to draw them, but the curse within inflamed to a near-insufferable level.

"I am Tal Dian, and we speak for the Tal," the man directly in front of them said. Though his voice was heavy with an accent, Tal Dian's handle on his language was refined. "You come to our lands seeking power. Who sent you to retrieve it, seer?"

Be brave. You have to do this. For Tele. For everyone. Navid took a small step forward. "My name is Navid Tevaad. I have come in response to the messages you have sent the prophets in Caldor."

A small wave of interest encircled him and spread as a few men worked to translate what he'd said. He was suddenly aware of how many villagers had joined in on watching in the background.

"You are a seer," Tal Dian said. "Are you also a Keeper of the Covenant?"

Navid shook his head. "No. But Tele …" He pointed to where she'd been carried off to be treated. "My friend is."

"Do you know anything about how to mend what is broken with the Seed?" Tal Dian asked.

"No," Navid admitted. "But is there anything at all that you can tell me? Perhaps there is something that you know that will change the problem as we see it."

Tal Dian slowly shook his head. "We know little of the Seed and its power. We protect it. We live with it. We do not understand it."

"Near two-hundred years ago," the woman beside Tal Dian said, "Wizard Titan came to us with a heavy heart. He could no longer carry the responsibility his power had thrust upon him. The beautiful works he'd built had become tainted by some. Others had caused war. He knew that in order to bring the world balance, he had to leave the mortal realm.

"So, he spun a bit of magic—magic that could tie off what he had started in the world. He then locked away his power with the Seed. Because he was a Wizard, the power was inseparable from his own existence. One could not exist without the other.

"But in doing so, he tied himself to our lands. The magic contained within the Seed was so vast that it could not be completely contained, and it spilled into the land around it, bringing magic to the life of the Tal tribelands."

She waved an arm to gesture to the village around them. "The power from the Seed has reshaped our lands and given us our way of life. But now it is dying. We fear that if we do not act, by winter's end the magic will drain away, destroying the new balance struck by over two hundred years of change. It too will destroy our way of life."

"But the seer has brought a Keeper of the Covenant with him," Tal Dian said, hope filling his voice.

"That is good," the Tal woman to his left said. "She will save our way of life, and balance will be restored."

"I'm afraid that won't be possible," Navid said.

"Not possible?" Tal Dian frowned.

"We—Tele, I mean—tried to find a solution to your problem, but we couldn't find one. There's only one thing that we know to do. Bring the Wizard back."

"That will not rebalance the power of the Seed," Tal Dian said. "It will only drain its power completely. The magic that infuses the Tal lands will die with the winter, and our entire way of life will be destroyed."

"There is an imminent war," Navid said. "A war that will even find its way here if it's allowed to occur. The Deseran Dominion has amassed an army. Caldor has fallen. Trade and communications have been disrupted. Every living Prophet and Seer, except me and the prophet in the Deseran Dominion, has been killed in a horrific twist of fate. A wedge between our lands is growing. War is coming. Wizard Titan is our last hope."

"The wars of your people are not our affair," Tal Dian said, "and we have no intention to be involved with it."

"The Creed—the religion that rules in Desera—demands

that all people must join their efforts to bring back the Wizard by being submissive to his divinity," Navid said. "It may not be soon, but eventually, the Dominion will find you here. And if you don't submit, they will destroy you."

"That is not the way Wizard Titan will return—"

"It doesn't matter," Navid waved a hand. "The Deseran Dominion has decided to wield their ideals offensively. Before they died, the prophets in Caldor were attempting to prepare for the coming war. Without their guidance or the unifying power of Caldor, we are more vulnerable than ever."

A low hum of voices surrounded him as the translation passed between the villagers. Tal Dian's expression hardened as he considered Navid's words, but it was the woman beside him who spoke up.

"If what this seer says is true, then we have no choice but to reincarnate the power of Wizard Titan."

Tal Dian gave her a sharp look. "Tal Eva? What are you saying? We will lose our entire way of life."

Tal Eva sighed. "Look around, Tal Dian. We are already losing our forest. Our time here has been long, wonderful, and prosperous. But it is at an end."

"People could die!" Tal Dian said.

"People *will* die," she countered. "But if we stop this war, far fewer will."

"But the Keeper. She can—"

"The seer has told you already. She has no knowledge of how to save our forest." Tal Eva regarded Navid. "Are you sure there is nothing she knows?"

"Nothing I'm aware of," Navid said. "But she believed that if she and the Wizard could work together, they might be able to write a new spell that could save your forest."

Tal Dian jaw worked with anger but his words came out even. "Elders. What is your decision?"

For what felt an hour of uncomfortable confusion, Navid waited as the Elders discussed their decision in their tongue, forcing Navid to wait, unsure which decision was gaining the most ground. Unsurprisingly, the debate was heated, but Tal

Dian and Tal Eva said the least, allowing the others to give their piece.

Navid's heart ached for them. The inevitable demise of their traditional home was a horrible fate. If he had any idea that Caldor would crumble before he'd returned, he knew he would have done all that he could to keep that from happening.

But fate is an ocean stronger than any man. And to willfully deny the future when it inevitably bares down on you is the act of a fool. These people had a chance to mediate the change to come. The Tal did not strike Navid as an unwise people. And so it came as no surprise when at long last Tal Dian turned to Navid and said, "We will take you to the Seed."

Unsure of the proper customs of the Tal, Navid dipped his head respectfully. "Thank you, elders."

"We will take you now," Tal Eva said. "You may need much time to put the world right again."

"Thank you," he said again. "But before I go, I would like to see Tele, my companion."

The elders agreed to his request, and then, with the slightest of glances, the elders dispersed the crowd. As Navid glanced about, he realized that a good portion of the village had paused to come see what he was about. A few hundred people now scattered, re-entering nest like buildings and picking up where they'd left off with their lives.

Navid crossed the village circle and stepped into the healer's cabin where he was shocked to find an even more bazaar interior. The pale glow of fungi tucked between the bands of wall, cast an eerie light across the simple furnishings. Dozens of clay jars were stacked with care along the back wall just behind a low bed where the Tal had laid Tele to rest. A Tal man and woman glanced his way momentarily but didn't spare him much time before they returned to mixing a dark paste with a pungent odor and sorting a strange tangle of vines that stemmed from the ceiling.

Assuming their disregard was a signal for him to come closer, Navid crossed to Tele's side. Her eyes were closed and she breathed at an even but slow rate. The purple that had washed her skin had deepened since the ardya's poison had first attacked her. In a strange, water-like pattern, the color rippled across her skin, alternating rings of contrast from light to dark.

"I'm so sorry," Navid whispered. "I have to go to retrieve the power from the Seed. The elders said they can make you better. Please hold on. I—" His voice broke, and a gentle sob unexpectedly tore away from him. "I'm sorry."

He reached out to take her hand.

"No!" the Tal woman said.

Navid quickly withdrew. "I'm sorry. I didn't know I couldn't touch her."

"The poison can be excited by the touch," the Tal man said.

Instead of asking how they planned to treat her if they couldn't even touch her, he respected their knowledge and gave them a short nod. He turned back to Tele. "I'll see you soon."

He waited a moment. In her state, he didn't expect her to acknowledge him, but he knew that if she could hear him at all, she'd have something to say, and it felt rude to walk away in the middle of it—as harsh as it was sure to be.

A man came to Navid's side. "The elders have chosen me as the new vessel for the Seed."

Navid turned to see Tal Aval next to him. "You must be honored."

"We go?" Tal Aval asked.

Navid met Tal Aval's eyes then nodded.

It was the event of a lifetime. The successor to Wizard Titan would finally come. This story might pass down for generations—how Tal Aval walked straight into a dark abyss. How he'd valiantly returned, all-powerful. It would make for an engrossing tale, a tale that Navid should be honored to be apart of—fully present for.

But all he felt was the fear that he might enter the forest and never return to see her again.

"Come then," Tal Aval said. "We journey."

Tal Aval placed a hand on his shoulder, turning away from the village. Tal Opas stood waiting ahead. When he approached, the two Tal men took the lead, but Navid stood still for a moment longer as the tug on his heart pleaded for him to see Tele once more. But eventually he resigned himself to the journey ahead and crossed into the unknown.

TWENTY-TWO

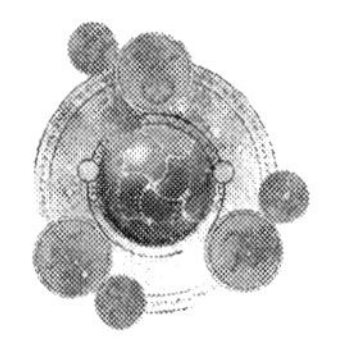

BLADED CASCADE

Gabriel fell back, keeping his opponent just out of striking range. Lurin sprung forward and swung his practice staff at him again. Allowing his form to slip, Gabriel stepped sideways to stay within the circle, then parried the attack.

He could see that Lurin was tiring. If he didn't manage to get in a good strike soon, even Gabriel wouldn't be able to make it look like they were on even footing. Lurin's fierce gaze met him with determination before he lunged again. This time he stumbled. Gabriel had to end this. He'd avoided Lurin's attacks as much as he could.

Trying to make his attempt look clumsy, he retaliated. Lurin's expression shifted from tenacity to uncertainty. Gabriel had fought defensively, as one who could barely hold his ground. Lurin fought back despite his change of tact, moving into a defensive cadence—one that could be easily maintained; one Gabriel expected.

Gabriel took the opportunity to push forward unconventionally, forcing Lurin to shift from his dominant footing to a weaker, submissive stance. With three sloppy but well-placed maneuvers, Gabriel forced him to the ground and ended the fight with a staff to his neck.

The Second League cheered as Gabriel backed a step and put away his practice staff. He offered Lurin a hand up, but he refused and rolled to his feet with a curse. He sheathed his mock sword and left the circle. Gabriel followed, breathing hard to feign exhaustion.

Mel clapped him on the back has he sat down. "Wisdoms, Gabe. I ain't see that comin'. You're gettin' good."

"Thanks," Gabriel said. "I've been practicing."

"Shows."

"Embarrassing," Cainan said to no one in particular. "This is what happens when our land relies on orphans and thieves to defend us. Pathetic."

"Bear, Jae," Captain Alden called out. "In the circle."

Bear and Jae drew their mock swords and faced each other. It was the fourth time in the past several days since Captain Alden began their close combat training that they'd faced off. Every time, Jae had won. The captain crossed his arms expectantly.

"*Two quarter marks says the westerner takes it in the face*," Paitin said to his twin brother in Armothean.

Urwell grunted. "*Three quarter marks says he takes it in the face and soils himself.*"

Paitin laughed and nodded toward Gabriel. "*Maybe some of the gentlemen here are betting men. The odds against Bear are almost irresistible at this point. I wouldn't mind going home richer than I left.*"

Gabriel blinked, smiled, then looked away. No one else in the Second League seemed to understand Armothean, so Gabriel pretended he didn't either in the interest of maintaining the illusion of his disadvantaged childhood.

"It's rude when you do that," Cainan said, frowning at the two brothers. "If you're going to talk, speak in a language we can *all* understand."

Paitin shrugged. "I thought I'd spare you our commentary on how different the weather in North Hzorah is from the South."

Cainan fixed him with a hard glare. "The weather has never been *that* funny."

Jae pushed an attack to test Bear's defenses. While Bear was much larger than Jae, his weight aided him little when held at staff point. Bear was nervous. Gabriel could tell by the way he gripped his practice staff. If he didn't loosen up, he'd lose again.

"You're in a High family, ain't you?" Mel asked Cainan. "You don't know any Armorth?"

"*Armothean*," Urwell corrected.

Mel gave Urwell a glance. "Really? Huh. Didn't know that."

Cainan's ears reddened as his frowned deepened. "There are more important things for a High Lord to learn than Ar*moth*un."

Urwell rolled his eyes. "*Armothean*."

"And if Captain Alden pairs me with you next, I'll show you first hand."

It had been like this for the past few weeks, and Gabriel had little more choice than to sit and listen to Cainan's insufferable bragging. As he prattled on, it took everything he had not to turn around and choke him.

His fatiguing affect on Gabriel wasn't lost to Cainan. He was fully aware. Even now, Cainan stood intentionally close to Gabriel and spoke just loud enough for everyone to hear, as if daring his cousin to question any of his claims or challenge his superiority as the son of a High Lord.

The worst part of it all was that Cainan wasn't entirely wrong. He *was* a good soldier in almost every right, except his unceasing tongue. Most of his stories and claims were true. He wasn't shy about proving it either. Luckily, Captain Alden hadn't forced them to duel. Gabriel wasn't sure he'd be able to resist putting him in his place.

Jae danced around Bear, compelling his opponent to retreat in circles. Bear tried to get in a strike, but Jae warded the effort. Before Bear could recover, Jae advanced again, cutting his way past Bear's defenses. Within moments, Jae conquered his giant.

"*Glad we didn't bet on that one*," Urwell said to his brother with a small shrug.

"And *that*, boys, is how *we* do it in the West," Cainan said, smirking. He clapped Jae on the back when he trotted up. "I didn't doubt you for a second, Jae. Keep that up and you'll be a scorching Low Lord when you get home, I'll see to that."

Jae smiled, but remained as quiet as usual as he scooped up his waterskin and took a long drink. Bear, red-faced and winded, sat next to Mel.

Mel handed him a waterskin. "You'll get him next time."

"Bastard's quick," Bear said before drinking. "I ain't that fast. I'll trip."

"You let him get too close," Gabriel said. "You're bigger than him. He may have you on speed, but if you don't let him get close enough, speed won't matter."

Bear nodded. "I'll remember that."

"Cainan, Aeron," Captain Alden said. "In the circle."

A long, swelling "oh" rose from the Second League. It was a fantastic pairing. While Aeron wasn't a phenomenal swordsman, he was a step above Lurin, Bear, Fabi, and Mel—the Second League's weaker fighters. But Cainan hadn't lost a duel yet.

With a final clap on Jae's back, Cainan stepped out with a wide smirk on his face. Aeron came from behind Gabriel and faced Cainan with a grim expression. Several passing soldiers from other divisions trotted over after hearing the rumored High Lord's name, trying to see if it was really true that West Hzorah's rising High Lord had graced them with his presence.

"I won't embarrass you," Cainan said. "I'll make it quick."

"*It's the blond beast versus the medicine man*!" Paitin said with dramatic flourish.

Cainan shot Paitin a glare. "None of that Armoth talk while I'm working. It's bloody rude."

"He's right," Urwell said. "Cainan knows a lot about rude behavior."

Gabriel smirked at that, but his humor fell away as he observed the two facing off. Cainan brandished his staff, letting it spin in his grip before forming into the stance he'd seen him take a hundred times before in their youth. Gabriel never particularly liked his wide side-stepping position, but it had a fantastic advantage for fending off fatal strikes.

Aeron shifted into a simple swordsman's stance. Though his form and posture was near perfect, his muscles looked tense and his staff dipped a sliver too low. It was a defender's stance. Cainan would be the first mover.

Accepting the invitation, Cainan pounced. Their mock blades met as Aeron warded against his attacker. With fluid calm, Cainan immediately switched tact and struck lower. Again, Aeron protected himself, trading a step of ground for leverage.

"*Three quarter marks on the medicine man,*" Paitin said to his brother.

"*Him?*" Urwell asked. "*He's barely attacking.*"

"*He's just figuring out the Lordling's approach while he tires himself out.*"

"*Fine. Three quarters.*"

Gabriel frowned as he scrutinized the duel. The Second League soldiers hooted and cheered as they watched the staffs fly, but none of them saw what Gabriel saw—the advantage that years of kinship had taught him about his cousin. Cainan liked giving a good show. He struck slower and with less strength than Gabriel knew him capable of. Keeping to the easily warded basics of offensive sparring, he allowed his attacks to fail.

With his first move of aggression, Aeron pushed Cainan away. Cainan fell back, stumbling back into his opening stance.

Cainan attacked again with keener dexterity. Moving from cadence to cadence, he gave a showing of his more skilled tactics. Aeron fought in stride, his form slipping under the patterns he was less familiar with.

"*Still want that bet?*" Urwell asked. "*Because I do.*"

"*Scorch it …*" Paitin grumbled then shouted at the battle ring. "Come on, Aeron! Do some damage!"

Increasing his speed, Cainan pushed Aeron into frantic defense. All sense of calm drained from his demeanor as he struggled to parry the fury of Cainan's charge. Cainan, in the grip of glory, took the opportunity to embellish his attacks with unnecessary theatrics, drawing out more chatter and shouts from his captive audience.

"*Bet's off, Urwell.*"

"*You can't call it off because you're losing.*"

With immaculate grace, Cainan descended the tree of cadences, driving Aeron back against the edge of the circle, then to a knee. His killing blow stopped just before Aeron's neck.

As if they were watching a Crown City cart race, the surrounding onlookers erupted in cheer. Gabriel was suddenly aware that the duel had drawn a large crowd of soldiers from other divisions. The applause of a good fifty or sixty men surrounded them. Soldiers shouted their approval, several turned about, attempting to mimic Cainan's bladed cascade with imaginary weapons.

Cainan gave his newfound fans a charming smile and a short bow of appreciation before withdrawing his weapon from Aeron's throat.

Jae clasped hands with Cainan as he stepped out of the circle. Aeron retreated back behind the Second League. Paitin fished out three quarter marks and reluctantly gave them to his smug-faced brother.

"That was an exceptional performance," Captain Alden said as he approached with his arms folded. "I'll have to remember to pair you with someone a bit more advanced next time."

Cainan smirked. "I doubt anyone here would fare much better, Captain."

"Perhaps," Captain Alden said then raised his voice so that the Second League could hear him clearly over chatter. "You all earned your dinner this evening. Go get rations. Meet back here tomorrow morning before dawn. Don't be late, or you'll be doing laps until you collapse." He shot a glare at Lurin. "I'm talking about you." He looked at Gabriel. "You. I'd like a word."

The Second League dispersed around him as Gabriel

approached the captain. Alden's arms were crossed as he watched him with a discerning frown.

"What happened out there?" he asked.

Gabriel glanced at the dirt circle. "I think Jae is much faster than Bear, sir. And Cainan—"

"No," Captain Alden interjected. "I mean what happened with you."

Gabriel raised his eyebrows and shrugged innocently. "I guess I figured out Lurin's weak point."

"Bosh. You could have beaten him at any time. You're as transparent as that High Lord's son."

"I've been trying—"

"I've been a soldier for a long time. I know the difference between an inexperienced fighter and one who's holding back. You may have the rest of the Second League fooled, but not me."

Gabriel met his eyes. "Alright, sir. You're right. But I've only been doing it because—"

"Scorch it," Captain Alden said. "I don't care *why* you're doing it. But it had better end. Can you explain to me where the honor is in what you're doing?"

Gabriel stood mute for a moment. He didn't have a reasonable answer. "No, sir."

"Then it had best end," he said. "I will accept nothing but absolute honor from you." He paused, considering. "And I want you to spend some time helping Aeron with his technique."

Gabriel looked at the captain. "I … Aeron and I don't really get along all that well."

Captain Alden fixed him with a stern glare. "Gabriel, it was framed as a suggestion. That was my mistake. You will spend the next few weeks after I'm finished with the group training with Aeron."

"Yes, sir."

"Excellent."

Gabriel met Aeron on a broad plateau that overlooked Hzorah encampment. The sun was large and orange as it approached the horizon, and the cool evening air felt wonderful after the day's relentless training.

"I don't need your help," Aeron said, rubbing his wrist. "I was just tired. It was a long day."

"Right," Gabriel set his pack on the ground. "But Captain's orders." When Aeron didn't look at him, Gabriel said, "Look, I'll let the captain know that you're progressing fine, and he'll probably let you stop doing it. But I have to at least say I sparred with you."

"You don't *have* to."

Gabriel shrugged. "No. I don't. But if I lie to him and you lose like that again, that's not going to look good on me. And I'm not interested in doing any more laps than I have to."

"Fine," Aeron said as Gabriel pulled a practice staff from his pack and tossed it to him. He took the same stance as he did with Cainan, flaws and all. "Let's get it over with," he said, then added: "It's not as though you're much better."

Almost before Gabriel could raise his own staff, Aeron charged. Despite the surprise, Gabriel countered his advance, disarmed him, and stopped just short of striking him in the throat. "Dead."

With a growl, Aeron picked up his staff and tried again, this time putting a bit more care into how he moved. Drifting into the third cadence, Gabriel sidestepped the first attack, parried the second, then dropped Aeron with a sweep of the legs.

"Dead."

"Scorch it!" Aeron rolled onto all fours and got back to his feet, returning to his sloppy form once more.

Gabriel waved his wooden sword away. "Never mind. You're not ready to duel yet. We need to work on your posture." Gabriel stepped up to Aeron and adjusted his arms, then pressed down on his shoulders. "Relax your shoulders. Don't lock your knees."

Aeron did as instructed, allowing himself to be maneuvered about but not without a grimace of humiliation. "If you're this good, why'd you keep losing when we practice?"

Gabriel circled him to make sure that his posture was just right. When he was satisfied, he paused just before him. "I don't know. Maybe I wasn't taking this as seriously as I should have."

Aeron stared straight ahead toward the Shadow Peaks as if focused on an invisible foe. "That's stupid. Shoved, even."

It was Gabriel's turn to feel the burn of embarrassment. "You're right. Captain Alden felt the same way." His posture corrected, Gabriel asked, "Do you feel it?"

Aeron gave a slight nod.

"Good. Reset and we'll do it again. This will be position 'one.'"

Aeron relaxed, letting his staff drop to the side.

"One."

Aeron moved back into position.

"Chin up a bit more," Gabriel corrected, and Aeron lifted his head slightly. "Good. From now on, 'zero' will be reset. Ready?"

Again, Aeron only responded with a small nod.

"Zero."

Aeron reset.

"One."

He shifted back into position, taking only a moment longer than optimal to find his perfect shape. Gabriel repeated the cycle over and over while he paced. He watched Aeron as he attempted to move into position with pristine accuracy. Being the son of a merchant hadn't afforded him the practice he needed to commit these movements to reflexive memory. But after some time, Aeron had tuned his body to do it just the way Gabriel wanted. Now it was time to allow his mind to start practicing it without all of his focus.

"One," Gabriel stopped pacing just beside him. "Why'd you enlist?"

"Same reason most people do, I suppose," Aeron said. "Because I had to."

"Zero. Is that why the others are here?"

"Lurin is. His family has been on the edge since his father died. He's lucky Lord Laonne allowed him to work his orchards, but that's only seasonal. If he returns a war hero, he can turn that respect into real prospects. If he doesn't … well … I guess it'd be the same if he never came. He and his younger siblings are headed for ruin."

"One."

"Bear's family isn't in rough shape, but if things go well here, they'd be in line for Low Lordship. Not that he wants to be here. He's under a lot of pressure from the farmers around those parts. Getting a farmer raised to the title will help change some of the laws. Bear's father served in the Dominion War. If he comes back home alive, they might have enough standing to move up."

"Zero."

"I'm not sure what Jae's story is. He's always so bloody quiet. All I know is he's already well off. His father's a Guardsman. Must be nice."

"One."

"Urwell and Paitin were both drafted. The draft is supposed to be random, but it got them both. They had a good life in the south. And their parents are too old to have more children. I guess it's something like that with Mel, too."

"Zero."

"As far as I can tell," Aeron said, "You, Fabi, and Cainan are the only scorching dolts that are daft enough to come out here voluntarily. Cainan's the son of a High Lord, so that makes a little sense—a status play. Fabi is on some masochistic quest for redemption, so I can kind of understand him. But you … You're here because you *want* to be."

Gabriel frowned at him. "I don't have anywhere else to go."

Aeron raised his eyebrows. "You could have entered an apprenticeship lottery. You could have tried to be a deckhand on a ship. Wisdoms, you made it all the way out here. You could have tried to find refuge in Caldor. At least you wouldn't be at risk of death."

He was right. He had other options. At least the Gabriel he'd invented had other options. Now that he'd thought about it, it was a pretty big flaw in his contrivance. Caldor wouldn't have been an option anymore, but he wasn't sure how widespread the knowledge of what happened there was at the moment. The information was probably only just filtering through the land. The soldiers out here would probably be the last to hear of it.

"We had soldiers before the Crown began drafting soldiers," Gabriel said. "Some people actually want to fight to protect our lands. Is it so strange that I want to do the same?"

"Sure." Aeron shrugged, then moved into form with Gabriel's prompting. "That makes sense. And I don't see anything wrong with that. Some of us, though, don't have a choice. Some of us want to actually make the land that's being protected a good place from the inside. You had a choice to do that. Maybe you should be here. But if it were me …" He shook his head.

Gabriel watched in silence as Aeron continued to practice. He'd always felt so trapped in the Crown Palace, restricted. Sitting through Samuel's lectures, being forced to learn other languages and geography, and, most recently, being forced to study the Crown's proceedings in person. It had never occurred to him that maybe other people felt the same—imprisoned. He'd always pictured a warrior as being the embodiment of agency. Lords argue. Warriors conquer.

He'd left the Crown City knowing that this was the right choice. Being a king was all wrong for him. He needed to step out and fight. Even Captain Alden didn't want him holding back anymore.

"Keep going," Gabriel said before sitting to watch. "You need to keep going until you can do it without thinking."

As Aeron continued the movement independently, Gabriel intended to eat the last bit of preserves from his pack. It'd been weeks since he'd had a proper meal, and it seemed to him that the food issued to the troops was prepared by cooks without tongues.

Gabriel pulled the preserves out of his pack, and the small jar clinked against the hilt of the Crown Sabre as his hand brushed up against it. And with that, it was like he'd escaped the bounds of the present and slipped into the memories of the past …

Gabriel pulled his sword ready to duel, but Jeremiah waved it away. "No. You're not ready to duel yet. First, you must understand what I'm teaching you."

Gabriel frowned. "You're teaching me to duel."

"Yes," Jeremiah said. "But being a warrior—a warrior king—is much more than the blade."

"What else is there?" Gabriel asked. "You see an enemy, and you …" He motioned across his throat with his sword.

"That, my son, is the action of a follower," Jeremiah said. "The passive complacency of a man who relies on the judgement of others to justify his actions. Every action you take is a choice—even inaction. And the very first choice you must make is leadership."

"But I just want—"

"If you do not choose to lead, then your blade will lead for you. And there is no more foolish a man than one who allows his blade to be his master."

Gabriel stared at the Crown Sabre a moment, shocked that he'd remembered something that he hadn't thought of in years. And with such vivid clarity. Not like the hazy meanderings of a dream. It was as if his father was standing right there before him, so close he could smell him, almost touch him.

Shuttering at the uncanny feeling, he pulled the jar free, opened it, and ate a mouthful of apricot. He savored the cool sweetness that was missing from his new warrior's diet. Sweet was just one of many words missing from the vocabulary of flavors that composed their rations.

Aeron continued to practice his form, his movements becoming more natural and relaxed. Gabriel had enlisted thinking that every soldier would be eager to fight, that they'd all be almost as good if not *as* good of a fighter as he was. But hundreds of them were like Aeron—just good enough but needing further instruction to be great. Thousands of them were worse.

Gabriel suddenly realized that Captain Alden had asked him to help Aeron because he saw that he was different, that he was already on track to be the kind of warrior the army needed. Gabriel had to accept that role. He had to choose to lead.

"Good," Gabriel said, stopping Aeron. "Just ten more forms to practice before we call it a night."

"*Ten?*" Aeron frowned. "That could take all night."

"I hope not," Gabriel said. "I want to get some sleep before Captain Alden has his way with us again. So, I hope you catch on quick."

"Good thing my father taught me how to make his sour tea," Aeron said. "I'm going to need it to be able to get out of bed in the morning."

Gabriel picked up his staff and stood beside Aeron and demonstrated the next form. "I hope yours is better than Nurse Ma—" He paused, catching himself. "Than the orphanage's brew. I'll need some, too."

TWENTY-THREE

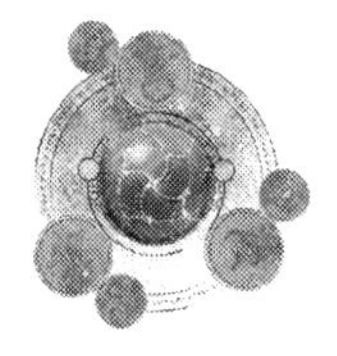

A TRUE CHALLENGE

Gabriel pushed Aeron back, then stepped to the side. He held his wooden blade between them while Aeron recovered. Rolling his shoulders, Aeron relaxed, took a deep breath, then took the time to reset his attack.

Smiling, Gabriel nodded to him, signaling that he was ready for it. Again, Aeron charged at an unnaturally slow rate. He attacked, moving from the first cadence to the fourth, to the fifth, then back to the first. Gabriel forced him away to repeat the cycle.

"Good," Gabriel encouraged. "Don't rush. Take the time you need to properly move back into form. Don't speed up your attack. This is about perfecting your transitions. Keep it slow."

Aeron gave a short nod, and stepped forward, moving from form to form, taking his time to make sure he'd executed each with precision. Gabriel felt a strong sense of pride at how well Aeron learned and how much he'd improved in such a short time.

In the distance, three dark silhouettes marched up the hill-side. Gabriel called for Aeron to take a break, then let his sword drop as Mel, Fabi, and Bear approached.

"Scorching fierce," Mel said, smiling. He looked to Fabi and Bear. "I told you it'd be worth it."

"What's this about?" Gabriel asked as he drilled the tip of his staff into the earth.

Bear nodded toward Aeron. "We saw how good Aeron was getting during training."

"You *saw*," Mel winced and rubbed his ribs. "You ain't felt it like me. The healer's got some punch."

"And we was wondering," Bear continued. "I mean … We saw you fixin' to go practice with Aeron and thought we'd watch is all. Maybe we could learn something."

Gabriel looked at Aeron, who shrugged. "They can watch me. But I think they might get more out of it if they practiced with me."

"If you three are serious about this," Gabriel said, "you can join in. But it won't do much good if you're not willing to push yourselves."

"I'll do anything to keep my ribs from getting cracked," Mel said as he moved to stand next to Aeron. Bear and Fabi stepped up beside them as well, both gave Gabriel a nod of confirmation.

"Very well, then." Gabriel pulled his sword from the ground. "We'll began with the basic formations, then move into common extensions tomorrow. The faster you get it right, the faster you can rest. Understood?"

Gabriel spent the next hour drilling them on their forms until their posture was flawless. He practiced with them, uncomfortable being a drill master who didn't participate. After he was sure they had these forms committed to memory, he began showing them how to use sets of forms to perform cadences, then how to move from cadence to cadence. Three hours later, all four continued to run his exercises without complaint before he called the night.

Half the night gone, they laid down on the hilltop for a few precious hours of rest before Captain Alden expected them ready for morning drills. Gabriel watched the clouds glow under the moonlight as they passed over the stars, racing the eastern winds.

"I think I just found a new muscle," Mel said into the darkness. "And it hurts."

"Is it your tongue?" Bear asked. "It ain't never stopped since we met."

Mel laughed, and the others joined in.

"Where you going after this, Fabi?" Mel asked. "I don't mean to put my nose in, but I can't stop thinking about it."

Fabi sighed. "I'm living one day at a time. If I make it out alive, I'll think of something."

"With Gabriel helping," Bear said, "I reckon we'll be some of the best swordsmen in the whole army. If we don't make it out, no one will. Ain't that right, Gabe?"

"But if the Dominion gets the upper hand …" Aeron snapped his fingers. "Just like that, it'll be all over. They only need to get the upper hand on you once. You have to win every scorching time."

"I heard we got almost twice as many men as they do," Mel said.

Aeron scoffed. "Where'd you hear that?"

"Around. They've been out in that desert. There can't be that many of them."

"Then why would they even bother?" Aeron asked.

"They're Deserans," Bear said. "They think they have a right to things. I know a family who's still devoted to the Dominion's Creed out by my farm. Pa won't let us tell others around about their religion because he don't think it right. People might try to do something to them. But they're like that. Always muttering under their breath about what's coming to them when the Wizard comes back."

"That's the worst kind of enemy," Fabi said. "Once, a man tried to kill my father because he thought that he'd touched his wife. My father is a lot of things—a thief, a cheat—but he never messed with anyone's wife. It didn't matter to this man. He fought like it was true, and if he didn't kill him, he'd be damned himself. I've never seen anything more fierce. If the

Dominion thinks they have a right to this, they'll fight like a nightmare."

"Then *we'll* fight like a nightmare," Gabriel said. "'Give the Creed a hand hold, and they will take the mountain.' We know what we have to lose. If we don't protect everything we love—our freedom to live a life free of single-minded, dogmatic tyranny—we'll lose everything that makes Hzorah beautiful. Our cultures, our beliefs, our histories will be choked out, blanched. That's a future that cannot be allowed to come to pass. We owe that to our mothers and fathers, our brothers, sisters, and descendants. We owe it to ourselves. Like a nightmare, we'll fight. And we will crush them before the mountains and burn their bodies where they lie."

After a moment of reverent silence, Mel broke it. "Wisdoms, Gabe! Where'd you learn to speak like that?"

Gabriel closed his eyes, remembering his father. "I don't know."

"Bear," Mel said. "What's the first thing you gonna do when you get back home?"

"Build a rope swing out near the lake," Bear said. "I'm gonna get all my brothers and sisters to go out and swim with me. It'll be about summer then."

"After this past winter, I don't want spring and summer to end," Mel said.

"Maybe you two can come out to the coast sometime," Aeron said. "The water there is perfect in summer."

The cool spring air relaxed Gabriel as they talked into the night. He smiled to himself as he listened to their stories—to dreams of a future lived in happiness—and vowed to do everything within his power to see them fulfilled.

Gabriel led Mel and Fabi across the field as he tracked the opposing team. Urwell and Paitin trotted behind Cainan as he moved into an attacking position. A few weeks ago, he would have been more concerned about the match up, but Mel and

Fabi had become much more competent in their dueling since they'd began their night sessions. As long as he held Cainan at bay, Mel and Fabi could handle the other two.

He glanced at Captain Vanik of the Third League who watched as Gabriel advanced up the field. At Captain Alden's request, Vanik had brought ten of his men to assist in the war game. While they had all improved in isolated combat, Captain Alden had devised a whole new way to push them.

Gabriel's father had taught him how organization must be found in the chaos of battle, and he'd picked Aeron, Fabi, Mel and Bear for his team for that very reason—he'd learned to trust them as they improved under his instruction. The Third Leaguers on his team were a different story. They were wild cards.

Keeping the wet, red dye that coated the practice staff well away from his body, he picked up his pace and charged straight for Cainan's knot of offensive scouts. Though Gabriel was certain he'd hidden his team's flag well, there was no reason to let the three break his defensive line.

"Fabi," Gabriel said as he slowed before Cainan. "You guard Urwell. Mel, you guard Paitin. I'll hold off Cainan."

Mel and Fabi grunted their understanding and split off. Cainan smirked as he stepped up to Gabriel. The blue paint on his practice staff blurred as he spun it before falling into an attack stance. Gabriel shifted into a counter-stance and glared at his cousin.

"Bet you wish you could have had me on your team," Cainan said. "We would have dominated if we were both together, don't you—"

Catching Gabriel off guard, Cainan lunged at him. Gabriel caught his attack and warded the flurry of combinations before breaking away. He took a beat to glance at Mel and Fabi to make sure they'd still held against the twins.

"Apart though," Cainan continued, "I'm afraid that I have the upper hand, especially with the lot you selected for your team. Honestly, Gabriel, what would possess you to select the dregs?"

"I wouldn't be so confident."

Cainan had continued to be insufferable and Gabriel was weary of the routine—the constant jabbing to edge him into revealing who he was or give up and desert. It was a game that Cainan didn't seem to tire of. Gabriel could hardly believe he used to be close with his cousin.

Gabriel pushed forward, attacking Cainan's defenses as his anger broiled. Invigorated by a true challenge, Cainan laughed aloud, pushing back with as much ferocity as Gabriel injected.

Cainan twisted away as he parried Gabriel's charge. "Don't think I don't see what you're doing. I've noticed you taking the thief and his company away at night. How amiable you're being with them. Don't forget who you are and where you came from. You don't belong with them. And if you're not going to tell them who you are, you need to fall in line behind me."

As the two team leaders faced off, Gabriel relaxed into the heat of the duel. It had been a long time since he'd been properly challenged. He'd almost forgotten the bliss of fighting an expert swordsman. He gave himself over to it, drank it greedily. Someone had to put Cainan in his place, and he was the only one who could.

Cainan pushed his weight into his next attack. Cainan was bigger than Gabriel and the force of it threatened to push him off balance. He dug in his heels as Cainan pushed against his staff, his face coming uncomfortably close to his cousin's.

"Dear Gabriel," Cainan sneered. "I thought you'd forgotten how to duel with how poorly you've been performing lately. I almost bought into your bosh duels."

"Dear Cainan," Gabriel said through gritted teeth. "I think you'll find that from now on, I'll be *quite* boshless."

"Unfortunately, your team can't say the same thing."

With a mighty shove, Cainan pushed him away. Before he could recover, Cainan's boot caught him in the chest. Gabriel's head smacked the packed earth. He struggled to breathe, but the impact took his breath. His head and chest burning, he rolled over to his hands and knees.

Cainan was charging down the field. Beyond, he could see Jae, sprinting back to his side, a red flag clutched in his hand. He'd found it.

Gabriel managed a breath as he pulled himself to a knee. "Fabi! Mel! Jae has the flag!" He staggered to his feet as Fabi came to Gabriel's call. "Where's Mel?"

"Captured," Fabi said as he helped Gabriel steady himself. "Are you alright?"

"I'm fine," Gabriel wheezed. "Just stop them."

Fabi nodded and ran after the duo. Gabriel took several, reviving breaths before he followed. He saw that Paitin also noticed Jae's find and was moving to defend his team's attempt.

Gabriel's eyes watered as he ran. His muscles burned, and his heart pounded. He hadn't taken the proper time to catch his breath. But if he didn't push on, Cainan would win.

Coming up from the rear, Bear dove for Jae. He didn't get a firm grip, but the weight of him slowed Jae to a stop. Seeing his chance, Fabi struck Jae with his staff, leaving a red mark across his shirt.

Gabriel tried to keep going, but his lungs refused to carry him any further. He slowed to a stop, panting, watching the scene helplessly.

Bear was up again. He spotted the flag, but before he could reach for it, Cainan cut him off. Their staffs met, and in short order, Cainan pushed him back from the flag while Paitin engaged Fabi. The snapping sound of wooden staff against wooden staff spotted the field.

Fabi managed to push Paitin back who fell backward into Cainan, almost edging his cousin into one of Bear's strikes. Cainan crouched and took hold of Paitin's shirt. The twin cried out as he rolled over Cainan's back. Cainan rose again, adding momentum and sending Paitin hurtling into Bear. The two collapsed in muffled grunts.

In a flash, Cainan spun, striking Fabi across the chest with his practice staff. All three soldiers down, Cainan snatched the flag from the ground and sprinted back to his side of the field. Several Third League soldiers chased him, but Cainan had too much of a lead. He held the flag high above his head, parading his victory as he carried the prize back to his side of the field. Cainan's defensive line of Third League soldiers sent up a cheer as their captain met them. Lurin ran headlong into him and gave him several celebratory claps on the back.

"Alright!" Captain Alden called. "That's game!"

"*The bloody shover,*" Paitin growled in Armothean as he rolled to his feet. "*Where is he?*"

Gabriel straightened as Paitin ran for Cainan and caught him from behind with a shoulder. Shouts rose from the soldiers as the two tumbled to the ground. Urwell and Lurin jumped into the fray, pulling the two apart.

"Bloody scorching mopper!" Cainan shouted as Lurin and pulled him away.

Paitin let out his own string of foreign obscenities as his brother pulled him back, trying to calm him. Captain Alden and Vanik stepped in, moving between the two. Vanik pulled Paitin into a headlock and shoved Urwell away when he tried to protest.

"Low-born dolt!" Cainan shouted, his mouth the only thing unrestrained by his team. "I won the bloody game for you, you bloody mopper. Armothean *idiot.* I bet your father's scrubbing floors back home while your sitter of a mother watches."

"That's enough!" Captain Alden yelled. "Go get cleaned up. And if I so much as suspect someone is thinking about fighting, all of you will be scrubbing the dungeons at the stronghold for a week."

Cainan shoved off Lurin and Jae and pushed his way through the rest of the soldiers as he stormed back to camp. Mel trotted up to Gabriel's side.

"You alright, Gabe?" Mel asked. "I ain't never seen anyone take a kick in stride like that."

"I'm fine," Gabriel said, as he watched his cousin shrink in the distance. "Just a bit winded. That's all. I need to walk it off."

Gabriel and Mel met with Aeron, Fabi, and Bear as they

followed the soldiers back to camp. Urwell and Paitin argued furiously in Armothean just ahead. Urwell kept a hand on his brother's shoulder, trying to calm him or keep him from running after Cainan.

"He's angry," Mel said.

"Is he?" Aeron asked. "I couldn't tell."

"I should be the angry one," Bear said, cradling his ribs. "That southerner is more solid than you'd think."

"I'll take a look at you when we get back," Aeron said then looked at Gabriel. "Both of you. Make sure you don't have anything broken."

Gabriel nodded before he turned to watch his cousin stalk away. He'd promised him he wouldn't allow him to hurt anyone in the Second League and he'd meant it. If Cainan couldn't pull his conduct together, he would jeopardize the unit. And that could mean death on the battlefield.

The cart shifted as it pulled off the main highway. Amie held onto the bars for support while the road tossed and jostled. Squinting against the low evening sun, she watched a few of the Dominion soldiers dismount and allow their horses to carefully navigate the path without added weight.

"Are we stopping again?" Amie asked one of the soldiers on horseback who pulled in close to the cart as the path narrowed.

He ignored her. They all ignored her. Mara insisted she not talk to them, saying that annoying their captors wouldn't bring them any good graces. Amie didn't listen.

They can't ignore us forever, Amie thought. And why should they? We can't do them any harm from in here. The least they could do is keep us company. She knew it was an absurd idea, but she'd held to it anyway. Nothing lasts forever. Not even silence.

It'd been over two weeks since they'd been torn from their home. Her father had been beaten and left incapacitated. While the soldiers shoved small bowls of water and morsels of bread through the cage bars when they remembered they had captives, it was hardly enough to sustain all three of them. She and Mara sacrificed the brunt of it for her father. He needed to have as much nourishment as possible.

But yesterday, Father had stopped eating.

Neither of them had any significant knowledge about healing. Father's injuries were far beyond their ability to treat, especially in the back of wheeled cage. It was only by Desolate's Hand that her father still breathed.

Mara sat up at the other end of the cart. It had only taken a couple days before they settled into a new rhythm of sleeping through most of the travel and waking in the evening when the soldiers slowed to a stop.

Amie avoided looking at Mara. She knew her sister was watching her. Every time their eyes met, she could almost hear what her sister wanted to say.

This was all her fault.

When they weren't caring for Father, her thoughts spiraled about Gavini and Tele and Navid. Was Gavini alright? Was he even alive? He shouldn't be traveling in his condition.

She replayed the memory of the soldier cutting into the two Azuri men again and again. The blunt hacking had kept her out of the kitchens at the inn. Even now, she could still smell blood in the mild spring breeze.

She couldn't stop thinking of Lana's mother either. Lana had always been so nice, but her mother … She would never have imagined that Lana's own mother was evil incarnate. The woman betrayed Amie's family, and she didn't even look like she regretted it.

And then there was Tele.

She'd assumed that Navid had rescued a noblewoman—perhaps the displaced daughter of a Hzorah Low Lord. Navid was a seer from Caldor, after all, and only a Lady would require such a high-profile escort. But Tele had revealed that she was from the Dominion. And, despite what Amie had thought of her, she wasn't heartless; she'd cared. She wasn't like these men or like Lana's mother.

"You should have come to me first," Mara said suddenly. "You know better than to go parading off to Gavini's like that after Father had explicitly told you *not* to. And with a strange woman, no less."

And finally, here it was: Mara's condemnation.

"I had to go," Amie protested, her fists tightened, rage building with the thought of what could have happened to Gavini. "It was only right. No one else would have helped him."

"You don't know that," Mara said, her eyes burning two small holes of red-hot blame into the back of Amie's head.

"No one *did*," Amie said, turning to her sister. "You saw how they burned the house. You were close to him too. How would you have felt if I hadn't done anything?"

Mara opened her mouth, but nothing came out; she simply looked away. And Amie went back to gazing out their prison window.

At last, Mara sighed. "What's done can't be changed."

"What are we going to do?" Amie asked. A question she'd asked herself several times over now. She knew the answer, but she couldn't help herself.

"I don't know," Mara said.

"Anchor down!" a soldier shouted.

The cart lurched, forcing Amie off balance. She grabbed hold of the cage bars to fight the prison's tilt. Then, when the cart stilled, light conversation between the soldiers broke out as they set to making camp.

Amie sat patiently. It wasn't a guarantee that they'd get fed, but the fact that the soldiers fed them at all was proof that they didn't want them dead until they got wherever it was that they were taking them.

"No … no no no! Amie!"

Amie turned to see her sister hunched over her father, her cheek close to his face.

"What is it?"

"He isn't breathing, Amie! He stopped breathing!"

Amie scrambled across the cart's floor. As Gavini had taught her, she found her father's voice box, then slid two fingers to the side to find his pulse.

Terror shook her to the bone. "He doesn't have a pulse." Without a second thought, she crawled back across the cage and gripped the window bars. "Help! My father isn't breathing! Please, help him!"

Two soldiers looked up casually.

"Please! He could die! Help us!"

One of the soldiers slowly rose and went to fetch their leader. It couldn't have been longer than thirty seconds before the soldier returned with the soldier in charge, but it felt as if time had ground to a halt like a drop of dew only just too light to drip.

Powerless, she watched as the soldiers opened the carriage and pulled her father out and onto the ground. Mara was shouting something, but she couldn't hear or understand it. Everything had become a swirl of color and sound—an unbreakable spell of horror. She could only see her father's slack expression. Nothing else existed.

The soldiers fussed over her father for a few minutes before they stood. Mara was shouting again ... something about the soldiers giving up. They ignored her.

Five of the soldiers lifted her father's limp form and carried him off into the forest while the commanding officer crossed his arms, waiting for their return. A few moments passed before they came back and sat again as if nothing had happened.

"I'm leaving you with these three," the lead soldier said to the one with spiky, white hair—the one who'd stood by as the leader killed the two Azuri men. "General Gareth will want a report of what happened here. I trust you can handle the transport of just two girls?"

The soldier nodded.

"Good. We'll split up in the morning. And Owen ..." the

commanding officer said. "I don't want any more accidents. Understood?"

"Understood."

Tears streaming down her face, she pushed back from the barred window and pulled her legs in close, burying her face between her knees as the realization that she would never see her father again struck her.

He didn't deserve this—to be unceremoniously disposed of like a vat of bad ale. She wished she had had a moment to say goodbye, just one last chance to tell him how much she loved him, how much she appreciated him. Her heart ached at the vile injustice.

"*My family died that way,*" Tele had said to her. "*They died victim to flame and steel and men who let hate destroy who they were.*"

As a roar of laughter erupted from the soldiers, Amie vowed to never let hate destroy who she was, to never become what had taken her father from her.

Standing atop the hill at the foot of the mountain, General Gareth watched his army stretch across the Deseran wilderness. And yet beyond, the lifeless expanse encircled the Creed's forces, hoping to consume them. The desert's bottomless appetite for any pitiful creature that happened into its wide-open jaws would gladly devour them if given the chance.

Midday rations were upon them, and the soldiers inched their way toward the cook tents. Only one man fought the ravenous tide of men, cutting against the current and spotting his general observing the camp from above: Lieutenant Farrin. Returned at last.

As Farrin approached, the general squatted down and opened a ceramic bowl. He pulled out a small brown rag that had been unfortunately stained with large blotches of red and squeezed it to release the excess cool water. He handed it to the lieutenant.

"My General," the lieutenant said, accepting the damp

cloth graciously and wiping his brow. "Even in the short time I spent in the south, I grew used to the moderate weather."

Gareth knew the truth of that. He'd spent the last fifteen years in the northern waste, away from the lush lands south of the Shadow Peaks where he'd spent his youth. And while his people had eventually found fertile ground in the far reaches of Desera, acted quickly to establish the city of Janamah, and cultivated land, he had never completely adapted to the harsh new world.

And now, as he stood in the bowels of the Deseran wastelands, watching his troops mill about like ants, the righteous anger that he carried just below the surface lit anew, threatening to ignite.

"Come," Gareth said to Farrin. Once he was on the move, the urge to release his rage would slowly dissolve. "Walk with me. I thought that I should have a turn at inspecting the troops today."

Farrin fell in step with his general. "Are you concerned that the officers are providing you with inaccurate reports, My General? If so, I can—"

"No," Gareth said. "It's nothing problematic. But there's only so much planning I can do before I reach a wall. So instead of idling in my tent, I find a way to keep myself busy. An idled mind grows lazy and dull."

"Of course, My General," Farrin said.

Gareth led his right-hand lieutenant on a winding path through the army camp with no specific destination in mind. At least, there was no destination until he heard the men in the distance, cheering on what sounded like a brawl. The dry air did that to troops. It was as if the desert heat had the power to ignite the passions that lay dormant in the hearts of men.

"I have come with a report," Farrin said as he followed close to his general.

"You found the Keeper's sympathizers?" Gareth snaked his way into the thickening crowd of jeering men who hadn't yet realized that there were high ranking officers among them. He wouldn't alert them. If he did, the fight would break up, and he'd miss the fun—the vicarious release of the fury that churned inside. "And you journeyed ahead to let me know that they are in transit to the war camps?"

"Yes, My General. However, there was an accident."

"Oh?"

"Yes," Farrin continued. "The sympathizers were a family of three and owners of an Azuri inn. A father and two daughters."

"Is that so?" Gareth asked, playing the fool. After he'd left Azuri empty-handed, he was forced to report back to Prophet Tristan in Janamah. Since he'd arrived back at his army's encampment, his prophet had replied, detailing what he might expect from Lieutenant Farrin's escapade.

Gareth broke through to the edge of the brawl and saw two young recruits trading jabs. It was unclear who or what had started the fight, but the surrounding soldiers didn't seem to care. There was little to occupy them in the endless waste, and tensions were reaching a fever pitch.

"The father was a rather large man," Farrin said. "He put up a good fight, and the soldiers struggled to put him down. Seems they overdid it a bit, and the man died not long after we left the town."

"And the girls?" Gareth asked, catching Farrin's eye. "Are the girls unharmed?"

"They were an easy capture, My General. They are fine."

"Good," Gareth said, turning back to the fight.

"I rode ahead because I thought you might want to cut your losses and have the soldiers return to camp without the burden of the prisoners. The girls are easy to manage, but prisoners always slow a journey to a crawl, especially with a cart as evidenced by my swift return. I doubt they'll arrive before we cross the Peaks. I can send a messenger back, have the girls killed, and return Owen and the three remaining soldiers in time for the siege."

"No, no," Gareth said. "It's not the man we want; it's the girls. I've already heard word from Prophet Tristan regarding the matter. He made it clear that the girls would be his subject of interest, not the father. Honestly, if you had reported that the father was still alive, I would have had you send a messenger to have them kill him if only to expedite their journey."

"Prophet Tristan is wise, My General."

"Wise, indeed."

Since they'd began their crusade, Prophet Tristan had always been one step ahead, his orders were often strange, but had always bore fruit. And after the demise of the prophets in Caldor, his orders had become ever more specific as if in the absence of the other prophets, his powers had strengthened. The prophet had mentioned something to that effect once—about how nature craved balance, demanded it.

Of course, there was little reason he should doubt that the prophet would lead them to victory. Fate is an ocean stronger than any man. The Creed sought justice and truth. It was their destiny to succeed.

A cheer rose as one of the soldiers tackled the other. Now that both were off their feet, the fight was in its end game. Whichever soldier had the best technique in the sand would end up the victor. Most street thugs didn't realize that your ground game was where the real contest was. They'd spend all their time learning how to throw a good punch and have no idea what to do when the fight inevitably ended up on the ground.

"How many years have you seen, Lieutenant?"

"I've seen twenty-one years, My General."

Gareth hummed. "Too young to really remember life before we were pushed into the waste. I was but a child in the womb when the war began, but I still remember some of what it was like before the war truly began in earnest. In those early years, the war was little more than the Creed putting down spontaneous rebellions among the most heathen tribes across the land.

"I distinctly remember the day the Creed ended construction on Wizard Titan's palace. I had seen five or six years. My father, a great general himself, held my hand as Prophet Odus officiated the ceremony. I'll never forget what my father said to me that day. He knelt down and looked me in the eye and said, 'this palace represents the pinnacle of craft, only made possible because of the blessings of knowledge provided to us by the great Wizard Titan. Son, never forget who we owe this day to. And one day, when he returns to us, we will stand here again, and watch him enter his new home.'"

Farrin looked at Gareth. "That's beautiful, My General."

Gareth's jaw clenched. "That was a few years before my father died, fatally wounded by King Jeremiah himself. And do you know who lives there now? The Desolate-bound heathen that *killed* my father. They've desecrated it, Farrin."

Gareth let his hand drift down to his father's sabre. *How long until I have the prince's head? How long until I restore the home of my forefathers? How long until I avenge my father's death?*

GIVE ME A TASTE OF VENGEANCE, KILL THE SPAWN OF THE HEATHEN KING, AND I WILL REWARD YOU WITH THE POWER TO RESTORE YOUR HOME. NO MAN WILL BE ABLE TO STAND AGAINST YOU.

Gareth sighed, the wisdoms' reassurances taking away a measure of the venomous rage that coursed his veins. He could see the prince in his mind's eye, slouching in the courtroom of Wizard Titan's palace as if the whole world were owed to him. *Soon, young prince. You will be mine.*

The crowd dissipated as only one of the Creed's soldiers rose to his feet. His friends steadied him and clapped him on the back, assuring him that he'd put the bastard down good. The other man was a bloody mess in the sand. His friends carefully tended to him while one ran for a medic. Like any respectable brawl, each clique had allowed the men to settle their differences without interference and accepted the outcome, even when it was clear who would end up the victor. *Respectable*. Not like the filth he'd found in Hzorah.

"My General!"

Gareth and Farrin turned to a soldier who approached from behind. "Yes, soldier?"

"My General," the man said, winded. "A message from our

great prophet. I apologize for not delivering it earlier. I had trouble locating you." He held out a folded and sealed note of parchment.

Gareth took the note and scanned the words, Prophet Tristan's instructions taking the remainder of his rage. He folded the letter. "Farrin, have my personal guard prepare my reading table in the Peaks. And are there any remaining Thief-Takers in our camp?"

"We brought one with us as instructed by the Prophet, My General."

General Gareth smiled. Always a step ahead. A wise prophet. "Very good, have him meet me at my reading table. There is another Keeper within our grasp."

TWENTY-FOUR

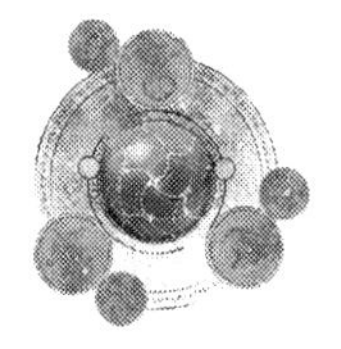

THE SOUL OF THE FOREST

The forest was dark, but alive. It wasn't the darkness Navid had been used to in Caldor—the dead feeling of a windowless room. Here, the darkness was alive. There were creatures that thrived within the shadow. He couldn't see them, but he could hear them.

Navid crossed his arms. He wasn't exactly cold, but there was a strange, uncomfortably cool stir about. The air shifted and churned. It was an odd sensation—like dew settling on his skin or being wrapped in a chilly, invisible blanket. He looked at Tal Aval and Tal Opus. They walked, unfazed by the breeze's gentle tickle or rocks that jabbed at their shoeless soles.

Probably have calloused feet, Navid thought. *I wonder if they even realize how mad this is. But they probably think the same. That I'm mad for letting myself become soft like an infant.*

The forest was thick with giant trees, making for a region of forest where the brush was thinner than the areas that preceded their arrival. If carved out, the trees could have made a suitable dwelling for a man if he didn't mind small spaces. The trees were ancient, spanning generations without calamity. The prize of immortality came at the cost of immobility. Navid wasn't sure if trees could think like men could, but he wondered if it was worth it.

You'll find out soon enough. Wizard Titan was said to be immortal. What roots kept him in place?

There were some trees that hadn't outlived the ages. They lay across the forest floor like city walls, thick and unmovable. Their corpses gave new life to glowing mushrooms and moss that draped over the slow rot, and the gap they left in the otherwise sun-choked canopy allowed for the saplings to rise up in its place.

After what had happened with Tele, Navid wished he could stay lost within the soul of the forest. Even with the uncomfortable chill and prick of small things beneath his feet. As much as he wanted to see her well, he feared that he'd destroyed their friendship.

Being a seer meant that courtships, marriage, and family were all off the table for him. He was not only forbidden by the code of the seers to engage another with thoughts of anything beyond friendship, but it was also illegal by the laws agreed upon by all lands. And even friendships were limited to the seers within the Sanctuary Calviere.

He should have known. The world had fallen apart, but what seers are would not change. *He* could not change.

He was Navid Tevaad, the cursed.

"We are close," Tal Aval said, with a pronounced reverence even Navid understood through his Tal accent.

"How do you know where we're going?" Navid asked.

"You do not need light when you can feel the pull of the Seed on your soul," Tal Opus said from the other side.

"How close then?"

"You do not feel?" Tal Aval asked. "Listen."

Navid quieted. He shut his eyes—pointlessly, perhaps—and opened himself to the world around him. Wings fluttered. Air whistled. Earth slipped between his toes. Gnats lighted on his skin. The faint smell of manure and wet wood wafted into his nose.

And the curse, calling to him.

Pulling back, he opened his eyes and said into the darkness: "I don't feel it or hear it."

The darkness didn't respond.

Navid prayed with every step that he wouldn't trip on a root or twist his ankle in a sinkhole, but the path was remarkably smooth with soft, cool dirt. Not even a rock interrupted his pace. It was odd, unnatural. Perhaps the Tal had done something to this place—created a smooth path for him.

Two centuries gone and they've still kept it pristine? That kind of commitment was unnatural. Any normal people would have abandoned guard long ago. But not only had the Tal stayed, they'd committed their entire existence to the task.

Suddenly, he saw a light ahead. Dim as it was, it glowed bright amongst the blackness where Navid's vision had become over-sensitive. It was like the gateway spell, appearing from the smallest prick of nothing and expanding into the void.

"There's a light," Navid said, then realized the two would have to be blind not to see it. "Is that what we're looking for?"

"It is," Tal Aval said.

Navid could see the outlines of the trees now. Their shapes were traced in blues and purples despite the milk white of the light beyond. He slowed his pace. At the corners of his ill-suited vision, he saw shadows of Tal Aval and Tal Opus pass in front of him. He stiffened, setting his jaw. He'd spent his whole life trying to fight the tide, but it is said that fate is an ocean stronger than any man. This was what he'd been born for. This very moment.

As if crossing a barrier, the light intensified then dimmed, bathing them all in shimmering violet. At the light's center was a deep black sphere. A black so deep, it was like a void in the world. More than just the absence of light—the very absence of existence. It hovered no more than four paces over the forest floor, resistant to gravity's efforts.

The two Tal men stood motionless—a gesture of reverence. Navid swallowed a scant sip of moisture as he waited. He looked to Tal Aval for instruction, but the man watched the Seed with a fixed expression of awe before he finally exhaled a long, slow breath.

Tal Aval reached out and touched the void.

A sharp hiss swept through him, bringing a surge of emotion—disappointment and fear. The emotions were not his own. They radiated from the Seed and siphoned what hope he had left from him. The trees shuttered and a chill set, raising goosebumps in his flesh.

"There has been an interference," Tal Aval said in a voice that was not entirely his own. "The power has been siphoned. There is but a drop left."

Siphoned? Navid frowned, trying to wrap his head around what it meant. "What does that mean?"

Tal Aval turned to him, an eerie shadow of light cast across his face. "*Much of the magic is gone.*"

"Gone?" Navid shook his head. "I don't understand. How could it be gone?"

"Life is balance," Tal Aval said. "The power was left for too long. Life seeks balance."

Navid grimaced as he stared into the void. He didn't understand what Tal Aval meant, but it wasn't good. "You said there is a drop left. What does that mean?"

"The Seed holds tight to magic," Tal Aval said. "The power leaves slowly, but there is little magic left. It will soon all be gone."

"What do we do?" Navid asked. His mind was beginning to spin in both worry and confusion. "How do we get it back?"

Tal Opus said something to Tal Aval in the Tal language, and Tal Aval responded. Tal Opus nodded, his expression clearly sorrowful even in the deep purple light.

"We do not get the magic back," Tal Aval said.

"But there's a drop left," Navid said, almost pleading with fate. "Can't we take that?"

Tal Aval nodded. "We will take it. If we do not, we will soon have nothing left."

The void spun under Tal Aval's touch before a flash of blinding darkness poured over him. It pulsed, rattling Navid's bones. The itch of his curse flared. The pain of it seared through his mind and burned every nerve in his body with such intense pain that he cried out and fell, tumbling through a vast abyss without end.

For a moment—or for an eternity—Navid lost all sense of himself. He didn't know who or where he was. There was nothing that separated him from the firmament but perhaps the scant notion of awareness that he fought to hold onto.

Existence struck him like a bolt of lightning. The buzz of it shimmered and swirled about his body until it rose above the chaos of his senses. He was on the ground, the dirt in a death-grip between his fingers. He opened his eyes and the world spun and flipped before settling. When he managed to get to his feet, he saw that Tal Opus too had only just picked himself up. Tal Aval still stood within the Seed's dark light. It churned about him, slowly dissipating like fog brushed aside by a gentle breeze.

Tal Aval stared at his hands as if he'd never before seen them. He let his arms drop to his side, then took a long, slow breath.

"Tal Aval," Navid whispered. "Are you alright? Did it work?"

He nodded, but did not speak.

"We must return and tell the elders of our success," Tal Opus said, gripping Navid's arm.

Together they turned to journey back to the Tal village. Unsteady on his feet, Navid panted, trying to comprehend what had just happened. He'd seen something that no one else would likely ever see for rest of all time. He wanted to feel honored, grateful. But what Tal Aval had said about their only being a drop left was sure to be problematic if they wanted to use it to win the impending war. The fear that all of this had been for nothing was the only sentiment that filled his heart.

Tele's eyes opened to the dim glow of violet against a brown churn of branches, surrounding her in a wide ring. Dozens of

… of something … pressed against her skin. Her vision blurred as she tried to glance down at her body.

Strangely, she was upright. Stranger still, her feet did not touch the ground. Somehow she was held aloft by … by what? As she struggled to regain the full measure of her awareness the memory of where she had been struck her.

She had been in the Borderland forests. And something had attacked them. She had fought them off and—

Her vision cleared as she focused on her body. Like a dozens of ropes, vines had wrapped themselves all around her. And where they met her flesh, they bit into her skin, sucking the life from her.

Tele remembered the rapid growing overgrowth, the chase through the forest. She remembered their plan to jump from the cliffs and pray that Desolate's Hand favored them in their fall. But the vines had caught her, and now they had her in her clutches, feeding off of her for sustenance.

"You must keep the Covenant safe."

The will to live, to break free overrode her reflections, and she tugged at the vines. The plant life wailed in distorted protest. She ignored it, squeezing her eyes shut as she concentrated on regaining control of her limbs. She had to free herself. She could not—would not allow this to be her end. There was still so much for her to do.

"Run, my child! Run!"

Tele redoubled her efforts to escape even as more vines took hold of her and held her in place.

"Wawa!" the plants droned. "Wawe!"

She jerked and contorted, mustering ever bit of strength she had.

"Wawe! Wally! Tele!"

Did the vines just call her name?

Her eyes shot open and when her vision again regained a measure of clarity, she saw that the extra vines that had taken hold of her weren't the rough textures of bark or the green of cellulose. They were arms—human arms.

"Tele!" a woman pleaded. "Please, calm! Do not struggle. We will free you."

Tele's gaze rose to meet the woman who spoke to her. She had kind eyes and gentle age lines that told of a life long-lived. She tried to respond to the woman, but tongue failed to move and all that came out strained moan.

As she resigned herself to their aid, they lowered her to a flat surface. Each vine that they removed was accompanied by a sharp prick of pain. They carefully cleaned the vine wound and bandaged them with strips of sticky green gauze. All the while, her senses and thoughts lost their haze.

The brown branches that surrounded them wasn't part of the forest monster. They were some sort of enclosure. The violet glow came from some sort of organic web that criss-crossed without about the branches. The vines that held her receded as the man and woman who bandaged her loosed them and the two helped her still up when they'd completed their work.

"Who are you?" Tele whispered, her mouth now working. "Where am I?"

"You are in the Tal tribe lands," the woman said. "There is much to explain, but first we must make sure you are well."

The woman nodded to the man and together they helped her stand. She was unstable for the briefest moment before she regained her bearings. The Tal man turned away and returned with one of her daggers. He placed it in her hand and the pair backed away from her before he said, "Lew."

Confused, Tele looked at the woman. "What?"

"He wants you to show us that you are better," the Tal woman said. "Use your weapon."

Still unsure, Tele looked down to the dagger. She felt fine, save the fading pain where the vines had punctured her skin and the faintest hint of a headache. But she obliged and took to running through a memorized pattern of manipulating the dagger, spinning it with fluid grace before falling into a defensive stance. She shifted to an offensive stance but didn't charge in the small enclosure. And, finally, she withdrew the weapon with a flourish.

"Good," the woman said and waved her to the entry. "You are certainly hungry."

Tele turned a questioning gaze to the man who only smiled and handed her pack. She thanked the man, and though she wasn't sure he could understand her, he again smiled before turning away to straighten his supplies.

As Tele walked to the entry, the Tal woman took her arm as though they were well acquainted. "Come," she said. "Allow me to show you our humble home."

Tele leaned forward, watching the Tal women practice their forms. She sat outside of a large dirt circle with her arms folded over her knees and the early morning's dew cooling her bare feet. In the circle, a few dozen women lurched, pounced, and twirled in tight unison. Several other women watched, scattered about the field. Most were mothers, some were daughters. The mothers watched with a spark of pride. The daughters watched eagerly, as if hoping they would be asked to spar.

Tal Eva had described her home as a "humble" village. And while there was nothing in the Tal tribe lands that Tele would describe as ostentatious, she couldn't quite agree with "humble" as a proper description of the endless wonders of their lost world.

With the Tal elder as her guide, Tele found that the people here lived in the canopy of the forest. The strange plant life—the ardya—that had attacked her was the same life form responsible for making their tree-top society possible. The ardya was harmless to the people that lived here, but fiercely defensive against outsiders. On one hand, Tele wanted to dig deeper and discover why that was, but there was much more to see.

A species of tree similar to the ardya called the cokawa was responsible for their many homes. Tal Eva had to some extent explained that its branches—when manipulated by a simple frame—can easily form a nest-like enclosure. And such a seemingly simple method of construction resulted in a vast variety of shelters. Some were like tree houses—organic cabins held aloft by the sturdy legs of the cokawa tree trunk—while others were unassuming like the medicine house.

After wandering the village for some time, she settled here at the edge of a dirt circle to study how the Tal trained. At first, Tele found their movements graceful and pleasing. Then, she found them disturbing. The movements were far too familiar. She recognized many of the forms as her own.

Her father and brothers had taught her self-defense while they hid away in the Dominion Desert. They'd said that every culture had found their own method of fighting, their own rhythm. Like art, no two peoples or individuals used the same methods, and, like art, each method was equally valid. Effectiveness was paramount. Style was subjective.

The Tal, however, seemed to take an oddly similar approach to what she was taught. A style that complimented her own. She watched as they stepped with arms raised, moving from shape to shape. Forms that, when properly engraved into their minds, would become reflexive. Despite your fear, reflex is what will save you when your attacker tugs on the thread of your existence.

Tele frowned as she wondered if Navid had any reflex for survival at all. She had felt something with Navid—something beyond the comforting warmth she usually felt with him—not like the feeling she had now while watching the Tal. It was more … exhilarating.

But then, when Navid failed to follow through on their plan, she was suddenly, violently pushed back into reality. Though they had lived different lives, she had come to believe that she could trust him. But now she knew that she could not. And that mistake had nearly gotten her killed.

While Tele risked everything to give Navid an opening, he had just stood there. Navid didn't have that instinct to survive, to act. He had become a detriment to the task at hand.

"Our women practice hard," Tal Eva said, approaching from the side.

Tele looked up from her spot in the grass, and Tal Eva passed her a small bowl of a green, curved, and leafy vegetable that she was unfamiliar with, then another with a light purple berry dressed in mint and seasoning. Tele watched how Tal Eva used the vegetable spoon for the berry filling before trying it herself.

"This is delicious," Tele said.

"Delicious?" Tal Eva asked, frowning.

"Good food."

She smiled. "Thank you."

"I've been wondering something about the healers here," Tele said. "The vines that you used to give me healing medicine—how do they work?"

Tal Eva gave a slight tilt of her head. "I do not know. They work fast to heal many ills. Even death wounds can be healed. It makes our people stronger to see death at least once. We no longer fear death so we practice harder. But I do not know how the healing works. Healing is not what I think on much."

Tele nodded. She knew that Tal Eva was still concerned about the future of her people's place here in the forest. Tele had found this hard to believe, but Tal Eva had insisted that the wonders that Tele saw all about them were fading away. She struggled to imagine how much more fantastic the lands were many years ago before the magic began to wane. And she couldn't imagine the pain of knowing that slowly but inevitably, everything you love would be taken away.

"Your people are very skilled," Tele said, smiling, hoping to distract her from her worries. She looked Tal Eva square in the eye, not wanting to betray the fact that Tal Eva's bare chest still made her uncomfortable. "Do the women here practice this way often?"

"All days," Tal Eva said. "Women do not where you live?"

Tele paused, taking the time to sift Tal Eva's words. She

was one of the few Tal who could communicate with her and, though Tele found her accent charming, her phrasings sometimes felt odd to her ear. "Do women train like this where I'm from? No. But I did."

"One woman to fight?" Tal Eva asked.

Tele shook her head. "I didn't live with others. I lived with only my family."

Tal Eva nodded slowly. She raised a hand to the women beyond. "Tal all fight. We are few."

"We were few, too," Tele smiled.

"We use our skill to find a fine partner," Tal Eva said. "Sword dance finds a good match."

Tal Eva pointed to the far side of the circle. A few youths, all boys, watched. They sat still near the edge of wall, avoiding notice.

"You use combat as a courtship ritual?" Tal Eva's brow raised, so Tele added clarification. "You marry this way?"

Tal Eva nodded. "Do you fight good?"

"I do," Tele said, feeling odd giving herself a blatant vote of confidence to a stranger.

Tal Eva, a light taking her eye, stood and pulled Tele to her feet. "You practice."

Tele resisted. "I couldn't."

Tal Eva ignored Tele and pulled her near to the dirt circle, stopping to lift one of the Tal's wooden blades. Like much of their community, even their weapons were extraordinary. Unlike the wooden practice staffs that were common elsewhere, these weapons were sharp and, from what Tele had seen, somehow just as capable as the metal swords she'd seen elsewhere.

She placed the sword in Tele's hand, and it shifted in her grip, adjusting to the span of her grasp—even changing its balance and length to adapt to her proportions. The weapon itself was alive and Tele became a creature in symbiosis with it.

"Tal Vai!" the elder called.

A young girl paused after ending a spin. She looked at Tal

Eva and raised her eyebrows when she saw her pulling Tele along toward her. Tele yielded, allowing herself to be led.

Tal Eva spoke with Tal Vai with a small smile. Though Tele couldn't understand, she knew the look of conspiracy. Tal Vai nodded, the corners of her own mouth beginning to rise.

"Tele," Tal Eva said, turning back. "You dance. Tal Vai teach."

Tele opened her mouth for one last objection, but Tal Eva walked away without another word. Tele turned to watch her leave and even caught Tal Eva looking back to be sure Tele stayed, sharing an encouraging smile.

I've been through worse, Tele thought. But even as she did, she realized that she didn't hate the idea of trying this. It was something she knew, if only a little.

Tele pulled into form, allowing her arms to flow into position and let her intuition and reflex pull her to safety. Tal Vai mirrored her with a smile creeping onto her face. She remembered her brother, Gib, falling into a similar configuration. Night after night, he'd taught her how to defend herself. Then, after she'd gotten a handle on defense, he'd taught her how to kill.

Tal Vai charged. Tele allowed her muscles to relax. Light and dark do not fight each other. They yield, knowing they need only to shift to where the other once was.

Tal Vai's blade swept from below. Tele caught it with her own, leading its sweep and allowing it to pull upward before she pushed back, breaking contact. Tal Vai immediately dropped into a second attack, this time lunging for her vitals. Again, Tele met wood with wood and redirected the blow, forcing Tal Vai into a vulnerable position. Tele spun, letting Tal Vai's momentum pull her forward then used the flat of her blade to shove her away.

Tal Vai stumbled, but recovered, turning back to meet Tele's smirk. Though Tal Vai's attacks were true, Tele could see that she held back, unsure if an outsider could actually hold up against her people's skill. Tele's smirk grew into a grin before she gave Tal Vai a nod.

Tal Vai smiled back, recognizing Tele's permission to unleash.

Tele let her movements flow, pushing when Tal Vai's attacks stilled and falling back when her attacks stirred. It was a pattern of survival. Life and death in constant tension.

After a few minutes of intensity, Tal Vai pulled back and put her blade to rest. She smiled at Tele.

"You fight good!" Tal Eva said from behind.

Tele turned to see her approach. She touched Tele's arm before passing to Tal Vai. They exchanged a few quick words before Tal Vai turned back to the rest of the women and began practicing her forms again. Tal Eva inclined her head for Tele to follow.

"Tal Vai says you fight good," Tal Eva said as she led Tele back to the grass. "I want you to come watch the sword dance."

"I'm sorry?" Tele said. "This wasn't the dance?"

"Only half," Tal Eva said. "Whole dance is with a man. We choose tonight. You fight like the Tal. You may dance and find a good match if you choose."

Tele nearly laughed out loud when she realized what Tal Eva was suggesting. "No, no! I couldn't. I don't know any of the men here. And even if I did, there are far more important matters at hand."

She withheld the further notion that she'd known Navid for some weeks now, and despite their commitment to be friends, he'd already betrayed her. How could she expect someone she knew from a mere training exercise to fair better when they lacked the same familiarity?

"I appreciate you thinking of me," Tele said, hoping that Tal Eva didn't think her rejection to the invitation an insult. "But I don't think my time has come to find a husband."

"Come watch," Tal Eva. "You will like. It is nice to watch."

Tele nodded and smiled. "That is something I *can* do. And I'd be honored."

Tele followed Tal Eva around the crowd of men and women who gathered after sunset. Torches surrounded the tribe's center circle, aiding the starlight and the rows of glowing fungi that patched the edges of the paths. The entirety of the Tal stretched before her, chattering away excitedly as children ran between the legs of their elders while playing games of chase.

Three deer cooked over fires off to the side where fire pits had been dug out. Several adolescent boys and girls served the people small portions of deer meat and the same sweet berry Tal Eva had offered her earlier. Tele almost turned down the food when a girl offered her some but thought better of it. Everyone had taken some. She didn't want to disrespect by being the only one who didn't participate.

Twenty men filed into the ring of torch fire. Their eyes were outlined with a black face paint that made their gazes pop. A short time after, the twelve women from earlier filed in. They stood in front of the men with the same eye-lined paint. All of the men and women held a razor-sharp wooden sword like the one she'd used when she'd sparred with Tal Vai.

A Tal elder, Tal Dian, stepped into the circle. He wore the warrior paint scheme—black lines that striped up the length of his torso, neck and face. The Tal fell silent as he appraised his people. His expression was serious at first, but as the crowd calmed, he smiled.

"You do not know our tongue?" Tal Eva whispered into Tele's ear.

Tele turned to her and shook her head.

"I will make my tongue your tongue."

Tele smiled. "I would like that. Thank you."

Tal Dian began to speak, and Tal Eva translated. "Many years ago, the Wizard gave us a duty. We protect the Seed, and we have had a good life. Tonight, we sword dance on the night the Wizard returns. Tal Aval will return and complete our duty. It is an honor. We were strong. We are rewarded."

When he paused to allow the people to cheer, Tele perked as she recognized Tal Dian's words for what they were. How the hard sounds melted into the soft, the specific intonations and rhythm. It was the same language that she studied to build the spell forms.

The language wasn't dead. It was very much alive.

"We dance to match husband and wife," Tal Eva said, continuing to translate. "But we dance to protect, to be strong. When the time comes to protect, we will protect. First blood is an end. Not a perfect end, but an end. Love for the Tal and love for our enemy protects us."

Tal Dian stepped away so that the ceremony could begin. While he'd spoken, a couple dozen others with instruments joined the ceremony behind the circle of men and women. With two mallets in hand, a drummer made two slow but powerful strikes to his drum before the other drummers joined in unison. The beat engulfed them, pushing air and reverberating from the trees. Exhilarated by the sound, the glowing fungi's color shifted with the rhythm, casting shades of red and blue and violet.

The drummers' beat split, two of them taking a quicker, urgent pace that fell in and out of step with the other. The Tal in the circle split too, men and women to either side. They summoned their wooden arms from the ground beneath them. Shooting up like trees growing out of the earth in a moment's time, their weapons rose out of the ground. As the young Tal men and woman pulled strange plants from the ground, they shifted into the wooden blades Tele had seen them use earlier in that day.

A guttural chant began, and the dancers ran toward each other. Their blades met and they began what looked to be a miniature battle. They ducked, spun, and struck with forceful grace, but not one drop of blood spilled. There were moments when a few of the men stepped out of the conflict, unable to find a woman to attack, but as soon as they spotted a woman who'd split off from the fray, they reentered.

Tele watched, trying to make sense of the chaos. They were relentless, never giving each other quarter. Never stopping to recover. Always vigilant, always moving. Always.

Tele spotted Tal Vai in the maelstrom of bodies. She

stepped with grace, perfectly in tune with another young man, smiles on their faces. They flirted with death, without much thought of what might happen if the other faltered in their defenses. Tele flexed anxiously when Tal Vai favored a styled attack instead of a more practical one, but her form was flawless and executed with precision.

The pulse of the drums increased in speed and the dancers reacted accordingly, as if time itself accelerated. Tele could hardly believe how well they kept pace. They didn't even appear winded.

She looked beside her where Tal Eva watched with a fond smile and pride etched on her face. She looked at the other villagers. They all watched, enveloped in the moment. Then she found herself smiling as she too became rapt in the beauty of the dance.

Tele wasn't sure how long the ceremony persisted. Even as she was aware of the affect, the rhythm and lights lulled her into a timeless state of mind. But eventually, in what felt like an abrupt awakening, the drums ended, and there was a short pause before the dancers relaxed. The Tal elder crossed back into the circle. His eyes welled with joy and he smiled with the pride of a grandfather who'd watched his grandchild take their first, timid steps.

"These are the new Tal to protect what the great Wizard Titan left behind," Tal Eva translated. "And they have found matches."

He then began listing pairings. Each couple took their place, side by side before the village. Some looked at their match with fond recognition, some of them with burning passion. Some, though, stood nervous—almost fearful. Tele's heart went out to the nervous few, praying Desolate's Hand would lead them to happiness.

Tal Dian called Tal Vai's name and she stepped down with the man she dueled with for the majority of the fight. A small group of villagers cheered as she took her place. She smiled to them, staying composed while appreciating the moment with her family. The man that stood with her watched her with a love so kind, she could almost feel it in her core.

As the tale of her grief—that so often intruded on her thoughts—again reared its ugly head, she repressed the longing to see her mother, father, and brothers once more. She remembered how proud her parents were at even then smallest accomplishment, and even as she was grateful that Tal Vai had that same measure of love about her, the prick of its absence in her own life couldn't be clearer.

Perhaps she could come to accept that she, Tele Gavina, Keeper of the Covenant, could not have the simple pleasures of family, of friends, of love. She had had them once, and now must forgo her indulgences so that others might have a chance at them.

An icy wind cut through the village center. Tele shivered at the strange temperature drop and joined a chorus of villagers that looked into the heavens for some sign of rain. The stars had disappeared, leaving the sky black but strangely turbulent. Above, she could barely make out clouds, churning in the beginnings of a terrible storm.

"Do we go inside?" Tele asked Tal Eva. "It looks pretty bad —" She paused. Tal Eva had a troubled look on her face. "Tal Eva?"

"Not rain," Tal Eva said.

Tele looked around, taking in the other villagers' responses. They all appeared as troubled as Tal Eva. "Weather can be unpredictable. Perhaps it's a quick storm that will pass."

"No," Tal Eva said. "Different."

Tele looked back to the sky. The clouds rippled over the stars, bulging as if she were watching from the underside of a whirlpool. The billows writhed as they condensed tighter. Then, the cloud expanded, seeming to take on shape and forming extremities from four sides before growing lighter in color. Squinting, Tele realized the mass was not growing, but descending. She took a step backward as the mass took an avian form.

TWENTY-FIVE

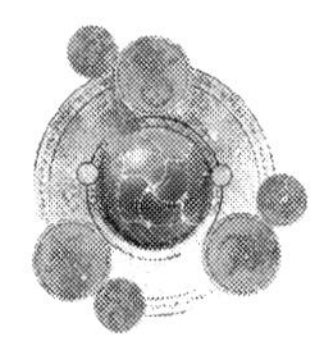

A CHANCE AT REDEMPTION

Panicked chatter erupted and accelerated into shouting as the clouds morphed over the firelight. Wings stretched out as the clouds took a reptilian form before its descent upon the village circle. It cried out with a shriek that cut through the air and sent ripples down Tele's spine.

The pale scales, lizard head, and white wings … Tele knew this creature. It was the same creature that she'd seen and studied deep within the Sanctuary. Or, at least, it appeared to be the same species.

A dragon.

Tele's breath caught as she took Tal Eva's hand. "We have to move."

She pulled Tal Eva through the crowd while trying to reason why the creature would show up here and now. Glancing back over her shoulder, she watched the dragon descended on the village with a black-robed man on the beast's back. A singular red band wrapped around his arm—A Thief-Taker.

Tele didn't want to believe what she saw. It was impossible. Why would a Thief-Taker be riding atop such a beast? What was a Thief-Taker doing here, so far away from the Deseran Dominion?

Tal Eva pulled away from her grip.

Tele took hold of Tal Eva's hand again. "Come on!"

Again, Tal Eva wrenched free. "No. We protect."

Tal Eva cast out her hand and, in a moment, a branch grew out of the ground. As she took hold of it, its shape transformed into a sword. The elder charged back into the chaos, leaving Tele behind in her astonishment. Tele held out a hand to stop her, but Tal Eva slipped away.

There was a rush of air as the reptile's dive pulled up from a close impact. Ghostly white legs stretched outward and caught the ground, quaking earth and scattering dirt and rock.

The dragon turned. Claws on heavily muscled legs dug deep into the ground. Its snout shot forth a geyser of smoke and water that condensed and rained down droplets of moisture.

The Thief-Taker held tight to the dragon's back as it reared its head. Like a striking viper, it lurched forward, and a pillar of crystal white shot from its open mouth. The fires that surrounded the lizard winked out, suffocated by its—

A chilling wave of air passed over her. *Ice. It's breathing ice.*

Darkness settled across the village. Shrouded by clouds, the full moon's light dimmed. Billows of water vapor steamed from where the fires once burned. Their thick plums glowed with the light of the remaining fires out at the village perimeter.

Village children screamed and cried out. Bowls of food clattered to the ground as men and women shouted orders to each other. Confusion swept the gathering while the dragon's ice-blue eyes glowed, and it stretched its wings as if welcoming the chaos.

Tele turned away and her gaze locked on to Tal Eva's small home. Her pack was in there. Her weapons and the books her father had left to her was there. She had to protect them. But then, what would she do? The only way she could protect them was to run.

She watched as the dragon raised its head and let out a wave of ice across the far side of the village. Spears launched into the air, then descended onto the creature. Though most of the spears were deflected by its thick, skin armor, it cried out and swung its tail. Several men were launched into the air, many more were toppled.

I can't leave them to die, Tele thought. Her books were important, but she couldn't just run without trying to help. But how could she fight something like this? The dragon was hardly phased by the Tal's weapons.

She gritted her teeth and tried to ignore the panic all about her. There had to be something from when she'd studied the creature in Caldor that would give her an edge, a clue.

Several villagers pushed past her with torches. They held them high to lend light to their warrior counterparts as they pushed through the throng of scattering villagers. When they neared the lizard, it recoiled shot ice at the fire wielding Tal, freezing them solid where they stood.

Fire.

Tele remembered how the dragon simply dissolved while she observed it in the water. How it appeared out of condensing clouds just moments before. When it landed in the village, the first thing it did was to put out the fires that were nearby.

All animals were, in part, made of water. This one seemed to be singularly made of it. That was the only way she could think to explain how it appeared and disappeared like it did—why it reacted so strongly to fire.

An idea began to coalesce.

Tele dodged men and women running the opposite direction, each carrying a wooden blade or spear and charging for the village center. She turned back a moment to track the monster.

Over the amassing Tal villagers, the dragon took flight. Its massive wings beat in wide arcs and it spit ice at defenders that came in close. The Thief-Taker sat tall in his mount at the base of the creature's long neck. He held its reins and pulled up, leading the lizard to rise many spans above the villager's heads.

She could smell blood. Already, the night's breeze was damp with it.

Tele slipped into Tal Eva's home and scanned the hut. She found a flint and a small jar of oil and stuffed them into her pack before she stepped back outside. She had what she needed to start the fire, but that wasn't enough.

Taking in a deep breath, she stilled her mind and held out her hand. Disregarding everything around her, she whispered one of the few Tal words she knew how to say. "Lew."

As if it had been awaiting her command all along, a branch twisted out of the soil and directly into her grip. When she took hold of it, she pulled it from the earth. And as though it knew her plan as well as she, the branch shaped itself into a bow and a quiver of arrows.

Tele sprinted for the edge of the village and to one of the tree houses near where the dragon had landed. She put the bow and quiver over her shoulders and climbed the long ladder to the high-perched home without hesitation. At the landing, she turned to the village to make sure she had a clear view of the beast. Satisfied, she pushed aside the thick deer hide that covered the tree house entrance.

A chorus of screams shocked her still. Inside, several children huddled in the corner. When they saw that it wasn't a monster from the clouds, they quieted, but began crying and trying to say something to her in their language.

Tele couldn't understand what they said, but it was clear the children were afraid and weren't sure if the stranger who had come to visit them had something to do with the monster's attack.

"You'll be alright. Quiet now," Tele said in her most reassuring voice.

When the children settled to sniffles, she fished out the flint and oil from her pack. She opened the jar, tore a strip of cloth from her sleeve, rolled it into a cylindrical wick, and soaked it in the oil. She handed a boy that looked to have seen ten or eleven years the flint and oil.

"Fire," she said, pushing the stones into his hand.

The boy looked up at her. Though he was the oldest in the tree house, he was as terrified as the children who clung to him.

He looked at the flint stone in confusion. He didn't understand her. Tele knelt down, held his hands, and showed him how to strike the stones together.

"Make fire," she said again and looked into his eyes to make sure he understood her.

The child nodded, seeming to understand but still confused. As the child worked to make the fire, Tele pulled the bow from her shoulder and tested the string's tension. It was a perfect match to her strength and size.

The child caught Tele's attention as the tree house lit the flame of the small, makeshift lamp. She smiled and told him that he'd done a good job. The boy appeared to catch her meaning.

Again, Tele tore off strips of her sleeves and—careful to avoid the flame—slipped them down into the oil beside the wick, then tied each to a shaft of an arrow near its point. She placed each of the six arrows back into the quiver, shouldered it, and took the lamp and bow back out to the ledge.

In the darkness beyond, the Tal fought on. Dozens of bodies lie sprawled before the great lizard. Dozens more were frozen in place. But the village did not retreat.

"Where is she?" the Thief-Taker demanded from atop the dragon. "Tell me where the girl is!"

The Tal responded with a flight of spears.

Stark realization took her breath. The Thief-Taker was looking for *her*. Somehow Prophet Tristan was behind this and, somehow, he'd found her. This was all her fault. She'd brought this to these people.

And she had to be the one to end it.

Tele pulled and arrow from the quiver and lit its oil-soaked cloth over the lamp. She knocked the arrow, took careful aim, and let it fly.

The arrow fell to the ground, a few dozen spans short.

Wasting no time, she pulled the next arrow from the quiver and lit it. Tele adjusted her pull on the string and the trajectory of the arc. When she felt confident that she'd made the proper compensations, she shot.

The creature lurched forward, causing the arrow to miss its mark.

Panic touched a nerve as she reached for another arrow and put it to flame. If she didn't pull it together, the Thief-Taker would destroy the entire village. She had to focus.

Tele pulled back on the bow string as she aimed. Fire danced at the arrow's tip. Through it, she could see the dragon beyond, see men and women dying under the cruel injustice of the Dominion—just like her family.

She let it all disappear. The screams, the village, the haunting memories, it all sloughed away until there was but the arrow and her target.

As if the arrow had loosed itself, it left her fingers.

The dragon jerked as the arrow struck its wing. Fire raced across its skin, searing and boiling. The reptile screeched in pain—a deafening reverberation that rattled Tele's skull. Her vision blurred with the buzz of it, and her ears rung as it faded away.

Tele shut her eyes tight against the pain, forcing it away as she reached for another arrow. She had found a way. No matter how painful it was, she had to keep shooting.

Another arrow knocked, another loosed.

It struck the dragon's exposed chest. Steam wafted into the heavens as the fire tore through its abdomen and up its long neck. Its pale hide thinned, becoming transparent as the skin excited and began to evaporate.

Again, the beast pulled forth a terrible scream, but Tele knew what to expect and braced herself for the pain. It hit her, causing her hand to fumble over the next arrow as she reached for it.

She lit the arrow and shot again.

The villagers were beginning to respond to what Tele was doing. Several lit and shot their own arrows. Others drove spears into the reptile's weakening body.

Tele retrieved the final arrow. She held her breath as she aimed, the flamed tip wavered in slow cycles—back and forth as she waited for the Thief-Taker's head to move into position. When there was nothing but calm, she shot.

The arrow caught the Thief-Taker in the throat. His arms spread open as he fell backward off of the dragon's body and into the steaming mists below.

Tele worked with rote precision—checking for a pulse, binding a wound, speaking soft words of comfort that relied on her tone more than the words themselves. At the surface, she was aware of the men, women, and children dead before her. She smelled blood and the pitch of fires that still burned. She communicated as best she could with the two Tal healers that she assisted, systematically assessing each of the injured for those at the most immediate risk.

She wanted desperately to watch closely as the Tal healers used the vines that they seemed to be able to summon from the landscape to administer medicine to those that they'd judged needed the healing most.

But her mind drifted elsewhere.

Clouded in a haze of dolor, Tele replayed the assault over and over and tried to piece together the meaning of it. She didn't understand how, but she'd led a Thief-Taker to these people. Beyond all reason, that Thief-Taker had found and ridden the giant lizard she'd seen beneath Caldor.

When she'd inspected the Thief-Taker's body, it was half-charred by the flames. His face wasn't one she'd recognized, but she wasn't familiar with any one Thief-Taker. He had only one red armband—the First House of Almirav.

Tele had just finished treating the wound of a spearman when Tal Dian approached her. Though he appeared unharmed, his eyes looked as though he carried a great weight.

"I'm sorry," Tele said, standing to meet his gaze. She hated that that was all she could think to say, how completely absurd it was.

He placed a hand on her cheek and smiled a sad, knowing

smile. "Do not say sorry. You are not at fault for the wrongs of others. The Tal are strong. We will go on and be stronger."

She nodded against his palm.

"I saw what you did," Tal Dian said. He looked to the tree house where Tele had mounted her attack. "You are clever. Even our best did not see the weakness of the beast. Without you, we would be lost to it. We are forever in your debt."

"I only wish that I'd discovered it sooner," Tele said.

"And I," Tal Dian said, "wish that you could stay here with us. Warriors with your mind are rarely grown."

Tele wanted to say that she'd stay. These people had felt more like family than anything she'd ever experienced. They'd accepted her and made her feel at home. Even Tal Eva—

Tal Eva.

"Where is Tal Eva?" she asked, but when Tal Dian looked away, she knew what had become of her. "She's gone."

"Tal Eva died to protect," Tal Dian said. "We *all* protect. We are *all* rewarded. Weep not."

"Tele?"

Tele whirled at the sound of his voice. There, amid the sea of death and trauma, stood Navid, accompanied by two Tal men.

As she faced Navid's dim, yellow eyes, she was overwhelmed with relief. She wanted to hug him. She wanted to press her head against his chest and release her anguish. She wanted to thank him for not being another who'd left her alone —who'd crossed into Desolate, never to return.

But she restrained herself as the memory of their forest chase renewed.

"What happened?" Navid asked.

"A Thief-Taker came. They were looking for me."

"A Thief-Taker? A Thief-Taker caused all of this?" Navid asked. He approached her. "Are you alright? Were you hurt?"

"I'm fine," Tele said. "Fortunately, I managed to escape this time."

"Tele is too modest," Tal Dian said from behind her. "She saved us all. She discovered how to stop the monster."

Tele inwardly winced at that. If it hadn't been for her, the creature would have never come here in the first place.

Navid's eyes darted about, taking in the destruction. He shook his head. "How? And the ice …" Navid turned to Tal Aval. "I don't understand. Your people were protected from danger."

"We are," Tal Aval said. "But our duty has ended. And so has our veil of protection."

"Does that mean …" Tele looked the length of Tal Aval. "Have you taken the power of the true Wizard?"

Tal Aval shifted uneasily. "Yes. But it is not so simple."

Navid looked her in the eye. "Things didn't go as we expected. I'm not sure that what we have done is going to make a difference."

Tele frowned. This made all the difference. Every last bit.

With the Wizard returned, they could perhaps stop the Dominion in their tracks, find the lost Gateway spell, perhaps even restore the Tal's village to the splendor they would soon completely lose. But before she could respond, a Tal man trotted up to them.

"Tal Aval," he said, catching his arm, then exchanged a few urgent words in the Tal tongue. Tele watched as Tal Aval took in the news. His eyes welled and his fists clenched.

He turned back to Tele and Navid with pursed lips. "I must see to my mother."

"Do you need help?" Tele asked.

"No," Tal Aval said. "I can see to this."

"May I come then?" Tele asked. "Your mother was very nice to me. Not many people have been in my life. I would like to see her to the end."

Tal Aval paused, considering, then nodded. "Thank you, Tele. I would like that."

The flames were all too familiar. Like the fires that had frisked about in the distance as Tele fled her family's camp, they frolicked even now in the pyre of the fallen Tal. The inferno crackled, snapping branches and dreams, laughing as it devoured the aspirations of the perished.

The Tal spread out the dead in the village center. The same circle that had once been the start of new lives had now become the end of many more. Within the mass of bodies was Tal Eva. None of the bodies were identifiable now, but Tele still watched the spot where she'd been laid carefully with love by her son, Tal Aval, and his friend Tal Opas.

The amber flames dominated the village, and the light of the fungi waned in submission to the fire's overbearance. The waves of heat ate away at the layers of ice that glazed the grounds and nesting homes, smearing the air with swirls of angry mist. Every remaining villager attended the funeral and watched as their mothers, fathers, children, brothers and sisters were exhaled on waves of smoke and into Desolate.

You will never have anyone ever again, the fire breathed. *I will take it all.*

Navid stood at Tele's side. He dipped his head with a silent composure of respect. She'd said little to him since his return. She had found it easy to avoid conversation amid the village disorder. But even though her reservations about him had not been resolved, she still needed to work with him until it was sensible for them to part ways.

"It all makes sense now," Tele said. "What happened to Caldor, the creature we saw in the water, what happened here … A *Thief-Taker* rode the flying lizard. The Deseran Dominion was behind the fall of Caldor. Somehow, the Dominion has control of these creatures, and they're using them to ascend to dominance."

Navid nodded slowly, though he remained silent.

"Such power," Tele whispered to herself.

If there were as many of these creatures as the Caldor Guardsmen had described, then Caldor never had a chance. Even if they had figured out what she had about using fire to stop them, there would have been too many of them airborne to stop it.

"And the Hzorah army is walking right into that," Navid said, finally looking to her. "It's going to happen all over again."

Navid was right. If the Dominion had this power, they would certainly use it against the Hzorah troops. The army wouldn't see it coming. They'd have no defense against them.

"We have to warn the army," Tele said. "And then maybe I can help Tal Aval construct a spell to stop the creatures. The language I've been trying to reconstruct was the Tal language all along. Tal Aval should be able to help me make sense of the runes and—" She paused, remembering what Navid had said. "What did you mean about the Seed's power not making a difference?"

Navid looked away, his long, dark hair shading the glow of his eyes. "I meant that Tal Aval was granted the power, but only a drop of it. It was somehow drained from the Seed."

"Drained? How could it be *drained*?"

"Tal Aval said something about life seeking balance," Navid said. "That eventually the power could no longer be contained."

"Entropic pressure," Tele said. "It applies to life and energy alike."

Navid shrugged. "I'm not sure what that means. But it is as I said. We only have a drop. It may only be good for one use."

This is just another step, Tele thought.

Anything appreciable takes considerable effort. She'd just have to work with Tal Aval to create something within the constraints of his power. The limits on their ability to affect change was no longer an issue of impossibilities. Now it had been reduced to an issue of improbabilities. It was a design problem now.

After what she'd witnessed with the dragon, even the infinitesimal hope of a simpler problem kept her from buckling under the grief of all that was now lost to her.

She had allowed herself to feel safe here. She'd thought that somehow, she'd found a place where she belonged and people who might understand her—just as she had thought she'd found with Navid—a new family. But belonging was not what she would find in this new world—not now, perhaps never.

Though she couldn't bring back the dead, she could make sure this kind of destruction never happened again. If she could stop the Dominion, she could stop them from hurting more people. Now, they had only to get to the Hzorah Army as fast as possible.

In time, Tal Dian and Tal Aval approached them. Tele gave her best condolences to Tal Aval. He accepted it, but Tele knew that any measure of sympathy would not dull the pain of separation.

"I am ready to leave when you are ready," Tal Aval said to them.

"Are you sure we shouldn't stay awhile longer to help?" Tele asked.

Tal Aval shook his head. "My people needed me when they were being attacked. Now they need me to end the threat. We go."

Tal Dian nodded his agreement. "Yes. You must end this terrible evil."

"Tonight, then," Tele confirmed. "I will gather my things."

"I have a gift for the two of you," Tal Dian said before he held out a hand and summoned forth two branches from the ground. As he pulled them free and handed one to Tele and the other to Navid, he said: "We cannot all go to protect you on your journey, but we can send a small piece of the magic here to help you."

As Tele held the branch in her hand, she again willed it to become a bow. Then, with the lightest push of intent, it reshaped itself into a short sword.

"Very good," Tal Dian said. "You are quick to learn, Tele. The växarot is very special. It can change to be the tool the wielder desires. But it cannot be used forever without being renewed. The växarot is a living creature and must rest and eat. You must replant it, but it will regrow where you desire."

Their departure was a somber affair. Tele and Navid

retrieved their belongings from Tal Eva's home that was somehow ever more still with the loss of the kind elder. Together, Tele, Navid, and Tal Aval left the Tal village behind, and Tele hoped that this would be the final place she'd leave that fell victim to fire and ice and men who let hate destroy who they once were.

Amie shifted her weight from one side to the other—a cycle that continued over and over during her waking hours and became much more uncomfortable during the couple hours of sleep she gleaned throughout the journey. Mara's light, restful breathing needled her. She made sleeping in the hard, wooden coop look easy.

She looked to the space between her and Mara—a vast canyon of separation where her father once slept. The glue that held them together as sisters was now gone. Amie didn't know how to be a part of the Kruv family without Father. While she and her sister weren't exactly enemies, they weren't close either. Without the elder Kruv to keep the peace when tensions rose between them, Amie feared things would get hostile. They were just too different. Without Gavini or Father, they may as well be co-workers—civil enough to each other to keep the Kruv House running, but when the day ended, they returned to their own lives.

Amie wiped away a tear as she thought about her father's warm smile for the thousandth time that day. Without him, she was utterly alone. His death had broken her heart, and she couldn't stop the reflexive thought of *I should talk to Father about this*. And that broke her heart all over again, knowing that the only person she wanted to talk to about her pain was gone.

Through the cage bars, she could see a fire burning, but it was too far away for her to feel the warmth of it. The soldiers could have at least afforded them a blanket.

If we freeze to death tonight, then they'll be sorry, Amie thought, remembering their commanding officer's final orders for "no more accidents."

By the position of the sun, it had become obvious that they were traveling north. Her observation had been reinforced when she'd heard two soldiers talking about the Shadow Peaks and how they might skirt the plains to the north. When she'd told Mara, she'd shrugged—almost uncaring—and said, "They're Deseran soldiers. Where *else* would we be going?"

It made sense. The Deseran Dominion was mounting an army. And the only way they could possibly move any sizable number of troops into Hzorah was by way of North Hzorah. Gavini had shown her a map of the known world a few years back. Desera was to the far north, beyond a great belt of mountains. The map had ended just past the Shadow Peaks. Gavini had told her that no one knew what was north of the mountains and most cartographers expected there was only wilderness beyond—an infinite desert, devoid of life.

But the Dominion had survived.

As if he'd suddenly popped into existence, Amie noticed the white stalk of hair. That Dominion soldier—the one who'd been with the commanding officers at the ruins of Gavini's cabin—was leaning against their wagon. She slid across the cage floor and peered over his shoulder. He held a book, muttering to himself as he read.

"What are you reading?" she whispered. She sucked in a sharp breath when she realized she'd actually asked him out loud. *What am I thinking?*

Startled, the man jumped. He frowned at her then turned back to his book, ignoring her.

Amie let out a slow breath. Even though she realized her asking him this was bordering on the insane, she felt compelled to do so. Yet he hadn't given her the simple courtesy of a response. She did *not* like being ignored, and there was a whole lot of ignoring going on as of late.

There was something different about this man—Lieutenant Owen, she'd heard him called. He didn't have the same look as the other soldiers. In fact, Amie wasn't really sure where he was from. Obviously not from Hzorah, but most of the Deserans had a similar appearance to the people of Hzorah, and Owen didn't share it. His white hair despite his obvious youth was the most striking difference. And his is dark skin—darker than South Hzorah complexion—was near the color of a dignitary from Roanne that had once graced the dining hall of the Kruv House.

But it wasn't just his appearance. The way he carried himself and the way he sat now, reading while the others talked—she'd watched him do it more than once. It was as if he tried to fit in by wearing the same outfit but was only playing a role.

"My words aren't poison," Amie said. "They won't hurt you. I just want to know what you're reading." She paused, considering her words. "It just looks interesting. That's all."

Lieutenant Owen glared at her. "I'm practicing."

"Practicing?" Amie repeated. "Practicing reading?"

"Yes," he said, his unidentifiable accent still evident through his clipped responses.

Amie waited for more of an explanation, but he didn't give one. Maybe he was new to reading. It probably wasn't a requirement of being a soldier, or whatever it was that he did before this, but he's a Lieutenant now. She didn't know what that really meant, but it was *some* rank. Maybe this was part of his job now.

Amie listened quietly as he began to mumble words again, somewhat quieter now that he was aware of Amie's observations. She read the words on the page as he did, trying to figure out what it was that he was reading. It was too long to be mission orders. Perhaps it was a novel. Gavini had had one, and she'd read it over and over until she'd nearly memorized every word.

Owen stumbled over a word. He re-read the passage—with a bit more grace than before—but again struggled with the word in question. He tried again but was no more successful.

"Permutation," Amie said when she finally realized what word he was trying to say. "The world is 'permutation.'"

Owen stood and pulled his sword. He pointed it at her, the blade's tip crossing just beyond the metal bars. Amie leaned out of the weapon's immediate reach. Her heart sped. Had she crossed the line?

"Sit back and hush up," Owen said. "Or else I'll cut your throat."

Amie slowly slid back across the carriage. She'd wanted acknowledgment. She'd gained that much. But she didn't want it so much that she'd lose her life.

Owen, satisfied with her retreat, returned his sword to rest. He opened the book, gave her one final glare, then sat and continued reading in his low, staccato tone.

"You want us killed, don't you?" Mara whispered.

Amie turned to her sister who'd sat up. "No. I just want to talk. Maybe they can be reasoned with. We haven't done anything wrong."

"We don't *have* to do anything wrong." Mara said. "They're Deserans. We're of Hzorah. There's no more reason for them to capture us than that alone."

"That's absurd."

"Of course, it is, because we both know that the reason why we're here is because you and that woman couldn't help but meddle."

"You mean Tele?" Amie said. "We weren't meddling. We were trying to help."

"And look where it landed us." Mara swept an arm about the small cage. "Stop meddling. You're just going to get yourself hurt. All of us, more likely."

Amie looked back to the man. She remembered how he'd helped kill Lana's father. How he'd invaded her home—

No … *He* hadn't killed those men. The other soldier had. Owen had faltered. And while Owen had invaded their home, his men had done most the work for him—resulting in her father's death. And, over the past few weeks, as they neared the North Hzorah Plains, Owen hadn't said much to his soldiers beyond the occasional general order. She imagined superior officers were supposed to maintain a sense of authority rather than friendship, but Owen all but avoided his men.

Over past several weeks, what Amie thought to be true had continuously shifted. Foreigners became friends. Townsfolk they'd trusted had sold out people they'd known for years. And she'd failed to see it coming every time.

She squinted, looking to the men beyond the carriage who stood about the fire. One of them—one of the largest with the broad scar across his chin—still wore his sword and leather breastplate. He thumbed the metallic hilt, his eyes darting about, searching for signs of danger.

Another lankier soldier waved his hands frantically above his head while he told some lewd tale about a woman back home. He watched for the soldiers about him to respond. When they did, his eyes flashed in the firelight as he recalibrated his story to suit them.

Yet another laughed heartily at the soldier's story, nearly choking on whatever it was he shoved into his mouth. He uncorked a waterskin and poured a stream of blood red liquid down his throat. He squinted at the strength of it, then continued laughing as if he hadn't almost died.

All the while, Lieutenant Owen sat alone, back against the carriage, struggling to read the next line of text.

I didn't see it coming because I wasn't watching, Amie thought. All the signs were always there, waiting for her. She had only to open her eyes and pay attention.

Amie slid back across the floor of the carriage cage. Mara called for her, but she ignored her. She gripped the metal bars and pressed her face against the gap between them. "Listen, I—"

Owen looked up at her, shut the book and pulled his sword. "I told you to sit back!"

"Amie..." Mara warned.

"I can help you," Amie said. "I can help you with the words. I know how hard it is. Just let me help."

Owen walked forward, and his sword stretched outward until it paused just under her chin. Amie flinched backward despite her want to stand—or, sit, really—firm. She looked him the eyes where anger burned, likely fueled by his own frustration.

"I don't need your help," Owen said. "Now, sit back and shut up."

The commanding officer wanted "no more accidents." Even if Owen wasn't different from the rest of these men, he certainly wasn't about to kill her because she offered to help him.

"You most definitely need my help," Amie said. "Unless you enjoy feeling like a fool."

"Amie!" Mara pulled her back to the far side of the cage.

Owen turned, picked up the small book, and walked back, flipping it open. "Read this."

Amie made to re-approach, but Mara held her in place.

"Mara—"

"Let the girl go," Owen ordered.

Amie looked back to Mara's angry yet worried eyes. "It's alright, Mara."

Mara's grimace didn't soften, but she did let her go. "Be careful."

Amie slid across the cage again to where Owen pressed the small book against the bars. His finger tapped the first line of the page. Amie squinted in the dark, trying to see the words despite the lack of light inside the small enclosure. She cleared her throat.

"Well?" Owen demanded.

"'Buytric substitute for a fatty layer, isolating the polypeptide bonds that …'" Amie read, then paused. She looked up at him. "Where did you get this?"

"You'll help me read it?"

Amie considered her options for a moment. Was this even really an option at this point? "Yes."

Owen pulled the book away and signaled to his men. The three soldiers jogged over with spears. Owen pointed to Amie.

"Get her out," he said. "Careful. Only her."

"Lieutenant," the scarred soldier said. "I'm not sure that …"

Owen rounded on him. "She's only a girl. I have a sister that looks like she could put up a better fight."

The soldiers eyed each other for a brief moment before taking to the cage doors. Amie swallowed with anticipation.

Mara perked. "This could be our moment."

The doors opened, and several inches of steel pushed into the opening. Amie and Mara flinched back as one. Then, between several swords and spears, a soldier waved her forward.

"Come on, lass," the drunken soldier said. "And don't bother trying anything foolish, or I'll slaughter the lot of you."

Amie gave Mara one last look before sliding across the wooden floor. When she got close enough, the man grabbed her leg and pulled her the remaining distance. Amie cried out until her feet met the ground. Mara cried out behind her.

"The girl's fine, sitter," the soldier said. "Stop your crying."

"You're a brute of a man to pull me like that," Amie said and maneuvered her thin shift of a nightgown back below her waistline.

The man looked her over. "It's not the least I could do to you, lass."

The soldiers chuckled while they shut the carriage cage behind her. Amie felt her face redden, more of rage than embarrassment. *What have I worked myself into?*

"If you so much as touch me, I'll—"

"Don't bore me with your hollow threats," the soldier said and shoved her forward.

Amie stumbled, but found her balance. Her legs tingled with thousands of tiny, cold pricks. She'd sat on them for far too long. Longer than she'd ever remembered sitting in her whole life.

"Put her over there," Owen said, he pointed to a large, flat rock. "Tie her ankles. I don't want her running."

The men nearly lifted her off the ground as they guided her. They forced her down on the rock, and Amie winced at the pain in her buttocks. It had felt so good to stand. Even for that short moment. Somehow, that made being forced to sit again all the worse. The scarred soldier fetched a dark brown rope and secured it around her ankles.

"Careful," Amie said, as they pulled the rope tight. "I'd like the keep those. You're about to saw them right off."

The soldier looked at her with a cold scowl, as if she was the very dirt beneath the rock she sat on. He gave the rope a tug, then walked away. It was just tight enough that she couldn't move, but it didn't cut off her circulation. *At least there's that.*

Amie looked back to the carriage cage. It was so small. How had she spent so much time in there without losing her mind, or, at least, her ability to stand?

Now that she was outside of the small cage, she had a thousand new opportunities to escape where inside she had none. Instinctively, she glanced about and searched for an escape route, weapons, any weakness she could exploit.

Nothing ...

Unless she could somehow shove one of them into the fire ... that might distract them long enough for her to get off the path and into the woods. Her legs were tied, but she could still hop or roll. Then she'd need a large dose of luck that she'd find a hiding spot just off the path.

Mara watched her through the steel-barred window. Amie tried to give her a look that said: "I'm fine. Everything is fine." She wasn't sure what that look was supposed to be, but she willed her face into an expression that felt appropriate.

Even if she found a way to escape in the moment, she couldn't simply leave her sister behind. Any plan to escape had to include Mara. Her sister could be cold, but she didn't deserve to be left alone with these brutes.

She then looked into the fire, remembering how Tele lost her family. *No. I couldn't possibly push one of them into the fire, no matter how horrible they are. I have to find a different way.*

Owen crossed to the rock with the small book. "You're going to help me read this. If you don't cooperate, I'll put you back in the cage. If you try anything funny, I'll end you and your sister. Is that clear?"

Amie nodded, watching his eyes. There was something there. Something that didn't quite match the words that came from his mouth. It was that same intuition that compelled her to speak to him in the first place.

"Good," Owen said. He sat beside her, opened the book to the page where she'd left off and handed it to her. "Read."

TAL TRIBELANDS

The Fourth Movement

TWENTY-SIX

THE WEDGE

Thick beads of sweat collected along Gabriel's hairline and slowly dripped over his nose and eyelids. The day was unnaturally hot for this time of year, and, as if he'd not realized it, Captain Alden had them running the perimeter of an offshoot hill from the Shadow Peaks.

A cloud passed over the warpath of the evening sun, and Gabriel let his muscles relax just a bit to enjoy it. The small relief that the clouds gave in these brief intervals felt like a cool bath in sharp contrast to his mounting exhaustion.

"If we keep this up," Aeron said between measured breaths, "we won't have the energy to fight when the time comes."

"It's the right way," Fabi said, just as winded. "You want to be ready, don't you?"

"Burnout isn't ready," Aeron said.

"You won't burn out," Fabi said.

"*Pass* out, then," Aeron retorted, then added: "At least then I won't have to run anymore."

Gabriel couldn't help but smile at Fabi's willpower. He'd taken Cainan's abuse with as much stride as could be expected, and now he was out-performing almost every recruit in the

Second League. *If these are the lessons you learn as a highwaymen, maybe more men should steal.*

Mel, just in front of them all, turned, jogging backward along the dirt path. "Don't you got somethin' in those trousers?" he said to Aeron.

"I do," Aeron said. "I just don't want them over-jostled."

The path wove to the right between two flag posts that Captain Alden placed to mark a full circuit. Five laps down, five more to go—two more than they'd ran last week. Gabriel had always kept himself in top shape, but he understood Aeron's complaints. Annoying as they were, he was beginning to feel it himself.

Urwell and Paitin joined them from behind.

"I think I'm going to die," Paitin said. "I'm going to scorching die mid-stride."

Urwell managed a chuckle. "This is why we stick to the southern reaches of Hzorah where the weather is cool." He looked at Gabriel. "Paitin is always going on about wanting to travel the world, but whines whenever he is the least bit uncomfortable."

"It won't be like this on the road," Paitin said. "I'd have horses."

"He also can't ride a horse."

"With a carriage!"

Gabriel smiled to himself. The twins still kept to themselves for the most part, speaking privately in Armothean. But after the incident with Cainan during their game of capture the flag, they'd spent less time talking to Cainan, Jae, and Lurin, and more time warming up to the rest of the team.

Gabriel glanced behind to see Cainan pacing himself with Jae and Lurin. Cainan caught his eye as Lurin went on about something Gabriel couldn't overhear. Jae, quiet as ever, manned Cainan's opposite side, watching his feet to navigate the terrain.

"Watching the royal warriors?" Aeron asked when Gabriel turned back. "Probably talking about us behind our backs."

Aeron had taken to calling Cainan and anyone who

frequented his company the "royal warriors"—a title that had actually caught with the rest of the Second League. Gabriel refused to join in. He didn't try to stop it either.

"Like we're doing now?" Gabriel asked.

Aeron smirked. "Something like that."

"Can you blame them?" Fabi said. "Cainan's family is the most powerful in all of Hzorah. I've heard it said they're even more powerful than the Crown—that the Crown turns to the Bendeths when they really want to get things done."

Gabriel frowned at that.

"I *do* blame them," Aeron said. "It's not too much to ask to be decent."

"Jae ain't that bad," Bear said.

Aeron looked genuinely surprised. "You've talked to him? I have a wager with Paitin that he's taken an oath of silence."

"*Really, Paitin?*"

"*What are the odds he has a vow of silence? He's probably just shy. It's a good bet.*"

"Well, no," Bear said. "I didn't really talk to him. We ... drummed together."

"Drummed?" Fabi asked. "What's that supposed to mean?"

"I brought my cajon from home," Bear said. "A few days back, I was sitting out, playing before we got together to practice forms. I had my eyes closed while I played. That's how I like to do it. Then, all of a sudden, someone joined in. I opened my eyes and Jae's sitting right there beside me. I ain't even hear him come up. He was playing a djembe, and he was good. We kept playing together, taking turns leading the groove. I ain't never drummed with someone so talented."

"And that's why you think he's decent?" Aeron asked.

Bear shrugged.

"You can't play music with someone and leave without some of their soul," Mel said. "I ain't that good at it—not like Bear—but I know what that's like."

Gabriel hadn't had much of an opinion of Jae either way. It was a bit unnatural how he didn't talk, even when directly addressed, but this did humanize him a bit. Maybe there was something he could do to bring him out of his shell.

"Soldier!"

Gabriel looked toward Captain Alden's voice. The man stood at the hill's summit with a wooden ledger. He did so often and was likely taking notes about the Second League for future reference. Sometimes, though, when a fanciful smile took his lips, Gabriel imagined that he might instead be writing letters to a lover back home.

Captain Alden waved him to the top of the hill as the sun spilled past the clouds. Gabriel slowed and looked to the soldiers who'd ran on ahead. The captain had definitely signaled to him. He continued to wave him over in case Gabriel couldn't see him well at such a distance.

He noticed me slowing, Gabriel thought. *The one time I allow myself to falter, and I get called out.*

Gabriel climbed the hill, picking his footholds as carefully as he could while still maintaining the pace he'd had just moments before. He tried to form an argument for why he'd allowed himself to fall behind the group.

My foot has been killing me the past few days and ... Well, that was just a lie.

The others were complaining about the run, and I just needed to clear my head so I could ... And now he was blaming his crew.

Gabriel slowed, taking the last few, uphill strides. He saluted, but his mind drifted elsewhere. From here, the view of the land stole his breath. The Hzorah army stretched over the gently sloping hills. Men and tents vibrated like a carpet of ants. How many were there now? Twenty thousand? Forty thousand? More? It was hard to tell. He didn't know how to quantify that many men.

"What do you see?" Captain Alden asked, jarring Gabriel's attention. He pointed to the line of Second League soldiers circling the wide hill.

"I see men running, sir," Gabriel said.

Captain Alden nodded. "Yes. What else do you see?"

Gabriel shrugged. "I'm not sure what you're trying to get

me to say, sir, but if this is a lesson of war, I'd have to say that the Second League is still undisciplined."

Captain Alden smiled. "Exactly. They're strong, fit, and haven't backed out of my training. They have potential, but they're not united in will."

Gabriel shifted uncomfortably as the moment of silence swelled.

"Is that all, sir?" Gabriel asked. "If this is about me slowing, I—"

"What do you think about that one?"

"Fabi?" Gabriel asked. "He's a good recruit. If we could have two of him, I'd take it."

Captain Alden nodded and continued to point out soldiers. Gabriel gave him his honest thoughts. Aeron was headstrong but competent. Bear and Mel had improved considerably.

"And what about those two?" he said, pointing this time to Lurin and Jae.

Gabriel winced. "I don't really know much about them."

"And the big blond one?"

"Cainan ..." Gabriel said, hesitating to say anything negative. He didn't think it was honorable to speak poorly of his teammates. "He's alright, I suppose."

"From what I've seen," the captain said, "he's just as good as Fabi. Better even, no?"

"He is good, sir. It's just ... I don't like his attitude."

"Oh?"

Gabriel paused again, not wanting to say what he truly thought—that Cainan was the biggest shoving looger the Second League had. That wouldn't be the right thing to do. On the other hand, if he said it in the right way, he could possibly get Captain Alden to remedy the situation.

"When I first met him," Gabriel continued. "I found him in a brawl with one of the other recruits. Fabi, in fact. I don't care how good you are, there's no place for that kind of behavior on the field," Gabriel looked back out to the Second League. "There's too much at stake."

"I had my own encounter with him," Captain Alden said.

"Really?" Captain Alden raised an eyebrow. His heart quickened. Had Cainan decided to give him away? "What sort of encounter, sir?"

"He came to me a week ago and petitioned for a rank. And also pointed out that Fabi was a thief in case I wanted to do something about it."

"Is that why you asked?" Gabriel inquired. "About Fabi, I mean. You think you should do something about him?"

"It doesn't matter much what a man is before he joins my crew," Captain Alden said. "What matters is who he becomes after joining it. He has your vote of confidence?"

"He does, sir."

Gabriel tried to imagine what the encounter with Cainan must have been like. His cousin could be intimidating, but that was the extent of his persuasive skill.

"I'm raising you to ranked status," Captain Alden said.

"Sir?" Gabriel said. "I'm not experienced enough to—"

The captain looked at him. "And I also presume you're not experienced enough to tell me who I should and shouldn't promote."

"No, sir," Gabriel said. "I'm not."

"Your job will be to unify the group. Make them of one mind—of one spirit."

"Yes, sir."

"Good," he said. "I'll have the paperwork sent through, and you'll be getting a set of armor that will note your rank."

"There are others," Gabriel said. "I'm not the only one giving it my all out there. Why me?"

"I'm not sure what it is," Captain Alden said, squinting against the evening sun. "Perhaps it's your ability or the fire I see in your eyes whenever you drill with the rest. Perhaps it's because I gave you a job to help Aeron improve, and you went above and beyond and helped the others, too. Don't think I didn't notice."

Gabriel looked away. "I'm just trying to live with honor like you said, sir."

"Did you know that Cainan is the son of a High Lord?"

Gabriel considered for a moment whether to admit it. But Cainan hadn't been shy about letting anyone know who he was. He would have had to be deaf not to know. "I did."

"His father was instrumental in the Dominion War," the captain said. "The house of Bendeth deserves that much respect. Does it make you nervous to give orders to someone who, in every other case, could make your life very difficult?"

It *did* make him nervous. Not because of Cainan's family power, but because Cainan knew what everyone else didn't know about him. Cainan could still cluck at any moment if he wanted to, and there was nothing he could do about it.

Gabriel was surprised that Cainan hadn't *already* clucked on him. There was a time when he wouldn't have doubted Cainan's friendship, but now …

"It doesn't," Gabriel lied.

"Good," Captain Alden said. "I just want to make sure you won't buckle under the pressure of what he might tempt you with when this is all over."

"There's no guarantee I'll be coming back from this," Gabriel said. "Even so, I won't gamble the fate of my land that way. It wouldn't be honorable."

"It wouldn't be fair of me if I didn't admit to you that I felt tempted by such prospects."

Gabriel frowned. "Sir?"

"I'm only a man, soldier. We all are. The good graces of a High Lord or a Lord-to-be is something many men would kill for. There are those of us who haven't had their shot. We labor away with the life that we want just beyond our reach." He smiled. "I'm not saying that I've sold my soul. I'm just admitting to my own fallibility. You're young, Gabriel. But perhaps one day you'll understand what I mean."

"No, I believe I do understand. You see the life that you want just beyond a transparent glass, but Desolate's Hand holds tight to your collar. It's suffocating. You want to get out."

"There are a lot of men here who aren't here because they chose to be. They haven't been indoctrinated with a warrior's mind. They're young and afraid—vulnerable to temptation.

You need to offer them something else, something bigger. Something that they can only receive by joining together."

Gabriel understood. He, at least, had his father to help him learn what he needed to be a warrior. Aeron had told him that most of them weren't here because they actually wanted it. Gabriel had to make them want it.

"I think you have what it takes to be a leader here. You can handle this, right? Am I making a mistake?"

Gabriel considered the question seriously. As much as he wanted this, he wanted what was best for the Second League above all else. *If I take this, I can't ruin it. I'll never forgive myself.*

"You're not, sir."

Gabriel scratched at his growing stubble as he watched his crew run his drills. He hadn't been allowed to grow a beard at the palace. Only his father wore one—a show of rank or something according to Samuel. He needed to find a razor.

Still several hours before high noon, the Second League had already worked up a day's sweat. Thankfully, the previous night's rain had cooled the air and left the sky overcast in white and gray. Now, all they needed was a cool breeze.

Captain Alden had met with Gabriel in his private tents to go over the drills and techniques he needed the Second League to learn. This was in addition to their combat training, and with their accelerated timeline, Gabriel pushed the crew to their limits.

His father's sword was an unusual but welcome weight to his normal garb. The sabre's blade was supernaturally light yet unmatched in strength and power. Most of the weight came from the pommel and scabbard, making the Crown Sabre strangely unbalanced but significantly advantageous in combat.

None of the Second League had received their war attire, including Gabriel, and it was Urwell who'd recommended that he wear the weapon while they trained because it made him look as though he were actually a ranked officer—so that

Cainan remembered his place. Gabriel took the suggestion. Less so because he thought he needed to look distinguished but because he'd wanted an excuse to feel closer to his father.

Gabriel watched as the Second League soldiers jogged across the plain. Heads down and mock shields high, they charged straight into their invisible foe. Gabriel whistled two sharp tones and the company shifted, turning left. Someone cried out. Another stumbled. The wedge failed to reform and collapsed on itself.

Sighing, Gabriel walked across the open field. "Formation!"

The Second League found their feet and stood in line.

"Anyone know what went wrong out there?" Gabriel asked.

Silence. Then Cainan spoke. "We lost our footing … *sir.*"

Gabriel knew it was painful for Cainan to address him with such formality. Every muscle in his face resisted forming the appellation. Gabriel felt a certain amount of guilt for being addressed in such a manner. But it was nice to see Cainan swallow his tongue for once.

"Clearly," Gabriel said. "But why? Why did you lose your footing?"

Cainan stepped forward and pointed down the line to Fabi. "The thief failed to turn in time."

Fabi's face twitched, but he didn't deny the accusation. He stared ahead, giving his attention to the Shadow Peaks beyond.

Gabriel stepped closer to Cainan. "Fabi is a part of this squad, just the same as you. You will not refer to him as a thief. Only as a soldier. Is that understood, *soldier*?"

Cainan's top lip twitched as he met Gabriel's eye. "Yes, *sir.*"

Gabriel stood there a moment, to be certain that Cainan's insubordination had reached its apex. He'd worried that after Captain Alden had promoted him to take the lead in the Second League's training, Cainan would have simply clucked and told someone who he really was. Cainan had agreed to keep his secret as long as Gabriel stayed out of his way. He wasn't exactly "out of his way" anymore.

But Cainan hadn't clucked. There was honor in that, and Gabriel tried to remind himself that Cainan wasn't all bad.

They had been close once, hadn't they? He was just sour because he wasn't the one the captain had chosen. He'd get over that.

Gabriel walked across the line to stand in front of Fabi. "What was the issue, soldier?"

"I was caught unaware and failed to turn in time, sir," Fabi answered without hesitation.

Gabriel took a slow breath to calm himself. Though clumsy, they'd ran the drill three times in a row without major mishap and suddenly the group had completely lost its coordination. It wasn't entirely strange. It's expected that a group of men would lose their rhythm at a certain point, but here, on the field, a small misstep like that could be the end of them all.

"You need to pay attention, soldier."

What else could he say? Captain Alden may have punished the group with a drill, but Gabriel hadn't been able to pull together whatever it was that gave the captain his latitude for torment. Moreover, it felt disingenuous. He was still part of the Second League, wasn't he?

Gabriel turned and walked back to his position on the field. "Run it again. No mistakes this time."

The soldiers grouped into the same arrow-like formation and waited for Gabriel's signal. When Gabriel was sure they'd settled, he whistled once, and the charge began. One whistle started and stopped the maneuver, two and three cued left and right turns respectively.

Gabriel whistled in three, quick successions. The charge cut right. It wasn't quite as graceful as Gabriel hoped, but at least they hadn't stumbled.

Packed so tightly together, even the smallest misaligned soldier could topple the charge. Given the proper practice, the wedge would prove effective, but anything less than extreme precision might spell disaster.

After two whistles that sent the Second league charging left, Gabriel looked back to the encampment and spotted Captain Alden in the distance, walking toward him. Instead of his usual officer's uniform, he sported sleek leather armor, dyed black and embroidered with his rank insignia.

Gabriel saluted and Captain Alden nodded his greetings.

"How are the troops this morning, Sergeant?" the Captain asked.

"We've run the wedge drill several times," Gabriel said. "I think we've made a good amount of progress. We should still test it. Perhaps with a few soldiers in the other divisions. I'm not sure if that's even a possibility, but it would help a lot. There's only so much we can anticipate when running it without any sort of resistance."

"Agreed. And what about morale?"

Gabriel turned back to look at his team. "Well, there is still some bad blood. A few arguments here and there. But nothing serious. At least, not like what I've seen out there." Gabriel pointed with a thumb to the army behind them.

Gabriel whistled and the wedged turned. Flawless. He tried not to show the relief on his face.

"This is why I'm depending on you to whip the Second League into shape," Captain Alden said. "With all these new, untested recruits flooding in after the draft, General Rollins is depending on me to assist the other captains in advancing their training. If you hadn't happened into our camps … well, I guess that doesn't matter now. Desolate's Hand has blessed us with your talent."

Uncomfortable with the heaping praise, Gabriel swallowed. "I'm doing my best, sir."

"The first few rounds of armor have finally arrived," Captain Alden said. "I'm not sure when they'll make it to the Second League, but your crew should be one of the first divisions to receive them."

"Thank you, sir." Gabriel gestured to the Second League. "We'll need to practice this in full armor. It'll be different once there's a bit more resistance and we need all the time we can get."

Gabriel whistled again. With a collective grunt, the Second

League collapsed. Gabriel felt his face heat as he turned to Captain Alden. "As I said, we'll need the time."

Captain Alden didn't frown, but his barring shifted. "I can trust you to get them functioning. Am I wrong?"

"No, sir."

The Captain stepped back. "Then they're all yours, Sergeant."

Gabriel turned and walked back to the Second League, calling for formation. He stopped before the line of men, then walked the length of it, considering each of the soldiers. *There has to be something … Something I'm missing.*

What would his father have done?

He glanced down to the Crown Sabre. Back when he trained Aeron, he touched it accidentally, and he'd recalled a precious morsel of advice King Jeremiah had given him. Before that, in the palace, he'd touched it and his father had visited him in memory then, too. Each time it had been so real. Each time he'd desperately needed his father's good council whether he knew it or not.

Are you there, Father?

He let his hand grip the sabre's warm hilt and closed his eyes.

"Tie his hand," King Jeremiah said.

Gabriel smiled. He pulled his mock sword and held out his left hand for Samuel to bind behind him. It would be a challenge to duel his father without an arm. More so for balance than as a tool of combat.

Samuel took his arm and wrapped it with thick fabric.

"No," his father said. "His right arm."

Gabriel frowned. "What? My right hand is dominant."

"Exactly," the King said, and circled his son. "Now, his eyes."

"You can't be serious," Gabriel said as Samuel slipped a black strip of cloth over his eyes. "Now I can't even see you."

"Seeing isn't your problem," his father said and then surprised him by thumping his chest, just over his heart. "Feeling is your problem. Combat is a dance, an orchestration of blood and bone and blade."

His father struck, catching him against his backside—not hard enough to seriously harm him, but hard enough that he didn't want it to happen again.

He cried out in surprise. "I can't feel you if I can't see you."

"I've allowed you to use your sight as a crutch and your dominant hand as a foundation, grounding you in place," the king said. "your vision masks the inherent rhythms around you. Your right hand anchors you to what you believe rather than what you sense."

Again, his father struck him. He recoiled then turned to the direction of the strike, lashing out but only catching air.

"You must feel the tempo of battle rather than see and react to your opponent."

His father struck again from the darkness. Gritting his teeth against the pain, he sought to quiet his mind. He listened closely to the slow drag of his father's boots against the tiled floor, felt the whispers of air over his skin as the wooden staff waved through the air—up, down, outward … and recognized the form as practiced experience met instinct.

He turned, sweeping his staff up to meet his father's. Like a downbeat following an expectant upbeat, their staffs met in resolution to the pattern of combat.

Gabriel opened his eyes and called out to his soldiers. "Take off your shirts!"

The soldiers hesitated for a moment. "Off with them!" Gabriel added with more authoritative flair. "Aeron will now lead the change." The Second League removed their shirts. "Formation!"

There was a wave of confusion, but none of the soldiers spoke out of turn. Once the League had arranged themselves into a solid wedge, Gabriel crossed between them, taking their shirts and using them as rope to bind their hands behind their backs.

Gabriel crossed over to Aeron, then held out his hand, beckoning for his shirt. Aeron complied, but not without a befuddled frown. Gabriel stepped behind him and used his shirt to blindfold him with a quick and just-tight-enough knot.

"The rest of you," he said, "are to follow. Same exercise but slower."

"And just how is he supposed to lead while blindfolded? Sir," Cainan said.

"It doesn't matter that he's blindfolded," Gabriel replied. "What matters is that you follow him to a point. As long as you do so, the wedge will still work. The reason you keep falling apart is because you're not in sync. You're relying on the predictability of a clean turn at the perfect angle. Now, you must pay close attention and become one."

"And these?" Cainan asked, lifting his bound arms. "How is this helping?"

"Oh, those?" Gabriel said. "No. Those aren't helping. They're just making this whole thing more difficult. So, mind your balance."

Unsettled looks passed between the soldiers, but Gabriel ignored them. He turned and walked back toward Captain Alden, who watched with arms crossed and a look of curiosity. Gabriel turned back to stand by his side.

"Unconventional," Captain Alden said.

"Quite," Gabriel said. "An unconventional exercise for an unconventional group of soldiers."

Gabriel whistled. The Second League pushed forward, gracelessly at first, but soon fell into a stable charge. Gabriel whistled twice, and the soldiers instantly fell in on one another.

"Formation!" Gabriel shouted.

The crew struggled to stand without using their arms for support.

"I'm not sure which is *more* cruel," Captain Alden said. "Making them run laps for failure, or effectively cutting off their limbs, even temporarily. Can't catch themselves if they fall."

"Then perhaps," Gabriel said, "they'll avoid falling all together." He smiled. "Or, at the very least, it's more entertaining to watch."

"Your way is more cruel," the Captain affirmed.

"Let's hope it's also more effective," Gabriel said.

"The poor bastards."

Gabriel smiled again. "You're not going to stop me?"

Captain Alden turned and began walking back to the camp. "I said that I trusted you, Sergeant. It's time to make good on my word."

After the captain left, they ran the drill a dozen more times, but their ability to coordinate didn't improve. On the most obvious level, it was clear why their movements were clumsier. He'd hampered their ability significantly. It had worked for him, but with the Second League, it didn't work at all.

As the midday heat intensified, Cainan shifted from irritating to furious. Even Jae looked as though he might scream through his mask of silence. Gabriel rubbed his forehead as he tried to come up with a new idea. He'd taken what his father had done and applied the same exercise directly to the wedge formation drill. Where this could have worked with each of them individually when training with hand-to-hand combat, in a group like this, it exacerbated the problem.

"*Feeling* is your problem," his father had said. "You must feel the tempo of battle."

"Great!" Cainan said, just short of shouting. "Just scorching great! I think I have low-born foot in my ass."

"You can shove it," Fabi growled.

Furthermore, I've damaged whatever comradery they've woven.

"Combat is a dance," Gabriel whispered to himself. "An orchestration of blood and bone and blade."

What was it that Mel had said several days ago? That you can't play music without leaving without some of their soul? It was a saying in step with the tradition of the tribes of North Hzorah. There, music was not just a form of entertainment, but a means of communication. In his time in the court, he'd even seen High Lord Eddings have his Low Lords accompany him with light flurries of musical accents when he presented his ideas before the other lords. It was always an odd form of speaking, but it wasn't without affect.

Gabriel trotted closer to the Second League. Expecting their sergeant to run the drill again, they reluctantly struggled to their feet and prepared to reform. "Bear, run back to camp and grab your cajon. Jae, go with him and bring your djembe."

Bear and Jae shared a confused look as Gabriel untied them. A smile took Gabriel's lips as his plan took further shape. "Anyone else bring instruments?"

Mel raised a hand as best he could from behind his back. "I got a conch and a mirliton in my pack."

"A mirliton?" Gabriel asked.

"It's like a kazoo."

"Go get them," he said as he untied Mel.

As Gabriel untied Paitin and Lurin. "Untie the others. I have a different idea."

He sent Urwell, Paitin, and Aeron to retrieve their dueling staffs, and not long after the Second League freed themselves from Gabriel's contraption, Mel, Jae, and Bear returned with their instruments.

Gabriel asked Bear and Jae begin playing together just as they'd done before, setting a groove while Mel played his mirliton.

"Anyone know how to play the conch?" Gabriel asked, holding it up.

Lurin shrugged. "I don't know how to play it well—"

Gabriel handed it to him. "Good enough for me."

As the four played, Gabriel took one of the practice staffs and began cycling the forms he'd taught the soldiers in rhythm with the music, changing cadences as Mel's melody progressed. He paused, looking to the other Second League soldiers. "Well? Grab a staff and join me. It's not fun out here all alone."

Cainan crossed his arms. "Gabriel, you scorching dolt …"

Paitin stepped out and grabbed a staff and turned to his brother. "Remember how you said you could dance circles around me? I guess you get to prove it now."

Urwell grinned and picked up a staff. "How many times must I embarrass you before you accept that you have two left feet?"

In step with Gabriel's movements, Paitin and Urwell joined. But it wasn't enough to have just the three of them participating. "Fabi, Aeron! We're about to move to the fifth cadence. Get in here!"

Shrugging, the two grabbed staffs and joined the group. Together they climbed the tree of cadences, locking into each form in tempo with the music, allowing the cajon and djembe be their guiding pulse.

"Cainan!" Gabriel shouted over the music. "Would you rather do laps or dance? I think you'd rather dance!"

"I'd rather do laps, sir." Cainan snarled.

"Really?" Gabriel said as they stepped into the forms of the eighth cadence. "Because nonstop laps for thirteen hours with the clock resetting whenever you take a break doesn't really sound like your definition of training. Mine either. Probably more like torture. And I'm sure none of us wants to watch you do them. We'd have to take shifts to watch you fail over and over. And really, that just means none of us will be prepared."

"How will we be prepared doing *this*?" Cainan yelled.

"Fine," Gabriel said. "Have it your way. I don't envy your legs, though."

"Scorch it!" Cainan snatched a staff from the ground and joined them.

As they cycled their forms, Bear and Jae took the liberty to add touches of complexity to their grooves, slowing the tempo to a crawl, then gradually increasing the beat to a frenzy. Staggering into polyrhythmic bliss, the soldiers' forms misaligned as each soldier chose which drum to take their cues, but masterfully, they united again as the two players realigned.

Together they danced the evening away, often dissolving into laughter as the impromptu song took unexpected turns. Gabriel allowed them to take breaks, but someone always danced their forms, eventually adding ornamental flourishes where unnecessary in practice but jived to the mood of the lighthearted exercise. And though Cainan was the most resistant to participate, he had impeccable rhythm, inspiring the others to jump back into the circle to try to be his better.

Eventually, Gabriel had to call the fun to an end, and as they headed back to camp for evening rations, Lurin hung back to talk to him, allowing the others to move ahead and out of earshot.

"Sergeant Gabriel, sir?"

"Well, that just sounds strange. Gabriel is fine."

"Strange?" Lurin said. "Strange is what we just did for the past three hours."

Gabriel smiled. "Fair enough."

"I just wanted to apologize if I've been cold to you. When I came here, I kind of had an agenda. My father died a few years ago and since then I've been doing everything I could think of to keep my family together. It's been kind of hard."

Gabriel nodded. "I understand."

"I thought that if I came here to prove myself on the battlefield—"

"You could return a hero," Gabriel finished for him. "Maybe gain favor with the High Lords?"

"Well, when you say it so bluntly like that, it sounds crazy. And selfish." Lurin ran a hand through his hair. "I just want to do the right thing for my family. I made a favorable agreement with Cainan not too long ago. And I'm afraid that if I don't stay close with him, I'll lose all that. If I die out here and I have nothing to show for it …"

Gabriel stopped and turned to Lurin. "I can't tell you what's best for your family, Lurin. I can't tell you who to make friends with. I can only tell you to be true to your sense of honor."

Lurin nodded, and Gabriel gripped him by the shoulder. "Urwell told me you're good with the bow. Is that true?"

TWENTY-SEVEN

THE BAMILEE

Navid ducked another attack. It'd come so close to taking his skull that he'd felt it graze his hair. Turning, he fell back further toward the treeline, struggling to find his footing and fend off the next attack.

There was a moment of silence.

The fire puffed a thick column of smoke and flurries of glowing ash into the air, blocking his view of the threat beyond.

Come on, Navid thought. *You're not fooling me this time.*

Tele fell through the smoke. Her sword held high, she attacked with a swift, downward swing. Navid caught her växarot with his own and pushed with all his strength, forcing her back to prevent a counter-attack.

Surprisingly, she didn't fall down. Instead, with a free hand to the ground, she arched backward, flipped, and landed cleanly, just shy of the fire. As quickly as she'd recovered, she recomposed into perfect attack form.

"That's new," Navid said, breathing heavy.

"You'll find that I'm full of surprises," Tele said. "Catch your breath. You're getting sloppy."

Navid let out a sigh and relaxed his muscles. He instantly realized that he'd been too tense. Both Tele and Tal Aval had warned him against seizing his muscles in fear.

I'm not made for this.

He sat on the ground and allowed his växarot—which he'd willed to become a staff—bury into the ground. They'd sparred for no more than fifteen minutes, but Tele had a way of making fifteen minutes feel like an eternity.

"Don't sit," Tele said. "Stand up. Walk around the fire."

"Right," Navid said.

Navid stood and began to walk around the flames, looking up into the heavens and trying to even his breathing. She was going to be the death of him. He couldn't keep up. She was too skilled, too fast. It was as if she could see what he was going to do before he could do it. She'd assured him that it wasn't the case, that his moves were just predictable and sluggish.

It'd been two weeks since Navid, Tele, and Tal Aval left the Tal village behind. They'd traveled south through the Borderlands and back into West Hzorah. Navid wanted desperately to just return to Caldor. Or, at least, he wanted to return to the Caldor he'd known before the world had gone mad.

He didn't voice his thoughts lest he sound selfish. Tele and Tal Aval must also miss their homes. They had also lost people they loved. But their ability to put aside their heartache made him feel as though he was alone in his grief. It was all he could do to force himself to stand for another day of travel.

Tele pointed her sword at the fire as she circled it and said: "Fire. That's what we used to defeat the dragon in the village." She looked at Tal Aval. "What's the Tal word for fire?"

"*Aear*," Tal Aval said.

"*Aear*," she repeated. "I'll need to know that."

Navid couldn't believe that even while Tele taught him, she was continuing to work out how to speak the Tal's language of magic. The revelation of that made him feel even more inferior to her talents. Did she ever stop?

Before they'd arrived at the Tal tribe lands, it had been *their* project. Now that she had Tal Aval along, she didn't need him and spent most of their waking hours talking to Tal Aval in his own language, insisting that immersion was the best way for her to learn it as quickly as possible. But it didn't take Tele's brilliance to know that she used it as a convenient excuse to avoid talking to him as much as possible.

Tele hadn't forgotten what had happened in the forests—how Navid had failed her when they had been attacked by the ardya.

He was weak. He wasn't like Tal Aval or Tele. Both of them had lived their whole lives preparing for the very moment they found themselves. Navid wasn't meant for this. Happenstance is what drew him into their quest. Just as could be expected of him, he'd failed Tele in the Tal tribe land. And he knew she'd never forgive him for it.

"You are fighting better, Navid," Tal Aval said. He sat on a log just before the fire, carving a piece of wood he'd picked a few days back. Slowly, it had begun to take the shape of an animal, though Navid wasn't sure what yet, and Tal Aval wouldn't tell them.

"Am I?" Navid asked, looking down at him.

He frowned. "I just said that you are, Navid. Why ask after I say it?"

"Good point," Navid said as his path around the fire caused Tal Aval to pass behind the smoke. "I don't *feel* like I'm getting any better."

"You only died seventeen times," he said. "A few days ago, you didn't last more than a moment."

"I suppose."

"You need to stay focused," Tele said. "I can see your mind elsewhere. You don't have the skill to let yourself think of anything but the battle. There is only you and your staff. Nothing else."

How am I supposed to focus? The pain of pushing back the darkness inside him was difficult. It stabbed at him, digging deep into his gut.

"Time's up," Tele said.

Navid turned to Tele who had already begun to advance on him. He summoned his växarot, and it immediately twisted out of the earth in response to his call. He then shifted into a defensive posture to block her attack.

She didn't follow through.

Tele spun—the opposite direction he'd always known her to—and swung low at his ankles. The flat of the växarot's blade slapped his bones and he staggered backward, half-limping.

It didn't hurt severely. Somehow, Tele was able to measure the pain she dealt him while attacking with the speed of a striking serpent. But it hurt well enough. Enough to spark his attention and inflame his curse to a sharp pain.

Thump.

Navid gritted his teeth. *To allow it to take me is to take a path of evil. To allow it to control me is to take a path to destruction.*

"Fight back!" Tele insisted, stepping forward and swinging her blade.

Navid fell back again and turned on heel to avoid falling out of the bounds of the campground. "I'm trying!"

He was.

"You're evading," Tele said. She took two more swipes, this time connecting with his växarot and rattling his grip. "Unless your plan is to wear me out, evasion does little to win a fight. It's a delay tactic at best."

Navid took another strike to his backside before he wrenched out of her striking range. He turned and held his staff with a two-handed grip between himself and Tele's warpath. With a calm, sure pace, she continued to walk toward him.

Thump. Thump. Thump.

"Straighten up," Tele said. "Relax your muscles."

How am I supposed to straighten and relax at the same time?

Navid stepped backward. He wished that he could stop time. Let himself think of what to do next. He couldn't win, and Tele didn't appear interested in giving him any quarter.

He backed a bit more. Tele held her staff in one hand, off to her side, leaving herself completely open to attack. She was giving him that. She wanted him to take a chance at attacking.

The itch caught fire.

Thump. Thump. *Thump. Thump. Thump*!

To allow—

Tele charged.

Sensing danger, Navid swung his staff and caught Tele's attack before it could land. A surge of awareness poured into him, and before he could choke it off, he was spinning past her and countering her advance. Their växarots cracked like thunder and blurred against the fire light. When she struck again, Navid found that he was in place to meet the attack. It was as if he'd gained extreme competency in an instant.

He could see Tele's eyes light up as she fought back. Her expression shifting from surprise to satisfied to irritated as he began to force her back.

Navid pulled back. He had to get a grip on his emotions. They ran free as they had when he was a child, like they had on the fragile ice of Caldor.

To allow it to take me is to take a path of evil. He breathed with renewed calm as he backed away from Tele's advances. *To allow it to control me is to take a path to destruction.*

Tele attacked again. This time, she only met his staff once before a sharp twist of her växarot disarmed him. Before he could react, she kicked his leg and brought him to a knee. She swung her sword, and it stopped just short of smacking the side of his neck.

Panting, Navid bowed his head, resigning to his defeat. Tele withdrew with a flick of her växarot, spinning the weapon away from his neck before she cast it back into the dirt. Navid looked at her, and she turned toward the rising sun.

"That's all for this morning," Tele said as she walked away. "We may as well break camp for today."

Navid looked back to the ground. He watched small orbs of sweat slip down his long dark hair and drip onto the ground below his chin. He'd lost control, allowed it to break free. He'd taken the path to destruction.

Not long ago, Navid had crossed time and space to find Tele in the Dominion Desert. At the time, he'd thought that was the most afraid he'd ever been. The burning isolation and incomprehensible magic had terrified him, but this …

this was altogether different. To lose control was to damn his soul.

Too many had died at the hands of seers in ages past. They had become monsters drunk with power, and few dared to challenge their warpath. And though the Prophets were no longer alive to help him temper the curse, he had to keep it contained lest it destroy their chance to warn the Hzorah troops.

He stared after Tele, watching her dark form disappear into the sunrise. She'd tried to convince him that he had to let go, that he had to forge his own path forward. Yet she still kept her distance.

Because she knew the truth. She knew what he was.

A monster. A coward. No truc friend.

He clutched the pendant through the thin fabric of his shirt and thumbed the smooth metal through the shroud of cloth. He tried to imagine what his father's face would look like. How happy he'd be when he was reunited with his long-lost son. How happy he, himself, would be to finally be free of this wretched curse.

I have to keep pushing on. For you, father. No one else would dare have me. With a sigh of exhaustion and tentative hope for the day he might reunited with the last vestige of his past, he dismissed his växarot, and watched it replant itself into the soil.

"Come," Tal Aval said from behind him. "It is time."

Navid stood and helped Tal Aval break camp. They doused the fire, stored away the leftovers of their breakfast, and packed their supplies. All the while, Navid watched the trees, waiting for a sign of Tele's return.

"You are fighting well," Tal Aval said as he secured his pack.

"You *really* think I'm getting better?" Navid asked.

"Is that not what I just said?" Tal Aval frowned. "Why do outsiders do that?"

"I mean that I don't feel like I'm improving."

"Your form looks better. It is more natural to you."

"There's nothing natural about it," Navid said. "I don't feel right. I'm not a fighter, Tal Aval. I'm not even a traveler."

"When Wizard Titan came to the Tal and asked us to protect his power, there were those of the Tal who did not want to fight," Tal Aval said. "Some refused to fight. Many people shunned them—called them weak and spineless. I do not believe they were weak. I do not believe they were spineless. They were different. We found different things for them to do that other Tal did not want to do, and they did these things with joy. None of these Tal called us weak or spineless because we did not want to do these jobs."

"But everyone I saw in your village could fight."

"Not long after, there was a sickness that took many of us. We were few. The elders were forced to ask those who could learn to protect us to practice with the växarot. The Tal who did not like to fight refused, saying it was not what they believed to be right. The elders said that it was our duty to protect ourselves and the Seed from covetous hands, from those who might try to steal the power for evil. In the end, they parted ways with us because we could not agree."

"Do the Tal know what Wizard Titan was like?" Navid asked. "The world still speaks of Titan as if he was the most important man to have ever lived. The Deseran Dominion revere him so much that they've militarized in his name."

"He was one of us," Tal Aval said. "He spent much of his time with the Tal when he was not traveling the world and solving its problems. My grandmother told me that he was the fountain of youth. That no matter how old he got, he still had the flame of a child behind his eyes. Children were attracted to it even more so than adults.

"He had a nickname among us: the falcon. He was independent. Not many—even those of the Tal—understood him completely. And though he was alone, he still was fiercely loyal to those who depended on him."

"How old was he?"

"I am not sure," Tal Aval said. "I do not think anyone

knew. But he knew my grandmother, and my great grandmother, and so on as far back as anyone could remember."

"He was immortal. I've always been taught that he was. But I wasn't sure if it was true or simply a legend because immortality is impossible."

"Everything he did was impossible," Tal Aval corrected.

Navid nodded. "That's true. What about when he locked himself away with the Seed? Did he say why he did it?"

Tal Aval shook his head. "Only that he felt that his time here was done. My grandmother said that youthful spark that she had always seen in his eyes was gone. It was as if the centuries had finally caught up with him."

"And that's when he gave up his life."

"There is more to the story," Tal Aval said.

Navid perked. "What is it?"

"I do not know," Tal Aval said, smiling. "But from what I know of the man, he would not have just given up the way he had. He had the will of a falcon. Wizard Titan was not the kind of man who would give up unless he had been broken somehow."

"I know what that feels like. Feeling broken."

Tal Aval placed a hand on his shoulder. "Someday, you will find your wings."

Amie wrote another set of words in the dirt with her stick. Satisfied, she stood and backed away so that Lieutenant Owen could decipher them. She watched his brow wrinkle, and his mouth work as he deciphered the characters.

"Air, hair, chair."

"Good." She pointed to the second set. "Now this one."

"Air, lair, flair."

"And this one?"

"Air, pair, repair."

"Exceptional!"

Owen frowned. "I wouldn't say *exceptional.*"

Amie rolled her eyes. "Will you just take the compliment?"

Owen's lips twitched with the smallest of smiles. "Alright."

"Here," Amie said, handing him the stick. "Copy the words yourself. It'll help you learn and remember."

Owen accepted the branch, squatted, and set to work. It was odd watching him struggle to shape the words. Amie had never thought of herself as smart; Mara was the smart one. But she had become so far removed from the difficulty of reading and writing that it had become as natural as walking.

She glanced at the carriage where Mara watched her silently. Though she didn't say anything, she felt like her eyes were pleading for her to figure out some way to help them escape. That had been her intention, but now that she was outside of the small prison, she found that she had no follow-up plan.

During the day, Amie walked. She'd thought she'd enjoy that more than the confined and uncomfortable cage ride but found that barefoot travel wasn't pleasurable either. Still, she didn't dare slow the men down. If she got put back in the cage, she'd have no chance at escape.

Amie glanced down to check Owen's progress. The first line was complete, but his handwriting was abysmal. *So much for any dreams of being a teacher.*

Lieutenant Owen's hair transfixed her. White, spiky, and bald on either side, it was unlike anything Amie had ever seen. People often commented on how bright her hair was. Some people even adored it, even a few handsome boys … not that Father ever let them near her.

And there it was. Every thought always found a way to lead back to her father. In the past, it wasn't a stumbling block but rather the bridge to yet another thought. Now, it was a pathway to sorrow.

Finishing the last line, Owen stood and sighed with a decidedly frustrated huff. "I'm finished."

"You did—"

"It is not good."

Amie shrugged. "You just need some more practice."

Lieutenant Owen tossed the stick to the ground. "Not tonight. I am done for now."

He gathered the small book and packed it away. Amie swallowed when she caught another look from Mara. She had to do something to get them out of this. So far, she'd only played at being teacher and a poor one at that.

"Does everyone have hair like yours?" Amie asked.

Owen turned. "What?"

"I mean where you're from," Amie amended. "Your people. Do they all have white hair like that?"

For a moment, Amie didn't think he would answer her, but eventually he did. "Yes."

He turned away from her again, as if insulted that she'd asked. She realized he has probably had to answer that question over and over and was tired of answering it. She'd heard that kind of question about her own hair at least a dozen times.

Good approach, Amie thought. *Make him hate you. That should work. Maybe I should ask to touch it, too.*

"Do you miss it?" Amie asked. "Home, I mean."

Owen paused a moment before slowly turning and eyeing her with curiosity. "I … I do miss it."

"What's it like?"

"Warm," he said, "and flat. There's lots of tall grass and bison to hunt. We learned to grow crops, and that made us stronger until the Dominion came."

"Why?" Amie encouraged. "What did they do?"

"They made our people slaves." Owen lowered his voice, though the pain it held could not be concealed. "We are forced to labor day and night so that the Dominion can grow—so that they can fight this war."

"Why didn't you tell them 'no?'" Amie asked. "Why didn't you fight back?"

Owen shook his head. "The Bamilee—my people—do not believe it is right to create violence."

"Even if it means you will be slaves?"

"Even then. To create violence begins a circle, a circle that cannot be ended. All people must only help one another, for only in that way will we thrive."

Amie opened her mouth to object again, but snapped it shut. She'd said—though not so eloquently—something similar to Tele. She'd thought that anyone who'd be willing to buy such terrible weapons must be evil.

She had vowed not to use violence—to not become the kind of person to begin the circle of violence, even to escape these soldiers. But when it was someone else—the Bamilee—Amie had immediately assumed fighting back was the answer.

I can't argue the point further. Not only will I risk insulting his beliefs, I'd be a hypocrite myself.

"But what about—"

Lieutenant Owen waved a hand and turned away. "No more questions." He stalked toward his men.

Amie sank to the ground before the words she and the Lieutenant had written. The misshapen figures were not unlike her own when she was younger. Jagged and sharp, the lines were without muscle-memory or grace. Luckily, Amie had had Gavini to help guide her hand—to help her grow. She was no Gavini. How had he managed to connect with her so that she learned?

The memory of him almost made her smile, and she prayed silently that he was safe.

TWENTY-EIGHT

A SECOND CHANCE

Tele slowed as they approached the long, stone bridge that stretched across a broad stretch of river. She paused, allowing Navid and Tal Aval to cross over ahead while she watched the surging water breaking over jagged rocks.

It had been weeks since she'd first seen the Drunn river, but the appreciation of it hadn't dimmed. She remembered her first bath after she'd left the Dominion Desert. How she'd watched it carry away sands of her past.

"Tele?"

Navid stood at the far side of the bridge, waiting for her. He beckoned for her to cross so that she would not be left behind. Deciding to keep her attention to the river below rather than give him more than a moment's attention, she sighed, crossed over, and skirted past him to avoid meeting his eyes.

"We should probably replenish our water reserves here," he said.

He was right, but Tele wasn't about to admit it. As uncomfortable as the silence between them had become, she would not allow herself to be taken in by him again. There was too much at stake to risk it all for friendship.

She turned back to him, untied her waterskin from her pack, and pushed it into his grip a bit more forcefully than was necessary. He didn't react, which somehow annoyed her even more.

Tele stared at the back of his head as he disappeared off the road. Slick after a late morning rain, he carefully navigated the rocky descent to the creek below.

Slip, she thought.

It wasn't what she really wanted. What she wanted was to be able to turn back time—to come up with a different plan in the forest that didn't involve her risking her life to save him. Perhaps they still may have escaped, or perhaps they both would have fallen, but she wouldn't have to endure the pain of his betrayal.

But wasn't it better this way? To know now what would happen when the stakes were high? The next time he failed to act, it could be their lives, perhaps even the lives of the entire world.

"*You look as if you are trying to cut his throat with your eyes*," Tal Aval said, stepping up beside her and speaking in the Tal tongue.

Instead of entertaining his comment, she asked him how to say river, stream, watergate, and other variations of water-based words in the Tal language. Besides allowing her to avoid talking about her frustration with Navid, it helped her as she continuously ordered the information in her mind—just as she used to do when she learned from her parents in the wilderness. Like how a new understanding of *Small Life* emerged from the various chemical processes that she'd learned from *Element and Reaction*, her command of the Tal language had begun to pull together across disparate groupings of information. She methodically filled her gaps of knowledge as they traveled, rapidly weaving a web of associations to push her toward fluency.

Tele forced her expression to relax, and she watched as Navid climbed back up to the road. When he rejoined them, he handed out the waterskins before pausing to take a drink.

"We're traveling east instead of northeast," Tal Aval said. "We would do better to take a more direct route."

"You're right," Navid agreed. "This isn't the most direct route, but I prefer to make a stop in Azuri for supplies. It's not too far out of the way, and there's an innkeeper there that I trust."

Tele sighed again. "Shouldn't we just keep moving?"

Like the suggestion of refilling their waterskins, Tele searched for a reason to refuse to go back through Azuri. In truth, she'd considered the same thing and would have probably suggested it if she hadn't realized several hours back that Navid was leading them back toward the town. Her objection was irrational. Still, she couldn't resist being the contrarian.

And then *that* infuriated her. She prided herself in being quick to act in the most practical manor she could think to behave, but her relationship with Navid had diluted her ability to reason.

"Look." Tal Aval pointed. "Someone is ahead."

Tele squinted, staring into the distance. Three men paced in lazy circles down the trail. Dressed in forest browns and armed with swords at the hip, they watched the road expectantly, as if waiting for someone to meet with them. One of them pointed with his sword, signaling the other two of their approach.

"Well," Tele said. "They've seen us."

"They don't look like the loveliest bunch," Navid said. "Perhaps we should turn around."

A whistle sounded, and though she could plainly see that it came from one of the men ahead, the sharp tone felt as though it came from no direction at all. A light crunch of boots from behind them made Tele and Tal Aval spin on heel. Five other men followed up the rear with the same attire and weaponry.

Tele turned back to see the first three slowly trotting up to them. "No turning around now. Perhaps they're reasonable."

"I do not think so," Tal Aval said and called forth his växarot. It shaped into a sword.

"One can dream, no?" Tele said. She summoned her

växarot and with a thought, it divided, forming into two daggers. She then looked at Navid, curious to see how he would handle himself.

He reached out and reluctantly pulled his växarot staff from the dirt path.

"Well!" One of the men called from a good distance away as they slowed to a casual walk. "The three of you look mighty lost out here in the woods. No horses or carriages and those heavy packs." He shared a facetious smile with the other men. "We offer a free service for people like you. Let us take those heavy packs off your backs so you can get to where you're going with ease."

"We aren't lost," Navid said. "We're travelers on our way to North Hzorah with urgent business. If you'd let us be on our way, we'd—"

"Urgent business?" The man said. "Well, I wouldn't want to hold you up any longer than *absolutely* necessary. Why don't you hand us those packs of yours, and you can be on your way to your business."

Navid looked at Tele, and she shook her head. They were *not* going to just hand over their belongings. The few clothes she had was of little consequence if she lost them. The food and water would be a much more dire hit. But she had books she'd sworn to protect, and she wouldn't allow a petty thief to take them from her. Not without a fight.

"No," Tele said.

The men laughed. Tele expected it, counted on it even. They weren't particularly clever men. Were they so, they'd have more than just swords. And with a quick glance about, she couldn't see any more to the threat than the men who surrounded them. Eight men wasn't a trifle, but employing just two of them as bowmen would have given them a distinct strategic advantage.

"You're a spicy lass, aren't you?" He looked her up and down as if her unflattering travel garb were transparent. "What's a pretty thing like you doing with these two? Surely, you can do better."

"I will fight," Tal Aval whispered. "We have a chance to win."

Tele watched the men slowly close in. She could tell that they were exhausted by the way that they paced themselves. They must have been out here for days, pulling in whatever they could until they retreated with their spoils to the hole they came from.

"They're not at their best," Tele whispered. "I'd say we have a good chance."

"A chance, yes," Navid hissed. "But is it a chance we should take? None of what we carry is worth more than our lives." He looked at Tele. "Right?"

Tele shook her head. "They don't have a right to what we have. Amie told me about these men. They've hurt enough people. It's time someone took a stand." She looked at Navid, challenging him with a glare. "Are you ready to take action?"

The eight thieves stopped a few spans short of them. Half of them smiled with greedy eyes while the other half wore a mask of stone-faced intimidation. The one who'd been talking stepped forward, smiled with a few rotten teeth, and groomed his neck-length hair back behind his ears.

"Go on now," he said. "Just drop your things and you can be on your way."

Tele's blood heated. "No."

Unanimously, all eight of them pulled their swords.

"Now, I've been civil and patient with you three," the man said. He rested the flat of his sword on his right shoulder. "And we're thieves, not murderers. But I can assure you, Lady Spice, that we will do whatever is necessary to get what's owed to us."

He looked straight into her eyes where Tele saw the twisted sincerity of his words. When his gazed passed to Tal Aval and Navid, Tele took the time to assess each of them. One had a bandaged knee and leaned heavily on one leg, another was left-handed, and yet another was tall and strong.

"I'm going to ask you nice like one more time," the thief said. "And if you don't drop your things, we're going to have to take them *and* your lives."

Tele let her muscles relax and prayed that Navid could handle himself without her instruction.

Just play defensively, Navid, she thought. *Let us do the rest.*

"Drop your things," he said. "The weapons, too. And move along."

Tele pulled in a slow breath as she shook her head. "No."

"Well," the highwayman said. "I'll see you at Desolate's gate."

The men advanced, and Tele backed a step before raising her växarot daggers. The closest thief stepped forward and swung his sword. Tele countered and redirected his attack, leading him off balance. Catching his dominate arm, she made a quick and precise cut to the flexor tendons on his inner arm before she kicked his side—more to push him out of her way than to inflict any further damage.

Another highwayman replaced him—the one with the bandaged knee. He attacked, but this time Tele dropped and struck him at the knee with the butt of her weapon. He cried out as he began to topple, and Tele's dagger caught him in the shoulder, just barely clear of a primary vessel. The weight of him shifted her balance, but as he fell, Tele rolled and rebounded to a crouched position.

As she recovered, she saw Navid block one of the highwaymen's advances, then the second, then the third before he gave ground—all in perfect step with her instruction. Still, Tele pushed herself between Navid and the threat before he had the chance to falter any farther. She countered two attacks before her växarot caught his vulnerability.

Her side of the trail clear, Tele and Navid turned to where Tal Aval had been left to fend for himself. Three bodies writhed at his feet. The last of them—the tall one—backed away slowly as Tal Aval advanced on him.

"Stay back!" the man yelled. "Scorch it.... ... Stay *back*, I said!"

The thief's sword shook in his hand, and another retreating step caught on a rock and tipped him backward. His head smacked the dirt road, but he was up on his elbows again as if it'd barely phased him.

Fear had taken over.

Tal Aval stepped close, his växarot formlessly twisting in his grip. But as Tal Aval towered over the man, the weapon snapped to the form of a sword and pressed against the stubbled flesh beneath his chin. The man shook. His breaths were sharp and labored, but he managed to utter a small, desperate whine. "Please …"

"Let him go," Navid said.

Tal Aval glanced back at Navid but left his sword at the man's throat. "Why? He is a thief. He tried to kill us."

"Everyone deserves a second chance."

"No," Tal Aval said. "Not *all* men."

Navid turned to Tele. His eyes pleaded for her to take his side. Tele was inclined to agree with Tal Aval, especially after all she had witnessed at the hands of evil men. They were all hurting and longed for justice, but the desperation in Navid's gaze turned her heart to pity.

She had strategically spared the others a quick death, and it was not her place to deliver a death sentence to these men. Even if she believed they deserved it.

"Let him go," Tele said. "He's not much without his friends anyway." She caught the thief's gaze. "There are healing herbs in this forest. I'm sure you're familiar with them. Bind the wounds of your friends before it's too late."

For a moment, Tal Aval didn't move. Then, as swiftly as he'd pinned the man, he backed away. "Go," Tal Aval said. "Do good for the rest of your days."

The man twisted to his feet, paused, and stared at them in confusion. He looked at each of them in turn, as if expecting them to cut him down once he turned his back on them. After one tentative step backward, he turned and ran into the brush.

"Desolate-bound fool," Tele muttered before replanting her växarot.

Navid called after the man, but when he didn't return, he

looked at Tele. "Should we bind their wounds? I don't know if he'll return."

"*If we try to help them, they will put a knife in our back,*" Tal Aval said.

"*I agree,*" Tele said before reaching into her pack and pulling out their only jar of healing salve and a bundle of bandages. "We can't help them ourselves. But I don't think the man will completely abandon them. He'll wait until we leave. I'll leave these in case he doesn't have the supplies. Apparently, they have succeeded in stealing at least some of our supplies."

When she placed the supplies on the ground, Navid gave her an appreciative smile. Tele looked at Tal Aval. "We should continue."

Tal Aval dismissed his växarot and looked at Navid. "You fought well. Did he not, Tele?"

Tele clinched her jaw a moment before responding. "Your stance could use an adjustment. We will work on that at our next opportunity."

Tal Aval frowned at her response, but Tele turned away from them both. Navid was not a child. She was not going to coddle him. The Hzorah army depended on them, and if Navid couldn't get on without a compliment for managing to stay upright for more than a moment, he would serve them best if he returned to Caldor.

Navid again took the lead down the West Hzorah road. As had become customary to their travel from the Tal tribelands, Tele allowed Navid to walk a fair distance ahead while she walked with Tal Aval and spoke with him in his language.

"*Tele,*" Tal Aval said quietly in the Tal tongue. He drew close to her side. "*I would like to talk to you.*"

"*Yes?*"

"*When you came to our village, you and Navid were allies. And though I did not know you together, Navid was worried about your safety. I knew that there was something special shared between you.*"

Tele kept her gaze focused on the road ahead. "*And?*"

"*Since we have left,*" Tal Aval continued slowly, "*you have shown him little kindness.*"

She shut her eyes and crossed her arms. "*I just can't believe him sometimes. He's a seer. People like him are supposed to be competent. I can barely get him to hold a staff upright.*"

"*It takes time to learn.*"

"*Yes,*" Tele said, trying to restrain the true extent of her anger. "*But you've seen him fight. He's holding back intentionally, as if he might accidentally kill me, yet his form is as poor as I've seen it. It's almost offensive that he won't try harder.*"

Tal Aval shook his head as he watched her eyes. "*I do not believe you are angry because he does not fight well.*"

The feeling in the pit of her stomach stirred.

"*You are afraid,*" Tal Aval said. "*You are afraid that you can't protect him. That you are going to lose him.*"

Tele glared at him, her anger overtaking her. "*Of course, I'm afraid! I should have known better than to let myself care about someone. I should have kept him at arm's length. Wisdoms, I thought—*"

She shook her head and covered her face with her hands. Tal Aval walked quietly, allowing her to recompose.

"*When I'd had seen six years,*" Tele said. "*I trapped a desert scarpe in a small jar. My father, mother, and brothers warned me not to become attached to the scarpe, that it would die soon if I insisted on keeping it in the jar.*" She paused to breathe and laugh nervously. "*Of course, I didn't listen. I loved the hairy little arachnid. I thought it was cute. I named it Fredrick and fed it daily even though I couldn't figure out what it ate, but eventually, the scarpe slowed; its stinger stilled. It was dead within the week.*

"'*That's why I didn't want you to name it,' my brother, Gib, said. 'Because it makes it harder to see it die.'*"

Tal Aval touched her shoulder. "*Tele, Navid is not a scarpe. He will learn in time; he wants to.*"

"*Tal Aval ...*" She met his eyes. "*I lost everyone I loved. And as long as Prophet Tristan lives, everyone close to me will be in danger. I'm not capable of protecting everyone. I can barely protect myself. I can't care for someone who can't help themselves. There's too much at risk.*"

Instead of arguing, Tal Aval only squeezed her shoulder comfortingly. Tele appreciated that more than anything. She didn't need this to be any harder than it already was.

When they arrived in Azuri, they'd gather supplies. But then she'd have to tell him that they should part ways. She could handle the rest of it with Tal Aval. Navid could go back to Caldor, or find his father, or whatever it was he really wanted. But whatever it was he wanted he'd have to do it alone.

The procession halted once again as the guard at the border of Azuri's town proper stopped the pair of traders just ahead. Though the Hzorah Crown Guard had created a bottleneck for incoming travelers, they moved the line with quick efficiency. After a short assessment, the soldier waved the traders on and turned to Tele and her companions. She adjusted the cloak she'd tied about her shoulders as they drew near to the checkpoint.

"Halt," the soldier said. He approached them and eyed Tal Aval suspiciously. "Where are you traveling from?"

"The Borderlands." Navid shielded his eyes from the evening sun. "From Caldor."

Tele let out a breath of relief. At least Navid knew to bend the truth. She'd half expected him to say they were headed toward the North Hzorah Plains, right into the battlefield.

"Is that so?" the soldier said. "Caldor has fallen. Hasn't been any trade from there in weeks."

"I know," Navid said. "I wasn't in the city when the attacks happened, but I'm on my way back from there to the Hzorah Crown."

"And this one?" The soldier pointed to Tal Aval. "He doesn't look like anyone I've ever seen. I've been given the authority to turn away anyone that look suspicious."

"I have a Caldor pass," Navid said, fishing it out of his pack.

Of course, he doesn't have it ready. Tele sighed and rubbed her forehead.

"Hold on now. Slow down," the soldier said. "Go slow."

Navid paused, then slowly pulled out the parchment. He offered it to the soldier. The man took it, and his companions glanced over his shoulder to check the authenticity of the document for themselves.

The soldier handed it back to him. "You're on your way to the Hzorah Crown? What business do you have here in Azuri? This isn't the most direct path."

Navid nodded. "It's not. But we have friends here."

"Who's that?" the soldier asked.

"The Kruv family," Navid said.

The soldiers looked at each other. One of them let out a soft whistle while another shook his head.

"You knew Master Kruv?" the soldier asked.

Knew? Tele thought, only just managing to restrain herself from voicing it aloud.

"Yes. I know him and his daughters." Navid frowned. "Why?"

"Wisdoms …" The soldier shook his head. "They haven't been seen in weeks. Whisked away without a sign or trace of where."

"They're gone?" Navid touched his chest, taking a small bit of cloth between his fingers. "I don't understand."

"Neither does anyone else," he said. "It looked like there was some sort of struggle—a break-in. They didn't take anything. Folks here are starting to think they're dead. If you planned to stay at their inn, you'll have to go to *The Commons* or *The Dill.*"

After the Crown Guard waved them on, they did their best to blend in with the town. But between Tal Aval's strange hair and his awe at a community so different from his own, they couldn't help but stand out. Tele cautioned him to keep his voice low as he questioned them about what he saw.

She remembered the first time she'd seen the great city of Janamah in Desera, the first time she'd seen the Borderland Forests, and the first time she'd seen Caldor, and even when she'd first seen Tal Aval's own home. It was hard to contain her curiosity, and all things considered, Tal Aval did a fair job of keeping his astonishment inconspicuous.

Navid led them down a familiar street that would lead to the Kruv House, and when they came to the dead-end street near the courtyard, Tele's heart sank. The Kruv House was abandoned, and the door was barred.

Tele circled the building and found a small wooden crate. She dragged it to the building's wall and stepped onto it. Cautiously, she placed a hand on the lip of the window—careful to avoid the shards of glass—and looked through the slits of wood that boarded the opening.

Countless specks of dust spun and tumbled, trapped in sunbeams that slipped between cracks in the common room door and windows. A faint but sweet smell of ale lingered as if it'd been spilled then dried, leaving the sticky residue behind. Tele could see the table where she and Navid had sat when they'd first come to the inn. Undisturbed, it waited patiently amid the broken glass and muddy scuff-marks that littered the once clean floor.

"And these shops," Tal Aval questioned from behind. "They are open all the time?"

"No," Navid said. "Only during the day when most people shop."

"How do they know when someone will need?"

"Well," Navid said. "People plan ahead. They know when they'll run out of bread or meat or vegetables, or when they'll need something new. They plan ahead for emergencies, and, for all else, they have to wait until the time comes."

"And they are not allowed to hunt or grow themselves?"

"They are. But not everyone has time to hunt or grow for themselves."

Tal Aval chuckled. "No time to eat? The people here think I am a savage, but they do not make time to eat."

Tele stepped down from her makeshift platform. "I can't tell much from out here. And it probably wouldn't be a good idea to try to break in."

Navid ran a hand through his hair. "No, I suppose not. I just thought that maybe we'd be able to determine something."

"Well," she said. "We can't."

"Is there anything we can do?"

"No, nothing," Tele said. "And I have a mission to get back to. I need supplies."

Navid just stared at her blankly for a moment, as if he couldn't pull a thought together, before he looked away. "We'll rest at *The Dill*. There's not much for food there, but at least their rooms are decent."

"I could care less about the room," Tele said. "I just want to make it to the North Hzorah Plains as soon as possible."

Navid caught her eye with a tired, sad expression. "Right."

Tele turned away and shouldered her pack. "Good. Can you handle the supplies? I did it last time."

"I can," Navid said, then pointed up the road. "*The Dill* is about a half hour walk that way. You won't miss it. It has a sign."

"Be quick," Tele said.

Tele watched *The Dill*'s patrons from the corners of her vision. Most of the men looked to be traders or hardened travelers—a more working-class crowd than the Kruv House served. But a few wealthier travelers isolated themselves at a table near the entry, warily watching the room and likely wishing the they'd found a more upscale establishment.

She had given Tal Aval her cloak which he wore with the hood raised to hide his long, spiked, white hair. It'd worked, and no one seemed to notice that he wasn't a local as long as he was quiet so that his accent wouldn't draw the attention of the curious. Still, Tele judged that it would be better for them to retreat to a room rather than sit in the open.

Though they'd come without Navid, the innkeeper accepted Tele's daggers as collateral until Navid returned to give him the pass. The set was far more valuable than a night's stay at the inn, and he apologized that the finer rooms had already been taken.

Tal Aval dropped their packs in the small room, and Tele lit a candle. The Kruv House had been Tele's first experience with West Hzorah hospitality, and while the staff here were adequate, she found that she missed the shining walls and jovial smiles.

And there was an undeniable sense that something terrible had happened to Master Kruv, Amie, and Mara. Master Kruv was not the kind of man who would just leave his establishment. He'd cared deeply for his work and seemed to enjoy it. Moreover, he wouldn't have left it in such disrepair. He took too much pride in his work for that.

Something was wrong. *Wisdoms. Please let them be safe.*

Tal Aval took to his usual evening activity of carving. Tele had originally planned to spend the evening reading more from *Element and Reaction* but found that the day had left her too scattered to focus. She'd spent every spare moment of late learning the Tal language or reading through her uncle's notes and diagrams—memorizing formulas and struggling to wrap her mind around the concepts it detailed. A night away from all of that would allow her to digest it.

She placed her pack against the wall to use as a pillow while she lay on the floor and tried to clear her mind. But thoughts of her family, the Kruvs, and the injured in Caldor and the Tal tribeland snaked their way into her meditation.

Searching for solace, she opened her pack and set about the rote task of checking off each item that belonged there. Everything was in its place, save her daggers.

She pulled out *Small Life*. One of the books that her mother and father had left to her. A book that she'd vowed to protect, improve, and return to the true Wizard. And, now, she sat at the threshold of accomplishing her life's mission—the dying wish of her father.

Tele opened the book to see her father's handwriting once more. She removed the map of the Dominion Desert and set it aside, but instead of seeing the words she'd seen a thousand times over, she saw the parchment that she'd placed there before she'd left Azuri. The beginning of a chronicle without her family.

After my father, mother, and older brothers—
Huvil, Abigail, Gib, and Simon,
respectively—died

The sentence left incomplete beckoned for conclusion. Since Tele started the thought, she'd met her uncle, journeyed to Caldor where she'd entered the Keeper's vaults, and found the Tal who guarded the power of Wizard Titan.

But before all of that, at the very beginning of that journey, there was a catalyst—a single event that had opened a world of possibility. Dressed in white, a golden-eyed mad-man, his hand outstretched, offering deliverance.

Navid had been there through it all, patient and kind. He'd trusted her when she'd insisted Gavini journey with them. He'd saved Gavini when the ice broke and swallowed him in its icy currents. He'd helped her heal the sick in Caldor and process the new ideas she'd learned since she found the catacombs beneath the Sanctuary. Even now, he risked his safety to journey to the Hzorah army and warn them of the dragons.

After her father, mother, and older brothers—Huvil, Abigail, Gib, and Simon, respectively—died, she'd met Navid, who, in turn, helped her find the life she'd always wanted.

And now, Tele was going to turn him away.

She looked at Tal Aval as he carefully carved what was now clearly a bird. He had been right. It was true that Navid had made a severe mistake when he froze on the cliff, but perhaps it was unreasonable that she'd allowed that *one* moment to disregard everything he'd done.

Tal Aval caught her watching him. He smiled, but only for a moment, for there was a loud shout outside of their rooms.

The low hum of talk from *The Dill*'s common room stilled. And just as she and Tal Aval shot to their feet, their room door burst open and a large, blond Hzorah soldier stepped in. Just behind him were eight other men, armed to the teeth. They scanned the room before their eyes settled on the two of them.

The soldier in front crossed his arms. "We have a directive from the Crown to inspect our cities. There is war, and we must make sure that all people within our borders are citizens."

Tele wanted to melt through the cracks in the floor or become invisible.

"We were told that there was a fellow who looked suspicious had come into town about two hours ago," the soldier said. "Had strange white hair and clothing … We asked around and a woman said she saw someone like that come to this inn."

Tele spoke up. "I think there has been a misunderstanding. We—"

The soldier stepped forward, ignoring her. "You. Take off that cloak." When Tal Aval hesitated, he added: "Now!"

Slowly, Tal Aval removed the cloak's cowl and revealed his white hair.

Tele quickly scanned the room for a way to escape, but their room was windowless, and there wasn't even a finger's width of space for them to slip though the door.

The soldiers stepped forward.

They could fight, but there were eight soldiers and only two of them. And these soldiers were nothing like the thieves they'd encountered earlier. They were coordinated, armed well, and larger than most men she'd ever seen. Additionally, they were in close quarters. The room was too confining for the odds they were against.

Still, she'd have to try.

She summoned the växarot, but it didn't come. Tele looked to the floor and realized that there was no dirt beneath her. The weapon must not be able to rise through the building's foundation.

Three soldiers took hold of Tal Aval, and the soldier in the lead looked at Tele. "Let's see your mark."

TWENTY-NINE

A WALKING PARADOX

Navid passed another cart of leeks and rhubarbs—the fourth since he'd arrived at the Azuri market—before he gave up on variety. The wide, cobblestone street was lined with vendors, all pitched in battle for the attention of the village folk who flowed down the street's downhill incline.

As long as there was a halt in trade with Caldor, there would be slim pickings for Hzorah. The Hzorah-Armoth Trade Agreement would assure that the selection would be even more sparse. Caldor had fallen, but the deal between Hzorah and Armoth traced back further than Caldor's rise to prominence—back to when the southern tribe of Juvok began trading with their mighty southern neighbors. And, with a looming war, that agreement would likely hold fast as the Crown and the Dominion held tight to their allies.

Navid kept the cowl of his cloak pulled low over his face so that the people here wouldn't see his eyes, but it was inevitable as he gathered supplies that a vendor might catch a glimpse of what he was. All he could do is limit the number of times he'd cause a stir.

The curse needled him, but he pushed it away.

Navid couldn't remember the last time he'd felt so hurt by

someone. When he'd first met Tele, he'd thought her disagreeable and cold, but he'd learned that she could be quite kind. She'd been distant with him for days, and now she'd crossed back into callousness.

He'd made a grave mistake by not following through on their plan in the Borderland forests, he'd even attempted to explain himself several days ago, but Tele wasn't interested. She'd silenced him with a glare and told him that an apology wasn't necessary.

He'd only faltered because it was too dangerous for him to be overtaken by his curse again. How could she not see that?

The traffic thickened as he neared the street's end. There was someone causing a commotion. Several men shouted, trying to drown out another—a woman. Navid slipped between the crowd, trying to find his way through the throng.

"There is only *one* way to avoid damnation!" a woman shouted. "There's only *one* way to save the lives of you and your children. You must let go of the heathen beliefs of the Hzorah tribe and align yourselves with the wisdom of the Creed. For the true Wizard comes, and all who do not serve him will be destroyed."

There was laughter in the crowd—others who shouted for her to be silenced. There was even a man who threw a handfull of leeks, causing the woman to flinch, but she did not stand down. She gripped the leather collar at her neck and gently rubbed its engraved surface with a thumb before she continued.

Almost without thinking, Navid did the same, finding the pendent beneath his shirt. The itch still burned within him, but the comforting hope of the necklace helped him endure its calling.

"You've heard what became of Caldor," she said, pointing to the north. "You've heard of the Dominion gathering at the Shadow Peaks. The Crown has lost its king and the prince has abandoned his post. The signs of what is upon us have never been clearer. We must turn from our wickedness—"

A rock, thrown from the crowd, struck the woman on her

shoulder. Navid turned about, searching for where it originated, but couldn't quite place where it'd come from. She was going to get herself killed.

He squeezed in closer to the woman. Another rock struck her, followed by others that missed their mark, then another few that didn't. She fell and covered her head and neck with her arms.

Navid pushed further into the crowd until he slipped into the small space between her and the enraging congregation. Several rocks pelted his back as he stood over the woman.

"Stop!" Navid shouted back at the group.

He turned around and waved his arms, but it didn't seem to pacify them. The woman had spoken out against the crown and the values of the Hzorah people. She was openly supporting the very army that threatened to take everything from them.

His curse coursed through him, pleading to be set free.

Navid turned back and lifted the woman by her shoulders. "We have to move!"

The woman stared into Navid's eyes before a rock slapped the back of his head. His vision blurred then faded to black as he slumped to the ground.

"I bet he's a drunk."

"Or a lush."

"That's the same thing!"

"No it ain't!"

"Yes, it is! Mama told me so."

Navid's head ached. His eyes were heavy—his thoughts clouded.

"Here," the voice said. "You do it."

"Why me?" the other voice replied.

"Because you're the oldest."

He was on the ground. He could hear people and carts move about. The sour smell of—

A sharp pain stabbed into his side, bringing sharp awareness. His eyes shot open, and he sat up.

"Ahh!" A small boy with a stick in his hand jumped back and screamed, wielding the stick like a ward to protect the small girl behind him.

"His eyes!"

"Run!"

The two sprinted out of the alley, then took a sharp left onto the main street.

Groaning, Navid felt the back of his head where he'd been struck. His hand came away with blood, but it wasn't as bad as he'd feared. The woman, though … He didn't know what became of her. She wasn't in the alley, and Navid feared she may have met an unfortunate end.

Navid climbed to his feet and shuffled out of the alley. His pack still lay on the ground, open with supplies loosed across the cobblestone street. Several of the rounder vegetables had rolled down the road. On shaky legs, he chased down the ones he could see, then climbed back up the hill and secured his belongings.

He should have run a quick inventory. Odds were that something had been stolen. It was a wonder that anything was left at all. But he needed to get back to *The Dill* and set out as soon as possible. Azuri wasn't the safe haven he'd once thought it was.

Navid shouldered his pack and headed back up the street. When he reached the inn, he first searched the common room for Tele and Tal Aval, but when he couldn't find them, he asked the innkeeper if he'd seen them.

"Was she with a fellow dressed up strange?" the innkeeper asked, then held up a hand. "Around this tall. Strange hair?"

"Yes," Navid said. "Did you give them rooms?"

"Yes," he said. "They didn't have money because they were waiting for a friend. Which, I'm guessing, is you. They let me have their weapons to hold until you arrived." He squinted at Navid. "Is that blood on your shirt?"

Navid ignored the question. "Where are they? Did they leave?"

"They left alright," the innkeeper said. A young server who listened from behind paused his sweeping, as if something unprecedented was about to occur. "They came in, said they were waiting to meet with a friend who had a Caldor pass for rooms and food. Then, not long after they arrived, the Crown Guard passed through with a directive to check for the Hzorah Mark. With the war going on and the king dead, they've been searching for insurgents. Your *friends* didn't have a mark. And the one with the strange hair didn't help much. He was for sure not from around here with that accent of his." The innkeeper frowned at him. "What business does a seer have here anyway?"

"Where did they go?" Navid asked, urgently. "I need to find them."

"They were arrested for interrogation," the innkeeper said, his voice taking the tone of accusation. "Perhaps if they hadn't made a wild claim of having a Caldor pass—especially with the rumors of Caldor in ruins—they may have been let go … Or maybe they wouldn't have. But that's a poor story if you can't back it up."

Navid pulled the pass from his pack. "We *did* have a pass!"

The man's eyes widened. "Wisdoms … where *were* you then?"

Navid turned and looked around the small inn's common. One couple sat in a corner, covertly glancing in his direction, and another at the opposite side—both speechless as if a wind had drawn the life from the room and replaced it with nervous consternation.

"Listen," Navid said. "I don't have a lot of time. Can you help me? I need to find them."

"Calm down, now," the innkeeper raised his hands. "No need to get all flustered. If they're innocent, they'll be fine."

"I need to find them," Navid insisted. He ran a hand through his hair, gathering more blood on his hands, and a rush of dizziness hit him anew.

"I think they're headed north," the boy sweeping the floor nearby said. "At least that's what I heard."

Navid glanced to the boy. "North?"

"To Stronghold Aear," he said, then pointed vaguely north. "Near the Shadow Peaks where the troops are."

"I don't pay you to stand around!" *The Dill*'s innkeeper turned to the boy, and he hopped back to clearing the floor of wayward debris. The innkeeper looked at Navid again. "I'm sorry … uh—"

"Navid."

"Navid, I'm not sure if the boy is telling the truth or not. He can hardly make it to work on time. And can hardly come up with an excuse worth his value." The innkeeper pointed across the common room floor. "Those are the rest of their belongings."

Between two tables were Tele's and Tal Aval's packs. Navid walked to the table and stuffed the empty waterskins inside. He shouldered the packs and turned back to the inn's entry. If he was quick about it, he'd catch up with the soldiers who took them into custody. The soldiers would see their mistake after he showed them the Caldor pass, and they'd be back on course.

"Thank you for your trouble," Navid said to *The Dill*'s innkeeper as he crossed to the door.

"No trouble at all," the man said, then muttered under his breath: "At least none that *you* caused."

When Navid left *The Dill*, he turned and immediately jogged toward the city's edge. The chances were slim that he'd be able to catch up with Tele and Tal Aval. But he worried that even if he did, there was little-to-no chance that he'd be able to free them.

But one thing was clear: if someone didn't warn the troops about the magic that the Dominion wielded, the Hzorah Army was going to fall. He had to push on.

Amie sat at the path's edge, waiting for instruction while the Dominion soldiers made camp for the night. She wasn't sure how far they'd traveled, but today had definitely been the longest day she'd had since she'd been allowed out of the cart.

She inspected her feet. Her legs were dead tired, but her feet were the source of most of her discomfort. Blisters had formed, and she was almost limping by the time they'd stopped. Slick with blood, about a dozen cuts and blisters covered each foot. If she ever got out of this alive, she was going to buy the best pair of boots she could find and never take them off again.

She'd hoped that Lieutenant Owen would want to learn a bit more tonight, but after camp was set, he didn't come. Maybe he was as tired as she.

Instead, two of the soldiers—Scar Face and Ale Breath—approached with the ropes they'd used to tie her up at night. Ale Breath spun the rope playfully, as if it was a delight to bind her. Scar Face grimaced as if annoyed by Amie for needing to be restrained and by Ale Breath for not being peeved about it.

Armed to the teeth as though they were expecting Amie to jump up and wrestle them to the ground, Scar Face glanced around, searching for a tree stump or something in the clearing that he could tie her to. Unfortunately for the soldiers, they were no longer in a wooded area, and the land was scant of any features for as far as she could see.

We must be in the North Hzorah Plains, Amie thought, remembering Gavini's maps. She'd never been to the plains before, and she wasn't sure what to expect. Maybe that's why they were called "plains"—she could hardly imagine anything *more* plain.

"Over there," Scar Face growled and pointed to the cart.

Slowly, Amie stood and half-walked, half-limped to the cart. They were going to put her back in. This was exactly what she'd tried to avoid. From inside the cart, she'd have absolutely no chance of escaping with Mara—not that she was doing much anyway.

She glanced about, hoping to find an excuse not to get

back into the tiny cell. "Um … Why don't you tie me to the cart? That way, when the Lieutenant wants me again, it'll be easy to retrieve me. You'll have to risk Mara fighting back if you open those doors again." She nodded to the barred window. "My sister's pretty scrappy."

Scar Face paused, considering, and Ale Breath shrugged.

"Alright then, lass," Scar Face nodded to the ground near the cart's wheel. "Sit there."

Amie let out a quiet sigh of relief as she hobbled over to the spot. Scar Face knelt down and glared at her, a clear threat should she fail to cooperate. She held out her hands and let him tie them.

"Ouch! Not so tight!"

"Quiet, lass," Scar Face growled.

"You tie them so tight," Amie complained. "How small do you think my wrists are?"

"I could tie them tighter," Scar Face warned.

"We don't need to try so hard," Ale Breath said. "The girl's a twig at best, barely even a woman. She can't give us too much trouble."

"We can't be too careful." Scar Face looped the length of rope through the wheel and tied it. "We shouldn't have taken her out in the first place."

"Just because *you* can't handle a woman, doesn't mean no one can."

Ale Breath grinned down at Scar Face, but Scar Face didn't look at him. He merely let out an exasperated sigh before standing and walking away. Ale Breath winked at Amie before following him.

Twisting in the restraints, Amie tried to position herself in a posture that was moderately comfortable. Experience had taught her that there was no satisfying position. No matter how she arranged herself, it wouldn't take long for it to become painful, forcing her to squirm until she found something else that resembled comfort.

With his pack swung over his shoulder, Lieutenant Owen

approached. He knelt beside her and began to rummage through his belongings.

"You're late to class," Amie said. "We'll need to reschedule as I'm a bit tied up at the moment." She tugged on the rope to make her point.

"I saw you limping today," Owen said. "Let me see your feet."

Amie frowned, but complied. After he inspected the damage, he pulled a glass jar filled with a light brown ointment from his pack.

"This is a salve for wounds." He released the thick cork. "It'll ease the pain and help your wounds heal quickly." He looked at her as if to ask her permission to use it.

Amie shrugged as best she could. "Fine."

The salve stung at first, but after the initial pain, her foot began to numb, leaving only a cool, soothing sensation. After he applied the ointment, Owen pulled out a long spool of bandage and began wrapping her feet.

"This will help too," he said as he worked. "And it'll help a bit tomorrow. It won't be as easy to get cuts. Your feet are so small. I don't know how you manage to step on everything."

"Your feet are so large; I don't know how you manage not to trip over them." Owen looked up at her with a questioning glare, and Amie sighed. "I'm sorry. This isn't exactly what I expected my first journey north to be like."

Owen didn't respond. Instead, he continued to wrap her feet. As Amie watched him work with such delicate care, she couldn't help but wonder why he ended up here with these filthy soldiers. The man didn't seem to want to hurt anyone, he'd even said his people were completely non-violent. Still, here he was, a lieutenant in the Deseran Dominion's army. He was a walking paradox.

There must be something more to him. It just didn't make sense for him to be here. Something—or someone—was keeping him here.

"Alright," Owen said, as he stood. "Try to get some sleep. Maybe we can do more lessons tomorrow."

Amie merely said "Right" before Lieutenant Owen left her alone. Her feet were already feeling better. A pair of shoes is what she needed, but short of that, he'd wrapped her feet enough that tomorrow was sure to be much better a journey. The blisters, however … Those were still going to torture her.

"Amie!"

Amie looked up to see Mara's nose poke out of the bars above. "Oh, hello, Sister. How was your nap?" She immediately regretted what she said. She was the one who'd gotten herself into this mess.

Mara ignored her question. "Have you figured anything out?"

"That shoes are man's greatest accomplishment."

"Amie," Mara hissed in a low whisper. "This is serious."

"I *know* that." Amie shot back. While she'd thought about what to do quite a bit—almost every waking moment—she hadn't come up with anything particularly compelling. "I'm working on it."

"Work harder."

"We could fight our way out," Amie said without thinking. "Tele fought off about a dozen men when we saved Azuri."

"And she taught you how to fight?"

She paused, again realizing she was suggesting something that she'd vowed not to do. Mara didn't know that, but she still felt guilty for reverting back to her base instinct—an instinct she knew that she wouldn't be able to stomach it if really came to it. "No, but—"

"Oh! So, the dolt who's playing tutor with you has promised to show you how to take them down?"

"No," Amie said through gritted teeth. "I'm just saying … that's the only thing I can think to do right now."

"Discard that idea," Mara said. "It's obviously ridiculous. We need a real plan."

"Please, Mara," Amie said. "I would *love* to hear your idea."

"Just keep your eyes open. We have to be alert and watch for the right moment."

"I'm always being watched," Amie said. "And when I'm not being watched, I'm tied up. What am I supposed to do with that? This is impossible."

"I don't know," Mara admitted. "Just stay vigilant. If we are to have any chance, we can't just give up. They think they're in control. Eventually, they'll slip, assuming they have the upper hand. *That's* when we strike. We might have to fight a little, and it might get bloody, but it can't be on their terms."

Strike? Amie had no idea what they'd even do with the right moment. She said it as if Amie would clearly know what to do when that moment came. At best, she might be able to escape into the woods. But she wasn't as fast as any of the soldiers, especially with her feet covered in cuts and soars. Amie wished she was Tele. She would definitely know what to do.

First of all, Amie thought. *Tele wouldn't have gotten herself caught.*

Tele would have fought back better. And even if she did manage to get caught, she would know what to do when the moment came. She'd kick them in the head … or … or … something impressive.

No, Amie chided herself. *That's not how I do things. I'm not changing that now. I won't break my word.*

Even being Mara would be preferable. She was at least smart. She'd figure something out. Amie was pretty certain Mara couldn't fight, but she'd find something even more clever.

I should have had convinced Mara to trick Owen into letting her out, not me.

But there was no going back now. Amie was the one outside, and she had to be the one to fix this. She didn't know *how*, but she had to try.

THIRTY

A HAZARDOUS REACH

Gabriel stood just behind Lurin, bending over slightly so that their eyes were level. The morning sun to their backs, the target glinted as the racing clouds pulled away and brightened the plains once again.

"Keep your bow level," Gabriel encouraged.

"I can't," Lurin said through a tight jaw.

"You can. Hold your breath. Missing isn't an option. Let everything else fall away."

Lurin did as instructed. Gabriel held his breath too, lending the soldier his own focus. Though Lurin had proven the hardest of the Second League to find common ground with, Gabriel's discovery of his interest in archery turned out to be just the linchpin to connect with the soldier. And it wouldn't hurt to have a good shot among them.

To his surprise, Lurin was a much better shot that he'd expected—at close range. He admitted that he practiced shooting arrows in High Lord Laonne's orchards where he worked to provide for his family. When Gabriel showed an interest in training him, he became nervous and resisted. Gabriel didn't have to ask him why he was so reluctant to work with him one-on-one. It was obvious.

Cainan.

Instead of forcing Lurin into working with him during the day, Gabriel reduced his late night training with Aeron, Fabi, Mel, and Bear to only two days a week. He told them that they were good enough to work on their own, and he expected them to continue in his absence.

In the cover of night, Gabriel began his training. He never brought up Cainan through their sessions. Whatever agreement Lurin and Cainan struck had clearly frightened him. Rather than threaten the deal his bastard cousin had made with the soldier, Gabriel decided to take the path of least resistance, hoping it would earn him an additional measure of respect.

Lurin lowered the bow and exhaled. "I can't do it."

Gabriel breathed again and the world rushed back in—the sound of Bear and Mel dueling in the circle, Urwell and Paitin chattering on in Armothean, Cainan's razor glare as Gabriel worked with Lurin for the first time during the day.

"You can do it," Gabriel insisted. "Stop saying that you can't."

"The light keeps changing. The clouds are distracting."

"You've shot at night," Gabriel said, straightening to his full height. "You're just nervous because you know that Cainan is watching us."

Lurin didn't respond.

"I don't know what he has over your head, but that doesn't matter out here. Remember your honor. Remember why we're out here."

Lurin sighed and nodded before raising his bow once more. Gabriel watched as the breeze responded as if intent on adding complication to an already difficult shot. Lurin didn't waver. His aim shifted to compensate, and then he let the arrow take flight.

The arrow struck the wooden block on the platform.

"*Yes! Pay up, Urwell.*"

Gabriel clapped Lurin on the back. "Well done."

Lurin let out a sigh of relief before a toothy grin washed away his stress. And despite a gruff snort from Cainan as he turned away, he raised his arms triumphantly as Paitin, Bear, and Mel chanted his name.

"Sergeant Gabriel," Captain Alden called through the cheer.

Gabriel turned, meeting the Captain's urgent expression. He stood at the edge of their training ground in full armor, clearly uninterested in joining the festivities. He jogged to his captain's side and the celebration died down to an orderly silence.

"Sir?" Gabriel asked.

"Follow me," Captain Alden said. "The rest of you: as you were."

Gabriel looked at his squad as the captain turned and headed back into camp. "Drill the wedge again while I'm gone. Cainan, you're in charge."

He rarely had to leave when training with the Second League, but when he did, he gave his cousin command. Not because their relationship had strengthened over the past several weeks, but because he thought it important that the Second League get used to taking orders from Cainan as well. There was no guarantee that something wouldn't happen to him out on the battlefield, and though Gabriel wasn't a fan of his cousin's arrogance, he would be the best suited to lead them if it came to it.

Gabriel had to trot to catch up with the man's brisk pace. "Sir, is there something wrong?"

Captain Alden held up a hand, and Gabriel fell silent. They dodged past several supply lines as he cut into the center of the encampment. They were headed for the General's command tents.

Gabriel's gut twisted. He'd never met any of the Hzorah Generals, but they'd attended formal events in the Hzorah Crown—sat across the room from his family. His hair was significantly longer, and his usually clean-shaven face was now partially masked by a beard. Still, they might recognize him.

Gabriel tried to run every possible scenario through his

head. Would he try to deny his parentage, or would he simply admit to it? Would it even matter?

I've shown my worth here. And I'm nearly king. Would they really force me to go home?

There were always consequences to his actions in the palace. Fairly, he got away with much more than the palace's workers ever could, but his father had tasked Samuel and Marium to do whatever they "saw fit" in the discipline of him and his brother.

But Father was gone now. They couldn't force him to leave; he'd enlisted willingly. He was his own man. It was within his rights to fight for the Crown.

He was his *own* man.

Until he took the crown. Then, he was a slave.

A pocket of dirt surrounded the command tents. As if there was an invisible barrier, no one crossed closer than twenty spans. Gabriel wasn't sure if it was an issue of respect or if enough men had seen the results of another wandering too close to risk their own lives over such a careless misstep.

Captain Alden waved off the guards posted outside of the general's tents. They compiled without giving them a second look.

The tents beyond stood taller than any other structure on the plains, save Stronghold Aear. A large, white banner swayed in the slow breeze, displaying the Hzorah Mark. Under it, a modest-colored brown canvas tent with a half-open entry flap awaited them. Instead of lifting the flap, Captain Alden ducked under it. Gabriel followed his example.

Inside, the tent was no more extravagant than its exterior. Though pitched sturdy, nothing lined the walls, and there were little furnishings save a few simple chairs without cushioning and a large, round table in the center of the room. Several light vents checkered the higher reaches of the tent walls, and a single doorway—similar to the one they'd just entered—was at the tent's opposite side, flap closed.

Another man stood over the center table, reading a map.

Noticing their entry, he straightened into grim acknowledgment. Then, he smiled when he met Gabriel's eyes.

It was Lieutenant Gaphe, the man who carted him to the Second League's corner of the army encampment. Like Captain Alden, the man wore dark leather armor as if he were about to march into the battle within the hour.

"Is this him?" Lieutenant Gaphe asked. "Somehow, I should have known. He's got the eyes of a warrior."

"You've met?" Captain Alden said, looking to Gabriel.

"We have, sir," Gabriel said. "He assigned me to regiment when I first arrived."

"And," Lieutenant Gaphe said, "he tried to get me to quit and go home."

"Did he?" Captain Alden said. "Did you think him too old to be here, soldier?"

Gabriel swallowed. "No, sir. I—"

"He *is* too old."

"Sir?" Gabriel asked, frowning.

"As priceless as his expression is," Lieutenant Gaphe said, "we do have pressing matters to deal with."

Gabriel let out a discrete breath. Perhaps Mel was right. He took things too seriously. He'd been so worked up worrying that his identity would be questioned that he'd missed the obvious joke.

It was only the three of them. His identity was safe.

"The General should be along shortly," Lieutenant Gaphe said.

Scorch it.

"Our scouts spotted theirs here," Lieutenant Gaphe said pointing at the map, then slid his finger to another place on the mountain range. "And here. Now this one …" He moved back to the original point. "Is likely abandoned already. It's a poor place to camp and the team will have likely discovered that by now. No good for gathering intel."

"But this one," Captain Alden said and pointed at the second point. "It has a clear view over the entire plain if they're high enough. And it'll take them another day or so to descend if they've already reached it."

Lieutenant Gaphe nodded. "Which gives us no more than twenty hours to intercept them coming back down. They're about twelve hours from here on horseback."

"Little good that will do us in this area of the peaks," Captain Alden said.

"We don't need to ascend far," Lieutenant Gaphe said. "It should be more than reasonable with horses—for the first seven or eight hours at least. We're waiting for them to meet *us*."

"True." Captain Alden crossed his arms, then looked at Gabriel. "Soldier, what do you think?"

Gabriel looked at him, trying to absorb the sudden barrage of information. "It all seems reasonable enough. I haven't seen a map like this," he lied, "with the land height noted. So, I'm afraid I'm a bit out of my depth."

"The fact that you picked up on what the map says is more than proof enough for me," Captain Alden said. "I'm sending the Second League to capture them."

"Sir?" Gabriel's breath caught. "The Second League? I thought there were scouts—experienced scouts—for this sort of detail."

"I didn't bring you here to casually discuss geography, soldier," Captain Alden said. "This is a briefing. I want the Second League on this job."

"I can have the horses sent within the hour," Lieutenant Gaphe said.

"Sir," Gabriel said. "I'm not sure that everyone in the Second League can ride. It wasn't part of the physical aptitude testing. We may have to walk."

"Can you ride, soldier?" Captain Alden asked.

"I can."

"What about the one smart with medicine? Can he?"

"I believe so, but—"

"The High Lord's son? He's got to know how."

"I'm sure he does, sir."

"Between you all, at least half of you must have some experience. Those that can't will have to double up. The horses here are strong enough to carry two men and won't have a fit about it."

"Yes, sir," Gabriel relented.

The light of the tent dimmed as someone approached the entryway. The man ducked under the tent flap and approached him from the rear. Gabriel turned away and fixed his gaze on the map, hoping to become suddenly invisible.

Though Gabriel hadn't met him directly, he'd heard of him from his father. He was an East Hzorah man who lived near the Crown City, yet rarely attended any palace functions.

General Rollins.

"Captain Alden," General Rollins said. "Lieutenant Gaphe. Any developments?"

Captain Alden spoke first. "We've narrowed down our efforts to this group of spies here." He pointed on the map, then looked at Gabriel. "I'm having the Second League investigate the matter."

"And is this," General Rollins said as he began to circle the table, "The young soldier you've spoken so highly of?"

"It is, sir." Captain Alden said.

General Rollins squinted at Gabriel as he crossed into his field of view. The man wore a tightly creased, green military uniform with a Hzorah Mark and a General's insignia across the left half of his chest. The green continued down to his black boots but was fractured by a thick, black belt that supported his sword.

Gabriel held his breath when their eyes met.

"My name is General Rollins. What's yours, soldier?"

"Gabriel, sir."

Gabriel wished he could have lied and gave a different name, but both Captain Alden and Lieutenant Gaphe knew his name. He couldn't go back on that now.

"Gabriel …" General Rollins let the name roll about his tongue. "You look familiar. Who's your father?"

"I don't know, sir," Gabriel said. "He's dead."

"Your mother, then."

"Also dead," Gabriel said. "I'm an orphan. I grew up in an orphanage in the Crown City. That's the only family I ever knew, sir."

General Rollins opened his mouth to respond, but then closed it, frowning as he studied Gabriel's face.

Come on. Let it go, he thought and then pointed to the map again to divert the general's attention from his face. "I'm sure that the Second League can accomplish Captain Alden's plan."

General Rollins broke his stare with Gabriel and turned back to the Captain. "It seems a waste of the Second League to task them with this, but I trust your judgement."

"I'll see it done immediately." Captain Alden saluted, then turned to Gabriel, giving him a slight nod to the entry.

Gabriel bowed then turned, eager to save himself time under General Rollins's scrutiny. As he and the captain exited the tent, he looked at his commanding officer. "The general does have a point, sir. I don't understand why you're having us do this."

"I've sent our scouts to capture Dominion scouts twice before," he said. "They returned without a capture. I don't want another failed attempt."

"With all due respect, sir, I don't think sending a crew specializing in war field special operations will do much better."

"I've taken a number of ill-advised risks with you, Gabriel." Captain Alden looked at him with a confident smile. "And so far, you haven't failed me. The Hand of Desolate has blessed you, soldier."

"I've heard that it is not wise to test Desolate's Hand, sir," he said in the most respectful tone he could muster.

The captain crossed his arms. "I'm not testing Desolate's Hand, soldier. I'm testing you." And with that, the Captain Alden withdrew, leaving Gabriel the find his own way back to the Second League's tents.

He took a deep breath as he walked back to his crew, relieved that General Rollins hadn't recognized him as the

Crown's heir, yet nervous at the prospect of leading the Second League on a mission that was outside of their expertise *and* before their training was complete.

That had been Captain Alden's way with him since he'd arrived. It'd been his way with all of them. As soon as he'd demonstrated himself capable of one thing, he immediately set him to task with proving himself with another. It was frightening, but he was getting used to that feeling, comfortable with it even.

And he wouldn't allow fear to let him fail the captain now.

Gabriel stood and handed the map back to Aeron. "We're going to have to scale this one."

Aeron slipped the map into its vial and sealed it. "Do we have enough rope?"

"I think so," Gabriel said. He turned and waved over the other Second League soldiers who waited in the clearing. When they saw his signal and started over, Gabriel turned back to the rock incline, inspecting the best method of ascent.

They'd made good time hiking up the mountain, but they'd underestimated the amount of time it would take to intercept the party of spy scouts. Between their being slowed by thicker brush than they'd hoped and a navigational error that cost them three precious hours, they'd fallen behind.

Gabriel faulted himself for both issues. He'd allowed the Second League to rest longer than needed when he should have had them leave early to tackle the mountain wilds. There was no way to know how bad the mountain thick would be, but he could have anticipated that.

He'd also made the heading error himself. The miscalculation was a seemingly small error on paper, but it had that cost them dearly before he realized the mistake. His father had taught him how to use a map, star chart, and ticker, but despite his training and the additional guidance Captain Alden had given him before they'd departed, he'd fallen off course.

The sandstone before them rose dozens of spans. Gray, brown, and deep red sedimentation packed tight to form a wall that was pitted in some places and smooth in others as if Desolate's Hand had chiseled out a clean bit of rock with a large pickaxe.

Gabriel placed a hand on the rock face. It was cool, still untouched by the morning sun. Looking up, he saw three sections of rock near the top ledge that could be used as anchor points. At least Desolate's Hand had offered them this one favor.

"How's she look?" Mel asked. He and Fabi stopped just to Gabriel's right and squinted up with him.

"It's high and steep," Gabriel said. "But we have enough rope. I'm not sure how long it will take to make the ascent, but it'll certainly be faster than going around."

"I got to tell you," Mel said. "I ain't never been one for heights. All I know is if you don't look down, you'll keep your stomach."

"I'd say that's good advice," Gabriel said, then turned to the others. "We're going to make the climb. It won't be easy, but it won't be as bad as you think. There are three anchor points that we'll need to secure."

Fabi raised a hand. "I'm good with knots. My father taught me a lot of tricks that few people know about. Not that we used it for anything like this."

"Good enough," Gabriel said. "Fabi, Mel, Aeron—I want you to tie the ropes. Cainan, I need you to help me plot a safe climb."

Fabi, Mel, and Aeron left to gather the ropes and Cainan joined Gabriel at the cliff's face. He guided his cousin off to the side, out of earshot of the other soldiers.

"Finally decided to trust me instead of the *children*?" Cainan asked.

"This is a risky move," Gabriel said. "I need a good eye and a skilled climber. I know you're good at this—better than me."

Cainan smirked and pointed up and to the right. "Too risky. There's little to grip here."

Gabriel nodded.

"We'll want to send everyone closer to the left here," Cainan said, pointing out the path upward.

"Agreed," Gabriel said. "The right side is too smooth, and it looks as if the rock has broken off recently. But there are too many of us to go one at a time, and far too many of us to all fit into that narrow of a path."

"We'll go three at a time," Cainan said. "We don't have time for less than that. Should be four to be safe, but that just won't happen. The fourth would be practically carried up."

"I think you're right. One more thing. I need you to make the climb and secure the anchors. You're the only one of us who has any real experience with climbing. I'd do it myself, but I don't trust I'd do it better."

"I can see why Captain Alden chose *you* over me," Cainan said. "Your bravery surpasses that of any man I've ever known—fit for a king at that."

Gabriel stood his ground. "You refuse, then?"

"And risk discharge for insubordination?" Cainan crossed his arms. "You have a real mind for blackmail. Perhaps politics is your game after all. I'll do it. But I want you to remember who risked his skin for the Crown. Perhaps you'll remember where your allegiances belong and stop groveling to the likes of these moppers."

Gabriel held Cainan's cold stare a moment before Cainan broke it to study the rock face once more, a slight, smug smile taking his lips. Gabriel turned and crossed back to Mel and Aeron. It had taken all he had not to jab his cousin right where his lip had hinted at a sneer. *That'd teach the looger.*

"Have you finished three?" Gabriel asked them. He forced an even tone, despite the rage that boiled just below his skin.

"We've got three here," Fabi said, pointing down to the three lengths of rope at his feet. "We're just about to start another."

"Don't bother," Gabriel said. "That's all we'll need."

"We already tied off the ends for harnesses too," Mel said, then looked up to the summit. "I don't know how we're gonna get them up there though."

"Cainan's taking them up," Gabriel said.

Before he could respond, Cainan approached, scooped up the rope ends and draped them over his shoulders. "You'll want to watch closely, ladies. I'm only going to do this once."

Taking another short moment to examine the climb, Cainan took his first hand-hold and pulled himself up against the rock face. A moment before, Gabriel had wanted to level him. Now, his breath caught as he watched him inch his way up the cliff.

For a moment, Gabriel thought he moved too quickly—either out of a reckless need to show off or fearful need to out-climb the nervous jitters that could be the death of him. He couldn't help but marvel at Cainan's grace. He found his mark each time, only slowing once to reconsider a hazardous reach.

Cainan grew small as he ascended. Like a spider, defying gravity on the flat of a wall, he scaled upward until one last haul of his core saw him over the edge. He disappeared for a brief moment, but reappeared with his arms raised high above his head and let out a cheer of victory.

"I wasn't sure if the Desolate-bound fool would pull it off …" Aeron said, staring up, a hand guarding his eyes from the sun.

"He's a fool," Fabi said, "but a bold one."

Gabriel gave Cainan his moment of victory before he called up to him. "Alright, alright. Anchor those ropes. We don't have much time."

Cainan disappeared again for a moment then reappeared with the harness end of a rope. He tossed it down over the edge. Mel let it drop before grabbing hold and stabilizing it. Cainan repeated the process twice more before calling down to them.

"Come on up, ladies! The rock won't carry you up!"

Mel, Bear, and Lurin were the first to couple themselves to

the cliff face after the anchors were secured. Single file, they followed Cainan's lead.

"Stick to the general path Cainan took," Gabriel said. "Don't take any risks."

Anxious, Gabriel watched as the three ascended. They weren't nearly as quick or sure as Cainan, stopping every few spans or so to navigate their next move. Gabriel resisted encouraging them to hurry, even if taking too long to move further risked sapping their endurance. What was most important was keeping them confident.

They reached the summit without any major faults and let out their own cheers. Gabriel smiled as he watched Mel and Bear embrace with joy. The endurance training Captain Alden had put them through certainly paid them back. As strong as the Second League recruits were, he couldn't imagine them pulling this feat off without it.

Gabriel began his climb with Aeron and Jae. He slipped the black rope around his waist and thighs, pulled the knot tight, then prayed Desolate's Hand had been with Fabi's.

The first few feet were simple. He'd watched Cainan, then the first three soldiers take their foot and hand holds on small protrusions and that were spread randomly across the crag. As he climbed higher, the options became much more limited. It at some points, he needed to pause a few moments to find the best way to proceed while the soldiers he'd been paired with waited below.

Gabriel's heart raced with both the effort of the task and the danger he felt as gravity clung to his back, hoping for him to let go. He risked a glance to the ground a few times just to check if the theory of not looking down held any weight. It did.

Between the nervous testing of rock grooves, Gabriel marveled at the size of the rock they climbed. While it couldn't rival many of the steep climbs the Shadow Peaks offered, he'd never seen a wall of anything that could compare within his city upbringing. A fall would mean his end. This was no garden wall or watchtower.

The scale of the Peaks gave him a small taste of what the Ghayan mountains might be. He'd never visited the land to the far north, but he'd seen breathtaking paintings of what the Ghayan mountain ranges offered. Vistas of snow-capped behemoths with cities set within their reaches. Samuel had told him—though he hadn't personally seen them either—that the mountains in Ghaya could make the Shadow Peaks blush in their majesty.

Mel smiled over the ledge as he neared the top. "Looking smart, sir."

"Feeling relieved," Gabriel said.

Mel reached down to help him. Gabriel took the assistance, then swung a leg over the rock face to find solid ground. Before he stood, he reversed and peered over the ledge. Fabi, Urwell, and Paitin stood far below, waiting for the ropes to be tossed back down to them.

"Wild, right?" Mel clapped him on the back.

Gabriel removed the rope and tossed it down the slope. He suddenly realized how extremely reckless this idea actually was. He'd known it was risky, of course. But it only just hit him how mad the Second League must think him now.

They're taking orders from a madman. I'm the one who lead them off course, and now, I ask them to do this.

A sharp snap from behind caught his attention. Gabriel to whirled in reflex, fists and teeth clenched. A tree that held one of the anchors in place folded over, and without further warning, it loosed, ripping chunks of out of the mountainside.

Gabriel jumped, barely dodging the unearthed projectile. He fell to the side with a thud that nearly pulled every wisp of breath from his lungs. He flopped over to watch the roots of the harness anchor clear the cliffside.

THIRTY-ONE

COLD DISHONOR

A startled cry followed by shouts from the last three soldiers sounded. Gabriel flipped over onto his hands and knees and crawled to the cliff edge. The tree that anchored one the ropes had tumbled down the slope and caught between two small protrusions in the rock.

Below, nearly halfway down the precipice, a small figure of a man dangled, swinging back and forth, taking heavy blows to his head and extremities as he buoyed across the rocks.

Cainan took Urwell's hand as he reached the top and helped pull him over. Gabriel shook himself out of the horror to help Paitin.

"What happened?" Gabriel asked to no one soldier in particular. "Is he conscious?"

"Knocked out cold," Aeron said, peering below him.

"He's bleeding," Urwell said. "Bad. *Wisdoms* ..."

"It's Fabi," Paitin panted. He held a hand against his head to stop the bleeding after getting caught by falling debris. "I'm not sure how it happened, but a good chunk of rock came down with him and caught me on the head."

Gabriel squinted back down the rock wall. He was so far down. *Is the blood on his head? Scorch it.*

"We've got to help him up," Aeron said, looking to Gabriel.

"I can bind his wounds, but I can't if we don't get him up here."

"Have you gone mad?" Cainan said, standing. "You can't go back down there. If you thought climbing up was a challenge, I wouldn't *dare* attempt climbing down."

Aeron stood and met Cainan's glare. "Listen, shoveboy. He's one of us. Someone needs to help him. You can't leave a man to die like that."

"Have you any idea how many have died climbing because they tried to help someone who'd injured themselves?" Cainan asked, but didn't wait for an answer. "I don't know of *any* who came back. The thief is on his own now."

"Didn't you tie the knot?" Bear asked Cainan.

"Yes," Cainan said through gritted teeth. "But I didn't anticipate that the whole scorching tree would uproot. Are you trying to blame this on me?"

Bear stepped up to him. "Maybe I am."

"Stand down, Bear!" Gabriel shouted. "This isn't the time to place blame."

Aeron turned to Mel. "Hand me the rope. I'm going back down for him."

"Wait." Gabriel caught Aeron by the shoulder. "Just wait a moment. We have to think this through."

Aeron frowned. "I don't know what we need to think about here. The more time we spend standing around, waiting for Desolate's Hand to bring salvation, the more time Fabi is bleeding out of his head."

"He's stopping you because he knows I'm right," Cainan said. "He's responsible for keeping us alive. It's his call. It's not an easy one, but it's the *right* call." Cainan looked at Gabriel. "Isn't it?"

Gabriel nodded. "Give me the rope, Aeron. You're not going down there."

"But—"

"That's an order!"

Aeron stood on the cliff a moment, the wind gently tossing his hair as he stared with the eyes of a cobra at Gabriel.

Gabriel held out his hand and Aeron dropped the length of rope in it.

Gabriel slipped the harness on. "I'm going to go down for him. I got us into this mess." He pointed a thumb over his shoulder. "Aeron help the others hold the rope to lower me down. Cainan, help me plot a way back down."

Both Aeron and Cainan eyes widened in disbelief, but only Aeron's expression broke into a half grin.

"Yes, sir," Aeron said, and crossed over where the rest of the Second League had already begun to form a human anchor.

"What's the matter with you?" Cainan said. "Have you gone completely daft? Your father—"

"My father's dead," Gabriel finished for him.

Cainan scoffed and crossed his arms. "I won't help you get yourself killed. Daft or not."

Gabriel didn't wait for him to complete the sentence before he turned back to the cliff edge. He'd had enough of Cainan. If he wouldn't help, then so be it. Gabriel squatted down and gripped the rope with one hand.

He looked at the rest of the Second League, who all held tight to the rope, waiting for direction. "Just lower me slowly as I climb down. There's seven of you, so it shouldn't be too hard. But if the weight becomes too much for you, don't let yourselves be pulled over."

Gabriel stopped to consider what he'd just said with complete confidence. *It won't be too hard?* He'd just assured them of that going up.

Letting his left leg fall over the cliff edge, he slowly leaned backward, testing the strength of his support. The soldiers tensed, but they remained in place.

Gabriel slid over the rock and searched for a foothold but couldn't find the one he'd seen directly below. He slid a bit further, catching the ledge with his hands, until he finally found his mark. He let out a breath, then glanced down to where Fabi hung.

I can do this.

While the descent felt less frightening than the climb up, navigating his way back down was at least twice as hard. Like before, it was about finding the next safe grip, but now his entire body was in his line of sight, and every glimpse below felt as if he were falling backward.

Mel had taken to watching to make sure the rope was fed to him at an even rate. If he lost his grip, the worst that would happen is that he'd have to reposition.

No … that wasn't the worst that could happen.

The worst that could happen is they would tire, or find that after he got hold of Fabi, they wouldn't have the strength to pull them back up.

Gabriel glanced at the tree that had served as the third anchor as he passed it to the right. It rocked and whined, protesting the human pendulum it supported below. The tree had caught in a section of rock that could only be explained by Desolate's Hand. Or the Windbringer's hand, if the Ghayan gods had any truth to them.

"Careful," Mel called from above. "Stay to the right. You don't want to get your rope caught up in roots of that tree."

Gabriel glanced back up and saw that his rope brushed against the fallen tree. If he pushed it even a little, it might send it tumbling over. A short shiver passed through him as he tried to find a hand hold that would take him further to the right.

Only a few spans away, Gabriel called out to him. "Fabi!"

No answer.

"Fabi, if you're alright … or at least alive, say something. A moan or a hand wave will be just fine."

Nothing.

Gabriel lowered himself to Fabi's side where he slowly swayed. Gabriel reached out with his left hand and grabbed at him but missed. Fabi rocked away from him then back. He took another grab at him, but again didn't catch him. Instead, he bumped him, adding to the width of his swing.

His attention immediately shot up to the tree. It wobbled in place, longing to fall to lower ground. Gabriel pulled his attention back to Fabi. He watched him swing. He had to take his time to get this just right.

Gabriel had put them all at risk by leading them the wrong direction, then added to it by having them make a risky climb. If he wasn't careful, he'd also lose one of them forever.

No more mistakes.

His third reach caught him by the wrist but pulled Gabriel off the rock he held. His heart stopped as he felt himself begin to fall, then he felt the harness tighten. He let out a painful grunt and his men groaned from above, catching his fall.

"Watch out!"

Gabriel looked back up to see the tree falling. Fabi's weight jerked against him. The tree—just barely clearing them—fell toward the ground below.

Gabriel's mind whirled as adrenaline surged through his veins. The tree was going to pull him and Fabi over the edge … and the rest of the Second League with him if they didn't have the sense to let go.

He closed his eyes, still holding tight to the dangling soldier, waiting for the tree to pull them both to their deaths.

There was a deep thud and the sound of wood snapping. Then … silence.

Gabriel opened his eyes.

Below, the tree rested on the rocks, and the rope harness around Fabi's waist hung slack. The rope had been just long enough for the tree to hit the ground before it pulled them with it.

Fabi groaned, and his head shifted from his left shoulder to his right.

"Fabi!" Gabriel said. "Are you awake?"

Fabi slowly lifted his head and his eyes focused on Gabriel. "I'm never climbing anything again."

Gabriel smiled, then reached back down with his left hand as his feet found a place to grip. "Grab my hand. We have to get you some help. You're bleeding something awful."

Slowly, he took Gabriel's other hand.

"That's it. Put your foot there."

"You dead yet?" Mel shouted down the cliffside.

"Not yet," Gabriel said. "And coming up."

Gabriel slipped between two trees—one that stood tall, and the other dead and leaning against the other for support. There was a clear line of sight to the clearing many spans below. Any moment, he'd know for sure how many of them he was dealing with.

The Second League filed in from behind. Three men down, Gabriel had begun to worry that there might not be enough of them to intercept the spies if anything were to happen. He'd left Aeron behind with Fabi and Paitin to treat their head wounds. There was no use in bringing them along. If anything, they'd be a liability.

"There," Gabriel said. "Four. There's four of them."

"Seems about right," Mel said. "Ain't no reason to bring many more."

Gabriel retrieved and opened the map. "We'll encircle them. We'll have to move fast, but there's another small clearing coming up at a higher elevation. They'll pass this way as it's the quickest and safest route back. If we wait until they reach this last, larger clearing, it'll be much harder to catch them off guard and properly spread with only seven of us."

Gabriel looked back to the rest of them. "Let's head west. Quickly, but watch your step. We've had too much go wrong already."

While the Second League considered this, Cainan exhaled, as if bored.

Gabriel stood as he slipped the map back into the vial. "Follow me."

He slipped under the overhanging branches with a brisk, ducking trot. He cut left to lower ground where there were more rocks than trees. They'd need to be even more careful about their step, but their target would be reached faster with a more direct line instead of trying to navigate the mountain brush.

His muscles ached from making the rock climb—all of them must have felt it, but he had made the climb twice, the second time with a passenger. All the drills they'd done during their training still hadn't prepared them for that feat. Apparently, there were still muscles they'd neglected.

The spring air felt like bliss as it brushed his face and filled his lungs with the sweet hints of amberdashes, in full bloom and fresh, and mountain water that cut sharply down the southeast face of the Peaks. The evening sun stared him in the face as he charged the horizon.

In the thrill of the run, he couldn't help but remember the simple joy of running the courtyard at the Crown Palace—dodging gardeners and runners alike and hiding under well-pruned shrubs while playing spy with Seth. It was a distant memory, but he let it rule his imagination to keep his mind off how sore he'd be in the morning.

With a quick signal, Gabriel beckoned his men to cut North. To his satisfaction, the unexpected formality was answered with the quick discipline he'd worked to instill them with since Captain Alden had ranked him. Another signal, and the crew split off in pairs to find their positions along perimeter of the clearing they neared.

Gabriel slowed to approach without drawing attention. His hand found the hilt of his sword and he wished he'd brought the Crown Sabre with him. Not because it was smart to bring it—he'd wisely chosen to leave it behind—but because he wouldn't have minded trying for another memory. Perhaps there was something his father had said about what to do after he'd spent the first half of his day trying to kill the soldiers under his command.

"You were wrong, you know," Cainan whispered from behind.

Gabriel turned to Cainan's frown. He'd almost forgotten that he'd paired himself with his cousin. It was a good choice. They knew how each other approached tactical situations based on years of familiarity. It was supposed to be a perfect match … at least on parchment.

He turned back, ignoring the comment.

"You've managed so far with Desolate's kind Hand," Cainan said. "But you could have gotten yourself killed. You've been treating me like I'm the enemy, but I'm the only one who is actually on your side."

"Because you want an ex-thief off of the team?" Gabriel asked.

"Because I'm flesh and blood, Gabe," Cainan said, tapping his chest. "What we are—who we're supposed to be—is something these lowborn soldiers can never understand. It's a dishonor to us to have a thieving shoveboy stand with us. How do you think that will look when they find out what you've done?"

Gabriel glared at him. "What's that supposed to mean?"

"Oh, come now," Cainan said. "I promised my silence. But it's not as if they didn't notice you gone. And when you go back and they find out what you did, do you think it sets a good example to the people of Hzorah—the *law-abiding* people who follow the order that we've established? You're supposed to be their king. You're supposed to keep them safe."

Gabriel rounded on him but kept his voice to a low hiss. "That's exactly what we're doing. I didn't come to the northern plain because I thought it'd be nice to get some fresh air. I came because the people need a king who can lead them into this war with some backbone."

"But what about principle?" Cainan said. "What about the law? What about what's right? What about your honor? You're *just* like your father—following some idealistic sense of self-righteousness instead of using his head to rule."

"You don't know *anything* about my father."

"Oh? What about how he abandoned the High Lords to lead the final charge the during the war? What about when he was offered the chance to unify Hzorah and Armoth, but he turned it down because he was 'in love'?" Cainan stepped closer. "What about when he put all his trust in that scorching prophet and got himself killed in Caldor, leaving you, your brother, and the entire kingdom alone and leaderless? Your father should have *never* been king."

Gabriel clenched his fists tight. Cainan had become tiresome at the palace, and, in the encampment, he was a thorn in his side. But this time … This time he'd gone too far.

Voices cut through his fury. Gabriel turned to see the Deseran spies cross into the clearing.

"Shh!" Gabriel held up a hand, as he watched.

"You can't silence the truth, Gabe," Cainan whispered. "Sooner or later you'll—"

"Shh!" Gabriel repeated sharply, then pointed.

The Deseran spy at the lead turned, walking backward. "You think she'd take a proposal seriously from a looger like you? All puffed up with a balding spot on top?"

"You think you could have her?" the following spy asked. "Think *you're* the looker, eh?"

"Don't have to be," he tapped the side of his head. "I got the smarts. Here's what you do. You go to Dargin's Underground market. Buy some of that sweet ale. The kind with the ruby seal."

"What kind of money you think I have? That'll cost me at least a month's worth!"

"Will you let me finish? You buy some of the sweet ale. And give it to her when you see her next. She probably never had the taste of ale, won't know what it'll do to her. Once she's good and mellow, that's when you make your move."

"My move?"

"If there's someone dafter … You *bed* her!"

Gabriel felt his insides turn. *Dominion scum …*

He whistled eight times, summoning the Second League's advance. The four Dominion soldiers paused in the knee-high grass, turning about, trying to place where the distinctly human call originated.

The spy at the lead pulled his sword, then turned to the three behind him. "What? Are you waiting for Desolate's scorching Hand to pull them for you?"

As if finding their senses, the other three spies pulled their swords as they huddled together, checking every side as not to be caught unaware.

Gabriel stepped out of the clearing with Cainan. One of the shoulders flinched as he saw them appear out of the brush. The three other pairs of Hzorah soldiers stepped out, nearly in time with Gabriel.

"Stand down!" Gabriel called to them. "Drop your arms and we won't cut your throats on the spot." Gabriel let the rage Cainan lit inside him blaze. When they didn't comply, he pulled his own sword and added: "Care to call my bluff?"

The whole of the Second League followed his lead, pulling their swords.

"Looks like some heathens wandered away from the fold," the Deseran soldier said. "Found themselves some swords and fancy themselves warriors. Ain't a one of you seen more than fifteen years, have you?"

Taunting—buying time for his men to gain the confidence to fight back. He was scum, but smart scum. Gabriel walked straight for them man, his sword extended, meeting his taunt with bold opposition.

"Hold up now," the Deseran said. "You don't wanna—"

Gabriel didn't slow. He struck, but the Dominion soldier caught his swing and pushed back. The Second League moved in, choking their ability to fight or flee. The spies huddled closer.

As quickly as he'd struck, Gabriel reformed and took a second strike. Too slow for his attack, the man froze as Gabriel's sword stopped just short of cutting his throat. The Deseran held his hands clear, signaling his surrender.

"Try me again," Gabriel said. "I'd *love* a reason to end you."

"Don't get eager," the man slowly lowered to the ground, and placed his sword before him. Then, on his knees, he held his hands open again. "We'll play fair."

The other three spies gave up their weapons. A slight tilt of his head gave Cainan all the signal he needed to move in and gather the weapons. Another to Mel, Bear, and Lurin and they took to binding their hands.

"Looks like we're seein' the camp up close, boys," the Deseran spy said.

Gabriel glared into the man's eyes. "Listen carefully, because if you don't do as I say, I will kill you without a second thought. I don't want to hear another word out of your filthy mouth. If I do, I'll make sure to remove whatever small bit of manhood you have below that belt."

The man smirked but said nothing.

"Good." Gabriel looked at the Second League. "Let's go home."

Somehow, the way back down the Shadow Peaks felt shorter than the way up. It was more than just the help of gravity pulling them back to camp, it was as if a weight was lifted from Gabriel's shoulders, and finally, for the first time since he'd left camp, he felt in control.

They found Aeron, Fabi, and Paitin where they'd left them. Aeron had managed to stop their bleeding, and, surprisingly, both were in good spirits. While Fabi insisted he was fine to travel despite a slight limp in his step, Aeron insisted that he stay by his side to provide an aiding shoulder. Fabi waved off the offer but retracted his refusal not long into their journey.

Though they needed to pace themselves slower for Fabi, they would have had to regardless as their captives were far less than willing to meet their fate with a skip in their step. The spies remained quiet as Gabriel had ordered. Cainan taunted them at first, hoping to get a rise, but Gabriel called for him to back down. Questioning was a specialized job. At least that's what his father had taught him. And it was about as much as he'd say on the matter before turning his attention to other topics.

The sun and exhaustion both set before they'd cleared the mountain, but Gabriel pressed on. They were ill prepared to spend too much time away from camp. This wasn't supposed to be a long excursion. They were all tired, but it wouldn't be so bad once they retrieved the horses.

Gabriel turned to the sound of shuffling from behind. In the darkness, a captive shouldered one of his men. They toppled, falling into the brush. Whoever the spy had pushed ended up under him. With a sharp movement, the spy lifted his bound hands.

A knife glinted in the moonlight followed by a blunt thud that echoed through the peaks and chilled the night before the Second League tackled him. They wrestled the captive to the ground and landed a few well-placed kicks to keep him there.

Gabriel pushed his men aside, mentally checking off the safety of each face he saw on his way to his fallen comrade. He knelt and stared into eyes that grew distant as his life faded away.

Mel.

Gabriel held his hands over his friend, looking for some place to clot the injury, but couldn't quite find the right way to apply pressure. There was so much blood. The cut had completely severed the artery in his neck. He hadn't even had a chance to scream.

Aeron fell to Gabriel's side, then took to looking the soldier over. Mel gurgled blood through what was left of his neck. His head twitched to the side and his mouth parted, pulling for air.

Gabriel's hand warmed as life poured over it and soaked into the ground he leaned against. Slowly, Aeron stood and backed a step.

He turned to the medic, his blood heating in panic. "Well?"

Aeron shook his head. "I'm sorry."

Gabriel just stared at Aeron as realization slowly penetrated his awareness. When he turned back to Mel, the soldier lay slack-jawed and unmoving.

Just like that, he was gone.

A good soldier, a friend—perhaps one of the only friends he'd really ever had outside of his family and the palace staff—taken by the a filthy, foul-mouthed, Deseran dog.

Gabriel rounded and stood. The Second League parted, letting him through to the spy that Bear held at bay. He watched the man's sick eyes, his satisfied grin. Reaching down, he wrenched the knife from the spy's hand. He was on the razor-thin edge of completely losing control and—

He looked at the knife under a thin patch of moonlight and saw the Hzorah Mark branded into the knife's handle and beneath it was the symbol of a tree and a hammer.

It was one of their own.

Gabriel turned, scanning his men. Only one of their knives were missing: Cainan's.

Suddenly recognizing what had occurred, Cainan felt for the knife that should have been secured to his right hip. He looked back to Gabriel, with an expression that blended horror with rage.

Gabriel crossed over to him and handed him his weapon. "I believe you dropped this into the wrong hands."

Cainan looked at Gabriel. He didn't apologize, but he didn't feign innocence either.

"Take Mel over there," Gabriel said, pointing to where the rocky crags split apart to reveal a large patch of vegetation. "We're going to bury him before we continue. We can't carry him back."

It was practical—*too* practical. Pragmatism that bleed into cold dishonor. But what else could be done?

"What about this bastard?" Aeron's voice growled with rage. "Let's cut his throat and be done with him. More than what he deserves."

"Leave him be," Gabriel said. "We have a job to do. He'll get what he deserves. More if I have a say." He looked the spy in the eye. "I promise you that."

THIRTY-TWO

UNDER THE SKY'S BLACK FATES

Tele caught the man's eye again—his only eye—and he smiled a wicked, toothless smile. She'd long ago set aside the idea that the man was merely curious about them. Tal Aval's appearance was far short of commonplace. And Tele ... well, she was the only woman that sat chained among them. All the other captives on the long prison cart had lost interest in them within a day or so. The one-eyed prisoner hadn't wavered.

His filthy gaze made her bones want to crawl right out of her skin, and all sympathy for his disfigurement had fallen away. Apparently, it only took one eye to flood the long, wide cart waist-deep with impropriety.

"*Do not look at him*," Tal Aval whispered. "*It will only make his thirst for you grow*."

Tele looked at Tal Aval. "*If I avoid looking at him, he'll think I'm afraid. And it's not as if I'm returning his less-than-subtle gawking*."

"*Your bravery is lost on him*," Tal Aval said. "*He does not know your intentions*."

Tele shifted. She'd avoided doing that as long as she could. Somehow, the Hzorah guard had managed to tighten the cuffs at her wrists too tight, perhaps fearing that her slimmer, more feminine arms could somehow shrink and allow her to slip away into the night.

"*I'm tired*," Tele said. "*I know that he's locked in place over there, but I can't help but fear he'll find his way over here if I let my eyes rest.*"

"*You think that I would let the man touch you?*" Tal Aval asked.

Tele inclined her head his cuffs. "*Yours must not be as tight as mine.*"

"*If the one-eyed man can free himself, I certainly can.*" Tal Aval turned to the stronghold in the distance. "*This is our … prison?*"

Tele looked to the near-black structure that grew out of the plain. Green and red vines wound the fortress, reaching the apex of hardened watchtowers. Either the stronghold suffered from lack of upkeep or the lord, king, or whoever lived in this place enjoyed the aesthetic. A man at the stronghold's wall signaled down to someone unseen inside and the wood and metal gate that barred the path lifted.

Tal Aval had hesitated in his use of the word "prison," because Tele had needed to create a word for it during their captivity. Apparently, there hadn't been a word for their particular fate in the Tal language.

"*It appears so.*"

"*I do not like it*," Tal Aval said. "*Men were not meant to sit behind walls.*"

"*We will be fine*," Tele reassured him. And herself if she were honest … "*As soon as they realize that we aren't here to harm the Hzorah people, they will return our freedom.*"

"*We were not a harm to the Hzorah people at the inn, and they put us in these.*" He lifted the shackles.

Tele had replayed that moment a hundred times, trying to determine how she could have escaped. But they were in an enclosed space. The inn was small and full of people who may or may not take up arms to help the Hzorah Guard who, themselves, were well armed. And the växarot couldn't be relied upon indoors unless it had already been summoned while out in nature.

Considering all possible options, she'd made the best decision she could. Still, she insisted on revisiting the moment, as if her obsession might allow her to change the past.

Tele turned her attention upward as the cart passed under the stronghold wall. Layers of thick rock swallowed then expelled them into the belly of the stronghold. The walls weren't as thick as what she'd seen in Caldor, but the amount of labor it must have taken to erect the partition reeled her mind nonetheless.

"*Take careful note of your surroundings,*" Tele whispered. "*If the opportunity comes for us to escape, we'll need to know how to get back out.*"

"*I will try,*" Tal Aval said. "*But I do not know much about these buildings and walls. I know how the world is given to man. But this … This is not how I know it.*"

"*I don't know it well either. My experience is nearly as limited as yours. But we have to try.*"

Tal Aval nodded. "*This is the reason why we have Navid.*"

Tele's stomach sank at that. If she spent a hundred times imagining what she could have done differently when they were taken captive, she must have imagined Navid's fate ten times over.

She'd let him search for supplies on his own. She shouldn't have let them split up. She shouldn't have thought that they would be fine alone in an unfamiliar place. She'd let herself become too confident because she'd passed through once and nothing had happened. At least, nothing had happened to *her*.

But really, she'd let it happen because she was furious with him. Somehow, her anger with him now felt trivial.

Tele caught the eye of the man at the end of the cart again. He smiled at her. She sighed and turned her attention back to the stronghold's courtyard where Hzorah soldiers trotted here and there, milling about supplies and adding to the white noise of chatter.

The cart slowed and halted. About a dozen strong soldiers approached the cart and took hold of the chains linked to their shackles. With little concern for the prisoners' balance, they pulled, forcing them off the cart in rows.

Tele marched in line as they guided the prisoners into a long passage and onto the docking bay, then down long, broad stairs that tunneled underground. Under torchlight, she caught glimpses of each of the prisoners chained in the line. Some wept silently, others stared ahead indifferently.

At the bottom of the stairs, another hall ran the length of the dungeon, meeting with subsequent halls at perpendicular intersections.

One, two, three, four, five. Tele silently counted as they passed each branching hall, trying to commit their location to memory. *Six, seven, eight.*

Her chain pulled left. She and several prisoners turned down either corridor, splitting the procession in half. Tele looked behind her to check if Tal Aval had taken note.

Tal Aval wasn't there. A torch faded behind them as guards led half the inmates down the opposite side. The torchlight was then eclipsed by the head of another prisoner. He smiled toothlessly at her; his good eye locked with hers.

Navid awoke, screaming. He summoned his växarot staff and swung in a wide arc, but the spirits of sleep faded, unscathed. Panting, he stumbled backward and fell back onto the patch of grass under the aging willow where he'd made camp.

He tried to use his shirt to dry his brow, but it was drenched in sweat, as though a heavy rain cloud had passed over him and only him. Navid sniffed to clear his sinuses. His heart drummed in his chest. His head felt hot, and his body cold, like all of his blood had pooled in his skull.

A gentle wind pushed against blades of grass. In the distance, a foreground to the breaking dawn, a trip of goats slept, huddled together in a brown and white patched mound. One of them raised its head, checking if Navid had suddenly become a threat. A few moments of observation gave the animal the confidence to settle back down.

Navid checked his belongings. He hadn't been robbed in

the night. That was good. He stood watch as long as his body would allow every night. Not just out of fear of travelers who were looking for quick supplies, but out of fear of the nightmares that increasingly plagued his mind.

He was alone—truly alone for the first time in his life.

Navid looked to the sword in his hand. At least the "warrior response" Tele had wanted from him had set in enough for him to try and fight the dreams off.

She'd probably give me a curt speech about only attacking what's real and how dreams can't hurt me. She'd be right, and it'd make him feel like a fool child. He wished with all of his heart that she could make him feel that way right now. Because at least she'd be here. At least she'd be safe.

Navid took a short drink from his waterskin before standing to break camp. He was still a few days from the North Hzorah plains, and those few days may turn into a week if he dallied.

The beaten road to the Hzorah army was clear and straight, running perpendicular to the Drunn river. Navid didn't take that route. The less people he encountered on his way, the safer he'd be. Instead, he took roads that cut around farmland in a narrow course made for farmers and countrymen who needed to pass between their lands and the lands of their neighbors. Eventually, all roads led back to the Drunn and its offshoots at the delta, but Navid circumnavigated that eventuality, favoring the view of flat fields and the ripe smell of cattle.

A shadow shifting to his left, drew his attention. He turned, but didn't see anything or anyone. An artifact of loneliness—every little movement became more than what it really was.

Overhead, the birds chattered incessantly, unwilling to hear out the reply of their kin. It all made him feel more alone than he'd ever felt before. He didn't think he'd miss Tele's company as much as he did. It was a terrible silence without her. He even missed the periodic questions that Tal Aval pitched at each unfamiliar junction.

Another shift from the corner of his eye caught his attention. He turned again, this time pausing in the path, and watching the field closely. Navid knew that there were wild animals out away from the cities, but he'd always been told that more often than not, they'd stay clear of people. The curse flared within and Navid clutched the växarot, praying that *this* was more often rather than not.

Another shift against the flow of the breeze, and Navid raised his staff. He swallowed hard, then moved to back away. Whatever was in the tall grass was best left there.

A man stood out of the grass.

Grimacing, he stalked out onto the path. "Well, now," he said, pulling his sword. "Fancy meeting you out here all alone."

Navid backed a step and looked the man in the eyes.

"Where are your friends?" he said. "The one with unfortunate hair and that sitter who killed my brother."

Navid took another step backward as a chill ran the length of his nerves. "Stay back …"

"So …" The man glanced about the path, and took another step to him. "You're alone; they got tired of fighting for you, did they?"

"I let you live."

"*Let* me live?" The man sneered then spat. "Boy, a rabbit would escape you sick and footless."

"I called them off. I let you live, so step back."

"Now, normally I'd agree with you there. A life for a life or whatever they teach you before bed on the pillow you were raised on. But they probably forgot to tell you about one small exception …"

The curse lit anew within him.

The man lunged, swinging his sword. Navid managed to raise his weapon in defense. The pain of the strike against his växarot stunned him, and the strength of it pushed him off balance.

"Hurt a man's brother, and you've made an enemy for life!" the man snarled.

Navid tried to roll out of the thief's gait.

The curse raged.

This is it.

As soon as he turned over, the thief kicked him. Navid grunted as his body jerked across the dirt path.

The itch of his curse burned ever more, a fire that coursed through his veins.

This is my end.

The thief kicked him again before backing away and letting lose a wicked, vengeful howl. Steel flashed against the morning sun, and the blade's point pressed the soft beneath his chin.

He'd failed. He was going to die. The Hzorah soldiers were going to die. Existence would fade to Desolate, and the war would be lost before it began just as the prophets had said.

The thief grinned. "I'll see you at Desolate's door."

Navid shut his eyes. He was a failure—a monster. He'd never see another day of happiness, never see his father, never see Tele again.

Tele.

She was the one person who had believed in him. He wanted his last memories to be of her. He conjured the memory of her in her mind. Her soft brown hair, tossing in the breeze. Her sharp, green eyes gazing into his against a background of the Borderland forest. Time stood still here, the perfect memory—his last thoughts were perfect, happy.

"Forget everything that the prophets told you," she'd said. "Forget everything that you've read about seers. Forget all of it. The prophets, the seers … They're all dead now. You are the only one who can decide if you are cursed. *You.*"

As he stared into her pleading gaze, the itch buzzed at the edges of his awareness, inviting him to take control, to take hold of his destiny, to damn his very soul.

I'd rather damn my soul than let the world fade away. I'd rather be a monster than to never see her again.

Navid reached out, plunging through the barrier in his mind. It splintered and fell away. Awareness rushed in. His mind filled like a lung desperate for air. He opened his eyes to the world around him and saw—truly saw.

Sensing his opening, he kicked. He caught the thief in the shin. The man cried out and fell back. The tug of fate drew him to the right. He rolled, dodging the thief's retaliation, just barely dodging decapitation.

Imminent victory rang through his nerves, compelling him to his enemy's weakness. Dozens of possibilities hung just before him.

His växarot staff had fallen just several spans away—moderate odds.

A rock, large enough to easily wield waited in the grass—a near split odds at best.

The thief's ankle, twisting in the dirt road—high odds.

Navid shifted a quarter turn on the ground and drove his boot as hard as he could just above the man's ankle. Every eventuality shifted as the man screamed out in pain over a sharp, shattering crack.

Sensing opportunity, he tackled the thief and gripped him in a headlock.

His odds shifted once again.

He twisted the man's arm, forcing him to release his weapon.

Cool waves of relief pulsed through him, rewarding him for apprehending the threat. But danger still burned beneath it all.

The man's face burned red as he struggled, mouthing for air, mucus bubbling from his nose. He flailed and jabbed, trying to free himself. Sensing release, Navid struck the man's face. Then again, and again, and again, until he stilled, limp in his arms.

Like a cool mist on a hot summer's day, his body sung with rapture, with victory—whole for the first time. Like hot, molten lead poured onto his heart, his soul cried out with sorrow, with defeat—fractured into countless shards.

Amie sat back and closed the book. "Should we end for the night?"

Owen yawned and nodded and took the book from her. Amie allowed her back to rest against the tree positioned just off the northbound road. Her wrists and ankles burned in anticipation of the ropes cutting into her flesh.

When Owen began packing away his books, Amie glanced at the cart to see Mara watching her. Ever since they'd talked several nights ago, she'd been continuously watchful. And now that she thought about it, Amie wasn't sure that she'd seen her sleep since then.

When they'd continued onto the plain, Mara had been quick to notice and point out that they were moving through the western reaches North Hzorah. How Mara figured that out, wasn't clear to Amie, but she felt reassured by Mara's discovery. Not because it gave them any real advantage, but because knowing where they were somehow made the procession less frightening.

But that was before they reached the Shadow Peaks.

Though the mountains still appeared to sit in the distance, she'd overheard Scar Face say that they were in them. The land had become less flat, making their traveling more laborious, but the mountain's most threatening reaches were still some days travel off.

Amie worried that they'd have to cross over the Peaks. She imagined slipping and tumbling down rocky crags before snapping her spine at the base of a mountain. She shivered, the thought of it so vivid in her mind that her neck hurt.

But she couldn't think about that right now. She had to come up with a way to escape. And the only leverage she had was Owen. He was the only soldier who bothered to talk to her. And though he kept his distance, he'd at least softened to her.

"Lieutenant Owen," Amie whispered. "Can you tie me tonight? Scar Face always does it too tight."

Surprisingly, Owen laughed. "Scar Face?" He turned and pointed to the soldier. "Him? That's Sergeant—"

"I prefer Scar Face," Amie said.

"Alright," Owen said. "I'll tie you. Sit still."

Amie nodded, and Owen left to retrieve the ropes. Amie sat quietly. When she looked to the cart, she caught Mara's eye again. Her eyes were wide, as if to say: "this might be your chance."

And she was right. This was perhaps the first time that any of them had fully turned their back on her. But Amie didn't have a follow up plan yet. If she ran off, she'd be caught for sure. And she still had no way to unlock Mara's prison carriage.

No. She had to continue to cooperate—keep earning his trust.

When Owen returned, she held out her wrists so that he could easily do his work without resistance. He tied the restraints with a bit more give than Scar Face. Not enough to slip away, but enough that they didn't cut into her skin at night.

"Too tight?" he asked.

Amie shook her head. "Much better. Can I ask you a question?"

A hint of suspicion crossed Lieutenant Owen eyes. "Yes?"

"Can you tell me more about your home and your people?" Amie swallowed. "I've lived in one place my whole life. I always wonder what other places and people are like."

Owen shrugged. "It's hot many days of the year, though not as harsh as the wilderness to the east. We don't live in places like you. Our homes are smaller. Some of them are in trees—"

"Your family. What are they like?"

Owen hesitated. "I have a younger brother. His name is Bam Po. And a younger sister—Bam Jaddi."

"Their names," Amie said. "They both begin the same. Why?"

"All the Bamilee names begin this way," Owen explained. "It is to remind us that we are all of one people."

"Bam Owen?" Amie's nose wrinkled at the strange construction. "That's your name?"

"My name is Bam Rav," Owen said. "Owen is the name

given to me when I joined the Creed's army. It is so that I fit in."

"Why did you join the army? Your people don't like violence, and you don't strike me as someone who would like to hurt anyone."

"That is my business," Lieutenant Owen said, standing.

She was losing him. *I can't let him walk away.*

"Right. Of course. I'm just wondering because I know your family would be concerned to see you hurt others, especially another family not so different from your own. I just don't understand. Why would you want to do that?"

Owen watched her for a moment, his eyes burning with fury. She could have been a bit gentler and she may have overplayed her hand. But Owen never talked to her long before walking away. She needed to know what pushed him to do something that felt so against his nature.

"I was forced to join," Owen said. "No Bamilee would willingly join, and the Dominion do not bother forcing us to fight for them. They are content with us slaving for them. I am the only Bamilee man they asked to join."

"They have asked no other?" Amie frowned. "Why you?"

"One day, soldiers came to my home. They asked me to join, saying that I can represent my people in the war. I said 'no.' They insisted, but I refused. They left my home. The next day, they returned again. The soldiers offered me freedom. They told me if I served, I would never have to work again. Again I said 'no.' No Bamilee man would lift his hand against another people. When they saw that I could not be swayed, they left. They came again the next day. The offered me money and promised me comforts that I couldn't even imagine for me and my family. I said 'no.' And I told them that there was nothing that they could do, nothing that they could offer me that could make me abandon the teachings of my people."

Owen paused and looked away toward the Shadow Peaks. "A week passed, and they did not return. I worked in peace, farming the land. But the soldiers returned while I was hard at work. When I came home, my mother, father, brother, and sister were tied to poles. Around them was a large pit of wood. They told me that if I did not join, they would burn my family before me.

"I begged them to please let my family go, but they refused, saying that I was the only one who could save them. My mother and father pleaded for me to not abandon our way, but I could not bear to have them killed—to see harm come to them. I told them that I would join."

As if returning from a faraway place, Owen turned back to Amie. "I do not know why they chose me. But I do know that I must do this. If I do not, I will lose my family."

Before Amie could digest what he'd just said, before she could reply, Owen—Bam Rav—turned and walked away, leaving Amie alone with her disbelief.

She was horrified at the actions the Dominion had taken to force Owen into their army. It didn't make any sense. Why would they want him to join, but no other Bamilee person? And why would they put him through all of that pain? Couldn't they have simply captured him and carted him away just as they had done with her?

Regardless of their reasons, what they'd done was barbaric. She'd vowed to never do what the Dominion was doing to the people she loved, but she wasn't sure that she wouldn't have broken that vow when faced with such an impossible choice.

Amie watched as Owen's silhouette snuffed out the last of the campfire's flames before he lay down to rest. He rolled this way and that, trying to find a place of comfort under the sky's black fates.

A prisoner. Just like her.

THIRTY-THREE

WHAT SEPARATES US

Gabriel watched the Second League climb the small hill, keeping pace even as the incline steepened. After Mel's death, he'd had to rearrange how their formation drill would work. He reconfigured them as a wedge of nine, and despite being two men short, their form remained impeccable.

He'd also doubled down on combat and saw a month's progress in mere days. Gabriel's relentless drilling had been a worthy an investment. His crew hadn't resisted his intense regimen. Though they no longer used music as a means of building their comradery, losing one of their own had forged a bond that he couldn't manufacture.

Gabriel whistled, calling the Second League in. He wanted to push their practicing late into the night, but he knew they needed sleep if they he wanted them to stay sharp. Meeting the four spies had made the Dominion army on the other side of the Shadow Peaks feel all the more real. He couldn't see them, but he somehow *felt* them now.

The Second League formed a tight line and filed into camp. Fabi, insisting that he make himself useful, worked with Bear to light the fire pit while Aeron, Lurin, and Jae fetched their rations. Fabi's absence from most of their training was temporary. He'd heal with time.

But Mel would never return.

Gabriel sat and watched them eat, still too sick about the last several days to stomach much of anything. He knew this was the nature of war. Many who laid foot on the battlefield never left it. He wasn't so naive that he believed this would be a civil affair. But to lose someone so unexpectedly had snuffed out some of the flame that doing what he thought was his destiny had ignited.

The screams from the spies tents had reinforced the business he'd become about. He'd stood just outside, listening to the men plead for mercy and shivered when their inquisitors somehow unleashed new heights of pain. He'd thought he'd like to hear them scream after what they'd done. They'd threatened his people … killed his friend. He wanted them to suffer. Wanted them to pay for what they'd done. But he didn't feel any comfort from it. Just numb horror.

Worst of all, Captain Alden hadn't stripped him of his rank for losing one of his team. Every one of the Second League soldiers were worth at least a dozen normal recruits, and the captain hadn't even batted an eye. He didn't even reprimand him.

Gabriel glanced to Cainan across the fire. Since the incident in the Peaks, he'd lost Lurin and Jae as companions. Whatever it was that kept those two loyal to his cousin was outweighed by how he'd behaved in the mountains. He sulked alone—almost as silent as Jae—speaking to no one if he could avoid it. Though it had been a priority for him, Gabriel didn't feel any satisfaction that he'd managed to gain the support of Cainan's friends. He had wanted to unify the Second League. He'd almost succeeded.

Gabriel stood when he saw a wagon round the Second League's camp. While the horses that pulled it didn't appear labored, the cart creaked, sharing its age. Gabriel approached the officer and soldier in the wagon.

“Are you in charge of this crew?” the officer asked as he hopped off the rear. “The Second League?”

“Yes, sir.”

The officer nodded before rounding the wagon and helping the other soldier unload two large, wooden crates of armor. When the crates were set in place, the man looked down to his list then back up to the Second League behind him. “Says here I’m supposed to be delivering ten sets of armor. There’s only nine of you. Is someone missing?”

“There were ten of us, sir,” Gabriel said. “Mel of North Hzorah was killed in the field.”

“The Crown increased armor production by a lot, but we’re still short. If there’s only nine of you …” The officer reached into the crate and lifted out a bundle of armor. Mel’s armor.

Gabriel waved off the request. “Of course. The extra set won’t do us any good here.”

The officer checked his list once more—making an adjustment to his tallies—before giving Gabriel a short nod then climbed back on the cart again to move on the next group of soldiers. Gabriel turned back to the Second League to see eager and curious expressions.

“I think we become warriors today,” he said.

Gabriel reached into crate and picked out the first set of leather armor. It was a dark stained, hardened and reinforced leather. Leather shin guards, pauldrons, gauntlets, and the other components of the armor were held together between breast and back plates and bound with twine. Adorned on the left breast was the Hzorah mark.

Gabriel tossed the armor to Fabi. He caught it and smiled. Gabriel picked out the next set and continued to pass the armor to all of the Second League. Spirited conversation and laughter broken out between them as they began unbinding the armor and trying it on.

The last set of armor was a bit different. Red trimmed the outer edges of the breastplate. The leather, fingerless gauntlets were also red. And, under the Hzorah mark was a round, metal insignia that officially denoted his rank.

Smiling, Gabriel slipped the armor over his head. The armor fit well. He slapped his chest with a fist to confirm the leather's defenses. The leather didn't give. It was strong and light—the ideal combination.

Gabriel watched his men as they chattered, happy that their spirits were lifted. But then his smile withered. *Mel should be here.* A hand touched his shoulder, and Gabriel looked to see Bear and Fabi beside him.

"I miss him, too," Bear said, and squeezed his shoulder in consolation.

Gabriel swallowed back the lump in his throat. "He should have lived to get his armor."

Cainan snorted.

Bear shot a glare to Cainan. "What's your problem?"

"The country boy was a waste of armor," Cainan said. "And a piss-poor swordsman."

"Better than I can say for your family," Fabi muttered.

Cainan stood. "You want to say that again?"

"Your whole family is a set of loogers," Fabi snarled.

"Because *your* family is the beacon example of character."

"We never let someone take a knife from our belt, I can say that much."

Cainan lunged at Fabi, but Gabriel was ready for it. He caught Cainan at his middle, stunting his advance and driving him backward out of the circle. Stumbling backward, Cainan fell and Gabriel with him.

Before Cainan could get back up, Gabriel pinned him. "Stop this!"

"You heard what he said about my family," Cainan's brow drew tight and his eyes caught fire. "What he said about your *mother* at that." Though his voice was low, it wasn't entirely discrete.

"I'll deal with him," Gabriel growled. "But I won't have you attacking one of your own. Is that what you want as part of your legacy? The man who couldn't take an insult and killed half his own army?"

"Get off me."

The two found their feet. A few of the others blocked Fabi from attacking while Aeron attempted to talk him down. The others on the sidelines watched Gabriel as if to see how he'd handle this.

"Desolate's Hand was with you," Cainan said, pointing a finger at Fabi. "If Sergeant Gabriel here hadn't been here to save you, you'd be a dead man."

"We're one unit," Gabriel said, glaring at his cousin. "Of one mind and purpose. Differences in class, wealth, or lifestyle don't matter here. We left those behind with those we love back home."

"You say that there's no rank between us, but there is." Cainan pointed to the insignia on Gabriel's breastplate. "We're not all equals here. No matter how much we wish it. Not here, and *certainly* not when this is all over."

Gabriel tapped the insignia on his chest. "This? This is what you want? This is what's causing the division between us?"

He pulled the dagger at his hip and carved the insignia out of the armor leaving a rough outline of where it'd been. Gabriel held the insignia high and turned to be sure they all saw it. Then, he tossed it into the fire.

"If a single piece of gold is what separates us," Gabriel said, "then I gladly give it up. We are *one*. That is the honor of a Hzorah soldier. A united stance is what will defeat the Dominion. If we allow ourselves to be divided, we will fail."

The Second League stood silent.

"I will stand with honor," Fabi said.

The Second League all repeated the pledge. Cainan turned away and stalked off.

"As you were," Gabriel said.

For a moment, he watched to the insignia burn in the flames before he turned way. He had to deal with Cainan's attitude before he destroyed the group. He wasn't sure how he'd bring him into line, but he had to find a way.

Gabriel sat on the only patch of grass that had escaped the daily traffic of the Second League during the Second League's relentless training. The hill overlooked the Hzorah army. Hundreds of campfires speckled the land as if in answer the twinkling signals of the stars above.

Even in the few moments since they received the armor, the sun had already nearly fallen beyond the horizon, and Cainan had slipped into the darkness between tents. He'd searched for his cousin half an hour before he'd given up. The Hzorah camp was a hoard of men. He could spend another half hour and find him, or he could search for ten more days and never catch wind of him. It wasn't worth it. He'd be back. And Gabriel would be waiting.

Gabriel breathed in the warm, night air. He still couldn't quite believe that he sat there, overlooking his army. The experience felt surreal. He'd imagined what this would be like over and over since he was a small child, and his daydreams hadn't touched the reality of it. But the feeling was shadowed by Mel's death.

A lone silhouette of a man climbed the hill. As he neared, Gabriel made out his sleek leather armor, a wooden crutch, and eventually his face—Fabi. He approached without a word and eased himself down next to Gabriel on the narrow patch.

"I didn't mean to dishonor your strength by stepping in again," Gabriel said, still staring at the encampment. "I hope you can forgive me."

"No," Fabi said. "You saved me from dishonor and probably a solid beating considering I barely made it up here on this leg. We can't afford division in our ranks. What's between me and the High Lord's son isn't important. Thank you for reminding me of what my duty is—why I came here to begin with."

"I'm truly proud of the Second League and how well we've learned to work together. The Dominion army will leave a trail of piss back into the wastelands."

Fabi chuckled. "Mel insisted that you weren't funny, but I think he just doesn't see your humor." He reached into his breastplate and pulled out a dark blue cloth and offered it to Gabriel. "Here."

"What is this?" Gabriel asked as it took it. It was hot.

"Open it."

Gabriel unwrapped the cloth. The golden glimmer of his rank's insignia dimly reflected starlight. Though mostly whole, its edges and surface were subtly distorted, but he could hardly see the flaws under the moonless sky.

"We fished it out," Fabi said.

Gabriel shook his head. "I don't want it anymore. Tomorrow, I'm going to Captain Alden and requesting he demote me. If Cainan having the position means we'll finally be united, then so be it."

"No," Fabi said. "You deserve the rank. It was unfair of Cainan to make you feel as if you didn't deserve it or that you having it somehow made you not one of us."

"I'm not sure I believe it, though. I haven't completely unified us. I almost got you killed climbing a cliff. And I already lost one of us before the war even started."

"They *like* you, Gabriel," Fabi said. "*I* like you. Cainan … well … he's an ass."

Gabriel laughed then, and Fabi joined in.

"For what it's worth," Fabi said. "Mel believed that Sergeant Gabriel is a leader worth dying for. And so do the rest of us."

Gabriel looked at Fabi. "You really believe that? Even if that means some of you might die?"

"Even then," Fabi said. "Dying was something we'd already accepted—even expected—when we came out here. But we didn't expect you. *You* made us into warriors. And *you* made us brothers. Cainan taking your place would break that."

A moment of silence passed between them.

"Come back down?" Fabi said. "I saved your rations. I haven't seen you eat the last few times. You need to stay in health."

"I'll be down in a moment."

"Good enough."

When Fabi was nearly back down the hill, Gabriel looked down at the insignia before he clutched it in a determined fist. He had chosen to lead. And now he must choose to follow through.

A few days later, Gabriel entered the tent to see Captain Alden tugging the laces tight on a saddle that sat draped over a wooden stand. He looked up to Gabriel when he stepped in and gave him a smile before circling around to him.

"Soldier."

"You sent for me, sir?"

Captain Alden nodded. "I did. Just one moment …"

The captain circled the mount, securing a few more items and tested the strengths of their bindings. After he was satisfied that they were secure, he lifted the saddle and tested its balance.

"Sir," Gabriel said. "You don't have someone to prepare your mount for you?"

Captain Alden set the saddle back in place. "I do, but I still prefer to prepare my own. Just because you're a leader, doesn't mean you can't get your hands dirty. General Rollins is ready to brief us on this week's battle."

This week? Was it time already?

Gabriel frowned. "Us?"

"I want you there, Sergeant, because you've been working with the Second League and know them better than I do now." Captain Alden clapped Gabriel on the shoulder. "I need to make sure you're on the same page as me."

The captain ducked out of his tent and ventured out into

the camp. Gabriel fell in line, knowing that the Captain Alden wouldn't turn back to see if he had followed.

The Crown's army had reached its full capacity. Gabriel wondered if there was one extraneous body back south that hadn't been rounded up and carted north. There would be a strain in the civilian population, but Gabriel was certain that the High Lords had found a way to restructure their own lands so that the pressure was tolerable, if only temporarily.

At least he hoped that's what they'd done.

Since he wasn't back home, there was no way that he could be certain that they'd taken all the proper measures needed to deal with the inevitable economic downturn. There would have to be a heavier intervention in free trade within the kingdom. They'd also likely need to borrow from Caldor under the terms of the Caldor Convention and install a plan to repay the debt they'd amount.

He smiled realizing that despite his best efforts, Samuel's tutelage had managed to slip through. *You've won this round, Samuel. I hope you're enduring court better than I did.*

In the distance, supply trains and what looked to be prisoners filed into Stronghold Aear. His father had told him that there were often an influx of prisoners during war times, either from suspicion of treason or desertion of the army. Another strain on the resources of the country.

It would be worth it in the end. Samuel had talked at length about the sacrifices they'd endured during the Dominion War, a war that now seemed to only have been in brief remission. But it would seem that the moral of all their trials is that freedom was worth the strain.

And freedom would be worth it again.

The guards stepped aside as Captain Alden lead Gabriel into the General's tent. Inside, Captain Vanik of the Third League stood with two other men, fully uniformed and bearing the rank of Captain stood with General Rollins.

The General nodded his acknowledgment of Captain Alden and then raised an eyebrow at Gabriel. "You have a recruit trailing you, Captain."

"Sergeant Gabriel is my right hand," Captain Alden said. "I need him here. Unless, of course, you find it objectionable—"

"I trust your judgement on this," the General said, looking down to the place where Gabriel's insignia had been gutted from the leather. "And even I can't ignore the stand-up job the Second League did with the spies. I haven't forgotten about that. You'll be rewarded for it."

Gabriel's stomach fluttered. Part of him wanted to admit that he'd not done a good job. That he'd endangered his crew and one of them died. The other part of him wanted to shrink back and hope that the General wouldn't notice his mistakes.

Captain Alden nodded to the other captains. "You've met Captain Vanik. This is Captain Savrin of the Fourth League, and Captain Krush of the Fifth League."

Captain Savrin smirked at Gabriel. "We've heard of your work."

Not too much of it, I hope, Gabriel thought.

"Speaking of which," General Rollins continued, "those spies were worth the effort it took to intercept them. It took prying, but we broke them." He stepped to the map on the center table and pointed along the Shadow Peaks where three small markers edged close to the peaks on the Dominion's side. "The Dominion army is positioned at three locations. Each of which holds roughly one-third of their troops. They've split their forces in order to maintain tighter control over so many soldiers."

"They plan to attempt encirclement? While crossing the peaks?" Captain Savrin asked. "How could they possibly expect such a feat with the mountains choking their efforts?"

"It's not for encirclement," Captain Alden said. "That would be a fool's strategy for them."

General Rollins nodded. "I agree. I believe it's purely logistical. With an army of their size, moving their troops into position to invade in one mass would mean half the army would still be on the move while the front lines begin a siege."

"What are their numbers, exactly?" Vanik asked.

"From what details we could extract from the spies," the general said,. "there are perhaps six or seven men to ten of ours."

"Splitting the troops into three won't completely solve their issues, but it'll help." Captain Alden pointed at the map. "What I find curious is the places they've chosen to make camp."

"It makes perfect sense," Captain Krush said. "There are valleys at each point."

Captain Vanik nodded. "Right. Going around the peaks is a far easier task than over. With an army, marching over the peaks is near impossible."

"But they still have a fundamental problem," Captain Alden said. "Split up as they are and unable to make significant use of their agility once they cross into our lands, they're setting themselves up to be crushed."

"Yes, and here," General Rollins said, again pointing at the map. "The passage is so narrow near the middle that they'll be slowed to a near trickle. Without spot on planning, they may not all arrive at the same time."

"Good," Savrin said. "They're rolling the dice. And the last thing we need is another extended war effort. The King is dead; his son's missing. If I ever get my hands on that boy ..."

Gabriel tried to keep his gaze focused on the map for fear that if he met Captain Savrin's gaze, he'd give himself up.

"What's worse," Captain Alden added, rubbing his chin, "is that they will need to capture two Strongholds to cripple our defenses."

"Exactly," Rollins said. "Stronghold Aear near the encampment and Stronghold Gordal further to the east. They have a shot at Aear, but if they split their forces again—another miracle act of coordination—we'll be hot on their heels to the Great Sea where they'll be crushed between the Gordal's walls and the pressure of our forces. We must assume that they'll be aiming for Aear. It's a much better target for them. One they actually have a true chance at."

"I wouldn't call it much of a chance," Captain Savrin said.

"Six men to ten? The veil of the Shadow Peaks dividing them into three?"

"There have been battles won with worse odds," Alden said. "We can't allow ourselves to become smug with confidence."

"We'll cut them down as they drip into the plain," Captain Vanik said. "Split our forces three ways and meet each army at the mouth of the valley. Six to ten and having them measured out to us, we'll eliminate them with ease."

"Won't work, sir," Gabriel said.

General Rollins and the Captains turned to Gabriel's interjection.

"Sergeant?" General Rollins frowned.

"Letting them trickle in," Gabriel said. "It won't work."

"Heel your soldier, Alden," Captain Krush snarled.

General Rollins held up a hand. "Let him speak."

Gabriel looked at each of the men in turn before continuing. Though speaking up about their plans might call to question his unassuming origins, he couldn't simply stay silent when there was so much at stake. "Well, it may work, but I wouldn't count on it. It seems to me that the best method is to fall back closer to Stronghold Aear and allow them out of the valleys as much as possible. This way—"

"Are you *insane?*" Vanik said, then looked at Captain Alden. "He's not serious, is he? Don't waste our time, boy."

"I'm not insane, I—"

"If we *allow* the Dominion *in*," the Third League captain said, "our difficulties are increased many fold. Keeping them in the valleys will allow us to control them."

"If you'd just listen," Gabriel said, then added, "sir, I could explain what I mean."

"Let him explain," Captain Alden said.

"The Dominion isn't completely daft," Gabriel said. "They won't allow you to simply siphon off their men. They'll pull back, luring us into the valleys where the odds are much more even. We may win this way still, but only because we hold the advantage of numbers. But it'll be a bloody effort, we'd lose many men, and that would be a tremendous tax on Hzorah, leaving us vulnerable after the war is won. The safer bet is to allow them onto the plain."

Nearly unanimously, the Captains opened their mouths to object, even Alden, but Gabriel continued before they slipped a word in. "Allowing them onto the plain will give us much more leverage to use our numbers against them. They will be split into three smaller forces. We will corral them together here." He pointed at a spot on the map. "Then, like at the walls of the stronghold, we crush them against the mountains, attacking from three sides instead of one narrow one."

General Rollins rubbed his chin. "I can see such a thing working. But where this may fall short is at the mountain walls. We'll have more leverage, but the numbers lost may not be significantly different."

"That's where we come in," Gabriel said, nodding to Captain Alden. "I've trained hard with the Second League. We'll be able to penetrate to the heart of the Dominion Army to axe its head—the commanders. Once we've taken the head, the rest of the army will fall into disarray. If we allow the commanders to remain in the valleys, it could take days before we reach them."

The captains looked at the general, as he rubbed his chin, considering how each scenario might play out.

"I like your thinking, Sergeant," General Rollins said. "When it's presented this way, it makes a lot of sense. What's more is that we can keep them from retreating on their terms—an advantage they'll want to hold considering the disadvantage in numbers."

"I like it." Captain Krush grinned. "I prefer to *crush* over chasing."

The other captains groaned.

General Rollins smiled. "Captain Alden, I don't know where you found this boy, but you may have struck gold."

Captain Alden placed a hand on Gabriel's shoulder. "His kind is scarce."

Gabriel felt a wave of relief followed by a cool air of joy when Captain Alden squeezed his shoulder.

"Alright," General Rollins said. "Let's see to it we drive these bastards back into the waste."

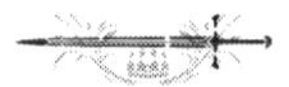

A heavy clank of iron pulled Tele from the brink of deep sleep. The door swung open and the stronghold's prison guard slipped into the dark cell. Tall and portly, he towered over his captives, blocking the only sure escape and, more importantly, the fresh air that the rancid, stone room needed.

To her left, the six men who shared the cell with her averted their eyes from the torchlight. Tele joined them. Within the dungeon depths, the light of a torch felt as luminescent as the sun itself.

Then, Tele allowed herself a small peak, hoping that she could catch a glimpse of hope. Perhaps Navid had come for her. Perhaps they'd come to move her to a cell by herself or one with Tal Aval. Perhaps they'd brought food.

Two other prison guards followed him in. They danced around shallow puddles of urine before stepping to the sides of the tall, dark guard who held the light. He appraised the lot of them, as if trying to decide which of them he thought would make the best questioning.

"Excuse me, sir," the short, frail man to her left said. He was near bald, with short white hairs warming his head just above the ears and forehead. "I believe you've made a mistake. I'm not supposed to be here, I—"

"Quiet, inmate," the torch-wielding guard said, cutting the man off. Then, he pointed to a man next to the short one. "Bring him."

The two guards bent down and uncuffed the man before pulling him to his feet. Stumbling, the man was half-led, half-dragged across the cell floor to the door. Once outside the cell, the tall guard, gave them another short look inside before turning and ducking out.

The thick door shut, the lock snapped into place, and Tele braced for the tightening.

Through two small holes to either side of the door—the only narrow windows to existence beyond—the guards pulled the chains that each captive was linked to. All together, they were forced tighter together so that the chains remained taut. Tele was forced from her own cold, damp, and soiled spot to the colder, damper, soiled spot of the man to her left. The chains rattled on the cell's exterior as the guards secured them in place. And then silence, save the gentle tapping of the chains as they swung, dragging along the stone floor.

The tightening gave new intensity to the rank odor of the cell. She wanted nothing more than to wash the short man's waste off of her—wash her own waste off of her. Tele swallowed the bile that rose to the back of her tongue. The only thing that kept her from completely losing her stomach was knowing that the stench would only intensify if she did.

Tele closed her eyes and imagined the smell of the Hzorah acrids in bloom. How wonderful it smelled when she'd first stepped out of the Gateway and into a world she'd never known before. A world that now literally dragged her through excrement. When that imagining failed her, she pivoted to the smells of the Kruv House, then to the Keeper's lab beneath the Sanctuary in Caldor.

Her wrists—cut open from the metal cuffs—stung as sweat salted the open wounds. Her neck ached from resting against a wall so uneven it couldn't possibly have been constructed by men with sight. But she didn't dare risk lying on the cell floor.

Worse was the darkness. It forced her to actively conjure imaginings so that her mind wouldn't conjure them for her. She knew far too well what terrors her mind would construct while she idled.

Though she couldn't see the men around her, she was acutely aware of the one-eyed man to her far left. He'd found little else to stay his attention for the duration of her captivity. Even now, in the darkness, Tele could *feel* his attention. The feeling wasn't something that she couldn't explain by any logical means. It was like expecting lightning to strike when your hair stands on end.

She gritted her teeth, trying to remember how awestruck she'd been when she'd seen the underwater world beneath Caldor—how it teamed with life and wonder. Her parents would have been so proud if they'd known that she would be the one to re-enter it after centuries of abandonment, proud that she'd brought back a Wizard.

Tele closed her eyes. *I have to survive this.*

She couldn't let this break her spirit, her will. She was still alive, and so long as she was alive, there was hope.

I have to believe that.

In the solitude of her mind, she opened to the first page of *Small Life.*

THIRTY-FOUR

A BETTER KING

Gabriel squinted against the late morning sun. The smell of wet grass and dirt and Hzorah acrids tickled his senses. He'd managed to round up several archers from Captain Savrin's Fourth League. He'd requested his best, but Savrin responded with a prompt "shove off." With Captain Alden's intervention, he'd managed to borrow ten average bowmen. Gabriel wanted more, but he got the sense that he was lucky to get even that many.

Lurin gave a short nod to the Fourth League archers. In unison, they nocked soft-tipped arrows and raised them. In the distance, the Second League responded by raising their shields. The archers let their arrows fly, and the Second League cut left to dodge the assault. Just as Gabriel had taught them, they maintained their forward momentum, and readjusted their charge to continue their onslaught.

Not one of them slipped on the wet grass. They were quick, accurate, graceful. Dangerous. Gabriel felt a tinge of pride. He couldn't believe these were *his* men. He couldn't even take credit for their ability. They'd done the work. He merely helped them fine tune their deficiencies.

The Dominion army was less than two days out according to Captain Alden's morning brief with him. This had been his last real chance to prepare them to take out the enemy commanders. He'd run the drills necessary for weeks, but the past couple days with the archers were the first time he'd given them a real dress rehearsal. It wouldn't properly compare to the reality, but he hoped it would be close enough that they wouldn't buckle under the pressure once they were really out there.

He clinched a fist as he watched his crew charge onward. *Less than two days. We'll be ready. We have to be.*

Gabriel stepped forward as the Second League neared and gave an approving nod to the archers. "Good work, gentlemen. I believe that'll be all for today. I appreciate your help. Dismissed."

The Fourth League archers dissipated, trotting down the field to retrieve the arrows before returning to their camp. Lurin joined the Second League as they formed in a tidy line before him. Though winded, they stood erect and proud, eyes focused on their Gabriel and attentive to his every word.

Gabriel paced before them a moment before stopping and appraising his men. "I wish I had the right words to express how proud I am of you. When you were selected to become part of the Second League, you'd already proven yourselves to be among the very best new recruits Hzorah had to offer its people. Over the past several weeks, you've transformed. You're not only among the very best. You *are* the very best. You work together like a creature of one mind. You react then counteract with the instincts of soldiers twice your age.

"I don't say this to decorate your accomplishments; I say it because you need to understand the kind of honor expected of such high achievement. There is nothing that will stop us from cutting off the Dominion's head—nothing. There is no anger, no anxiety, no fear. All of these emotions will only serve to distract you, they will keep you from achieving your true potential, from fulfilling your duty, from living and dying with honor."

He paused, taking in their calm composure. "In a few hours, the Dominion will be upon us. There is no more training that I can do to prepare you. From now until we stand at Desolate's door, we must now prepare our minds. We must make peace with our destiny. For fate is an ocean stronger than any man. We must meet it and accept it if we are to become the men we are meant to be." He gave them a muted smile. "Dismissed."

Gabriel watched as the Second League left for midday rations before turning and heading back to the camp alone. When he arrived at camp, he set to securing and checking his equipment. He re-laced his boots and shin guards, reset the angle of his pauldrons, and adjusted the boldric that held his sword and dagger. He then placed it all in a neat pile next to his sleep pallet.

He reached for his sack and pulled out the Crown Sabre. His gaze and fingers caressed the red and silver sheath, wandering down to the blades hilt. Gabriel knew that the coming battle may be the only opportunity he'd have to use his father's sword. He'd carry it into battle and slay Dominion's commanding officers. It's why he'd come out here. His honor demanded it. And it was the only fitting use for a blade of its kind.

Help me bring honor to your name, Father, Gabriel thought as he gripped the Sabre's hilt.

And there he was, standing on the North Hzorah Plain, his father just beside him, contemplating to the mountains beyond. His father had asked him to join him out here on the plains, and Gabriel had hoped that his father would share war stories with him. Instead they stood out here alone and silent for what felt like hours.

"Do you miss it, Father?" Gabriel asked, breaking the hush. "The challenge, the rush, the freedom?"

When his father didn't answer, Gabriel looked at him. King Jeremiah gazed across the plain and to the Shadow Peaks beyond as he hadn't heard him.

"No," his father said. "I miss your mother."

Gabriel looked to his feet. "Is it true what they say? What Samuel told me about that last battle? That you turned away from the final charge and came back home before the battle ended with the final charge north?"

"Yes."

He hadn't believed it when Samuel had told him this during his history lessons. It wasn't uncommon that rumors about what his father had done was blemished by inaccuracies. Some made his father seem superhuman. Others were clearly told to discredit his father. Gabriel had always hoped that this one was the latter. How would Samuel know something like that anyway?

But he always trusted his father to tell it to him straight. Some of the feats were true, as well as some of his failings. But King Jeremiah always owned up to them.

Even this.

"But why?" Gabriel asked. "You must have known that the Ehrel tribe would have considered that a forfeit of the Crown. Those are the codes they live and breathe."

"When you duel, do you continue to climb the tree of cadences when it is clear that following the standard structure will gain you nothing?"

"No, but—"

"Son, there are times when you follow the rules and take the well-trodden route because it's the right thing to do. It's well-trodden for a reason. Law and code are how we keep peace in our land. They provide justice and peace. They're a means to forge trust across the land where otherwise it would fall to anarchy. When a people have a common identity through these codes, they can come together and forge a new identity.

"But then there are times when you must follow your heart, your instincts. Because sometimes the traditions we hold dear will fail us. In fact, they are sure to fail us at some point or another. And when they do, you will only have the true source of your actions—your honor. That's what it means to be a Hzorah warrior: to live and die with honor."

"Sergeant."

Gabriel stuffed the sword back into his sack before standing to meet the messenger behind him. "Yes?"

"You're needed in the command tents," the man said, then slipped out of the tent.

Taking a moment to ensure everything was in its place, Gabriel arranged his belongings in the most efficient picking order he could think of in case of a midnight raid. Satisfied with his preparations, he ventured out into the camp.

Gabriel marched straight for the command tents, and the savory smells of evening rations made him wish that he'd taken the time to eat. A quick glance to the soldiers about the camp told him that General Rollins thought it might be best for morale if their last few meals were good ones. The smell of sweet and spicy sauce poured over rice and a north melon warmed him, reminding him of the comforts of home. It was possibly the most decadent meal a soldier could expect on the battlefield. How the cooks managed to serve so many this kind of dish was perplexing. It was wildly impractical considering their priorities, but sometimes certain impracticalities were a means to a greater end.

All of the guards in front of the command tents were unfamiliar, yet they stepped aside when he approached. *Odd.* Perhaps they'd known he was coming or what he looked like.

Gabriel ducked under the tent and froze.

High Lord Bendeth stood alone behind General Rollins' map table, hands clasped behind his back.

"Ah, Gabriel," he said. "Please, come in."

Gabriel didn't move. "What are you doing here?"

Bendeth's eyebrows rose. "I'm here to oversee the war like a king should."

"*You're* not king."

"Yet."

A challenge? Gabriel's hand instinctively felt for his sword, but he'd left it behind. *Scorch it.* Cainan had promised him that he wouldn't cluck. And yet, here his uncle was, waiting for him, expecting him. *I should have never trusted him.*

Bendeth glanced down, taking note of Gabriel's hand, then smiled as if unconcerned. "Your time of playing soldier is over, boy. I'm taking you back home. There, you'll answer to your crimes, bend the knee, and submit the kingdom to my hand. And maybe, if I'm feeling generous, I'll let you live. You are family, after all."

"Crimes?" Gabriel grimaced. "I've committed no crimes."

"Abandoning the throne? Circumventing the council of High Lords to take matters into your own hands?" Bendeth circled the table. "You idealists are all alike. Your father got away with it; his father got away with it. But I'm putting a stop to it. Someone has to."

"My father—"

"Your father was a *traitor*," Bendeth's eyes flamed. "He left his Generals to fend for himself—left me to do the work he should have done. *I* should have been king. The epics never tell of how House Bendeth led the final charge. It's always Jeremiah. But your father was a coward, a traitor. And then he robbed me of my right to the throne." Bendeth stepped closer to Gabriel. "Never again. Guards!"

Several soldiers spilled into the tent.

"This soldier is to be placed under arrest for treason."

Gabriel tried to run for the tent's opening, but the guards caught him in short order. He struggled against their grip and earned himself a blow to the gut before they forced him to the ground. One soldier pressed a knee to his backbone while another wrenched his hands behind his back.

Gabriel grunted against the pain but managed to lift his head enough to see Bendeth's boots. "You won't get away with this."

It was a desperate reaction. As if stating that would change his uncle's mind. He let his head drop to the ground and struggled to breathe under the weight of the guards.

"I won't get away with it?" Bendeth squatted. "No one in the camp knows who you really are. Be honest with me, Gabriel. Deep down, you know that I'm right. You know that you weren't right for the throne." Bendeth grabbed him by the hair forcing him to look into his eyes. "You've always known it, no?"

Gabriel wanted to meet his eyes and tell him that he was wrong, but he couldn't. Gabriel only knew how to fight. He would be a terrible king. He didn't deserve the throne. He'd always known that. That's why he'd ran away in the first place.

And yet, now that it really came to it, he found that he suddenly cared who held the Crown. Maybe he wasn't the right person to be king, but it certainly wasn't High Lord Bendeth.

Bendeth let go of his head and stood, smoothing the wrinkles from his uniform. "It's time for new leadership in Hzorah. And if you care about your people, you'll know that you're not fit for the job. Hzorah deserves a better king." He strode back to the table. "Take him to my tent. Keep him restrained. I want guards posted. No one goes in or out with their head on their shoulders."

The guards lifted Gabriel and dragged him out of the tent.

Tele coughed and spit, trying to force herself to finish vomiting so that the dry-heaving would stop. The stinging taste of bile coated her tongue and teeth. The layered smells of acid clung to her hair and induced another vicious cycle of retching.

Breathe through your mouth, she encouraged herself, Gib's voice taking the place of her own thoughts. *If you keep vomiting, you'll dehydrate.*

She could hear her brother's voice as if she stood next to him. She felt ashamed that she'd allowed herself to get caught. If he or Simon were to see her like this ...

Though her eyes burned from the fumes of the chamber, Tele managed to control her breathing and restrain her gag reflex. She shut her eyes to mitigate the pain, and again tried to conjure images of joy.

Dust tumbling over dunes set beneath stark blue skies. The cool, refreshing taste of water under the shade of her tents. Her mother reading from her journals and explaining the healing properties of various plants from far-away lands.

She managed to smile when remembering her mother. She, like her father, protected the Covenant, and her interests lie in medicines. Her father's work had mostly come to an end once they had gone into hiding. Tele's mother's work expanded. When her brothers entered a city or town to find what goods they might be able to steal, Abigail Gavina always had a list of items she wanted to experiment with; new plants and potions that she wanted to test.

Tele's interests were more to her father's work, but she found that there was much crossover between the two. They both studied life and what affects conditioning had. Tele often wondered if they had fallen in love because of their mutual interest in the study of life. When she had asked them, they only smiled, meeting each other's eyes lovingly. Her mother's response still resonated with her: "Our interests may have sparked the fire, but love crosses all barriers. Sees no faults. Where there may be an ocean of difference between two souls, love is big enough to fill that gap and bind one heart to another."

Tele thought of Navid. She'd come to understand how much Navid had done for her, how he'd helped her piece together the Tal language as she struggled to learn before they'd met Tal Aval. How he'd helped her achieve everything she and her family dreamed of, then she'd pushed him away out of fear. Navid had bridged the gap between them. Tele had refused to cross it. He kept trying for her, despite his fears.

If my brothers hadn't been so patient with me, I would have never survived. I could have been more patient. I could have been more understanding and considered the circumstances and pain he carried. Instead I was cold. He didn't fail me. I failed him.

The cell door opened.

A moan accompanied her recoil from the prison guard torchlight, and, with the same silent musing, the guard looked at the five of them as if considering which pastry contained the most fruit. This time, the man to her left didn't request his freedom.

After a short moment, the torch-wielding guard inclined his head. "That one."

Again, the two accompanying guards uncuffed and ushered the man out of the cell. Tele turned to see the missing slot. They'd picked the man from the center again, this time—by convention of the chains that ran between them and out the two small holes—rebalancing the difference between the two halves of the cell.

This was either by coincidence or design. The latter appeared more likely as it was far easier to keep the chains tight when you merely have to pull from the center like laces. The considering and suspense put on by the guard was just a fun game played—a cruel game.

It also meant that Tele would be nearly the last one to be questioned, second to last, in fact. How long had it been since the guards had last pulled a prisoner? Five, perhaps six hours? There was little in the dark dungeon that gave her a measure of time. Her review of the Keeper's work was the best metric she had, and that was imprecise at best, perhaps completely useless. When she was in the state of mind that allowed her to reassemble what she'd committed to memory, the world seemed to fall away, leaving only absolute focus on the work at hand.

The guard turned and stepped out of the cell. Before he shut the door, before he could order the guards to pull the chains, Tele leaned forward, to see who had the unfortunate fate of being the last out of the prison.

At the left end of the cell, Tele met the single left eye of the man from the cart before the door shut and cast them into darkness.

Amie slipped on a rock that broke away from the steep incline. She yelped as she fell, entirely certain that she'd tumble back and fall into Desolate's grip. Instead she fell into someone else's.

"Easy," Owen said, holding her upright. "Step there. That's right."

She leaned into the climb again, tentatively placing her foot where Owen suggested and was rewarded with a firm foothold.

"Thanks," she whispered.

Owen didn't reply.

The horse pulling the cart seemed to struggle at least as much as she did. She glanced at it as it struggled up the hill, the stallion's eyes fearing what faltering would mean.

You can do it, she silently encouraged. *We both can do it.*

They'd taken a wide berth around the North Hzorah Plains and into the Shadow Peaks to avoid getting caught by any Hzorah troops in the area. And though they weren't exactly summiting a mountain, the Shadow Peaks proved to be a beastly traversal nonetheless. Amie had thought that her body couldn't ache any more than it did back on relatively flat land. She should have savored it. It was all she could do to keep from crying.

"Whoa, now. Ho!" Scar Face shouted as the horse stumbled, shifting sideways.

"'Let's take the short way,'" Sir Lanky mocked. "'I can get us there.'"

Scar Face didn't dignify the soldier with a response. Ale Breath chuckled as he shielded his eyes from the dirt kicked up by the horse and cart.

"We should have taken the safe way in," Sir Lanky said. "We'll probably take just as long to get there this way. You're gonna wear out the horse."

Scar Face continued to ignore Sir Lanky's taunts, and when they reached the plateau, he turned to him and spread his arms as if to say: "I told you so." Sir Lanky quietly scoffed but didn't complain further.

The cart bumped along, juggling its prisoner. Amie hoped that her sister was alright. And though she envied her for not having to hike the mountains, she knew that her confinement was a torture in its own rite.

Scar Face had informed them they were perhaps only a day away from the camp now, and if they pushed hard through the mountains, they'd reach the Dominion forces in time for tomorrow's evening rations. It seemed a call to haste meant to inspire Sir Lanky and Ale Breath to not request a mid-day break. But for Amie, it was a declaration of just how soon she'd meet her fate, and she was nearly sick with fear.

A sharp crack from the cart pulled her from her thoughts. Sir Lanky and Ale Breath shouted. Scar Face took hold of the horse. The whole cart began to tip.

Ale Breath and Sir Lanky ran to the cart's rescue but backed away. Any attempt to stop the tipping would result in them being crushed in the act. Scar Face cursed as he tried in vain to save the horse from falling, but instead fell with it.

Ale Breath ran to Scar Face's side. Lieutenant Owen and Sir Lanky went for the cart.

Amie stood in mute horror.

Run, she told herself. *Run right now while you can.* They might not notice her gone for a few moments, giving her a decent enough head start to truly get away. They might not even bother to chase her. They might have bigger problems than one girl on the run who'd likely get lost and die anyway.

And they'd be right. She *would* get lost and die. Amie had no idea where she was going. And even if she somehow survived, what good would it be if she still lost Mara? She couldn't live with herself if she just abandoned her.

Another part of her still urged all the same. *Run. Go now!*

Owen turned to her and caught her eye before gesturing to Sir Lanky. "Bring the girl over here."

The soldier marched over and grabbed her by the arm, pulling her from where she'd taken root. She stumbled over numb feet until Sir Lanky forced her down beside the cart. Amie peered into the sideways cage. Inside, Mara struggled to arrange herself into a comfortable position. She was bleeding from her head. That was never a good sign.

"Are you alright?" Amie asked.

"I'm fine," Mara answered without looking up. "Just a little lightheaded."

Fear clutched at Amie's heart. She didn't know what to do. She felt so powerless, so weak.

"The scorching shaft broke," Sir Lanky said. He stood from where he was inspecting the cart and turned to Lieutenant Owen. "What are we supposed to do now?"

"We can fix it if we can get some wood," Ale Breath said.

“Have you ever repaired anything before?” Lanky asked. “Even once?”

Ale Breath stammered. “Well, no …”

“What are we supposed to use to cut the wood just right?” Sir Lanky demanded. “How are we to bind the parts together?”

Ale Breath shrugged. “We have rope.”

“I say we just walk the rest of the way,” Sir Lanky said. “Take the other sitter out and walk them both back to camp. Leave the carriage here.”

“It’s already risky enough that we walked one of them all this way,” Scar Face said. “She’s slowed us down considerably, and the one inside hasn’t walked in so long, I’m not sure she’d be able to. And if she can, it’s much harder to chase down two girls than one.” He knelt down, looking inside the cage. “And she’s bleeding bloody everywhere. Who’s going to carry her?”

“We send for help,” Owen said, cutting off Sir Lanky before he could retort. “But first, let’s get this cart upright.”

“Wisdoms,” Mara growled. She looked at her hand to see it covered in blood before pressing it against the wound again.

“Can you go slow?” Amie asked Owen. “My sister—”

“We can *only* go slow,” Owen said, nodding to the other men.

Scar Face disconnected the cart from the horse and took the stallion’s reins as it found its feet. The animal stumbled, shying away from a leg. Scar Face urged the horse on, but he was clearly in too much pain to move much more.

“Stop it!” Amie cried out. “Can’t you see he’s hurt?”

Scar Face glared at her, but at least he stopped. He let the horse be and joined the other three around the Mara’s cage. Together the soldiers took to righting the carriage.

As they began lifting it, a glint of silver caught Amie’s eye.

A dagger.

There was a dagger lying in the dirt just behind Ale Face’s heels less than two paces away. None of the soldiers had seen it yet. It probably fell from the carriage’s trunk when it tipped over.

A dagger could cut her ropes. A dagger could be used to pick the lock that jailed Mara. A dagger could be used to defend herself if she was caught. And they'd never see it coming.

Faster than she'd ever remembered moving before, she fell to her side, snatched the weapon and stuffed it under her night shift. There was nothing that would hold it in place, so she pressed it between her legs, hoping she'd be able to hold it there without it falling. Masked by the sound of the creaking carriage, grunts of effort, and the soldier's own focused lifting, none of them noticed what she'd done.

She had a weapon now.

She had a chance.

The carriage tipped upright with more force than Amie thought necessary, but at least they'd moved slowly, allowing Mara to ease back into place. Detached from the horse, the cart leaned at a hard angle, but it was stable.

"Please," Amie said. "She's hurt."

Owen nodded to Ale Breath who set about finding a bandage for her sister's wound. "How far are we from camp?"

Scar Face shrugged. "I'd say about eighteen hours on foot. Maybe twelve if I ride."

"I don't think you can ride the horse," Sir Lanky said. He leaned over to look at the stallion's leg. "I don't think it's broken, but she'll need rest."

"He," Amie said.

"What?"

"You two," Owen pointed at Sir Lanky and Ale Breath. "Get ready. You two will go to camp and bring back a few soldiers and a new cart for the prisoners."

The two nodded. Sir Lanky began gathering travel supplies, and Ale Breath opened the carriage and began binding Mara's head wound. Owen circled the cart and looked inside to check on his captive. Satisfied that she was alive, he turned away.

"Are you really going to send *those* two?" Amie asked, her voice low.

Owen turned back. "What?"

"Those two," she said. "The frail one and the one who can't go an hour without a shot of ale. They're sure to get lost. I don't want my last days to be out here in the dark forest, alone and starving. Do you?"

Amie held his gaze, hoping he believed her. After considering a moment, Owen walked back around the cart.

"Landon, you go with the Sergeant Dalick," Lieutenant Owen said. "Farrow, you're staying with me."

So much for not learning their names, Amie thought. Now she'd be forced to see them as a bit more human, and that wasn't particularly useful for her right now.

Amie sat quietly as the Owen made camp, and Sergeant Da—

No. They don't get proper names. They're horrible. Proper names are for good people.

Scar Face and Sir Lanky set off after preparing their packs. They'd have a good four hours of travel before it got too late to continue. Though she wasn't sure if they'd bother to stop at this point.

Once they returned with even more soldiers, it'd be next to impossible to escape. Their fate would be sealed. That meant Amie had to find her opening within the next few hours. If she didn't …

She caught Mara's eyes, and knew that she was thinking the same thing. Amie had never seen her sister cry. Not once. But she could have sworn she saw a tear escape her eye before she turned away.

"Looks like it's me and you," Ale Breath said after he'd tired her arms and legs. He plopped down beside the campfire, pulled out his ale, and swigged.

Her back against the cart, Amie pulled her knees close and wrapped her arms around her knees, the dagger pressed firmly between her thighs.

THIRTY-FIVE

TRUDGING THROUGH MISERY AND DESPAIR

Fabi shut his eyes as a gust of wind pushed waves of smoke over him. While the camp's ambient noise was ever-present, the Second League sat in numb silence, watching the flames consume its kindling.

It'd taken him weeks to learn to sleep with the new assortment of sounds in the camp, but, eventually, they'd become like the sounds of the night—the buzz of spring's dkricas was like the chatter of men, and the chirps of forest frogs was the shuffling of equipment, replacing the sounds he'd known since childhood.

As the wind died down, he opened his eyes again to see Bear poking at the fire with a stick. Urwell and Paitin sat together but were uncharacteristically quiet, refraining even from speaking alone in Armothean. Lurin sat in somber contemplation with Jae, who was quiet as ever. That, at least, was a bit of normalcy.

Only a few hours back, High Lord Bendeth had paid them a visit. He'd told them that Gabriel had been arrested for treason and promoted Cainan to Sergeant. The bastard and his son left together to "inspect the troops."

Fabi wasn't willing to believe that Gabriel had betrayed them. He was honorable, probably the best man he'd ever met.

His own father certainly wasn't a shining example of character, but everyone he'd encountered who'd found out what kind of family he'd come from had treated him like dirt. But not Gabriel. Gabriel had given him a chance, fought for it even. He only wished he could be that kind of man someday.

It was painfully clear that Cainan had asked his father to remove Gabriel after their scuffle. And it wasn't at all lost on him that if he'd held his tongue, maybe Gabriel would still be here. He wished he could do something to fix this injustice.

But he was just a soldier and a thief. No one would listen to him over a High Lord.

Aeron pulled an aleskin from his pack. "A parting gift from my father." He unstopped the aleskin, downed two swift gulps, then squinted. "Like bottled lightning."

"Is that a good thing?" Fabi asked, then beckoned for it. "Never mind that. I'd prefer to check for myself."

Aeron tossed the aleskin to the him. "My father makes his own. Cheaper than getting over-priced imports."

Fabi took a drink. It wasn't the strongest he'd had, but it did have a kick.

Good. We need it.

"Not bad," Fabi said, then tossed it to Bear.

The circle fell silent again.

Mel's absence was never so acutely apparent. The northerner could make him feel light of heart no matter how much he fought it. Fabi wished he had that kind of inner joy. If not that, he wished he had whatever spark it was that gave other men the ability to light a flame in the hearts of the downtrodden.

Fabi wanted to stand up and say that he didn't believe the High Lord, and Gabriel wouldn't sell them out. He wanted to assure them that it was all some misunderstanding. He wanted to tell them not to give up hope, that even in the darkest of times, there is always hope. But he didn't know how. Those words never came out the way he wanted.

And so he drank. His brothers in arms drank. And the night wore on, trudging through misery and despair.

He didn't know how long he sat there before courage came or how much he drank before the light of hope burst forth. Piercing heartache and extinguishing fear, Jae's ethereal song took hold of his heart.

All along the cobbled path
Stained with blood and sweat and pain
Sorrow song of bottled wrath
Washed away by cleansing rain

Dust and grime and flea alike
Crusted on the saddle skirt
Rider comes and tack does strike
To brush away and free the dirt

Hot of head and thick of tongue
Child lay sick and spelled with pox
Herb of red breathe into lung
Fever breaks and blood detox

Father slain and Mother struck
Stripped of poise, a fallen house
Spark to brush to burning luck
Again, the rain, the fire doused

Drink to dander, drink to pain
Drink to slander, drink to strain
For when chaos dares threaten flame
Know that soon then comes the rain

Tele pulled herself from sleep at the sound of muted footsteps. With an elbow, she lifted her sagging weight from its slow descent into the impurities of the stone floor. The door unlocked, and the prison guard stepped in, his torch illuminating the dank cell.

"Him," the man said, picking from the middle again.

The two accompanying guards leaned down to unshackle the small, thin man that sat next to her.

"Thank you, kind sirs," the man croaked, his feet clearing the ground as the men carried him by the shoulders. "Thank you."

The guards maneuvered the man out into the halls, turned right, and disappeared. The torch-wielding guard followed them out and shut the door behind them. Darkness blanketed the room along with a brief moment of silence.

Then the sound of cold metal against aging rock as the shackles were again tightened, pulling the three prisoners into a tight knot. The frail man had left Tele another fresh batch of unpleasantries. Tele shivered as she slipped into the waste, her damp clothes absorbing the stale liquid.

The bile came, but she swallowed it back. The last thing she needed was to start the chain of vomiting again. She couldn't afford dehydrating. She had to keep some air of strength about her.

Desperate to pull her mind away from how the scent made her feel, she slipped into the pages of *Element and Reaction*, trading her disgust for the comfort and neutrality of the analytical.

Vomit: composed primarily of food and water … that's not so bad … acids, bile, small life …

How long had it been since she'd entered the cell? How long since she'd eaten? She was dreadfully thirsty.

Stool: composed primarily of water, with appreciable concentrations of small life, fat, cholesterol …

Questions seethed about her mind, prying into her focus. Where was Tal Aval? Was he alright? Had he been pulled and interrogated? Had they freed him? Or had they sentenced him to some terrible fate? He had an impressive grasp of the common tongue of Hzorah, but there were times when things Tele said was lost on him.

No! Focus!

Urine: composed of primarily water, with appreciable concentrations of urea, sodium, sulfate, ammonia …

And Navid … her throat locked with pain when she thought of him. He was vulnerable, alone. What if he got hurt? She should have been with him. They should have all stayed together. If they had, she and Tal Aval wouldn't have been at the inn when the soldiers came. Or, if they were, they would have had Navid and his pass.

"Pretty girl …"

Tele started at the whispered voice, his tongue letting the last sound of the phrase linger in the cell's gloom.

"Pretty girl …" the voice said again then softly cackled.

Left-eye had given a voice to his advances. Tele twisted in her shackles, readying herself for an attack. But Left-eye was cuffed and another man sat between them. She was safe. He couldn't reach out to her. At least for now.

"Pretty girl …"

Fabi took a deep breath of the North Hzorah plain air. Grass, pollen, dirt, sweat, leather, steel—they all congealed into a thick musk of agitated, sun-baked anticipation. The sun had nearly reached its apex, triumphant in its defeat of the darkness, cutting through the tumble of tall clouds that remained to threaten its preeminence.

Fabi worked his fist around the hilt of his sword before turning to see the Second League in wait just behind him. He wanted to say something to encourage his team—give some sort of speech. That's what Gabriel would do, wouldn't he?

Scorch it. Where was Gabriel? Was he really gone for good? He'd thought that as long as Gabriel was leading them, they might have a shot. Instead, they were alone with the High Lord shoveboy.

Aeron nodded to Fabi, a gesture that was both reassuring and affirmed his understanding of the maddening silence. Not the stark silence of an empty plain—it was impossible to have so many men together without there being any noise at all—but a silence that cut through the ambient noise, and the low tremble of Dominion troops in the valley's shadows beyond.

It was fear at its highest potential, awaiting galvanization.

To the far left, a rider galloped across the army's front line. "Ready arms!" the man cried as he crossed them. There was a unified shuffling at the final warning of the Dominion's approach. Though Fabi was sure that he was as prepared as he could be, he took stock of his weapons. The sword at his hip, the dagger at the opposite side, the small shield across his back, completing the circle. In the face of an impending hoard, he felt stripped down like a naked toddler, defenseless despite his armaments.

Scorch it, Gabriel. He'd let the bastard make him feel confident. He'd come into this prepared accept his fate—prepared to walk through Desolate's door. Instead, Gabriel fed them hope and he'd eaten it greedily. He'd known better than to dream, and now …

Ahead, a soft murmur passed through the ranks. Soft as each individual soldier was, it rumbled, like the sound of the Great Sea crashing against the shore. Then there was pointing.

Fabi craned to see the mountain line before them. Like a slow leak of molten glass, the Deserans spilled onto the plain. Further down, the Dominion filed into the plain from another point, and, further beyond, yet another. Somehow, they'd timed their journey through the mountains with sophisticated precision.

Unsettled, their troops' grew louder. Urgent chatter between small groups of soldiers who had banded together over their time on the plain meshed over the lone weeping of soldiers who had finally crossed from courage to crushing panic. This wasn't the part the epics of ages past ever spoke of. They were all just men—men whose time had come.

Captain Alden, atop his war horse, trotted through the ranks. In his right hand, he carried a long pole flying a red banner branded with the Hzorah Crest that tossed with the rising breeze. In his other hand, a small brass horn. The troops split as he passed to the front line and crossed several spans in front of the Hzorah defenses. With a firm stab, he rooted the banner in place, marking their final stand.

Across the length of the troops, several other riders placed banners. Then, Captain Alden raised the horn to his lips and trumpeted a loud, high call to battle. The other Captain's joined the call, and the Hzorah army advanced.

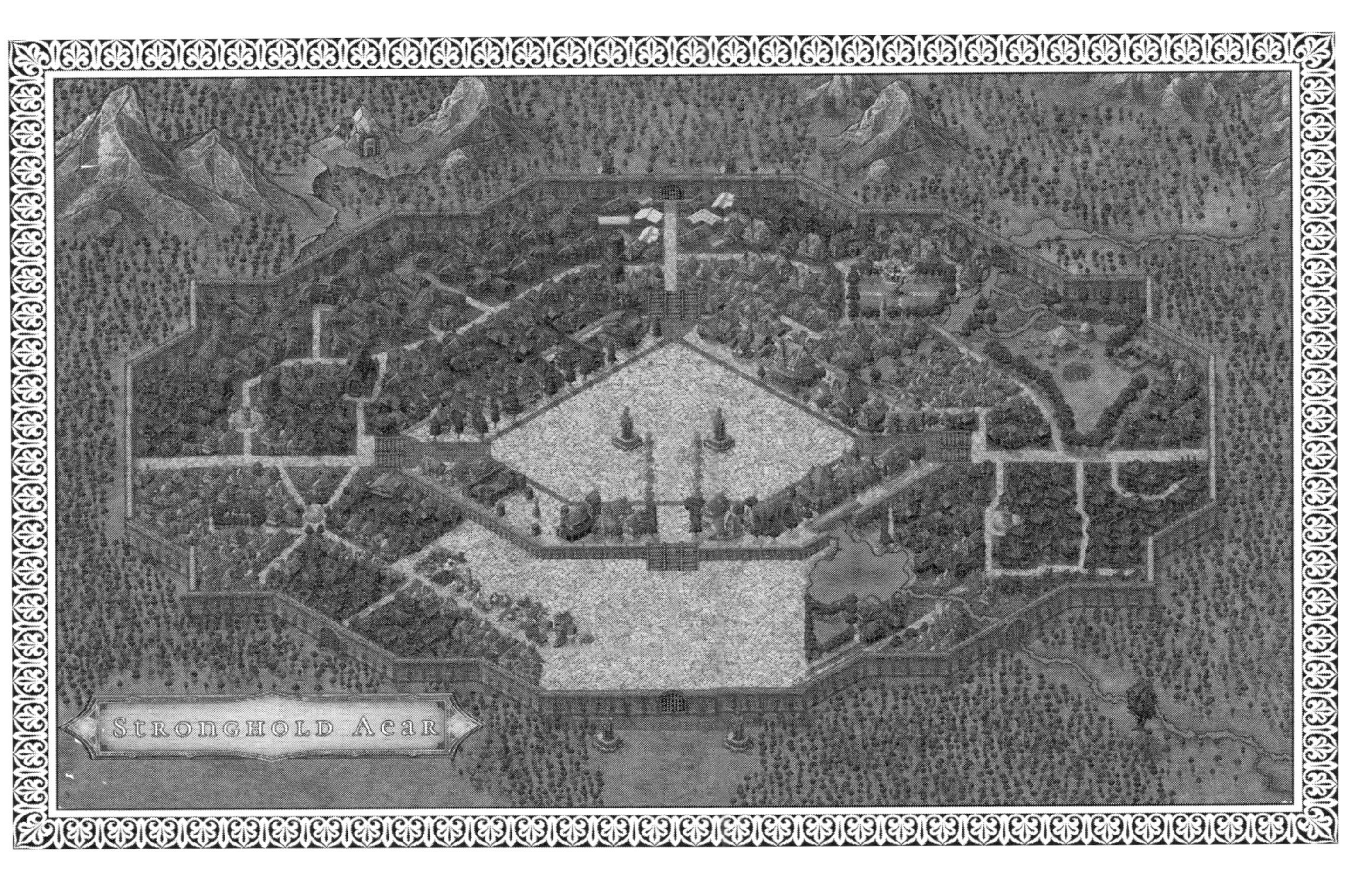
Stronghold Aear

The Fifth Movement

THIRTY-SIX

DEATH'S SHOWER

Cainan whistled, and the Second League cut right, slipping past a small band of Deseran soldiers who charged them. Another whistle, and they pulled back on course and into a measured trot toward the heart of the Dominion army.

At first, when the front lines of each standing army clashed, both the Hzorah and Deseran troops were locked tight, pushing the Dominion army back against the mountain wall. But, as strict coordination degenerated into chaos, the front lines loosened, breaking into smaller patches of battle. While far from graceful, this is where the Second League's core strategy became key.

His breath heavy but even, Cainan pushed the Second League as hard as he could. There wasn't a morsel of himself that would accept defeat—not one scorching sliver of his soul. He wouldn't fail his father. He wouldn't fail his kingdom.

A fist of arrows took flight from behind a group of pikemen that inched across the plain. Cainan whistled again, pulling the Second league out of death's shower. The arrows fell within an arm's reach of them.

"Shields up!" Cainan shouted.

Without missing a step, the Second League raised their shields, shading them from the heavens. The Deseran archers released another burst of arrows, and they responded again with a change in heading. By Desolate's Hand, the arrows missed their targets, and, in swift retaliation, Lurin launched five arrows of his own. Not one failed to kill.

Even in the heat of battle, Cainan couldn't help but let a smile edge onto his face. The weeks of training had clearly earned them a small but razor-sharp regiment.

It's a shame what we had to do with you, Gabriel, Cainan thought.

Though Cainan knew that he was the best leader for the team, he couldn't deny that Gabriel had shaped the Second League into something to be proud of.

You at least did that right, cousin.

Instead of charging forward again, Cainan allowed the wedge to continue sideways. Their charge found them climbing a large, slow-pitching hill. Cainan whistled them to a halt, just as they crested the hilltop. Due to the sheer size of the North Hzorah Plains, the battle had sprawled as each army attacked then relented to an unclaimed foothold. A higher vantage point had become necessary to plot their next trajectory.

Ahead, the Dominion continued to spill onto the plain, their numbers multiplying steadily as the Hzorah troops cut them down. They were staying ahead of the Dominion—a good measure ahead. And, as long as the Hzorah army held their stamina, they would crush them.

Hope swelled within his chest. He would finally receive his birthright, and the dignity of the Ehrel tribe—and rule of law—would finally be restored. Too long had Jeremiah bowed to the sovereignty of Caldor while Ghaya and Armoth took advantage of his naivety. This was the first day of Hzorah's—no, the Kingdom of Ehre's prominence.

Following the brunt of the Dominion's army, several men sat atop large, brown beasts with white horns that protruded aggressively from under a long, mouth-like appendage. *Elephants*. Behind the beasts were the large war tents, still erect, carried on the shoulders of Dominion troops. They stopped, set down the tents and began anchoring them in place.

"Bold bastards," Fabi said. "You'd think they'd keep camp within the safety of the narrow valleys."

"They would have if we'd allowed them to hide inside," Aeron said. "Now that they're out of the valleys, they're forced to face us head on. Just where we want them."

"What are they?" Fabi asked. "Those creatures?"

"Elephants," Cainan said.

"How'd they tame such a beast?"

"So, how are we doing this?" Aeron interrupted.

"Those elephants are armed to the tusks," Paitin said. "I'd like to avoid them if we can."

"I don't think we'll have much of a choice," Aeron said. "They're hanging back near the tents."

"Where the officers are," Fabi finished.

Aeron nodded. "Exactly."

"But what good will it do getting ourselves killed?" Paitin said. "Wouldn't we be twice as effective out here, cutting down their forces?"

Urwell grunted. "Anything is more effective than dead."

"Well?" Aeron asked, turning to Cainan. "What's *your* command, my liege?"

And with that, seven sets of fearful and furious eyes turned to him. Cainan could care less if they liked him. He wasn't like Gabriel. They could all get shoved. He wasn't here to be their friend. He was here to win. The women and children back home wouldn't ask if they became fast friends when they returned. They would only ask if their families were to die.

Still, their success depended on the team remaining well-coordinated, and if he didn't keep them in lockstep, things would get dangerous fast. His fool cousin had gone and built their unity on top of hope and friendship instead of iron will and fist.

And that's why you're losing the throne, Gabe. You can't be trusted with it.

"I know you hate me for what I did to Gabriel," Cainan

said. "I don't expect you to understand it, and it's not *for* you to understand. I do expect you to finish what we came to do here. There's no room for us to fracture. We owe it to our families back home—to every man, woman, and child depending on us. And if it makes you feel like a scorching unit again, you owe it to Gabriel. Understood?"

The crew nodded, though not without a glares of begrudging distaste. They hated him, but they couldn't disagree with the logic of his argument. They were at least soldier enough to admit he was right.

"Alright," Aeron said. "What's our move?"

"We stay the course and take out their commanding officers." Cainan squinted and held up his shield for shade. "We'll circle around the east. There's less resistance to that side. We'll surprise them at the rear. If we can't get in there, we'll keep circling until we find a crack in the wall of men and cut our way through." He looked back to the Second League. "Clear?"

"Clear," they said in unison.

Tele sat straight when the clap of prison guard boots approached the cell. Her heart raced. The door unlocked. The torch-welding guard stepped inside. His two accomplices followed.

Pick me! Tele thought, her will reaching out and demanding attention. She looked the guard in the eye. *Pick me!*

The guard took her in, frowning at either her urgent expression or the unconventionality of there being a woman as his ward. Regardless, his eyes slipped passed her and fell on the man to her left.

He pointed. "Take him."

The guards unlatched the man and pulled him to his feet. Stumbling, the man fell forward, splashing the waste and giving the vapors a renewed sting to her nose. Fortunately, the guards caught his misstep before he could topple and pulled him to his feet.

"Please," Tele said, just above a whisper. She swallowed her dignity and looked to his eyes. "Take me, too. Don't leave me with him."

The guard considered her before he glanced to the one-eyed man. Then he smirked before he turned away and sealed the chamber, leaving them once again in darkness.

But the chains didn't tighten. There was only a shared, horrid chuckle between the guards before they dropped the chains and stalked out of the dungeons.

Silence.

"Pretty gi—"

"If you touch me, I swear I'll be the last woman you ever set eye on."

"Pretty girl …" Left-eye said, almost in a soft coo. "*Tsk tsk tsk.*"

"Stop it!"

Silence.

She felt his hand. It traced the arc of her inner thigh, then gripped the thin fabric of her pants. Reflexively, Tele lifted a hand to push him away, but the cuffs stifled her defense. She pivoted, letting her back fall to the cell floor and kicked, pushing the man.

Left-eye fell away but not far. The chains clanged as they pulled tight, dropping him sideways into the cell floor slop.

"Just a taste, pretty girl. Just a—"

She kicked again, hard, but the chains held him taunt in place. A wet hand caught her calf. His fingers slipped before jagged fingernails dug into her skin and gripped her in place. Tele jerked, twisting to let her other leg find a vulnerable spot, but it touched only air before she fell back into place.

Desperate, she turned again, this time the opposite direction. Even as she did, she realized that it was a useless maneuver. The chains on her cuffs tightened, keeping her from turning completely, and she fell to her stomach.

Tele lifted her head as high as she could to keep her face out of the excrement below. Left-eye's grip receded just enough to allow his hands further beyond the fold of her knees. The gashes he left behind stung as the cell's rank fluid dripped over her skin.

Given leverage from her position, he pulled. Tele fought him. She pulled back, folding her arms up to her chest. She kicked again, but he'd snaked his way between her legs where her kicking did little to cut off his advances.

The weight of the man fell atop her. The pressure pushed her face into the shallow urine. It was all she could do not to gasp in pain. She jerked her head back out of the waste and gasped for air.

Left-eye struggled atop her, fumbling with his chains and struggling to pull her into submission. Tele pulled her knees up to her middle and pushed herself upward into a small ball. The man rolled off her. Seeing her chance, she slipped to her back to loosen the chain's twist. She kicked with as much power as she could muster, and the man's form fell away.

She kicked again, pushing him as far away as the chain's slack would allow.

Tele kicked again. Then again. Then again. Then again.

A tin clamor resonated, accompanied by a sharp slosh of liquid, then a loud hissing and crackling. Tele paused, unsure what she'd disturbed. A foul odor caught her nose. Tele coughed and sputtered. The rancid smell burned her lungs and stung her nose. She pulled on the iron shackles, trying to pull herself as far away from the poison.

Tele felt dizzy. She turned away as best she could with her hands still anchored in place. Squinting, she scanned the edge of the cell, searching for the source of the odor. Her eyes slowly focused on Left-eye's dark outline. He slowly writhed on the floor, coughing. Between them, Tele could just barely make out the dim reflection of a metallic surface—a bucket.

The astringent smell … the hissing. It had reacted with the wet floor—with the urine. In a flash, Tele remembered the women who'd come to clean the Keeper's lab in the Sanctuary.

"Pretty—" Left-eye coughed. "Girl—"

"Don't call me that," Tele warned. "If you move, I'll make sure you choke to death."

The man groaned but didn't move for her.

Tele looked to the cell door. *Come on …*

THIRTY-SEVEN

THE SHADOW OF WAR

Blood. It was all blood.

The grass, pollen, dirt, sweat, leather, steel—it was all gone. Only the smell of blood remained.

Fabi exhaled and pulled his attention back to the Second League's tight march, but there was little he could do to ignore the smell of copper, and the unending war cries. If he shut his eyes, he could almost feel Desolate's Hand pulling the lives of the dead beyond its cold threshold.

Ahead, against the Shadow Peaks, the Dominion general's first guard were so tightly packed together that it was hard to see where one Deseran bastard ended and the other began. With a whistle, Cainan ordered the team to cut left, drilling directly into the fist of guards. A dangerous move, but it was their only option.

Several Deseran soldiers leapt out of the way of their charge, but before they could press much further, several men locked together in an effort to push them back. Fabi pulled his sword and swung at the man just before him. He caught the assault with his shield, pushed back, and followed with his own attack. Fabi shifted, allowing the man's poor technique to leave his backside vulnerable. He struck the man at the base of his skull with the hilt of his sword, dropping him to the ground.

As fast as the Dominion soldier had fallen, another was upon him. Fabi cut him down with the same swift efficiency, tearing into his exposed calf. The scent of blood was on him now, and the Deseran soldiers swarmed at the smell of it, forcing the Second League out of their tight formation.

Fabi met steel with steel. Like Gabriel had taught him, he fought like a nightmare, trying to take on the center of the attackers to ease the weight on the others, but the Second League responded bravely, taking up the front line with him and peeling off the Dominion one at a time.

Ducking a beheading, Fabi lost his footing in the small hole pitched in the dirt. He tumbled before finding balance on a knee. Before he could rise, a Deseran tackled him from the side. His head smacked the packed earth as the full weight of a man near half-again his size fell on his chest.

Fabi sucked in a shallow breath. His vision blurred with a pain that rattled his body. He pushed at the soldier but found him far too heavy to maneuver. He squinted, trying to refocus.

I have to focus. I can't let them win.

The man had a knife.

Fabi jerked to the right as the soldier stabbed at him, then again to the left to dodge a second blade fall. Before he could take another thrust at him, Fabi jabbed him in the mouth. Soldier's head flicked backward, and a sword caught him at the neck, half-severing the man's head from his shoulders. Aeron kicked the man from atop him.

"We don't have time to play on the ground, Fabi," Aeron said, then offered him a hand.

Fabi took it. "Thanks."

When he found his balance, Cainan whistled, calling the Second League back into formation. After they fell into position, Fabi realized that someone was missing.

Fabi turned. There, face down in the dirt, was Urwell, skewered in the gut with a spear. He wanted to stop. To try to get the man back to the stronghold. If they were fast, he might live. He'd seen men with worse. He could survive.

Paitin fell to his brother's side, a wail of anguish broiled from the pit of his soul. "Urwell! Brother! My muse …" His words slipped into an Armothean tongue as Cainan drew him away.

"Compose yourself, soldier!"

But Paitin wept on, his brother spent on the accursed plain.

"Paitin," Aeron took Urwell's face in his hands. "We have to push forward. If you don't stand and fight, you'll die here."

Through the tears, Paitin managed a short nod before stumbling away from the grip of his fellow crewmen. "I'm alright," he lied, his gaze still transfixed on his brother's unblinking gaze.

Cainan turned away, his expression a measure from stoic indifference. "Let's go."

Dawn didn't bring warmth to the mountain chill, but it did bring the sounds of war.

Amie sat with her legs tucked close, her arms and legs still bound together. She watched as Owen and Ale Breath ate a silent breakfast over the coals of the dying fire. Neither had slept that night. And Amie had decided it was too risky to try much with both of them wide awake.

The broken cart had meant a day without travel, so she wanted to allow herself to feel relieved. Instead, with inactivity came a new kind of horror. Though they were far from the battlefield, Amie could still hear the echoes of conflict as it reverberated through the Shadow Peaks. Dulled by stone, the sounds stretched into inhuman moaning—like the shadow of war from ages past, still haunting the valleys below.

She could almost imagine it. Fires like the one at Gavini's cabin. Men killing one another. Horses stuck in the mud where they'd suffer and starve. She shuttered.

Though Amie had only spent a brief time with Owen, it'd been long enough to tell when something was bothering him.

She could see that he was having a hard time with the sounds, too. He put on a brave face for Ale Face—who was hopelessly oblivious—but the distant agony in his eyes was unmistakable.

Ale Breath stood and wiped his hands clean on his trousers. "I'm gonna go see if I can see the battle from up top. You want to come?"

"I want to guard the prisoners," Owen said.

"They aren't going anywhere," Ale Breath said. When Owen didn't respond, he shrugged. "Alright … I'll be back in a bit."

Amie looked to the broken cart and met Mara's dark gaze. Though her sister didn't say anything, her expression said it all. This was their moment.

"I didn't think it would sound like this," Amie said in Owen's direction. "The killing. I didn't know it would sound so miserable. I don't know what I expected it to sound like … I guess I never truly thought I'd ever have to hear it."

Owen sat with his back to her. He didn't respond, but she knew he could hear her.

"My father had bards come to our inn from time to time. I was always interested in the love songs, but men were the majority of travelers and for some dumb reason they enjoyed hearing songs and tales of war.

"The songs always told of the glory, the conquest, the victories, the men who were so valiant even Armothean women would travel for weeks to be their brides. There was even one about a woman who had fought. *That* one was interesting, but no one ever requested it."

She was rambling now. *He'll start ignoring you soon if you didn't figure out what you're trying to say.*

But then it struck her. Did she really want him to be paying attention to her when she did what she knew she must?

"The songs never talked about how frightening the sounds are. They didn't warn of how fear and hate and hurt caused men to do terrible things to one another. They never talked about those who weren't meant for such things. Some of us would rather live in peace. Some of us would rather spirit away with our loved ones than make our rivers run red with blood."

Owen turned away, his eyes focusing on something distant.

And Amie let the dagger drop from between her legs and into her hands.

THIRTY-EIGHT

THE PERIMETER

Fabi paused to wipe the sweat from his hands. Looking down, he saw that he hadn't wiped away sweat, but smeared blood across his leather armor. It wasn't his blood. At least he didn't think it was.

Further down field, the Second League cut into the remaining Dominion troops that had arced north. To their advantage, there'd only been a few dozen men who'd stormed the field without bowmen to back their charge. Fabi hadn't been sure what their plan was, but seeing the chaos that surrounded them, he wasn't sure that any of it was well coordinated.

The Hzorah troops had the discipline to segment their ranks and divide into well portioned units. The Deseran troops fought with blunt force—a losing strategy for an army so comparatively small. They'd leaned too heavily on the idea of the Shadow Peaks offering them refuge and leveling the battlefield.

Now that Desolate's Hand had given him a moment of respite, Fabi turned to watch as his regiment hacked away at the wave of Dominion troops who thought to slow down their advance. He held his breath and counted.

Six. There were only six of them left.

Lurin.

Further back, Fabi spotted the leather armor—his hand still outstretched, clutching his bow. It hurt deep to his core, vibrating his very bones. These were all good men. They didn't deserve this fate.

Give the Creed a hand hold, and they will take the mountain.

Cainan whistled, calling the Second League to heel. "Let's finish this. We'll cut into the General's tents. There's not much of a guard left. We'll need to be swift and efficient. This is what we came for. Let's take back the mountain."

"How?" Aeron asked. "We still can't get into the tents without penetrating their first guard. And it's just as strong on this side as the other."

"And Lurin—" Bear began. "Well, we ain't got an archer now. We gotta go in blades brandishing."

"Bastards are brash to put up their tents right here," Paitin said, his voice deadly serious since what had happened with his brother.

Cainan turned to survey their target. Flags were erected now, and the command tents were secured in place. Just ahead of the tents, an elephant swung its head, clearing a fist of Hzorah troops with its tusks.

"I have an idea." Cainan pointed downfield and pulled his sword. "Follow my lead."

Cainan fell into a full sprint, going straight for an elephant. Fabi pulled his sword and gave chase. While Cainan didn't bother to give direction to his team, a tight formation for what Cainan appeared to be attempting would only hurt their chances.

As Fabi approached the enormous, brown beast, the archer stood on the animal's back, knocked an arrow, and took aim at him. Fabi watched the man carefully, then turned just before he let the arrow fly. The shot deflected off of the shield on his back. Fabi turned again to meet another nocked arrow.

This time, Fabi crossed behind the elephant, falling out of the archer's line of sight. Instead of crossing to the other side, Fabi stopped, turned and headed back in the same direction he'd come. The archer's back was turned to him, expecting to catch him on the opposite side.

Fabi bounded and caught hold of the large saddle strapped to the elephant. It tugged, shaking the archer's balance. Fabi pulled himself upward and swung a leg up and over onto the creature's backside.

The Dominion archer, regaining his composure, turned. Before fear or gravity could take him, Fabi stood and advanced on the soldier. He caught the man with a quick jab before he could lift his bow. The archer fell backward to the ground below.

Fabi turned back and settled himself behind the elephant's massive head. Around him, Cainan and Bear had taken to eliminating the men to his right while Aeron, Jae, and Paitin dueled at his left.

Just like a horse ... a huge horse, Fabi thought, and searched for the reigns. There were none. *Oh, shove off.*

"Come on, Elephant," Fabi coaxed. "Turn around."

Fabi pushed his right heel into the animal's side, and it turned. He applied a bit more pressure—not enough to hurt the animal, but enough to redirect him back toward the Dominion general tents. The elephant turned, and, when he had him lined up with the tents, he pressed both heels into its thick hide. The elephant charged forward, first at a walk, then faster at a trot. Fabi held tight to the saddle, his heart pounding.

Ahead, a few Dominion soldiers waved their hands for Fabi to stop. When the realization that he didn't intend to stop his charge hit them, they scattered, shouting orders to stop the beast.

Fabi pulled the elephant around to disperse the perimeter. To avoid being trampled, soldiers fell out of the way to the left and right. Fabi turned to see his five teammates engage with the fallen, cutting them down where they lay. After taking a full lap around the tents, he dismounted the elephant.

"You Desolate-bound fool," Aeron shouted, half-smiling as

he and the Second League approached. "That'll be one to tell the girls when you get home."

"Let's get home first." Cainan's glower focused on the command tents. "There's only six of us, but that should be more than enough to cut down a few old men. Just leave the general to me. He's mine."

Several men filed out of the tent, swords in hand. Then, another row followed. Then, another—archers. At least forty-strong swept around the Second League. Fabi turned, allowing the others to take his backside.

How had they fit so many soldiers in those tents? Had they known they were coming?

"Any other ideas?" Aeron asked.

A tall man in a black uniform stepped out of the tent. His long gray beard tugged in the breeze and the scar on his forehead creased as his brow cast downward. He wore a dark gray, pristine uniform in contrast to the dirt, destruction, and death within his swath. He, surveying the damage, then appraised the six Hzorah soldiers. Finally, he raised a hand, and an officer came to his side.

The officer knelt—a fist to the ground. "My General?"

"Lieutenant Farrin, have the injured brought to the healer's tent in the pass, then meet me at the base of the mountain."

Farrin shouted orders while the general watched the Second League, his gaze passing over each of them.

Shove off, Fabi thought as the general's satisfied gaze made eye contact with him.

"And what of the heathens, My General?" the Lieutenant asked.

"Kill them," the general said.

With another commanding nod from Farrin, several soldiers stepped forward, their swords glinting in the sunlight. The general turned back to his tents.

"Coward!" Cainan shouted. "Pick up a sword for yourself! Where's your honor?"

The general paused and turned. His eyes settled on Cainan. Then he started for him. He didn't pull a sword. He just looked him straight in the eye, recognition contorting his expression.

"Those eyes," the general said. "That hair. Tell me, soldier. Why do you look so familiar?"

"I am Cainan Bendeth, son of High Lord Bendeth and heir to the Hzorah Crown."

Heir? Fabi shot a glare at Cainan. How was he the Heir? King Jeremiah was dead, but he had a son, didn't he? What's he playing at?

A smile curled the general's lips. "Now this *is* interesting ... I suppose I shouldn't expect heathens to maintain stable structures of order. I'd hoped to have my battle with Jeremiah's son, Prince Gabriel. I find that my blade may not be satisfied with anything less than the spawn of the man responsible for stalling the return of Wizard Titan."

"You're looking at him," Cainan said. "It was my father who pushed you scorching zealots into the waste. Jeremiah and Gabriel aren't the ones you want. It's me. How about you show me what you're made of—man to man. Right here, right now. Let's see if your Wizard returns to save you."

"You dare blaspheme?" the general's face contorted with fury.

"Your Wizard can shove it," Cainan growled.

It was brash of Cainan to so blatantly insult the general and his beliefs to his face. But then again, what did they have to lose? It isn't as though they would be any more dead when the soldiers cut their throats.

The Dominion soldiers, raised their weapons, but before they attacked, the general raised a hand, and the soldiers stepped back.

"My General?" Farrin said.

"On second thought, Farrin, don't kill them. Bring them with you. I want them to see this." He looked at Cainan again with piercing eyes. "Especially this one."

Tele lifted her head at the sound of a distant thud and faint footsteps. She turned to listen for Left-eye's breathing. He'd been silent since she'd given him her heel, save a few instances of turning in the dungeon floor slop. She squinted to see him in the darkness but couldn't make out his form against the stone.

Another thud. Closer. More footsteps.

Tele sat up. Startled, the man flinched, ringing the cuff-linked chains. Tele turned, giving her back to the cell door. She edged forward until her foot touched something cool, smooth, and round—the tin bucket.

Left-eye moaned, "Pretty girl," then winced in pain.

"I told you not to call me that," Tele whispered. "I won't say it again."

He moaned his reply, followed by a sharp grunt. She must have roughed him a bit more than she'd thought. A broken rib from the sound of it. *Good.*

The guard's footsteps moved from the stairway to the hall. Tele slid forward just a bit more—close enough to feel the bucket with her foot. She would have gotten closer if the chains permitted it, but it was enough. Closing her eyes to the world around her, she focused her will, and forced her breathing to slow.

The cell's door clanked as the guard worked the lock. Light illuminated the enclosure, and the guards stepped in. Tele didn't turn to them.

"Take the girl," the guard said.

The guards sloshed over to her. The one to Tele's right side bent down and jerked her wrist over to expose where the cuffs connected to the chain. The one to her left circled to watch and bent over close to her face.

"She's a fit sitter, ain't she?"

Near the edge of her restraint, she bit her tongue to keep from giving him her mind but spared a sharp glare.

The guard chuckled. "Saucy, too."

The chain fell away, and Tele gritted her teeth, hardening her resolve.

"Up with you."

Tele kicked the tin bucket. The pail rattled as it smacked against the stone wall before falling back toward her, spilling a light green liquid. The fluid hissed as it reacted with the excrement on the cell floor, and a thick, gray cloud of vapor filled the room.

Resisting the reflex to inhale, Tele cried under her breath when the fluid washed over her ankles. The burn felt as though she'd been cut with a thousand razors. It pulsed, shooting its way up her thighs.

Tele stood as the guards coughed. Freed from the cell chain, she swung her still-cuffed arms, slamming into the back of the jailor and knocking him to the cell floor. Another double-fisted attack caught the second in the jaw. He stumbled backward and tripped over Left-eye.

From behind, the torchlight winked out as it fell to the cell floor. Tele turned and leapt over the prison guard who knelt on his hands and knees, suffocating in the toxic gas. She turned around in the cell's entrance. A guard had already found his feet, one hand waving away the fumes, and the other pulled the fabric of his shirt over his nose. When he caught her eye, he charged for her.

Tele slammed the cell door. The guard crashed up against it, nearly pushing the heavy door back open. She leaned against it, but the guard was heavier than she was. If he got one good push in …

Tele looked to her left, then to her right where a wooden latch balanced against the door frame. Tele reached down and lifted it.

The guard crashed against the door again, shoving Tele off balance. She fell back against the door and pushed back with everything she had while fumbling to balance the latch between her bound wrists. The door shut just long enough for her to turn and drop the latch in place, barring the door.

Again, the guard crashed against the cell door. It rattled against the wooden latch. It wouldn't hold long. If all three put their weight into it, it would fail. But the gas should do its work. They couldn't hold their breath forever.

Tele looked down the dungeon corridor. Keys hung on rings on the wall across from each door. She had to find Tal Aval before someone came looking for the guards.

THIRTY-NINE

ONE RADIANT BEACON OF HOPE

Navid ran the rest of the way up the grassy hill. When he reached the top, he looked out at the North Hzorah fields. Where the land should have been green and golden with crops, now they were dark, wet, and littered with the fallen.

Navid allowed his senses—his instincts—to reach out. Like tendrils lighting about his focus, they brushed over the land, searching for potential. Countless pricks of danger and tugs of safety washed over him. Effortlessly, each wasted opportunity faded away as if filtered by a net, leaving behind the only choices that mattered.

The land crawled with Hzorah troops, pushing the Deserans back and slowly encircling their ranks. The terrible roar of battle pressed against his ear drums in a thick wall of sound. Steel scraping against steel, the wailing of men in pain —it was the sound of all he'd feared mankind could become.

I could help them. Push forward with their primary charge. Single-handedly tip the scale in favor of the Hzorah troops with violent disproportion.

His awareness fanned out further. Stronghold Aear sat across the flat of the plain. Thick-walled and fortified, its safety was hard to resist. While his heart was with the Hzorah troops, his instincts—his seer's eye—drove him toward self-preservation. Resisting it was a dissonant echo of pain.

That's where she is. Trapped and alone, waiting for Desolate's Hand to deliver a miracle.

As much as Navid wanted to save Tele and Tal Aval, as much as he wanted to hide behind the fortress's battlements, there was one more eventuality that must be considered. He had to reach the Hzorah army's leaders and warn them of what the Dominion wielded—the terrible destructive power that had been unleashed on his home.

At least you're safe there, Navid thought. *You would have wanted me to warn them first. You would have wanted me to choose to protect the world's future.*

His senses fell over the general's tents. Lifeless and void of any present eventuality, only one radiant beacon of hope persisted. It outshined all other chances of a proper warning, and Navid knew that if he wanted to save the army, he would have to find the officer waiting there. Before he knew it, he was charging down the hill, sprinting, carried away by his ability's unwavering focus.

Doubt pried at the corners of his mind. Years of suppressive training rattled against the walls of its prison. Guilt ravaged with the image of the dead thief's eyes as his life slipped. Navid gritted his teeth against everything he'd leaned on and trusted.

Where were the prophets when his fellow seers were killed?

Why couldn't his ideals protect an entire village that fell prey to Tristan's murderous intent?

How did his allegiance to the old way protect the only person who'd ever treated him like he wasn't a monster—like what he had was a gift?

Sensing hope, he pushed forward. He set aside what he'd been taught, for it offered him nothing that could help him now.

Navid slowed as he approached the tents. The weight of the necklace around his neck felt heavy, and he clutched the pendent through his shirt.

As he neared the tent where the officer waited, he felt something else … an overwhelming sense of *kinship*. Navid paused. Dread, betrayal, and disloyalty all fought for his attention but they were but a slim concern as he came to realize what he sensed before him.

His father was in that tent.

Navid pushed aside the tent flap and stepped inside. A tall man, clad in armor and bent over a table, studied a map with his back turned to away from the entry. Navid stood frozen, overwhelmed with a fury of emotions.

"Father?"

"Cainan? What are you—" The man turned, his blue-eyed gaze surprised to see someone he didn't expect.

Who was Cainan? *Do I have a brother*?

"I …" Navid swallowed, trying to find the words. He glanced down to see the man's rank. He was marked higher than a general—a High Lord. *Wisdoms*. His father was a High Lord. "You … You're my father."

"What are you doing in here, soldier?" The High Lord—his father. His *real* father—examined him. "Why aren't you in uniform?"

Navid took a tentative step forward. Navid didn't have the same blond hair as this Lord, but he could almost see that he had the same eyes—albeit, his were no longer blue. He pulled the necklace from over his head and held it out.

"My name is Navid—Navid Tevaad. You knew my mother. She was your—"

Navid didn't know what to call her. This man was a High Lord. There was no possibility that his mother and this man were ever married.

"What are you going on about?" Then the High Lord saw it—his eyes. "Scorching Wisdoms, boy! Why aren't you in Caldor?"

Navid lowered the pendant as he sensed danger. He watched the High Lord look off to the side where his sword sat, as if judging whether or not he could make it to the sword before Navid pounced. He couldn't, Navid could feel that, but that wasn't important right now.

"Caldor was destroyed," Navid said. "That's why I'm here, Father. It was the Dominion who destroyed Caldor with flying beasts from the sky that spit ice."

The High Lord backed away, edging around the table. "You're deranged."

"I came to warn you," Navid said and stepped forward. He locked eyes with the High Lord, trying to make him see the severity of what awaited them. "We have to do something to curb the odds. This whole battle is a trap to crush the Hzorah army in one, swift blow. Father—"

"Stop calling me that," the High Lord said. "I'm not your father. I'm High Lord Bendeth of West Hzorah, and you—"

"You *are* my father," Navid said. "The prophets told me I had to find you. You and my mother—Tevaad—had a child."

Grimacing, the High Lord continued to circle the table. "That's impossible. Gwendlyn was a whore, I—" He shook his head. "You're a seer. You aren't my kin. You're one of the cursed—a monster."

"Father—" Navid felt as though his throat might close, that every remaining hope was about to fall apart. "Let me help you. The Dominion has a magic we can't easily fight. We have to—"

"I am *not* your father," he spat. "And if you lay a hand on me, you'll sorely regret it. Now step aside."

"I'm not here to hurt you." He held his father's gaze. "Please. Let me help you."

"Step aside," the High Lord growled.

Before Navid could move, something new pulled his senses. He turned his attention to the small cage in the corner of the tent. And as he focused on it, the odds of survival narrowed to a fine point. *This* was the key. The man inside had to be freed.

Navid pointed to the cage. "You have to let him go. We need him to win this."

"Boy, you must be shoved if you think—" His father shook his head as he regained his countenance. "Listen …"

But Navid's mind had already drifted away. His gaze swept the tent and he saw that the High Lord had hung a banner. The Bendeth family crest: a tree and a hammer. The same symbol on his pendant.

Their time was short, and there was but one way that he could tip the scales of the army in their favor. The odds were slim, but he had to try. There was no other way.

He lifted the pendant again. "My mother stole this from you, didn't she?"

The High Lord's mouth snapped shut.

Navid looked to the pendant as it swayed. "You had her killed because you didn't want it to come out that she bore your child. It would complicate things for your son. Cainan, isn't it?"

The momentary shock of Navid's deduction passed and High Lord Bendeth sneered. "Now, you look here, boy—"

"I propose a trade," Navid announced, cutting him off. "I know it wouldn't be good for your family to have a *seer* in your bloodline. And this pendant proves my connection to you. If you let the man in the cage go, you can have the pendant, and you can be done with me forever. Otherwise, I think I may have to make myself known. After the Caldor attack, I'm without a home, and perhaps it's time I redeem my birthright."

High Lord Bendeth's glare danced between the pendant and the cage. Swearing, he dropped a key on the map table and snatched the pendant from Navid's grip.

"Out of my way, seer."

Navid stepped away from the tent's entry. On his way to the exit, the High Lord retrieved his sword. Sensing temptation, he watched as the Lord considered attacking him then reconsidered, thinking better of it.

"Today is a day of grace," he said pausing beside Navid and smoothing his uniform. "I will allow you to live. Go back to Caldor and speak no more of what you think you know about your parents. If I hear of anything that remotely resembles your failing to do so, I will find you and kill you."

Then the High Lord brushed past him and hurried out of the tent.

It hadn't taken as long as Amie imagined it would. The dagger was much sharper than the rope was thick. Amie's hands were free, and she now worked at the rope around her ankles.

She glanced to Mara. Her sister watched her work at her binds, her eyes wide with shock. Amie hadn't had the opportunity to tell her sister about the dagger. The two remaining soldiers may not have heard them if she had whispered, but she was too nervous that she'd lose her one chance at freedom.

Amie nearly cried out in relief when the ropes at her ankles fell away, but she held her tongue. She looked at Owen again to ensure he hadn't noticed her work. He still watched the dying embers, the breeze tossing his tall white locks.

She pulled the rope back across her ankles and secured it again with a single, loose knot that would break away without much pressure. She then placed the dagger between her legs again and rebound her hands, securing them by holding the ends of the rope in her palms after she realized tying them was near impossible.

"Good work, Amie!" her sister mouthed when Amie looked at her again. Amie gave her sister a forced, weak smile. But even as she smiled, the tears came. She knew what she had to do. She knew what she had to become. Her sister, understanding her pain, nodded sympathetically—an expression of both sorrow and encouragement.

It had to be done.

She turned back to Owen. She was free now but was too far away from him to make use of her weapon. Slowly, Amie inched closer to him, making sure to maintain the knots that would fall away with too much agitation.

Owen looked up to see her move closer. He watched her warily but allowed her to push herself across the camp and sit next to him. When she settled, he sighed as if comforted by her presence before looking back to the charred wood.

Amie let out her own ragged breath. "It's funny how small the world is when you place yourself at the center of it. Back at the inn, I tried so hard to take control, to live my own life. I wanted so badly to find adventure. I just never imagined this would be the way I'd do it.

"Isn't that what you want, Bam Rav?" she pleaded. "Don't want you want to break away? To live free and to let others live free?"

Owen looked to the sky. "I can't betray everything I love and lose it all. I won't be a traitor."

"Yes ..." Amie bit her lip. "Yes, but sometimes you have everything to gain from letting go of your current course. Sometimes there's more than one way to get what you want. What you're doing now may be the easiest way to save the ones you love—the way of least resistance." Under her shift, she released the weapon and allowed it to drop into her hands, her resolve taking hold. "But maybe the difficult way is the only way to live with yourself when this is all over."

FORTY

THE PRETENSE OF DARKNESS

Navid, the cursed.

Numb with despair, Navid stood in his father's tent. He sank to his knees as grief took him. His ability was but a distant buzz amidst a flood of tears. All that he'd done, all that he'd sacrificed to reach his father and claim his freedom was for nothing.

But even as the grim reality of it all tore at his heart, Tele's voice splintered the pretense of darkness. Hope radiated through to his soul, disrupting shadows and melting away a lifetime of shame.

"*Forget everything that the prophets told you. Forget everything that you've read about seers. Forget all of it. The prophets, the seers … They're all dead now. You are the only one who can decide if you are cursed.* You."

"He's a real looger, isn't he?"

Navid looked up, disarmed by the voice. Cast in a shadow, the man inside the cage watched him, his back reclined against the crate's wall.

"Who are you?" Navid asked.

"A fool," he said. "Just like you. A fool who believed he could change things."

"I thought that if I found my father …" Navid began.

"Well, I don't really know what I expected to happen. I just didn't expect *this*."

The man laughed, but not unkindly. "Some say that the family that you're born to—flesh and blood—is what's important. That at the end of the line, your kin is all that you have left." The man's blue eyes turned to him, piercing the darkness. "Piss on that. Flesh and blood doesn't make a family, love does. If you ever find true friendship—true family—that's where you should put your loyalty." He nodded toward the tent entry. "Bendeth can shove it. That man's my uncle, but look where it landed me."

Navid's ability, no longer choked under layers of woe, whispered futures.

"You're Jeremiah's son." Navid's breath caught. "You're the king."

The man—the king—snorted. "And you're a seer. I suppose we all have our faults."

"No." Navid shook his head, the shame of years of repression cast away. "I used to think of myself as flawed, as cursed—destined for a life of misery. I almost didn't make it here because of it. Fortunately, there was someone—family—who helped me realize that I have to let go of what others said of me. That I had to fulfill my birthright in order to affect the most good." He looked at the Hzorah king. "We both have a right to who we are, and to reject it is death."

"'Every action you take is a choice—even inaction. And the very first choice you must make is leadership.'" The king sighed. "My father told me that."

"I wish it was *your* father that I'd found here."

The King chuckled. "Here's to shoved up family."

"I suppose it's time to take action," Navid said. He took the key from the table and crossed the room. "Let's get you out of that cage. I wouldn't want you to be stuck in there, unable to relieve yourself for hours on end."

Navid approached the cage and tested the lock. With a satisfying click, it fell away. He stepped back to give the king the room to crawl out.

The young man emerged, clad in a soldier's uniform with disheveled blond hair. He held out his hand. "My name is Gabriel."

Navid took his hand. "Navid Tevaad."

The last few minutes had been an uncomfortable silence like Amie had never experienced before. She felt as though she might vomit in anticipation of what was coming—what *she* was becoming. But what was she to do? As long as Owen stood guard, they would die. And if she didn't do this before Ale Face returned, her only opening would be forever lost.

The only thing her captor was concerned about was keeping his family safe. And could she blame him? That's exactly what she was doing. Who doesn't love their family?

Bam Rav certainly loved his. He wouldn't want to let them down, to disappoint them.

"I do wonder what your family will think," Amie said as she tugged on the ropes that bound her feet from beneath her shift. The ropes fell away. "What will your little sister think when you tell her that you fought in a war?"

He stilled. "I have not fought."

"But you will. And then what?" Amie let go of the ropes that wrapped around her hands, leaving only the dagger. Her hand tightened around its hilt. "They won't look at you the same, will they? It would be as if you were dead to them."

"I'm an officer," Owen said. "I may not have to fight, only command."

"But you're commanding men to do evil, right? Your commands move their hands."

"I—" He swallowed hard. "I am not responsible for the evil others do."

With focused stealth, Amie slipped her hand that held the blade behind him.

"Yes. I agree. You are not responsible for the evil that others do." She lowered her voice as if to assure him the rocks wouldn't hear what she said next. "But my father died. *You* didn't hurt him. It was those other horrid men. But you *command* their hands now. You *allowed* him to die. You allowed those people at Gavini's home to die, too."

Surprisingly, Bam Rav turned from the fire's ashes and looked at her with streams of tears in his eyes. "It was not my fault what happened to your father." His voice broke as he wept. "I am only doing what I was commanded."

Amie watched his eyes while the dagger hovered just behind him and out of sight—inches from the nape of his neck. Her heart pounded in response to what she was about to do, and it ached knowing how much what had happened troubled him. Owen was a cold and detached soldier, but Bam Rav was a broken man. It was Bam Rav who looked at her now.

"Yes," she said, her own tears welling in her eyes. "But who is responsible if not the soldier who commands the sword and if not the soldier who thrusts the sword?"

Bam Rav had no answer. He simply closed his eyes.

"It's not too late. You can still make things right. You can still save my sister. You alone have that power. You alone have the heart."

"But my family—"

"You can go back and free your family," Amie said. "Take them away from the Bamilee, away from slavery."

"I will have to fight to free them."

"Yes, perhaps you will. But sometimes you have to fight so that you don't have to," Amie said, recalling what Tele had told her, "when the stakes are even higher."

"And where would we go?" Bam Rav asked. "There is nowhere for us. The Bamilee Plain is our home."

"You can live with us in Azuri. We have a place for you. You'd have beds, and meals, and work. Believe me, there's no end to the work there, but you'll never be a slave again. No one will ask you to hurt another again." She caught his eyes. "But, Bam Rav, none of that will be there for you if you don't let us go.

"It takes courage to turn away from the easiest path. It takes honor to do what's right. You have the key."

Amie dropped the dagger to the ground behind him. Bam Rav turned at the sound and saw the weapon in the dirt. And when he turned back to her, he exhaled with resolution and gave her a short nod.

FORTY-ONE

ESCAPE

Cainan kept his head held high as the tight knot of Second League soldiers were guided up the hill that leaned against the base of Shadow Peaks. Encircled by sword and shield, the Dominion general's guard didn't give them an inch of room to try for an attack or escape. Compressed as they were, Cainan could almost hear the racing hearts of the remaining Second League soldiers.

He gritted his teeth and his mind raced trying to devise a plan to slaughter the general before he himself could be cut down. It was like trying to climb a perfectly smooth wall—his thoughts couldn't find a handhold, slipping back to down before he could form even the simplest idea.

"What you said," Fabi whispered. Pressed up against each other in a prison of metal, it felt as though the thief was right in his ear. "About being heir. How is that possible? What of King Jeremiah's son?"

Cainan didn't look at him, but answered: "He won't be king, not after what he did. My father will take the throne."

"What he did?" Aeron asked. "What did he do?"

I guess it doesn't matter anymore, Cainan thought. He and his father were already on their way to securing the throne, and now that they were marching to certain death, a promise made to his cousin meant little. "Gabriel—your former Sergeant—was the Prince of Hzorah, Jeremiah's son."

"That can't be true," Bear said. "He's an orphan, he said so."

"And you told us he was a traitor," Aeron said.

"He *is* a traitor," Cainan hissed. "He abandoned his throne in the face of war, groveled at the feet of thieves and commoners instead of manning the throne as a beacon of strength and leadership to his people."

"Bosh! He was fighting to protect his people," Aeron said. "Scorch it … How shoved up are you?"

"A king fights as a leader," Cainan said, "as a commander. Gabriel abandoned that. Every man has his place, his role." Cainan looked at his regiment. "Just like you had a role here in the army, Gabriel's was to his people on the throne."

"Shut it," a Dominion soldier threatened as they neared the top of the hill.

Preset for the General's arrival, the hill had a small table set with several objects adorning it—some parchment, a map perhaps, and a leather-bound book. Cainan could see the entire battlefield from here. In the distance, the war continued in his absence. Their separation from the conflict failed to diminish the rumble of death.

Though their neat and coordinated battle lines had descended into mixed chaos, the trained eye could see that Cainan's army owned the battlefield and would carry the day with persistence. And in the face of his own death, that truth sustained his pride.

General Gareth sighed as he looked upon the forces below. The way he clasped his hands behind his back with strict discipline was unsettling. How could the man fail to waver in his defeat? Couldn't he see the inevitable outcome?

"It was here," Gareth said, "that the Creed made its final stand against your filthy lot. Moved by compassion, the Creed tried to align you with the truth through charity. We built your cities and your strongholds using the powers given to us by Wizard Titan. We brought you food, codified your language to strengthen relations and trade, carved roads so that together we might prosper. All these things were made possible because of the True Wizard. Without him, you and your kingdom would be no more than beasts roving the land, killing your neighbors and hunting your fellow beasts until there was nothing left. You would have *starved* in your savagery."

Cainan glared at the back of General Gareth's head. He wanted to leap up and stab him through the back. He wanted to pull out his spine from his neck and beat him with it.

"It was the Creed that built the kingdom that you claim to inherit, and how do you repay us?" Gareth paused, allowing the torrent of fevered battle to fill the silence. "Again, we came. In peace, we offered to make things right—to once again help guide you to the light, to truth, to redemption. For the Wizard left us because of our disregard for his sovereignty and only after we submit to his will can he return to us."

It was madness. The dribble of a Desolate-bound fool. Cainan gritted his teeth and struggled in vain against his restraints.

"I entered your lands, hoping to find that it was merely your king who forced his savage ways upon you. I believed that the hearts of the people here still believed, still held on to truth and the hope of his return to us. Instead, I found roving highwaymen and traitors willing to kill their own neighbors.

"It was *your* father," the general said, turning back to Cainan, "that turned me away, that insisted on this pointless loss of life. We offered a peaceful union—a return to righteousness—and we were rejected. It was then that I realized that my hopes were but the dreams of a fool. You had lost all ability to see reason."

Cainan nearly laughed. How deluded was this scorching fool? A peaceful union? Did he forget who had initiated the aggression?

"And when the few reject truth at the detriment of the many," General Gareth said, "tolerance ends and force begins. No longer will you reign in wickedness. No longer will your perverse ideals scorch the land. No longer will the Creed stand by, hoping that you will accept truth so that Wizard Titan can return with his blessings. It ends here. I will gut your lands of malfeasance. And in its place, hope will flourish."

"You haven't won," Cainan said. "Your army will be crushed. You may kill us, but Hzorah has won the day."

"Oh?" General Gareth turned again and took four quick strides to the table. He lifted a small leather book, then turned back to him. "Do you know what this is? This is the Abbreviation that will end this war. Do you know what it does?" He waited a half-moment, before continuing. "This book holds the spell that will end your little resistance. And, from here, you will have the best view of your army's demise."

General Gareth turned back to gaze out at the battlefield below. He opened the book, then, with a harsh, staccato lilt, he began to chant.

Tele fumbled with the key. The cuffs that bound her wrists were a handicap to what should be a simple action. She unlocked the cell door and poked her head inside. "Tal Aval?"

"Let me out!" a voice called. "I ain't done nothin'! I swear it!"

Tele squinted in the darkness. She saw three figures silhouetted against the prison wall.

"Tal—"

"I said let me go!"

Tele slipped back out and pushed the door shut, muffling the continued shouts of the prisoner inside, then hung the key back on the wall. She moved to the next cell door and unlocked it.

"Tal Aval? It's Tele."

Silence. She stuck her head inside and called to him again. Tele jerked her head back when a wet spray of saliva struck her between the eyes. She pulled back, wiped a cuff-linked arm across her face, then slammed the door shut. The sound reverberated down the corridor, rattling the doors of the cells below.

Tele jogged to the next cell and unlocked it. "Tal Aval?"

"Tele?"

"Tal Aval!" Tele slipped into the cell and crossed a new batch of urine. "Where are you?"

"Here," Tal Aval said. "Did they release you? We are free to go?"

Tele lifted her hands so he could see the cuffs. "Not exactly. Hold still."

With the cell key, Tele unlocked the chains to the cuffs, then the cuffs themselves. She gave Tal Aval a hand as he stood. "We have to find our way out before more guards come down."

"What about us?" The man beside Tal Aval lifted his cuffs. "I didn't do anything wrong. Don't leave us here."

Tele paused for a moment to look to Tal Aval, but he only lifted his eyebrows as if to say: "your call."

Tele tossed the key into the man's lap. "Good luck!"

A cheer rose as Tele and Tal Aval exited the cell.

Tele nodded to the right and switched to Tal to explain herself clearly. "The guards always come from that way. I don't know what's back down the other direction, but I'm betting it's a dead end."

"*And those*," Tal Aval said, looking to Tele's bound hands. "*Why did you not unlock them?*"

"Didn't quite work out," Tele said. "I tried some of the keys on the walls, but they must be unique to the cell. And my key is locked in with the guards."

"That is a bad place to put it," Tal Aval said.

"Can't argue with that," Tele said, then began walking to the end of the corridor. "We'll have to figure that out later, but first, escape."

FORTY-TWO

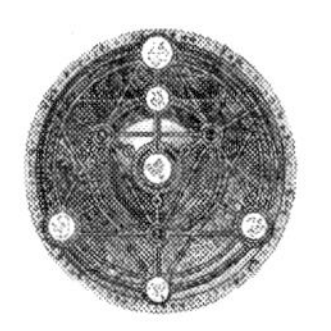

A PATH PAINTED RED

Deep within the thicket, Gabriel crept forward. His stomach twisted in rage as he listened to the Dominion general go on about his "righteous goals." Were it not for landscape's resistance, he would charge in and—

"Patience," Navid whispered, just behind him. He placed a hand on Gabriel's shoulder. "We have to wait for the right moment."

"This *is* our moment," Gabriel couldn't imagine a better moment to attack than right in the middle of his pompous monologue.

"No," Navid said. "You must trust me. The time has not yet come."

Strapped against his back, Gabriel could feel the Crown Sabre get heavier as if requesting to be drawn. He envisioned the zealot swallowing his tongue in shock when he drove his father's sword through him. He should have done it when he'd first seen the bastard when he'd disguised himself and entered the throne room. If only he'd known then …

Gabriel tried to count the Second League's numbers through the legs of the guards that surrounded them. Thick as they were, Gabriel couldn't tell how many were there, but he knew that it was fewer than there should be.

Let them have escaped, Gabriel prayed. But something deep within his soul told him that they wouldn't have abandoned their brothers, and that stoked the fire of his rage into a fever pitch.

"You haven't won," Cainan said. "Your army will be crushed. You may kill us, but Hzorah has won the day."

"Oh?" Gareth turned and lifted a small leather book from the table. "Do you know what this is? This is the Abbreviation that will end this war. Do you know what it does?"

Gabriel focused on the small, leather-bound volume while Gareth continued bragging.

"An Abbreviation," Navid whispered. "That's how they're coordinating the spells without Wizard Titan. Just like the Gateway spell."

Gabriel didn't know what an Abbreviation was, but he didn't have to. He'd heard all that he needed to know: magic. Whatever that book was, it had magic and nothing good would come of it.

General Gareth opened the book and began to chant. Above, the clouds swirled, agitated by the general's strange words. Gabriel watched in awe as the clouds divided and took the shape of birds.

Gabriel stood. He was done waiting for the right moment. He had to put a stop to whatever evil the man had planned. He charged out of the clearing, ignoring Navid's call for him to stay.

Hearing his approach, several of the soldiers guarding the Second League turned and drew their swords. Gabriel released a short sword from the scabbard at his hip without slowing his charge. Momentarily shocked by his unexpected attack and brash behavior, the soldiers paused. That brief moment allowed Gabriel to pick out the weakest link in the guard.

The first soldier met Gabriel's sword and parried. Falling into the third cadence, Gabriel re-doubled his attack with blunt force. If he had any chance of breaking through to Gareth, he'd have to sacrifice economy of motion for strength. Once he'd penetrated the barrier, Gareth was the only target that mattered.

Driving his blade through the man's gut, the first soldier fell, but not before Gabriel leveraged his body as a battering ram. He grabbed the soldier by his leather breastplate and put his shoulder into the effort.

To Gabriel's surprise, the guard responded and immediately recognized his strategy. They returned the push, overwhelming him with the force of three men and drove Gabriel off balance. He fell backward with the dead soldier atop him.

I'm dead, Gabriel thought. *It's over.*

Before a single sword struck, a figure leapt over him.

With a grace beyond anything he'd ever seen, Navid fought off the soldiers, his deft work with a quarterstaff preferring to render them unconscious over a clean death.

Gabriel pushed the fallen soldier off of him. When he got to his feet, he was shocked to see all but one soldier left. Navid had struck every single soldier down in the time Gabriel had killed one man. He was like a force of nature.

"Navid ..." Gabriel whispered.

Panting, Navid turned to Gabriel, his golden eyes locking with his. Gabriel looked past him to where Gareth had stood, but he was gone.

Gabriel turned back to the Second League who sat near transfixed at the sight. He strode over to them, cut Cainan's restraints, and inclined his head to him to get on with the untying. Cainan set to freeing Paitin.

A sharp, otherworldly shriek drew his attention. Out over the battlefield, the monsters that General Gareth had summoned—at least a dozen of them—swooped over the land. He watched as one targeted a group of Hzorah soldiers and projected thick threads of white from its mouth. Its prey smothered, it turned away to find its next victim.

"Where's Gareth?" Gabriel asked.

Aeron lifted his chin downhill, and Gabriel turned to where the hill rolled into the mountain base near the valley passage. He watched Gareth traverse the uneven ground, the small book clutched in his right hand.

He'd have to catch the bastard, but first …

Gabriel turned to his men. Lurin and Urwell were both missing. His chest burned with anger as a hundred memories of their smiles, their voices, their dreams washed over him. His desire for vengeance was renewed tenfold as he turned back to the Shadow Peaks.

"Is it really true?" Fabi asked. "Are you really Prince Gabriel, son of King Jeremiah?"

Gabriel nodded looking back at them. "It's true."

"All this time, I've been talking … eating with a prince." Fabi frowned. "Not a prince, a king."

"Still a prince, technically," Gabriel corrected.

"Why?" Fabi asked. "Why leave your palace? Why come to this nightmare? To this horrible end?"

"Because it was right," Gabriel said. "Because I'd rather die protecting my people than hide behind a throne. Because I'm no better or deserving than you or any of the others. And I'm just awful at politics."

Cainan stood after cutting free the last of the Second League. "How'd you—?"

"No time," Gabriel said. "Fall back to the Stronghold. I'm going after Gareth."

"We're coming with you," Aeron said. "We've come this far."

"No, Gareth is my battle." Aeron opened his mouth to protest, but Gabriel shot him a look that took the words from him. "Find anyone that looks healthy enough to survive and help them back to Stronghold Aear. Report to Captain Alden. Is that clear?"

The Second League stood silent for a moment before Cainan broke the silence.

"Your *prince* has spoken," Cainan said, holding Gabriel's eye. "Let's go."

"I can help you get through to the Stronghold," Navid said. "I'm a seer."

Cainan frowned, slightly squinting as he looked into Navid's eyes. "Scorch it! The bastard's got golden eyes. Just like the legends."

The soldiers packed in, trying to get a good look for themselves. When they'd each confirmed that he was what he said he was, they looked at Gabriel, as if unsure if they could truly trust a seer.

"Take him with you," Gabriel said. "You can trust him. He saved my life. You'll need as much help as you can get."

Aeron nodded, taking Navid's hand. "If Gabriel trusts you, so do I—seer or not."

The others nodded in agreement.

"I'm Cainan," Cainan said, stepping up to Navid, "son of the High Lord Bendeth. Your kind doesn't belong here, seer." The edge in his eyes softened for an instant before he added, "but if you can do what the legends say you can, and you can help us get to the Stronghold, I'll see to it that my father rewards you."

"Quite unnecessary. He's done enough," Navid said, then turned to Gabriel. "That book that Gareth has. You must get it. It's a powerful spell, and without it, you'll lose this war."

Gabriel nodded as he tracked Gareth's movements into the Shadow Peaks. "Look, I have to go. Get them to the Stronghold."

Reluctantly, they turned, and headed down the base of the mountain, and Gabriel turned to vengeance.

Tele paused by the stone archway while Tal Aval peered around the corner. She took the moment to examine her legs. Red and blistered, the wound was a fire to her skin, and stopping like this gave her the pause to consider the pain. She shut her eyes and held her breath before exhaling again, somehow hoping it'd help the pain recede. She needed to clean the wound and find a salve.

"Well?" Tele asked.

Tal Aval held up a hand, then turned back to her. "There are two guards at the next door, but I cannot know what is after."

"We'll find out when we get there," Tele said, almost snapping.

"If we walk to them, they will know we are prisoners," Tal Aval inclined his head to Tele's cuffs.

"I think they'd know by the way we look and smell right now. The cuffs would only be a garnish."

"Then we need your hands free to fight," Tal Aval whispered.

For the third time since she'd escaped the cell, Tele tried breaking the cuffs by wrenching them apart. It was crazy, she knew. Even at her best, she didn't have nearly enough strength to escape the bonds. And what little strength she had left wasn't worth wasting on the effort.

She scanned the hall. "If I could just find something to break them."

"And break your wrists?" Tal Aval frowned. "Not a good plan."

"I'd suggest something different if I thought there was the option," Tele said, then winced. She just wanted to get moving. The more they idled the more her leg burns stung. "We have to get the key."

"Good idea," Tal Aval said with a hint of sarcasm.

"Alright, but we can't just go in there. That cell is a death chamber right now."

"I can hold the air in my chest."

"And it burns," Tele said, and lifted a leg.

Tal Aval glanced down at the burns. "It is better than broken wrists."

"And—"

"*We are wasting time.*"

Tele led the way back to the cell door. She pressed an ear

against the door but couldn't hear a thing. She took hold of the slab of wood that barred the cell door, then looked at Tal Aval.

"Ready?"

Tal Aval nodded. "Yes."

Tele lifted the latch and leaned it against the frame, then took hold of the door's heavy handle. She gave Tal Aval one last look of confirmation—the signal to hold his breath—took in her own deep breath and opened the cell door.

The thick fog of poison tumbled out of the cell. Tal Aval fanned it away as he stepped across the cell's threshold. Tele caught his arm, pointed to the pool of water at their feet, and shook her head. He nodded, understanding her meaning.

Tele squinted in the dim light, searching for the key. The guards and Left-eye were unconscious on the cell floor. Each of them were burned as severely if not worse than Tele. She tiptoed around them, trying to avoid the bodies.

Her foot brushed against something wet, and she jerked it back. She examined it, but there was no burning. Tele almost let out a sigh of relief but held fast to the air in her lungs which had begun to burn. They needed to find the key quickly.

Tele looked to where Tal Aval searched. He stood near Left-eye, his legs spread wide to avoid the floor's waste. He shoved the half-blind man aside and pulled a thin, leather cord from under him. With a gentle yank, he freed the other end. A thin, key swung on the cord's end. Tele's hopes swelled.

She turned and stumbled out of the cell, before letting out what was left in her and took a quick breath. The breath stung painfully, and she instantly regretted it as she began coughing in fits. Tal Aval exited the cell behind her.

"Give me your hands."

Tele held her hands out to him, and Tal Aval turned them, searching for how to key fit into them to unlock the cuffs.

"It's there," Tele said. "At the top."

Tal Aval searched a moment longer before he saw the small hole for the key. He slipped it in and pulled.

"*No*," Tele said. "*Turn it. No, the other way*."

Tele turned to the sound of someone approaching. Down

the hall a man stumbled toward the guard post. Another man stepped out, shoving the first out of his way.

"Freedom!" the man shouted and limped toward them.

Tele turned back to Tal Aval, who'd paused to watch. "Get these things off of me."

Tal Aval turned back to his struggle with the key and the cuffs fell off her wrists. Tele stepped back as the man stumbled by, heading toward the dungeon stairs. Several more men stumbled into the light and began running toward the exit.

"We may not have gotten by the guards before," Tele said, "but I'm not sure they can stop us all."

Tal Aval nodded, and Tele followed him up the dungeon stairs. The guards at the end of the hall had already begun to strike down the captives, but they were being pushed back into the corners of the hall. They bolted down the corridor, and through the unguarded door.

Tele paused to remember the way that they'd come down—the left passage. "This way!"

"*No, wait.*" Tal Aval turned down the opposite way and crossed into the first room. Before Tele could follow, he reemerged with two swords. He tossed one to Tele. She caught it and smiled. It wasn't the nicest weapon, and it was certainly no växarot, but anything more than their bare fists gave them a much greater advantage.

"Brilliant," Tele said.

Tal Aval smiled grimly. "I do not know this word. *Come.*"

Tele led Tal Aval through the dungeon until they emerged from the depths of the stronghold. She took a moment to appreciate the dry, but fresh air. Nothing smelled sweeter. She wanted to stand there—to revel in the moment—but she thought better of it. They weren't safe yet.

Tele and Tal Aval paused to gaze out of a tall, narrow window that faced the stronghold's courtyard. The entire fortress was in a state of panic and high alert. Men and women crossed back and forth, carrying armaments and weapons. Officials shouted orders, and children were herded into buildings. Beyond it all, nearly unheard in the chaos, were distant screams and war cries.

Several Hzorah soldiers crossed the courtyard, carrying one of their own, his arm severed and bleeding out. One of them called out for a healer, but no one came to their aid. More soldiers filtered in, many were injured, but still limped to safety. Others were carried in but were dead—the soldiers just didn't realize it.

Within the stronghold's catacombs, Tele hadn't heard the commotion. She had no idea how long the battle had raged above her head. She didn't even know how long she'd even been locked away. It couldn't have been more than a week. Or was it longer? She'd lost her sense of time within the darkness.

"The Dominion?" Tal Aval asked.

"I believe so."

Tal Aval looked out to the soldiers filling the courtyard. "If we escape, we will walk into death."

"Yes," Tele said. "But if we stay, they'll put us away again. With how we look, and smell? We can't hide in here. And after what I did to those guards—"

A shout from down the hall cut Tele short. They both turned to see several men and women cross the intersecting passages, but she and Tal Aval went unnoticed in the panic.

"I think death will even come to the stronghold," Tele said.

Tal Aval sighed. "I believe you are right. But how are we to escape?"

"Well," Tele said, turning about. "The way we came in. I don't know any alternate ways out of the stronghold. There must be some other way out, but we don't have the time to search for one."

"And they will let us leave?" Tal Aval asked.

"Honestly, in all the commotion, I'm not sure they'll notice." She inclined her head. "This way."

Tele swung her legs over the window's edge before pushing off and falling two spans to the courtyard below. She turned to check if Tal Aval followed. The window had been quite narrow, and Tal Aval was wider than she. Perhaps she should have waited to see if he could fit. Tal Aval slipped through the window with little to spare for wiggle room. He dropped to the courtyard and gave her a nod of reassurance.

Tele turned and straightened. *They won't even notice*, she thought as she began walking straight for the tall stronghold gate. *Just walk straight for the entrance. Two people walking about in this chaos are nearly invisible.*

Countless men and women brushed past them. None of them stopped to even consider her. Several times, Tele turned back to look for Tal Aval, and each time he walked just behind, keeping pace within the river of bodies as they plodded upstream.

A low rumble of a horn sounded at the stronghold's walls and men who trotted along its perimeter rushed to the gate and began cranking the large wood and metal doors shut. There was a rush of men through the gateway that rippled back to where Tele carved the crowd, forcing her back in a sharp torrent.

"They're closing the gate!" a soldier near her shouted, along with a wave of similar sentiments.

Tele pushed against the crowd as she attempted to increase her speed. She slipped sideways between two arguing soldiers then ducked under others shouldering long spears. Then another few who carried a long-dead soldier.

In her brief surfacing to see above the crowd, she saw the large gates. They were half-way shut now, but men still poured in between their folds, desperately trying to find safety before the refuge was cut from them. If the yard was clear, they would have reached the gates within moments in a full sprint, but at her pace, they were far beyond a quick reach.

A stiff shoulder pushed her off balance, and Tele fell to the ground. Several other men fell over her, unable to stop in the unwieldy pressure. She tried to find her footing but couldn't rise above the mass of legs as the soldiers corralled into the courtyard.

"Tele!"

It was Tal Aval. His hand took hold of her arm and

wrenched her off the ground. Tele tried to compose herself as she found her feet but was soon pushed further back as the crowd of soldiers compressed enough to carry her off her feet, still upright.

As the pressure let up, she slipped between soldiers to catch the door before it closed, but, just as she and Tal Aval neared the gate, it shut, securing them inside.

FORTY-THREE

A TASTE OF REVENGE

Gabriel slowed his sprint when Gareth vanished into shadows behind a wall of rock. Gabriel was fast, but the general had a large lead on him. If Gabriel had kept his pace, he would have been atop the Deseran, but caution caught up with his intent. His journey into the Peaks had taught him that many of the narrow steps of the mountain came paired with danger. It'd be a pity to break his leg just before for he clutched victory.

Gabriel stepped lightly and followed Gareth into the darkness. Vines draped between the protruding rock and the mountain face, casting only glimpses of illumination. What the light afforded revealed a pathway that wound up the mountain like stairway carved into the stone itself.

General Gareth was nowhere to be seen.

Proceeding into the dark, he inclined his head to steal glimpses around jagged rocks pitched at harsh angles where the small light that trickled through the growth skirted shadows. Each crevasse he inspected was accompanied by a skip of his heart and twist to his gut.

I'm not afraid, Gabriel thought, letting his hand rest on the Crown Sabre and hoping the affirmation would alleviate the reflex of fear. The warmth of the sabre's hilt reassured him.

The climb cut to the left as it wound the mountain, and Gabriel considered turning back. How had Gareth disappeared? Perhaps there was some strange path he'd taken that Gabriel had overlooked in the darkness. Apart from growing winded, he'd become tired of the game that the general played.

There was a shift—a crackling of leaf or rock. He'd almost missed it, but something had moved. It may have been simply been a small animal, but if Gareth was waiting for him on the path ...

The Desolate-bound fool would show his shoved-up face—

Gabriel just barely noticed the flash of steel in the dim light before he leapt from under the sword's deadly gate. He slipped on the loose gravel and tumbled to the side. The Crown Sabre holster's belt tore from his waist and slid down the mountain path. His father's sword rang a metallic whine as it clashed against rock and into the darkness below.

The general revealed himself, crossing from the rock's safety and onto the path. He attacked again, but Gabriel dodged the stroke, slipping further down the incline and tumbling until a rocky landing halted his fall. By a miracle, as if it were placed in his hand, he found the Crown Sabre's hilt and pulled it defensively.

"In my time in Hzorah," General Gareth said, his blade spinning skillfully between nimble hands, "I have only seen two kinds of filth: traitors and fools. From the moment I set eyes on you, I could see that you were no traitor. The Wisdoms did not need to tell me that, which only leaves that of the fool. Tell me, boy, how did you come to walk so squarely in your father's footsteps?"

Gabriel ducked and spun as the general struck again. His sword bounced off the mountain wall, tearing away a layer of dirt. The sword again between them, Gabriel recovered and evened his breathing.

"How," Gareth continued, "have you allowed yourselves to fall into the prideful trap of self-sovereignty? There is only *one* we are to serve—the true Wizard. And, instead, you've deceived a multitude into blasphemy."

Gareth attacked, but this time Gabriel caught his advance and parried, pushing him back. The general's effort was only momentarily countered as the weight of the path's incline gave the man an overbearing advantage. Gabriel turned at the next strike, trying to shift the duel a quarter turn to give himself at least the footing for a fair fight, but the Deseran blocked his attempt and pushed him further down the path's slope.

Gabriel fought for his footing as surely as he fought off General Gareth's blade. The crunch of his sliding boots mixed with the scrape of steel brushing steel. He met each assault with its counter—each cadence with its complement.

He let the whole of his soul pour into the duel. He had nothing else to lose as the world turned to ice below.

General Gareth smirked as they pulled apart. "It's pointless, you know. You think that this fight is what will win this war? That taking the life from me will crumble what is just and true? Come now, *prince*. Are you really the fool?"

Pointless? Avenging his father was pointless? Avenging his people was pointless? Mel, Lurin, and Urwell's deaths were pointless?

Gabriel fixed the Dominion general with a glare. "Perhaps you're right, but you'll do fine for now."

He charged, stepping into the ninth cadence with the second extension. General Gareth blocked the thrust, but fell back a step, losing ground to the mountain path. Gabriel pushed forward, contorting his form to suit the all-but-fair odds.

Gareth pushed back and forced Gabriel into the fourth cadence; the fourth to the fifth, then the sixth, then back to the fourth. The forms revolved, with Gabriel losing ground with each turn. Gritting his teeth against the inevitability of the risk he knew he had to take, Gabriel lurched into the seventh cadence.

Gareth took a swipe at his middle, cutting into the leather armor and splitting it in two. Gabriel spun to the right, a quarter-turn that placed him on level footing with his opponent. Their blades met again, close enough that he could smell the general's breath.

"You're talented with your father's sabre," Gareth said. "But you haven't unlocked its true power yet."

Gabriel risked a glance down and realized for the first time that Gareth's blade was strikingly similar—the same silver metalwork with incomprehensible runes etched across the blade. Gabriel had been told that his father's sword was one of a kind, unrivaled in its beauty in strength. Legendary.

"It's a pity that you'll never behold it's true potential," the Dominion general smirked at Gabriel's confusion. "You don't even know, do you? Your heathen father didn't even tell you what it could do?"

"My father is *not* a heathen."

Gabriel leaned into the next attack and General Gareth fell back a step but kept his back from falling to the rock face. Their swords met again and again, but the general never failed to thwart his every move. Gareth surpassed even the most skilled swordsmen he'd ever encountered. His form was impeccable, and his grace was as elegant as any youth. He warded Gabriel's attacks with the slightest of hand, even within the confined space.

Stilling his mind and allowing his reflexes to take control, Gabriel searched for his out. The general's swordsmanship left nothing to be desired, and he didn't appear to have any ailment that accompanied a man who sported gray in his beard. His uniform was air-tight and looked to be reinforced with leather down to the—

Then Gabriel saw it. At the general's waist, a small, square pouch bounced in rhythm with his movements.

The book.

The book he'd used to call down the vile magic that had scarred the land and destroyed his troops. The book that had crippled the treaties forged by Caldor and brought them to war.

The book that had taken his father from him.

Navid had told him that it was important that he take the book from Gareth. He wasn't sure what he'd do with it, but if the book could trigger the magic, there was likely something in it that could stop it.

Taking advantage of Gabriel's instant of distraction, the general cut into his left shoulder, and pulled his sword away, wet with his blood. Gabriel wrenched back, wincing as the pain rattled his nerve. He cursed himself for allowing his mind to wander.

Gareth stepped away and brandished his sword. To Gabriel's shock, the sword began to glow as if the blade had re-entered its smithing fires. A guttural purr accompanied the sword's pale light that resonated across his flesh.

"Finally," Gareth grinned. "A taste of a revenge, but now we desire the whole meal."

As if responding to the general's sword, the ground rumbled, excited by his sword's hum. Small rocks danced about the mountain's surface. Even the air churned to the rhythm of vengeance.

Instinct reclaimed control, and Gabriel stepped forward again to catch the next round of fury. General Gareth countered his charge. Buzzing, the general's sword rattled his bones. The man's attacks had strengthened.

Loosed in the chaos, rocks slipped beneath their feet and pulled Gabriel and General Gareth several spans down the mountain path. Gabriel tipped, losing balance, and Gareth—seizing his opportunity—swung his sword. The flat of it struck Gabriel's hand hard enough to knock his blade up through the vined canopy.

Gabriel found tentative footing and spun on an uncertain heel. He pulled the dagger at his hip and swiped at the general's left side, freeing both the book and a gushing stream of blood.

Gareth cried out. He fell to a knee, then tumbled as inertia carried him down the mountain. Gabriel followed, carried down the mountain with the avalanche of unearthed sediment.

He leapt over loose rock and streaming dirt. If the quake continued, they'd both be buried beneath the rubble.

By Desolate's Hand, he managed to stay upright, and ceased the opportunity to leap over Gareth to where the path evened. He bent over and snatched the book from the rubble, then stepped away from Gareth, gripping the small volume close to his stomach.

General Gareth rolled to his side and propped himself up with his sword like a glowing cane. He reached out toward Gabriel with desperate hand. "No!"

In response to the Dominion general's outcry, Gareth's sword glowed ever brighter, and the world beneath them roared in chorus, splitting the ground between them. Gabriel backed away from the chasm, but Gareth, still on bended knee, was caught between the splintered rock.

At the corner of his eye, Gabriel saw the glint of steel, and he turned to it. There, not more than a few strides away lay the Crown Sabre. Moving slowly to keep his balance as the world rumbled, Gabriel reached his father's weapon and pulled it from under a thin layer of dark earth.

Gabriel stuffed the book in his knife belt and took up his father's sword. The scabbard warmed under his touch, as if inviting him to free it from its slumber—to allow it to breathe for the first time in years.

Gabriel turned back and approached the edge of the newly erected cliff before him. Below and just out of his immediate reach was the Dominion general. Trapped under a layer of rubble, the man glared at him with as much hate as Gabriel had ever seen.

"So, prince," Gareth growled. "This is how it ends?"

He could reach him. He'd done it when he had to reach Fabi. Even if he lost his footing in his descent down the cliff face, the fall was shallow enough that he would recover. And trapped under the rubble, Gareth would be helpless in the face of his vengeance. He could finally finish what he came here to do.

He would avenge his father's death.

"Go on, then," General Gareth spat. "Strike me down. Spill my blood. End it. It's the last, small victory you'll ever know."

Gabriel shoved the blade back into its scabbard, then turned and started down the mountain path.

"Where are you going, boy?" General Gareth shouted after him. "Have you lost your nerve? Not only the fool, but a weak fool?"

Gabriel didn't turn back. He didn't need to kill the man. He was as good as dead anyway. It would accomplish nothing of true value. The only thing that was important now was figuring out how to stop the magic. That was what his honor demanded, and he wouldn't risk it all for vengeance.

"Come back and finish your filthy work, prince! Don't walk away. This is your only chance to do what your father failed to do!"

Gabriel jogged down the path and into the light. *To Desolate with you, General.*

FORTY-FOUR

OCEAN OF ICE

Navid sprinted just behind Aeron as they navigated around the long, curved streak of ice in the middle of the Hzorah plain. Near white with the frozen water, it was as if a glacier had jutted from the earth below and grew straight up into the air as high as twenty spans. And where the ice was transparent, Navid saw Hzorah soldiers, frozen in mute terror.

Above, the dragons circled, diving occasionally but had all but ended their first attacks. Hundreds of Hzorah troops had been swept aside by the rivers of ice, encapsulated into a quick, cold death. Many of the remaining soldiers had crowded into Stronghold Aear. Others retreated east to Stronghold Gordal. Several of the winged beasts had followed them above, nipping at their heels and shaving off their numbers. Navid doubted many of them would make it there alive.

The ice wall that they circled curved toward the Stronghold. They'd been forced along this indirect route when it became apparent that this was the only path they could take without plunging into a hoard of Deseran soldiers and risk being devoured within their ranks.

Navid nearly tripped over the man in their path that Aeron jumped over without a second thought. Trapped by ice from the waist down he raised a hand, pleading. "Help … don't leave me here. Help me! Help!"

Cainan pushed past Navid to follow Aeron. "Keep up, seer."

"Don't leave me," the soldier's words slurred and his eyes rolled back in his head. He was losing consciousness. "Please. Mercy."

Pulling together every bit of will he could, he stepped over the man and followed the Hzorah soldiers. Despite the cold air that tumbled from the ice, his face warmed, and before he could stop it, a tear slipped down to his chin.

I'm doing the right thing. He was. It had to be the right thing.

Stronghold Aear stood out over the labyrinth of ice and fallen soldiers, its walls promising refuge against the supernatural threat above. Aeron slowed as he rounded the icy partition.

"We're shut out," Aeron said.

Navid trudged through the thick ice as he approached the stronghold's entry. The gate's doors were large enough to fit two carriages abreast and tall enough to allow more than twice the height of a man. As accommodating as they were, the gates were sealed with nary a guardsman to grant them access.

Undeterred, Bear stepped forward and pounded his fist on the thick door. "Open the gate!" He repeated it several times over, but was met with abject silence.

"We're too late," Aeron said. "They're not going to open the gates now. It's too dangerous."

"Scorch it," Fabi said through a clenched jaw.

Navid turned back to see a fist of Dominion soldiers—at least one hundred—marching toward them. A couple dozen of them carried a thick battering ram.

"Wisdoms," Paitin whispered. "That will get us inside."

"They're going to crush us against the walls," Fabi said.

He was right. The ice around them left them little room to maneuver out of the way. And this was the enemy. They wouldn't let them live in return for them politely stepping aside.

As if to multiply the certainty of their doom, another mob of soldiers began to file around the ice like a swarm of ants out of an ant hill.

"What do we do?" Bear asked.

All eyes turned to the High Lord's son.

"We fight." Cainan drew his sword. "'To live with honor and to die with honor.'"

The rest of them drew their swords as one.

Navid summoned his växarot. This would be the end of them. This was the day that existence faded to Desolate—the day that the war was lost before it began.

Terror rattled his nerves. Cainan gave instructions, but Navid couldn't hear them over the earth-rumbling march, the war cries, the pumping of his blood. Normally, this would have been a point where he would begin his mantra to quell the itch. Instead, he let Desolate's call fill him.

He looked to each of them, trying to find where his greatest advantage was. None of the men were particularly small or appeared incapable. In fact, they all seemed savage, as though the battle had revealed the animal beneath the man.

Navid's chest tightened. He could feel the odds of his survival slipping away. He could *literally* feel it. It was an unpleasant sensation—like his stomach growing ill. But it was more than that. It rang every nerve within his being. The same feeling he'd felt at Dunham Lake as a child as the frozen lake fell to pieces and threatened to steal his life from him.

Navid stepped backward, before pulling into form—the forms Tele had taught him.

Another circled.

Three. There were at least three dragons out there.

Tele had seen first-hand what these creatures were capable of. Twice, she'd walked among the death and destruction they'd wrought. Caught in the warpath of such fierce creatures, the Hzorah army would suffer the same fate.

The Dominion had won.

No. Tele frowned as she watched the dragons circle overhead. *No. There's still hope.*

"Aear." She turned to Tal Aval, when she recalled the Tal word. "That's how I stopped the dragon that attacked your village. I stopped them with arrows of fire."

Tal Aval squinted, and he looked to the sky. "These dragons are too far for arrows. Too far to reach."

He was right. Tele had stopped the dragon with fire arrows. And she had just barely achieved that. She wasn't an expert shot. Her victory was likely due to the fact that she had such a large target. Even if she were an expert shot, she couldn't shoot an arrow the required distance—no one could.

Tele suppressed a flinch as a thud shook the stronghold gate. Fear crawled across the soldiers in the courtyard. Many of them had watched their fellow soldiers slaughtered in battle, or frozen like the thousands in Caldor. Some worked frantically to bind the wounds of those who'd hobbled through the stronghold's gate. Others stood, watching the gates, praying that they were safe behind the thick walls, and that Desolate's Hand would hold back the Dominion long enough for them to be satisfied with their victory and regroup.

Another thud. The gates clattered. Dust loosed from cracks packed with years of wind-flung dirt. All around, the soldiers shouted, some wept, still others stood silently, awaiting death.

"They're using a battering ram," a soldier, a few spans away, explained to someone Tele couldn't see. "That's why they brought those beasts with the horns in their mouths with them."

Tele frowned. *Elephants? They brought Elephants?* She'd always wanted to see an elephant in real life.

"*How long?*" Tal Aval stared forward, eyes locked with the large gates. "*How long before the door falls?*"

"*I don't know.*"

Her hand rubbed the hilt of the sword. She would fight. She would fight to her very last breath. Only in life was there hope. Only in life could she do what she'd been tasked to do.

"*You must keep the Covenant safe. Find the true Wizard and deliver it to him! Run, my child! Run!*"

She was still the last vessel for her father's work. She and Navid had found the Wizard—at least a version of him. And now, she had to use the one chance she'd been given to win.

"A spell," Tele said, she turned back to Tal Aval. "We'll write a spell. You have the ability of Wizard Titan. We could write a spell and you can bring it to fruition."

"I have a small portion of ability," Tal Aval said. "If the spell does not work or is insufficient, we will lose it forever."

I can do this. I have to. Tele's fingernails dug into her palms. This was a chance at survival. "*I'll gamble doubt over certain death any day.*"

Tal Aval gave a grim nod. "*So be it.*"

Her resolve established, her mind began to work. "I need something to write with."

FORTY-FIVE

A FLOURISH WITHIN THE CHAOS

The battering ram shook the ground as it struck the gate once more. After only two strikes, Navid's ability now anticipated it. He compensated for the distraction by leaning into his attack at each strike while the Dominion soldiers were caught off guard each time.

Their first priority was to strike down the wave of soldiers behind the battering ram. The danger wasn't in the gate opening. The danger was the soldiers who might get inside if the gate opened.

In the interval between strikes, Navid fell back a step, twisting about their ranks, appearing before one set of soldiers then another as the continuous wave of soldiers pressed ever forward.

He varied the pattern to keep the soldiers unsuspecting. It would be risky to let them think this through. He needed to have them confused, unorganized. Their inability to work together would be his greatest asset. He couldn't explain that intuition, but he knew it to be true.

Navid was the only defender to the battering ram's left. He'd allowed the rest of the Hzorah soldiers to defend the other side—insisted on it, really. His eyes open to the most imminent eventualities, he knew their best chance of survival would be to have them stick together. They understood each other as a unit. And with so many soldiers bearing down on them, splitting the group raised the danger exponentially while increasing his chances by a negligible measure.

The ram struck once more and Navid took another step backward. Sensing death, he gritted his teeth. If he didn't do more than repel the soldiers, he'd soon be overwhelmed by exhaustion and killed. He was nearing the end of his ability to spare their lives.

There is only you and your staff. Nothing else.

Navid relaxed and allowed the weight of the växarot meld with his hand, let it become a part of him. As he calmed his mind, he felt the odds shift again. This time in his favor. It was a near blissful sensation, filling him with confidence.

Sensing opportunity, he stepped forward and struck left, the växarot staff instantly reformed into a blade and cut through the necks of two of the soldiers. The unexpected move paused the group with a moment of precious confusion. But even that passed as the soldiers fell, and the remaining three started for him.

Navid turned, parrying the first strike from his left, then turned again to catch another from his right. Danger pressed in on him, but he warded it back, letting the forms Tele had taught him keep the odds even. Before a soldier could strike, he felt the blade's approach, like the memory of being struck down. As if he had been given the opportunity to turn back time and correct the mistakes he'd made. And he corrected each, his växarot becoming a blur between the soldiers.

The växarot twisted, alive in his grip and shifted from form to form as Navid willed it. A staff, a sword, a spear. Every swing of his weapon stilled a heart. Every turn of his body cheated death.

But even as he pushed them back, he could still feel his fate edging toward the precipice of Desolate. If he didn't strike them all down, they would win. There was only one of him, and, eventually, he would make a mistake. If it wasn't a mistake, it would be exhaustion. There was no other way.

Navid felt the odds shift once more, moving from imminent failure and back toward the light of hope. He pushed away from his attackers and stumbled back, then fell before rolling to a crouched position.

He looked up, expecting the three Dominion soldiers to continue their attack, but they'd halted in their steps, looking just behind him. Navid turned to see Cainan charging across the plain.

Flanking from the right, Cainan tore through the line of soldiers. Their ranks split, the soldiers fell back, forced into a brief retreat by the blockade of death the soldier created.

"You look like you could use a hand," Cainan said without looking to him. He held his sword to the enemy—ready for their retaliation.

"You shouldn't have left your men behind," Navid said.

"They don't need my help. They can handle themselves just fine. If anything, my ego was in the way." Surprisingly, he chuckled. "Jeremiah, you damn fool."

"What?"

"I've never fought with a seer."

"I've never fought with a High Lord."

"Try to keep up, will you?" Cainan said then launched himself at the enemy.

Navid joined him. Sensing where danger met opportunity, he let his instincts drive is actions. While he couldn't control what Cainan did, he could complement. He became a shield or distraction where his half-brother needed it—a wedge in a tight place, a lever against oppressive odds.

But there was something wrong. He felt it through every fiber of his being.

Danger.

Navid grabbed Cainan and pulled him back behind the ice wall as an avalanche of white roared across his path. Where the frost failed to catch them, the cold air did, pushing them backward as the warmth was siphoned from their blood.

Pelts of ice sprayed Navid's face and the field darkened as something large eclipsed the sun. Over the wall of ice, a large white lizard craned its head to look down at them with fierce, ice-blue eyes. Its head swayed before turning to the sky and letting out a screech that tore at his eardrums.

The dragon rose into the air, but instead of taking flight, it dived. He turned to run, but just as he managed his first step, the beast landed. The weight of it shook the ground, tossing Navid off balance and into the ice wall.

Navid tumbled as he fell. Rolling to his back, he found himself face to face with the reptile's cold gaze and a row of sharp teeth. Rattled, he crawled backward, his hand already reaching for his växarot. He gripped it.

Where was Cainan?

Gusts of frozen mucus misted from the lizard's nose. It quickened, as if the dragon was winded. This close, he could see the dragon for what it was—shards of crystalline water. They locked into an unbroken pattern down the length of the creature's body. Light, though faint, actually passed right through its body, though most of the light seemed to reflect back away before reaching the other side, giving it a near radiant glow.

Navid emptied his mind and opened himself to what his senses were trying to tell him—what his ability was trying to tell him.

Cainan's form fell from the sky. Screaming with his sword raised high, he struck at the dragon's head. The beast recoiled as a chunk of ice fell away from its snout.

No. Sensing death, Navid found his feet.

The dragon attacked with a jet of ice. The force of it cleaved Cainan in two, scattering his remains about the snow.

Tele scribbled another set of runes across the parchment. She'd been lucky enough to steal a bundle from a war scribe. He'd protested at first, but in the air of terror, he didn't put a grand effort into getting his materials back after she'd snatched the bundle from his arms.

"*You should hurry*," Tal Aval said from behind her.

"*I'm trying*," Tele snapped. "What's the Tal word for glass?"

"Glass?"

"It's like transparent rock." Tele looked up and scanned the area, but there was nothing close that she could point to. "It's like ... *Remember in Azuri when we went to the first inn? The windows had been broken. The clear rock that they'd placed in their windows.* That's glass."

"We do not have glass," Tal Aval said. "But we have seen rocks that are clear. 'Lastruk' it is called."

"*Lastruk*," Tele whispered to herself as she wrote. She'd harness the power of the sun to focus a beam of heat. "A large convex lens could do it."

That could overcome the distance problem, but she didn't understand how to forge glass, meaning she couldn't build one with a spell.

The hand lens. I could write a spell that expands the size of it. That way I don't need to understand how to forge it. It's already made for me.

She reached for the lens in her pocket but came up empty. It was in her pack that she'd left back in Azuri.

But would it have mattered? She still needed to angle the lens correctly to focus the light. The dragons were above. She was below. She'd need two spells. One to expand the lens, and one to somehow hoist it above in a way that they could direct it.

The plan was flawed from the start. They had but a drop of magic to use. The spell had to be elegant, simple. She needed to accomplish this in one step.

From the sound of it, the gate fractured at the next thud.

"Tele ..." Tal Aval warned. "I think we have run out of time. It is now time to fight."

No.

Another thud.

No, scorch it, no!

She could have done this. She was so close. She just needed more time. She needed everyone to stop chattering so she could think clearly. She needed the burns on her legs to cool—

The burns on her legs were from the dungeons. The cleaning agent they used down there had reacted with the excrement to a dangerous effect. But there was something else that compound could do when mixed with water.

Tele discarded the parchment she'd been working on and began a new set of runes as her idea snapped into place. Her studies with her father's and uncle's work converged, giving light to a solution.

"The spell that conjures the dragons must rely on collecting water from the atmosphere," Tele told Tal Aval. "The cleaning agent's basic chemical makeup should be available in the atmosphere in ready quantities, but the water that's in the air naturally dissolves it. The spell that created the dragons has already removed the water, meaning the element that I need is easy to collect. The other necessary compound is organic—expelled from crops and livestock—all abundant on the plains."

"*Tele*," Tal Aval backed into her as she wrote. "*This is not looking good*."

Tele took a beat to sketch an equation to the side of the spell to ensure she didn't miscalculate. "When put together—element with compound—then mixed with the condensed water used to create the dragons, an endothermic reaction occurs."

She lifted the parchment and scanned the runes to check her work.

"And that means?" Tal Aval asked.

She turned to him. "They'll melt."

At the gate, several stronghold guards backed away, clearing the way for the flood of men. The soldiers quieted, and Tele tensed, expecting the final blow to the stronghold gate to be the one to tear it to splinters.

But the final blow never came.

Tele turned her head, listening. There was shouting, then screaming. Not that of efforts being coordinated by a commanding officer, but confusion and hysteria. Something wasn't right. She looked at Tal Aval and he met her eyes with the same bewilderment.

The cries from outside died, and frightened whispers broke out among the soldiers. Tele stood on the tips of her toes to see the stronghold's guards slowly approach the gate as if unsure if it was safe. A guard slid open a small window and looked outside. For a moment, he stood there, unmoving. Then he backed away slowly before turning and waving at the others. The guards sprinted back to their cranks.

"They're opening the gates again!" a soldier shouted along with a wave of panic.

The crowd shifted, pushing Tele forward again. She stumbled before she slipped between the two men in front of her then again between two to her right. She passed another set of soldiers before encountering a knot of men too compressed to separate until she used the handle of her sword to pry them apart. Unnerved by the strange woman's passage, they shifted, allowing her to pass. Tele turned to see Tal Aval, not far behind, following her as she parted the mob.

The gates swung outward as Tele neared the edge. A harsh, dry draft of cold air swept inside, forcing her to shut her eyes in pain. When she reopened them, she gasped.

The fields outside of the stronghold were completely frozen—as frozen as Caldor had been when she'd journeyed to the city. Thousands of men were covered in snow and ice a span high, caught in what appeared to be a sudden avalanche. A large wooden battering ram protruded from the ice, unmanned. Snow churned about, obscuring how far she could see beyond the gate.

Tele pushed the rest of the way to the front of the soldiers, their whispers and confused swears falling behind her. She walked straight toward the gate, and her gaze locked on the ocean of ice beyond.

Then, Tele saw five figures in the distance, sprinting toward the stronghold. She couldn't make out who they were, but they appeared to be soldiers. As they drew near, Tele could see the leather armor of the Hzorah troops.

Further beyond, she saw another figure. Växarot in hand, he danced amidst a small swarm of Dominion soldiers. He was death itself, a flourish within the chaos—a viper in a field of mice.

It was Navid. *Navid.*

Tele could hardly believe what she saw. *This* was the seer the legends spoke of: fiercely lethal and majestic in his element.

A shadow crossed behind, and a large winged lizard—a dragon— landed behind them.

No!

"Behind you!" Tele shouted, but Navid was too far away to hear her warning.

Tele burst into a sprint. A guard caught her arm as she crossed the gateway, but Tele wrenched free and climbed onto the mount of ice. She thought she could hear Tal Aval following, and turned to his approach.

She handed him the parchment. "We have to activate this spell. It'll attract the compound in the air to ice—the dragons—causing the reaction needed to stop them."

Tal Aval nodded as he squinted at the runes she'd written in haste. She wished she'd had to time to write them clearly. He was new to reading his language, and this was hardly the time for error.

Tal Aval began to chant, and Tele watched with anxious anticipation as Navid fought on. The dragon before him gazed at his minuscule form as if waiting for an opening to isolate Navid and attack him alone.

Navid prevented the Dominion soldiers from splitting, corralling them into a knot. One moment he was to the left. The next, to their right. The dragon twisted its long neck and struggled to lock onto Navid's ever-changing position.

He can't possibly keep this up forever. Tele chanced a glance at a chanting Tal Aval. *Why isn't it working?*

Just as she had the thought, the dragon drew back. Clouds of vapor shed from its skin, and the creature cried out as it slowly expanded into tiny, iridescent droplets of water. She watched until the animal evaporated into the clouds.

Tele looked to the skies where the creatures lost their form, stretched out as the counter spell weakened the icy bonds that kept the creatures solid. The clouds churned and darkened as the reptiles rejoined with the sky.

The ice across the field began to melt away. In its need for stark simplicity, the spell had been constructed to attract the required compounds to ice rather than the dragons specifically, and it had worked beautifully.

Tele sprinted the distance to Navid, sloshing through half-melted snow and slowly evaporating puddles. The air itself glowed as it filled with moisture and light refracted about the field. Shades of red and orange arced over the skies, tenting the world in warmth.

She slowed as she approached the seer. He knelt in the mud with his växarot planted in the dirt—a stave to his slumping form. She knelt beside him and slid under his arm to help him to his feet. He accepted her assistance.

Tele gazed into his golden eyes. "Are you alright?"

He smiled, his eyes aglow with new life. "I am now."

"Don't get ahead of yourself," she said, fixing her tone to reprimand, but couldn't stop herself from smiling.

"Here," Tal Aval said, as he trotted up to them. "Let me help."

With Tal Aval as Navid's second crutch, they walked together back to the stronghold. As they neared the gate, Navid had already begun to walk on his own, but Tele didn't let go. With him near, she felt whole again. And she never wanted that feeling to go away.

When they crossed into the stronghold, the guards watched them in terror. The soldiers in the courtyard backed away, giving them a wide berth for fear that the seer might again unleash his wrath but on them this time. Navid dismissed his växarot as he paused before the soldiers inside.

"I'm not going to hurt you," he said, his voice horse in his exhaustion.

The soldiers' defensive stances didn't shift.

"Try offering them a waterskin," Tele suggested.

Navid turned and frowned at her.

"It worked with me," Tele said, smiling.

A Hzorah soldier approached them from behind. He clasped hands with Navid before drawing him into a hug. "I ain't never seen anything like it."

Another few soldiers came into the stronghold, the one at the fore spoke first. "Wisdoms, Bear! Let the man breathe!"

Tele allowed the soldiers to approach. Their approval was infectious. The courtyard's soldiers relaxed, returning to the injured while others cheered and chatted about the spectacle that Navid had shown them.

Lightning flashed and thunder rumbled. And, as if the magic summoned were no more than a dream, the heavens parted, and the rain fell.

FORTY-SIX

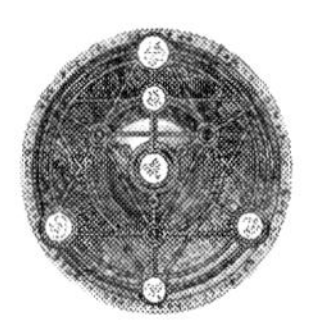

HOPE ENOUGH

Amie gritted her teeth as the path turned uphill. The incline was slight, but it was the first significant pitch against gravity since they'd left the Shadow Peaks. Even with the favorable terrain thus far, her aching feet and legs demanded that she stop.

Mara's head injury made it hard for her to walk for very long before she became too lightheaded to continue. Mara insisted she was fine whenever Amie caught her stumbling, but Amie would immediately find a place to rest whenever she faltered. Better they rest often than risk a fall that could break a limb. Then they'd really be in trouble.

Moreover, it was too dangerous to have Saleh—that's what Amie had named the horse—pull the cart in his condition, so they had had to leave the cart behind and walk, pacing themselves slow and taking frequent breaks to make sure that his injury didn't completely cripple him. Amie had promised Saleh that she'd make sure he got better, and she intended to see that through.

True to his word, Bam Rav had helped them escape, freeing them both before he abandoned his own post. Bam Rav left the book he'd been tasked with learning with Amie after Mara convinced him that the book could be dangerous and he couldn't risk it falling back into the Dominion's hands. Amie and Mara were the perfect guardians of the text. No one would suspect them of carrying it.

The three reasoned that it was best they find alternate routes out of the Shadow Peaks, covering their tracks for at least the first several hours to give the soldiers no solid leads as to which way they'd gone. The soldiers would return soon and could travel swiftly. But it wouldn't matter how fast they could travel if they couldn't decipher what direction they'd gone in. They split the supplies, leaving only a small ration of water for Ale Face for when he returned.

When Amie had asked Bam Rav when she might expect him to visit the Kruv House and perhaps take her up on the offer for a place for he and his family to stay, he smiled sadly before he said "soon," but his eyes betrayed the truth of it. He didn't intend to return, or at least he didn't believe he would.

And with that, they went their separate ways.

Beside her, Mara stumbled. Before she fell, Amie caught her arm.

"Don't slow," Mara winced. "We need to keep momentum on these hills."

Amie shook her head. "No. We can rest. Saleh needs a break, too."

Mara relented and allowed Amie to prepare a place for her to sit. It was still a few hours until sunset, but she'd intended to stop for the night within hour the anyway.

"Do you hear that?" Mara asked as Amie passed her a half slice of bread and a bit of cheese she'd carved into a meager meal with the dagger.

Amie tuned her ears to her surroundings. A gentle breeze whistled as it fought the evening heat. Several swift arrows danced about the branches of sparsely distributed trees, their spring mating calls blending with an emergent summer song. A camouflaged toad chirped away, confident its mate would arrive with haste.

"Not really," Amie said.

"It's quiet." Mara glanced over her shoulder. "The sounds of battle are gone."

"That's good."

"Perhaps. But that could also mean that soldiers might begin to scatter in the disorder. We might have soldiers to contend with."

Amie forced herself to smile. "Well, I wouldn't mind a few handsome soldiers giving us a hand."

"It's not the Hzorah soldiers I'm concerned about finding us."

She'd gotten used to the feeling, but she now felt quite exposed in her nightshift. Boots *and* a good dress. That's what she'd be buying when she got back home. And she was never taking any of it off ever again.

"So, where do we go from here?" Amie asked.

"We keep going until we can find a place to truly rest. Perhaps a farm where someone kind will be willing to help us. And then back home to Azuri."

It was overwhelmingly practical. That was Mara's way. And in this case, Amie couldn't deny that was the right thing to do. However, something pricked at her—almost a bit of sadness that they were to return home. The Kruv House could return to prominence if she and Mara put in the same care her father had, and they'd again have more patrons than time. She'd get her boots and dress. She'd wait tables. She'd clean and cook and retire to her chambers.

It was all so … normal.

"And then," Mara continued, "when Uncle Reese and Aunt Bell are ready to take over the Kruv House, we will need to go to Caldor and find Gavini."

Amie looked up at her. "What?"

"The entire world has changed. Our king is dead. Caldor has fallen. Hzorah is at war. Every bit of stability our lives are built on depended on the order of our previous life. And that book we took from Bam Rav could be important to keeping the Dominion from destroying everything we know and love. Gavini left to help hold the world together, but he's not a young man, and if anything were to happen to him, I need to be there to take his place." She looked at Amie. "*We* need to be there. It's what we were trained for."

Amie nodded. She wasn't at all Mara's equal when it came to what Gavini had taught them—not by any stretch. She wasn't sure that she was really needed at all. "I understand."

Mara took a bite of the cheese before she sighed. "I hate the Dominion. They're all filthy, irredeemable dogs."

"They're not all irredeemable," Amie said as she used the dagger to cut herself a piece of cheese. "There's at least one that has turned to good. And that's hope enough for me."

Gabriel led the procession over another short bridge. It wasn't the most direct way to the Crown Palace, but he preferred the road because it skirted the thick of the market in favor of a long stretch of river taxi docks. The route circled the palace and its courtyards where several gardeners worked to arrange the yellow roses, Hzorah acrids, and blue-eyed dandies, and yet another dozen gardeners tamed the shrubbery into artificial but pleasing shapes.

Though the Crown City was alive with activity in the distance, his party had grown suddenly quiet as they neared the palace. At first, they'd all been silent, but soon enough, they'd warmed again and became something like the Second League he'd loved being a part of.

The last few hours worked to revert them back to silence. Bear's never-ending curiosity about South Hzorah and Armoth had kept Paitin going on and on about the marvels of his mother's homeland, but now they simply stared about, taking in the city. Aeron and Fabi were generally more somber during their journey south but now looked about as reserved as Jae. And Jae … well, Gabriel wasn't sure he could be less intrusive if he disappeared altogether.

Gabriel looked at Fabi. When he caught his eye, Fabi looked away. "You can look at me, you know."

"Of course, Majesty," Fabi said before putting a forced effort into turning back to meet his gaze.

"And don't call me that."

"Yes, Your Ma— Yes, Sergeant."

"Scorch it ..." Gabriel turned, walking backward toward the final bridge that crossed over to the palace grounds. "Will you all stop treating me like a king? The whole reason I left this place is so that I wouldn't have to be subject to that. Can we just go back to how we were?"

Aeron shook his head. "It can't be that way."

"You're the king, Gabe," Bear said. "Ain't nothing gonna change that."

Gabriel was relieved to hear his nickname being used instead of "majesty." He sighed, still walking in reverse. He'd walked this path countless times and was certain there was nothing to obstruct him. "Listen, I'm going to need friends here—real friends, not subjects. I need people I can rely on because we're bonded by trust rather than subjugation. Can you be that for me?" He looked at each of them as they looked at each other with uncertainty. "Please?"

"We can be that," Fabi said. "If you can overlook where I came from and treat me like a friend, we can do the same for you."

The others agreed.

"Good," Gabriel said. "I know it seems strange, but you'll understand once—"

Gabriel collided with something solid. Its armed gripped him and turned him around. It was a palace guard. The man's eyes widened when he realized who he held in his grip.

"Wisdoms!" The soldier let go of him as if his hands would surely burn, then turned to the First League guard behind him. "It's the king! Form up! Send a runner ahead! Right bloody now!"

Gabriel glanced over his soldier to the Second League soldiers. "See what I mean?"

With practiced order, the palace guard executed the command, and before Gabriel had time to interject, a dozen soldiers had formed around them as they entered the palace grounds.

"It's too bad you're not going to be able to tell everyone that you slayed the Dominion general," Fabi said.

"Attempting it would have been too risky," Gabriel said. "It wasn't worth it."

"So was risking your life that day on the cliffside," Fabi said. "That was just me. That general was an important target. It was worth the risk, Gabe."

Gabriel shook his head as his hand found the Crown Sabre's hilt. "Not to me."

In the days they'd spent traveling back to the Crown City, Gabriel had replayed what had happened in the Shadow Peaks over and over in his head. When he turned away and left the Dominion general at the cliff's base, he was following his instincts, listening to the natural rhythms of battle. If asked back then, he wouldn't have been able to explain exactly why he chose to do what he did other than the fact that he'd gotten what was most important: the magic book the general used to summon those wicked ice monsters.

And, really, that was reason enough.

But there was something that Gareth had said in the Peaks that had shaken him—about the Crown Sabre. He'd said that Gabriel hadn't unlocked the sword's true potential. The stories told about his father and the sword were mythical, and even his father had confirmed some of them to be true. But he'd never actually seen is father use the sword, never truly experienced how—as it was said—he transformed into a god of war when he wielded it. He'd only ever seen Jeremiah the king, never Jeremiah the warrior.

More than that, something strange had occurred within the mountains. Gareth's sword—which as strikingly similar to Gabriel's—had actually *glowed*. When Gareth struck, it was as if the strength of two men bore down on him. And when his wrath was ignited, nature itself responded to his call. That sort of thing wasn't natural. Gareth's sword was something fearsome and unparalleled.

If asked now why he'd turned away from finishing Gareth off, his answer would be altogether different. Something deep inside rejected the idea—warned him that it wasn't safe, that the time had not yet come. But he couldn't tell Fabi this. It would sound as if he were simply afraid.

Gabriel's thumb rubbed the hilt of his father's sword again. He'd always known the sword was special. And when he'd taken it from his father's study, the sword helped him remember things that his father had told him with such vivid clarity that he felt as though he were living it once again. At first, he thought it was coincidence, then it seemed as though he could intentionally use the sword as a catalyst to aid him.

He didn't know what this all meant, but if his father's sword was anything like Gareth's, then there was power yet to be tapped—abilities that had lain dormant for years as his father ruled in peace.

As they entered the palace, Gabriel was vaguely aware of the palace staff gaping at him and whispering, but he ignored them. He trained his attention on marching straight for the palace courtroom. Recognizing his intent, the palace guard lead him to his destination. A guard pushed open the large doors and Gabriel continued inside without missing a step.

It was time to face his fate.

And for the first time, Gabriel didn't fear what that meant for him. He only feared what might happen if he didn't.

He was impulsive. He let his passions guide him. He was idealistic to a fault.

The very best of his father.

Tele nudged the pot back a finger's width to make sure it was perfectly aligned with the other planters. It had taken a few days to discover exactly how much earth their växarots needed to properly grow, but she still needed to perfect how much water and light they required.

The Keeper's lab was a perfect controlled environment for

her investigation. While it seemed that the växarots restored much faster outdoors, the lab had powerful lights that could imitate sunlight, and she discovered that with a prompt in the Tal tongue, the conditions within the room would adjust to almost any setting she requested.

Tele stepped to the side and dipped her pen before she took a few more notes.

Växarot A's response to Light 13 has resulted in a significant decrease in response time to the thoughts of the wielder. Växarot B's response to Light 14 has resulted in a moderate increase in recharge time. Växarot C's response to light 15 has not yielded any change that my measurements can detect.

She closed the book and brushed a thumb over the title: *The Everwisps: The Undiscovered Life within the Tal Tribelands*. It had always been a dream of Tele's to add something to the work of the Keepers of the Covenant, something she could point to and say she was responsible for. It was perhaps vain, but she'd only wanted to follow in her parents' footsteps.

And though she could still feel the pain of losing her family gently burning, often just beyond her awareness, she knew that if they could see her now—a Keeper in the Keeper's lab again after two hundred years—they would be proud of her. It was a bittersweet realization, but it was infinitely better than enduring all of the suffering with nothing to show for it.

Setting the book aside, Tele crossed to the glass wall that separated the lab from the waters below Caldor. Though she'd watched for the dragon's reappearance, she hadn't seen it since she'd returned. She was sure that it was still out there. The spell she'd activated on the North Hzorah Plain was too far away to dissolve the dragon here. That was evidenced by the fact that Caldor was still covered in icy slush that seemed resistant to the sun's attempts to melt it.

She could wait. She had all the time in the world now.

"*Evres*," Tele said, and the glass shifted from transparent to opaque. She then crossed to the lift in the room's center and stepped on the platform. "*Ret'en*." The lift opened and Tele stepped inside. "*Nescht*." The lift descended.

Moments later, the lift stopped, and Tele stepped out into a vast library—a chamber so large that she was sure it could consume the whole of the sanctuary above. At a few dozen landings high and floor area she hadn't yet dared to completely traverse, its immensity was dwarfed only by its unparalleled splendor.

Row upon row of bookshelves that disappeared into the distance were outlined by white marble archways. Aisles with polished wooden floors and unreal paintings checkered the soaring coffered ceilings. Ladders, stairwells, and lifts paced the expanse, providing ample access to every corner of the library without having to deviate too far from one's path. Comfortable nooks, tables, and desks peppered the library, each stocked with a supply of paper, ink, pens, and a number of instruments Tele didn't recognize but were inviting, nonetheless.

Sitting at one of the long tables not far from the lift was Gavini, Navid, and Tal Aval. They turned to her as she entered, and with welcome smiles, they called her over. A warm feeling of acceptance fluttered in her stomach as she smiled and crossed to her friends.

Gavini had found extensive maps of Caldor that detailed the city in ways the Caldor Guardsmen's maps couldn't possibly match. They were spread across the largest table Tele had ever seen. And it appeared Navid and Gavini were discussing the secrets they revealed.

When Tele sat next to Navid, he turned to her and said, "Gavini was just saying that maybe the spell you wrote can be repurposed to finish melting the ice in Caldor."

Gavini nodded. "The damage the ice has done to the city is substantial, and if we can remove it, then we'll be in a much better position to redistribute the survivors to their new homes and attempt to reestablish some semblance of normalcy."

"There is one problem," Tal Aval sighed. "The magic from the Seed is gone. The spell we cast to melt the dragons took it."

Gavini rubbed his chin. "Are you sure it's all gone? All if it? Not even a small bit left?"

Tal Aval shook his head. "All of it."

A silence fell over them.

"It is strange," Tal Aval said. "When I took the power of the Seed, it felt as though I carried something beautiful and powerful. But now that it is gone, there is an empty place inside. I do not know if the empty feeling will leave."

"So," Tele said, finally broaching a subject she'd avoided these past several days. "When will you be returning home? Perhaps Navid and I can make the journey with you."

"I think," Tal Aval said. "That I will stay here for a time and continue to help you learn my tongue. If that is fine to you."

A rush of relief passed over Tele. "Of course it's fine with me!"

"This is good," Gavini said, smiling. "There are many books here, and there may still be spells here that function much like the *Gateway Abbreviation*. We will need your expertise if we are to use them to help rebuild Caldor."

"Or help with the war with the Dominion," Navid said. "Hzorah only narrowly survived the encounter. This won't be the end of it. In a way, the Dominion still achieved a great victory by crippling the numbers of the Hzorah army."

"And let's not forget the dragon spell," Gavini said. "We still don't know how the Dominion got their hands on such a powerful incantation. If they have one, they may have others."

Though Tele had had that same thought, hearing Gavini say it out loud chilled her to the bone. "But the Dominion has shown their hand, and now that we know what they're capable of, we can begin to imagine what weapons they might use in this war." She looked at Navid. "Did the Gateway spell ever surface? I still want to study it."

Navid's eyes flashed golden yellow before he looked away. "The guardsmen haven't come up with anything. We had to call off the search. They needed those resources elsewhere."

Gavini placed a hand on Navid's shoulder. "Don't burden yourself with guilt. I'm sure it will turn up. Sanctuary Calviere is an enormous place." He nodded to the expansive library around them. "Probably much more enormous that you ever imagined it could be."

Navid gave a weak smile. "You're right. It will turn up."

With a final pat to Navid's back, Gavini turned to Tal Aval. "If you're going to be staying here, you'll want a private room. Come, let's find some place where you can settle in. And while we look, you can explain to me a bit of Tal syntax that has been troubling me for years now."

As Gavini and Tal Aval entered the lift and disappeared into the Sanctuary above, Navid turned back to the maps spread before them. "This is insane. We might need an entire team to properly examine all of this."

Tele swallowed. Tal Aval's departure wasn't the only thing she'd been fearing. "Navid, I've been meaning to apologize to you for how I treated you after we—"

Navid looked at her, his golden gaze taking her voice. "Tele, there's nothing for you to apologize—"

"I disagree. My behavior was unacceptable. I—"

"You felt betrayed. I get that. You don't—"

"And I just want you to know that I truly value our friendship."

"I too value our friendship."

He smiled at her, and Tele smiled back.

"There are still a lot of people to help in Caldor," she said, "but now that things are a bit more under control, I can help you find your family. I said that I would."

"No, thank you." Navid took her hand and gave it a gentle squeeze. "*You* are my family now. You and Gavini and Tal Aval. And that's good enough for me."

Tele raised an eyebrow. "Is that what you *really* want? I did promise to make trouble for you."

"And I wouldn't have it any other way," Navid said.

And neither would she.

POSTLUDE

POSTLUDE

A long shadow snaked over the plain, passing over smoke and airborne dust, sweeping over soil and sediment and wayward flurries that flitted about even as the beasts that had breathed them drifted away. The frost amassed and thawed where the dry grass subsided at the base of lofty rock, and the dead piled where the ice failed to devour them. The Shadow Peaks held tight to its victim, brushing its jagged fingers across his red and black face and flaunting regal indifference to the affairs of men.

Filth.

Gareth gathered his will and called out to his father's sabre. The earth about him shook with the fury of vengeance. His blood boiled, and his breaths grew hot. And with a scream that was not entirely his own, he released his passions.

Layers of dirt and rock that had buried him drifted into the air as if held aloft by Desolate's invisible Hand, spinning and tumbling about, cradled among the firmament.

The Dominion general slowly rose and brushed himself off. He looked to the sky as the rains began to fall, slipping between the rocks and ice that hovered in the air. Countless droplets splashed about and washed away the red of blood and the black of soot.

VERY GOOD, GARETH.

He looked to the sabre in his hand. He had given the blade just one taste of the wicked prince's blood, and the power it granted him was already far beyond what he imagined it could be. The strength of it had overwhelmed him, breaking the mountain, and carrying him away in an avalanche of rage. But as he fell into the opening rift, and the rubble buried him below, he'd gained a measure of dominion over the sabre's magic as his mind began to comprehend the breadth of it.

He had only to trick the prince into finishing him off—to walk right into the clutches of his power and meet his fate. But for some reason, the fool boy didn't take the bait.

As the rage of his failure washed over him, he released yet another scream and cast away the floating debris, flinging it in a thousand directions and clearing the path for his descent from the mountain.

There was but one thing left to do now. He had to return to Prophet Tristan and report his failure. The prophet hadn't demanded that he take the heathen's head, but Gareth had desperately wanted to accomplish the feat. Not only to prove himself to his prophet but to avenge his father's death.

But as he began his journey back to the war camp, the wisdoms came to him again.

YOUR TIME TO RETURN HAS NOT YET COME.

Gareth gritted his teeth. What else could he do? Though he hadn't achieved perfect vengeance, he'd crippled the Hzorah army and cleared the path for the Dominion's return to their ancestral lands.

THERE IS ANOTHER. THE BAMILEE MAN.

Why? Gareth asked of the wisdoms. *Why him?*

HE IS A TRAITOR. HE WILL SUFFICE FOR NOW.

After stumbling over the slick earth and righting himself, Gareth wiped his face clean of the rain. He'd always known the Bamilee man was a traitor. If not to the Dominion, to his own people. And once a traitor, a traitor you will forever be. He could never fathom why Prophet Tristan insisted that the man be placed as his left hand when there were many more men his better. Untrained and weak, Owen could not be trusted.

HE HAS BETRAYED YOU. WHEN YOU RETURN TO THE CAMP YOU WILL KNOW THE TRUTH.

He didn't know how the wisdoms could know this. Gareth clutched the sabre's hilt and again allowed the power to surge through him.

Such power.

IT IS BUT A TASTE. GIVE ME THE BLOOD OF THE TRAITOR, AND I WILL GRANT YOU THE POWER TO DEFEAT THE HEATHEN PRINCE ONCE AND FOR ALL.

As long as the source of Hzorah's wickedness was allowed to reign, the Wizard would never return to them. There would never be peace. He had to do everything within his power to purge the world of the prince's filth.

And then vengeance would finally be his.

Queen Frey stood before her elegant, red-cushioned iron chair in an intimate chamber as fourteen young girls reverently filed before her. Their graceful strides lightly clacked against the white marble floors. She appraised them as they arranged themselves to sit on the red carpet before her. Their eyes were bright with energy and their hair had been tended with such care that she could hardly imagine how many hidden pins had been required to tease it into their intricate braids and patterns.

Like the queen herself, they wore the thin chambray dresses in the warm colors of summer that crisscrossed with innocent, lacy whites. Armoth's capital city of Zel es Klath was situated in the northern reaches of the Armoth Queendom, and though her palace's design accommodated the summer winds cooled by Brayavera Lake, the drawing room was largely isolated from the palace currents. Spring had been warmer than usual, and Prophet Lilith had predicted a particularly sweltering summer this year.

It still pained Frey that her prophet's body had not yet come home to be buried with their ancestors in the tombs in the Frozen Waste. She still wasn't sure if Prophet Lilith's body had ever been recovered after the calamity in Caldor. And as the young girls sat quietly before her, she silently prayed that the traditions Lilith deserved would be upheld.

Letting go of the melancholy thoughts before it overcame her royal countenance, Queen Frey gave a warm smile to the girls. Each was a daughter of several prominent Baronesses in Zel es Klath, and each could one day be the woman who would succeed her as queen if the Baronesses of the land found them worthy of the title as she had been elected to duty twenty-two years ago.

And though it would be likely that her own daughter would have been elected to be queen, Frey's ambitions to wed Hzorah's King Jeremiah had postponed the continuation of her lineage. Even now, her matchmakers were no doubt working tirelessly to find her a proper suitor before winter fell upon her womb. All of which, she'd likely reject as she had done time and again.

When word of the fall of Caldor reached her, she knew before her messengers reported it to her that Jeremiah had died along with her hopes of forging a Queendom of unprecedented power. She knew that Jeremiah feared what their union would mean for his people, but Frey held no ill intent for his people or Jeremiah. And as much as she knew such an arrangement would be politically advantageous, cementing her legacy as the greatest Armothean queen to have ever lived, she was fond of Jeremiah and found him desirable.

Jeremiah was rough around the edges, and he and his people held destructive and repressive ideas about women, but she knew he could be molded into something better—in the way only she could force him to grow.

But all of that was lost now.

Queen Frey sat and opened *Ul Senamp Braya*, the book of Armothean oral traditions. It was not the original transcription of the oral traditions. That book was kept safely in the vaults of her palace. Instead, the version she held was a beautiful leather-bound edition, full of colorful illustrations that she used for such occasions as this. Each parable was accompanied by several of their Queendom's most revered artists' impressions of the stories of their people, and each of the stories contained within the volume was meticulously curated by Armothean scholars as the best written retelling of the story in Armotha. Of course, with the caveat that this specific volume was meant for the queen to read the tale to girls who had not yet come of age.

"I am pleased to see you all here," Queen Frey said to her captive audience. "It is my greatest pleasure to read to you from our most sacred stories. The Armothean tradition is great, and the principles established by our greatest stories are the foundation of our prosperity. Is there a tale you'd like for me to read to you?"

Immediately, the girls erupted in a chorus of requests.

"*Sunrise, Sunset, Always*!"

"*Crescent Moon*!"

"*Omaai and the Great White Wolf*!"

Frey was overjoyed to hear some of her favorites, especially *Omaai and the Great White Wolf*. She caught eyes with the girl who'd made the request and gave her a kind smile before she opened the tome and searched the table of contents for Omaai's story. She knew it well enough to tell it herself, but the words of the storyteller of this book were specifically tuned for a younger ear.

But before Frey could flip to the appropriate page, another story caught her eye—one that none of them had requested: *The Midwife*.

Queen Frey herself had not heard the story in quite some time. *The Midwife* was most popularly told to girls during their ceremony of womanhood. Because of its niche purpose, it was rarely requested by young and old alike. It had become a story that was quite out of fashion to tell in modern retellings and songs. Some of the Queendom's oldest artists still endeavored to attempt it, but Armoth's younger artists knew better than to adapt it if they were searching for fame in their performances or illustrations.

It was an old tale that taught the value of a level-headed approach to situations of great risk. And she'd almost forgotten the value of its lessons.

Perhaps the young Hzorah Prince Gabriel is worth my attention, Queen Frey thought.

He was young and without proper guidance. His army had been crippled by the Deseran Dominion. His entire kingdom was at risk of spiraling into decades of economic decline.

But she could save him.

If Prince Gabriel was anything like his father, he certainly would not have taken the lessons of *The Midwife* to heart—if he'd even heard the tale in the first place. Hzorah was horribly uneducated, and it was a wonder that they survived in spite of themselves.

He needed her.

And she needed him.

"All of the tales you have requested are great and important," Queen Frey said to the young ones. "But today, I will tell you one that is often overlooked—one that will prepare you for the throne."

Bam Rav paced himself as he hiked through the remote mountain pass. Though the path back to the Dominion Desert was remote and far from the passes that the Deseran army had used to cross into the North Hzorah Plain, it was still lucky that he had not yet encountered retreating soldiers.

He would eventually, and Bam Rav was not sure how he would respond to them when he did. Would he raise his hand against them? Would he hide? Would he allow himself to be captured? Would he allow himself to be killed?

He did not want to return to the Dominion army and had resolved to go back to the Bamilee Plain and rescue his family from slavery. They would never free themselves, but he had already crossed into the murky waters of violence. He had not harmed anyone with his own hand, but Amie had shown him that his ethics required a greater measure of responsibility for his actions. And now that he had already compromised on his beliefs, he would risk one last act of violence to liberate his mother, father, and young siblings.

Bam Rav was not sure where he would bring them. Life in the Dominion Desert was harsh, and he did not want his family to suffer in the wilderness any more than he wanted them to be slaves. But as long as they were slaves, they could not make a better life. In the desert, they would at least have a chance of making a better life. And perhaps he would take up Amie's offer to live with her in Hzorah.

Thank you, Amie, for showing me hope.

The narrow mountain pass opened as he turned along a curve of exposed rock. He paused as he came upon the opening of a cave behind a wooden carriage covered in canvas. Bam Rav's grip tightened on his pack. He should keep moving before the soldiers in the cave noticed him. Be it Dominion or Hzorah soldiers, neither would be good news.

Just then, he spotted a small boy that had seen perhaps seven years appear in the mouth of the cave. He watched Bam Rav curiously, his head tilting ever so slightly before he turned and fled into the dark cave.

Bam Rav shook his head. It was the strangest thing he had seen since he had left his home. And as much as he wanted to investigate why the boy was out here all alone, he thought better of it. It would be best if he continued his journey. If word of his desertion reached the Bamilee Plain before he did, there would be Thief-Takers watching for his return.

But before he could continue on, the boy re-emerged, this time accompanied by an older man with black-and-white stubble and gray-streaked hair. The man smiled at him and waved him over. He was too old to be a soldier and seemed friendly enough.

"Supplies for your journey?" the man asked.

Bam Rav shifted the pack on his shoulder. He was about to

journey into the Dominion Desert, and he had only purchased enough supplies to journey from Azuri to the Dominion army just on the other side of the Shadow Peaks. If he were careful, he could have made his rations stretch the majority of the journey home, but he had already resigned to the fact that he would have to find food and water at some point.

He trotted over to the cart. "You are a merchant?"

The man nodded. "I am, yes, yes!" He looked to Bam Rav's Dominion uniform, then retrieved a bundle of clothes from his carriage. "Would you like clothes for travel? For comfort? They're the finest silks in the land. Yes, yes, the finest, I assure you of that."

Bam Rav shook his head. "No. I only need food and water."

With only a small look of disappointment, the peddler replaced the clothing and pulled out several pre-bundled bricks of mystery food and three waterskins. "Each bundle will carry a man for a full day—three if you must! The best rations in the land! Yes, yes, the best!"

Bam Rav reached into his pack and retrieved the small purse of Hzorah marks General Gareth had left with him to gather the supplies he needed to travel back to the Dominion army. "Why are you out here in the middle of nowhere with a child?"

The peddler smiled. "The boy's mother died several years ago. He comes with me on my travels now. A tragedy. Yes, yes, a tragedy, indeed."

Bam Rav counted out all but one final mark for the food and waterskins. "Do you get enough business in a mountain pass?"

"I haven't set up camp here in fifteen years!" the peddler said. "But there is war about." He leaned in as if to hide his words from the rocks. "A battle means abandoned supplies for a scavenger if he's quick. My father taught me that, yes, yes, he did!"

"Huh," Bam Rav said as he stuffed the rations into his pack. "Well, I must get going."

"Is there anything else you might need to make your journey easier. A sword? A dagger, I found many today, yes, yes, indeed! Fine quality too!"

"No—" Bam Rav said but paused. It was an unlikely request but … "Do you have anything I can read?"

The merchant cocked his head. "A strange traveler you are. Yes, yes, very strange." He looked at the small boy. "Quickly, bring me that book you found. Quickly!" The boy hopped into the carriage and reemerged with a small, blood red book. The peddler took it from the boy. "No one ever requests something to read. I began to think I'd never sell this. Yes, yes. A strange traveler."

Bam Rav handed the peddler his final mark, and the merchant handed him the book. "Thank you."

"Thank you, yes, yes. Off you go then!" the peddler said before smiling from ear to ear.

As Bam Rav walked away, he thanked Amie for saving his life once again, and this time added: *And thank you for teaching me to read. That will make this journey bearable.*

Once he was away from the peddler's cave, he rubbed his thumb over the book's black lettering before reading its title.

The Gateway Abbreviation.

ADVENTURE AWAITS

Continue your journey by reading the next book here:

https://emergentrealms.com/tcc1

ACKNOWLEDGEMENTS

I guess this is when the credits roll. I'd appreciate it if you pretend an epic orchestration is playing in the background while you read this. If you're not mentioned here, clearly I despise you.

My wife, Pamela: You are my everything. I would not have completed this story without you, and the fact that you allowed me to sit alone and work on this for so long is a testament to your long-suffering care and abiding love. Thank you for following me into the dark.

Adryanna: I have no idea how you've endured my rambling and strategic missteps so far. I'm afraid to list how many times I was totally wrong. If I were to write it all out, you'd probably seriously reconsider talking to me ever again. We're still at the beginning of our journey to fulfill our ambitions, but I'm already so proud of what we've accomplished. I can't promise to not be wrong anymore, but I can promise that the best is yet to come.

Kate Watts & Spencer Hamilton: You two have helped transform this story and make it something far more complete and beautiful than I could have done alone. Thank you, Kate, for helping me learn the basics and encouraging me for years. Thank you, Spencer, for helping me tidy up my loose ends and for being every bit as enthusiastic about this project as I am. You both are champions, and every author should have the opportunity to experience working with at least one editor of your caliber.

I would also like to thank:

Nefarious Press, Billy Christian, and Nell Fallcard for helping bring my stories to life with your amazing visual art skills. Seriously. Wow.

Noel, Cher Armstrong the speedy fan of hobbits, Jennie B., Mira P., and the Walpole Writer's Group (RIP) for being fantastic alpha readers.

Megan G., Mercedez R., Jean L., Stacie M., and Mira P. (again) for beta reading this novel and giving me the dirt.

Lisa Bryan for jumping in at the last minute and helping us with editing.

My friends. You know who you are. You're the very best.

Massachusetts Public Libraries and their librarians for allowing me to sit, write, and research for hours. Also, pretty much every Dunkin Donuts and Starbucks in the state where I spent way too much of my money to use their WiFi for an hour.

The Emergent Realms team. Emergent Realms is pretty small at the time that I'm writing this, but it's sure to grow, and you guys have to figure out how to sell this book once I'm done typing. Suckers.

That cashier at Borders bookstore (RIP) that looked me over, shoved a fantasy novel in my hand, told me to buy it, and changed my life forever.

And you, dear reader.

For without you, my stories would be lifeless and forever incomplete.

ABOUT THE AUTHOR

Jim Wilbourne is a creative at heart. If he's not writing a novel, he's writing and recording a song, or once again trying to learn how to draw. When he's not working on the next project, he spends his free time working on another project. He totally has a life. Jim lives in the deep south with his wife and son and doesn't miss the snow at all.

 facebook.com/jimwilbourneauthor

 twitter.com/jimwilbourne

 instagram.com/jimwilbourne